THE NAZARENE

BOOKS BY SHOLEM ASCH

THREE CITIES
SALVATION
IN THE BEGINNING
MOTTKE THE THIEF
THE WAR GOES ON
THE MOTHER
THREE NOVELS
SONG OF THE VALLEY
THE NAZARENE

THE NAZARENE

by Sholem Asch

TRANSLATED BY MAURICE SAMUEL

G·P·PUTNAM'S SONS NEW YORK

Designed by Robert Josephy

MANUFACTURED IN THE UNITED STATES OF AMERICA
BY THE HADDON CRAFTSMEN, INC.

PART ONE

CHAPTER ONE

NOT the power to remember, but its very opposite, the power to forget, is a necessary condition of our existence. If the lore of the transmigration of souls is a true one, then these, between their exchange of bodies, must pass through the sea of forgetfulness. According to the Jewish view we make the transition under the over-lordship of the Angel of Forgetfulness. But it sometimes happens that the Angel of Forgetfulness himself forgets to remove from our memories the records of the former world; and then our senses are haunted by fragmentary recollections of another life. They drift like torn clouds above the hills and valleys of the mind, and weave themselves into the incidents of our current existence. They assert themselves, clothed with reality, in the form of nightmares which visit our beds. Then the effect is exactly the same as when, listening to a concert broadcast through the air, we suddenly hear a strange voice break in, carried from afar on another ether-wave and charged with another melody.

I stood before the door on which I could perceive, even in the half-darkness which reigned in the corridor, the three letters I.H.S., written in chalk: a circumstance which did not fail to impress me, leaving no doubt in my mind that this was the residence of a Christian, more specifically, of a Catholic. He himself opened the door for me.

Thick air was wafted out upon me, laden with the mildew of old things long stored away, and of rotting papers. In the darkness which filled the front room on that wet and cloudy autumn evening I was aware by feeling rather than by sight of the dynamic figure which confronted me. Not that it was powerful and imposing; on the contrary, it was small and withered. And yet there was the feeling that in this vague little blot of a man there was concentrated a tremendous electrical charge which was liable to explode at any moment. And indeed, I approached him with the utmost care; it was in the most modest and respectful voice which I could muster that, in answer to his astonished look, I explained my presence there.

"Oh . . ." Deep breath passed through his horribly bony, thin, aristocratically chiseled nose—the only hint of form standing out from the dim, featureless blur which was his face. I heard the echo of the change of air in his lungs. Without uttering a word, without even looking at me properly, he waved to me to follow him.

We passed through the long, narrow front room, the walls of which, on either side, were covered with bookshelves. The books did not stand in rows; they lay in bundles, corded up as if to be carted away. The walls of the studio were likewise covered with shelves, and on these too the books lay tied up in packages. I had ample time to observe him in this, his habitat, for the man had no sooner brought me into his room than he promptly forgot about me and calmly seated himself at his writing desk, from which I had torn him away by ringing the bell. He not only did not ask me to take a seat, but ignored me completely, as if I were not in the room at all. I had, before coming here, made up my mind to react to no insult and not to lose patience under any provocative remark. I was well acquainted with his attitude toward the nation and religion to which I belong; but I had resolved to pay no attention to irrelevancies and to pursue the single purpose which I had set myself, which was, to make the closer acquaintance of this man. I therefore did not let myself become perturbed, but used the interval of time in order to observe him from my corner. His writing desk stood near the single window, which must have looked out upon a narrow yard, for the light which managed to seep through the double windows, stopped with cotton-wool, was faint and dim, as though it had passed through a sieve. And yet, in spite of the heavy onset of twilight about us, a luster as of yellow parchment rested on his face. The head, steeped in the colorless atmosphere of the room, looked like the head of a Caesar on a worn-out Roman coin. The thin, bony nose was like a delicate instrument with two finely carved wings; sharp-pointed, it hung over the paper like the beak of an eagle. It dominated his face, repressing all the other features. The big head, hovering above the desk, was naked; only a thin border of yellow-white hair lay like a circlet about his baldness. There was so much energy in the nervous, trembling hand which he pushed across the paper, that the pen protested with a loud, scratching noise. But I was puzzled to know how he had managed to find room on his table for all the things that lay there: there were positive towers of dictionaries, encyclopedias and handbooks; and quite apart from the volumes, pamphlets, journals and stacks of papers belonging to the writer's craft, there were also piled up innumerable objects apparently unrelated to it; I saw a Roman helmet, a sword, innumerable bronze and earthen vessels and other archaeological fragments, spikes, buckles, fragments of old pottery, bronze and marble pieces of Greek or Roman figurines. And, beside these, enormous numbers of stones with a variety of inscriptions.

Finally he recalled my presence in the room and rose. With him rose likewise a single fly with which he had been waging war without interrupting his writing. Now it pursued him and circled about his head. He chased it away with a handkerchief, and with energetic steps came over to the corner where I had stood immovably waiting for him to call me to mind. He began to talk to me as if he had known me for years, and as if we were resuming a conversation which had only just been broken off:

"They're a frightful pest, these flies! Do you know with whom the historian Tacitus compared them? With that noisy and tumultuous people, the Jews! Har-r-r, ha-r-r!" His laughter ended on a long, sharp rolling *r*. "And do you know how the Emperor Domitian used to pass the time, days at a stretch? He used to catch the flies in his palace and tear off their wings so that they could not fly. Har-r-r! Har-r-r! A lofty occupation for a Roman Caesar, what? But it was symbolic, young man, it was symbolic. He was, in fact, fit for nothing else. His campaign against the Germans was an empty bluff, nothing more. He did not even cross the Rhine, though he was one of the Vespasians who freed the world from the Jewish plague, and burned that nest of the Pharisees and Sadducees, the Temple—har-r-r! Har-r-r! . . ."

I answer him calmly: "Sir, I have come here on the recommendation of Madame B. . . . I am ready to place my knowledge of the Hebrew language at your disposal."

He looks at me in astonishment, comes a step closer as if to see me better, takes a step back, and answers, seriously:

"If I have in any way offended the zealot in you, I beg your pardon, grandson of the Maccabees and of Simeon bar Giora! And still they say that the lamb, Jesus, came out of the lion's den of Judah! I'm at one with Nietzsche—I'd give away the whole New Testament for a single page of the Old. The latter deals with men, the former with nothing but females; the latter deals with a God of vengeance, and the former with nothing but feminine forgiveness . . . ."

Afraid that he was off again on a wild flight, I once more ventured to interrupt him:

"On the recommendation of Madame B., I have the honor . . ."

"Ah yes, ah yes, Madame B. told me that you were ready to impart to me the mysteries of your holy tongue, which I need in connection with an important matter. I thank you for your offer, and I must confess that I admire your courage, young man. And may one know what motives impel you to make the enemy of the chosen people privy to your conspiratorial world? Perhaps the price you will set for it will be too high, and I shall not be able to pay it."

"The price?" I repeated, astonished. "I hope Madame B. informed you that any material return for my co-operation is out of the question."

"Har-r! Har-r! I am much more afraid of the spiritual variety."

"Sir, the only payment I am ready to accept from you is the opportunity to partake of some of your rich knowledge of the classic literature of antiquity. It is your fame as a scholar and investigator in the field of ancient Rome which has attracted me. I must admit that I too feel drawn toward the epoch in which you are so deeply interested, and concerning which you have, by your discoveries, placed the world in your debt. Please believe me when I say that I have long sought the opportunity of making your acquaintance."

The soft words soothed him as a raging bear is soothed by sweet syrup, and he lapsed into silence; but it was a suspicious silence, for he again sprang back a step and looked at me searchingly. The eyes became screwed up, the nose seemed to be thrust forward like a prehensile organ, and altogether it was as though he was investigating me with the sense of smell rather than with that of sight. And then, having as it were approved of me, he seated himself once more at the table and switched on the electric lamp swinging above him. It was as well that he did, for by now thick darkness had settled in the room. True, the single electric bulb, shaded by a piece of scorched paper closely covered with writing, was not strong enough properly to illumine the room, but enough light fell on the table and on his head —and above all on his features. He motioned me to sit down in an old armchair which stood facing him at the table. My compliance with the gesture was accompanied by an uncomfortable little surprise. I did not notice that the armchair was already occupied by an old tomcat, and I did not become aware of his presence till he was awakened from his sleep by the weight of my body. However, he did not dispute possession with me, but took himself off to another corner of the room from which the darkness had not been driven.

"My achievements in the field of objective science would have been greater, and of higher importance, if I did not have to carry on a perpetual struggle against certain forces in whose interest it is to prevent the truth from coming into the light of day," he said, and passed his fingers over his gray-yellow, short-cropped mustache. "I will refrain from mentioning them by name, in order to spare your sensibilities, but you cannot be unaware of their identity. . . ." But now a singular opportunity has come into my life: there has fallen into my hands a document which has been hidden from the world for nineteen hundred years. This documents contains the complete truth concerning that world-tragedy which was enacted in Jerusalem, and which has unfortunately become the most important factor in our history of the last two millennia. The document, which is in my possession, will revolutionize our attitude toward the accepted truths. The consequences of its publication are incalculable, and I need your assistance, young man, in order to make a thorough and objective analysis of the script. For you must know that this particular document, unlike the others which were prepared for the benefit of the gentiles, is not written in Greek, but in the original and authentic Hebrew, as its purpose, namely that of internal or family use, dictated. What I ask and expect of you, young man, is that irrespective of your obligations to the Jewish community, to which you are bound by secret oaths and interdictions, you shall place the interests of pure science above those of your own sect, and without bias help me to decipher the text of this epoch-making original document which a happy chance has brought into my possession."

I already knew by repute this man's habit of exaggeration and of self-inflation, yet I could not help being impressed by the earnestness and sincerity of his words. I really believed that I was about to be confronted with something important and hitherto unknown. The low tones in which he addressed me, and the serious expression which lay on the extraordinary parchment-yellow face, were devoid of any hint of the trickery or practical hoaxing which was his habitual attitude toward his own discoveries. I was convinced that this time an issue of first-rate importance was at stake. I answered him in all seriousness:

"Please let me assure you, professor, that only one impulse brought me to you—the thirst for knowledge; for me science and absolute truth take precedence over all other considerations." I then went on to thank him with genuine feeling for the confidence he was prepared to show in me, though our acquaintanceship was so short and he knew so little about me.

"Yes, you have my confidence. I do not know how you have awakened it. I believe that you have toward these things an attitude which differs completely from that of your co-religionists. Actually, the little that we know of the life and acts of that personality with whom we are concerned, and who has unfortunately molded our history of the last two thousand years, we owe to a couple of your 'fellow-countrymen'—or shall I say your co-religionists?—who have left us their accounts of that life and its activity. They were not free from partisan passion and sectarian interests. These tendencies, ranged on either side of the struggle, have created the figure of that personality; they gave it birth and fashioned its form. You will certainly know"—and he pointed a finger at me—"that in the beginning, before the Graeco-Roman genius introduced a little order into the labyrinthine chaos of the Pharisaic mentality which dominated the Christian sect, this entire matter of the new faith was a purely Jewish affair. The followers of the new faith and its opponents were both of that human material out of which God had created the chosen people."

Despite my preliminary resolution to remain untouched and unmoved by any observation of his, I could not help seeing that theologic disquisitions of this kind threatened to break off our relationship at its very beginning; for he could hardly utter a sentence which was not provocative. I forced myself to answer in the softest and gentlest tones of which I was capable:

"Professor, I believe that it would be of mutual benefit if we were to avoid theological discussions which might lead to unpleasantnesses. It would be better for us to confine ourselves to Hebrew instruction and to the factual material."

A look of astonishment and anger came into his face, as though he could not understand where I had found the impudence to interrupt his discourse. He muttered something unintelligible between his teeth, then he lapsed into silence, his searching gaze still fixed piercingly upon me, as though he was at a loss as to what to do next—throw me out without an instant's delay, or first blast me out of my chair. Finally he burst out:

"For the sake of science I will put up with everything—even with the insolence of a Jewish whipper-snapper."

In the literary circles of our provincial city there was one man on whom his intimates had bestowed the title of "the theologian" or "the professor." Himself not a professional writer, he was the friend and counselor of writers, an aesthete, a philologist of the classic languages. However, from time to time he did put his extraordinary erudition to use and published observations and brief essays in journals devoted to Roman and Greek history and literature. If, for instance, some scholar had made an error in the name of a Roman general or jurist or philosopher, had given a wrong date, or misspelled the name of a tribune—in brief, if any sin of inaccuracy had been committed against one of the major or minor heroes of antiquity—at once a correction appeared in the following issue. In the majority of cases the editors had either to rewrite the letters or throw them into the trash basket because of their fantastic style. In the first place his style was "severely classical," that is to say, he threw in so many Greek and Latin words that it was quite difficult for a modern reader to know what he was driving at. And then it was his peculiar delight to unearth, from God alone knew which sources, the names of classic heroes of whom no one had ever heard before. There were some who said that many of the names contained in his observations and essays were unearthed out of nothing more substantial than his own imagination. Others, less rash, tried to check up on him, ransacked the various anthologies, dictionaries and encyclopedias, and arrived at unsatisfactory conclusions; apparently there was something in the names, though exactly what they could not determine. It was as though this man was in exclusive possession of a peculiar library of Greek philosophers and Roman statesmen, accessible to him alone. Whenever he wrote it was invariably behind the mask of a pseudonym, which was never the same, but varied from occasion to occasion, always however retaining an outlandish and unexpected character. These peculiarities might have passed as harmless eccentricities; but the worst feature about his contributions was his habit of introducing into purely scientific notes violently controversial observations on contemporary individuals and events. He used his brief notices for the purpose of settling his accounts with all his enemies, and in particular he would direct his fury against his bitterest foe—the Jews. On the slender pretext of a newspaper correction he would hang all the list of their shortcomings. If he had occasion to mention the jurist Cicero, he would never forget to add: "He it was who, two thousand years ago, already alluded to them as a 'noisy and tumultuous people.' " It need hardly be added that in consequence of this monomania his communications were not particularly welcome to the various editors.

As against this, however, it could not be denied that he had his coterie of eager listeners in the cafe which he frequented. In keeping with the practice of the philosophers of antiquity, he used the spoken rather than the written word in the communication of his wisdom to others. Like some prototype of his in Athens of old he would take his place at the center of a circle of young listeners who hung on his lips and gathered up eagerly the pearls which fell from them. I do not know what such a circle, assembled about a Socrates or a Plato, must have looked like, but among those who surrounded "the professor" were to be seen such as had already lost their first youth, some of them, in fact, displaying the baldness of advancing age. Smoking innumerable borrowed cigarettes, he, an unshaven figure, sat in the cloud of smoke which went up from the gnawed and battered pipes of his disciples. These were drawn principally from the ranks of the untalented and the unsuccessful. It is no exaggeration to say that whosoever had failed in the literary or professional world was attracted to the table in the cafe in which was mirrored the intellectual life of the provincial city.

In the Polish language there is a word *kaval,* meaning a piece of trickery, a hoax, a canard. For the sake of a *kaval* he was ready to sell his father and mother or to destroy half the world, and if he managed to put it over successfully he was indescribably happy, and tears of sheer joy would run down his cheeks.

It was in connection with such a *kaval* that his name had at one time appeared in the world press. The incident was connected with the report of an Ethiopian manuscript of the New Testament which he claimed to have discovered in a monastery on Mount Sinai, with the help (as it appeared later) of a notorious literary forger. Whatever the external upshot of this epoch-making discovery—it ended in a scandal of world-wide proportions—it clothed the man in a mantle of local fame. From that period on he was for ever astonishing the learned world with new, unknown manuscripts of antiquity which he had brought back with him from his long research travels in the Orient. The numerous falsifications contained in these documents had ruined his reputation as a scholar; and yet the attitude of the academic world toward him, essentially suspicious as it was, did not lack an element of interest, for in the midst of these very falsifications there were always such strange, mystic and unintelligible evidences of authenticity, that he seldom failed to divide the ranks of the learned. Time was needed to establish beyond the shadow of a doubt the falsehood of his claims. And somehow this was never done completely, for there always remained behind a lingering suspicion of authenticity. Here and there individual opinions of weight considered the discoveries genuine or, in any case, thoroughly mysterious. When it so happened that he was caught red-handed in a falsification, his excuse was that he was putting over a "kaval" on the learned, in order to show how essentially unreliable they were.

More recently he succceeded in imposing on scholars a deception which made a great stir in the press, and which almost landed him in jail, while his reputation sank to its nadir. One fine morning he issued through the newspapers a statement that he had found in an old church an unknown Josephus manuscript, written in ancient Slavonic, which derived from the tenth century and which had escaped the censorship of the church. In this manuscript, he claimed, there was a passage, not to be found in any of the known Josephus texts, relating to the person of Jesus Christ and shedding on it a peculiar light which vindicated the claim of certain anti-Semitic scholars who would have it that Jesus Christ was an Aryan. It may easily be imagined what storms were roused in the ecclesiastic world. The sequel might have been anticipated; it was established that not only was there no such passage, but that the very story of the manuscript was a wild exaggeration, for what was actually produced was a two-page fragment of an early Slav chronicle, the genuineness of which could not be definitely proved or disproved. In any case, the incident trailed off into mystery. High representatives of the church prosecuted him for blasphemy. The trial cost him much effort and suffering, but he did not seem to mind. It was at this trial that he first revealed the symptoms of a strange mental disease; he suddenly astonished the judges with the statement that he was a contemporary of Pontius Pilate, the Procurator of Judea, and had a first-hand knowledge of the incidents which occurred in Jerusalem at that time from his own participation in them.

As will readily be understood, this extraordinary sickness remained a "strict secret." The court at once perceived that it was confronted with a case of mental aberration; it was profoundly reluctant to make public fantastic statements which could only add to the damage which the incident had inflicted on the church. The trial was suppressed. But hardly had the tumult raised by this *kaval* died down, when he tried to provoke another sensation: this time he claimed to have unearthed, in the shop of a Jewish antiquarian located in the Old City of Warsaw, nothing more nor less than the papyrus of an unknown Version of the New Testament, in which were contained many new sayings and parables of Jesus of Nazareth, as well as a new account of the crucifixion. Coming as it did after the story of the Josephus text, this discovery of an Evangelist did not produce the effect it might have produced. Two sensation-mongering papers gave space to it; the learned world ignored it. He himself attributed the attitude of the latter in part to the jealousy of the learned and in part to the world domination of the Jews, who were determined to keep his discoveries from the light of day lest the real nature of the tragedy which was enacted at that time in Jerusalem become generally known. Nor was there anyone, anywhere, who knew as much about the subject as he himself. . . . For various reasons, which he was not able to reveal, he would keep the document secret while he continued to prepare it.

At the time in which this account opens, that is, when I made his acquaintance, his star had almost completely set. Personally too he had declined; he was no longer as witty as he had once been, his inspirations were less frequent and less interesting. It appeared likewise that he had at last exhausted the discoverer's well of unknown sources. He had become old. He was seen more seldom in the cafe; it was reported that he was now subject to long fits of depression; he remained locked in his room, or else he passed entire weeks in the University library, rooting among books and manuscripts.

I cannot quite explain the reasons which drew me so powerfully to this man, and which made me determine to win his confidence and to hear him speak about those days. All I can say is that I have always been profoundly attracted to that period. Hearing that he stood in need of a man with a sound knowledge of Hebrew, I obtained a recommendation to him. I knew that the contact might be far from pleasant; that he would in all probability insult me at every step. But my mind was made up. And the beginning was, in fact, difficult. There seemed to be no genuine contact between us. I swallowed his insults, and wondered whether it was worth while. Then, when the character of his mental condition was borne upon me, my determination was strengthened. The fact that I had before me a contemporary of Pontius Pilate, a man who had lived in Jerusalem and had personally participated in the repression of the rebellions, a man who had been a first-hand witness of the tremendous events of that time—even though this might be nothing more than illusion —held me bound to him. And I must confess that I even asked myself whether this was not, perhaps, a case of metempsychosis, a reincarnation of someone out of that period, flung across the centuries into ours.

CHAPTER TWO

THERE is no human intimacy which can compare for closeness with that which results when two men divest themselves of their divisive beliefs and convictions, and make their contact solely on the basis of their common human needs and weaknesses. Concerning the fearsome "theologian," or, to give him his actual name, Pan Viadomsky, the following facts developed: with all his haughty and chivalresque bearing, with all his Roman-warlike character, he was nothing more than a weak and sickly child of our day. Born into a not particularly well-to-do family (his father was a poor provincial doctor), he had in his childhood shown an extraordinary gift for classical languages. For reasons I never learned he broke off his academic studies in the middle, became an independent student, and began to travel. When his reputation was ruined by the repeated forgeries in ancient documents, he took to teaching, his pupils usually being students of the classics, the children of wealthy parents. His independence and pride stood in his way, and he never did well at his profession. On more than one occasion, invited to a country estate during the summer in order to prepare a student for the fall term, he was sent away before ending his contract, as a result of his arrogant behavior. Nor was this all; there were adventures with the parents of the students, there was a good deal of litigation in the courts—and the consequence was that people began to avoid him. Now he was living from the sale of the remaining fragments of the huge library which he had accumulated and of the dubious "original" documents which he had brought back from his travels. Still, this did not cover even his modest needs. He "helped" himself out by living in a state of semi-starvation. The apartment he occupied had been his since before the war; the tenant-protection laws prevented the landlord from throwing him out though he had not paid rent for years. There he was, occupying an apartment owned by a Jew who did not dare to do anything against him. Now and again he delivered a lecture arranged for him by old acquaintances of his, mostly gymnasium teachers. At rare intervals he was lucky enough to get one of his notes on some classical subject—he still flooded the editorial offices with them—printed and paid for. The wife of the janitor, an old woman, cleaned his rooms for him twice weekly, not for the occasional, pitiful pay he could offer, so much as for charity's sake. Such meals as he took he cooked for himself on a primus stove which stood in the kitchen; this room, like all the others, was chock-a-block with packages of books, newspapers and documents. Everything seemed to point to the probability of a first-class fire. But if anyone had dared to point this out to him he would have had his head snapped off for his pains. . . .

He was a lonely man, and with all his bitterness—so I convinced myself later—not a bad man. Certainly he hated the common people, the "plebs," and he never failed to buttress his contempt for them with relevant quotations from the thinkers of old, in the original languages; but it could not be said that he displayed any particular sympathy for the rich. In fact, if anything, he had an even greater hatred for the opulent and mighty of the earth. Against them he quoted the words of the New Testament, in the original Greek: "It is the rich who oppress ye, who bring ye before the courts." His keenest contempt was reserved for modern times and for modern life, and no level of the population, no system of society, was to his liking. Contemporary life refusing to offer him a place within, he felt himself to be an outsider. He had, if one may so put it, taken refuge from our age and fled to the age to which he belonged, to the men he knew best, to the circumstances and incidents with which he was intimately acquainted and which interested him most.

With regard to the history of the Roman age he had a wide knowledge which must have been derived from sources known to him alone. To classic episodes the records of which are strictly limited to definite sources, he added a wealth of details from his own imagination, but these were so much in keeping both with the incidents and the characters to which they related, that they seemed, like his doubtful documents, to be partly authentic. He imparted to his stories a verisimilitude which destroyed the interval of two thousand years and brought them so close to our own time that he might very well have been a participant or spectator. Thus, for instance, he would weave something queer into his recitals of events concerning Germanicus and "us, the Secunda Italica."

"What do you mean by 'us'?" I asked in astonishment.

"Oh, I am speaking of the Second Legion, which consisted entirely of Romans," he would answer, and a faint tide of color would creep up his withered cheeks.

After a time we dropped this subject.

Just as every anti-Semite has his Jew, of whom he is prepared to make an exception, so I became Pan Viadomsky's "personal Jew." He found a new name for me: Josephus. This was, in fact, a title of distinction, for Pan Viadomsky thought the world of Josephus. He could hardly have lived without me. If I missed one evening's visit, I was sure to receive a letter from him the next day. And I must confess that I too became greatly attached to him. In the first place, I loved to listen to his stories. His reading was immense, and I learned a great deal from him. Even the remainder of his library constituted a huge collection of classic literature, both in the original and in translations, and he was glad to give me access to it and even to find for me the passages which I needed. In spite of the polar difference in our outlook on the events of that period, our common interest in the time of the Second Temple held us close together. Over and above all this, his character, bitter, sharp and obstinate—I might say his Quixotic refusal to compromise—which had brought him so many enemies and isolated him from his contemporaries, aroused in me, in spite of frequent hurt and irritation, a definite respect. I became convinced that his sensational "discoveries," which had done him so much harm, were not the result of deliberate fraud and dishonesty (what, after all, had they brought him?) but sprang from a naïve and fanatical enthusiasm for the subject in which he was interested. Like quite a number of anti-Semites he had a special relish for Jewish delicacies; they were probably spiced for him by the feeling of forbidden fruit. I used to bring him, from the Jewish quarter in which I lived, little presents: Jewish white bread, Jewish black bread, a piece of herring, a pickled cucumber, or even a slice or two of Jewish sausage; and we used to eat these dainties together over the tea which we drank during the long evenings. He never failed to express his thanks; not in so many words (a kindly word could not get past his lips: it was as though a psychological filter prevented its passage) but by his looks, or by a smile—and that, too, was seen seldom enough on his face.

On one occasion he fell sick; he caught a cold and ran a temperature. I took care of him for several days, and brought a doctor who prescribed for him. I sat up with him a couple of nights. He was so touched that he actually said something pleasant: he confessed that he had never suspected that a Jew could be capable of playing the Good Samaritan.

And thus, without our willing it (or did we, on the contrary, actually will it?) there developed between us an increasingly friendly relationship. There was something curious about it; we were like two fellow-countrymen who, in their old home town, had always lived on the worst of terms, and who now found themselves thrown together on a wild and savage island at the other end of the world. Just as every lonely man fastens on the first person who shows a sign of friendliness, just as every sick man catches at the hand held out to him and tries to enslave the entire body of his rescuer, so Pan Viadomsky clung to me with convulsive fingers and would not let go.

I really do not know what happened to me: the moment I heard that he was sick and could not leave his bed, I became uneasy and felt I had to hasten to his side. And then, before I knew it, I found myself with a broken old man on my hands and I was the one mainstay, such as it was, that he had in life. I felt that I was bound to the man and could not liberate myself. The worst moments occurred in the late evening, when the time came for me to leave him and return home. It transpired that he was afraid to remain alone through the long, sleepless nights; and he used to hold on to me until the small hours. He was proud; it was hard for him to betray the fact that he was dependent on somone else; and yet he did it. When I began to intimate that I had to leave him, something childlike came over him, and he almost begged me to stay on.

He began, during that period, to take a closer interest in me, in my personal life and my studies; he even expressed the wish to re-educate me. The first thing for me to do, he intimated, was to subject myself to the Roman discipline—and in this connection he naturally did not fail to remind me that if the Roman character had vanished from the world it was the fault of us, the Jews, who had introduced into the ancient empire the disintegrating principle of a Judaizing Christianity; he desired to re-create in me, the unfortunate individual, the greatness that had been Rome. I listened with a show of sympathy, for I could not help feeling the warm rays of friendliness and even of love (to whatever extent this concept could be applied to him) which were breaking for the first time through the cold iron walls in which his soul was encased.

But I still did not get a glimpse of the famous manuscript which had been the subject of our first conversations. It had simply dropped out of the picture. I was determined not to be the first to refer to it again. It would seem that his interest had shifted. He questioned me a great deal concerning the life of the Jews in the period of the Second Temple, and I was astounded by the range of his own knowledge in that field. His information was, to be sure, such as is to be found in our Jewish sources, but he added to the various incidents on which we touched a color peculiarly his own and a wealth of unfamiliar details. He was acquainted with the ceremony of bringing the first fruits to the Temple, likewise with the rituals of the Day of Atonement and of the Day of Water Pouring. I asked myself more than once where he could have obtained this knowledge, whence came those details which were unknown to us. On one occasion he even inquired of me concerning the relation of the Jews to the High Priests, and he spoke of the old High Priest Hanan, who had had five sons and a son-in-law, all of them High Priests. It was in the time of the incumbency of Joseph Kaipha, the son-in-law, that Yeshua of Nazareth had been condemned, and "the old man was not without guilt in the business . . ."—this last being added with a smile.

On another occasion, as we sat on a cold winter's night over glasses of hot tea and some Jewish white bread which I had brought with me, he asked me suddenly if there existed anywhere in the Jewish sources a list of the Ciliarchs or governors who ruled Jerusalem from the Antonia fortress. "Ciliarchs?" I asked. "Yes," he repeated, "the officers in charge of the Temple." "I have never heard of such a list," I replied. "We have the names of the High Priests, transmitted by Josephus; we also have those of the Procurators, but the Ciliarchs. . . ." "Is there no mention anywhere in your sources," he asked again, "of the Ciliarch Cornelius?" "No," I answered, "that name occurs, as far as I know, only in the New Testament, as being that of the centurion in Caesarea. I have the impression that Cornelius was also the name of the centurion of K'far Nahum." "No, no, not the centurion of K'far Nahum. Him I knew well, personally. We met often. I am speaking of the Ciliarch Cornelius who commanded the Antonia fortress and was charged with the supervision of the Temple in the time of Pontius Pilate."

I looked closely at Pan Viadomsky, and I was aware of a queer change in his appearance. The few hairs on his head were in wild disarray; his eyes glittered strangely, sending out rays of feverish light from their deep sockets. It occurred to me that the man was ill. I wanted to soothe him, to make him stop running fiercely back and forth. I suggested that perhaps it would be better for us not to pursue this topic; he ought to lie down and try to sleep. In fact, I rose, as if to go. Then, to my utter amazement, he grabbed me suddenly with his bony fingers, making me feel that a corpse had laid hands on me, and in a tone of stern command cried: "Stop!" He forced me to return to my chair while he himself sat down again in his accustomed place at the table opposite me and fixed an eager, penetrating glance on me. His face had taken on what was an extraordinary pallor even for him; the cheek-bones stood out with the sharpness of a skeleton through the thin, withered skin; the eyes, blazing in their sockets, dominated the dead face. A long time that piercing stare was fixed on me, then finally he addressed me again, calmly, but with another voice, a voice which I did not know, but a voice which I recognized as one accustomed to the issuing of commands and the utterance of sentence:

"Jew, do you not know me?" he asked. "Look well at me. Have you never seen me leading my cohort into the inner court of the Temple to restore order among you Jews?"

I was silent.

"I am Cornelius, the Ciliarch of the cohorts stationed in the Antonia; Cornelius, the lieutenant and representative of Pontius Pilate in Jerusalem. Answer, Jew! Do you not know me? Have you not seen me in the Court of the Gentiles, in the Temple, when all of you fled from my path?"

An eerie sensation filled me. I was not afraid of him, of course; there was only a feeling of pity and discomfort at this unveiling of his secret. And yet a profound curiosity as to the identity of this man held me fastened to my place; and deliberately ignoring the possibility of fantastic consequences, I went along with him, as it were, encouraging him to sink deeper into the incomprehensible role born of his sick imagination.

"Why, yes," I mumbled. "I recognize you, Cornelius, of the Antonia fortress."

"Is that the way to address me, Jew? The Jews of Jerusalem called me only by my title: Hegemon Cornelius."

"Yes, Hegemon Cornelius."

He looked again into my face.

"And have I not seen you? The curly black hair, the young, sprouting beard and the pale face—they are not unfamiliar to me. Were you not among the ringleaders of those who dared to lift their voices against the High Priest, against Pilate and even against Rome, when we were dragging Yeshua of Nazareth, with his crown of thorns, to the cross at Golgotha? Were you not among those who tried to break through our ranks in order to liberate that rebel of yours? Did not our gallant legionaries have to draw their broadswords in order to hold you back? Yes! I recognize you! For I remember that later on you were brought before me. What was your name then? Jochanan! Yes! Jochanan! The same face! I remember it till this day . . . ."

The game had gone a little too far, and consumed though I was with eagerness to hear what he still had to say, I repressed the impulse to exploit his sickness in order to uncover his secret. I tried to awaken him:

"Pan Viadomsky, Pan Viadomsky, what are you talking about, wake up, you are dreaming. . . ."

There were suspended before me two wide-open, wakeful and terrified eyes. The wakefulness did not come into the eyes all at once, but gradually, as if a mist were dispersing from before them; and the pupils, motionless of themselves, broke through, emerging from the unknown realms of night to surrounding reality, and shining more and more clearly. The more life they took on, the larger and more terrified and damper they became. It was as though Pan Viadomsky was weeping, but that the tears were falling within him. His face seemed to grow longer, and an unfathomable sorrow lay in the deep folds of his forehead and still more in the tear sacs and in the countless wrinkles about his eyes. The withered cheeks sank deeper, the jaw stuck out further, the mustaches lay like shorn wings over his drooping lips. The eyes were turned toward me, but it was only when they were cleared that he saw me. He opened his mouth to say something; the jaws remained apart, but no sound issued. The upper half of his set of false teeth, in which there were several gaps, fell on his lower gums. He lacked not only words, but breath. I could see how he was trying to draw in air through his big, distended nostrils. I could mark the passage of air into his lungs by the quiver of the Adam's apple behind the hanging skin-folds of his throat. He stretched out his convulsive fingers toward me, and drew them back. At last he found his breath, and stammering with excitement and fury, he babbled:

"Are you here?"

"Yes."

"And you heard what I said?"

"Certainly."

He was silent for a moment, while he pierced me through with his glance, which grew sharper and sharper.

"You can't leave this place any more."

"What do you mean?" I asked.

"You have heard my secret. You cannot go from this room."

"What secret? You revealed nothing to me."

He found strength enough at last to seize the arms of his chair and to lift himself erect.

"I assure you," I said, "that your secret will be sealed within me as within a tomb, and that no one will ever hear a word of it."

"That secret can be sealed only with your death," he said dramatically and, as it seemed to me, in a false, assumed tone which broke in with devastating effect on the comedy he had been playing. But what was more serious was the fact that he was moving toward the door.

"What are you doing?"

"You are remaining here, with me."

"What are you talking about?" I cried, and hastened to intercept him before he could reach the door.

Nervous, convulsive fingers and nails fastened on my flesh.

"I have said that you are remaining here, with me!"

"But what are you talking about?" I repeated and freed myself with an energetic gesture, thrusting him from me in a sudden burst of anger.

He tottered drunkenly on his feet, and would have fallen if I had not rushed to support him.

"I did not ask you to unfold your secret to me. You did it of your own accord. Go to sleep. That will calm you."

"Stop! Stop! Where are you going?"

"I don't want to remain with you," I said, standing at the door. "You are not well."

"The Jew has robbed me! The Jew has robbed me!" Pan Viadomsky began to scream.

I closed the door again, lest the sound of his voice reach the neighbors. I took him by the hand, led him to his chair, and made him sit down. He was as weak as a child, and offered no resistance.

"Pan Viadomsky, you are ill, you must calm yourself. I assure you by everything that I hold sacred that I will not reveal your secret to anyone. Calm yourself."

He remained seated, and buried his face in his hands.

I waited two or three minutes before I left the room. Once outside, I paused at the door and listened. I heard a low weeping.

I returned, went over to him, lifted him up, placed him on his bed and covered him. He suffered me to treat him like a child.

At last I was out of the house and in the open air. I hurried homeward, my mind made up that our relationship was definitely ended. I would not see him again.

CHAPTER THREE

I WAS not a little astonished when, a few days later, I was handed a letter from Pan Viadomsky. Written in a lofty, severe style, it stated that although I had behaved toward him in a manner which could only be expected from a member of my race and had filched his secret from him, he was nevertheless prepared to act toward me as a Christian and to forgive me; he therefore asked me to come to his apartment, as he needed me for an important purpose.

I naturally sent no answer.

A few days later a second missive arrived, very different in content as well as in style. There was no mention this time either of filching or of forgiveness. In fact, the whole incident was ignored; instead, he addressed me in a tone which was downright sentimental. I was surprised and, I must confess, touched. He stated frankly that he had become "accustomed" to me, and that our meetings had become a necessity to him, both on personal grounds and for reasons related to his scientific work. The exchange of ideas between us had been particularly useful to him in that they had served to refresh his memory. He therefore begged me to renew my visits. He closed the letter with the "complimentary" observation that I had proved to him the truth of the old proverb: there is no rule without its exceptions. Indeed, he added, the very exception proves the existence of the rule; the lower the general level of a community, the finer and higher are the individual exceptions.

I need hardly say that this letter, too, remained unanswered.

Then, early one morning, when dimmest twilight still reigned in my room (the snow which had fallen in the night covered my skylight window completely), I was astounded and terrified to hear footsteps on the narrow stairs—heavy, stumbling, dragging steps accompanied by a thin, racking cough. The stairs led to one door only—mine, on the top floor of a wooden house in the heart of the Jewish quarter. I could not think of a living soul who would be seeking me out at that hour; in any case, the uncertain steps and the tubercular cough recalled no one of my acquaintance. Breathless, I remained in my bed, for my room was exposed on every side to the wind, which penetrated the wooden walls, and it was too cold to get up. I lay waiting, and racked my brains in a vain effort to guess who might be approaching. Finally there came a knocking at the door. I recognized the voice which answered to my query as that of Pan Viadomsky.

I begged him to wait a moment until I could restore a little order in the room. I did this very hastily, and when I opened there fell into my arms an old man frozen almost to death.

I half carried, half dragged him over to my own chair, which stood by the stove. I thrust paper and faggots into the stove and lit a fire. Icicles hung from his wet mustaches and from the tattered and mangy fox-skin coat in which he was wrapped. He sat there, a broken old man, his eyes red and swollen, as if he had not slept for several nights. His bluish, bony fingers trembled as he held a handkerchief to his lips in an effort to keep back his coughs, and the sunken cheeks expanded and fell as the breath came and went.

"What is it, Pan Viadomsky?" I asked, deeply perturbed by his appearance. "What brings you out in such weather?"

"I came out in such weather because you would not come to me, and we have to see each other—I have to see you," he corrected himself. "I have something very important to talk over with you."

"Pan Viadomsky, move closer to the stove. You're shivering, you're ill."

"I am not ill, and I have come to you in order to talk with you concerning that matter. . . ."

"We will talk later. Calm yourself. I will put the kettle on—you will freeze—" and as he had left his place by the stove I led him back and forced him to sit down before I filled the kettle.

"I did not come to drink tea with you. I have come to discuss with you a matter which is of the utmost importance for both of us."

"If you have come here to talk about that matter, I want to assure you again that what you told me that evening has long since passed out of my memory. I know that gifted men with rich and active imaginations are subject to visions, sometimes in sleep, sometimes in their waking moments, but that is in no way a reflection on your person. I beg you to give up, once and for all, the idea that I am the guardian of your secret. There is no secret involved; it was a passing visitation or chimera which I have completely forgotten." Preparing a glass of tea for him, I used every device at my command to reassure him.

But when I held out the cup and saucer to him, he thrust them angrily away.

"I am not suffering from sick delusions, and you are not a doctor to offer me advice. This matter is much more serious than you seem to suppose. That which I told you the other evening is not the product of a diseased imagination. Do you know who I am? Do you know who sits here before you? I am the man who, under orders from Pontius Pilate, my superior officer, and according to sentence passed by the High Priest in Jerusalem, directed the execution of that mysterious personality whose nature has remained unexplained down to our own day."

"What are you talking about? Whom do you mean by 'that mysterious personality'?" I stood aghast, and my hands must have trembled, for I could feel the hot water pouring over them from the saucer.

"If you insist on knowing the name, I will pronounce it: Yeshua of Nazareth, he who is called Jesus Christ."

"But in God's name, what are you trying to tell me, Pan Viadomsky?"

"Do not call me back into this miserable world: leave me in the world to which I belong."

"But for God's sake, what are you telling me?"

"And not only did I direct his execution, but I tortured and insulted him before his death. I am the man who played the spy against him, and I bear the chief guilt for his death—I and no other."

"Pan Viadomsky, you are ill. Come, I will lay you on my bed, you must calm yourself."

"I killed him, and I kill him again every day of my life, I kill him again and again in the long, sleepless nights."

I stood benumbed. A little time passed, and Pan Viadomsky seemed to revive. He fetched a deep sigh, as if a fearful load had been lifted from his heart.

Then came a fit of coughing, after which, in a hoarse voice which betrayed something of the agitation through which he had passed, but was comparatively calm, he said:

"I suppose I can go now. I have entrusted my secret to my enemy. I have delivered myself into your hands. You can do with me as you will. There is nothing more that I could have done," and he crossed himself piously three times.

I could not find words with which to answer him. He sat, or rather crouched, like a man whom a thousand furious winds threaten to dismember. A great pity welled up in me. I did not know what it was that actually ailed him, the identity or name of his sickness; but his words had unveiled for me the boundless depths to which he consigned himself when he lay down to sleep at night, the torments which crushed and strangled his soul. I tried to say something, but the words died on my lips; it was as if a physical seal had been laid on my mouth. I was silent in my compassion.

It was he who released me. For he suddenly seized my hand, clung to it, and exclaimed:

"We have made a pact today, you and I. We are bound to each other by the common possession of the secret I have just entrusted to you. Now we can never again be separated, for we belong to each other. You are the only living man to whom I have felt it necessary to uncover my oppressed soul."

"Pan Viadomsky, be calm. This is self-delusion. When you awaken you will regret having admitted a stranger to the secrecy of your self-created fantasies. Quieten yourself. You are feverish; I can feel it in your hand. Come, I will put you to sleep in my bed,

I will cover you well"—and as I spoke I looked around in embarrassment, seeking something that might serve as a cover. "Here, I will pour another glass of tea for you. You will warm up and forget everything."

But Pan Viadomsky still clung to my hand.

"What will I forget? That which I am? That which is the purpose of my life? That to which destiny has consigned me? Do you indeed believe that all you have just heard from me is a wild and empty imagining? 'Self-created fantasies' was what you said. Can you not see that this is my veritable life? I brood on it every waking moment of the day. It is my outward life which is false, a perpetual mask. The other life, the one I lived over there, is the true and eternal one. It is with me the instant I am alone. I hear the voices of that time calling me. At night, lying in the sleepless hell which is my bed, I am transformed into the reality of my person, and I live endlessly through the life which was mine. Then I am once again in the ancient cities, I pace their streets, I encounter the faces of old. What is it you want me to forget? My life-long studies, the papers I have written, the research journeys I have made, the dangers which I have confronted, all the discoveries of unsuspected sources, the eternal ransacking of old books? Why do I pass day after day in the libraries? Why do I shut myself off from the light of day and the faces of men? And why have I confided in you, a Jew, my enemy? In order that I might forget? You are a part of that secret! You were with me in that time! When I look at your face, I remember everything. You are, like myself, the ever-enduring person among these creatures of a moment which crawl like insects about the streets; today they are here, tomorrow they will be wiped out. Who will know of them fifty, twenty-five years from now? But you and I are eternal, eternal in the flying whirlwind of dust, because we were together in that time and we live in all times, in all eternities. . . ."

I let him talk himself out, for it seemed to me that this was what he needed—to empty himself of all that had gathered in him during these last days or—who knew?—during all the days and all the sleepless nights of his life. I remained silent.

"You are silent, Jochanan?" he said, looking at me.

"What shall I answer, Pan Viadomsky?"

"Why do you call me by that false name? For you I am Cornelius, Ciliarch of the Antonia in Jerusalem."

"So be it: Cornelius. But later you will regret it."

"What will I regret? Before you there is nothing for me to regret. You and I are not of the life of today, but of the life of the past. In that far-off time there were not yet born the circumstances and prohibitions of this age, which move us to shame, which make us choose between denial and admission, and therefore create regret. You are my contemporary; you are of my family, and even more than that: you are my only companion soul. For the rest of the world, for all other men, I wear a mask. For you I am myself; from you I have nothing to hide. You and I are the only ones who have passed without loss through the sea of forgetfulness. That is why I have sought you all my life, that is why, meeting you, I entrusted my secret to you. That is why I will uncover to you all that is hidden in me, all that must remain unuttered before the rest of the world. I will uncover, and you will write down every word, every detail. For it is only through you that I become wholly myself. Only when I meet with you do I become truly timeless. That is why I am drawn to you and cannot release myself from you. I must always have you about me, and if I cannot love you, I must hate you, for without you I am dust, without you I am the pitiful Pan Viadomsky of today, crushed under a burden of sin. Then I am ashamed of Cornelius, the thought of him in me lashes me with the whip of conscience, lies on me like a millstone. But through you and in you I acquire a meaning; I am filled then with the assurance that what I did I had to do; duty dictated it. Through you and in you I become proud to be what I am—the true Cornelius. Speak! Who am I? Who stands before you? Do you recognize me?"

"Certainly I recognize you, Cornelius! The Hegemon Cornelius, commander of the Antonia fortress, before whom Jerusalem trembles like a leaf. When he passes at the head of his cohort through the Court of the Gentiles in the Temple, the crowd hides from him in terror."

These words, it seemed, calmed him more than every other device I had tried. They affected him like an opium injection into the veins of one frantic for nicotine. He took his seat again in the chair near the stove, exhausted, but relaxed and relieved.

"But now," I said, "come, I will lay you in my bed, I will make you a glass of tea; or perhaps I'd better go down and get you a piece of the Jewish white bread you like so much."

"Not before you have sworn to me, by the holy vestments of the High Priest, as the Jews were wont to do in Jerusalem."

"What shall I swear to you by the holy vestments of the High Priest?"

"That you will come to me every evening, and take down in writing what I have to tell you. You will inscribe, word by word and letter by letter, the things that happened in those days; you will set them down as they were, illumined by no other light, no other age, and no interpretation added by mankind to those events. There are many truths, and all truths have verity in them. Truth is flung into the heart by a thousand means, by the sword and the word, by tradition and faith. Only that truth is the real one which is anchored in its time, in the temporal vitals of its being. We two must rise clear out of that ocean of accepted truths which seek to pull us along in the currents of their time-justification. We must strike back to the first beginnings, of which you and I were the witnesses. You too—I know you again, Jochanan; I have taken hold of you; this time you will not escape from me—" and, as once before, he held his clenched fist at me—"and we will set down once more the record of men and events as they are for ever inscribed in the tablets of our souls: all of them, as they return to me in the nights, my old friends, my old enemies—no, not old, but of today, eternal, veritable, unchanged. Do you promise it to me, Jochanan?" And he clung to my hand as if he would never release it.

"Yes, Cornelius, I promise it, and I make an oath by the holy vestments of the High Priest."

Pan Viadomsky uttered a deep sigh.

"But now," I continued, "I believe it would be best to see you home. You need rest, and I will come to you tomorrow."

"No, not tomorrow, but this very day. I will expect you this evening. For you remember the little proverb current among you in Jerusalem: 'The time is short, the work is great.'"

"So be it, Hegemon. Your will shall be done."

CHAPTER FOUR

HE who sat confronting me at the other side of the table, steeped in the light of the hanging lamp, did not belong to our day. Outside this illumined circle the night swallowed up the surrounding room and all that was in it. We were suspended in a fathomless universe of shadows. I had before me a face of unnatural parchment-pallor which had lost all suggestion of association with a living and contemporaneous human being, but belonged, instead, to a ghost, an evocation. Past and present fused in his brain, and the fusion was reflected in his speech. In his recital he sometimes used the past tense and sometimes the present, as though the incidents were still unrolling. I set down the words exactly as he uttered them.

I am the commander of the Antonia fortress. My titular rank is that of Ciliarch; the Jews call me Hegemon. The importance and delicacy of the task entrusted to me—that of keeping a restraining hand on a people as strange and rebellious as the Jews—called for the appointment of a commander who united the abilities of the soldier with those of the administrator. I also fulfilled the functions of liaison officer and am attached to the political section belonging to Pontius Pilate, together with whom I came into this wild country. But in the course of my official duties I made numerous journeys between Jerusalem and Caesarea, also between Caesarea and Antioch, where I visited the legate Vitellus, who is our ruler and commander-in-chief. It was also in line of service that I proceeded to the neighboring Tetrarchs. I was in Caesarea Philippi, and in Tiberias. On one occasion I even found myself as far afield as the Tetrarchate of Galilee, where Herod Antipater maintained his fortress Machaerus on a stony mountain beyond the Dead Sea, surrounded by an ocean of sand and wilderness. I was the witness, in that place, of a scene which accorded well with its atmosphere of heat and desert winds. But I shall have occasion to speak of it again, in its proper place. . . .

My acquaintance with Pontius Pilate dates back to the time when we were both serving in the legions commanded by Germanicus in his war against the Germans. Pilate's rank was then no higher than mine, though he had the advantage of precedence. We were both centurions but with excellent prospects of promotion. I served throughout that entire campaign under Germanicus, took part in the fiercest battles, accompanied him on the most difficult marches, helped cut a way through the thickest, blackest and most tangled forest of that wild country of the German barbarians. I still bear on my body, to the glory of Rome and the honor of Caesar, the mark of wounds inflicted by spears and arrows sped from the shelter of trees and thickets by barbarian hands. I was with Germanicus when we took ship on that unknown river whose waters are as dark as the forests that border it; I was with him when the storm carried us to unknown shores where wild and warlike hordes awaited us. There were times when our commander led us through the blackness of the damp undergrowth and death lurked all about us, either in the hidden swamp whose treacherous surface, covered with moss and leaves, could swallow up whole legions, or in the overhanging branches whence the battle-axe might suddenly descend to fling the marcher into eternal night. And yet we thrust forward into the lightless unknown, and had it not been for the jealous and cunning Caesar Tiberius, who begrudged our commander his victories, we would have carried the Roman eagles through the black forests and planted them among the peoples of the east, who have only one eye in the middle of their foreheads and horns on either side.

When we returned to Rome with our legions we found ourselves in the shadow of the disfavor which fell upon our neglected and abandoned commander. But even then Pilate already harbored high ambitions. He had, in fact, heard that the post of Procurator of Judaea had fallen vacant, and without delay he set himself in motion to obtain it. True, the province of Judaea is a small, dull place, and its inhabitants are restless and warlike; risings occur every month or two. But he had heard that in Judaea the Procurators became rich suddenly. Gratus, the displaced Procurator, who had been recalled to Rome, acquired great wealth there as it were overnight. The noisy Jews of the country have a habit of competing among themselves for the position of High Priest. And a wonderful position it is, too! The gold of all the Jews of the world flows into the treasury of the Temple. There are four families entitled to fill that high office, and there is a wild scramble among them when it falls vacant. Brother betrays brother, son-in-law betrays father-in-law. Gratus put the High Priesthood up for auction every year among the four wealthy priestly families, and let them run like racehorses for the juicy morsel. When Pilate learned that Judaea was a cow with inexhaustible udders he set his heart on the post and resolved to let nothing stand between himself and possession.

And yet how was he to go about it? His family connections were obscure and undistinguished. He was a Spaniard by birth. His father had entered the Roman nobility by betraying his countrymen, having been among the first to go over to the Romans. Family rank did not entitle Pilate to a place in the Senate, and he could not, therefore, aspire to a Proconsular position. True, the Procurator of Judaea did not have to be of Senatorial rank, but to become the Procurator of any province one had to be a somebody.

He soon perceived that in Rome he could reach his goal only through two methods: flattery and treachery.

In the court of Caesar Tiberius there was being "brought up" at that time his stepdaughter Claudia. . . . Claudia was the daughter of Tiberius's wife, Juliana. This same Juliana, after she had acquired a third husband in Tiberius, abandoned herself to such orgies with slaves of the Imperial court that her father Augustus, the reigning Caesar, began to fear an open scandal and banished her from Rome. It was in exile that she gave birth to an illegitimate daughter, sired by some Roman knight. This was Claudia. When the girl attained her thirteenth year, her mother sent her to her husband, Tiberius, to be "educated," the latter having in the meantime inherited the purple from Augustus. Well, what "education" and "upbringing" meant at the court of Tiberius is known to all. That dissolute and treacherous fox, whose eyes were always lifted to the gods, affected to play the role of saint, and when the Senate offered to confer upon him the title of "Father of his Country," piously rejected it, and even pretended that it was against his will that he had assumed the heavy burdens of the Roman Empire. A slave of the Roman rabble, who never had the courage to take a stand against it, but victimized the aristocracy instead, Tiberius was a dissolute rake. Sick lust was written on his face, on the low forehead, the drooping lower lip, the narrow, truncated jaw: all in all, the face of a bird of prey, expressive of cunning and base passion. No one in Rome ever knew what was in the Caesar's mind; even his intimates were never certain how they stood with him, could not tell from day to day whether the trap had not been laid, the ruin prepared, as it was for the noble Germanicus. Such was the secretiveness of the man. And one of the passions of this Tiberius was to maintain at his court a "school" for little girls, whom he himself gave an "upbringing." . . . It is not hard to guess into what a pure soul little Claudia grew under his guidance. Her mother, the corrupt Juliana, had of course sent him the child of set purpose, hoping that this gift would restore her to the favor of the Caesar, her husband. Naturally all Rome knew the story, which was repeated wherever the higher social circles assembled. Dignified Senators in session whispered the details of Tiberius's "educational methods" in each other's ears, to while away the tedium of the long speeches. Ho, it was rich material for the scurrilous matrons of Rome! When they assembled in the peristyles of their villas, or in their gardens, they sent away their slaves—not because they were ashamed to talk of such matters in the presence of slaves, but rather because they were afraid of being reported—and abandoned themselves to delicious conversation concerning the Caesar and his "school."

Obviously, no Roman noble with a grain of self-respect would stoop to pick up the leavings dropped from Tiberius's table. . . . The aristocracy trembled at the thought that any day the old Caesar would order one of them to marry little Claudia, so that her reputation might be considered re-established. At this pass there suddenly appeared a volunteer—none other than our Pontius Pilate.

Pilate began by manifesting a tender and most respectful regard for the little Claudia. He could stand for hours under the columns of the Imperial palace on the Palatine or by the exit of the Circus Maximus, waiting till her slaves carried her by in her litter, for an outing or a visit to a temple. He ordered from the goldsmiths of Rome the most exquisitely wrought rings and bracelets, not only for the hands of Claudia, but for the neck of her little cockatoo. He resorted to the use of soothsayers and Chaldaean witches, of which there was no lack in Rome, as well as Alexandrian snake charmers; he hired them to stand at the gates of the palace, and to cry out to the little Claudia, whenever she emerged, that a Roman knight of Spanish origin had been decreed for her in the stars.

But his greatest help toward the fulfillment of his ambition and the conquest of Claudia's heart came, as it happened, from the Jews of Rome themselves.

A Jewish community of considerable importance had existed in Rome for ages past. How had the Jews established themselves there? Futile question! Where have they not established themselves? It is said that Pompey brought large numbers of Jewish prisoners to Rome. The unity of the Jews, an ancient and characteristic quality of theirs, led the already existent community to purchase their liberty. In the time of Caesar they even played an important role. Like all great men, Caesar had his whims, and one of them was the Jews. He encouraged them to excess, so that the great Cicero already found cause for complaint. There was again a large increase in their numbers in the time of Augustus, so that by now Rome was full of them. They were, as a matter of fact, expelled from Rome by the Caesar Tiberius for having extorted money from a Roman matron for their Temple, but within a short time they were back again. The truth is that they were not so numerous as they were visible. They crowded into the forum at every public assembly. If a favorite of theirs happened to be speaking, they were thrown into such an agitation of joy that the Roman rabble was dragged along in their enthusiasm. But if, as against this, it was an enemy of theirs who ascended the rostrum, then, the heavens defend us! there rose such a tumult, such a sneezing and coughing and whistling and interrupting, that the speaker trembled to attack them publicly. Even the great Cicero was afraid of them, and when he had something bad to say about the Jews he lowered his voice and spoke in an aside.... What a sight they were when one of their favorites came marching in triumph through the gates of Rome and up the Capitol, or when one of their supporters died: what music of lamentation pealed through the city! I remember once seeing them as they received a Jewish deputation from abroad, or it may have been one of their princes who was visiting Rome: it was as though the city was inhabited by nothing but Jews. The streets were a-flutter with their gaudy national costumes, donned for the occasion; they led forth in parade their parchment scrolls, which they called their "Holy Books," and the sound of their singing and jubilation deafened the city. I could only wonder that the authorities did not interfere. But all this was in the days of Augustus. Augustus stood by the traditions of Caesar, and therefore by the privileges he had accorded the Jews. That was the time when Rome belonged to them.

But the most pernicious influence in Rome was that of the Jewish women. These had insinuated themselves into the highest society, and served the Roman matrons as purveyors of love-philters compounded according to secret recipes, amulets and precious oils; smooth of tongue, they became secret advisers to the higher Roman circles. Side by side with their love-philters they smuggled into the Roman palaces their alien faith, propagated the greatness of their God, sang the glories of the Temple in Jerusalem, and instilled in Roman matrons the belief that all dreams would be fulfilled for one who sent a sacrifice to the Temple. Women have always been the propagators of alien faiths and cults in society. They fall easily into the toils of exotic religions—attracted by incense, miracles and the other tricks employed by the priests. Oh, those Jewish women had garnered in more than one Roman matron, set her against the gods of her country and enrolled her among the worshipers of Jehovah. They were a plague, a visitation in the imperial city, those Jewish women.

Among these purveyors of drugs and perfumes and devotees of the Jewish religion there was one who had achieved high popularity. She was known as "Dark Hannah," because she went about swathed in dark and mystic veils, like a vestal. She said she had taken a vow that as long as the sea separated her from the Temple of her God, she would not put on colored fabrics and shawls. She stood out among the other women of her kind for her wide insight, her practical cleverness and her physical beauty. The veil which fell over her face did not quite hide the shimmer of the olive skin beneath and the luster of her large, dark eyes, in their long, finely-molded sockets. She had become the special favorite of the ladies of the Roman aristocracy. It was told of her that she had an inexhaustible store of recipes, brought with her from her own mysterious country, for the mixing of love-philters. But these were of less effect than her intelligence and human insight. She had a mind as lucid as sunlight; men, no less than women, sought her out for her counsel. I too had occasion to meet her more than once, but this was later, when I was stationed in Jerusalem, and in the midst of vastly different circumstances.

This Dark Hannah played a role of some importance in Rome through the mere fact that the matrons of the city consulted her in their love difficulties. She advised them how to act in various situations. She was quiet in her bearing, listened long and patiently, spoke little, just throwing in a word or an observation from time to time, all with such skill that the matron scarcely observed the intrusion of the other's thoughts, and attributed the ideas and suggestions to her own wisdom. Frequenting, as she did, the homes of the most prominent Senators, Dark Hannah was thoroughly initiated into the complications of Roman politics. Often she was in possession of facts to which even the Senators were not yet privy. The best informed asserted that Dark Hannah was an agent of the Jewish Prince Agrippa, who had sent her to Rome to work up good feeling for him at the court in Senatorial circles.

Dark Hannah had won the confidence of little Claudia, whom she supplied with perfumes, unguents and potions. It is said that she was an evil influence over her, for while Claudia was still a child Dark Hannah filled her with the confused and confusing mysticisms of her religion, teaching her, for instance, that God was going to send down a deliverer who would lift up the Jewish people. That same bad influence Dark Hannah likewise exerted on many Roman matrons, and in particular on a famous beauty, who was pursued by all the Senators and generals, a certain Poppeia, who later became empress and was secretly converted to the faith of the Jews.

Dark Hannah came to Pilate's help.

It is said that he made her a definite promise; if she, on her side, would help him to make the match and he would become Procurator of Judaea, he, on his side, would treat her people with special consideration. He would, for instance, return the sacred vestments of the High Priest, which were being kept in the Antonia fortress. There were other favors which he promised, but this one in connection with the vestments of the High Priest was the most important, for the Jews believed that the vestments had been brought down from heaven. It was due to Dark Hannah, in the end, that little Claudia turned her affections toward Pilate.

But even then, the post of Procurator of Judaea still remained to be won. He had taken only the first step. The cunning Caesar Tiberius detested flattery; it was not the proper approach to him. Action alone could convince him, and in exchange for so important a position it would have to be action of special value.

Before long Pilate found the opportunity to demonstrate his devotion to the Caesar and to win his regard. Germanicus, the general who had fallen out of favor, went to Alexandria. We, his former soldiers, persuaded him to this course. Pontius Pilate insisted that he, Germanicus, should seek somewhere outside of Rome, and preferably in the great city of Alexandria, that field of effectiveness which Tiberius had taken away from him in Rome; and I, following Pilate's lead, took up the argument. We kept on repeating to him: "Make good use of your popularity throughout the Empire while it lasts; your fortune lies outside of Rome." He was reluctant. We urged again: "Alexandria is the training ground for the great of Rome." "Yes," he said, "but remember Pompey and Antony. And Caesar too would have been caught in the tangles of Alexandria, if it had not been for Herod. . . ."

We went on talking, and he finally walked into the trap which the subtle Tiberius had prepared for him—Alexandria. And there, in Alexandria, he was, as you know, poisoned by the Governor of Syria, on command from Tiberius. When the knowledge of his death came to Rome, the rabble rushed into the streets, and called upon Tiberius and the Senate to give them back Germanicus. The Emperor, a coward by nature like every traitor, took fright, not having foreseen that the death of Germanicus would stir up such resentment. He tried to cleanse himself of guilt by arranging an imposing funeral for his victim. He was loudest in his lamentations for the dead Germanicus. But even at that moment, before the earth had covered the murdered general, Pilate was circulating among the Senators and the plebs the rumor that Germanicus had been plotting to wrest the Empire from Tiberius, and had gathered an army to that end in Egypt and Asia. It was a dangerous thing for Pilate to do in those days, and he had to proceed with the utmost caution; for the general love for Germanicus still ran high, and only here and there could Pilate drop his poison into receptive ears. But Pilate was resolute. He had even prepared forged documents which supported his contentions and asserted that Germanicus had drawn him, as well as myself, into the conspiracy. He brought me before Tiberius to testify that Germanicus had hired me to proceed to Asia in order to enroll in the Asiatic legions. Pilate succeeded; he washed Tiberius clean; and in the process he trampled underfoot the name and reputation and memory of the hero, his own commander, who had led him and me through the dark forests of Germany to glorious victories for Rome.

Pilate's reward was not long in coming. A few months after the death of Germanicus, when the rage of the plebs had been soothed with the sight of much blood shed in gladiatorial shows—all of them arranged, of course, to this end, by the Emperor—the marriage of Pilate with the Emperor's stepdaughter Claudia was celebrated with much pomp in the Temple of Diana.

After the wedding, when the bridegroom wanted to enter the litter of his young bride, he found his way barred by the Emperor. Instead of his wife, Pilate was handed a parchment scroll with the Emperor's orders to proceed at once to Caesarea, and thence to Jerusalem, where he was to take up the office of Procurator of Judaea.

"And my wife?" asked the new husband.

"For the time being you will leave your wife at Caesar's court. You know that it is not the custom for Procurators or generals to take their wives with them into the provinces. Later on, perhaps, I will send her to you," the old fox answered, and the shadow of a cruel smile trembled on his sensuous, overhanging lower lip.

When Pilate came to pay his last respects to Caesar before leaving Rome, the latter gave him his final instructions.

"Pilate, you have no doubt heard that I do not like to change my officials. Do you know why? The officials who settle in a country are like flies settling on a body; when the flies have had their fill of blood, they become quiet and peaceable. See to it that I don't have to send a new, thirsty fly to the province of Judaea. . . ."

When Pilate set out for Judaea he took me along, because of our old friendship. I received the post of chief councilor to the Procurator, liaison officer, and commander of the Antonian fortress guarding the Temple in Jerusalem.

CHAPTER FIVE

FOLLOWING the Caesar's orders we took boat for Caesarea, but our stay there was very brief; we hastened on to Jerusalem. To make our entry into the city as imposing as possible, we drew into our train a cohort from the garrison of Jericho; another came to meet us from the Antonia, supported by German cavalry; and with Pontius Pilate at the head of the procession we marched into Jerusalem. In accordance with the privileges of the Jews, special orders were issued by Pilate before the cohorts entered the city: the eagles and the other ensigns of the cohorts, the bundles of arrows, the likeness of the Emperor, were to be covered and hidden! We were astounded by this act of *crimen laesae majestatis.* Were we to hide the emblems of Rome, the visible evidences of our triumphs and glories, at the behest of a crowd of Jews? Everywhere else in the world the legions carried them proudly in the light of day, nations hailed them with frenzied cries of admiration and respect, the gates were flung wide open to receive them—and here, before the gates of Jerusalem, they disappeared!

But what could we soldiers do? The order was given, it had to be obeyed. The religion of the Jews had been granted official recognition by Rome. The strategy of Rome was to grant the barbarians every liberty in connection with religion. Augustus Diva had confirmed the privileges of the Jews, which had been established by Caesar; and Tiberius was scrupulous in his observance of all the laws and customs followed by his predecessor Augustus. There was no help for it! But where, we asked, were the deputations from the country and the city, where were the representatives of the religious and civic authorities, the wise men and the law-givers, to receive and greet Rome's representative, the deputy of the Caesar, the Procurator of Judaea? We waited in vain for them at the Hebron gate. I saw Pilate's face turning wax-yellow with rage. And then, at last, there came toward us, in undignified haste, a handful of Jews in white robes; some of them had their heads covered with shawls, some of them had their hair dressed high, in the Chaldaean style, still others had curled beards after the manner of the Persians. The leader was an old man with a long white beard descending in ranged curls. He, as I learned later, was Hanan, the father-in-law of the regnant High Priest; he had himself been High Priest in years past. This old man passed as a friend of Rome, and he constituted himself the High Priest's representative at official receptions. I shall have much to say in the sequel concerning Hanan, who not only knew how to handle the Jews and to retain the power in his hands, but by his cunning maneuvers even exercised an enormous influence on the Procurator himself. Here it is sufficient to set down that among all the notables of Jerusalem he alone came to greet us at the gate of the city. The others were, without exception, hired "representatives," that is, men paid for taking on themselves the degrading task of greeting Rome! They were chosen for it because of their fine figures and their long, curled beards; apart from this, they represented nobody. There was not among them a single teacher of the law, at any rate, not a single distinguished one. There were present, indeed, two or three "notables" of sorts, minor figures, even members of the Sanhedrin, but they were of Hanan's inner circle, of the Sadducees. The old man had always found it difficult to put together a decent, representative deputation for official Roman celebrations; and he had hit on the device of paying a few men of fine appearance to fulfill the role; just as the Jews in their religious practices pay those individuals who have the dubious honor of reading forth the Section of Curses from their Holy Scroll. . . .

All this, of course, we did not know until afterwards. Meanwhile we were under the impression that the high notables of Jerusalem, the sages and the scholars, had come forth to greet us in the name of the city. It did not take us long to discover our error, in fact no longer than it took us to enter the city. The streets were empty, as if after a plague. We understood, of course, that only a few minutes before our arrival these same streets must have been swarming; indeed, the dust of innumerable footsteps had not yet had time to settle, and the last murmur of an excited multitude still seemed to hang in the air. Suddenly, as if a great hand had swept them all away, or as if the approach of the angel of death had given them wings of terror, they were gone! The columned arcades of the houses of the aristocracy, which at that time of day were usually thronged with men and women seeking shelter from the sun, were now utterly deserted. The shopkeepers had put up their shutters to hide their merchandise, but the jars filled with oil and honey remained standing on the steps; they were too heavy to be moved in a hurry. There was no living being to be seen. In one spot a dealer in pots had left his earthenware jars and plates on a wooden stand in the street; he himself had fled. Our legions marched straight on the rows of earthenware and trampled it into fragments. In another street we came upon donkeys laden with skins of wine and jars of oil, and no one in charge of them. In the Street of the Spices the spice-grinders were silent, the dried spices and roots lay spread on the tables, and no person was about. It was the same in the Street of the Weavers. Motley woolen and flaxen fabrics were stretched on the looms, and not a person near them. . . . So we marched, as through the empty streets of an abandoned city: except that from behind the high fences which surrounded the houses, from behind the pillars and the curtains stretched across the galleries, there came to our ears the ominous murmur of an excited throng, like the rush and beat of waves heralding an approaching storm. . . . Now and again, indeed, we could glimpse, behind the lattices shutting off the flat roofs, agitated groups; from time to time we could catch the flash of hostile eyes directed into the street. And doubtless thousands of eyes filled with hatred were trained upon us as we marched past. We could hear behind us the multitude pouring out again from their houses, from behind walls and pillars.

That first entry into the city taught us what we could expect from its inhabitants. The pealing of our trumpets died without an echo in the deserted streets. And so we marched between the dumb walls which sheltered a hidden enemy until we reached the upper section of the city. Here the population was friendlier; laughing faces were turned down upon us from the casements; cheerful groups in the shadows of the formal arcades greeted us; and finally we came upon a place which may be compared to the Palatine Hill in Rome.

This, I guessed, must be the place of residence of their kings, princes, High Priests and nobles. We were astonished by the sight of an antique-looking building with mighty towers, all in an alien style of architecture. This was not a palace, but a fortress with gigantic walls composed of enormous blocks of dressed stone fitted into each other at the edges, and so massive in appearance that they suggested less the handiwork of human beings than some sort of unnatural growth out of the earth. Ionic columns built into the walls kept guard like dead sentinels around this mysterious structure. There were neither lattices nor windows, neither loopholes nor balconies, to break up the stern uniformity of the exterior. Only high up, above the arched entrance, a stone lattice sat like a crown, with places for a lookout: and up above these shot a conical-shaped tower, rising into the skies. It was one of the loftiest buildings in Jerusalem. As we learned later, it was an ancient royal edifice, dating back to the time of the Hasmoneans, and even today, when one of the Tetrarchs or Herodian Princes came up to Jerusalem, this building was reserved for his use. Around this tower of the Hasmoneans palace after palace sprang from the earth, sheltered by high cypresses and surrounded by mighty gates. Loftiest and mightiest was the palace of the reigning High Priest or, as they called it, "The Tower of the House of Hanan." I had occasion later to spend hours resting in its pleasant gardens or bathing in its refreshing pools and basins; much of the dreariness of my stay in Jerusalem was made tolerable by them. But of this I shall have more to say later.

Beyond these towers and palaces were still rows of imposing edifices; there was the Council House of Jerusalem, with the national archives. That abutted on the bridge leading from the higher part of the city to the place of the Temple. From afar off we caught a glimpse of the friendly, familiar images of the great theaters, in the form of the Circus Maximus, built by Herod: an echo of home, awakening home-longing. Oh, how those Jews hated the magnificent theater buildings, rising magnificently toward the sky with their circular, temple-like architecture. Every time a Jew went past a theater he muttered a prayer thanking his God that he was not called upon to sit there, or to visit the temples of the Olympian deities. What miserable ignorance! But I shall keep my observations on Jewish intolerance for another occasion.

The upper part of the city was encircled by a wall set with towers. These were the three towers which the great Herod had erected as monuments to the three who had been closest to him in their lives—his father, his brother Feisal and his wife Miriam. Actually these structures were not just towers; they were enormous buildings with many underground caves, prisons, garrison quarters, slave and servant quarters and vast rooms which could accommodate great numbers. The most magnificent as well as the most interesting of the buildings was the Miriam Tower, dedicated to the memory of Herod's wife, whom he had had legally murdered out of jealousy. As if to recall to life the womanliness of his victim, he erected a monument in the form of a palace with graceful and noble lines suggesting the image of woman. The Miriam Tower, like the other buildings, was constructed of the regular rock on which Jerusalem stood; but the structure had so been modeled that it brought to mind the noble curves of a Greek vase. He had poured into the stone all his vain longing for his dead wife. The entire, massive façade of the building consisted of nothing more than a lofty and gigantic platform above which a conical tower, whose shape suggested a woman's breast, rose into the heavens. Hard by the Miriam Tower the mighty Herod palace lay like a sprawling Hercules, shutting off the chain of the tower palaces. This was less a single palace than a cascade of stone structures, marble columns, stairways, lookout posts, pouring westward and linking up with the wall which encircled the city. We knew that the Herod palace was the largest and most magnificent in

Jerusalem; it was surrounded by halls and by Corinthian columns, so that it could well have taken its place in the very heart of Rome and competed with the best in the Forum of Augustus. The Herod palace was the official seat of the Procurator whenever he was in Jerusalem. With its complement of a cohort of men it was our most important strategic point of power in the city.

From his litter Pilate issued the command that we were to continue on our march across the bridge which connected the uppermost part of the city with the place of the Temple. But before we could pass under the one gate which leads into the mysterious area of that Temple concerning whose sanctity and wealth we had heard so much, we had to pass by an unusually large edifice built into the wall which encircled the Temple. On the roof of this edifice rose a tower surmounted by a dome so that, except for the absence of columns, it looked like a Temple of Diana. The palace was constructed, again, of large blocks of stone fitted cunningly into each other. This was their great hall of justice or, as they called it, their Sanhedrin. Actually, as we learned later, it was their Senate. But soon we found ourselves in the midst of an opulence and magnificence which amazed us.

Our military procession had now entered the outermost court of the Temple, called by them the "Court of the Gentiles," because to it the uncircumcised could still be admitted. If the place of the towers might be likened to the Palatine Hill of Rome, this Court of the Gentiles could be designated the Forum of Jerusalem. It played for the capital of the Jews the role played by the Roman Forum for us.

I should never have imagined that behind the massive walls which surrounded the outer court of their Temple there was room for such tumultuous movement as we encountered. But it was here that the real life of Jerusalem was mirrored. We found ourselves between two walls or, more correctly, between two rows of columned arcades. The section leading toward the outer wall was studded with four rows of Corinthian columns; the floor was worked throughout in mosaic, while above us stretched a roof of cedar wood. Here we found a multitude of shops, stands and moneychangers' tables, among which circulated an enormous and motley multitude. Along the line of columns which followed the wall of the inner Temple court there were countless balconies, labyrinths of buildings which must have housed innumerable inhabitants; we saw, through the apertures of the balconies, the gleam of unfriendly eyes. We did not have time to take close note of our surroundings; our faces were turned forward in the direction of our march, which now led us toward the fourteen rows of marble steps which barred our approach to the inner entrance of the Temple.

The gateway was open, but across it stretched a golden chain on which still hung the fragments of a broken eagle. That eagle had once symbolized the might of Rome; it had been placed there by Herod the Great in honor of the Caesar, but the fanatical Jews had broken it off. Herod had punished the Jews with a massacre for this act and had restored the eagle, but the Jews had removed it again. The blood grew hot in our hearts when we saw this evidence of lèse-majesté, and it was with feelings of mingled anger and sorrow that we approached the fourteen steps, where we were awaited by a deputation with the High Priest at its head.

The High Priest was not wearing his official vestments. He was wrapped from head to foot in a glittering mantle of silver thread, the symbol not of his religious but of his civil power. He was a man of lofty stature, like his father-in-law; again like his father-in-law he wore his beard in the double-pointed style, but in his case the beard was more curled. On his head he carried a crown-like tiara, and on his forehead flashed a diadem. But most striking in his appearance were the heavy curls which flowed from under the tiara. They had been woven with such extraordinary art, so delicately and minutely, that the headdress resembled the product of an unimaginably fine loom. The suite accompanying him was not particularly large, and contained very few Priests. These could be distinguished from the other members by their pure white garments, their trousers and tunics, their colored girdles and their cap-like headcoverings. As we learned later, they were his brothers-in-law and the officials of various departments, treasurers and overseers.

The High Priest excused himself before Pilate for not having appeared with as large a retinue as was fitting for a reception to the Roman Procurator. He explained that the Priests were having a busy day in the Temple. The Jews of Babylon, of Persia and of northern Africa had sent in large consignments of cattle to be offered up as sacrifices in the Temple, and the Priests were occupied in the holy services. As against this, however, he could report that there were present in his suite the first representative of the Temple after himself, a former High Priest, and all the other high functionaries. These, the sons of Hanan and his brothers-in-law, represented not only the Temple and the Priesthood, but likewise the highest court, the Sanhedrin. He alluded also to another two or three old men, whom he introduced as important interpreters of the law, sages as it were. They too, he said, were friends of the Romans, for they belonged to the party of enlightenment which wanted peace with the Romans, to wit, the party of the Sadducees.

Pilate's fleshy nose sank downward; he glanced at the party furtively from under his heavy eyelids and said, briefly:

"That we shall see. It depends on good will."

"On one side at least that good will always exists," answered the High Priest.

"That will have to be proved by deeds," said Pilate, and made a sign to the trumpeters to continue on the march. They began to ascend the steps toward the gate leading to the inner court of the Temple.

The face of the High Priest turned pale under the flashing tiara. "The residence of the Procurator is in the city," he cried, terrified, and pointed outward. "In the Herod palace."

"I know that. But I plan to pass this night with my troops in their quarters in the Antonia," answered Pilate, and signaled to the trumpeters to resume their march.

Suddenly there came a wild pealing from the rams' horns of the sentinels posted in the balconies about the gate, and the two massive, gold-covered doors swung to from within. We were shut out.

The High Priest, pale as death, his eyes glittering like the blade of a sword, stood in the middle of the closed gate, and without uttering a word pointed to the two bronze tablets in the wall on either side of the gate; on these appeared, in Greek and Latin, the following inscription: "Beyond this point none of the uncircumcised may pass, under penalty of death."

"Ah, yes . . ." said Pilate, and I observed the trembling in his thick lower lip, while an angry color mounted his face. "I had almost forgotten. And yet, if I am not mistaken, Romans have passed under that gate. I should like to know how Pompey captured the Temple, undeterred by those inscriptions."

"He made use of the Sabbath, Procurator, when the Jews may defend themselves but are forbidden to attack. Today we are a little more advanced. In any case, he received his punishment from God, and the great Caesar took vengeance on him for us."

"It appears that your God is quite powerful, to have such strong alliances."

"All the greatest men of Rome, with mighty Caesar at their head! And it is our hope that the new Procurator of Judaea will be among them," said the High Priest, with a disarming smile.

"That will depend on the attitude of his believers. Centurion, lead the cohorts back to the Procuratorium."

Pilate himself, accompanied by a small detachment, made his way to the Antonia through the Court of the Gentiles.

We passed between two columned walls. Under these columns were the stalls of the merchants who sold the smaller sacrifices for the Temple. There were dealers in turtledoves of a special kind fit for sacrifice, dealers in spices and incenses, dealers in fine white meal and in precious oils, dealers in all such objects as could be brought before the priests as offerings for purification from sin, or in payment of the tributes laid by their God Jehovah on his chosen people. And besides these there were the moneychangers, sitting at their tables and accepting against the currency of the country the currencies of many lands. What an extraordinary assortment of men and of costumes was to be seen here under the columned walls! There were Jews from Abyssinia with white sheets about their bodies, and barefoot; Jews of Alexandria or the noble Greek islands in woolen and rough sheepskin garments, with palms and golden circlets on their curled heads; Jews from the desert draped in camel hides or even lion skins; men of Galilee in simple working garb consisting of sackcloth, their faces hardened like rock by sun and labor; there were the poor, whose wretched clothes scarcely hid their nakedness, and the rich, with gold rings on their hands, and gold stripes on their mantles of fine linen woven and dyed in Zidon. There were also Jews from remote Babylon, where the legions of Rome have never penetrated, and Jews from the cold west, where the footsteps of legions have been heard; and Jews from the Rhine with heavy head coverings of wild skins. I did not know, until I saw this vast diversity of faces and costumes in the Court of the Gentiles, that the Jews were so widely scattered throughout the Roman Empire and beyond its borders. I became convinced of the wisdom of Cicero who warned us against the evil influence of this people, which fills all the markets of east and west and has footholds in all the known and unknown lands. I must confess that when I gazed on the multicolored crowds, the riot of costumes, the varieties of racial shadings which swarmed through the gates of Judaea's Temple, I began to appreciate the foresight of the Roman rulers who had always exerted themselves to remain on friendly terms with the Jews, had respected their religious cult and had accorded them special privileges. . . . A people so diffused throughout the world, able everywhere to exert influence, must enter into the calculations of every ruler.

I paid close attention to the people and to the commerce which went on about the Temple. I knew that I should long continue to have dealings with them. I could not help being impressed by the religious ecstasy which they manifested even in this place, outside the Temple wall, as they made their purchases for their little sacrifices; I noticed with what infinite care they examined the doves, choosing the sleekest, the richest in feathers, the most perfect in appearance. I noticed with what rejoicing they exchanged their good gold for precious oils and essences, compounded of the most exotic incense plants, and for the fine white meal; it was as though they were choosing gifts for a beloved or a present for a mighty ruler whose favor they sought; not at all as though these tenderly chosen objects were to be dedicated to some imaginary deity, whom none of them had ever seen and to whom no artist had yet given eternal form in marble or bronze. As far as I could make out, their religious service actually began there and then with the purchase of their sacrifices. They did not bestow a glance on our cohorts, marching through their midst. They did not manifest the slightest interest in their new Procurator, being carried past in his litter. They were too deeply absorbed in the purchases they were making for their God. I observed one poor woman, whose only dress was a covering of sackcloth through which showed glimpses of her skin; she was engaged in purchasing—it must have been with the last of her money—two turtledoves; and when she had obtained possession of them she kissed them, she pressed them to her bosom, she caressed them; she murmured to them with an expression of such extreme piety that she seemed to be entrusting them with a message which they were to deliver into the ear of her God. I saw a broad-shouldered and powerful man holding in timid and tender fingers a twig of incense; he seemed to be afraid of crushing it; he gazed on it with imploring eyes, as if the plant had the magic power to lift off his shoulders the burden of sin which crushed him. I saw youngsters hurrying by with pans of white meal and cruses of oil. There was a universal and happy absorption in the service of the Temple, and no one had a glance to spare for the man who had been sent from the center of the Empire to wield over them the power of life and death. Deprived as we were of the emblems of our legions, of our eagles and shields, we did not look like a Roman legion marching through a city subject to Rome, like the entourage of a Procurator sent out to govern a province, but like a loose band of wandering mercenaries in the camp of a foreign army. I looked from time to time at Pilate lying in his open litter, and I saw that his heavy face and thick neck were flushed with blood, that the veins on his temples stood out and throbbed. His will rebelled; he was brooding on revenge. But his patience seemed to cost him so much effort that I feared he would have a stroke of apoplexy.

At one point we came upon a large crowd gathered before a speaker, no doubt a teacher or interpreter of the law, who stood leaning against a pillar under the wooden roof of a shop and addressed himself to the assembled. So absorbed were they in his words that they did not hear the sound of the trumpets which heralded our coming; either that, or else they deliberately ignored us and did not get out of our way. It was as well that we were not accompanied at this point by our German cavalry! A couple of our legionaries sprang from the ranks and with the points of their broadswords reminded the Jews of the presence of the Imperial representative.

They simply scattered the mob and opened up a way for the litter and its cortege. Looking again at Pilate I could see that he was no longer red with anger; he had turned almost blue! But soon the flame of his rage died down; the promising glitter of gold soothed his fiery mood.

We were marching along the eastern side of the Court of the Gentiles when we came suddenly upon a gate which made us open our eyes with speechless amazement. We had heard a great deal concerning the immeasurable opulence of the Temple, but the sight of a huge gate of solid Corinthian bronze staggered us. This was the entry to the Court of the Women, which was densely crowded, for access was afforded here to gentile as well as Jewish women. The gate had been left open, whether by inadvertence or not I could not tell; and scarcely had we taken in the sight of this incredible mass of Corinthian bronze when we caught, from the other side of the Court of the Women, a blinding glare of gold; we saw, not a gate, but an enormous tower, covered with gold, leading from the Court of the Women into the inner Temple. As we learned later, this was in fact the "Beautiful Gate," of which we had heard even in Rome, a gift to the Temple from just one rich Jew of Jerusalem. Above that Tower Gate hung a huge golden cluster of grapes, the emblem of the Jews. But the quick glimpse which we obtained of the glories beyond that gate was beyond all our imaginings. The Temple was built in the form of a pyramid; there was an ascent of high steps from one hall to the other, and the inmost temple stood like a mountain of gold on a lofty marble platform. Whichever way we looked, gold, always gold, flashing in the light of the afternoon sun. Our eyes watered with weariness, astonishment and appetite. But soon the alarm sounded, blown on huge rams' horns by the sentinels on the outlook posts, and the huge bronze doors swung to before our eyes. We saw now only the nearer gates, and we observed that on their glittering and fine-wrought surface there appeared no image of man or beast; it was as though their God Jehovah was jealous of the imaginations of men and would permit no adornment in His Temple, demanding to be served with that which He alone had created, the bare material given to man. And indeed, these gates, like the Temple as a whole, produced an overwhelming effect. It was as though the elements themselves had wrought this structure, which seemed therefore to have risen out of the earth.

And looking now at Pontius Pilate I saw amazement written on his face.

"Procurator," I said, "the first thing you will have to do on reaching the Antonia, is to send for leeches, to have the bad blood drawn from your veins."

"I am thinking of very different methods for ridding myself of my bad blood."

"I know it, Procurator. By drawing the blood of the Jews."

He tried to laugh.

CHAPTER SIX

THE Antonia Fortress lay on the northern side of the Temple; reared on lofty rocks, it dominated and overshadowed the Temple area. It consisted of several buildings, among which were our regular barracks, enclosing a yard large enough to contain a place for exercising the troops, a gymnasium, and swimming baths. In the center was the citadel proper with its four towers. It rose on a pyramid-like base framed about the summit of the rock. From the galleries of the citadel there was a clear view of the Temple area, and we could always see what was going on there. Ho, there was discontent enough among the Jews about that fact; and there were rebellions expressing that discontent. Whenever our guards became visible to them in their march around the galleries, the Jews would shake their fists, white cloths would flutter, and the cry would go up: "Away! Away!" It need hardly be said that our guards paid little attention to these demonstrations; if at all, they lingered for a moment in their stride, to take the scene in better. There was also direct access from the Antonia to the Temple area, two flights of steps separated by a partition wall; but this wall could easily be taken apart, and there was no serious obstacle between us and the Temple area. And, unknown to most, there was a secret passage, built by Herod, leading straight from the fortress not into the Temple area, but right into the Temple itself.

Arriving, we took over the command of the cohort stationed in the Antonia, changed the guard, and went to refresh ourselves in the baths. Pilate had dinner served in the citadel gallery, whence, leaning comfortably in his chair, he could observe at his leisure his new, unruly subjects in their own Temple Courts. Cooled by parasols which shielded us from the light of the setting sun, we sat near him and could look down on the Temple, the city of Jerusalem, and all its hilly surroundings. It seemed to us as though the sunlight were melting into the hot, sandy walls of Moab's mountains, visible on the other side of the Dead Sea. The clarity of the air brought them close to our eyes. Sunlight was reflected, on the other side, from the countless golden thresholds, lintels and gates of the Temple; at that moment one would have said that it was not built of stone and metals but consisted of a single flow of molten gold. Among the golden flames fluttered blue and purple hangings. A thousand beams of light, in as many colors, shone back from the fantastic structure, massive in the simplicity of its construction, yet light and aerial in its effect by reason of the many walls which consisted of nothing more than fluttering curtains in reddish purple and light blue. As we learned later, the colors of the curtains were supposed to symbolize the four elements out of which the world was made: fire, air, earth and water. The entire building stood on foundations of white marble; and all about it, as though to guard it tenderly, and as though to accentuate its unique sanctity, countless courts were grouped, sundered from each other by fantastically high towers and gateways, rows of columns and niches; and these again were, like the Temple itself, separated from each other by walls and pillars. In a sense more interesting even than this extraordinary Temple and its surroundings was the life that filled the courts. There seemed, to the hasty view, to be nothing but confused motion down there; the white-robed Priests, walking barefoot, with pious and measured tread, on the polished marble and granite, seemed to be moving over the waters of a lake; the entire mass of human beings seemed to be single and undifferentiated; but more careful observation dispelled that notion, and it was seen that the Priests were kept apart from the rest of the multitude in strictest discipline—one might have called it military discipline. After the first dazzle had passed, we could observe clearly the court in which the women were massed, the court of the men, the steps on which were ranged the musicians; there was a separation, again, between the outer court of the Sanctuary, where the Priests assembled between services, and the inner court of the Sanctuary, where the Priests were occupied with the sacred service. All this, we perceived, was severely and exactly divided, as though we had before us not a nation of believers gathered in its temple, but a military organization ready for inspection. We discovered later that the Priests and the Levites and all the other Temple servants were indeed disciplined like the members of a military organization. The doormen, the night watchmen who made the rounds with torches in their hands in order to control the doormen, the nightmen who called the hours, the trumpeters, the first, second, and third divisions of Priests, the Priests in service and those that were off duty, the overseers, the lamplighters, the women weavers, the overseers for the sacrifices, which had to be passed and stamped, the innumerable ceremonial attendants—in brief, the entire vast and complicated activity of the Temple—represented a highly disciplined association, subject to the authority of the High Priest and his many delegates, who constituted his immediate entourage.

We lay stretched on couches in the gallery of the citadel, cooled by parasols and by oriental fans; we drank wine of Cyprus and ate Jericho figs and gazed down into the Temple of Jehovah, whose jealousy was such that no mortal might look on his face. The Temple with its incalculable treasures of gold, with its costly vessels, its Priests and Levites and proud scholars, lay, side by side with the entire city, at our feet. We were fascinated by the spectacle. From the height of our observation post the swarming thousands had the aspect of helpless pygmies; they, together with their God, were delivered into the mighty hand of Rome, our hand—mere booty taken as the lion takes up his prey. We could not understand from what source they derived their pride and self-assurance. One word of command, one cohort of Askelon legionaries supported by a detachment of German cavalry, and the silly game of divinity and independence would be over; the Holy of Holies would be violated, the treasures seized, the Priesthood scattered like chaff before the wind. And they knew it. We read it in the glow of hatred which showed in the eyes of a white-robed Priest, of a long-bearded scholar. Yes, they knew they were as firmly in our hands as toys in the hands of children. And we found incomprehensible their pride and their senseless delusions about their God.

Marcus Petronius, the old centurion of the Antonia, who had served under the first Procurators and had been in the country many years, knew all the manners and customs and beliefs of the Jews and explained them to us. He it was who informed me first concerning the severe discipline which reigned in the Temple, the queer guard changes of the Priests and Levites, the night watchmen marching in military formation with their torches, and the sentinels exchanging the watchword "Is all well?" When the sun's first rays appear the rams' horns are sounded. A detachment of Priests proceeds in marching order to the first service. Marcus told us further concerning the vestments of the High Priest, which they consider so sacred that they swear by them. The vestments are kept in one of the towers of the citadel, and the lamp burning at the top proclaims that they have not been touched. They lie under the seal of the Procurator and of the High Priest. Just try to put that lamp out, and see what happens! Marcus related more regarding the Holy of Holies, which no mortal may enter save the High Priest in his holy vestments—and even he only once a year. And what a tremendous occasion it is for them when the High Priest issues from the Holy of Holies unblasted by its sanctity!

Pilate, who listened with keen interest to this description of the exotic customs of the Jews, asked Marcus Petronius whether in his opinion there really was, in the Jewish sanctuary, a mystic inner chamber which it was dangerous for a mortal to enter; and whether this inner chamber contained an ass's head, as the Roman legionaries affirmed—this same ass's head being the object of all these Jewish devotions and ceremonies.

"An ass's head? Pompey, who penetrated into the Holy of Holies, saw no ass's head. Indeed, he saw nothing whatsoever, and I do not know what it contains. I myself have only been in the outer halls, to which the sacrifices are brought; I broke in on the morning of a festival, when it was necessary to restore order. What I saw there was an incredible quantity of gold, golden tables, a gigantic golden altar, on which a tremendous fire burned, a golden candelabrum, countless golden jars, tongs and other vessels and instruments necessary to their ceremonies, and two mystic birds covered by their own wings. I saw everywhere the glitter of gold."

"It seems that the Jews do not begrudge their deity gold. I should only like to know where they get so much of it."

"Where? All Jews throughout the world pay taxes to the Temple as to a Caesar. For that matter, it is exactly what they say: God is our Caesar. And the joy with which they pay the taxes! Not one of them evades payment, not one of them is late or in arrears, no matter on what wild, distant island he lives. And not only the taxes. You should see the free-will gifts they send to the Temple. Do you see that tremendous gate, with its turrets overtopping all the other gates—there at the entrance from the Court of the Women to the inner court? That gate is worth a kingdom. On one side the doors are covered with silver plates, and on the other side with plates of gold; and it is the gift of one man. But there are others like him. You should see from what remote places of the earth they assemble here! Sometimes you would not believe that they are Jews; and then again, sometimes you come across men of obviously civilized bearing. But I personally doubt whether they are Jews. They are non-Jews, attracted by the mystic power which their God radiates, so that they bring him their prayers, their sacrifices and their gifts. The gold which you see here on the Temple doors is nothing. They have secret treasuries in which are accumulated the gold gifts of all the generations; and no matter how often they are bled of their gold, it flows back again from inexhaustible sources."

"The Jews are not without influence in the Caesar's court," said Pilate.

"It is hard to tell how far their influence goes and what circles they have penetrated; you never know, either, whom you affront if you happen to fall foul of the Jews. More than once sacrifices have arrived here sent—secretly or openly—by some of the highest personages in Rome; worse still, they tell me that the Jews have created much sentiment in favor of their incomprehensible God among the ladies of the aristocracy."

"Yes, I know it; I know, too, the methods they use to create this sentiment."

A spasm passed across Pilate's face; unseen by the others he twitched my toga and made as if to say something; but he suddenly bit his lip and remained silent.

"That," said someone, "is the way of women: they are always ready to be victimized by unintelligible mysteries."

But before Pilate left Jerusalem to go up to his capital, Caesarea, he said to me:

"We have learned from Marcus Petronius that the Jews do make use in their Temple of figures of mystic birds; so their opposition to the Roman eagle is based on political and not on religious grounds; their religion does not forbid them to gaze on the Roman symbol of power; their aversion springs from their enmity to Rome. I say that the Roman eagle is our emblem throughout the whole world, and wherever the power of Rome has spread, the emblem must not be absent."

"Is that a command?" I asked.

"As you understand it."

With Pilate's departure from Jerusalem I assumed command of the citadel. On one side of the Antonia, facing the new section of the city, there was a deep cleft. I ordered my German horsemen, for whom the Jews had a particular hatred, to take up their position along the cleft. Then I ordered my men to pour oil and fat on that side of the citadel rock which faced the Temple, so that the covering of marble blocks became slippery to the foot. At night, when these orders had been carried out, I commanded that the shields with the emblems of our cohort and the images of the Caesar be hung out along the gallery of the citadel. I also had them extinguish the lamp which burned at the summit of the tower where the vestments of the High Priest were kept, and substitute in its place the Roman eagle.

Early next morning, before sunrise, I stationed myself, together with my guards, in the citadel gallery, to see how the Jews would respond to these dispositions. When the first rays of the sun broke out from behind the eastern hills we heard the pealing of their trumpets. We saw the first detachment of the Priests advancing in regular formation; they were returning from their ablutions to put on the vestments of their office and take over the service. Suddenly, as if at a word of command, they came to a halt. The first sunlight was being flashed back by the eagle and the shields. What a change came over their faces! What a howl went up! It was as though a thunderbolt had smitten their Temple and laid it in ruins. Hundreds of trumpets and rams' horns sounded the alarm. Priests and Levites streamed out of the innumerable halls of the Temple; many of them were still half asleep, many were only half dressed in their service vestments. I had not imagined such numbers; they came swarming out like flocks of birds; old men with curled beards, young men of powerful build, and then youngsters, children almost, innumerable youngsters, neophytes and students of the priestly schools. The Levites continued to blow their trumpets and the assembled multitude of Priests grew larger and larger. Gradually it drew nearer the citadel; a forest of clenched fists was lifted toward us, and from its midst rose wild shrieks of rage. But before long the alarm had wakened the city and new crowds poured into the Temple area. The women, who did not dare to pass the limits of their court, wailed and lamented at the top of their voices, as if an enemy had broken into the city and was slaughtering their young ones in their sight; a deeper, more ominous roaring came from the men, whose packed masses were drawing nearer and nearer to the citadel. From the side of the cleft there was no approach; the German horsemen were stationed there, and a rain of arrows kept the space before them clear. On the other side, however, the Priests, advancing where the common people did not have permission to follow, made the attempt to crawl up the citadel rock. They lifted each other up, they stood on each other's shoulders, they laid themselves on their backs and tried to work their way up. But there were no cracks in the covering of marble blocks, no holds for finger- or toe-nails; they slid back from the oiled surface. Meanwhile our good Askelon legionaries, mixed with Samaritans who had been brought from the Jericho garrison, stood in the shelter of the turrets and were overjoyed at this opportunity to teach the insolent Jews a lesson. They shot the climbing figures down, one by one, like birds, and we watched the Jews rolling over, tumbling, to shatter their heads on the stony rock of the platform. Such was their persistence, however, that some of them actually managed to reach the upper rock, and from time to time a hand was laid on the lattice of the gallery. Then an Askelonite would draw his broadsword; the hand would be severed with a single stroke, and the body would go rolling like a pea down the slope. Sometimes, again, the Askelonite would put the climber out of his misery by bringing the blade down on his head. Before the sun had emerged properly from behind the hills, the rock and the walls of our fortress were liberally besprinkled with Judaean blood—as liberally as their own altars with the blood of animals—and at the foot of the rock lay a pile of Jewish carcasses.

Meanwhile we saw emerge the High Priest, in the midst of his entourage. I recognized him by his imposing figure and by the respectful attention evoked by his appearance even in that tumult. The Priests, the old men, and the sages assembled about him. They began to calm the hotheads, to recall the men who were trying in vain to storm the citadel. Among the sages and scholars there was one of younger years, yet obviously their leader; tall, strong of build, he seemed to command universal reverence. Surrounded by his pupils, he addressed himself to the infuriated throngs, and they listened. As I learned later, this was one of their spiritual leaders, one Jochanan ben Zakkai; he had been the pupil of one of their greatest scholars, who had died at a very advanced age. This Jochanan ben Zakkai restrained the hotheads, assisted by old Hanan, the father-in-law of the High Priest; I at once recognized Hanan as the head of the deputation which had met us at the gates of Jerusalem. Surrounded by his five sons, he approached the citadel walls and made signals that he wished to address us. I sent down a messenger and asked him what he wanted. An audience, was the reply. But I had not power to grant him an audience. I came out into the open on the gallery, though there was danger of being hit by a stone or by the arrow of some hidden marksman, and asked him what he wanted. He spoke Latin with difficulty, but had a good command of Greek. In a poor Latin, mixed with many Greek words, he alluded to the exposed eagle and shields and, as the Jews always did, appealed for their ancient privileges: the great Caesar, and after him the Caesars Augustus and Tiberius, had recognized the Jewish religion and had never transgressed its laws.

I had no intention of entering into long arguments with him. I answered in Greek that we in the citadel had not power to alter the orders of the Procurator; if the Jews had anything to say, let them address themselves to the Procurator in Caesarea.

That day a vast concourse of Priests and Levites, headed by old Hanan and accompanied by half the population of Jerusalem, men, women and children, set out for Caesarea. Jerusalem looked like a deserted city; within the Temple there remained only the Priests and Levites needed strictly for the regular service. Avoiding the hostile city of Sichem, the home of the traditional enemies, the Samaritans, they poured across the hills and fields; they did not use the open road, but approached Caesarea along the by-paths. There they were joined by the local Jews, and the united multitude beleaguered the house of the Procurator. Five days and five nights Pilate let them camp in the white marble streets of Caesarea, the city built by their own king, and would not give their leaders audience. They had time enough to study the spectacle of the alien heathens dwelling in the marble houses which King Herod had built, with their money, in honor of the Caesar. They looked on the rich harbor, the gymnasiums, the theaters, the colosseums, the cavalry schools and—worst of all—the temples, particularly the magnificent Temple of Augustus, which the king, with taxes squeezed from his own people, had erected for their enemy. A rabble of children of Caesarea followed them through the streets and threw stones at them. But they bore all these trials and humiliations with infinite and loving patience in the name of their God. During the day they wandered, hungry and thirsty and weary, through the streets; nights they wandered in the parks and along the alleys by the shore; they lay down to rest on the marble steps of the harbor, and they rose wearier than they had lain down. Still Pilate would not receive them. In the city which their own money had built, in the heart of their own country, they had to drain to the dregs the cup of bitterness held to their lips by a population of strangers and enemies. On the fifth day Pilate had them driven like sheep into the big cavalry school, which he had surrounded by mounted German troops; he then admitted into the midst of the Jews detachments of Askelonites and Samaritans, headed by Greeks. This done, he sent word to the Jews that if they did not disperse quietly to their city, and pay honor to the Roman eagle and shields, he would have them trampled like worms by the hoofs of the cavalry. What think you was their response? All of them, from their spiritual leader and the priests down to the women and children, threw themselves on the ground like one man and cried: "You may send against us not only the wild Britons and the German riders, but even the fiercest beasts. We will welcome death a thousand times before we will pollute our sanctuary with alien symbols!"

"Pollute our sanctuary!" Pollute it with the Caesar's picture and the triumphant eagle of Rome! The incredible insolence of the Jews! Had I been Pilate I would have taken them at their word. But Pilate had in mind something other than the honor of the Caesar's picture and the Roman eagle.... He admitted to private audience cunning old Hanan and remained closeted with him for two whole hours. What passed between them I do not know, but orders came to us in Jerusalem to remove the images, the shields and the eagle from the citadel. "Rome honors the laws!" he wrote to us. The Jews had triumphed.

I heard that after the interview between Pilate and the old former High Priest Hanan, the former bought his first estate in Sicily and built himself, on the shores of Pompeii, a villa which he presented to his wife Claudia, who was still at the court of Tiberius.

They said in Rome that rain falls seldom in Judaea, but when it does fall it is not water, but gold....

CHAPTER SEVEN

I ACQUIRED by slow degrees a knowledge of the people into the midst of which I had been exiled; I began to penetrate into its life and into its manner of thought, to find my way through the labyrinth of its party divisions and to become familiar with its customs and manners. It was no light task, for the Jews are a people who close their life behind seven seals, especially in the presence of a Roman functionary. Months passed, years, before I could prepare a substantial report for Pilate. It was enough for them to see the flash of my armor when I was about on official duty, or to catch a glimpse of my toga on other occasions, and they made themselves scarce as if I were the carrier of a pestilence. But by dint of patient effort I made the acquaintance of individuals, and accustomed them to my presence. I cannot say how it was, but this people which repelled me also had a curious attraction for me; it awakened my interest from the first moment of our meeting. My duties brought me into frequent contact with the higher officials of the Temple, and I was a regular visitor in some of the more aristocratic homes in the Upper City. I also contracted a number of friendships in the higher social circles. In particular, I was greatly obligated to the two youngest sons of the old High Priest for their assistance in guiding my first steps among those strange and hostile crowds. I gathered a great deal of information which was not without value to me in my official capacity.

Apart from these personal contacts I found much pleasure in circulating through the city and observing its life. I did not confine myself to the richer quarter of the palaces, but went down into the most miserable sections of the lower city and made the acquaintance of the Jewish masses. It was here that I found the market place, and here I could touch the pulse of the city. It was not, strictly speaking, a market place, but a long, wide street which cut a path from one end to the other of the old city. It contained most of the shops. Here the fishers of the Sea of Genesaret and of Acco brought their goods, fresh and salted, for sale, and found ready and appreciative buyers among the Jerusalemites. Here the farmers of Sharon marketed their vegetables. There were varieties of greens and fruits such as are not to be seen elsewhere. The gardens about Jerusalem sent their honey-dripping figs, soft and rounded like full udders; some of these gardens had grown fat on the blood of the sacrifices drained off from the Temple, hence their fruits were peculiarly rich and juicy. Such clusters of grapes as I saw in this market have not their equal anywhere else in the world. And along this street, under coverings of dried palm leaves, or in booths made up of sacks stretched on poles, or in niches under the columns of arcades, the artisans worked in the open. The dyers, the oil-pressers, the weavers (the younger men among the weavers were a fierce, quarrelsome lot and gave us endless trouble), the tailors, the sandal-makers, who took foot-measurements on the spot, but would never glance up at the faces of their women customers (most of the sandal-makers were exceptionally pious), were here; so were the saddle-makers and tentmakers, and perfume sellers; these last were generally regarded among the Jews as frivolous idlers, because, having to deal almost exclusively with women, they could easily be led astray. Along the street stood endless rows of oil cruses and honey jars; there were countless skins of wines of every variety, from the local provincial wines of Sharon to the precious and costly wines of Cyprus; there was every grade of grain, including the famous wheat of Ephraim, thick-eared, heavy, and rich in flour; there were the far-famed dates of Jericho.

Every man's trade could be recognized, even when he was not engaged at it. Dyers went about with colored threads drawn through the lobes of their ears, tailors had needles stuck in their clothes. There were scribes without number! With goose-quills behind their ears they sat at every corner before little tables, selling their services and little parchment scrolls bearing excerpts from their sacred writings; they wore little leather boxes on arm and forehead, and these contained passages known as the *"Shema"* from their code of laws, which they taught the children to repeat by heart. For in every street of Jerusalem the Jews had their synagogues and study chapels whither they brought their young to be instructed. If a mother went out to buy oil for her night lamp (the women had to provide this from their own earnings) she would not forget to procure at the same time a *"Shema"* or some other sacred parchment for her little ones. Often enough there would occur loud disputations between scribes and scholars, in the very midst of this clamor, as to the manner of writing a certain phrase. And almost as numerous as the scribes were the moneychangers. It was impossible to shake them off, for they were everywhere, with dinars dangling from their ears and jingling bags of coin in their hands. In and out of this tumultuous mass moved the tax collectors with the badges of their office on their breasts and the Temple officers with leather straps in their hands, taking in tithe and heave offering for the High Priest. The officers addressed themselves to the peasants and gardeners, and if any countryman had failed to pay his dues to the Temple, his produce was declared unclean and untouchable, and no purchaser dared come near.

Every trade also had its own separate side street. In the street of the dyers one often came across precious purple stuffs from Tyre and Zidon, white sheep's wool from the Syrian and Lebanonian hills, and gorgeous silks of Persia; in the street of the spice-dealers the air was laden with innumerable perfumes. There was no end to the variety of oils they used, from the coarser kind for softening the leather of their sandals to the costliest kind reserved for brides on the marriage day and for the embalming of corpses. They had scores of names for their oils. In the street of the goldsmiths one might come across masterpieces of artistic work from Mesopotamia, Alexandria, Antioch, or even one of the Greek islands. Nor was it a rare thing to encounter implements and weapons and stuffs, stone, fur and hide, originating in the remotest provinces, Gaul and Britain and Spain.

Jerusalem was a world city. The Temple drew pilgrims from every part of the Empire and beyond, and these brought with them the produce of their respective countries. It was amusing enough to wander about in this chaos of men and materials and color, but it would have been more so if it had not been for the restless and turbulent spirit which pervaded it.

The life of the foreign visitors to Jerusalem was mirrored chiefly in the Court of the Gentiles, which encircled the Temple and through which I had frequent occasion to pass. My personal quarters were, of course, in the Antonia, but our tax offices, military administration, quartermaster stores and police precincts were scattered in the vast, formless buildings of the old Herodian Palace where the Procurator lodged when he came to Jerusalem on the holy days. As a matter of fact there was a shorter path, through the new city, between the Antonia and the Palace (we had cut it through for strategic reasons), but I preferred to pass from one to the other via the Outer Court. Within the city one might be surprised by the sight of a caravan of camels, drawing in from a distant province and carrying on their proud, humped backs rich gifts to the Temple, while on the foremost of them sat swaying an outlandish figure in exotic garb; but within the Temple courts there was a fascinating concentration of the spiritual life of the Jews. For apart from the sacrificial commerce in doves, fine flour, spices and incense, apart from the chaffering of the moneychangers, one always encountered, either in the open between the pillars on sunny days, or in the shelter of the arcades and balconies on days of rain, the scholars and interpreters of the law, the preachers and visionaries and foretellers of the Messiah. The throngs they attracted consisted of all manners and conditions of men, the poor and the rich, workers in rough sackcloth garb and pilgrims in colored linens; all of them listening in pious silence. But they were at their most interesting on their Sabbath, that is, on that recurrent seventh day which they set aside for rest.

I was never able to grasp the idea of their Sabbath. Imagine an entire people taking every seventh day in its life and turning it into a day of rest! The entire country comes to a standstill; there is no movement, no labor, no work of any kind. Nothing to do but rest! They all rested, they, their wives, their children and even their animals. For on that day nothing is done with the animals beyond leading them to drink at the wells, or throwing some fodder into their troughs. At first I was under the impression that this seventh day of rest, or Sabbath, which as an institution is equally unknown among the civilized and the barbarian peoples, was nothing but a concession to laziness—a day of complete and pointless idleness. But I soon discovered that this was by no means the case. To begin with, whatever one might say of this extraordinary people, one accusation could not be brought against it—that of laziness. If anything, these Jews are a trifle too active. Had they only known how to be idle on occasion, had they only taken themselves and their work and their God and their Temple a little less seriously, they would have spared themselves, us and the rest of the world a good deal of trouble. They were, as a matter of fact, an exceptionally industrious people; the hard and niggardly soil which was their portion had taught them this lesson, they had to wring their livelihood from the rocks, and their God had not spoiled and corrupted them with an overabundance of gifts. It became evident that they had taken their Sabbath upon themselves, with all its duties, proscriptions and prohibitions, not as a period of rest but as a heavy burden. They did not dare to walk beyond a certain distance lest they desecrate the sanctity of the Sabbath. This was a day not of repose but of sacred service, a day of self-giving and of self-sacrifice to their God. On that day they sundered themselves from this world; they went about as if they had been translated to another life, their eyes, hearts and heads fixed on the heavens. On that day they belonged solely to their God.

And yet they were by no means so alien to this worldly life, and such deniers of its worth, as the foregoing might imply. With all their somberness they had quite a capacity for rejoicing. There were, first of all, their holy days. On one of these they brought their earliest ripened fruits to the Temple. It was amusing to look down from the Antonia and watch the peasants of Sharon and Galilee, bowed with constant stooping over the soil, carrying their first fruits to the holy place. From what I hear, they choose the offerings, the dates, the pomegranates, the grapes, while they are still on the stalk. They go out into the fields, they observe what fruits are beginning to ripen, and they wrap them round with little twigs to mark them off. It was strange to see with what piety, what fanatical faith, they bore the baskets with their tributes to the dwelling place of their God. The delegations from the various districts and provinces arrived in separate formation, rich and poor from each locality marching together. First came an ox with a golden crown thrown over its horns; this was the sacrifice, whose steps were accompanied by the sound of music as they entered the city limits. Rich landowners, and even members of the aristocracy, carried their own offerings on their shoulders, in gold- and silver-plated baskets; the poor bore their gifts in baskets of straw and twigs. The officers of the Temple and the population of Jerusalem came forth from the city to receive them; the workers and artisans of Jerusalem lined the street and invited the pilgrims into their homes.

During these festivals of theirs the Jews were even capable of wild ecstasies of joy. What a sight they were, for instance, on the night of the ending of their most solemn sacred day, the Day of

Atonement, when their High Priest issued from the mysterious Holy of Holies unharmed by his contact with supreme sanctity!

The bitterness which they felt throughout the whole year against the High Priest and his acolytes was forgotten and forgiven on that day. They arranged, in his honor, a procession worthy of a conquering general returning from his campaigns. They conducted the High Priest to his home with music and singing, the Levites played on their harps and flutes, the flower of the Priesthood danced before him. Then came a cortege of aristocratic, Priestly families, the venerable sages of the city, the scholars, the interpreters of the law, the people at large, the regular inhabitants of the city, mingling with the multitude of pilgrims. Dressed in their richest and most colorful clothes, carrying torches in their hands, singing and rejoicing, they conducted him home.

They were a remarkable sight, again, on that festival which they called the Holy Day of Water Pouring. On that day they offered plain water as a sacrifice to their God. That was a festival for which I find the nearest parallel in our own Bacchus celebrations. To begin with, they illuminated Jerusalem in such a way that one would have believed the city to be in flames. They assembled on their roofs, they pulled the threads from their old clothes, dipped them in oil and set them alight. The essential celebration occurred in the Temple courts. There the great throng of pilgrims from the countryside was gathered, and the Priests were ranged on the Temple walls, the gates and turrets; they too brought their worn-out robes of office—vestments which could not be assigned to any other purpose—soaked them in oil and set them ablaze. Among those vestments, so consigned to the flames, there might be some of the costliest handwoven stuffs of gold and silver thread, of blue and purple wool, made specially on the looms dedicated to that labor within the Temple, or brought as pious gifts by wealthy women of town and country. We gazed down from the Antonia tower on the flood of flame which rose from the Temple walls and was reflected from the roofs of the city. One might have thought the city was being sacked; but the crackle of the flames was drowned in the singing, in the joyous shouting which accompanied the wild dancing of the frenzied crowds in the Temple area and in the narrow streets.

What a sight, too, were the young Priests or, as they were called, the flowers or blossoms of the Priesthood. Their white robes and white hats shone out of a sea of flame, their naked feet moved in a rhythmic dance to the accompaniment of harp, flute, trumpet, and cymbal played by the Levites on the marble stairs. All bonds seemed to be loosed that night; the people felt that on this night of fire and water even their God Jehovah had burst the confines of His eternal loneliness to mingle with His jubilant worshipers. They were drunk with His invisible spirit; every moment He might lift them up in a flaming cloud and carry them off to the secret fastnesses of His heavens. . . . Such was the rejoicing that even grave, solemn, and meditative sages and interpreters of the laws were pulled into it, or actually became centers of radiating and delirious gaiety. The old were transformed into children. We saw bearded and reverend scholars juggling with flames like prestidigitators with spheres. Young men danced between swords and young girls among flames. Some of them did magic tricks, for all of them were magicians after a fashion. What more need I say? On that day, or rather that night (for the chief celebrations began with nightfall), the grim city of Jerusalem and its somber and solemn Temple were transformed into one gigantic altar on which the opposing elements of fire and water were offered in a single sacrificial gesture to their God.

Astonishingly enough, their spiritual leaders were not their High Priests, but their interpreters of the law or, as they called them, their Rabbis. Their influence over the masses was enormous, and the people followed them blindly. On the surface it would appear that they had nothing against us, that is, against the power of Rome, so long as we did not interfere in their internal life. Inasmuch as their internal life consisted of their religious service and their study of sacred lore, we had neither reason nor inclination to interfere. But we could never tell what their intentions were and what they were plotting. Looking at them in their shops or booths between the columns in the Temple courts, looking at their Rabbis, with the long ritual fringes hanging from their clothes, with the leather straps bound on arm and forehead, observing them as they argued fiercely about some point of law, I could not help feeling that they were not the innocent lambs they pretended to be. The one good feature of the situation was this: however deep their hatred for us, the alien power, still deeper was their hatred and contempt for the power of their own. They had rather, a thousand times over, submit to the rule of Rome than to that of the House of Herod, which they despised.

But what love, what reverence, what inmost devotion they accorded their Rabbis, their Yea- and Nay-sayers! Their Rabbis always moved amid throngs of pupils, like kings amid their bodyguards. The pupils kept their eyes fixed on the lips of their Rabbi, so as not to lose a single word of interpretation and exegesis. Often these Rabbis were sprung from the lowest ranks of the people. I saw among them such as lived in the most miserable section of the city, in huts consisting of plaited twigs. Round one of these huts scores and hundreds of pupils would gather, waiting for the Rabbi to finish his work, and issue forth to interpret and teach the law. Others, again, were day laborers and field workers, paupers who had not so much as a decent garb to throw about themselves, and they would have gone naked if not for the generosity of their pupils. Some of these Rabbis were lean with starvation. One that I saw was so withered that one could follow the descent of each bite of food down his throat. I was told that because of some vision of calamity he had taken the vow of fasting on himself. But others abstained from food simply because they had nothing to eat! They took no payment for their teaching, no matter how rich their pupils. More than once I saw, amid the throng which followed such a pauper or day laborer—and he might not be venerable with age—riders in fine linen on richly caparisoned asses. Sometimes the Rabbi would be quite a young man, and old people would be following him and listening to his words with the utmost respect. I have never been able to understand wherein lay this profound power which they wielded over the people. For the people as a whole, and not only the following of pupils, was prepared to obey them in all things, no matter what dangers were entailed. We were, frankly, afraid of the power of the learned, and we kept close watch on them.

It did not take me long to discover that our most natural allies in this atmosphere of hostility were the members of the higher aristocracy, with the High Priests at their head. They belonged, moreover, to a party which psychologically approached our manner of thought. I shall not enter here into a detailed discussion of the differences between their parties; the subject may not be without importance, but the pursuit of it is invariably accompanied by a headache. I do not know whether this party was really as fond of Rome as it pretended to be; but I do know that the situation of the aristocratic families was such that they fell naturally into our hands. Without our help they could not have remained where they were for a single day, and their need of us was greater than ours of them.

By no stretch of the imagination could it be said that they were beloved of the people, all these High Priests and their retinue of servants, Levites, singers and sycophants. They were no light burden of rulership, and they took themselves with immense seriousness. I shall tell you more of this later, but here let me say that you Jews have nothing to be proud of in your kings and High Priests and other state-mongers. It was with our strength that they were able to apply the whip to the people. However, I shall return to this subject....

The people hated the High Priests, but could do nothing against them. The Priests guarded the Temple—and the Temple was the center of the religious life of the Jews; their religion, in turn, was the central nerve and organ of their spiritual and physical existence. They lived in and for their religion. I have seen a world of men and lands. I was with Germanicus in Germany for four years; I learned the manners and customs of the barbarians beyond the Rhine; I have been in Gaul and Spain and Africa; I have delved into the mysteries of the Egyptian priesthood, of the magicians of Chaldaea and of the snake charmers of Abyssinia, but I had never yet encountered a people which did not dedicate its energies to fighting hostile neighbors, to acquiring the means for luxurious living, to displaying prowess and wisdom, to accumulating wealth, to indulging, in whatever manner it might be, the natural human passions. But in the case of the Jews, their interests, their whole life, their thoughts, their love, their prowess and everything else were dedicated to a single passion—their God. On him they concentrated their being, and on how to carry out his commandments down to the minutest and strangest ritualistic details.

And since the Temple was the center of their religious life, it naturally became the center of all their activities, their meditations, dreams and wishes. There was no other life for them. Thus the High Priest became not only the director of religious functions but the ruler, in effect, of the whole people. He was the highest religious functionary, and, at the same time, the uncrowned king. He could send out his messengers to arrest Jews even beyond the frontiers of Judaea. And the Priesthood was like a leech, sucking the blood and marrow out of the people. The High Priests were bloated with wealth; for apart from the tithes and the first-fruits, payable in kind, they imposed additional taxes on the people. With every sacrifice brought to the Temple there was a fee to be paid for the Priestly stamp. When the poorest of the poor came bearing their doves, or a twig of incense, or a jar of wine, or a cruse of oil, or a measure of flour, there was something to be paid to the Priests. And then the meat of the sacrifices! What their God received was a little blood, part of the fat and a fragment of meat; the remainder went to the High Priests. All these tithes went into the hands of a few families who divided among themselves the highest Temple offices. The lower ranks of the Priesthood, members of obscure families, lived in poverty. Theirs was the work—one might compare them to a slave class. There were also, among the lower levels of the Priesthood, rebels and trouble-makers who had a hand in every uprising.

CHAPTER EIGHT

BEHIND our Antonia fortress dropped the wall of the city. It happened that once, descending the slope, I turned aside from the regular path, and was startled and terrified by the sight which my eyes encountered. I heard at first a tinkling of bells, as though sheep and cattle were browsing about me. But I soon observed that the bells or clappers were carried by human beings who maintained a continuous crying as they walked. *"Tama, tama,"* they cried, which (as I later found out) signifies, in their language, "Unclean! Unclean!" I was about to approach one of those figures, to discover the significance of this curious behavior, but one man who was repeating the cry stopped me. I asked him what was toward, but before he could answer there began to stream past us hordes of cripples, the halt and the blind. They fled in a panic, some of them crawling on all fours, others holding up broken limbs, still others being carried or else dragged along on wooden sleds. The blind tapped the ground before them with their sticks and screamed helplessly to be led away. In their frenzy they ran around in circles, and there was no one to set them on the path, for all those that could see and move were fleeing as from a pestilence. I held on to my man, and with the utmost difficulty managed to obtain from him an account of what was happening.

It appeared that this extraordinary disturbance had to do with a small natural spring whose waters issued to the surface near the summit of the slope. The people believed that from time to time an angel appeared and smote the waters, and anyone who could then draw near and throw himself into the spring as it gushed up would be healed of his sickness. Until that day the spring had been the natural resort of the sick and the cripples of the city, but now the lepers, who were kept outside the walls in the Valley of the Kidron, had burst through the cordon of chains, swept up the hill and occupied the spring. Hence the mad flight of the crippled and the sick.

In spite of the throng bearing against me, I drew nearer the spring, running the danger of infection, and I saw, rolling about in the thick, splashing mud the last remnants of human beings, creatures on whose skeletons the flapping flesh hung loose like filthy rags on the bodies of beggars. Men and women of all ages, children too, fighting desperately with the stumps of their limbs for a place in the mud, which they lifted up as best they could and spread on the raw and gaping flesh. I turned and ran—I could bear the sight no longer. The air was poisoned with the stench of putrefying human flesh.

So it was! On the heights Jerusalem shone to the heavens with its golden Temple, its High Priests, its aristocracy and its towers, but down below it was rotten with poverty and decay. Wherever one turned in those alleys one encountered beggars, cripples, outcasts from every corner of the land. One needed only to catch a glimpse of the Lower City, of the filthy tangle of streets around the wall, in the Vale of Hinnom, and by the waters of Siloah; one needed only to explore the region in the Valley of the Kidron at the foot of the Mount of Olives and see the gutters where the lowest servitors of the Priestly clan washed the hides of the sacrificed animals, or pass by the midden mounds where the poorest of the poor scraped desperately in the refuse. One had to see all this, and then to reflect on the life of the wealthy contractors who farmed the taxes, on the palaces of the Priestly aristocracy in the Upper City, on the pleasure gardens which they had laid out on the Mount of Olives and in the new quarters. There was an abyss between the levels of the population, between swollen opulence on the one hand and grinding poverty on the other.

Moreover, the city swarmed with tax and tithe collectors, big and little. There seemed to be no end to the varieties of tribute exacted from the poor. The chosen people, living in its own land, had been compared to an ass which patiently carries a double burden for its own and for alien masters. There were, first, the levies due to us, the Roman rulers. We had, together with the mastery over the province, taken over the taxation system of the Jewish princes and Tetrarchs in its entirety, and we saw no reason for diminishing by a hair's weight the exactions which had been instituted by the native princes. We collected head tax and water tax, excises on food produce, meat, salt and bread, and road tolls; on top of these we demanded and obtained special levies from each city separately. Then followed a series of taxes on natural produce being taken to market; the Galilean farmer, the peasant of the Valley of Jezreel, the vine grower of Sharon could not carry his basket of vegetables, fruit or grain to market before he had given the Roman his dues; at every ford and crossroads stood the booths of the tax gatherers. All this was payment to Rome, and when that was done there began the series of religious exactions, the Temple tax, the first and second tithes for the priesthood, redemption of the first-born, sending of first-fruits and the like. The state tributes were farmed out to special contractors, who maintained gigantic staffs of collectors; these were to be seen everywhere with their staves, their knotted cords, and their lead-weighted sacks, at their task of harassing and squeezing the people. Woe to the farmer who fell in arrears! They took away his last cow, his last ass, his vineyard and field, and often enough he was thrown into prison. Farmers were seldom sold as slaves; Jews would not buy Jewish slaves because of the queer laws governing their possession. The fact was that their slaves retained practically all the rights of freemen. To begin with, the term of slavery terminated automatically at the end of seven years, even when the purchase had been "for life." The purchase, moreover, extended to the slave's labor, but not to his person, so that he was in effect nothing more than a day laborer. What Jew, under these conditions, wanted to acquire a Jewish slave? There was a folk saying which ran: "He who buys a slave buys a master over himself." This situation, as may easily be seen, aggravated the problem of poverty. On the one hand the tax contractors accumulated vast wealth, adding field to field and farm to farm; on the other, countless masses were torn from their land and flung into the cities. Stripped of the last of their possessions, they had not the possibility of earning their livelihood even by slavery.

We Romans were greatly concerned by this state of affairs. It was quite clear that the unrest which perpetually plagued the country was rooted, at least partly, in the system of taxation and the poverty of the masses. Many of those who had been driven from their soil gathered into patriotic bands which would stop at nothing in their efforts to overthrow the legally constituted authority. They went by the name of Zealots, but in reality they were nothing better than bands of robbers, who lay in ambush for travelers and sometimes descended on entire towns and villages. The many caves which dot the hill country of Palestine offered them shelter and security. Herod himself had had to carry on unremitting war against these hordes, which robbed the rich and divided the proceeds among the poor. There rose among them daring leaders who were ready to defy the power of Rome not less than that of the High Priest. Frequently enough they were joined by groups of poor Priests, whose fanatical oratory, directed against the stranger in the land, inspired them to attempts on the Roman soldiers. To suppress them was no easy task, and our methods were severe; we were determined to wipe out the bands; we crucified every leader who fell into our hands, and the followers, when taken alive, were sold on foreign slave-markets or sent to feed the beasts in the amphitheater at Rome. And still these robber bands were not the most difficult to deal with. Numbers of the poor sought refuge in religious ecstasy; they fled to the wilderness and formed themselves into a sect which regarded poverty not as a misfortune, as a cruel visitation, but as a high virtue which every man should seek to cultivate. Their scholars and interpreters of the law excogitated for them a system of belief which included the idea of an after-life beyond death, a survival of the soul. They held that punishment for evil deeds, reward for good ones, did not belong to this world, but to a second world beyond the grave. It need hardly be said that the reasonable Jews, like the High Priest and his party, had not the slightest use for this nonsense. But the folk of which I speak regarded this legend of another life beyond death with the seriousness of a proved reality; the life of this world, they contended, serves only as a preparation for that life beyond, or, to use their own language, as "a vestibule to the great dwelling place." Bearing this in mind, they were for ever purifying themselves, for ever avoiding evil. They drank no wine, and ate no meat. Many of them subsisted on figs and wild honey, which they found in the wilderness. They shared their last bite with each other and their last shreds of clothing. They were formed into closed brotherhoods, and they ate at common meals, every meal being the occasion for a religious ceremony. In joining these societies they relinquished all their earthly possessions—this being a condition of membership. Property ceased to belong to the individual and was held in common. When one of them came from the wilderness into the city he sought out one of his brethren in the faith and stayed with him; they were, in fact, like one great family. We Romans knew that the most dangerous elements were recruited from among them, and we dealt with them accordingly.

On the surface they could easily be taken for the meekest and mildest of mankind, gentle as lambs, constituting not the slightest danger to the state and the rulership of Rome; for they even had a saying: "It is forbidden to oppose the will of God; every government rules by the will of God, and therefore it is forbidden to rise against any government." Harmless as this sounded, it was more dangerous to state and government than the rebellions and attacks of the road robbers. The latter were the open enemies of the High Priest and of Rome; they declared freely that their only salvation lay in destroying the power of the foreign ruler, and their God Jehovah would help them to achieve this end. We knew what confronted us. But the pretended meekness of the others was a piece of Jewish cunning. They did not rise up against authority; no, not they; they only waited for the coming of their Messiah. We Romans were never able to get a clear picture of what they meant by the word "Messiah." Who and what was Messiah? Was he something more than a Jewish king who would liberate Judaea from the rule of Rome? Was he also to be a world ruler? They said of him that he would do away with all the evil in the world, and introduce goodness everywhere; he would, according to the words which they quoted from the hallucinatory visions of one of their poets, "cause the lion to lie down with the lamb, and the lion shall not consume the lamb." He would likewise cause the nations "to beat their swords into plowshares." Or else, according to the illusions of another of their poets, he would conquer the world not with the sword, as we Romans had done, but with the spirit of God. And suppose I grant that their deliverer, or Messiah, as they call him, conquers the Roman Empire not with the sword, but with the spirit. What difference does it make to me by what means they conquer Rome? I was always trying to make this clear to Pilate. The High Priest, too, agreed with me, that these pious little fellows, these Jews with the sanctified faces, who did not war on Rome, but waited for their Messiah and hastened his coming, were a thousand times more dangerous than the open rebels. The latter wanted, at most, to drive us from Judaea; the others wanted to transform the entire world into one Judaea, and have all the heathen circumcised into Jewishness! The boundlessness of Jewish insolence!

For these Jews I had nothing but hatred from the moment I set eyes on them. I looked on them as the bitterest and most subtle enemies of the ruling power, dark moles undermining the security of Rome. Whenever, from the height of the Antonia, I saw one of them in the Temple court, my blood boiled up in me: wild creatures, almost naked, a leopard or sheep skin thrown over their bodies, unshod feet, fierce tangles of hair, faces burned to a cinder by the desert sun, leanness, hunger, eyes blazing with dark fanaticism, bony hands stretched out toward the sanctuary as if invoking spirits as mad as themselves. They, with their mystic spirits, were to overthrow the Caesar and wipe the name of Rome from the face of the earth in order to make room for their Messiah!

The first impression they produced was that of men not belonging to the world; they were incomprehensible and unearthly in their fanaticism. Any other people which had had to put up with such humiliations for the sake of its faith would long ago have abandoned its gods and sought out for itself mightier and more dependable ones. For the life of me I could not understand what they saw in their God, and in what manner He had ever helped them. A small, poor people in an obscure, desolate country, sewn with hills and deserts and subject to the power of Rome—they lived their tortured and uncertain life on sufferance; at any moment we could wipe them out, trample them into the dust. What sort of life was that? . . . I would not subject the unruliest of my slaves to such a ritual as their God imposed on them. No joy, no love, no beauty: He had taken everything from them. And yet look at the devotion, the incomprehensible faith they bestow on Him, the exalted love they feel for Him, the voluntary enslavement they suffer for Him. And what is their reward? Often I had the feeling that the relationship between them and their God resembled no other relationship between a people and its gods; it was not based on mutual obligation, but on a love without bounds and without conditions. For their God they were prepared to risk and endure everything; for His sake they would even pit themselves against the might of Rome. Therein lay the danger.

Jerusalem was full of these fanatics. It often happened that a peasant, coming up to Jerusalem for one of their three High Holy days, would stay over until the next. In this respect the inhabitants of Jerusalem were very hospitable to their provincial brethren, and this was particularly true among the poor. Artisans among the pilgrims could obtain work at their trade during the period of their stay in Jerusalem. In the section of the Temple area which was reserved for the people, every trade had its reserved location. A goldsmith, a weaver, a tent maker coming up to Jerusalem had only to seek out his fellow craftsmen in order to obtain employment. A place was also reserved for farmers and poor land laborers below the Temple area, between the pillars which supported the Temple platform. It also happened that because of the great crowding of families which occurred here during the High Holy days infectious diseases broke out and spread rapidly.

But the stream of pilgrims brought with it not only the poor, the homeless, the unemployed and the dispossessed, but large numbers of Galilean rebels, revolutionaries and inspired fanatics who found in the discontented mass the perfect element for their destructive activities. The congenitally poor, and those who had been dislodged from their foothold on the soil by the weight of taxation, were equally sympathetic material for the dangerous agitation of the Zealots. There were frequent altercations between myself and the High Priest on this subject. I insisted on the necessity of expelling the accumulated provincial rabble from the city, and of limiting the pilgrimages to the High Holy days. The High Priest, interested in the receipts of the Temple treasury, would not hear of it. For the Priesthood a steady, all-year-round flow of pilgrims and strangers was a matter of great importance. This was, moreover, a purely internal religious affair—such at least was their contention—and lay presumably beyond the competence of the Roman jurisdiction.

On nights when I could not fall asleep I would sometimes go out on the gallery of the Antonia and look down from a turret on the Temple area. In the quiet night a rain of starlight came down and was reflected from the golden thresholds, lintels, gates and plates. The Temple area, which during the day swarmed with hosts of men and women, was now silent. No voice was heard, no face was seen; only the movement of the torches betrayed the presence of the night watchers making the rounds. I was of course not intimidated by the unknown God who had chosen, out of all the width of the earth, this place upon a rock, to dwell behind coverings of gold and curtains of purple, surrounded by the eternal fire of His altars. Yet I was ill at ease. It was the unknown and invisible in Him which disturbed me and awakened my curiosity. I was greatly tempted more than once to enter the secret passage which led from the Antonia into the sanctuary, to steal quietly past the curtains which cover the place of His abode, to enter the Holy of Holies—to surprise Him, to discover who was there, who it was rested between the wings of the mystic birds, to see the unseen and obtain knowledge of the unknown. But I must confess that I lacked the courage. When I looked down on the roof of the Holy of Holies, which rose into the sky above all the other buildings of the Temple, and reflected that under it was concealed that unknown God which, according to the Jews, rules over the destinies of the world, a strange feeling came over me. I was quite certain that our gods were more powerful, Jupiter, for instance, with his thunderbolts. There the proof of it was, the things he had done to the followers of the other. And still the unknown in the Jewish God made me uneasy. A God who does not embody a single passion, who contains everything within Himself, and yet cannot be represented. He does not incarnate a single human quality, He fills the entire universe—and yet He stands above it and enslaves to Himself a people which worships Him with the extremest measures of devotion and love. Who is He, this Jewish God?

CHAPTER NINE

BUT at last I became sick of those Jews. In the first place they were for ever squabbling, even in the Temple area, where the Priests were at loggerheads with the interpreters of the law. The clamor of their arguments reached high heaven. On one occasion they even came to blows, and we were afraid of a revolt; I had to send my Askelonites down into the outer court to do a little pacification among the Priests and the scholars. I thought heaven knew what high philosophic principle, what crucial religious problem, was dividing them. But the matter at dispute was thoroughly trifling—one of the minutiae of their ritual. Would you believe it? The fight broke out over the question whether the Jew bringing his sacrifice was supposed to place his hands on the head of the sheep and confess his sins, or whether he had to confess his sins without placing his hands on the head of the sheep! I was utterly at a loss as to the significance of it all. I know only one thing: I suffered the extremest torments of boredom up there on the Antonia.

One fine morning there appeared before me in the citadel a young man of excellent appearance; he wore a Roman toga in the best metropolitan fashion, and were it not for a suggestion of an Alexandrian accent I might have taken him for an authentic Roman noble, so perfectly did he speak the language. He had a fine figure, athletic, but not muscular; his manners were distinguished. He addressed me as follows:

"Hegemon (this was my official title among the Jews)—as long as you find it necessary to stay in our modest city of Jerusalem which, because of the severity of our religious laws, lacks the Graeco-Roman diversions to which you are accustomed, my father, the oldest High Priest, begs that you do him the honor of considering his house with all that it contains at your disposal. He has further entrusted me with the honorable mission of offering you this laurel wreath, made of the finest gold, in token of invitation to the supper which he is arranging for you for tomorrow. My father, the oldest High Priest, my brother Eliezer, former High Priest, my other brothers and myself, will exert ourselves to provide some modest compensation for your labors for the peace of our city."

I must admit that the young man produced an excellent impression. I had not expected to encounter among the Jerusalemites this educated type. After brief reflection I accepted the invitation.

At the appointed hour I was admitted into a residence—actually not one house, but a series of structures. From the outside, as in the case of all these palaces of Jerusalem, nothing was visible; the place might have been taken for a barracks. The house was constructed of blocks of Jerusalem stone, with watchmen's turrets. Within was a paradise. The first sight within the gate was the so-called external court. This was paved throughout with slabs of white marble, and about it were grouped the numerous official buildings of the High Priest. Here lived the tax collectors, as well as the administration officers. There was likewise a court, in which, at the instance of the High Priest, meetings were held of the inner or small

Sanhedrin, which consisted largely of the members of his own family and his intimates. From the outer we passed to the inner court, which contained the gardens of the High Priest, his private residence and the residences of his relatives. In between, however, lay a smaller court, or passageway, on either side of which were the rooms for his private bodyguard.

When we emerged into the interior court our nostrils were assailed by the intoxicating odor of countless unfamiliar trees and shrubs grouped, in a well-laid park, about several swimming pools. Tall cypresses, oleanders and ethrog (citron) trees cast their shadows over the water. The rose, it appeared, was the favorite flower of the Jerusalem aristocracy, for the entire park was aflame with rose bushes of various hues. Outside, in the city, the population was parched with thirst, water was a luxury, the cisterns were almost dry in the summer heat; and when the wind came in laden with the heat and fine sand of the desert, the inhabitants of the city crowded about the troughs which brought thin trickles of water from the streamlet of Siloah. They snatched the skins from the hands of the water carriers bringing meager loads from the wells about the city and from the Pools of Solomon. Up here, however, in the court of the High Priest, the water gushed freely from many fountains which, in the shape of bronze lions, were grouped about the swimming pools. A special pipe conducted the water from the source in the Temple to the garden of the High Priest, just as special pipes led the blood of the sacrifices, which spouted into the troughs, to the gardens of the High Priest and of other members of the aristocracy, to fertilize the soil. The double supply of water and blood nourished the garden so well that it blossomed with indescribable beauty; the oriental plants shone in their broad flowerbeds. The water not only supplied the trees, bushes and plants, but flowed also into the swimming pools. Above the surface of the pools fluttered flocks of white turtledoves.

Like all other large residences in Jerusalem, the house of the High Priest consisted of huge blocks of stone, with no exterior decoration, so that the effect from the outside was one of extreme severity. Triangular windows, set with deep-colored Phoenician glass, admitted a dim light into the rooms. On the northern side, facing the Temple, a flight of fifteen steps, pure white marble, led up to the hall of columns. There were three rows of columns, on three sides: Corinthian throughout, their capitals supporting the huge cedarwood beams of the roof, which was covered with other fine woods and adorned with mosaics. The floor, too, was one tapestry of mosaic, its blending colors woven into various Jewish religious symbols. At the top of the flight of stairs, and above the ceiling of the hall of columns, towered a pyramid, which closed off the façade on this side of the house.

I was received at the entrance by the chief steward of the house, accompanied by a group of slaves and servants; he conducted me through the outer court. At the entrance to the inner court there waited for me the young man who had brought me the invitation, namely, the youngest son of the old High Priest. He was dressed in a mantle of silver thread, and a laurel wreath was placed on his artificially curled locks. At the foot of the hall of columns I was received by his brothers, clad in similar mantles, with similar laurel wreaths on their heads. All of them were tall and of manly aspect; some of them had beards combed and woven in the Chaldaean style. They conducted me ceremoniously up the flight of marble steps to the hall of columns. Servants and slaves in light, transparent tunics came to conduct me further, and though it was still bright day, they carried oil lamps in my honor. We passed through the hall of columns into the great reception hall, and there, on thrones, there waited for me the High Priest and two companions, former High Priests—his father-in-law Hanan and his brother-in-law Eliezer.

To tell the truth, this whole business of the reception ceremony rather startled me. These Jews, it appeared, took themselves very seriously. I knew that according to their custom a former High Priest had all the privileges of a reigning High Priest, and these privileges were almost regal. He had the right to wear a tiara, and honors had to be accorded him as to a king. Here, however, I saw not one king, but three—and that was a bit too much for me.

The reigning High Priest offered me greeting in Hebrew or Aramaic. The third son of the old High Priest, Theophilus, translated it for me into Greek, and I responded in the same language.

Attendants brought in a couch for me, and when I had taken my place the High Priest asked me how I was enjoying my stay in Jerusalem. He expressed the hope that although I was deprived, by reason of the religious scruples of the Jews, of the institutions to which I was accustomed in my own country, I would find in Jerusalem enough of general interest, likewise a large enough circle of educated men, to render my sojourn pleasant. I answered that we Romans did not leave the capital of the Empire and take up posts in remote provinces for pleasure or amusement, but solely to perform our duties to our Emperor. The audience, Jupiter be thanked, was a brief one. The regnant High Priest excused himself, saying that he was compelled to proceed to the Temple, where the evening sacrifices were being prepared. He left me in the hands of his family, his father-in-law and his brothers-in-law—for which I was duly grateful.

The meal was served according to the oriental custom, outside in the hall of columns. The slaves carried out couches covered with linens of Zidonian dye. We took our places at the tables and looked down upon Jerusalem.

The hall was open on three sides to the city, which unrolled its vistas under our eyes. Opposite us was the bridge which led from the Upper City by the Sanhedrin building to the Temple area, and which was crowded with men and women proceeding to and from the area. The vantage point was so high that we could also look down direct into the Court of the Gentiles; what lay beyond was concealed by the high, turreted golden gate on the fourteen steps and the adjoining galleries. It was pleasant to sit in the hall of columns; from behind the colored curtains which sheltered us from the blaze of the setting sun was wafted a delicious odor of roses which interpenetrated the fabric of the curtains and cooled the air. Servants in light transparent tunics handed us golden salvers with rose water, and we dried our hands on Zidonian serviettes. There Jerusalem lay before us, like an enormous, overheated oven. In the lower part of the city, where the poorest inhabitants lived, the clay huts looked like heaps of stones rolling down the slope to the wall, and beyond it to the Kidron valley, whence they began to climb the further slope toward the Mount of Olives. It was only from this point in the house of the High Priest that I perceived how the city spread itself upon the hills. It might have been compared to a hare, springing from hilltop to hilltop. The hills were covered with descending terraces of roofs in close contiguity, and on these were ranged water cisterns alternating with artificially planted shrubs, trees and flowers. I had not suspected that Jerusalem was so large; it spilled over far beyond its walls and covered with its new quarter the entire area of Mount Scopus, on the side of the Antonia and down as far as the sheep gate and beyond; on the other side, to the east, it climbed up to the Mount of Olives and northward it stretched to the Vale of Hinnom, the quarter of the poor.

All the roofs, between the fences, balconies and lattices which encircled them, were occupied by human beings; the inhabitants of Jerusalem sought relief from the heat beating up from the terraces of baked clay. Here and there the eye struck on a spot of green—a little cypress wood set in the midst of a cluster of houses. There, we knew, one of the aristocrats of Jerusalem was taking his ease among the shadows of his garden. But beyond the city walls these green interludes of cypress and olive grew wider and denser.

The meal proceeded in quiet dignity. There was little conversation; the actual eating seemed to have a religious character. On the right hand of the father Eliezer, the eldest son, reclined on his couch; he was treated by the slaves, the guests, and even his younger brothers, with special respect, almost equal to that which was accorded to his father. My own couch was placed to the left of the old man. Opposite us were ranged the other four sons. We lay at little tables covered with linen, and the serving of the dishes was accompanied by the soft music of harp and flute proceeding from behind a curtain. There were no women to be seen. All the guests—the servitors, too—were men.

I observed once more that the dishes, plates and ewers were hammered out of raw material into their necessary shapes, and were devoid of adornment and design; it seemed that in these utensils too the Jews sought to imitate their God, making use only of native and primitive matter. The courses, including the baked stuffs, were prepared by a Syrian cook. After the ceremonial washing of hands, the old High Priest pronounced a benediction on the bread which was placed before him on a golden platter, and the ritual was repeated by the other High Priest his eldest son. Thereupon the blessed bread was passed round among the reclining guests. Apart from the flesh of the swine, which their religion forbids, nothing was lacking. There was Egyptian fish, fish from the Sea of Galilee, fish from the city of Akko, prepared in a variety of styles, baked into pastry or pickled—and in the latter case the peculiar Jewish weakness for garlic and onion was abundantly evident. Every course was followed by wine. It was extraordinary how these Jews knew exactly what wine to serve with each dish. Thus, after a course of oily fish, they served a drink distilled from white grape seeds, which refreshed the palate with its keen tang and sharp body. The meat dishes were of countless variety, but mostly fowl. There was dove, chicken and duck; also wild fowl, like pheasant; but in no instance was the bird served up intact and as though still alive, in the manner much loved by us Romans and brought to a high pitch of perfection by the Alexandrian cooks, who specialize also in the serving of whole sucking pigs. After every dish the servitors passed round the golden ewers with rose water. In addition to fish and meat, there were plentiful supplies of greens, boiled and in raw salads. Among the greens were some unknown to our Roman tables, plants and spices which cleanse the palate and assist the digestion.

After the meal the ewers with rose water and the fine linen serviettes were passed round again, and the pleasanter half of the evening began. The rather severe bearing at table, during the meal, which was in some sort a continuation of the official reception, relaxed. The slaves lit the oil lamps on the capitals of the Corinthian columns, for the night shadows had enveloped Jerusalem. The light of great stars, pouring down from above, mingled with the softer glow of the oil lamps and the candelabra. Thus we lay on our couches and listened to the gentle melodies of the harp players behind the curtains. When the remnants of the meal had been removed and smoking censers distributed between the columns to freshen the air, I had the opportunity to make the closer acquaintance of my dinner companions.

The five sons of the old High Priest were all men of the highest education. Apart from the official training which they had undergone in preparation for their high positions in the Priesthood, they had had the benefit of a wide range of education by private Greek teachers, slaves purchased for that purpose by their father; the range included Greek history, mathematics, astronomy and rhetoric. They had a perfect command of the Greek and Latin languages and literatures. Were it not for their Jewish habit of gesticulation and their Alexandrian accents, it would have been difficult to recognize them as Jews; they would have been taken, instead, for Askelonites, or even for Greeks.

The old High Priest had rounded off the education of his sons by sending them to Alexandria, where they had also taken a part in all the sports. Though they were not particularly muscular, they were tall, and their bodies were the bodies of athletes. Hanan, the youngest, who bore his father's name, was likewise his father's favorite. He bore a closer resemblance to the old man, too, than the others; he had the same energetic lips and jaw; with his thick, curly hair thrown back from his forehead he, like his father, called to mind a lion. The hair of his beard and head was thicker than his brothers', and he was especially proud of his beard.

He questioned me concerning the most recent political developments in Rome, a subject in which, it appeared, he had a particular interest; he asked for news of the Caesar, who had withdrawn to Capri, and wished to know who was likely to be his successor; and whether Sejanus, Tiberius's chief adviser, was much spoken of in this connection. His brothers were more interested in sport, and what they were intent on was the latest sporting news from Rome; they asked me the name of the most popular gladiator in Rome, and wanted to know if I had ever seen him in the arena; they also inquired eagerly when the Emperor planned to arrange the next games. I cannot say what their Priestly qualifications were, but I cannot imagine that these cultivated young men could have been profoundly interested in the severe, unfriendly and complicated ritual which their difficult calling made it essential for them to know; nor can I doubt but that they were thoroughly wearied by the monotonous ceremonial service which consisted of preparing sacrifices and of watering the sheep from a golden laver before bringing them to the altar. They were weary, too, of that eternal singing and flute-playing by men musicians only. I did not find it difficult to believe that if it were not for the great wealth which their Priestly office supplied them as long as they lived, they would gladly have relinquished the Priesthood for some other calling. They were, indeed, not without sympathy for our gods and our customs.

The dying rays of the sun poured over the sand bastions and shone back from the wilderness of white roofs; they twinkled on the clustered tops of the cypress groves and took on a silvery tinge as they were reflected from the shimmering olive trees. In the opposite quarter of the heavens a mighty hand was drawing a thin veil of clouds over the city, and a milky mist was diffused through the air. As the darkness deepened, myriads of lights sprang up among the houses, and the moving points of fire which were the torches of the watchmen illumined the bases of the towers about the Temple area. The wings of the night, suggestive of the wings of those mystic birds which they call cherubim, spread out gradually over the Temple itself; and above the canopy, as it seemed, glimmered the light in the summit of the Antonia tower. A shower of faint star-luster came down, with mournful and dreamy effect, on the stretches of the city and Temple....

The old High Priest had had his couch placed next to mine, and the desultory conversation finally settled on the troubled condition of the country and the difficulties he was having with the unruly Galileans. I became aware, gradually, and in a fragmentary way, that the Priestly power was again confronted with one of those possessed and fanatical individuals who believed themselves to be the carriers of a divine mission of prophecy and of a special message from on high. This time, it appeared, an exceptionally dangerous figure had emerged; by one means or another he had managed to persuade the common folk that he was the reincarnation of one of their ancient prophets, famous in story and legend for the wonders he had performed; and as such he had gathered about him an unprecedented following, which was persuaded that he was the bearer of God's promise of redemption and liberation.

Now, lying on our couches on the open hall of columns, we discussed the man Jochanan, who, because he called the people to dip themselves in the waters of the Jordan, had become known as "The Baptist." At first Hanan and his sons were, for some reason or other, loath to admit me to this conversation; apparently they wished to conceal from the gentile in their midst the story of the queer "prophet." During the early part of the evening the sons of the High Priest entertained me, as was their wont, with accounts of gladiatorial shows, Olympic games, and gladiatorial conquests; only the oldest son, the former High Priest, conversed earnestly with the old man on the disturbing events in Galilee and the Judaean wilderness, while the others distracted my attention with their idle chatter. But I kept one ear cocked toward the half-whispered conversation and caught much of its drift.

"Where did you say he comes from?" the old man asked in Aramaic. (They were not quite aware that I had already made some progress in this jargon, or they might have kept their voices lower.)

"Galilee."

"Galilee," his father said, and his beard shook scornfully. He repeated the contemptuous popular saying: "Can anything good come out of Galilee?"

I had been half listening to Theophilus; I had also been telling Hanan, the youngest son, vaguely about the latest scandals in Rome. But at this point I broke in on the conversation of the others, and asked:

"Have any disturbances taken place in the province of the Tetrarch?"

The old man answered. "Disturbances? By no means. And in any case it is none of our business. We are quite sure that Herod Antipater can handle the rebels in his territory; he has always done it quite well. We were talking about the trouble makers in Galilee, an abominable place, a hot-bed of rebellion; if not for the Galileans we could sleep comfortably of nights. But one day it's an outbreak of banditry, the next day it's a Messiah. . . . An impossible, credulous mob, ready to follow every adventurer. And it's not only the Zealots; we have those absurd super-pietists, the Hasidim, the Essenes, who are forever washing and baptizing. They baptize everything, their bodies, their vessels—they'll be baptizing the sun and moon next—"

and the old man finished with a burst of angry laughter, in which his sons joined him.

"Ho, ho, I know whom you mean," I said. "Those lean and hungry-looking creatures I sometimes see in the Temple courts, walking about in the skins of wild animals. But tell me, who are they exactly, and what are their beliefs?"

The old man answered wrathfully: "They ascribe all sorts of wretched human weaknesses to the eternal divinity. They drag down the Godhead to the level of petty human interests. They believe, for instance, that the Almighty, who has made His dwelling place in our holy Temple, has nothing more important to do than occupy Himself with the private affairs of every obscure individual. Instead of guiding the world and directing the destinies of the nations, with special reference to His own beloved people Israel, He is concerned with the tribulations of every little Essene—and not, mark you, in this world only, but in the world to come, where He has prepared a paradise for the good little Essenes, while He reserves for the wicked a flaming pit to which they have given the name of Gehenna. Drivel of this kind—about which there is not a word in the sacred Torah. But this isn't enough for them. They have provided the Eternal with a regular staff of beneficent and maleficent spirits who carry out His orders. They transfer the providential attention of God from the people of Israel in its entirety, the inheritor of Abraham, Isaac and Jacob, to the tiniest private concerns of the individual." Thus the old man, speaking in Syrian Greek.

"But surely," I exclaimed, "this is rank blasphemy. Why do you permit it? Why do you not proceed vigorously against those atheistic Jews?"

"Blasphemy? M-m, you cannot exactly call it blasphemy or atheism. Nor can we proceed against them on these grounds. Unfortunately they are not the only ones to be infected with such follies—with the belief, for instance, that every man lives a second life in an imaginary world and that his soul is purified in the heavens. There is among us, unfortunately, a big sect, in which you will find people of no little prominence, which shares these ridiculous views. It is composed of the Scribes, and of the Pharisees, who interpret the words of our Torah not according to plain sense, but inject into them their own thoughts, which are repugnant to the traditions come down from Moses our teacher. But I repeat that we cannot proceed against them. The unlettered masses are on the side of the interpreters of the law, and if we attempted to suppress them—and such attempts were made in the past—we should court the danger of splitting the nation, and this must be avoided. What insane, hysterical hopes they associate with their Messiah cult! And what dangers these boundless expectations can create! Perhaps I had better keep silent."

"You mean," I asked, "rebellion against Rome, a general rising?"

"I would not go so far as that," he answered, with a show of caution. "I will only say that their inflamed imagination transports them into very dangerous areas. One must not, of course, take their absurdities too seriously. You have heard it yourself: their Messiah will awaken the dead from their graves."

There was general laughter.

Old Hanan turned toward me. "As if the burden of the law were not heavy enough, we have the Pharisaic members of the Sanhedrin, who introduce intolerable difficulties into our criminal code. And in particular they complicate its procedure in the matter of capital offenses. They interpose so many scruples, they find such subtle and far-fetched objections to commonsense evidence, they uncover such hairsplitting interpretations of the law, that the criminal can always find a loophole through which to escape."

"In effect, then," I observed, "they are guilty of complicity with the criminal element. I should not be surprised if there is a secret understanding between them and the fanatics who stir up the people both against your religion and our authority."

"Not exactly," the old man returned, reverting to his habitual caution. "And still their tortuous subtleties are a direct encouragement to disorder, for they serve to weaken the law. Let me give you an instance of the new ideas which they read into the code. Our Torah states specifically that any man who assaults another and breaks off a tooth or gouges out an eye, must pay for it with his own tooth or eye. Along come the quibblers and tell us that what the Torah meant was not literally an eye for an eye and a tooth for a tooth, but compensation therefor. What is this but encouragement of violence?"

"Very true." This from one of the sons. And I added, at once:

"Well then, if the Jewish law is no longer capable of maintaining peace and order in Jerusalem, we, the Romans, will have to see to it."

But now it seemed that with all his caution the old man had gone further than he intended, for he turned pale at my words, and his sons looked at each other in alarm.

At this moment there came to us, where we lay in the open hall of columns, the sound of distant shouting, distinct words; but they were in Aramaic, and I did not catch their meaning. But it was clear, from the changed expression on their faces, that old Hanan and his sons had understood them, or at least knew that they were meant for the priestly family. Slaves hastened in and drew the curtains between the columns, to shut out the noise. For some seconds there was oppressive silence, then the old man addressed himself to me:

"This is because I invited you to eat at my table."

"What were they shouting?"

The sons stirred uncomfortably.

"Why should he not know?" asked old Hanan. "It is a sort of song they have, ridiculing the High Priests. To such a pass has it come, and to this level has the priesthood sunk. Theophilus, tell our Roman guest what they sing in the streets of Jerusalem against the highest authority, that is," he added hastily, "against the highest Jewish authority, the Priesthood."

Theophilus translated the words of the song into Latin. They ran approximately as follows:

> Woe unto us because of the House of Beitus,
> Woe unto us because of their lead-loaded whips,
> Woe unto us because of the House of Ananus,
> Woe unto us because of their betrayals.
> They themselves have become High Priests,
> They have made their sons into treasurers
> And their sons-in-law into high officers,
> And their servants whip us with whips of lead.

"And that," said the old man bitterly, "is our reward for our long and faithful service to the people."

"The time has come to restore order in Jerusalem," I said.

The old man nodded dubiously, his sons looked at me uncertainly, torn between gratitude and uneasiness.

CHAPTER TEN

IT was gradually borne in on me that among the relatives of the High Priest it was his youngest brother-in-law, Hanan, who exercised the greatest influence in the conduct of the affairs of the Temple. He was, in fact, the power behind the throne. The old High Priest had a particular love for his youngest son (all Jews have a special weakness for the children of their old age) and had called him by his own name. Hanan ben Hanan was not only the cleverest of the brothers; he was also pre-eminent in character. Young as he was—I guessed him to be in the early twenties—he had already set himself definite goals, and he thrust his way through to them with resolute elbows. I can still see him as if he stood before me: a tall frame, muscular limbs, a body hardened by athletic discipline and thickly covered with a hirsute growth; his short black beard, which was tended daily by a skilled Chaldaean hairdresser, ran up to mingle with his heavy locks, so that his long face was completely framed in the black growth. From this circle the powerful nose stood out, casting a shadow on the narrow lips. His smooth, lustrous forehead cut deep into his dense hair. His eyes were like his father's; they looked out from under the protective barrier of his brows with arrogant and far-sighted brilliance. . . . He was compact of energy from head to foot, and everything in him seemed to cry for immediate action. His hands were always clinched, as if about to take the offensive, his lips tense, as if about to utter a battle cry: he was in a state of continuous mobilization. One careless word, one unfriendly glance, and his limbs became rigid, the hair bristled on his chest as though to pierce like a forest of spears through the covering of linen.

Hanan ben Hanan was a born fighter, and there was occasion enough for fighting. It was no light thing either for us Romans or for the Jewish Priesthood to retain power in Jerusalem, and the boy was hungry for power. Hunger for power shouted from his person, as it did, for that matter, from the person of his father. But while the old man had learned, from long experience, to go about its satisfaction with infinite cunning and patience, contenting himself with the outward show of the civil authority delegated to him by his son-in-law, Hanan ben Hanan was too young, too impetuous, and too inexperienced to conceal his envy of the regnant High Priest.

He knew that much water would have to flow even down the meager Siloah river, before he could realize his dream. Three older brothers stood between him and the High Priesthood, and their ambition, if not as furious as his, still could not be gainsaid. Besides, in spite of his fondness for his youngest child, the old man wanted to live long enough to see every one of his five sons invested in the robes of the supreme religious office, and so far only the oldest, Eliezer, had achieved the distinction. And here was his son-in-law holding onto the position, apparently without intention of ever retiring to make way for his brothers-in-law. There was too much power and too much wealth concentrated in the High Priesthood for any man to relinquish it willingly. Under these conditions, it was natural that there should develop between old Hanan and the regnant High Priest a silent battle for the favor of the Procurator. On the surface it would seem that the High Priesthood was family property, its business was transacted by the group, and the income flowed into a common treasury; actually there was fierce competition for the office, expressing itself in the endless offering of bribes and gifts to the Procurator, the Proconsul Vitellius in Antioch and all the hordes of advisers and sycophants had the ear of the rulers. But still Joseph Kaifa hung on; in his own quiet way, with all his yielding of the civil authority to his father-in-law, he was the more cunning and insistent of the two. His gifts were fatter, the bags of gold he sent to Caesarea were heavier. The end of it was that he triumphed as no High Priest had triumphed before him: he clung to the office through the duration of an entire Procuratorship! While Pontius Pilate was Procurator, Joseph Kaifa was High Priest. The hidden battle went on, but old Hanan knew he was fighting, at least for the time being, in vain; and indeed, he concentrated most of his energies on the struggle to maintain the power of his sect, his class and his family. . . .

Young Hanan, who had inherited the greatest share of his father's gift for rulership, saw clearly enough that the office of High Priest in Jerusalem, like any other office, retained its power and significance only through wealth. Himself still far from possession, he was nevertheless interested in strengthening the throne which would some day be his. He had scarcely come to manhood when he set himself to organizing the income of the High Priesthood on a purely commercial basis. The tithe or tenth of wheat and of other natural products, reserved by the law for the Priesthood, is the exclusive property of the High Priest and his family. The mass of the Priests must be satisfied with the leavings of the sacrifices. The money income of the Priests is likewise the property of the High Priest, and he is free to dispose of it as he sees fit.

More than this: the produce consumed within the Temple itself, the flour for the holy bread, the herbs for the sacrifices, the incense and the distilled oils, the Egyptian flax for the looms at which the women weave the vestments and curtains of the Temple—all these are considered sacred and may be supplied only by the High Priest. And then there are the doves, which every woman must bring as a sacrifice for the birth of a child. They are not ordinary doves, obtainable anywhere. They cannot be trapped by anyone and offered for sale in the Temple market. They must be of a pure breed, well tended, guarded from ritual pollution; they must be specially fed with permitted foods. The breeding of such doves has been taken in hand by the High Priest, and they alone can be offered as a purification sacrifice by the women, who must pay for them the rate fixed by him. And what woman will not find the money for the doves which will purify her in order that she may once more fulfill herself in her womanly duties? Furthermore, the law which regulates the offering of a sacrifice of doves may be broadened, so that the demand increases; the price had already risen from a silver to a gold dinar for a pair of doves without blemish.

It was through the sons of the old High Priest that I finally entered the circle of the gilded youth of Jerusalem. I discovered at long last that the Judaean capital was not wholly the accursed and desolated city which I had imagined it to be. Behind the frontage of severe prohibitions which was the tribute to their stern and jealous God, the aristocratic youth found highly cultured amusements like those of the aristocratic youth of any heathen city; and their enjoyment of life would have done credit to any Greek metropolis.

This circle of the select was regarded with scorn and hatred by the populace, which gave it the contemptuous name of "the heretics" and accused it of atheism. But as far as I could see the youth was merely driving to its logical conclusion the system of views held by the parents—the Sadducees. This was the argument: "If all that life can offer us is the fate of the camel fallen in the wilderness, or the bird shot down by the hunter, what is the sense and purpose of restraining the natural impulse to joy and pleasure? Why should we not let the hours ripen happiness for us? Why should we hesitate to make full use of the position into which we have been born? If God has, indeed, placed you as a ruler over your brothers, is it not because he wants you to draw the reins tight, and increase the burden they bear?" They cited, further, the lines of one of their poets: "What is man that thou art mindful of him?" The manner of their life was based, as one of their prophets remarked bitterly, on the principle: "Today let us eat and drink, for tomorrow we die."

Thus they founded groups of young people which at first met in secret, and later without any precaution of secrecy, the avowed purpose of which was to destroy the bonds and prohibitions laid upon them by their religion. They discovered the world of beauty and pleasure which their cruel law had closed to them, and they threw themselves with all the fury of their starved and passionate bodies into our joys. They quickly became adepts in all the varieties of enjoyment which long experience and traditional institutions had planted among us Romans. They were rich; cost did not deter them. Soon enough their nocturnal banquets, on rose-strewn platforms, surpassed our own. There were gatherings of young men and women who, with their marvelously tended bodies, their education and culture, their singing and wit, would have graced the best society in Antioch, Alexandria or even Rome. I must concede that they did add to these nocturnal affairs a note peculiarly their own. These were not the wild and uncontrolled Bacchanalian revelries, free from every control of decency, and shot through with erotic indulgence, which were common in Alexandria and were carried over from that city into our Hellenism. They, the Jews, brought into Hellenism a note, a modest rhythm, which somehow suggested restraint and decency, and at the same time had a special and more refined touch of provocation, like their perfumes and incenses. Their women never forgot themselves, and even when the gaiety and excitement reached the highest pitch, never showed themselves naked but draped themselves in their long hair. But this was a draping of the body which touched the nerves more sharply, which was more naked than nakedness. Moreover, there was at all their banquets a perpetual mood of regret, subdued but insistent, breaking through the deliberate gaiety; a mood of elegaic meditativeness and recollection, as though it was impossible for them to liberate their minds completely from their ancient burden and they were under a compulsion to name the name of death:

> Like the passing shadow, such is our life.
> There is no returning after the end.
> Let us taste the joys that lie before us,
> Swiftly, while we still have youth.

The circle of the aristocratic youth of Jerusalem to which I was admitted, was frequented by a woman named Miriam, or Mary; and because she came from the city of Migdal, on the Sea of Genesaret or Tiberias, she was also called Magdalena—that is, Miriam of Migdal. The reputation of this woman was not without blemish. Or perhaps I should say that her reputation varied according to the class that spoke of her. In our circles she was loved and honored. When I met her she was no longer in her first youth; she was closer to that age of ripeness in which the Greek masters have always chosen to portray the goddess of love. She was the experienced mother type, with broad hips and full-developed breasts which peeped out like modest doves between the red veils of her hair. There was a mild motherliness in her treatment of those who were admitted to her favors. And she distributed her favors according to need rather than reward, for she was capricious, full of surprises and fantasies, like a true daughter of her people. There were men of wealth who loved her, who had flung away fortunes to please her, who would have fulfilled the most arbitrary demands for the breath that came from between her lips; these she often ignored, letting them wither for want of her. Instead, it was to such as had never had the courage—or the means—to court her, or even to dream of courting her, to the unimportant, the poor and the forlorn, that she offered her kindness. She distributed her favors as one distributes charity among the poor, that is, without seeking reward or return.

I had heard a great deal concerning Miriam of Migdal, even before I met her. But who had not? All Jerusalem spoke of the woman who was said to exercise a profound influence on the sons of the oldest High Priest, the leaders of the Jerusalem aristocracy. This had not a little to do with her popularity among the gilded youth, for anyone who aspired to social distinction in Jerusalem began by imitating the sons of the High Priest. Miriam of Migdal, or Mary Magdalene, was skillful in the management of her life; her favors were widely scattered, like the rain which falls on many fields; her lovers would encounter each other, they knew of each other, and yet, in a strange way, there was no jealousy between them. Instead of creating enmities she possessed the art of binding men together by their common love for her. I too, I must confess, fell somewhat under her influence, for at our first meeting she made an unforgettable impression on me.

The occasion was a banquet in honor of Hanan, the youngest son of the old High Priest. It was a glorious moonlit night; the heavens were covered with a pearly veil of light, and at our feet Jerusalem lay sleeping in a web of shadows. We were drunk with the manifold odors of flowers and sweet-blossoming plants which even in those hottest months had been richly watered. The jasmine and the towering iris, the rose and the lavender, troubled the air with the lure of their scent. We lay stretched on couches in the columned hall of Hanan's house, the perfumed head of my friend Theophilus rested on my shoulder, and we watched, by the discreet light of hanging oil lamps, the dancing of Abisheleg, the most beloved girl of Jerusalem, accompanied by the music of invisible harps. Her perfect limbs flowed before us in waves of rhythm. She was still very young, in the third lustrum of her age, and her body was still gathered up in itself like a bud before the moment of its opening. The alabaster shimmer of her skin broke through the delicate weave of Zidonian linen which hung in folds from her hips, and her body, almond light, compact of blood and milk, followed in close, severe discipline the harmony of her dance. Her belly, encircled with a wreath of leaves, trembled and twisted spasmodically, like the surface of an overflowing lake, and the bud of her breast sang in motion the song of her immanent ripeness. But what delighted us most was the snake-play of the line of her back; a cascade of whiteness was poured down into the soft and smooth double roundnesses, and the supple backbone trembled and bent through a gamut of serpentine motion.

And while our eyes drank in thirstily the welling harmony of the dance, so that we forgot the honey-rich grapes and the honey-scented pomegranates and the figs bursting with sweetness which the young Phoenician slaves offered us in baskets of woven gold, we heard suddenly, from a dim corner of the hall, a voice, filled at once with womanly allurement and disturbing sadness, raised in declamation:

> "Who can arrest and hold back the breath of youth which is on our bodies and which is like the night dew on the rose? Who can seal up the firmness of our limbs that they may not fall into ruin before the storm of time? Who can suspend even for the duration of a moment our progress toward destruction? Who knows as well as we ourselves the nothingness of our being? He has made us the witnesses of our own downgoing. He has made our bodies the nest of worms which we breed for our own destruction. What is beauty, which passes like a mist? The wind

takes it up and carries it away. Over what shall we rejoice—over that which once was, and now is no more? Are not our days like those of the hired laborer in the field? Like a slave who longs for the shadow of night we long for the shadow of death. . . ."

The girl suspended her dance, and we became silent and motionless. The head of Theophilus trembled on my shoulder. Then Hanan signaled to the slaves to withdraw. A dead, oppressive stillness rested on all of us. The girl Abisheleg, the beauty of whose body was a byword in Judaea, burst into hysterical tears, and at that moment the woman who had extinguished the gaiety with her song of lamentation rose from her corner. It was Miriam of Migdal. She approached little Abisheleg and took the girl under her veil, while she wiped away her tears with her kerchief and led her into the dim corner from which she had emerged.

Later I became more closely acquainted with Mary of Migdal. Indeed, she held us all like hounds on a leash; some she let approach her, others she held off implacably. There were also times when it pleased her to know not a single one among her many lovers and to permit no one to cross her threshold. The most favored man was never certain of her. Young Hanan, it was said, was one of her "official admirers," and she had cost him great sums of money. His brother Theophilus and his wife were visitors in her house, and marvelous evenings were passed there. Of one of these I shall tell later. One of the Askelonite officers of our garrison was desperately in love with Miriam of Migdal. Another man, Kalman ben Kalman, the son of a millionaire of Jerusalem, who had inherited possessions in farms and fields and forests of olive trees the extent of which was beyond his reckoning, had also been deeply affected and showered her with costly presents. But it appeared that the admirer whom she admitted most closely into her confidence was a Babylonian princeling who for her sake had converted to the Jewish faith. He made frequent pilgrimages to Jerusalem, where he offered sacrifices with a lavish hand. He had built for Miriam of Migdal a house in the Babylonian style, situated in the Lower City. She had, moreover, countless admirers among the Jewish merchants of

Alexandria, Antioch and Caesarea, who came on business and pilgrimage to Jerusalem.

It was a characteristic caprice of hers which had made her choose the poorest part of the city for her house and to refuse to live among the aristocracy of the Upper City or in the new quarter on the slope of Mount Scopus, beyond the Sheep Gate, a district which had of late become fashionable because it afforded room for gardens. She had made her home close to the wall which divides the city from the Valley of the Kidron.

It was not a pleasant quarter to live in. Indeed, only one other quarter could have been less attractive, namely the valley beyond the Dung Gate, the Valley of Hinnom, where the waters of Siloah ran through gutters and the lepers had made their camping ground. Not for nothing had the name Ge-Hinnom, or Valley of Hinnom, become the symbol of the pit of punishment reserved for the wicked in the world to come. Certainly it was not a fitting place for a lady of her standing. If there were no lepers, there were multitudes of men and women afflicted with other sicknesses; they gathered round the waters of the Kidron, and they filled the air with the stench of their diseases. Vast swarms of insects bred in the valley, for on the other side, at the foot of the Mount of Olives, the High Priest, or rather the house of Hanan, had its stalls and the storerooms for the hides of the sacrifices. The servants and slaves of the High Priest washed the hides in the Kidron, preparing them for the market. The filth which reigned in that part of the city was indescribable. All the garbage of Jerusalem was carried out through the Dung Gate and flung into the Kidron Valley. Beggars poked among the midden heaps, seeking the remnants of the meals of the rich, or rags with which to cover their shame.

Here, in this section, she had built her house; here, in the heart of Jerusalem's poverty, among the narrow fetid alleys, the walls of her house rose behind cypresses and olive trees. Thus her doors were for ever beleaguered by the armies of the poor, and her servants, under her strict orders, were for ever issuing with platters of food or gifts of money.

An overwhelming love of life impelled her to drain to the dregs the beakers of joy, but there always lingered on the rim the taste of poison, restlessness, and remorse, left there by the religious madness which gave her no peace. All her servants went about clad in the ritualistic fringes of their religion; no image of man or beast was permitted in the house; the appointments were of the richest material, but devoid of ornament; there was no trace anywhere of the art or the customs of the Roman and pagan world, and within the circle of her walls reigned the severe discipline of her faith. Even when I first became acquainted with her she was already subject to religious seizures—a general characteristic, I may observe, of Oriental peoples. She had surrounded herself with a band of interpreters of the law, scholars and scribes. They were not, of course, the authentic and accepted sages who preached and taught in the Temple courts; those would not have come within a hundred paces of her, and whenever she sent a gift or sacrifice to the Temple there was endless disputation whether it ought to be accepted, for her money was considered unclean. However, there were scholars enough of dubious standing who were troubled by fewer scruples in regard to her profession. They did not fail to threaten her with the fires and demons of Gehenna, but they gave her assurance of another life, too, because she devoted the wealth of her admirers to benevolent purposes, the most important being naturally the support of scholars. There were also the hosts of the poor, who transformed her house into a refuge of poverty, wretchedness, and sickness. The streets were black when she was carried forth in her litter, preceded by two servants with bags of dinars to distribute to the rabble. Beyond all this, she gave with a liberal hand to various institutions founded by the charitable women of Jerusalem; the range of benevolences was extraordinary, and stretched from the care of poor women in childbirth to easing the last days of condemned criminals. . . . I need hardly say that Miriam of Migdal was not admitted to membership in the institutions of "the noble ladies of Jerusalem." They were even reluctant to accept her gifts, but her "scholars" had managed to find an interpretation of the law which left the letter of it intact without interrupting the flow of money. And she, the proud and beautiful woman, did not take offense; on the contrary, she was overwhelmed with joy at being permitted to contribute the golden dinars given her by her lovers.

CHAPTER ELEVEN

AND it was in this gutter, in the heart of this noisomeness and filth, that Miriam of Migdal kept the collection of perfumes which she cultivated, according to her own prescriptions, in the flower garden she had planted on the Mount of Olives. It was as if she had entered into a contest, pitting her precious oils and essences against the mephitic stench which surrounded her. More than one king was envious of her collection.

The Jews have a weakness for oils and sweet-smelling herbs. In one of the many chambers of the Temple they had installed a laboratory for the extracting of essences from the rarest plants, to use in their holy lamps, and for other ritualistic purposes. They even had a special treasury of oils and perfumes, which they ranked not lower than their treasury of gold, and which had become the subject of legends. It was said to contain the strangest and most exotic growths, sent from the remotest corners of the world by followers of their cult. It contained likewise anointing oils of incredible antiquity and sanctity. One of these, the legend told, had been preserved from the time when the Jews were in the wilderness; their deity had sent it down from heaven, bidding them guard it until the coming of their Messiah, for whose special anointment it had been created. It was related, further, that certain other oils disappeared when approached by an unbeliever, and thus retained their purity; they had to be re-discovered and re-distilled by the priests. They had developed a complicated and incomprehensible cult round the herbs and oils and spices which they used on their various holy days and for the purification sacrifices. They used oils and essences for a great variety of occasions, for the anointing of bridegrooms, the preparation of brides, the laying out of the dead for burial. The rich anointed themselves with perfumes for festive banquets. Even the common people, the very poorest, smeared their bodies with oils at certain times. There were salves for sicknesses and for skin eruptions and perfumes to awaken love in the heart of the desired one. There were spices to be burned against the effects of witchcraft, and to ward off the evil eye, not to mention the innumerable oils used for cleansing purposes. The city was filled with little oil mills, which spread the savor of their contents through the streets. It seemed there was hardly a plant or herb or weed from which they did not extract an essence. And correspondingly, their language was rich in names of oils, according to the growths from which they were pressed or the ends to which they were devoted.

Every woman of the aristocracy had of course her individual perfumes and cosmetic oils, prepared from her own plants according to her own prescription, but Miriam of Migdal surpassed them all in the ingenuity, refinement and number of her salves. She was a woman of two lives, one belonging to her house in the Kidron Valley, the other, diametrically different, to her garden on the Mount of Olives. In the Lower City she was the woman of the world, who drew to her doors the rich and cultured youth of Jerusalem; there she received her wealthy admirers, and there she displayed herself draped in the flaming veil of her hair which her servants wove about her with such skill that only glimpses of her nakedness came through. But high up on the Mount of Olives, in the garden which was part of the village of Bet Eini, she had a house in which lived her sister Martha and her brother Eliezer. The garden went by the name of Gat Shemen, which in their language means Oil Treader, for there the unguents were prepared for her use. It was an extraordinary place, worthy of the reputation which it enjoyed in Jerusalem and beyond. She had brought together, from every corner of the world, an infinite variety of herbs, weeds, plants, and blossoms. Whenever she heard of some rare flower or cactus thorn growing in a remote wilderness, she sent for it and had it transplanted to her garden; nothing mattered but that she should possess herself of some new, delicate odor. She kept, for the pursuit of this passion, her own oil treaders, whose sense of smell was keenly developed, and who had secret recipes, transmitted in the tradition of their families, for the extraction and compounding of perfumes. It was rumored that there grew in her garden the fabulous plant called mar-d'ror, which the Jews had brought with them from the wilderness; from it had been distilled the original oil which, spread upon their altar, had been a sweet savor to their God. In time, however, the plant had been lost. Stories were told in Jerusalem concerning the scholars who had sent to Miriam's garden to find out whether it did indeed contain the unique mar-d'ror; and then there had been violent disputations as to whether it would be permissible to make use of her plants for the Temple. Her religious advisers, the scholars, were greatly exercised by the immense variety of the plants: were they being grown separately, according to the law, or was there grafting and mingling of species, which their religion specifically forbids?

The garden of Miriam of Migdal attracted the learned and the curious of all nations, and visitors from Rome and Greece and Egypt who happened to pass through Jerusalem would apply to her for permission to study her garden. She seldom accorded it, for she had reserved this place for herself. When she became weary of the tumultuous life of Jerusalem she withdrew to her garden of spices, and there she would pass whole days in meditation, casting up accounts with herself. She was haunted by the problems of eternity, of the ultimate end of man, and of the purpose of life. She could not be content, as we others are, with daily joys, with the fruits that fall from the branches of the hours. For the truth was that they did not stir her, and the brilliant banquets which she prepared in her city house were intended to make her forget herself in a kind of intoxication rather than satisfy a native appetite for pleasures. The weak flame of her desire would flicker out some warm summer night on her starlit terrace, and she would disappear for weeks at a stretch, to fast, repent and purify herself, and to seek the counsel of the bearded and black-robed Rabbis on how to wash away her sins.

And indeed her garden was admirably suited for meditation and self-communion, as I can testify, for I have been in it. Together with some friends who were as eager as myself to look on the famous retreat, I set out once, uninvited, to risk a visit. We rode up the slope of the Mount of Olives. Unexpected luck attended our venture: Miriam of Migdal was not at home. She had gone that day, as she so often did, to the Temple courts, to listen from morn till evening to the disputations of the scholars. We were received by a young man who, as it transpired later, was her brother. His extraordinary length was topped by a face the like of which I have never encountered elsewhere. The cheeks were incredibly drawn out, but they were irradiated by a queer smile of kindliness—one might have said an idiotic smile. But what was it, simplicity or goodness? At first I had the feeling that his mind was not wholly developed, for he did not cease to smile all the time he talked, and he seemed gratified to be able to do whatever we, complete strangers to him, suggested. I assured myself later that it was pure simplicity, of a kind which may be met with frequently enough among country folk in Judaea, and even more in Galilee. He did not once ask us who we were and what business we had in the place, but made humble obeisance and besought us to enter. He brought us basins of water and towels to wash our feet, though they happened to be well-encased in sandals. He washed our hands and, as the custom is among them in the receiving of visitors, approached to kiss us. Within, the house was scrupulously clean and simple; there was nothing that hinted at the great house in the city. We saw only the barest and most necessary of furnishings: two mattresses of woven straw on the hard, earthen floor, two cushions and covers disposed in the corners and partly shut off by screens of bamboo wood, a low table, two small mattresses by its side—and then a few clay or woven vessels and gourd bottles, a few jars, two large urns, some wooden boards, all homely work, in which they kept their daily supplies of bread, cheese, sour milk. As in every poor house, the stone oven was so built that its smoke did not escape by the roof, but poured out through the open door. Door and window were draped with curtains of woven straw. The man bade us sit, and asked us to be at ease, but I could not shake off the strange impression he had made on me. He spoke slowly and with frequent pauses, as though both his organs and his impulses were dull with heaviness, but at the same time his gentle smile and humble demeanor seemed to beg forgiveness for his labored speech and motion. I soon discovered that this dullness did not proceed from a defect in his mental growth; it was the result of a certain inner quietude. For later, when he conducted us through the garden, with all its complicated plants, he displayed both intelligence and knowledge. And yet at first the undisturbed faith which possessed him made me feel that he lacked something and was unable to grasp and analyze simple things and incidents; it was a curious and eerie effect, as though I had before me not a man, with will and nerves, but rather a strange, phlegmatic animal. The same strangeness, I would even say the same hint of death, rested on the whole peaceful house, for one would have believed, from the quiet, from the severe cleanliness and order which reigned in it, that only the dead dwelt here. Yet this was by no means the impression which one carried away from his sister Miriam, or from the young girl, Martha, whom he now called into the room; for the latter, in spite of her obvious nervousness and distress at our unexpected visit, retained enough vanity to throw a glance at her face in the urn of water as she hastened toward us. But he remained, with all his humility and submissiveness, as distant as if he belonged to another world.

He was just as remote from us and from this world when he led us through the garden. He was interested in what he was telling us and yet completely indifferent. We saw him standing before us, pointing to one object after another, speaking to us, seeing his surroundings, touching them with his hands; and yet he was not there, he was elsewhere, as though he had been partially awakened from a dream which was his real life.

There was, moreover, a disturbing congruence between his mood and the spirit of the garden. I had never seen such varieties of flora, I had not known that so many existed. It was not a garden of plants and flowers, but a necropolis of petrified foliage and color in the likeness of creeping things, animals and limbs of unknown creatures. In Judaea one becomes accustomed to the sight of new growths, plants and vegetables, not encountered in other lands. Because of the stringent ritualistic prescriptions which surround the preparation of meat dishes, the Jews rely largely for their food on the produce of their gardens; hence they have developed unusual varieties of plants. One finds here melons and artichokes in forms and sizes never encountered elsewhere. They have a sort of apple-melon which they call "k'sus" and which resembles an animal climbing on the leaves; the surrounding leaves are hard and black like old leather, and set with wild tongues. The fruit is a mixture, half flower, half fruit, with a strong taste of mint, which burns the tongue. There is also the artichoke, which they call "kineres"; this is not a vegetable, but a kind of cactus with the claws of a wild cat; under the claws lie pouches of magic powder which attracts insects on which the plant feeds by sucking out their juice. There are in this land rooted growths which are more animal than plant; and yet everything that I had seen till then in Judaea was as nothing compared to the contents of the garden.

On a sloping terrace in the shadow of dark cypresses there stretched four trellised lanes of plants. On this side, close to the entrance, lay four flower beds; one was a blaze of red poppies such as are common in Judaea only in the springtime; the second was a harmony of picked blue hyacinths, their heads hanging down in close clusters; the third was a bed of tremulous lilies of the valley; and the fourth a lane of violet irises. The four colors, Miriam's brother explained to us, represented the four elements of the creation, earth, air, fire and sea. This, as I recalled, was a repetition of the symbolic coloring on the strange Babylonian curtain which, according to young Hanan's account, covered the entrance to the sanctuary of the Temple, and which was woven in hyacinth, byssus, scarlet and purple. Between the four beds and the trellises in the shadow of the cypresses lay the actual garden of spices or, as I have called it, the necropolis of petrified or enchanted creatures: a field of fantastic figures, gaping mouths, contorted limbs, convulsive tendrils, black tongues, and protruding-swords, a confusion of heavy colors, close-locked and oppressive, from deepest violet to fieriest red. Side by side were beds of dragon-flowers like tangles of worms, beds of irises which held in their pistils captive flowers like butterflies, beds of carnations fast asleep in their stamens, beds of narcissus, beds of cummin and sharp peppermint, bushes of mild bluish lavender and stinging, intoxicating ginger, nutmeg bushes and branches of saffron, cinnamon plants with tiny distyll tongues. Scattered through all of these were countless field flowers. There was not only a harmony of color, but an almost visible exhalation of aromatic mists.

What I have described till now covers familiar names, the flora of all gardens. When we passed beyond these beds we came upon incredible eruptions of form and color, on twisted, root-like shapes, pointed and prehensile, which caught at our clothes and arrested our progress. These were the exotic plants which had been brought from remote places in the wilderness, such as the sharp-smelling helbonah and lebonah, which are used in the Temple services; they came from Syria and were dried and ground into incense. Now I saw where Miriam of Migdal obtained the odorous herbs which she burned in the metal and earthen censers scattered through the rooms of her house. We saw in her garden plants, which in form and color were replicas of the severed limbs of man and beast, a flaming red cockscomb, the erect ear of an ass, noses thrust up sensitively from the soil, trembling, one would have said, with inhaled and exhaled air; there were crippled plants which brought forth no flower, but consisted of fungus and naked, crooked roots reaching out with unearthly hands, fists and fingers as if in dumb prayer. I could have sworn that there went up from them a bitter lamentation, as if they were the earth-bound reincarnations of the accursed dead imploring release. And all these plants, flowers, thorns and cacti, familiar and unfamiliar, from the homely flower of the field to the remotest blossom of the desert, were there to yield up their hidden essences for the unguents and perfumes of Miriam of Migdal.

CHAPTER TWELVE

THE religious seizures of Miriam of Migdal were intermittent. When she was free from them she arranged in her house the most interesting evenings in Jerusalem, bringing together all that was illustrious in the city.

Here we Romans could mingle with the enlightened class of Jews and exchange views freely. We were united by our admiration for this extraordinary woman, cast under a common spell by the brown-tinted skin whose nacreous shimmer was visible here and there between the folds of her veils. Her close-knit body possessed all the mysteries of the love with which she was sated. . . . The high, proud neck, the immense dark eyes, crowned the benediction of her body, and these, together with the subtle perfumes in the midst of which she moved, held us all, Jew and heathen alike, in thrall. For every mood she had another perfumed oil, creating its separate accompanying atmosphere. She played with these perfumes as a snake plays with the colors of its scales. When she fell into dejection, in the first onset of an approaching religious seizure, her presence exhaled deep, quiet scent of heliotrope and iris, which threw a shadow on the spirit. When she wished to transmit to others a mood of delicate modesty she used an essence of innocent and refreshing violets mingled with lilies of the valley, reminiscent of spring showers. And when she was intent on breathing into you the uttermost desires of the flesh—wave upon wave of longing which subdued the will and made it the servant of her imperious commands—she sent forth from her veils and her thick-woven hair a ripe, sweet odor of roses, tinged with another distillation, sharp, penetrating and disturbing, whose nature was unknown to us.

She had set apart one room in her house for the storing of her oils and perfumes, and here she kept an extraordinary assortment of bottles, vials and flacons in mother-of-pearl coloring, delicate, rainbow-hued Phoenician glass adorned with designs of candelabra and clusters of grapes. There were tear-glasses with long, thin necks, which admitted and gave out liquids one drop at a time. Her costliest oils she kept in clay and earthenware jars, for the finer materials permit evaporation, with deleterious effect on the oils. She possessed likewise great numbers of tiny vessels of precious stone, turquoise and emerald, which she carried on golden chains about her neck. In the moments of sweetest graciousness she would anoint her chosen one with the contents of the precious vials.

Of the highly developed sense for perfumes and oils among the Jews, of the recipes which are transmitted in families from generation to generation, of the varieties of occasions which call for the use of unguents, and of the specialists in their preparation, I have already told you. The profession was one of the most respected and lucrative in Jerusalem. There was even a popular saying: "Oils love the voice of the mortar." I became acquainted in time with several of these oil mixers, and one of them I encountered under unusual circumstances in the house of Mary Magdalene. Of this meeting I shall now tell you.

We were seated one evening in the perfume hall of Miriam's house, a considerable company. The banquet had been arranged in honor of her rich Babylonian admirer, the princeling, who was on one of his visits to the Temple of the God to whom he had converted. It was a matter of importance to the Jerusalemites that the Babylonian, who came of a powerful and influential family, should be well received, and there were assembled that evening all the admirers of Mary Magdalene. Two of the sons of Hanan came, and with them several rich young men of the city, among them the son of the wealthy Kalman. There was present, too, the Askelonite officer of the garrison. Women were few. Miriam did not like the company of women, but she had invited for the evening little Abisheleg, for whom she had developed a warm friendship, and one or two other young girls. She loved to be surrounded by youth, which was one of the reasons why she did not keep in her house Greek and Egyptian musicians, as was the custom in all the distinguished houses in Jerusalem. For the Greek musicians and singers and the Egyptian flute-players who came to Jerusalem, either as freemen or sent thither as slaves from the markets of Tyre and Askelon, were no longer young; they had shining bald circles on their heads, and their bodies were without desire, for the years had taken away their charm and their lust of life. . . . Miriam kept as house musicians young Levites of poor families who had not been received into the Temple service; they had been trained in the music school kept by the Temple for the children of the Levites. Their upbringing and training had been severe and traditional, and they were useless except for their own kind of music. When Mary Magdalene danced, she was always accompanied by little Phiha, her beloved Egyptian flute-player.

The guests who assembled that night in honor of the Babylonian prince had put on their costliest clothes and jewels. There was, indeed, a spirit of competition among them. Pearls and other precious stones twinkled softly in the folds of every silken *ketonet* or robe. The prince himself was in royal attire and wore on his head a tiara of flashing jewels; but what held our attention most was the *ketonet* of delicate Babylonian weave, which he wore buttoned to the throat, and which was set with fringes of pearls. The brothers-in-law of the High Priest were scarcely less distinguished, for each one wore over his *ketonet* a rich mantle or cape of silver thread. The son of the magnate, whose rank was that of simple Israelite, was not permitted to wear such a mantle (that was a privilege reserved for a member of a ruling house, the flash of silver being associated in the mind of the Jews with their angels, the beneficent demons of their God), but he sought to outdo all the others with the rings he wore on his fingers, set with rare stones, some black as night, some blue as the mid-day sky, and with the chain of brilliants fastened about his neck. The glitter of the stones dominated the room, and all of us considered this display of riches on the part of a parvenu in very poor taste. We, the Romans, came in our centurion uniforms, and in breastplates on which were displayed our medals. But we wore these only during the formal part of the banquet. Later, when Miriam danced for us, and when the company relaxed from its stiffness and tension, the prince removed the diadem from his brow, the priestly scions their silver capes, while we Romans had the servants undo our breastplates and take away our togas, so that we remained in our tunics. For the house was hot with the mists which drifted from the glowing censers.

Little Phiha, who played for Miriam's dance, had a little, full mouth which stood out on her round face like a ripe grape; the almond shape of her eyes had been lengthened by an operation, and her pitch-black hair hung in scores of tiny locks over the curves of her shoulders. Ornaments twinkled among the locks, surrounding a comb of white ivory, and a white lotus blossom was fastened to her temple. Her neck ran in long powerful lines into the breastbone, and her arms, disproportionately long for her figure, were covered, like her naked feet, with rings and other ornaments. A delicate veil of black tulle, sewn with lotus flowers, was thrown about her well-formed body, and the lines of her hips and breasts filtered through its gauze. She rested on one knee as her fingers, with their yellow-lacquered nails, swept over the strings of the long hand-harp, drawing from it a strange melody. To the restrained tones issuing from the harp Mary Magdalene appeared before us, surrounded and draped by the rings of smoke from the glowing spices which the young Levites carried in censers. At first she was almost completely veiled from us, then, as the mists of incense were diffused from round her, she stood revealed. But in what a fantastic likeness! The nakedness of the body was draped in a shower of flame-red hair, and the strands were arranged and woven with such cunning that one would have said she was wearing a glowing tunic. The delicate weave of hair passed through a filter the dark luster of her body. For a moment there was uncovered the fullness of her rounded breast; it vanished, and the next moment afforded a glimpse of the rich-flowing back, the strong neck, the sensitive backbone. From the proud, turret-like throat hung, as always, the golden chain which supported Egyptian vials of precious stone filled with intoxicating perfumes. Her head was crowned with a wreath of fresh olive leaves, in the midst of which shone darkly an unknown jewel. Her eyes were ringed with black and artificially lengthened with cosmetics. And on naked feet glittering with rings she danced for us to the melody of the harp-player and of the young Levites who, kneeling as they held aloft their censers, added their voices to the music.

I was told later that this was a national dance of the Jews, a dance in which the women express their love-longings for the man of their choice. It embodies in its movements a love song of the people, a song widely beloved and heard on every hand. Tradition ascribed its words to their famous king, Solomon. At one moment in the dance movement, the woman stretched out her hands to her beloved, and her eyes were filled with longing and desire; at another she hid from him, like a dove taking shelter beneath its own wing, under the cover of her arms. So Miriam danced; her whole body was caught up in a fever, she writhed in agonizing ecstasy, drunk with the rhythm of melody which poured from the harp strings and the singers. In the intoxication of motion she seemed to forget our presence and existence. Or, if she remembered, she ignored us.

She uncovered her breast, her back, her shoulders, in the whirlwind of sound. Her mouth became like a sponge which soaks up kisses. Her arms were wound about her in self-embrace, she showered tenderness upon herself. When she began to chant the words of the folk song, and her voice was added to the ecstasy of music and motion and perfumes, we who watched her felt ourselves melt into one dark sea of desire. I glanced at my neighbor, young Hanan, lying on his couch, and I saw his lips tremble, I saw a pallor creep over his pointed nose, I saw his eyelids droop. I glanced at the Babylonian prince, and I saw him consumed in his own fire, I saw the thin dark face grow thinner. He had closed his eyes, his fists were clenched convulsively, one of them against his temple, to which he pressed a rose as if to cool himself. I glanced at my Askelonite officer, who stood leaning against a shadowed pillar; he was pale, like the others, but his eyes were wide open, hot, and moist, as though they were bathed in burning tears. I glanced at the son of the Jerusalem magnate; he had turned his eyes from the dancer and was staring in wild self-concentration at the black stone in one of his rings.

Then something happened which tore us suddenly out of the hot torpor of absorption: at the other end of the hall a man broke in through the long chain of servants. From the tapping of the staff which he held before him we perceived at once that he was blind. He was as thin and pallid as a dried root, and his body seemed ready to slip through the tattered sackcloth shirt about it. But the blind, dead face shone as with an inner flame; his bony limbs were sharply chisled. He tore through the hands of the servants who tried to detain him, thrust forward his bird-like face with its tangled beard, held out his arms in the direction of Miriam and sang, or rather howled, with her the verses of the folk song which referred to her unguents:

"*L'reach shemonecha ha-tovim* . . . —because of the savor of thy good ointments . . ."

We were paralyzed with astonishment. We did not know what had happened. Miriam suddenly suspended her dance and signaled to the house watchman, who approached and explained something to her.

And then, incredible as it sounds, instead of breaking out in fury, instead of having the blind beggar flung from the room, she burst into loud and joyous laughter which bordered on hysteria. When she had recovered self-control she ordered her servants to lead the blind beggar away, to wash and anoint him, to drape him in the finest Phoenician linen and to bring him back to the banqueting hall.

Then, turning to us, she explained, while interrupting herself with the same wild laughter, that this man was a certain Bar Talmai, once an oil mixer, the best in Jerusalem. "He caught the perfume of my ointments beyond the gate, and it drove him mad. He always goes mad if the perfume reaches him when he is passing the house, and then he breaks his way in. I hope you will have nothing against it if this unfortunate man takes his place amongst us. God has closed his eyes, but has opened up instead his perception of perfumes."

And this extraordinary command was carried out. The servants washed and anointed him, they wrapped him in fine linens, they brought him back and led him to a couch, and they placed before him the most delicate fruits and the rarest wines. But he neither ate nor drank. He hid his face in his hands, breathed heavily, and went on repeating the verses of the folk song.

Nor was this all. Nothing would do for Miriam of Migdal but she must repeat her dance for him; and since he could not see her supple motions, she passed close to him again and again, and from different parts of her veils and hair wafted upon him one perfume after another. They were innumerable and strong; they seemed to carry with them the color of the flowers from which they were pressed. And as often as her veil showered upon the blind beggar another perfume, he started with a cry of joy. He kissed the air, he stretched out his hands to the perfumes, he seized them, he spread them upon his body as though they were ointments, he spread them upon his face and his eyes, and he babbled his own words mixed with the words of the song: "Who hath comforted me as thou, my modest one, thou chosen of my heart; thy ointments comfort my heart like the taste of apples, they heal my wounds like a good balm, they wipe away the contumely of the despised, they strengthen the oppressed. See, they stretch out to me thy soft, desirous hands, they caress me as the mother caresses her only child. Sing to me, my beloved, sing to me of thy perfumes, for now they take me back to the garden of my mother when I was but a child and my eyes still rejoiced in the light of the sun. I feel now the fresh crocus which blossomed in our garden and I see the tender buds of the jasmine—so tender and modest and blossoming art thou, so little and so radiant with perfume. Now I am cooled by the wind of field and forest in the hot days of summer, the odor of the lilies of the valley washes me with the dew which falls on the morning rose, and the honey of roses is poured through my skin. O sadden me not with the storm of the cruel iris, frighten me not with the night of the dark rose, but soften me with the odor of violets, and stay my heart with the dripping honey of myrrh. O sing to me the song of thy ointments—" and the blind beggar babbled in ecstatic verses which escaped us.

And she, Miriam of Migdal, was wholly occupied with him, and forgot us utterly; neither by glance nor gesture did she acknowledge our presence in the banqueting hall. She circled widely before the blind one, pouring down alternating perfumes from her veils and tresses. And with him it was as if every change of perfume shot a ray of light into the darkness of his eyes; his open mouth gulped in the laden air, and returned it in cries of happiness, so that in the end the strange spectacle began to fill us with revulsion.

I saw the Babylonian prince writhe on his couch, spring to his feet and lie down again. Young Hanan's eagle nose had become still paler, and it curved in a white ridge over his lips. His eyes had narrowed down to points of flame. I was afraid that he would suddenly leap from his couch, fling himself on the insolent and revolting old beggar and tear him limb from limb. The same fury and hate burned in the faces of the son of the magnate and of the Askelon officer; it seemed to me that I heard the furious drumming of envy and loathing in their hearts. So it was with all of us. But Miriam, circling closer and closer about the recumbent, chanting beggar, shielded him from our rage.

One by one we left the banqueting hall. First it was the Babylonian prince who snatched up the diadem which had fallen from his brow, and the mantle which lay beside him, and called to his servant with a loud, impatient cry. But Miriam paid not the slightest attention to him. Then followed the priestly scions, the Askelonite, myself. If she was aware of our going, then her frenzied dancing hastened our departure. We left her alone with the blind, ecstatic-singing old man.

The next morning, happening to pass through the Court of the Gentiles, I saw her in the company of a woman servant near a booth of sacrificial doves. She was veiled from head to foot like a Vestal. I paused to wait until she had completed her purchase; a long time passed before she found a pair of doves to please her. When she caught sight of me she drew her veil hastily over the blue-iridescent heads of the birds, which she was holding most lovingly to her bosom, as if she was afraid that my glance would defile her offering. I approached her and said something concerning the incident of the preceding night, but she did not let me finish my remark; she made a vague gesture of acknowledgment and farewell, and turned from me. I followed her at a little distance to the entrance of the women's court. At the gate of Corinthian bronze she put off her outer veil, and donned another handed her by her servant. Doubtless she felt that the words I had spoken had contaminated her garment. She then lifted the veil which covered the doves to hide her own face; a twig of incense in one hand, she disappeared with little, singing steps behind the gate of the women's court.

CHAPTER THIRTEEN

THEN suddenly all this disappeared as at the wave of a hand. Thus it is with Orientals. You cannot be sure of them from one day to the next.

She took the blind man permanently into the house, and his influence over her was fatal; he unrooted her from the midst of her life as one might uproot a lovely plant in the midst of its flowering. He was one of those who believed that the dead would rise from their grave with the coming of their Messiah, and he filled Miriam of Migdal with his own faith.

The blind oil-mixer was one of the learned, well versed in the writings of the Jews. From that night on Miriam always kept him by her side at all banquets and receptions. His beard combed, his body washed, anointed and covered with linen, wearing the ritualistic fringes, he sat there babbling interminably the verses of their tradition. He spoiled completely every one of our assemblies, and transformed our banquets from amusing and pleasurable occasions into weary evenings of hair-splitting—and head-splitting—disputation.

Miriam became steadily worse in this respect, sinking completely under the blind man's influence. The latter developed, in time, into a follower of Jochanan the Baptist, the same Jochanan was being held in prison by Herod Antipater for blasphemy against the kingship, as I had heard from the old High Priest. For when the news spread that Jochanan had been thrown into prison for his bold attack on the Tetrarch, he gathered many believers. The common people believed that he, Jochanan, was one of their ancient prophets returned to life. The blind oil-mixer pulled Mary Magdalene with him into this faith. They awaited now great events, among them the coming of their redeemer, according to the words of Jochanan, and they were constantly purifying themselves in preparation. Miriam abandoned the life she had led until then, forgot her former friends, and on a certain day disappeared from the city. She was not seen even in the Temple. She retired for a long time to her garden of spices on the Mount of Olives, taking with her blind Bar Talmai. There they called together certain of their brethren in the faith, among them, it was said, even lepers and other sick folk. They changed the magnificent garden into a simple factory of spices, and they sold the oils and aromatics in the city and in the Temple. This was their means of sustenance; whatever was left over from their needs they distributed among the poor.

When a long time passed and she did not return to the city, young Hanan, impatient with love, and I, curious as to her fate, mounted our horses and ascended the Mount of Olives. We found the garden at last, but we recognized it with difficulty, so greatly had it been changed. In the place of the marvelous collection of exotic flowers and plants from every part of the world, there was now an ordinary oil and spice mill. A horde of tatterdemalions, young and old, infested house and garden. They weeded, tended, and ground, some in small hand mills, others in mortars. Much sickness, and that of a dangerous and contagious kind, was in evidence, for she had taken along to her retreat the most wretched of the beggars who had haunted the gates of her city house. There was one old man among them whom we were afraid to approach, for we were certain that he was infected with leprosy. Nor could we have vouched that all of those gathered by Mary Magdalene were free men and women, and not escaped slaves.

And in the midst of this human refuse she, Miriam of Migdal, moved with her proud figure and her pure skin, which still looked like transparent alabaster. It made the heart swell with indignation and pity to see that lovely body, which had been tended with the rarest oils and wrapped in the noblest silks and woolens of Zidon, thrust into sackcloth and raw sheepskin. For it was now late autumn, the dampness of the approaching rains was in the air, and it was cold in Jerusalem. Indeed, we saw her shiver more than once. Her hands, once soft with unguents and cosmetics, had been burned and blistered by the sun, hardened and calloused by labor. The one remnant of beauty which she had saved intact from the claws of the religious fanatics was her red hair, which still fell in cascades over her shoulders.

She saw us at once on our arrival, and received us as though she had not undergone the slightest change; nor did we betray by any sign our awareness of it. She asked us to come in and offered us stools near the blind man, around whom the work was concentrated. The workers brought him the dried flowers, plants and herbs, and he assorted them before redistributing them to those that worked with mills of sandstone and marble and mortars and pestles of metal. All this he did in blindness. His eyes, wide open, covered with a glimmering, dead-white film, seemed to have retained the perception of the colors of the plants handed to him. During the sorting and the grinding he did not cease to talk, and those about him listened with intensest interest. Sometimes they suspended the grinding and hammering and asked him to repeat. And he spoke as though somewhere in the distance, in a far mist, he saw clear visions. Even my companion, young Hanan, became absorbed in his words. Signs of his irritation and impatience were not wanting—the pallor of the nose, the narrowing of the eyes—and still he wanted to hear what the old man was saying. Miriam listened too, but not with the interest of mere curiosity; her face was radiant with happiness and salvation, and her soul was in her eyes. And of course the old man spoke of the theme which was now common everywhere in Jerusalem and Judaea and Galilee; he spoke of the Messiah, whose coming they awaited as though he were a real identifiable man. He might have been a king, who had gone out to battle, had conquered, and was returning, so that his triumphant entry could be momently expected. The outriders, the messengers who preceded him, were proclaiming that he was approaching the gates of the city. . . . So real, so simple was the expectation, among all classes, rich and poor alike.

Then Hanan lost patience and there broke out—as it always does when Jews assemble—a violent disputation. The silent contempt with which young Hanan usually listened to the babblings of the credulous rabble yielded to hot resentment. He forgot the dignity of his rank. I do not know whether the motley crowd knew that before them stood the omnipotent Hanan ben Hanan. Old Bar Talmai, as I guessed, knew it well, for it seemed to me, a little later, that he was deliberate in his provocation of the visitor.

And what did they talk about? Why, this: how much bread and oil, honey and wine, their fields and orchards and beehives would yield when the Messiah came! In what wealth and comfort he would steep them, what nations he would conquer—if they did not submit of themselves—and what miracles he would perform on the day when the skies would open and the earth tremble!

"But who will it turn out to be, this Messiah of yours who already stands at the gate and listens to your weeping? A mighty king who will fill your granaries with wheat and your cruses with oil and honey, provide you all with fields and gardens, clothe every man's nakedness and spread a roof over his head? Who is this in whom you repose so much faith? Where will he take all that is needed to turn such dreams into reality? Will he conquer so many countries? Where will he find the armies? Who will be his allies to help him subdue the whole world?" These were the contemptuous questions of the young son of the High Priest.

Laughter, sprayed with spittle from toothless mouths, sounded all about him.

"Do you think he will have to conquer lands? The nations will submit to him of their own free will."

"When God's appointed will appear, a single grape will pour forth so much wine that I shall be able to fill one cruse after another and drink and drink and drink," declared one man, whose eyes, gummed together with sores, stood dead in the midst of his transfigured face.

"A-a-nd I—" stammered another out of his tangled and filthy beard, "I—I will go out into my field, and I will c-cut one ear of c-corn and fill all my b-bags and have b-bread for weeks and m-months."

"Foolish one," another corrected him, "do you think you will have to cut ears of grain? The wind will thresh the grain, you will not even have to carry it to the mill. Or else you will eat it off the stalk, because the grain will grow as bread, ready to be eaten."

"And I," trembled another joyfully, "will lie all day long under my date tree, and the honey of the dates will drip straight into my mouth." His tongue protruded from his slavering mouth, as if it already licked honey.

There sat among them, all gathered up in herself, a hunchbacked woman. She had drawn her legs under her, so that she looked like a square stump. Her sharp, bony head stuck out in front of her humped bosom; she stretched forth her short neck and whined ecstatically:

"And every day I'm going to—every day I'm going to—I'm going to. . ."

"What will you do every day?" the others asked, eagerly.

And in a voice that gurgled, as though she were choking with a sweet drink, she managed to get out:

"Every day I'm going to give birth to a son."

But blind Bar Talmai silenced them. He looked as though he wanted to stretch out his hands, seize them all by the throat, and choke them into silence. They paid no attention to his eyes, the whitish films of which were turning red, nor to his face, contorted with long weeping, nor to the choking cough of his voice, so absorbed were they in the visions of plenty. At last he managed to shout them down.

"No, no, that isn't it, that isn't it, not just eating and drinking and living and having children. No, not that, not that! Neither with arms nor with strength, but with the spirit of the Lord—the holy spirit, as the prophet has prophesied. A time of pure justice, of pure truth, a time of the reign of God. . . ."

Now the rest of Hanan's patience vanished.

"But who will this be, I ask? A king of the house of David? Even King Solomon, with all his great wisdom, could not perform the wonders you ask of this one."

"A new Solomon?" the blind man took him up. "Surely he will be of the house of David, as the prophet has prophesied, but he will not be a king; not a new Solomon do we await, and not kings! For what, God save us, have our kings done for us? Have not the words of the prophet Samuel been fulfilled in regard to our kings? 'He will take your sons and appoint them for himself, for his chariots and to be his horsemen, and he will take your daughters to be confectionaries and cooks and bakers.' But it has been much worse. How long did the kingdom of David last? His own son Solomon made us into slaves, as Pharaoh, his father-in-law, whose daughter he took in marriage, did with the people of Egypt. What was our portion therein if he built a rich Temple for the Lord? The golden altar dripped with the anguish of the people. All the width and depth of the copper sea which the children of Zidon poured for the Temple could not hold the tears of the people. Neither an altar of gold nor a sea of copper does the Lord demand, but the heart of an upright man, and hands which do not oppress the widow and mistreat the fatherless. And as for him, King Solomon, the great Jewish king, did he not take to himself many strange wives, did he not set up altars for the idols and abominations of Moab, so that the people was split and shattered into fragments? Did his children follow better paths? Did not his son, Rehoboam, say: 'My father chastised you with whips, but I will chastise you with scorpions'? And did not he and all his sons chastise us indeed with scorpions, and serve idols, and do evil in the sight of the Lord, until the Lord despised us and cast us away, as one casts away a precious d'ror plant which has turned wild and brings forth no more sweet flowers, but thorns instead"—and here he flung away a weed, his face expressing contempt—"until the Lord made desolate his own house and drove us amid shame and pain into exile? And were the kings that came later any better? One generation the house of the Hasmoneans endured in righteousness, nay, not even that, and behold, they themselves placed in the Temple the uncleanliness against which their grandfather had carried on the war of a hero. See what came of the second and third generation of Hasmonean kings. With their unceasing quarrels, with envy of each other, they brought Edom into the land, and set over us as king a wicked man of alien blood. Such have been the Jewish kings which we have lifted up over ourselves—until, in the end, we were content to have a foreign power rule over us. And has the rule of the High Priests been any better?" (And here, at this point, I became certain that blind old Bar Talmai knew who his visitor was: he had doubtless recognized him by his voice, which he had heard more than once in the city house of Miriam. For a special venom now informed his speech, as though he had long waited for this opportunity to square his accounts with a scion of the Priestly house.) "Are the sons of Hanan any better than the sons of Eli? Do they not fish with their forks for the choicest morsels in God's caldron? And was not a voice heard but recently in the Temple: 'The sons of Eli know not the Lord . . .'?"

Hanan had turned pale.

"What was heard?"

One in the assembly hastened to answer: "A heavenly voice was heard crying in the Temple, the Priests heard it at their service and they spread the news of it throughout the people: 'The children of Eli know not the Lord,' and we all know that this means the sons of Hanan."

A second added his voice:

"I heave heard a Rabbi in the Temple court interpret as a sign to the sons of Eli the verse of the scripture: 'The days of the wicked shall be cut short!'" . . .

But by now young Hanan had recovered his composure. He seized me by the hand and cried:

"Come, Hegemon, we are among rebels!"

As we rode back he was silent for a long time, digesting his rage. Now we were both convinced that not only the blind man, but the others, too, had somehow known that the son of the old High Priest was in their midst. I tried to tempt Hanan out of his bitterness by conversation.

"What will you do with him? Have his tongue cut out?"

"Unfortunately we have no such punishment," he answered, regretfully.

"Ah, if he had said those things against the Caesar and our rule, you may be sure we should know what to do with him. But he insulted your kings and your religion; sentence for blasphemy against your religion and your temple must be pronounced by your Sanhedrin."

"But there's the curse of it," he answered. "Our Sanhedrin is rotten with Pharisees. What think you, Hegemon, they will do to him for having desecrated the sacred memory of our kings and the reputation of our High Priests? They will condemn him—at most—to thirty-nine lashes. Do you wonder that rebels and blasphemers multiply in our midst?"

"That is bad indeed. Only recently I reported to the Procurator on the lightness of your punishments."

"Let me but once mount to the place of power," groaned the young man. "I will know then what to do with this rabble."

"I am eager to hear your intentions."

"Over and over again I have pleaded with the High Priest to make a Sanhedrin only of the scholars of our party—a small Sanhedrin meeting in the house of the High Priest. Blasphemers of the Temple and the Priesthood will fall exclusively under the jurisdiction of this Sanhedrin."

By this time we had reached the city gate. There, among the tax collectors and the guardians of the gate, we came upon the agents of the Temple. We knew them by their appointments; they carried in their hands the lead-loaded whips of their profession, they wore high white headcoverings, and on their breasts were the badges of the High Priest. They recognized the son of the old High Priest, ran to encounter him, and bowed low before him.

Hanan ben Hanan spoke sharply:

"Go up to the Mount of Olives, to the village of Eini. In the garden of spices of Mary Magdalene you will find a blind man by the name of Bar Talmai. Bind him and bring him before the court. He is one of the most dangerous blasphemers in the land."

The words were scarcely uttered when the agents of the High Priest were already on their way.

It appeared later that when Bar Talmai came up for trial Hanan ben Hanan failed in his plan to have the blind man sent away as a slave to the oil mills. But he called me to witness the carrying out of the sentence pronounced by the court.

"What did I tell you?" he said, as he led me to the small judgment house which stood near the entrance to the inner court of the Temple. "Thirty-nine lashes. How can we discourage criminals and blasphemers in that fashion?" The guards had just carried out Bar Talmai, and laid him on the marble floor. They stripped his back. The lashes of the whip were composed of double thicknesses of ass-hide and ox-hide sewn together. And those white-clad servants of the High Priest knew how to ply the whip. One of them stood to a side and chanted, "One, one and two, one and three."

Not one cry of pain came from the blind man. Lying on the floor he beat his breast and confessed his sins.

Shortly after this incident Mary Magdalene disappeared entirely from the city. She had gone to Galilee where, according to rumor, a new visionary had declared himself to the people.

What became during that period of the blind oil-mixer I cannot tell. I was sent away from Judaea for a time on a mission of importance to the Tetrarch Herod Antipater, in Galilee. I met Bar Talmai again, and Miriam of Migdal, too, but in totally different circumstances.

CHAPTER FOURTEEN

IT was at this time that I became acquainted with Herod Antipater, and with his new capital, which he had built on the shores of the Sea of Genesaret in the vicinity of the warm springs. My visit was official. Relations between the Procurator Pontius Pilate and the Tetrarch were far from satisfactory. It all began with a question of etiquette and precedence: who had to pay the first visit to whom? The Tetrarch regarded himself as a friend of the Caesar Tiberius, in whose honor he had built the city (for that matter they all considered themselves friends of the Caesar, and they were never tired of stating the fact on their coins); besides, he was the ruler of a country, almost a king; and he looked down on the Procurator as on a Roman functionary. Pontius Pilate, on his side, simply ignored the Tetrarch. Herod Antipater was a man, moreover, who had not awakened much love; he was disliked by the Proconsul of Syria, Vitellius; his "friendship" with the Caesar was a dubious business. In reality he was much closer to Sejanus, the Emperor's powerful minister to whom he, like all the other provincials, sent costly presents in the hope of obtaining favors. The Tetrarch was a subtle and crafty Asiatic. In appearance he would never have been taken for a Jew; there was not a trace of his people in him. The characteristically energetic Herod face, the massive skull, clean-shaven, the steel-gray Samaritan eyes, penetrating and suspicious, might have belonged instead to a Roman commander (they all wanted to look like real Romans). His arms were muscular and powerful, he drew a good bow and was an excellent javelin thrower. He had distinguished himself in the chase, had cultivated good manners and even spoke a tolerable Latin and Greek. But all this was on the surface. His Hellenistic culture hung on him like a Roman toga on a wild German or British chieftain.

Not having been destined to inherit the throne after the death of his father, Herod had not, in his youth, been sent to study in Rome, like the children of Miriam. Later, however, when the older Herod had put to death Miriam's children, also his third son, whom he had originally chosen as his heir, for treason—this was what occasioned Augustus's famous quip: "I would rather be a pig than a son of Herod's"—the younger Herod, Antipater, who was the son of a Samaritan woman, became official heir to the throne of Galilee and Perea. But the Caesar Augustus would not let him assume the title of King; he had to be content with that of Tetrarch.

The god of the Tetrarch Herod Antipater was his father, Herod the Great, whom he not only worshiped—as his brothers did, too—but tried to imitate in all ways. Like the older Herod he called himself a friend of the Senate and the Caesar, and was for ever sending costly presents, squeezed out of his people, to the court and to influential Senators. Neither his protestations nor his gifts convinced us. We had him carefully watched, and we were fully informed as to his secret meetings with neighboring Tetrarchs and princes; for we had forbidden such gatherings—"social interchanges" was what he had called them. Subsequent events justified our suspicions. We discovered in his possession an arsenal of arms and armor. But of this later. For the time being we were content to know that he could not maintain his rule in Galilee for a single day without the support of our cohorts. He resembled, or imitated, his father again in his building mania; but lacking his father's means, he could not indulge it to the same extent. However, he did not lack his father's cupidity, for he laid a crushing burden of taxation, levies and contributions on his tetrarchate, and it was astonishing enough that he should have pressed from this inconsiderable province, which, fruitful enough to provide Judaea with grain, was nevertheless of small extent, and from the sandy stretches of Perea, enough for the building of one such city as Tiberias, his new capital. With the characteristic craftiness of a barbarian, Herod Antipater played a double game; to the Jews he gave out that he was a faithful follower of the tradition, a pious observer of the Jewish law. He would not, for instance, have the image of man or beast stamped on his coinage; like his father he made use for this purpose only of the regular symbols of the fruitfulness of the country, ears of corn and olive trees. On the High Holy days he came up to Jerusalem according to the ancient custom; he was a frequent visitor then to the Temple, and offered up in sacrifice the fattest sheep and cattle. In his interpretation of the law he was not on the side of the enlightened Sadducees; he held with the reactionary fanatics, the Pharisaic scholars. But he compensated himself by leading, in his residence of Tiberias, the life of a genuine heathen. First of all, to ensure himself a great measure of privacy from the intrusions of his Jews, he had had his new capital built on the site of an ancient cemetery; this led the Jews, in accordance with their law, to declare the locality ritually impure, so that they could not settle in it. He imported numbers of poor Greeks, Askelonites and Phoenicians from Tyre and Acco; they say that he even encouraged beggars and runaway slaves to settle in his capital. He brought colonists from Cyprus and Syria, gave them free allotments of land, and went so far as to build swimming baths, gymnasia and theaters for their use; nor did he fail to provide these with actors and gladiators from Antioch. He arranged Olympic games and offered high prizes to make it worth while for athletes to attend from Alexandria, Athens and other Greek cities; and in all this he was imitating his father, Herod the Great. Last, though not least, there was the famous Temple of Augustus, of white marble and with many costly columns, which he built in honor of the former Emperor. For all this his wretched Jews had to pay through the nose.

It was my honor to become acquainted during this visit with the first lady of the court, Herodias, a highly cultured and well-bred matron. Herod Antipater had taken her away from his brother, having met her on his way to Rome. The lady was ambitious, enjoyed a wide range of friendships in Rome, and was eager to obtain for her husband the title of King and larger territories—at the expense of his brothers.

She and her brother Agrippa had been brought up at the court of Augustus; hence her thorough acquaintance with the intrigues of all the leading families of Rome, and her friendships among them. From Tiberias she maintained a copious correspondence with the capital of the Empire. She exchanged letters with the Empress and with Agrippina, the daughter of Germanicus, who had begun to play a leading role in governmental circles. She introduced the Hellenistic culture into the court of the Tetrarch, surrounded herself with Greek philosophers and Roman actors and dancers, and maintained the court on a level of magnificence worthy of a great kingdom. She brought down to Tiberias Ptolemaeus, the brother of Nikolaus, to manage the business affairs of the state, to write the orations which Herod had to deliver on various occasions, and to conduct the correspondence with Rome. High Roman commanders often passed through the territory of the Tetrarch, important officials came to collect the taxes; all of them were received at the court with open arms. They were provided with the diversion of the theater and they were honored by sacrifices in the Temple offered to the Caesar in their presence. It was hoped that no visiting commander or official would fail to carry back to Rome or Antioch the report of this island of Graeco-Roman culture in the ocean of Jewish barbarism, and of the corner of love and friendship for Rome established in this hostile and tumultuous wilderness of Galilee.

I too, as the representative of the Procurator, was received in friendliest fashion. The Tetrarchess made me feel at home from the moment I crossed the threshold of her magnificent hall of columns. She took me by the arm and led me to see her superb gardens which sloped down to the shore of the quiet, glittering sea of Genesaret, the fine reservoirs set like jewels among the beds of exotic flowers, and the rare and marvelous birds which flew among the foliage. Once, as we walked in the great alley of Jericho palms which ran along the shore at the edge of her garden, she said to me, in the purest Latin:

"We are, alas, too far from Rome and its treasuries of culture. But we do all that we can to maintain here, on the rim of the wilderness, the spirit of the Roman genius, the only fountain of light and happiness for human beings."

She presented to me her little daughter Salome, a child by her first husband. The young lady cannot, at that time, have been more than nine or ten years of age, but her appearance was already remarkable. Thick curls of hair hung in wild playfulness over the young, trembling neck and shoulders. The two eyes which flashed up at me were very dark, with a glimmer of brown—almost of red—which suggested ripe cherries. Her body was as supple as a serpent's, as taut as a bowstring pulled by a strong arm; she looked like a trained and disciplined boy—in brief, a characteristically Oriental beauty, unfortunately a little too Jewish, touched with Jewish exaltation and excitement, with Jewish nervous sensibility. Covered with ornaments from head to foot, her very hair weighted down with them in the Arab fashion, she gave forth a continuous tinkling as she walked.

"She is a little wild still," her mother said, apologetically. "Until now she has had no real upbringing. We lived with her father in the heart of the desert and she grew up there like a wild gazelle." She fondled her daughter's locks. "From now on it will be different. We have bought for her a Greek tutor in the Tyrian market, a man educated in all the sciences and of the best Greek manners. Her education will be under the supervision of our friend Ptolemaeus. The Ciliarch has no doubt met our State Secretary—" she paused proudly. "He is the brother of the famous Nikolaus of Damascus, who so often represented our great father Herod at the court of Augustus. I do not doubt that with his help our daughter will acquire the best in Greek culture; before long she will have to take her place in society and play some part in affairs of state. Indeed, she will become a ruler, too, for her uncle, the Tetrarch Philippus, has expressed his wish to marry her." She turned to her daughter. "As a future Tetrarchess, my child, you will have to know how to mingle with people."

From what I have already said you will easily understand that we were not hampered, at Herod's court, by Jewish ritual and ceremonies, by Jewish restrictions on food, for instance. The kitchen was in the hands of a first-class Alexandrian cook. And then the distractions which accompanied the meals, the musicians, the men and women dancers—it was not easy to remember that I was at the court of a Jewish prince, in a remote province of barbarians; at any moment I could have imagined myself back in Rome. To the music and dancing were added the Sophist discourses of Ptolemaeus of Damascus. For my part they could very well have been omitted, and I do not propose to reproduce them, for in the midst of the entertainment and the heavy drinking they were extremely boring. I had occasion, during this visit, to renew acquaintance with the future Jewish king, Agrippa, who was at the time busily engaged in playing dice and accumulating debts. He was staying with his brother-in-law Herod, who had provided him with a lucrative post—that of overseer of the markets. I say lucrative, but we must bear in mind that not too much meat was left on the carcass after Rome and the Tetrarch had taken off their share. In any case, whatever he managed to squeeze out of the Galilean farmers and gardeners was not enough for the Jewish aristocrat Agrippa, and he was always short of money. He had surrounded himself with a large retinue and lived not like a future but like a present ruler. His upbringing at the court had accustomed him to a life of the highest luxury, and he borrowed on every hand, from his own pious countrymen and from wealthy Romans. He also applied for loans to his brother-in-law the Tetrarch—who was also his uncle—and these came, again, from the wretched peasants of Galilee.

We had met before, Agrippa and I, at official celebrations in Caesarea and at Antioch; indeed, we knew each other well. But he never recognized me; I was, it appeared, not important enough to be remembered by the Jewish prince. Then we fell foul of each other at the chariot races in the arena which Herod the Great had built near Neapolis, in Samaria. The institution, with its halls and temples, was too costly for the Procurator to maintain in good condition, and it was therefore beginning to fall into disrepair. But now and again, when exceptionally important visitors came from Rome and Antioch, he arranged in it athletic games, gladiatorial shows and races, in their honor. Agrippa, bored with his life at Tiberias and his post as overseer of the markets, attended every such occasion, both in order to meet with Romans and to satisfy his gambling impulses.

On the occasion of which I am now speaking, I found among the charioteers entered for the contest two sons of the High Priest, my friend Theophilus, who was extremely skillful in this branch of athletics, and his brother Mattathias. I placed my bet on Theophilus, Agrippa his against me on Mattathias, with whom he was on intimate terms of friendship. As we stood by our favorites shortly before the race, examining the impatient horses and encouraging their drivers, Agrippa suddenly raised the bet by a considerable sum of gold. I, who knew Theophilus's qualifications, was sure of his victory; but I was by no means so sure of the money which the Jewish prince was throwing with such prodigality into the race. I was bold enough to demand, instead of his word, cash. The prince took offense, the more readily, no doubt, because I had touched a weak spot. He measured me with a contemptuous glance which asked: "Who is this man who dares to doubt my word?" He turned to one of his friends and said:

"One never knows today whom one may rub shoulders with in the better circles. It used to be different. There was a time when we knew every man who was admitted."

Naturally I did not let this pass. I said, loudly enough to be heard by the group:

"There used to be a time when princes of the Herodian line paid out in gold and not in dishonored notes."

It need hardly be said that the bet was not placed. From that time on the prince had better reason than my unimportance to ignore me. When his sister presented me in Tiberias, slight astonishment ruffled his boredom; he took out his emerald, applied it to his eye, looked me over from head to foot, and said: "I did not know there was a Ciliarch in Jerusalem." I replied: "I have already had the pleasure of meeting you—at the chariot races in the arena at Neapolis." He pretended not to remember. His sister, court-bred, at once felt the tension between us, and hastened to add:

"But Agrippa, this is the good commander, Cornelius, the right-hand man of Pontius Pilate."

Agrippa was not greatly liked in Tiberias. He treated Herod not as a king, but as a person of inferior rank. The only adult male heir of the illustrious royal house of the Hasmoneans—with which he was connected through his grandmother, the ill-fated Miriam—the boyhood comrade of Tiberius's only son, who had died young, the close friend of Tiberius's cousins, the sons of Germanicus, Caligula and Claudius, Agrippa felt himself immeasurably superior to the Tetrarch, and showed it in his bearing. He never spoke of Rome without mentioning "my friend Caligula" or "my friend Claudius." He hinted, in gestures rather than words, that Tiberius was living too long; soon the Roman Empire would fall to one of his friends, and then new times would begin for him.

I disliked thoroughly this Jewish aristocrat who was for ever boasting of his friendships in the highest circles in Rome, who knew every turn and twist of the politics of the capital, and who was deeply involved in its intrigues. On the strength of his probable elevation to the kingship of Judaea, and perhaps of entire Palestine, he had pawned his friendship, against heavy loans, to the future Emperors among others. In appearance he was completely Roman; his round, fleshy face was clean-shaven. He sat at table, this Jewish princeling, toying in the Roman fashion with a polished emerald which he carried from time to time to his eye, in order to stare at the assembled company with a tired, indifferent gaze. He held himself aloof from everybody and expressed his boredom by leaving the banquets before they were half ended. I need hardly mention that I took special note of those significant gestures, those facial expressions, which indicated his dissatisfaction with the longevity of Tiberius, and I did not fail to report them in the right quarters. No, there was no love lost between me and your Jewish king, Agrippa the First. But his sister Herodias—all honor to her! What an intelligent and charming woman! She was witty, she was amusing, and she was always apologizing for her brother's boorishness. "You know him, Ciliarch; spoiled by the luxury of Rome, what can he find here, in this forsaken province? He is bored, and when he is bored he is irritated."

I had the honor to be invited by the Tetrarch to his fortress of Machaerus, in his province of Perea, beyond the Dead Sea. The occasion was one of his birthdays, which he wished to celebrate not in the capital, but at a distance, in the more select company of his family and its closer friends, among whom he now included me.

Machaerus was situated on a high hill, and its mighty walls dominated the desert which rolled its desolation to the very foot of the citadel. Hard by was the frontier of Arabia, the kingdom of the Tetrarch's former father-in-law and present enemy. The enmity sprang up when Herod exchanged his first wife, the Arabian king's daughter, for Herodias. The ascent to the fortress was laborious in the extreme; for a whole day the long caravan, with its rich trappings and appointments, its camels and asses and mules, clambered up the slopes, which consisted not of sand but of masses of rock fused together by the heat. It was as if a sea of lava had been poured out across the landscape, wiping out grass and tree; only here and there a miserable cactus shoot issued from a fissure in the rock. The Jews had given the name of Sodom to this region and according to their legends it had once been a flourishing land, but God had cursed it for the sins of its inhabitants and buried it under blazing rock and ashy sands. From the summit of the hill we could descry, far off, the refreshing green of the fat date palms, olive trees and vineyards of Jericho, enclosing one side of the Dead Sea and losing themselves in the rich Jordan valley. But the Dead Sea itself was sunk deep in the desert setting like an open eye in a wild face. Once in his own fortress the Jewish Tetrarch threw off the mantle of Roman culture which he wore—in part at his wife's insistence—in his capital of Tiberias and lapsed into his natural being, the true, undisciplined Asiatic tyrant. Here he maintained an Arabian harem with countless concubines, together with their men and women slaves—originally the gift of the daughter of the Arabian king. Here his life was utterly unrestrained; he did not feel the slightest embarrassment in the presence of his cultured wife or his guests. "He has to live himself out . . ." was what Herodias, clever woman of the world that she was, said to me, a good-natured smile on her lips. "After a few months down there in the palace, among civilized people, and in an atmosphere of culture, he begins to feel pent up; then he has to come up here to his barbarian stronghold. Here he can loosen all the bonds which irk him in Tiberias, he can have all the concubines he wants. A couple of days of it is enough to release the tension; he becomes calm again, and able to live with civilized people."

I learned on my arrival in the fortress that here in one of the prison cells, Herod was holding captive the strange fanatical figure whose name I had heard so often in Jerusalem, to wit, Jochanan the Baptist. It would have seemed that from the nature of the offense which had led to his arrest—his gross insults to Herodias, and his frantic prophecies of the evils in store for her—and for the other, more general offense of his anti-religious preachings, this Jochanan could have been put to death. And yet he was treated with extraordinary leniency. Herod had, indeed, removed the fanatic from the wilderness near Jericho, in order to decrease his influence with the hordes which visited him on the banks of the Jordan. But he wanted for nothing in his prison. He was permitted to receive visitors, that is to say, his pupils, who continued to take instruction from him in his incomprehensible lore. More than this: I learned that Jochanan was even permitted to send out messengers, who preached for him throughout the country. The fact is that Herod, like every tyrant before him, was profoundly superstitious; he looked on Jochanan the Baptist as a prophet. He felt impelled to circumscribe the preacher's influence, but he had not the courage to lift up his hand against him.

But Herodias interpreted this leniency as an offense to her person; in this she was correct, and she was equally correct in regarding the weakness of the Tetrarch as dangerous to the interests and security of the state. Religious blasphemy was one thing; an attack on the highest personalities of the state allowed to go unpunished brought all authority into disrepute. I was in thorough agreement with her. I made so bold as to urge this view on the Tetrarch, both as my own and as that of the Roman power. I said: "Even if you look on this affair as purely local, belonging entirely to the jurisdiction of the Tetrarch, we cannot ignore Rome's interest in the maintenance of civic order. Criminals, no matter what the nature of their crime, cannot remain unpunished." I took it upon myself to urge, in the name of Rome, the early carrying out of the right sentence against Jochanan the Baptist.

Herodias was not the only one to thank me. Ptolemaeus was grateful for my intervention and added his plea to mine. Our words fell on deaf ears. Precisely in this matter, which affected his royal dignity and security, the Tetrarch behaved with the obstinacy of a mule. He offered the most evasive excuses. "I shall wait until his popularity has decreased among the masses, so that execution of sentence will not stir up wide resentment." The absurdity of the excuse was evident in the fact that the long delay was bound to increase the popularity of the imprisoned—or rather detained—fanatic. The simple truth was this: the Tetrarch was afraid of the man. At heart Herod was the same superstitious barbarian as the rest of his people.

I was curious to see the extraordinary desert maniac who had inspired such terror in Herod, and I asked Ptolemaeus to conduct me to him. I wanted to hear, likewise, the words of the "prophet."

We found him in one of the cells of the keep, chained by one hand to the wall. Outside the window-hole of his cell were gathered some of his followers, to whom he was addressing himself. As he talked, he gesticulated wildly with his one free hand, and when Ptolemaeus and I entered by the inner door he paid no attention to us; either he had failed, in the frenzy of his oratory, to notice us or else he deliberately ignored us. I was confounded by this spectacle of free intercourse between a political prisoner and his accomplices, but I said nothing.

In appearance he was more or less what I had imagined him to be—one of the wild men I had seen so often in the Temple courts: tall, unkempt, lean, his bones standing out through the skin burned almost black by sun and desert. But for all his leanness he displayed a powerful musculature, and his build was that of a giant. He wore on his head one of the ritualistic leather boxes of the believing Jews, in which is contained a parchment with a declaration of love to their God. From time to time the gesticulating free hand caught at the box to prevent it from tumbling out of place, for the leather strap was too short for the thick tangle of his black hair. At the bottom of his sackcloth covering hung, likewise, the regular ritualistic fringes of the Jews. His blazing eyes were turned upward to the hole, around which crowded the faces of his followers outside. When we entered he was declaiming words which I could not understand, for they were not in the current Aramaic, with which I was now fairly familiar, but in their ancient Hebraic language, spoken by their prophets of old. Ptolemaeus, who knew both Hebrew and Aramaic, translated them for me into Latin. This, more or less, was their content:

He was chosen and hidden of God before the making of the world;
And he will be with God through all the eternities.
He will judge the hidden deeds of men,
No one will be able to conceal them from him according to his own will.

I was impressed by the rhetorical style of the man, and said so to Ptolemaeus. "If he were not so dangerous," I added, "we could use him in one of our theaters. What is he declaiming?"

"Those are verses from a certain book, 'The Book of Enoch,' one of their visionaries who lived in the time of the Hasmonean kings and prophesied the coming of the Messiah. The book has been a pernicious influence; it has unhinged thousands of Jews. Listen!"

The fanatic continued to declaim, ignoring the sound of our voices as he had ignored our presence, and addressing himself exclusively to the faces about the window.

> In that day I perceive the well of righteousness,
> And all are drinking therefrom.
>
> * * *
>
> Before the sun and the heavenly signs were created,
> Before the stars of heaven were fashioned,
> His name had already been pronounced by the Lord.
> He shall be a staff of support to all the righteous,
> That they may lean upon him and not fall.
>
> * * *
>
> The son of man, whom thou seest,
> Lifteth from their thrones and their places of power
> The kings and the men of might.
> He thrusteth the kings from their thrones
> And from their kingdoms.
> Their dwelling place shall be darkness,
> And they shall make their marriage bed with worms.

When Ptolemaeus had translated these words I protested: "But this is contumacy in the highest degree! This is incitement against the Emperor, the Senate and the world power of Rome!"

"That is why we have imprisoned him."

"But what sort of imprisonment is this? Do you always admit the followers of a political prisoner to his cell, so that he may continue to spread his dangerous agitation? Look! Not only can he preach to them; he can obtain all the information he needs from the outside world."

"So it is, unfortunately. He not only receives information—he sends out his messengers and apostles to all parts of the country."

"But in Jupiter's name, what sort of government have you?"

"Ciliarch, we can do nothing against him. Whenever the Tetrarch hears that voice from the cell he trembles like a child. You have spoken with him—you have seen for yourself."

"If there is no other way," I answered, firmly, "I shall have to ask for the intervention of the Proconsul in Antioch. You know that we are reluctant to interfere in the internal affairs of the Tetrarch, but if you have not the courage to safeguard the security of the land, others will have to supply it for you."

CHAPTER FIFTEEN

WHAT we, the diplomats, statesmen, high functionaries and whatnot failed to carry through, was effected by a ten-year-old girl.

That evening the official banquet was held on the columned terrace of the citadel, a celebration in true Oriental style. The rows of torches shed a fiery light on the wild surrounding scenery; beyond the glowing circle we saw dimly the shining level of the Dead Sea throwing back the glitter of the starry sky. The Tetrarch was in high good humor, his blood warm with the strong Cypriot wine, mixed with honey, which he had swallowed in copious draughts at the coaxing insistence of Herodias. He watched with comfortable satisfaction the dancing of the half-naked, bespangled slave-women, Arab and Negro, whom he had received with the marriage portion of his first wife. But as the wine mounted in him he began to find the contortions of these faded and elderly entertainers less and less amusing. The bloodshot eyes rolled in his swollen face as he looked for something spicier, and rested at last on little Salome, who sat at the banquet with her mother. The ornaments which weighted down her locks tinkled as she threw back her head in lively conversation. The Tetrarch's eyes filled with concupiscent pleasure, for she was a delight to look at. With her slender figure and her lovely dark skin she was worthy of a place not only at a provincial court, but at the side of Tiberius himself. It had become a habit with our barbarian princes to flatter the Emperor by imitating him in all things; they had suddenly become refined voluptuaries, with a passion for the noble and delicate love tastes of the Hellenistic world.... In those days you would find at the courts of all our subject chieftains the same pleasure-boys and pleasure-girls as in Rome. I really cannot tell whether the Tetrarch of Galilee and Perea had risen to such heights of sophistication, or whether he was merely acting from motives of policy. In any case he had for some time affected a distaste for Arabian dancers and Egyptian slaves and expressed an imperious preference for girls of tender years...

The eyes fixed on little Salome grew warmer; he did not even trouble to conceal in our presence the emotions which gripped him. Suddenly he cried:

"And now little Salome will dance for me!"

But little Salome was the only one in that assembly who dared to oppose the Tetrarch's will. With a childish gesture of caprice she shook her tinkling locks, and answered, "No, little Salome won't dance for you," then hid her head in her mother's kerchief.

The Tetrarch glowered for an instant, as though he was ready to explode into fury. But the wine had not overcome him completely, and he still retained some feeling of propriety in our presence. He mastered himself, and in a teasing voice called out:

"Oh, yes, little Salome *is* going to dance for the Tetrarch."

Again Salome shook her head and cried: "No, she won't."

"What? Not even if the Tetrarch of Galilee and Perea commands her?"

"No—she won't obey the Tetrarch of Galilee and Perea."

The teasing game had developed into something more serious; but it was the Tetrarch, not the child, who was trapped in the conflict.

"And if the Tetrarch of Galilee and Perea promises little Salome a palace in Tiberias, and a garden where young gazelles will walk about, accompanied by beautiful peacocks and beautiful parrots?" he asked now, in a somber tone which startled us.

"Even then she won't dance," Salome answered with childish obstinacy.

We burst into laughter, partly to relieve the tension, but partly in sheer amusement. It was really difficult to tell now who was the Tetrarch and who the child, for the game had lost all its playfulness.

Herod's eyes blazed with restrained anger. It was as though he considered it a matter of life and death to bend the will of the child by promises or break it with threats. And no doubt he was ready, at this instant, to resort to sheer violence; but he still wanted to have his way, in our presence, by gentle means, if possible. In all this he paid no attention to his wife; and perhaps, in an obscure way, he was seeking to wound her; perhaps the game was really pointed at her, and if he was indifferent in revealing before us the undertones of lust which accompanied his demands on the child, he derived a double pleasure from the taunt aimed at Herodias.

He tried again:

"And if the Tetrarch of Galilee and Perea promises little Salome that if she will dance for him he will fulfill every wish of hers, though it cost him half his kingdom?" he said, grimly, and he fixed his eyes sharply on his wife.

"Even then—" Salome began, but at this point her mother bent down to her and whispered in her ear. The child stopped, looked up, and questioned the Tetrarch.

"Will the Tetrarch of Galilee and Perea really give Salome whatever she asks for, if she dances for him?"

The Tetrarch burst into a great shout of laughter. The sweat poured from his huge head, and he answered the child, imitating her piping voice:

"The Tetrarch of Galilee hereby promises little Salome that if she fulfills his desire and dances for him, he will fulfill every wish she expresses!"

Without uttering a word little Salome left her place and walked across the terrace till she stood by the Tetrarch's couch. Unprepared, and standing thus in one place, she began to move her body to the accompaniment of a single drum beaten by one of the slaves. Childishly innocent and undiffident, she let slip from her the tunic which covered the upper half of her form, so that she was naked to the navel. Her feet fastened to one spot, she carried out the dance movements with her slender, dark-skinned childish belly, but every muscle in her thin body trembled. And every gesture, performed as it was by a child, sent a stronger impulse not only through the blood of the Tetrarch, but through the blood of all that watched her.

She herself, in the midst of these passionate movements, retained an expression of such innocence that we were in doubt whether the child was aware of what she was doing; and yet, the longer she danced, the more dissolute was the challenge of her cadences. She turned and twisted, presenting now her back, now her smooth, unformed bosom, and the muscles swam in light waves under the shimmering skin. Again the thought of Tiberius came into my mind: what a present she would be for the old voluptuary! Even when he retired to Capri, to meditate and philosophize on his life, he would be glad to be pulled back into the world by that bosom and that back. I turned to my neighbor, a Roman officer, and whispered the suggestion to him. But Salome's mother, seated close by, either heard my words or read my lips or guessed my thought, for she became, or affected to become, confused. She leaned over and said:

"I simply do not know where the child learned such things, unless it was from the Arabian women slaves. She does not know what she is doing."

"In any case," I answered, half jestingly, "I can assure the Tetrarchess that if the Caesar Tiberius saw the child, the Tetrarch's chances of obtaining the title of King, together with additional territories, would be greatly increased."

She took the remark in perfect good humor (oh, she was a thorough woman of the world), made a threatening gesture at me with her sweat-kerchief and answered:

"But, Ciliarch, such cynicism from you? I took you for a very serious man. . ."

But now the little one had become exhausted, and she seemed ready to collapse with the physical effort and the excitement. The Tetrarchess was about to rise from her place when Herod, heavy-limbed and half drunk as he was, sprang to his feet, lifted up the child and carried her to his couch, where he held her in his lap.

"And now, little Salome, you can ask the Tetrarch of Galilee for whatever your heart desires, and in the words of King Ahasuerus to Esther, when she found favor in his eyes, you shall have it, though it be half my kingdom."

And little Salome, fondling the face of the Tetrarch, answered:

"I want the Tetrarch of Galilee and Perea to have his faithful Germans bring me, on a silver platter, the head of Jochanan."

We heard the words clearly, and yet we did not understand them. We had listened intently, absorbed in this second part of the game between the Tetrarch and the child, and it seemed to us that the words could not have been spoken. And it seemed also that the Tetrarch did not believe his own ears, for he asked in a puzzled voice:

"Whose head do you want my faithful Germans to bring you on a silver platter?"

"The head of Jochanan the Baptist, the prophet whom you keep imprisoned in the cellar of the fortress."

"The head of the mad prophet?" stammered Herod, turning white. "What fantastic idea is this? What do you want with the head of a man?"

We sat rigid with astonishment. Only the Tetrarchess observed, mildly:

"Where can the child have learned such odd things? It must be her early upbringing in the desert."

"What?" asked little Salome, seated in the Tetrarch's lap and still fondling his face, "are you, the Tetrarch of Galilee and Perea, really afraid of him because he is a prophet?"

The Tetrarch threw a furious glance, like that of an enraged Zeus, first at the child's mother, and then at his secretary, Theophilus, who looked down innocently. From them he turned his gaze on me, and proudly, almost insolently, he replied, not to the child, but to the assembled guests:

"The Tetrarch of Galilee and Perea is afraid of no one. No, not even of—" he was about to utter something frightful, for his face turned a shade paler, but at the last moment he bethought himself, and ended up lamely—"not even of the King of Arabia, who threatens me with war because I thrust out his daughter in favor of my brother's wife." And now he fixed his eyes again on Herodias.

"Oh, but you're afraid of *him*!" the child cried, pointing downward.

"I have told you that I am afraid of no one, except—of course

—the Caesar, who has been my lifelong friend!" With this he turned his eyes back to me, as if to threaten me.

"Then why won't you give me his head?"

"Because a man's head is not a toy for a child," the Tetrarch answered, his baffled gaze seeking the mother once again, in warning that he knew well what was afoot.

"But you promised me that you would fulfill my every wish. Aren't you going to keep your word now, Tetrarch of Galilee and Perea?"

In vain the Tetrarch sought help in our faces. We avoided his eyes. He understood.

"Yes, you are right, little Salome, the Tetrarch of Galilee and Perea is the slave of his word, like every monarch, like the Caesar in Rome. Go, carry out her wish!" he cried to the German guards at the further end of the terrace.

Tense silence followed. We heard the footsteps of the guard descending the steps. The Tetrarch set Salome down, lifted his beaker to an attendant, who filled it, and cried:

"For the peace of Rome and its Caesar!"

We repeated the toast.

He was calm now. It was as though he had stilled his inner terror by invoking the aid of the Emperor.

In a little while we heard ascending footsteps, and two German soldiers entered, carrying on a silver platter the head of a man. It was the head I looked upon in life that afternoon, the same muscular face, turned now from deep sun- and desert-tanned brown to ashy blue. The soldiers had set on the severed head the phylactery, the ritualistic leather box. The eyes were open, the lips too; we were almost prepared to hear a voice issue from them.

As the soldiers offered the head to little Salome, who stretched forth her hands, the phylactery slipped forward and tumbled into the blood which filled the platter. The eyes suddenly closed, the lips too.

From outside, from the court below, rose a sound of wailing mixed with curses. I was amazed that at this late hour there should still be strangers in the citadel. We pretended not to hear; we tried, at least round the table of the Tetrarchess, to resume the conversation as if nothing had happened. But I looked at the Tetrarch, and I perceived that the momentary reassurance evoked by the mention of the Caesar had fled, and his face was pallid with terror. The effect of the wine had left him. He did his best to conceal his torment from us. He spoke loudly, he jested—but no longer with little Salome, whom he had pushed away with a look of loathing. He commanded the soldiers to remove the bloody platter with the severed head. Little Salome protested: the head belonged to her.... The Tetrarch glanced angrily at his wife, who caught up the child and pacified her. To us she said again, apologetically:

"Really, these wild ideas must have been planted in her head at the barbarous court of her father. Who ever heard of such a thing? A child wanting to play with the severed head of a man!"

Herod labored to continue the banquet. He ordered the slaves to fill the beakers of the guests, he drank again and again to the Empire and to his friendship with the Caesar.... It was a sorry performance. He could not even drown his terror in wine. The wailing did not cease to mount from the court below.

"Those are the followers and pupils of Jochanan," said Ptolemaeus, superfluously.

"Why don't you drive them out?"

"He would not want us to," and he indicated the Tetrarch.

After a time the lamenting ceased of itself. A suspicious stillness followed. Then a single voice was lifted up. It pealed out with the disquieting sound of one of their rams' horns. The clear, ringing sound cut through the air, and we heard every syllable distinctly. It was a verse from one of their sacred books, which they applied now to their decapitated prophet. The words had a shattering effect on the Tetrarch, and even the Tetrarchess seemed to be shaken out of her habitual calm and well-bred self-control.

"A voice cries in the wilderness: Prepare a path!"

"Have them driven out," said Herodias to the Tetrarch. "They are disturbing the banquet."

"Whom shall I have driven out? It is a voice crying from the wilderness. How shall I silence it?"

The Tetrarch rose hastily and without a glance even at his Roman guests fled from the banquet.

The Tetrarchess, herself again, made an effort to erase from our minds the painful impression created by her husband. She said to the table:

"What is the difference, after all? The rebel has been punished, the law has been satisfied. Rome may now be content."

"I shall not fail to tell the Proconsul," I returned. "Your little daughter has deserved well of Rome."

CHAPTER SIXTEEN

THE death of Jochanan the Baptist did not put an end to the expectation of the Messiah among the Jews; it became, on the contrary, stronger than ever. This was their interpretation of events: the darker they were, the nearer was his coming. They spoke of such a time as "the days of the Messiah." And sure enough we heard before long that in Galilee—as might have been expected—there had risen another, who called to repentance and to preparation for the Kingdom of God, now at hand. At first this new man was looked upon as a follower of the dead Jochanan. Then they said that it was Jochanan himself, resurrected. Others would have it that this was their ancient prophet Elijah, who had in his day performed many wonders. For it was reported that this one, too, who had appeared in Galilee, on the shore of the Sea of Genesaret, was likewise performing wonders, healing the sick, cleansing the leprous and driving out evil spirits. The name of Elijah was greatly loved and honored among the Jews; hence they were easily inclined to believe that he had returned.

I first heard the man mentioned by the old High Priest. On a quiet spring evening I was strolling in the garden of his palace, watching his sons disporting themselves in the swimming pools, when old Hanan approached me and said, with a sarcastic smile:

"Well, have you heard? They've got themselves another prophet to preach the kingdom of God to the boors of Galilee. This time he comes from Nazareth." And the old man broke into contemptuous laughter. "From Nazareth, you understand."

"What makes that so strange?"

"Of all the boorish cities of Galilee, the worst! Nothing but gross, unlettered peasants and carpenters, who are utterly ignorant of the law, and do not know how to guard themselves from impurity."

A desperately serious matter this was, of purity and impurity. It divided the people into two groups. A learned man, who knew the law, and the distinction between pure and impure, was called *chaver*, or comrade, or colleague, by other learned men. He was an equal, who could be invited to one's table, without fear of ritualistic defilement. But the unlearned man, not so equipped, was called *am ha-aretz*, which meant countryman, or man-of-the-earth; or boor; he was unfit to be received, or even consorted with.

Well then, Galilee, town and country, was the center of the "men-of-the-earth." In Judaea they referred to Galilee as "a confusion of peoples." And Nazareth was so typically Galilean that the idea of an interpreter of the law, a learned man or a genuine prophet arising there, could not but move a man like old Hanan to the utmost scorn.

The road which took me to Sepphoris, or to Tiberias when I visited the Tetrarch, led through Nazareth. The caravan route from the Great Sea to Damascus, by the way of the rich Valley of Jezreel, also led through Nazareth. The town lies among the hills, on a slope facing Jezreel. The tilled fields rolling like a sea between Tabor and Gilboa run almost to the foot of Nazareth, which is set in a framework of golden vineyards, dark cypress groves and honey-dripping date palms; but the landscape as a whole takes its coloring from the silver-gray olive tree. In my day the vegetable patches, the gardens and groves were closely cultivated. An industrious population filled the region; yet Nazareth was a poor townlet of farmers and craftsmen; the houses, or rather huts, were built of dried clay, with roofs and hedges of wattled palm leaves. Here and there one encountered in the streets a saddle maker, a tent weaver, a spinner, a potter, a shoemaker; but mostly one saw carpenters. Lying as it did on the highway, the town possessed a few wells for the watering of animals; and by each well stood booths affording shelter to the wayfarer. Wainwrights and wheelwrights had plenty of work from passing caravans; but they, like the carpenters, were employed mostly by the local farmers, who needed wooden plows, rakes, spades and other implements.

Out of this city came the prophet concerning whom I now heard from the old High Priest in Jerusalem. But I met him first not in Nazareth, but in the town of K'far Nahum. And it was by no means the laughing matter which old Hanan tried to make of it; on the contrary, it was, I regret to say, profoundly, even desperately serious.

K'far Nahum lay on the shores of the Sea of Genesaret or Kineret. (The Jewish name is *Yam Genoser*, the Sea of the Garden of the Princes, for the body of water is set in a valley which is one blossoming garden of grain and fruit.) It was a fairly large provincial center, a market for the produce of the surrounding countryside. It had a fishing harbor and a customs house. Flat-bottomed boats were loaded at K'far Nahum with the grain and fruit of the district and rowed across to the opposite shore, where began the territory of the Tetrarch Philippus. The two principal sources of income were the rich fruit gardens which surrounded the town and the fisheries. It was a marvelous sight to watch the fishers of K'far Nahum setting out on moonlit nights across the blue, crystal-smooth waters of Genesaret, the reflection of moon and stars glittering among a network of boats. The sound of their singing came back to the shore; they would sing passages from their beloved Song of Songs, or from their ancient psalmody. In the day time the little harbor was crowded with sails, women spread out the nets to be dried or mended. Most of the fishermen were in the employ of wealthy fishing merchants, who sold their smoked wares throughout Galilee and Judaea. The population was poor; taxes and excise made it difficult to conduct small enterprises, and therefore the fishermen hired themselves out. Labor was cheap in Galilee, and life was hard. The fish dryers did not eat the wares they handled, they had to content themselves with figs and dates and flat unleavened cakes baked on their open stoves. Were it not for the heavy tribute exacted from the fishermen and the fish dryers the little town might have lived comfortably. But there were two sets of tax collectors—

that of the Tetrarch, and that of the Roman power. The town swarmed with fishermen, fish dryers, fruit dealers and tax gatherers. However hard the population worked, it could not even put by enough to build a synagogue for itself; one of our centurions, stationed in K'far Nahum, had had to help them out in this respect. For when the tributes had been paid to the Tetrarch and the Romans, there still remained the exactions of the High Priest for the Temple, tithes and offerings for the Priests and Levites.

I was a frequent visitor to K'far Nahum. Whenever I stayed with the Tetrarch in Tiberias, I would not fail to free myself one quiet or moonlit evening and have myself rowed across to the harbor, where I would buy a stock of fish fresh from the water. The road to Antioch in Syria also passed through K'far Nahum, and it was by way of K'far Nahum, again, that I traveled on official missions to the Tetrarch Philippus.

The centurion commanding the cohort in K'far Nahum was, officially, at the disposition of the Tetrarch, but his superior officer was of course the Proconsul in Antioch. The town, lying close to the juncture of two tetrarchates, was an important strategic point; and an additional reason for maintaining a garrison there was the contribution K'far Nahum provided for our treasury. As I have already indicated, the centurion lived on excellent terms with the Jews and liked to frequent their company. I invariably stayed with him when I stopped in the town; and one spring evening, when I was visiting him, he told me a story of an extraordinary man who had appeared there—a man who had the power to heal the sick, drive out evil spirits and perform other miracles.

I was not particularly interested at first. I did not connect this wonder-worker with the new-risen prophet of Galilee mentioned by the High Priest. Moreover, I had seen enough of wonder-workers and exorcizers of demons in Jerusalem, which swarmed with them. All of them, it appeared, were adepts at magic; the members of the Sanhedrin had to practice the art in their capacity as judges so as to protect themselves from magicians. But they were all inferior to the Chaldaeans. It was only when my friend told me that he himself—or rather his young servant—had been the beneficiary of the wonder-worker's gifts, that my interest picked up. But I knew the boy well, a fine, lovable Greek youngster from the island of Rhodes. True, my friend the centurion, with his peculiar leaning toward the Jews, was himself liable to enthusiasms akin to theirs; I suspected him even then of secrt leanings toward their faith. Yet I wanted to hear the story, and he gave it to me in all its details.

"You know," he said, "how fond we all are of the lad Andros; as for me, I regard him more as a son than a servant. Well, one day he fell into a sickness. I could not tell what ailed him, but he was unable to stir a limb. I was greatly frightened, for the lad's life and well-being are precious to me; and I did not know toward whom to turn for help. We have no doctors here. The folk hereabouts apply, in such cases, to nature healers, of whom there is no lack. They cure the sick with herbs, incantations, amulets and the like. Then suddenly I heard of a man of miracles, who had only recently healed a certain leper, whom we had known and avoided a long time. He used to come to the synagogue for services, but of course stayed outside, at a distance. This leper had encountered the man of miracles and had said to him: 'If thou wilt, thou canst heal me.' Thereupon the man of miracles had replied: 'I will that thou be healed.' In that same instant the leper became clean, as if a new skin had grown on his body. The man bade him go to the Priest and bring an offering; he also charged him to say nothing concerning what had happened. But of course the whole town knew of it by the next day, and I too. Enough; when I saw the boy Andros lying like one dead before me—he had perhaps eaten poisoned food, unwittingly, or had been stung by some deadly insect—I went, in the heaviness of my heart, to the Jews, and said: 'I have always been good to you. I have even helped you to build a synagogue. Now you must help me. Go to your man of wonders and let him heal the youth.' They obeyed at once and set forth. I did not wait till they brought the man back, but followed them at a distance till we came upon him. And the outward seeming of the man already impressed me. I came up and proffered my request. He looked straight into my face, and read there all my pain, then said: 'I will come to your house and I will heal him.' I was moved by his goodness, that he should be prepared to come into the house of a gentile—for as you may know, Cornelius, their law forbids them to enter the house of a heathen. Therefore I said to him:

'What need have you to trouble yourself thus, to go to my house? You can command spirits with your words, as I do soldiers with mine. I know it.' The man was touched, and said to those about him: 'I have not found among the Jews as much faith as in this gentile.' And to me he said: 'Go home, and the thing will be according to your faith in me.' And let me say this to you," the centurion ended earnestly, "it was so, that when I looked at the man I was filled with faith in him, and did indeed believe he could command spirits as I command my men. And think of it! When I returned to the house I found my Andros on his feet, walking about and speaking, just as you and I are doing now."

My curiosity now aroused, I said: "Centurion, can I see your wonder-worker?"

"Assuredly. He is in the harbor every day. He consorts with the fishermen and the fish dryers. If you wish, we may go now and find him."

I went down with my friend the centurion to the harbor of K'far Nahum. It was a poor place, a curved inlet shut off from the lake by a dam of stone blocks, for though the waters of Genesaret are usually quiet, they are capable of violent storms which threaten the foundations of the houses near the shore. Fisherfolk sat in their boats not far from the waters' edge, and in one place on the sandy beach we saw a crowd gathered. All about the labor and commerce of the harbor went on. Women had stretched out the fishing nets of their men, and were mending them, while the men, naked to the waist—for it was full springtime, and it was hot in the low-lying region of Genesaret—dragged baskets and pails of fish from the beached boats to the land, spread them out on the flat stones covering the tables, salted them, then laid them to dry on beds of palm leaves on the ground. Other half-naked men carried on their mighty, suntanned backs sacks of grain, baskets filled with fruit, and bundles of vegetables—the produce of the rich Valley of Jezreel, brought to the harbor on donkeys—and loaded them on to the barges and sailboats. Tax collectors went about their business from group to group, buyers chaffered with farmers, overseers drove the fish dryers to work faster. But in the midst of all this to-do we observed how, from time to time, a man would steal away from his work and join the crowd which was assembled about a teacher or interpreter of the law; then someone from the crowd would steal back to the porters or fish dryers and tell them, with excited gesticulation, what he had just heard. I was eager to approach, but my friend warned me to be careful; for though we were in civilian dress, that is, the toga, they would take fright, thinking that we meant to attack them, and would scatter.

We therefore drew near very slowly, and took up our stations under a fig tree a little distance from the crowd.

To one side of the harbor, and close to the water's edge, there stood a few withered fig trees. At one time there must have been in this place a grove, or a garden alley, which the waves of the lake had gradually washed away. Nothing remained now but these wretched remnants. In the high spring, when nature blossomed out from under stone and sand, these fig trees remained naked; only a twig turned green here and there near their summits. The women hung their nets from the branches; farmers tethered their asses to them, and the patient animals nibbled at the bark. There is not a more desolate sight than a naked fig tree which stretches out crippled branches like the hands of a crucified man falling from the cross. Under such a tree I saw standing a young man, surrounded by fishermen, dryers, porters and even country folk who had just brought their wares to the harbor of K'far Nahum. They were a strange sight, these simple people, with the implements of their trades in their hands, the fishermen with their hooks, the porters with their baskets, the peasants with their staves, which they used on their donkeys. On every face that was visible from our vantage point joy was poured out; heads and beards nodded in happy confirmation; some of the men, for sheer delight, scratched their perspiring backs with hook or staff. They winked ecstatically at each other with their twinkling black eyes, and the nodding of their tangled beards and wind-hardened faces was a continuous accompaniment to the words. What astonished me most was to see that certain tax collectors stood in the crowd, and no one moved away from them. Among the Jews tax collectors are regarded as sinners, and few wish to consort with them; but here they were among the rest, in a ring of brotherhood about the speaker. The crowd grew larger from minute to minute. Workers seized a moment of leisure to run over and catch a few words, like a thirsty man running to a spring for a gulp of water. Close to the shore, almost grounded, were several fishing boats, in which men stood up, barefoot, their bronzed faces tense, their throats exposed, listening from a distance; others sat, their black-bearded faces in their hands. In the breathless absorption of the crowd our slow approach, the centurion's and mine, seemed to pass unnoticed.

I am compelled to admit that the first impression made on me by the young man was altogether extraordinary; it was a contradictory impression, compounded of equal measures of reality and unreality. There was, to begin with, his figure and pose, his manner of standing with outstretched arms under the spreading branches of the naked fig tree. I judged him to be some thirty years of age; his body was lean and hungry-looking, as Jochanan's had been, but it lacked the power and musculature of the enthusiast I had seen shortly before his death in the fortress of the Tetrarch. No, this man had the body of a strengthless child, even though he was taller than any of his listeners; for his head, set on the long and slender neck, rose clear above the crowd, as though he were standing on a little elevation. The face was of a strange pallor, the skin delicate, so that the veins of his temple showed clearly; but his expression was so lively that it imparted to him a look of extreme youthfulness. A young black beard, which mingled with the ritualistic ear-locks hanging down at either side, framed his longish face and accentuated its pallor. His garb, which covered him, after the manner of the learned, from the opening at the throat down to the feet, was white. Over it he wore the sleeveless blue-white tunic with the ritualistic fringes hanging down almost to the ground. Thus he stood under the naked fig tree and preached in the Aramaic jargon of the people.

I would have understood him much better if he had not woven into his discourse so many verses from their ancient scriptures in the original Hebrew; but it was clear that everything he uttered, whether in Aramaic or Hebrew, was meant directly for the poor people who surrounded him. They were words of comfort, as one might have guessed without understanding him at all, from the happy faces, the open mouths and the radiant eyes of his listeners. He told them that they were the salt of the earth and that salvation would come from them. "Blessed are the meek," he said, "for they shall have the kingdom of heaven!" (There it was again, the kingdom of heaven!) "Blessed are the poor, for they shall inherit the earth." Then he quoted something from their scripture, which the centurion translated for me. "The people that walk in darkness have seen a great light; those that dwell in the land of the dead have been illumined by a great light."

Then suddenly all the faces flashed into ecstasy. I could not hear what he said, but it must have been something unusually wise. "He is explaining a beloved parable," my friend whispered. And just as suddenly, the picture was broken up. On the further side from us a rain of blows descended on the heads of the crowd. Whips whistled in the air. There was a frantic scattering and scampering, and we saw the overseers flailing about them. Faces glowing with bliss changed their expression abruptly into one of terror. Fishermen and porters snatched up hook and basket and fled. But there were some who, whether they were not day laborers like the others, or were so transported by the preacher that they were oblivious to their surroundings, remained standing in their places, waiting for more. The overseers raised a loud outcry.

"Why does he come here to confuse and mislead the workers? Does he not know that they are day laborers?"

"The day of the day laborer belongs to his master," the chief of the overseers shrieked at the preacher.

"Thou hast said," answered the other, a smile breaking over his pallid face. "The day of the day laborer belongs to his master. But no one can be called master and lord, save the Lord of the world, and our days belong to him. To what may this be likened?"

He wanted to speak on, but the chief of the overseers shouted him down.

"If you have pretty sermons, keep them for the synagogue on the Sabbath. The working day is no time for them."

Another voice entered the dispute. It came from a dark-robed man whom I had observed out of the corner of my eye during the preaching. He had stood to one side, absorbed in the scene. He said, weightily: "It is against the law to disturb the day laborer during his labor even in order to preach the Torah." He was, as the centurion informed me, the chief presiding officer of their synagogue. On the Sabbath just past there had been a dispute between him and the present preacher, and now the populace were obeying the latter.

Encouraged by the support of the synagogue dignitary, the overseers became louder in their attacks on the preacher.

"We'll drive him out of here, the lawbreaker! We'll have him up before the court for damages."

I cannot tell how the scene would have ended if there had not suddenly appeared around the preacher a group of men making up a sort of bodyguard. One of them I had noted as he sat in his boat close to the shore, a black-bearded Jew with broad shoulders, of low stature but powerful build, compact and sinewy like a tree-root. He stretched out his veined and muscular arms in front of the young man. Several others like him, fishermen, with hairy, uncovered breasts and tangled beards, had left their nets, joined him and made a protective circle about the preacher.

"The harbor is a public place and belongs to everyone, and not only to the contractors," one of them yelled. "Whoever wishes to preach here has the right to do so."

But the man who was the center of the tumult stood there as though he had no connection with it and did not perceive what was taking place around him or hear the words meant for him. He had fixed his gaze on the first fisherman who had come to his rescue. I saw the great dark eyes scrutinizing the simple, commonplace countenance, and I saw the other shrink back as in fear from the scrutiny. The two men stared at each other for a while, in silence. Then the fisherman took the preacher by the hand, and led him away from the crowd as one leads a child.

A long time the fish dryers watched the two men as they moved off till they were swallowed by the shadow of a street. Then I heard them talking among themselves.

"All this because he befriends us, the poor folk. They hate him for it."

"He brings us comfort. Who else is there to talk to us as he does?"

"He is the prophet Elijah, for he heals the sick as Elijah did."

"Enough, enough!" shouted the overseers. "The rest of it you will hear in the synagogue. Back to work! You have wasted enough time today." But the men still looked longingly in the direction taken by the preacher and his friend.

"They are right, of course," I said to the centurion, whose eyes were as dreamy as those of the others.

"Who?" he asked me, starting.

"The overseers, of course. These men are day laborers. They are being paid for their time. And here one comes and makes them idle away the hours."

He turned on me a strange, mournful gaze. "Yes," he murmured. "He disturbs men at their work, as the sun and the spring disturb men with their joy and consolation."

I did not understand my friend. In any case, it was high time to leave, for the crowd of workers had begun to observe us. They were undecided in their attitude. My own face, a stranger's, alarmed them, but they were reassured by the presence of the centurion, a well-known and friendly figure in the town.

"Let us go," I said. "The Jews will begin to think we are going to convert to their faith. You know how they are; if we stay another moment they will become altogether too familiar with us."

CHAPTER SEVENTEEN

YES, I must admit again that from the moment I set eyes on him, surrounded by his eager listeners under the withered fig tree, I could not rid myself of him. There was in his manner of utterance a curious power to invest with reality whatever he said. His very appearance, his posture, his relationship to people, awakened a profound faith and boundless trust. I must go further in my confession; for all my jesting remarks to the centurion, little was wanting to draw me into the magic circle. If I did not succumb, if I did not fall a victim to that Asiatic magnetic force, as other Romans did, I have to thank my manly character and the severe discipline of my upbringing. And yet, I repeat, there was a time during which I could not quite free myself from the man.

Nor is it really to be wondered at. I have witnessed more than once the extremes to which the power of faith can go. We Romans, outsiders as we are, cannot conceive to what extent the Jews are the dupes of faith. One had to see them on the High Holy days in their Temple courts; they stood jammed against each other so that not a finger could have been inserted between body and body; nevertheless they persuaded themselves that when they threw themselves to the ground, to confess their sins, a miracle occurred and there was so much room around each man that his neighbor could not hear his confession! And for them it was actually so! What happened I cannot tell, whether the place was actually extended, or whether they shrank so upon themselves that one body did not touch the next. Again, they believed that in all the Temple, in which innumerable animals were being slaughtered continuously for the sacrifices, not a single fly ever appeared. I grant that faith exists for the purpose of making the incredible appear credible. Our gods too are not without power in this respect; Zeus can transform himself into a swan or a golden cloud. By the power which those Jews ascribed to their God, the faith which they reposed in him, had no parallel elsewhere; it was an art in which they had no equal.

I now learned that the man was widely known and loved in K'far Nahum. He was a prominent Rabbi, accepted not only by the fisherfolk of the little port, but also by the scholars of the vicinity—particularly had his reputation risen when he had declared solemnly in their synagogue that he had come not to "destroy the Law and the prophets, but to fulfill them." He was even reported to have used these words: "Sooner shall the heavens and the earth pass away than one jot or tittle of the Law," or words like them. This, by the way, was typical of the arrogance with which the Jews spoke of their sacred books. In this tremendous self-conceit the Rabbi, whatever his other differences with the official Rabbis, was wholly like them. All of them were convinced that divine power resided solely in their sacred books, which had been handed down from the heavens. In any case, if there had been friction between the man and the scholars of K'far Nahum and vicinity, it disappeared after he had made this extravagantly patriotic declaration in their synagogue. His performance of miracles did not affect them adversely; on the contrary, it was perfectly proper that the learned should assist the sick by prayers and miracles, and he was by no means the only Rabbi familiar with these practices.

He had his own pupils and disciples; true, they were not of the learned class; they came from among the poor, a few fisherfolk who had left their trade and their livelihood to follow him. He lived with one of them, the very man, in fact, who had rescued him that day from the overseers. This was his first disciple. I made the acquaintance of this fisherman. Simon was the name he went by at that time. A simple man, below medium height, but of tremendous strength, with a bearded face which storm and wind had hardened into stone. His mighty, squat body was filled from head to foot with a strange and tender love for his Rabbi. It sometimes happened that when the crowds of the poor and the sick pressed too close upon the Rabbi, threatening to crush him in their ranks, the fisherman would lift him up in his arms and bear him away as a father bears away a child. Simon lived only for his lord, and it was touching to see this hardy Cyclops standing among the fishers in the port or the worshipers in the synagogue and gazing with openmouthed and tremulous happiness at the preacher. Tears of enthusiasm gathered in his eyes. Among the other disciples there was a brother of this Simon, likewise a fisherman who had left his nets to follow his master. So it often was among the Jews; they held their Rabbis dearer than their own families. They could sometimes leave house and field, wife and child, trade and livelihood, in order to attach themselves to a teacher. There were two other brothers who followed the man; their names were Jacob and Jochanan; their mother was a rich woman of Bet Zeida, a little town not far from K'far Nahum. They had gone away from her to be with the teacher. A fierce couple they were, these two disciples, true Maccabaeans, stormy spirits; they were ready with fist and knife for anyone who dared to speak evil of their Rabbi. They were for ever at loggerheads with the other Jews, and their Rabbi had to hold them in check for fear of disturbances. But his most beloved—and most devoted—disciple was Simon, with whom he stayed, not actually in Simon's house, but in the house of Simon's mother-in-law.

On the occasion of another visit to K'far Nahum, not long after, I followed the Rabbi, with others, to his home. Whenever he appeared in the harbor or near the synagogue, he was surrounded by crowds of the sick and the poor who implored his help. They went along with him through the streets—and this time I followed the rabble at a distance till we came to the court where stood the house of Simon's mother-in-law. At the gate of the court Simon turned and with his burly figure blocked the way.

"Let him rest awhile," he begged of the importunate mob. "Do you not see that he is weak?"

Then, looking up, he perceived me. By now I was not unknown to him. He had seen me more than once in the company of my friend the centurion, in the streets of K'far Nahum, or standing on the outskirts of a crowd which his teacher was addressing. Out of respect for a Roman officer, he let me pass.

It was a poor courtyard, enclosed by a hedge of twigs intertwined with palm leaves. In the center stood a few lean, dusty fig trees and palms, such as you would find in every poor Jewish yard. (They could not do without palms, for they put these trees to a great variety of uses, including shelter; in the summer the leaves afforded shade, in the winter they were a protection against the rain.) The bark of the trees had been eaten away by deposits of fish-scales, accumulated from the nets which they hung there to dry. In front of the house there was a well-tended vegetable garden, another necessity among Jews, indeed their chief source of food. Apart from the house there was a small hut leaning against two old olive trees; the walls were of baked clay supported by logs and covered by a network of palm leaves. A little ladder led to the flat roof, on which there was a booth, woven of palm branches and topped by straw and twigs. The upper reaches of the olive trees shaded and protected the booth, which they had erected for the use of their Rabbi. The sweet peas which they had planted by the side of the house were now in full blossom; they had worked their way up the walls, and their tendrils, laden with blue-rosy delicate flowers, made a wreath about the booth. When I entered that day an elderly woman in a sackcloth covering was standing by the earthen oven, baking flat cakes over a twig fire. This was the woman concerning whom a remarkable story was current now in K'far Nahum. Some days before she had fallen sick, and had been on the point of death, when the Rabbi had healed her. All the town knew of the miracle that had occurred with Simon's mother-in-law, and crowds came to look at her. On one part of the hedge lay some nets, unused, the property of the fishermen who had left their trade to attach themselves completely to the Rabbi. A few young people—members of the household—were busy in the yard helping in the preparation of the evening meal.

I learned that they were going to hold that evening a sort of feast for a larger group of the Rabbi's followers, hence the unusual stir of preparation. The women baked unleavened cakes, the men put boards together to make a long table. In one corner a woman stood over a jar and washed the Rabbi's clothes. The work went forward amid quiet; instead of speaking, the men and women made signs to each other; they did not wish to disturb their Rabbi, who had ascended to the booth and was now sunk in meditation and prayer.

I saw that my entry into the yard had frightened the inhabitants, and I therefore withdrew. But that evening I returned in the company of my friend the centurion. We had exchanged our Roman garb for the simple, sackcloth coverings worn by many of the Jews, so that we might attract as little attention as possible. When we arrived we found numbers of people congregated about the gate, and we entered with them. We were admitted into the house of Simon, and found ourselves in a fairly large room, from which everything had been removed except the mats of woven straw and the long low table of rough boards on which I had seen them working in the afternoon. There were some fifteen or twenty people present; some of them sat on the floor, on the straw matting ranged about the table; others stood. Two earthen oil lamps hung down from the roof, but their dim light was scarcely needed, for it was a brilliant night of moon and stars, such as is common in the spring above the Sea of Genesaret, and a silvery light came in through door and window.

At the head of the table, half seated, half reclining, was the Rabbi; his pale face and white garb shone out from the circle of black-bearded and black-haired men. The guests were mostly fishermen of the town and peasants from the surrounding country, who had come that day to sell their wares; but having heard of the man of wonders they had found their way to Simon's house to see and hear him, and perhaps be helped by him. The women of the house brought in earthen platters with the food prepared on the oven outside, flat cakes, small fishes baked in a covering of dough (this delicacy was in honor of the Rabbi) and large quantities of green stuff from the garden. Other women had brought gifts to the Rabbi, one a cruse of wine, another a jar of honey, a third fruit, dried grapes, and dates.

Many children were present, young boys swathed in the *tallit* or prayer-shawl; thus fathers brought them before the Rabbi, so that he might place his hands on their heads and bless them. He detained the children and made them sit near him.

When the food had been placed on the table, and before any of the flat cakes had yet been broken, the Rabbi called out:

"Let us pray to our father in heaven!"

One of the men answered:

"Rabbi, we are ignorant men. We have not been taught to pray."

Thereupon he said to them:

"Is it not written: 'Ye shall be simple before your God'? You are more important in the eyes of God than the learned, for it is written: 'The simple and the upright shall comfort Me.'"

Another one said from a corner:

"We are sinners, Rabbi."

Thereupon he answered with a parable:

"There were two men went up to the Temple, one a sinner, the other a saint. The sinner stands with a broken heart before the sanctuary, and dares not lift his gaze, but lets his eyes fall to the earth; and he says in his heart: 'Father in heaven, thou knowest I am a sinful man, forgive me and have mercy on me.' The other, the saint, stands and says in his heart: 'Father in heaven, thou knowest me well; I am not like that man of sin who stands over there, but I walk in thy ways and perform thy commandments.' I say to you, the sinful man returns newborn, and without sin like a little child, and the saint is laden with sin."

When the company had calmed down from the ecstasy into which it was thrown by this parable, a man stretched out his arms to the Rabbi and said:

"Teach us, Rabbi, how to pray."

He answered:

"Do not think that your father in heaven does not know your needs even before you have prayed to him. Therefore pray in this manner—and repeat the words after me, one by one."

Then the Rabbi covered the bread with his hands, closed his eyes, and said the prayer, and the congregation repeated it after him, word by word:

"Our father which art in heaven, hallowed be thy name. Thy kingdom come. Thy will be done in heaven as it is on earth. Give us this day our daily bread and forgive us our sins as we forgive those that trespass against us. Lead us not into temptation but protect us from evil. For thine is the kingdom, the power and the glory for ever and ever."

Then he took the flat cakes, broke them into pieces and distributed the pieces to the assembled, to the women and children as well as the men. His own piece of bread he dipped in salt, then he closed his eyes and said something to himself. But as he was about to put the piece of bread in his mouth, a voice was heard from the further corner of the table:

"Rabbi, we have forgotten to wash our hands before eating."

The Rabbi looked toward the man and said: "To the pure all things are pure."

He put the piece of bread in his mouth and ate, and the others did the same.

I turned round to see who had had the impudence to interrupt the Rabbi and in the dim light I caught a glimpse of a face half hidden in the crowd; and I was startled, for I was certain that I had seen the face elsewhere. I could not recall where, or under what circumstances, so I turned and looked again. Those yellow tufts of beard on the long face—they could not be mistaken. But who was the man? Then it suddenly came back to me. Always as I passed from the outer to the inner court of the High Priest's house, a man had been seated on the steps, near the guard; and always I had been struck by the appearance of his beard, which consisted of long, yellow tufts growing separately out of moles, like knolls of trees on little hills. But I had been struck still more by his eyes, which were blue as polished crystal, cold and dry as if they had never been washed by tears, as if they were not made of flesh and nerves, but of stone. The light that came from them was gathered into thin, penetrating shafts liked sharpened spears. Even when my back was turned to him I felt the shafts on my neck, stinging the flesh. Nay, more; even when the man was absent, I could not pass his accustomed post without feeling that I was being observed from behind a door or an invisible opening in the walls. Now surely this was the same man, seated here in the company at the Rabbi's table. And yet it could not be. I looked a third time, and certainty continued to fight with doubt. This was indeed the man's nature, to sit, not openly among others, but half hidden, sending out the steely shafts of light from his eyes. What confused me was the face, which was so different now in its expression of sadness, that I seemed to see it for the first time. There came up in my memory my conversation with old Hanan, in which he had made mention of the Rabbi of Galilee. Could he have sent one of his men here, to observe and report?

"Cunning old fox!" I murmured to myself. "Your eyes and ears are everywhere!"

Meanwhile the feast went on. The company was made up of poor folk, and the meal was a meager one, such as these men and women were accustomed to. It consisted for the greater part of flat cakes and olives, greens and sour milk. They dipped their bread in honey. There was one delicacy, the little baked fishes. The Rabbi took one from the earthen platter in front of him, ate, and passed the platter round the table, and each one lifted a fish with his fingers and ate. The Rabbi did the same with the platter of dried figs and dates. Between one course and the next they repeated various psalms, following a leader who knew them by heart; and with the progress of the meal a great spirit of unity grew among them, so that they became, men, women and children, like a single body, with a single soul—their Rabbi. When the meal was ended Simon brought a dish of water to the Rabbi, who washed his hands; then the dish was carried round the table, and everyone did likewise. The faces of all the assembled glowed with intense joy. It was as if the presence and utterances of their Rabbi had opened for them gates of happiness which they had thought eternally closed to them.

And as they sat and stood thus, locked in one radiant expectancy, there was a sudden noise above their heads, as of something creaking and breaking. What was this? From the low balcony screened with palm branches a bed, with a sick man lying on it, was being lowered by ropes. The press of men and women made room. Two mighty hands were lifted up; they took hold of the bed and placed it near the Rabbi. What amazed me most was the composure of the guests, who accepted this strange procedure as if it were an ordinary thing. On the bed lay a living skeleton, which tried to lift its bony arms toward the Rabbi. The face was hairless; the head, too, had lost nearly all its hair, so that it looked like a disinterred skull, and the face was dead, except for the agonizing eyes in their dry sockets. The white lips moved, and from them came a whispering stammer:

"Help me, help me, man of God."

New figures had appeared in the doorway, the room had become more crowded, and now a forest of hands was lifted toward the Rabbi and innumerable voices implored:

"Rabbi, help him!"

The Rabbi stood up—I see him now, white-robed and barefoot —and took two steps toward the head of the bed. He bent down over the dying man, and their eyes met and fastened on each other. Thus several moments passed, while the Rabbi held the sick man's gaze in his own. The Rabbi's face was pale and strained, the veins on his temples worked like tiny snakes. Then he placed his hands on the withered body and said, in a loud voice:

"Mordecai, son of Isaak, dost thou believe with perfect faith that I have the power, and have been given the permission of our father in heaven, to heal thee?"

The sick man whispered, word by word:

"I, Mordecai ben Isaak, believe with perfect faith that thou, Yeshua ben Joseph, hast the power, and hast been given the permission of our father in heaven, to heal me."

The Rabbi straightened up, and it seemed then to me that his head reached to the stars. But he still kept his gaze fixed on the sick man, whom he now addressed in a voice of command:

"Mordecai ben Isaak, by the power of faith, I bid thee rise from thy bed!"

The sick man stared back as if he had not understood the words, but the eyes of the Rabbi remained fastened on him.

Then suddenly he moved his hands, gripped the sides of the bed, and tried to lift himself. The first time he fell back, but he tried a second time under the imperious and relentless gaze of the Rabbi. His face filled with terror, he rose a little and his head fell forward. Still the Rabbi held him transfixed. Spasms of pain shot through the body as the man turned and put one fleshless leg and then another on the floor. The legs trembled, as if the slightest weight would break them, but, as if they felt the command of the eyes shining down from above, they straightened out slowly. Slowly the man rose; he took two stiff steps forward and fell on the Rabbi's breast.

"Hosannah!" A wild cry of joy rose from the guests. Hands were stretched out to Mordecai, a sack was thrown over his naked body; they laid the man down tenderly near the table.

But now the newcomers filled not only every cranny of the room, but overflowed into the yard of Simon's house. They had brought all manner of sick with them. Two powerful men thrust their way through, leading a young woman possessed of evil spirits. They had tied her with ropes. The evil spirits screamed out of the woman in unknown languages, or imitated the cries of household animals. Others came, bearing their sick on their backs. A great clamor rose, wails of pain, sobs of entreaty, exclamations of prayer, mingling with the hideous noise of animals, a ceaseless clucking and barking and mewing, which issued from the possessed woman. I thought I had been trapped on an island of demons, or that I was being engulfed in a sea of putrescent humanity, of sickness and madness. An unbearable stench spread from the decayed bodies and distended mouths, and finally I did not know who was mad, they or I. And above all the tumult, the night rang with the sustained cry: "Hosannah! Hosannah!"

I wanted to flee from this witch's caldron, and I caught at my friend's hand, but there was no retreat through the screaming press of human beings. We perceived, also, that the Rabbi was exhausted and that in another moment he would sink down and become part of the writhing, weeping, crying heap of wretched bodies which surrounded him to the height of his waist; for they had made their way through to him, they kissed the hem of his robe, they called out: "Hosannah! Hosannah!" It was then that Simon suddenly bestirred himself. He lifted up the faltering Rabbi in his mighty arms, drew the white mantle down over the tired face, and treading on human bodies carried his burden out of that sea of misery and pain, as one might carry a drowning man out of the waves.

* * *

At the gate, as I was about to cross the threshold, I encountered the man with the yellow, tufted beard and sad face. I stopped him.

"Judah, man of Kiriot!"

He looked at me in astonishment.

"Who calls me?"

We looked straight at each other.

"Do you not recognize me, in spite of these clothes?"

"Who are you, then?"

"Judah, do you not recognize your Hegemon?"

His eyes pierced through me.

"How should I, a poor man, know the Hegemon?"

"Judah, have I not seen you in the court of the High Priest?"

"In the court of the High Priest? Certainly. I serve the High Priest, as every good Jew does."

"What are you doing here, Judah Ish-Kiriot?"

"I came to do honor to a great Rabbi, according to the Jewish law, and to sit at his feet and listen to God's word. But what is a Hegemon doing here among Jews?" he turned on me.

I must confess that I was compelled to retreat under his penetrating glance.

And still I could not quite make up my mind whether this was indeed the man who sat in the court of the High Priest, or whether I had come across a remarkable but accidental resemblance.

CHAPTER EIGHTEEN

THAT spring I spent several weeks on end in the town of K'far Nahum. I will not disguise the fact that my interest in the man led me to neglect my duties. It was a great folly. I put off my visit to the legate Vitellius in Antioch, whom I had originally set out to see, and sent forward the message that I was ill. I pleaded that the winter climate of Jerusalem had broken down my health and that in order to recover it I needed some weeks of rest in the warm valley. I cannot until this day explain what came over me, or what good or evil spirit imbued this man with such power to attract others, both his own—that was more comprehensible—and complete strangers, like myself. But stay I did, in order to be near him. By no means the smallest part of the folly lay in this, that my unconcealed interest in the man damaged my standing with the Jews. That distance between me and them which the dignity of my position demanded grew altogether too small. They came, in that peculiar way of theirs, to regard me practically as one of their own, an honor which they had already conferred on the local centurion. It is this sort of thing which one must avoid in dealing with the Jews; they are near enough a mile away. I was aware of the undignified consequences of my behavior; I even reproached myself with it; I decided more than once to leave the city immediately. But something had happened to my will—as it seemed to happen in the case of so many others who came under the man's influence.

Yes, I confess that it would have been difficult at that time to distinguish me from one of his crazed followers. And of these there were enough, for it was during this period that his name stood highest. Their numbers increased not only among the poor and ignorant. Jewish scholars and men of learning flocked to him. Every day boats landed in K'far Nahum from the territory of the Tetrarch Philippus on the other side of Genesaret, bringing the halt, the sick and the possessed—and bringing also others whom nothing ailed, who only wished to listen to his teaching. For this much that is natural must be conceded to him: he knew how to speak. I do not know where he obtained the gift, this simple carpenter's son of Nazareth, to clothe his thoughts in such visible imagery. Of Greek education he had nothing whatsoever; he was quite devoid of the rhetoric which enables a man to express himself with precision and learning, choosing one exact, short phrase after the other and stringing them together in polished discourse like pearls on a thread. His style was purely Jewish, formless, loose and scattered. But he possessed the art of uttering himself in vivid picture parables which broke through like lightning to the minds of the simple folk to whom he always addressed himself—whatever the composition of his audiences—leaving there an unforgettable image. The art of speaking in parables, by indirect and concealed expression, was also a fashion with the learned Jews. It had developed among a people long familiar with alien rule and afraid to give open utterance to its thoughts, after the manner, for instance, of a free Roman. With typical Jewish cunning they concealed their meaning in allegorical fables, by means of which they were able to convey the most subtle ideas not in so many words, but through allusive images.

On general grounds it would not have been at all foolish to spend a few spring weeks on the shores of the Sea of Genesaret. Something of my reluctance to leave the place may be ascribed to the beauty of the landscape and the gentleness of the climate. It was the loveliest time of the year, in the loveliest spot in the land. After the grim monotony of the Judaean landscape about Jerusalem, which withers the spirit and throws the mind back upon itself in gloomy meditation, eyes and nerves drank in with delight the idyllic restfulness and springing greenness of the Jordan Valley, of the cypresses, palms and olive trees, the vineyards and the long fields of wheat for which the region is justly famous. Here, where the land lies below sea level, fruit and grain ripen in advance of the other provinces. Innumerable flowers bedeck the earth; there is not a patch of soil, a stone, a house, a booth, a hedge, which is not covered with wild flowers; their tendrils creep up the walls and twine themselves among the trellised palm twigs which screen them. The lodges in the vineyards and the gardens are set in the midst of blossoms, and blood-red poppies are scattered thickly across the fields and yards. Oleanders spring up, whether planted or not, along the paths and about the water troughs. And loveliest of all is Genesaret itself, a blue and polished level surrounded by beds of green sprinkled with color. From afar the snow-covered crown of the highest of their mountains looks across the scene.

On such a spring day I once heard the man preach outside the city. I learned from my friend the centurion that a certain afternoon had been set aside—it was one of their holidays, if I am not mistaken, when they pray for their trees, a minor festival—for a sermon to be delivered from a hilltop in the vicinity. My friend and I, wearing civilian togas above our armor, accompanied the crowd that left the city.

The smaller hills in Palestine are molded like platforms. This particular hill cannot have been more than forty or fifty paces from base to summit, but there was room enough on its slopes for the two or three hundred men and women who had assembled to listen. The majority of them were his constant attendants, fishermen, fish dryers, day laborers and city workers; but there was a higher proportion than usual of scribes and interpreters of the law. They stood apart from the common people, in their own groups, distinguishable by their black garb and their headgear, the marks of their class. They too, it appeared, had heard in advance of the sermon that was to be delivered, for they had come prepared; some of them carried parchment scrolls and papyrus leaves, no doubt their holy books, for while they waited they consulted texts and engaged in earnest discussion with each other. I did not know that I was about to witness an event of great importance; it was at this assembly that he set forth in systematic form, as it were, the substance of his teachings. Perhaps the scribes and scholars knew of it, which would account for their numbers and the air of preparation. They had come not only from K'far Nahum, but from outlying towns and villages as far off as Naim. There were present many heads of synagogues, prayer leaders, Rabbis and judges of local religious courts. They kept at a certain distance, these *chaverim*, from the common men-of-the-earth, who might contaminate them; and the latter did not dare to approach them. But the plain folk felt that this was their day, for it was their Rabbi whom the learned had assembled to hear.

The hill slopes, like all the fields about them, were thickly sprinkled with poppy anemones; the delicate crimson robes swayed and fluttered on their stalks against the deep background of green. On the summit of the hill was a little cluster of cypresses, and one of them lifted high beyond the others its crown of dark foliage. Swallows had filled it with nests, for the mother birds flew twittering back and forth, carrying food in their beaks for the little ones.

When the crowd was all assembled we saw the Rabbi approaching from the lake shore, whither his disciples had rowed him across from K'far Nahum. His white robe set with fringes gleamed against the poppy-sprinkled grass on which he trod with sandaled feet. This time he wore a black headgear. His face was earnest. With slow, almost solemn steps he mounted the hill, greeting the scribes and scholars with their usual salutation, *Shalom aleichem,* to which they answered, *Aleichem shalom.* One of his disciples handed him a prayer shawl, which he drew over his head, while he made the appropriate benediction. Then, taking his station under a cypress, he lifted up his arms as if to shield the whole assembly, and began to preach.

He spoke long and earnestly, with frequent pauses; sometimes with extreme, deliberate slowness, by way of emphasis. Then the words came out of him not as if they were sounds which could be lost in the air and be no more, but rather as if they were external images transmitted direct from mind to mind. And with what power he spoke! The frail and slender body seemed to expand until it became a mighty human pyramid, until we felt that the hill beneath him was but a pedestal. Perhaps the afternoon sunlight, deepening into the fiery red of evening, imparted an illusion of immense height and width to his figure. But his voice too had taken on unearthly power; for it filled all the circumambient air. . . .

On the scribes and scholars standing in their separate group the sermon produced an extraordinary effect. Astonishment was poured out on their faces, and they lifted their arms in gestures of wonder, especially when the emphasis on certain passages seemed to deny any possibility of doubt or challenge. Very different was the reception accorded the sermon by the unlettered masses; they were prepared to accept every utterance before it issued, and they nodded their eager approval. Listening, they bowed their bodies, as if to take on their shoulders the burden of the laws which he placed on them. With blissful faces and liberated eyes they swallowed the words and nodded confirmation. But the scribes and scholars listened with such concentrated attention that the veins stood out like swollen muscles on their high foreheads, their faces and throats, as though the blood were hardening in them. Sometimes they frowned and bit their lips. Sometimes, during a pause, they consulted hastily with each other and nodded in acquiescence. Thus it was, for instance, when he said the following: "When thou bringest thy sacrifice to the altar, and rememberest there that thy brother is angry with thee, leave the sacrifice on the altar, go make thy peace with thy brother and then return to offer the sacrifice." After these words he waited a little while, as if to hear an echo from the learned. They stared intently at one another, as if they were analyzing this law in silence, but soon they indicated their agreement. On other occasions they did not wait, but with powerful gestures of their heads and hands gave their approval at once. It was thus, for instance, when he said: "When thou givest charity, let not thy left hand know what thy right hand doeth." And there were other sayings of this kind which seemed to be in harmony with their teachings and which they accepted with indications of great respect. But there were moments when their faces showed alarm and dissatisfaction. So, for instance, when he added to the rigor of the law and increased its severity, they said to each other in distress: "He follows the school of Shammai." On another occasion I heard them say: "Now he follows the school of Hillel." These were the two schools of their tradition into which they tried to fit the laws he enunciated. When he said to them: "Love your enemies; bless those that curse you; do good to those that hate you; pray for those that persecute you," —when he said this, they stretched out their hands to each other in bewilderment and despair, as if they had to go forth the very next day and fulfill the commandment. They exchanged frightened glances, and said in utter confusion: "Surely it were well if it could be so! But who can carry this out? An angel, not a man of flesh and blood!"

And again they were seized with confusion and fright when he uttered these words: "But I say unto you, resist not evil, and if a man smite you on the right cheek turn the left cheek to him also." They were as terrified as if they had to leave at once and put this law into immediate effect. Sometimes, however, it was not fear they showed, but a dark, cloudy resentment. In particular they raised their brows in angry astonishment whenever he used the words, "But I say unto you," and they expressed their feeling of outrage by lifting their shoulders and turning to each other with questioning hands. But their amazement reached its extreme when he said: "You have been told that he who wishes to put away his wife, shall give her a bill of divorcement; but I say unto you that he who puts away his wife except for adultery, causes her to commit adultery, and he that takes to wife a divorced woman is himself an adulterer."

"From what passages in the sacred writings does he deduce this?" the scholars asked each other, violently. "It is against the law of Moses. For Moses allowed divorce and he would forbid it. Is he greater than Moses?"

But one of the scholars sought to defend him, beginning: "Our sages, too, have said, that when a man puts away his first wife the altar in the Temple sheds tears."

"True, true, we do not dispute that it is a bad thing. Forty days before the woman is born a voice sounds through heaven, saying: 'Daughter of such and such a one, the Lord of the world arranges marriages, and you are going down on earth to destroy them?' But that which he preaches is against the law of Moses none the less."

This interruption lasted longer than any other. His observations and utterances on divorce had brought up a storm of disagreement among the scholars, and it was some time before they could compose themselves. There was heard in the meantime a crackling of parchment as they unrolled their scrolls and pointed out to each other the exact passage in which their ancient teacher, Moses, had given his permission to divorce. Their faces grew obstinate, and with violent gestures they shook their heads, saying, "No!" But as against this they were nearly all in accord with him when he bade them have faith in God and take no care for the morrow. He told them to look at the birds of the air, which neither sow nor harvest nor gather into barns, but which their father in heaven feeds. "And are ye not better than they?

"And why do you take thought for raiment? Consider the lilies of the field, how they grow. They toil not, neither do they spin, yet I say unto you that Solomon in all his glory was not arrayed like one of these"—and he pointed to the flowers blossoming at his feet. "If God so clothe the grass of the field, which today is, and tomorrow is cast into the oven, shall he not clothe you, oh, you of little faith?"

"It is a beautiful saying," I heard a happy voice; and the faces of the poor were filled with beatitude at the thought that they would no longer need to toil or spin, to sow or reap, or prepare against the winter rains, but would put their trust in God, who would feed them like the birds of the air and clothe them like the flowers of the field.

Some of the scholars were, indeed, moved to hostility, and their foreheads became covered with wrinkles; but others among them smiled, but more, I think, for the charming similes of the rhapsodist than for the substance of wisdom that lay concealed in them.

When he had finished preaching he came down from the summit of the hill. His face was pale with the sustained effort, but in his great eyes shone a light of release. He had become sad for sheer joy, and he was beautiful to look on, with a strange beauty which I had never seen before. A peace that was not of this earth rested on him. Then something happened to me which I remember clearly, but for which I have never been able to find an explanation. The moment he descended from the summit he was swallowed in a circle of Rabbis and scholars, who engaged him in discussion. Some unrolled their parchments and showed him the passages of holy writ which were in contradiction with certain of his utterances; but there was disagreement among the scholars, for several supported his views.

During the discussion the plain folk drew off respectfully, not daring to approach the scholars and interrupt the sacred occasion. But before long Simon, perceiving that his teacher was weary with the long strain of preaching, intruded boldly into the circle, and implored him to leave the others and rest himself on the grass; it may have been also that the disciple feared that the discussion would lead to a break. However, no sooner had the preacher withdrawn to a side than the common people left their places impetuously and closed in on him. Now their joy broke out without restraint; cries of love and admiration and delight filled the air; one would have said that here was a hero who had just returned from the battlefield, bringing victory. Some bent and kissed the hem of his robe, others were content if they came near enough to touch it. And suddenly there were youngsters also, children who had remained in the background till now. Their parents brought them forward to have him place his hands on them and bless them. Suddenly there were also numbers of the sick, who pushed their way frantically through to him. The disciples struggled with the multitude, particularly the sons of the woman Zebedee, but they could not clear a way for him. It was only when Simon lifted him up in his iron arms, and carried him off, that the circle was broken. Even so, the multitude streamed after them like a torrent bursting through a dam.

And the thing that happened to me was this: I repeat it with shame, but it is the truth: I, the Ciliarch of Jerusalem, forgot my dignity, my standing and my identity. With the centurion of K'far Nahum, who was in no better case, I had joined the enthusiastic multitude; and I ran with it now as if I were part of it and as if the sermon had been meant for me too! To this degree had I and my friend forgotten ourselves. It was less astonishing in the centurion, for he had long been subject to the influence of the Jews; but I, the commander of the Antonia citadel, the right-hand man of the Procurator Pontius Pilate—that I should behave in this incredible fashion! . . . I confess, here and now, that at the time of the sermon on the hill I came within a hand's breadth of yielding to the man's magic. Shall I go further and reveal the final details? Caught up in that atmosphere of wonder, I approached, and for the first time in my life made obeisance to a Jew. When he saw this he stood still and regarded me with an expression of pain and compassion, and I felt something in me breaking. What is most amazing in all this—I speak of it with difficulty—is that at the moment I was not even ashamed of my subjection to him. That emotion overwhelmed me later, but at the time I was aware of a struggle within me, evoked by the mournful and compassionate eyes which he bent on me, a struggle between anger and yearning. The pale face, fringed with the young beard, the frail body, the slender neck, the expression of infinite pity touched me so, that I felt very near to him. I was aware also of something beyond my comprehension hovering about him, so that I was not free from fear, too. Then I remembered myself, anger took the upper hand, I turned hastily and said to my friend:

"Come, let us go from here."

And I fled. It was the awareness of my fear which had pulled me up in time.

CHAPTER NINETEEN

IT was after this frightful incident that I first understood the extent of the danger which threatened my friend the centurion, and I must thank the gods that they came to my rescue at the last moment: a litle later, I tremble to think, it might have been too late. I had of course long observed that my friend had been deeply affected by the Rabbi; but I had had to learn from a brief though shattering experience that even I could under certain circumstances entertain the idea of relinquishing my rigid Roman discipline, that perfect molder of character, and of yielding to an Asiatic influence. It was at once a warning and a profound lesson.

The centurion had too long been removed from a Roman camp, he had too long been steeped in a Jewish environment. When a man lives for many years in a barbarian province, remote from the civilization of Rome, he becomes capable of the most fantastic and irresponsible acts. Such things have been before. Some of our best men, heroes of a hundred fields, victors over innumerable barbarian hordes, have fallen victims to the vanquished when they have been set over a conquered territory and kept away from Rome for many years. It calls for exceptional character to live in an alien environment, in loneliness, without yielding and losing oneself. Of such a character, alas, the centurion of K'far Nahum was not possessed. Long, long before the appearance of the wonder Rabbi he had betrayed serious inclinations toward the cult of the Jews. He had neglected the cultivation of our religious institutions in the subject land, and he was greatly remiss in his duty of encouraging the use of the theaters and gymnasia. He was rarely seen in the temples of our gods, and I do not except the temple of the Caesar which the Tetrarch had erected in his new capital, and which the centurion practically ignored save for official functions. As against this he had become a regular frequenter of Jewish synagogues. He had let himself be led astray by their mystic services to their invisible God; he had taken instruction from their learned men in the laws of their religion. He had compared the lore and philosophy of the Jews with ours, and the result was that instead of exerting himself to build a temple of Jupiter in K'far Nahum he had enabled the Jews to build themselves a synagogue! I saw this structure; indeed, he was so proud of it that he insisted on showing it to me. It was in the finest Graeco-Judaeic style, with a marble façade, with fine granite columns engraved with Jewish ornaments; nor did it lack a splendid mosaic floor covered with religious symbols. The gratitude of the Jews to the centurion can readily be understood, but our men murmured secretly.

He had surrounded himself with Jewish scholars, who were his closest friends. True, they could not visit his home, for the laws of purity forbid Jews to enter the dwelling place of an unbeliever. But he met them in the street and in their synagogues and study chapels, where he received religious instruction from them. Then came the incident of the wonder Rabbi and the boy Andros.

I believe that my friend had originally bought Andros for purposes of pleasure, for the lad was exceptionally beautiful, and I had often admired him when he had served us in the centurion's villa on the road to Tiberias. Later, under the corrupting influence of the Jewish cult, which is sternly opposed to this variety of love—as it is, indeed, to nearly every joy in life—the centurion renounced this source of pleasure, and his affection for the lad was transformed into paternal tenderness. It is possible that he even adopted him formally as his son. The love he had for Andros awoke in him as deep a love for the Rabbi who brought about the miraculous cure; but later, as my friend came to know the Rabbi better, his love and admiration and reverence for him grew beyond all bounds and quite swallowed up his love for the boy.

I should perhaps set it down, as a curious weakness and predisposing cause in my friend, that he had always looked for someone to love and admire. This form of nourishment was a necessity to his soul. And it is not without repugnance that I report a discovery which I made about that time. This man with the powerful body and the massive breast which had so often been exposed to the spears and arrows of the enemy, this man who had marched through the marshy German forests at the head of a cohort, this Roman could put off his silver armor, covered with medals won in a dozen campaigns, and conceal himself in a Jewish garment at the end of which dangled their ritualistic fringes! Or he could put on the sackcloth rags of the poor, and station himself at the doors of their synagogues and study chapels to listen to the sermons of their scholars. He was drawn into the religious life of an alien and subject people amongst which he was stationed as one of the conquering and governing race. He would rise respectfully before their old men. He sent gifts and sacrifices to their Temple in Jerusalem. All this became much worse after the appearance of the wonder Rabbi. Whenever he could, my friend would steal away from his duties to listen and observe. He ran to the synagogue to hear him preach. And that which had been a single experiment with me, was with him a constant practice: he would hide his identity in sackcloth garb and visit the house of Simon, the disciple, times without number.

Since that strange afternoon when the man delivered his sermon on the hill, the centurion of K'far Nahum had known no peace of mind. He often sat alone in his locked garden, near the statues of the gods, or else he walked, a solitary and absorbed figure, on the shore of Genesaret, meditating on the words of the Rabbi. He had had a copy of the sermon made on papyrus by one of the disciples, and he read the pages night and day, till he knew the whole utterance by heart. Sitting and walking, he repeated the words. And there were also times when he tried to win me over to the teaching of the Rabbi, and pressed insistently upon me the contents of various of his sayings.

So it was when we sat one evening on the columned terrace of his house, fronting the Sea of Genesaret, and looked at the play of moonlight on the waves. The moon had risen just as the sun had set, a blood-red sphere enveloped in clouds; and after a time her beams had dispelled the covering of vapors, and had troubled the waters of the lake. The lad Andros was there with us. My friend leaned his head on his hand and murmured something into the air.

"What is that?" I asked.

"They are words from the sermon of the man of miracles," he answered. "Hear them. 'Ask, and it shall be given; seek, and you will find; knock, and it will be opened.' "

"But I see nothing in that," I answered, "to add to the philosophy of the thinking man. The sentences rest on no basis of experience or reality or acquired knowledge. They reflect only the undisciplined moodiness of the dreamy Jewish spirit, which drives you to find happiness in the sea of nothingness."

"It is the beginning of all truths," the centurion answered, with the childish yearning of a barbarian. "The acquisition of knowledge should not stop with the narrow limits of our consciousness, no more than the world stops with the chimera of the sky, moon and stars, which seem so close to us now that we think we could touch them with our hands; or with that milky cloud which drapes the hills there on the other side of Genesaret. Our life does not stop at the narrow entrance to the grave. Above the clouds and above the heavens there are other worlds; and so there is a second life after death. That is the life of eternal being, the eternal conscious-unconscious, the everlasting searching and finding. And ever since these words sounded in my ears, I hear a voice from the other side, not of our time and space, but of the illimitable which has its dwelling place in my heart. I feel that I am at the beginning of a faith, that there are doors where you can knock, and behind the doors there is someone who can open for you. Since those words fell on my ears I feel that I have discovered an everlasting spring, which can never be exhausted. I have begun to understand faith."

I looked at him in astonishment and distress.

"These are fantasies, fantasies," I returned, vehemently. "Right sense, with its feeling for reality, can make nothing of them. Moods like these are fit only for fatalists who lack the will, energy, and power to command their own destinies. Such men have never known the privileges and never felt the characteristics which make up the Roman; they are devoid of prowess, and therefore do not know the delight of battle, and they have never drained the beaker of victory; they have never experienced the peculiar intoxication which comes with conquest and mastery by the sword. And just as they are completely alien to such joys, so their character is alien to discipline. Submerged in their passion of submission, they know nothing of the true will to love, will to mastery, to revenge, to combat. They know nothing of life and the world. How, then, should one of them render judgment? This people has been content to accept as its lot the sands and rocky hills of its tiny country. Earth is niggardly to them—so they lift up their eyes to the heavens and dream of a life above the clouds. What have we Romans to do with such things? Are our national heroes not enough for you? Would you exchange the great Marius, Sulla, Caesar, the god Augustus, our own commander Germanicus, who conquered the world for Rome, in favor of the Jewish patriarchs, so that you may sit with them in the kingdom of heaven?" I ended up jestingly.

But he answered me in full earnestness:

"The achievements of our heroes? Who can number them? They have planted the Roman eagles at the extremities of the world, they have brought under Roman rule countless peoples. Who shall deny their valor? But could they command spirits in the same way as they commanded their soldiers? Could they change their own destinies, determine new fates for themselves? Could they spread out a net beneath themselves to save them when they fell into the bottomless abyss of death? Could they with all their arms and armies dull the tooth of the invisible worm which is called time—which gnaws so insolently the bodies of the great and the small? Or could they, with all their valor, conquer for themselves a single day, a single minute of time beyond their share, or demand as war tribute one more breath than had been assigned to their lives? Could their triumphs yield them one second of pure joy unembittered by the sick remembrance of the end? What is all their wealth if it consists of the realities which are measured with the gauge of destruction? What are their victories, if victor and vanquished share the same fate, are flung together into the same pit of endless night? What are their deeds, if they are ground by the millstones of destruction and carried away by the winds of the past and extinguished by the nothingness of our limited being? Victory is that which creates eternal values, which are not subject either to time or to poison. Victory is that which creates the eternal joy of ever-enduring possession. Prowess is that which conquers evanescent passions and desires, those that satisfy without fulfilling. Victory over yourself prepares you to receive the great benediction of belief in one perdurable power, which in the fullness of its grace has taken you under its protection, and keeps guard over you in all the worlds, through all time, in all the forms and existences to which you are consigned. Oh, then they may crush my bones, my blood may run out on the battlefields of life: God will assemble my shattered bones and gather up my spilt blood, and weave them again into a single wholeness. What fires can destroy me then? What wars can prevail against me? I am the eternity in him. Only one kind of might can give me ultimate victory: the might which comes from fellowship in the union which the only eternal divinity has set up with man. And no one can assure me of fellowship in this union if I do not find it in the faith of the barbarians over whom we rule—the Jews."

I was staggered by this speech. I took my friend's hand; I said: "Centurion, what ails you? To whom do you belong?"

"Cornelius, you will not understand me. You are blind and you will not see. I feel that something is being born in me, a door is opening for me, and you cannot pass through it. The name of that door is—faith."

I said no more to him. I saw that he was a lost man. . . .

CHAPTER TWENTY

THAT night I did not sleep. I had obtained from my friend, before leaving him, a Greek translation of the sermon, prepared by him for his own use. There were certain passages which I had not quite understood when I had heard them in the original Aramaic. Some of them I had not heard at all, my attention having been fixed, at the time, on the effect which the utterances produced on the scribes and scholars. Further, the mood of that afternoon had not been adapted to a reasoned and objective hearing. Now I had the sermon before me in a civilized language. I analyzed it point by point and came to the conclusion that the activities of this man, however innocent their outward form (for he would have it that he sought only to guide human beings in paths of righteousness), could in time become extremely troublesome. Besides, he was by no means the helpless weakling which he pretended to be. His teachings could become dangerous to the religious regime of the Jews themselves (and we were interested in perpetuating the power of their present rulers) and therefore to our own rule. It was possible that he constituted a threat to the entire Latin civilization in the Orient. In that part of the world such ideas spread among the ignorant masses with the speed of fire in a dry forest; and among all the eastern races none is so inflammable as the fanatical and fantastically minded Jews. These things always begin very innocently, being at first only internal religious matters, and they always end up with revolts against the prevailing local power and against Rome. Oh, we have had our experiences! For however they conceal themselves behind the mask of religion, with which we do not interfere, they all have one ultimate purpose: to overthrow the foreign dominant power.

Those uprisings of the Jews were much too costly for us to regard them with indifference. We had to exercise care and remain perpetually on the watch. Once they adopt a cult, they cling to it to the death. Before Pilate and I came to the country, in the days of the first Procurator, Coponius, a man rose in their midst—Judah the Galilean was his name. He began, as far as I can make out, just like this Rabbi, with something purely religious. It had nothing to do with us. He launched among the Galilean masses a motto or proverb, something in their own language which meant: "To God alone belongs dominion." The phrase caught, it spread, it carried everything before it, for if dominion belonged only to their God, their duty was to oppose all foreign rule. And sure enough, they began to withhold their tax payments, they drove the tax collectors from the country towns, they raised the standard of revolt, they formed armed bands which took refuge in the caves, they attacked passing travelers and caravans and they nourished the idea of driving out our legions. It is hardly necessary to say that we soon disposed of them. The Procurator took swift and energetic action, the leaders were nailed to the cross, numbers of them were sent to the slave markets, others to various arenas and still others to the galleys. Many years later, traveling on a government ship from Alexandria to Caesarea, I came across a survivor of the rebellion. The captain informed me that among the slaves chained to the oars there was one, a phenomenal creature, who had outlasted twelve years of service. I was sufficiently interested to descend into the bowels of the ship and there I saw a giant of a man swaying back and forth among the others fastened to the oar in such wise that they could not move without dragging their heavy load backward and forward. His eyes, burned out, consisted of nothing more than two red holes oozing blood and pus. His body was covered with long tangles of gray hair gummed together by filth. He thrust his mighty breast forward and dragged it back to the rhythm set by the hortator, and the moment he lagged behind the tempo the lead-loaded whip descended on his body. An unbearable stench rose from the mass of human flesh. These slaves were a collection of the foulest murderers and rebels, and we let them putrefy in their own filth. They received just enough food to remain alive and fulfill their task of driving the ship forward. We were not so short of slaves as to be compelled to pay special attention to their condition. The truth is that we scarcely knew what to do with the huge numbers of war prisoners, rebels and criminals provided by our colonies. The Caesar Tiberius is not noted for extravagance, and he does not spoil either the provinces or the Roman plebs with too many shows. It is not a question of men to be thrown to the animals; those are plentiful enough; but the animals represent a considerable expense. Our largest outlet for men was in the galleys. "Except for him," the hortator told me, "I haven't met one who has lasted longer than six or eight months. But that man"—he pointed to the blind Maccabaean—"has been there for twelve years. We don't understand what power keeps him alive." Overcoming my revulsion I approached the slave, and I heard him muttering something to himself in his incomprehensible language. "That," said the hortator, "is the war cry of their fellowship. He keeps on repeating it to himself."

"And what does it mean?" I asked.

"It means, 'To God alone belongs dominion,' " he answered.

Thus he sat, blind, half rotted away, steeped in his own filth, chained to the oar, still murmuring their battle cry: "To God alone belongs dominion!" He would be repeating it with his last breath. And that is the nature of the Jews; once they get something into their heads all the whips and scourges in the world will not drive it out. This Rabbi, whose sermon I now hold in my hand, belonged to the type. He too proclaims the divinity as the sole ruler and admits of no other near it. There it was, in the text: "A man cannot serve two masters." He went further; he bade his followers give up the baneful habit of producing bread and raiment through laborious effort: "Take no thought for your lives, saying, what shall we eat, what shall we drink, or how shall we be clothed." What was this but incitement to laziness? And again: "Gather no treasures on earth, where rust and moths corrupt, where thieves break in and steal. But gather treasures in heaven, where rust and moths cannot corrupt. . . ." What was this but disorder and rebellion? It was an attack on the entire existing order and rule; it was worse, because more specific, than the slogan of the rebellious Judah the Galilean. It said: Refuse to work, break the forms of the system, sit with folded arms until your invisible God will send down bread from heaven. If such sentiments were accepted by the people, the land would sink into ruin. From whom would we Romans then collect taxes, with what would we support our soldiers? In effect, this man called on his followers to destroy life in order that we might be destroyed also! Why, I asked myself, was such a man permitted to run around free and to continue his dangerous work?

He attacked the very process of law. "If a man sue you at law, and take away your coat, give him your cloak also." Direct encouragement to lawlessness, contempt for the courts! No oaths to be taken, because "you cannot make one hair black or white!" But this was the destruction of the fundamental forms of legal administration. He would wipe out all codes, forbid men to resist evildoers: "If a man smite you on the right cheek, turn the left cheek also."

What is the goal of this man's doctrine? I asked myself. And the answer was clear: He seeks to undo and wipe out everything that man has accumulated by experience, whatever has been won in the struggle for mastery and supremacy, everything that tradition has ratified, whatever custom and law have validated, everything that has been cultivated and is controlled by institutions, rulers and spiritual leaders—and to create in their place a new world and a new order founded on diametrically opposed principles. The things that we regard as virtues, as the highest achievements of man's peculiar and separate greatness, he would condemn as vices and defects; and contrariwise, vices and defects are exalted by him into high moral commandments, the truly good which has subdued the world and laid it at the feet of man. Not dignity and pride, which have hammered out the character of man, but weakness and submission, lowliness, modesty and softness: these will inherit the earth, and theirs will be the kingdom of heaven. Not wealth, accumulated by industry and conquest, but poverty, the consequence of neglect and surrender—that is to be the ideal of mankind. To avoid anger and hatred, which are the parents of battle and victory, to renounce, to love your foe, to fly from the battlefield before you have set foot on it, to forgive your enemies their sins in order that your father in heaven may forgive you yours. Not to taste the pleasures of life and the glory and abundance of wealth, not to give free reign to the natural passions so that they may live themselves out in the fullness of their strength and marrow, but to repress and deny them, to burn them out. If your right eye offend, pluck it out; if your right hand offend, cut it off. Carry eternal sadness in your heart, but do not let your face betray it. When you fast, anoint your head and wash your face. . . .

I came to the conclusion that this man was wholly different from all the Jewish teachers and interpreters of the law who had preceded him. Those others applied the law only to the chosen of the people, whose character and condition made them fit for it, while they refused to concern themselves with those that were not of their own. But the doctrine of this Rabbi was baited for the simple and credulous of all peoples, even the heathens. For, to begin with, he did not confine himself to the narrow service of their Temple and their religious customs, like the High Priest and his class; he used words which spread out a net for all men.

There are altogether too many Romans susceptible to the mysticisms and spiritual savageries of our conquered enemies. It is a weakness with us that makes us bend our heads before the gods of barbarians and offer sacrifices in their temples: not to speak of the verminous and crafty Greeks who consider themselves our superiors with their culture, art and philosophy and despise us as imitative apes. They rule us, not we them; they instill their tastes and their outlook into us through the teachers and educators whom we purchase in the slave markets.

The Egyptians and Chaldaeans, too, have infected us with their magic, their fire-swallowing and their snake-charming, through their women. And it is no secret that the highest circles in Roman society have always been fond of toying with Jewish ideas. But the full significance of the danger came home to me only when I saw with my own eyes in K'far Nahum, how the magic wielded by a Jewish Rabbi could lead a Roman commander to deny the Roman gods, betray the Roman character and transform himself into a soft and sentimental Asiatic dreamer and visionary.

Nor was he the only one of his kind. Among the Caesareans and Askelonites included in the multitudes which followed the Rabbi I had caught, now and again, glimpses of officers. If as yet they had not gone as far as the centurion of K'far Nahum, they might well do so before long.

I saw in this man the epitome of all dangers, of all uprisings, of all the teeth-grinding and fist-shaking, all the impotent fury which the name of Rome awakened in the hearts of the Jews. I foresaw the destruction which they were capable of bringing on us. He was a more desperate enemy than Carthage had been of old, or any other hostile state since then.

This was the war which Judaea had declared on Rome, a war not of the sword but—to use their phrase—of the spirit of God. We would have to take them in hand, before it became too late.

CHAPTER TWENTY-ONE

NO halfway stand, no halfway measures, would do in such a case. Indifference was defeat. Either one succumbed to the man's doctrine—as the centurion had done—or one fought it with all available means, for the security and very existence of Rome. I resolved to take my own measures.

I began by trying to determine, once and for all, whether the man called Judah Ish-Kiriot—that is, Judah the man of Kiriot—had indeed been sent to K'far Nahum to keep an eye on the dangerous Rabbi. If he was the High Priest's agent—and what else could he be?—I would come to terms with him. Not that this would be easy. This is the way of the Jews; they stand by each other even among the lowest; whatever may be happening among themselves is their own affair, to be concealed from the eyes of a stranger. But the business turned out more difficult even than I had expected. To begin with, the man had disappeared. The last I had seen of him had been at the sermon on the hill. I heard that he had gone with his

Rabbi to the surrounding villages, and that some time would pass before they would return.

Then I was informed that the Rabbi, Yeshua, was back in K'far Nahum. If so, his pupil, or disciple, or pretended pupil and disciple —I was still baffled by his identity and function—must also be in the town. So it turned out. I sent a message to him with a tax collector, one of our inside, trustworthy men. But I did not tell him for what purpose I wished to see Judah Ish-Kiriot. Trustworthy or not, the tax collector was a Jew. One of the peculiar tricks of the Rabbi Yeshua, again, had been a special appeal to the tax gatherers, whom he drew to himself though they had always been hated by the people. (There was an extraordinary subtlety in his methods. His doctrines took away our most reliable men and turned them into secret conspirators against us.) I played the pious innocent with this tax collector. I told him that I was greatly interested in the doctrines and miracles of the Rabbi, and that I wished to learn more about him through one of his pupils, Judah Ish-Kiriot, whom I had known in Jerusalem.

This was the answer which came back: Who was he, the poor and obscure worker, to be known to the Hegemon of Jerusalem? No doubt the Hegemon was mistaken and had another man in mind.

He was continuing the game, then—if game it was—which he had begun with me in the house of Simon. I realized that I would have to think of other ways. I could, of course, have sent two Askelonites or Samaritans after him, but violence was not to my purpose. I wanted to win the man's confidence. For, assuming that he was the High Priest's agent, it would be an excellent thing to have a double control. Old Hanan was loud enough in his protestations of friendship for us, but what harm would it do if his confidential agent served the common cause by bringing us direct reports, so that we would not have to rely on a secondary source? I decided to seek out Judah Ish-Kiriot myself. He was staying, the tax collector informed me, with a certain potter in K'far Nahum, a man famous for his learning in the law, Chananiah by name. Judah helped him at his work, mixing the clay, heating the oven and baking the vessels; and while they worked the two men discussed the sacred scriptures and the new doctrines of Yeshua. I threw a mantle over my

Roman uniform and following the directions of the tax collector found my way to the little house outside the city, on the road to Naim. There I found them seated at the board on which the black clay was heaped, working and conversing quietly. I addressed myself without ado to the man I wanted:

"Come with me, Judah, I have something to say to you."

He did not even lift his eyes from the pot on which he was working. He answered, as if speaking to the pot:

"I have no secrets from this man. Whatever you have to say, say it here."

I tried again:

"What I have to say to you is of great importance. It concerns only you and me, and a third person may not be present."

But Judah still gazed steadily at the vessel in his hands and replied:

"I am a laborer hired by the day. I cannot leave my work. If you have something to say, say it here, or else wait until evening."

There was nothing else to do. If Judah was playing, in the presence of his friend, the role of a simple, innocent man, I had to sustain him in it. I waited outside until evening fell, and when he came out I approached him and said, in a low voice:

"Judah Ish-Kiriot, you know who I am, and you know that I know you. We have met in Jerusalem, where I am Hegemon, and we met but lately in the house of Simon, when your Rabbi was teaching and performing his wonders."

Quietly but obstinately he returned the old answer: "Who am I that I should know the Hegemon of Jerusalem? I am a common man of the people, and I consort with the common people."

"Judah, I am returning shortly to Jerusalem. There I shall see your lord, Hanan, the eldest High Priest. Have you no message for him?" And I tried to catch his gaze, but this time he kept his eyes lowered.

"Who am I that I should have the honor of knowing the lord Hanan, the eldest High Priest? I have told you that I am of the common people, and my lord is mistaken, I am not the man he seeks."

"Judah, I repeat that you are the servant of the High Priest. He has sent you here to watch the Rabbi of Nazareth and to report on all that he says and does."

"The High Priest is indeed my lord, as he is the lord of all pious Jews. But as to the rest, I understand nothing that my lord says."

My patience was now at the breaking point. I said, harshly:

"Judah, I am the friend of your lord, the High Priest. He and I are both interested in the words and acts of your Rabbi, Yeshua of Nazareth. This is the matter I would discuss with you. Do not hide from me."

But now a startling change came over the man. He lifted his piercing eyes to mine and they shone with a wild light. Insolently he threw back:

"My lord would speak with me concerning the words and acts of my Rabbi, Yeshua of Nazareth? Is my lord a Jew? Has he been admitted to the covenant of Abraham? Does he serve the one and living God of Israel?"

"I am a Roman, and I serve the gods of my country."

"If so, why does my lord seek to discuss with me the words and acts of my Rabbi? The words and acts of the Rabbi are meant only for the children of Israel, and not for strangers."

"I am the Hegemon of Jerusalem, and whatever happens in this land is of interest to me."

"The Hegemon of Jerusalem is set over the tribute which we must pay the Caesar. How does the Hegemon of Jerusalem come to be interfering in matters pertaining to our faith in the one and living God of Israel and in his laws?"

"Judah," I said, holding back my rage, "you do not treat your Hegemon with the respect which is his due. I shall have something to say concerning this to your lord, my friend Hanan."

"To the Hegemon of Jerusalem I will deliver the tribute due to the Caesar. With my lord the High Priest I will discuss matters pertaining to our faith."

And with this he turned and left me.

I understood now that all my efforts in this direction were wasted. I determined at once to apply to the highest civic authority in the land. A few days later, on my way to Jerusalem, I halted at the palace of the Tetrarch.

I turned first to the Tetrarchess Herodias, knowing that she, a woman of the world, would understand me better than her husband, and would help me with her influence.

"Tetrarchess," I began, after we had exchanged greetings, "in the Roman galleys which traverse the Great Sea we have, chained to the oars, not a few of your subjects; in our circuses and theaters hundreds of them have been thrown to the beasts. Your Tetrarchate furnishes us with more rebels, insurgents, religious disturbers of the peace and leaders of robber bands than the entire province of Syria. Your subjects cause us more concern than all of Egypt, with its great center of Alexandria. Every day we hear of new insurrections in Galilee. This matter has been mentioned more than once by the Proconsul in Antioch, and at the court of the Caesar. I tell you as your friend, Tetrarchess, that these repeated disturbances do the reputation of the Tetrarch no good in the eyes of the Caesar. The less so since your brother, the one pretender to the throne of Judaea, Agrippa, the friend of the Imperial heirs, has returned to Italy, stays close to the Caesar on Capri, and intrigues against you. I can assure you further that the standing of the pretender has risen considerably of late; and however extravagant he may be, there is no lack of such as will lend him new money, while the old creditors have become much more patient. Do you know why? Because his prospects of becoming king of a united Palestine are by no means to be ignored; there are some who expect them to be realized even during the life of Tiberius. I take the liberty of pointing out to you, Tetrarchess, that it is high time for you to prove to the Proconsul at Antioch and the Caesar in Rome that you are able—and willing—to suppress every insurrection at its beginning, and to tear out by the roots every attempt at rebellion which appears in your territories."

The Tetrarchess did not wait to hear more. She took me by the hand and conducted me to the Tetrarch.

"But Hegemon, what has happened?" he asked me, when I had repeated for his benefit the warning delivered to the Tetrarchess. His face had blenched.

"Tetrarch," I answered, "I have just come from K'far Nahum, where I spent some weeks as the guest of the centurion. It has no doubt reached the ears of the Tetrarch that in K'far Nahum there has appeared an extraordinary man who has won a great following among the people by the wonders he has performed. I have had the opportunity to become acquainted with the activities of this man on the shores of Genesaret, and to listen to the doctrine which he preaches. I have come to the conclusion that this man represents a great danger to the state and to the ruling order, and the sooner the Tetrarch puts an end to his destructive activities the better. But what he teaches is also directed against the accepted laws, customs and traditions of your own religion. I understand that his doctrinal utterances have aroused the bitterest hostility among your scholars and interpreters of the law. I would counsel you most earnestly, Tetrarch, to put an end to the threatening work of this most dangerous person, for he stirs up the people against labor and obedience and corrupts them with promises of a kingdom in heaven. And I have learned for myself that his power has begun to extend beyond the ignorant masses to high-placed individuals whose peculiar natures makes them susceptible to visions and illusions. I urge immediate action, if you are not to come too late."

The pallor deepened on the Tetrarch's face. He had to lie down on a couch which slaves brought into the garden, where the conversation was being held. He held his head in his hands for a long time, then he lifted it up, looked straight at me and exclaimed:

"Over that man I have no power, and none of us has any power over him, Hegemon."

"What do you mean, Tetrarch?" I asked, astounded.

"I have already beheaded him, have I not? and he has returned to life," he cried, and he trembled visibly with fear.

"I do not understand you, Tetrarch," I said, and turned my astonished gaze on the Tetrarchess, who had become pale at her husband's words. For the Tetrarch made the impression of a man who had lost his reason; he stared blankly into space and he shook from head to foot.

"You were present," he went on, with chattering teeth, "when the German soldiers went down into the cellars of the fortress and returned with his head on a silver platter which they placed before little Salome."

"You mean Jochanan, whom they called 'the Baptist'?"

"Why, yes, this is he, this is Jochanan the Baptist, who has risen from death and brings the message of repentance and the kingdom of heaven to the people. I closed his mouth once, and now he speaks again. I have no power over him. Hegemon! I cannot behead a beheaded man!"

"But Tetrarch, these are wild fantasies and empty dreams born in the imagination of the people. How can you give them credence?"

"Hegemon, our people have only dreams and fantasies; everything else has been taken away from them. What harm can the reality of your power suffer from dreams and fantasies which this man propagates among the poor? And what threat issues to the glory of Rome from a kingdom established in heaven? Is Rome jealous of treasures in heaven?" And with this question he rose and left us.

"Leave this in my hands, Hegemon," the Tetrarchess said, soothingly. "Never fear—it will be properly seen to. The Tetrarch has been affected by the stories circulating among the common folk concerning this man, and he has not been able to sleep of nights. He will recover his peace of mind before long, and the business will be disposed of to your and our satisfaction."

Hardly any better was the reply of old Hanan in Jerusalem, when I laid the problem before him.

The conversation took place in the hall of columns of his magnificent home, over a beaker of rich, tasty wine fermented from the juice of Jericho dates—a delicious beverage which I had never found anywhere else than in the High Priest's house. I gave him the full story of my encounter with the strange man of K'far Nahum, of the miracles he performed and the corrupting doctrines which he spread among the ignorant masses. I did not fail to exert on my listener the kind of pressure I had exerted on the Tetrarch; I told him flatly that if Caesarea got wind of the dangerous public state of mind which the man's doctrines had created, there might be uncomfortable consequences for the High Priests and the other local powers in Jerusalem. I observed then, as I observe now, that what astonishes me in you Jews is the sensitive jealousy which you display over the most trivial detail of your ritual and tradition when one of us strangers comes too near, while you leave your own preachers and interpreters to make a general assault on the foundations of your faith.

The old man listened with close attention, passing his fingers down the length of his white beard, tugging gently at his earlocks, caressing his majestic side-whiskers—all very thoughtfully and comfortably, as his manner was, while an expression of contempt flickered at the corners of his mouth. Then he answered:

"Idle dreams, Hegemon, idle dreams; nothing to grow hot at, while the danger is so remote. Our people cannot live without dreams, Hegemon, and in every generation it must have its dreamer, one who will play sweet melodies to it and put it to sleep. From the time of our father Abraham on our people has been living more on promises than on fulfillments. I doubt whether it even desires to give reality to its dreams; it is probably afraid of the test. It dreads to have the wings of its dreams clipped by the steel of reality. He who puts off to the remotest future the day of their deliverance, who transports to the remotest heavens the scene of their final happiness, wins their attention. Now as to the doctrine which you speak of—Hegemon, we are a strange people. Every one of us is his own Moses and law interpreter. In this respect we cannot be compared with the disciplined nations which accept and implicitly obey a fixed code; when it comes to interpretation of the law, we are independent, every one of us has the right to interpret according to his own light, as long as the interpretation remains within the framework and spirit of the accepted doctrine. But the framework is such that there is no limit to the varieties of interpretation which it can enclose, for the spirit is not the spirit of this world. Among us it may happen, without warning, without rhyme or reason, that a man will arise from the plow, or from tending sheep, or from baking pots, or from serving in the Temple, and declare that he has been sent of God. Yesterday no one knew him and today he is the accepted prophet to whose words we must listen. Our task is only to investigate and test whether he has really been sent of God. To that end we have certain signs and general rules indicated in our scriptures, whereby we may know whether his words are in the spirit of our doctrine, whether he strengthens our hands and our faith in God, or whether he weakens them. On this man too, concerning whom you have told me, we are keeping our eyes. We are investigating even now, we take note of every word and act, and you have my assurance that for the time being there is nothing to be alarmed at. All that I have heard of him so far consists, as I have said, of empty dreams. And should he really become a danger to our faith, which I do not believe will happen, then you may be certain that we shall know as well how to deal with him as we have known how to deal with others in the past."

"Yes, I know that you keep careful watch over him. I encountered, in K'far Nahum, your agent, your trusted emissary. He has even become one of the disciples, and if I am not mistaken, one of the most important. I have heard that it is he who is entrusted with the funds of the fellowship."

"My agent, my emissary? I know of no such man."

I stared at the High Priest, dumbfounded. The smile still flickered in the corners of his mouth, and I could not determine its meaning. Was he laughing secretly at me, or was it a smile of self-satisfaction and omniscience?

"Judah Ish-Kiriot, the man I often saw seated near the entrance to your inner court," I urged.

"Judah Ish-Kiriot? No, I am not acquainted with the name," the High Priest insisted. "It must be a mistake on your part, Hegemon. In any case, as regards the man's preaching, we are now prepared to send up from Jerusalem a commission of scribes and scholars to establish formally whether his utterances are as dangerous to our faith as you seem to fear."

"I should very much like to know the results of their investigation, High Priest."

"Ah, that, my dear Hegemon—that is a purely internal religious matter, and you know the jealousy of our people in regard to this point."

"It would appear," I said, dryly, "that your prophet of Nazareth must be very deeply implicated in anti-Roman conspiracy if even you, High Priest, whom we consider a friend, think it necessary to conceal the outcome from us."

"Oh, believe me, Hegemon that this whole affair of the prophet of Nazareth is not worth the attention and trouble you devote to it. If we were to take seriously all the prophets and Messiahs, all the teachers and dreamers, who rise in our midst, we should have to give them every hour of our time, to the complete neglect of serious business. We should for ever be fighting with shadows. The best specific for Messiahs and prophets is—to let them shout themselves out, let them choke and struggle with their own lunacy until they become weary of themselves, or their followers become weary of them. The moment you begin to persecute one of them you make a martyr of him, and he is transformed in the eyes of the people into a saint. Leave all this to us, Hegemon; we have had much experience. This is a land of prophets and Messiahs, and we have long ago discovered that the wisest course is to let them have their say. And as to the prophet of Galilee who causes you so much concern, be certain that if the investigation—which will be carried out with the help of the opposition, that is, of the Pharisees—should reveal any danger to the state, we shall not fail to advise you. For you know well that we can undertake no serious action without coming to you for your ratification."

Some assurance I did gather from the cautious promises of the old High Priest, even though I suspected that his long-winded utterances were a veil to secret purposes of his own. In any case, I resolved not to rely on him, and not to relinquish my direct participation in the affair.

* * *

Here Pan Viadomsky suspended the narrative of his experiences as Ciliarch of the Antonia fortress in the time of Pontius Pilate, which he dictated to me partly from memory and partly from notes, and which I transcribed word for word during the winter of that year. The interruption in our meetings was due to causes over which I had no control.

END OF PART ONE

PART TWO

CHAPTER ONE

RELATIONS between Pan Viadomsky and myself deteriorated again. The new unfriendliness came solely from his side, and it coincided with a great change in the outward circumstances of his life. He began to receive callers, and if I chanced to be in his rooms when one of them arrived, he was embarrassed beyond words by my presence. He would have liked to shove me under the bed. Several times I knocked at his door and he refused to admit me. Then once he ignored my salutation in the street. He was walking with one of his old admirers—the reasons will follow for this resumption of status—and as I lifted my hand to greet him an angry grimace distorted his features, as if he found my impudence intolerable. I took good care not to salute him again in public.

What had happened was this: a new wave of reaction was passing over the country, and Pan Viadomsky was once more coming into his own—at least in part. Several anti-Semitic periodicals which had completely dropped him took up the old scholar again and invited him to write theoretical articles. Pan Viadomsky's star began to rise, his material condition took a turn for the better—with consequent beneficial repercussions on his health and therefore on his spirits. Or perhaps these last two items should appear in reverse order. He recovered his self-confidence, his cheerfulness and his haughtiness. Even his external appearance underwent visible improvement. He became sturdier-looking. I attribute this expansion less to physical than to spiritual nourishment; he was able once more to feed freely on the bread of hatred, and it actually enabled him to put on flesh. For a time I thought, to my intense chagrin and disappointment, that all was over between us. But I was quite wrong. The first flush of triumphant disdain passed, and Pan Viadomsky suddenly turned up one day on the staircase of my attic. A secret visit, of course. He explained himself.

"Times like these, you know. . . . You understand . . . no connection with our historic work, what? Our 'mission.' That must not suffer—we must resume the task in the name of those unforgettable historic events. . . ."

Again Pan Viadomsky and I slipped into a double life; but now I use this phrase in another sense. His visits to me, and mine to him, were arranged furtively from occasion to occasion. During the day we did not know each other. If we happened to meet we avoided each other's gaze. The evenings—and not all of them, of course—were reserved for our secret conferences.

But he was not easy to put up with. His hatred of Jews had, under the stimulus of the times, developed into a possessive mania. I put on one side his published articles, which were one thick stream of scurrility, sparing neither the Jews nor anything that, being progressive, was according to this attitude automatically associated with the Jews. It was the man himself, in his personal contacts, who had become almost insufferable. Delusions of grandeur crowded into his brain. If he was not running down the Jews, he was boasting that now, at last, the time had come to reveal himself in all his greatness; the seed he had sown in tears was soon to be reaped in joy. He would lift himself up on his wings (the mixture of metaphors is his, not mine) and the world would be able to see who he was. . . . And so on, ad nauseam. What he meant, in brief, was that now, at long last, his great work would come into the light of day.

He talked so long, so wearisomely, so offensively, without ever coming to the point, that I began to lose hope; I even suspected that no such epoch-making manuscript existed. What with this suspicion, and the constant strain on my nerves, I was almost ready to withdraw from the queer partnership. You could not press him; he was as touchy and capricious as a high-strung, fading lady. And then he suddenly abandoned generalities and lapsed back, almost with a jolt, into the role from which he had emerged into his commonplace existence. He began to speak once more of those far-off days, simply and forthrightly. But a curious difference was this: he no longer spoke in a hypnagogic condition. The reversion to the dead self took place without a struggle or a transitional state. The past lived again without annihilating the present, so that when he lapsed into the personality of the Hegemon he kept an eye, as it were, on Pan Viadomsky the scholar and orientalist.

The revelation of his great secret, the uncovering of his priceless treasure, took place late one night in his apartment. He slipped back without warning into the narrative—with the result, indeed, that for the moment I did not know who was talking to me.

"During a certain period, the man's activities in Galilee escaped my observation. I have not been able to reconstruct them entirely even now. I tried to get a report on him from the old High Priest—without avail. What lay behind *his* secretiveness I have never been able to understand. Even when the Rabbi appeared in Jerusalem, and entered into vigorous disputations with the other Rabbis, the nature of the disagreements and the causes of the turmoil were concealed from us. To me, at least, the High Priest could have spoken, inasmuch as I had made some effort to grasp the principles involved. He chose otherwise. And meanwhile the expectation of the Messiah, the feeling of his imminence, spread to larger and larger numbers. It may very well be that I had failed to penetrate to the innermost being of the dispute. Later, when the matter came up for trial in the presence of Pontius Pilate, the latter was quite unable to understand the nature and the details of the charges. But of this I shall tell you later.

"However, I did manage to fill in some of the gaps in the lost record of his activities in Galilee. Only some of them, and that in a superficial and unsatisfactory manner. Individual episodes were reported to me here and there. The full account I shall now obtain—through you."

"Through me?" I gasped.

"Why, yes, through you, through your help, Josephus. It was for this purpose that I made a bond with a member of your race and faith—though you know well enough my attitude toward it. But I have told you once before—there is no rule without its exceptions."

"I thank you again for the compliment, Pan Cornelius," I said, so bewildered that I added the Polish prefix to his Roman name.

The mustaches bristled, the face became rigid.

"I beg your pardon," I corrected myself hastily. "Hegemon Cornelius."

"Have I not told you that for us the life that surrounds us is dead?"

"As you command, Hegemon. I am eager to help."

"I know it. I was aware of it from the beginning. And now, because of the solemnity and secrecy of what is to follow, I demand of you special assurance, and the most binding oath known to your religion, that whatever I disclose to you will remain between you and me in life and death. I want you to take this oath upon your Torah and by the light of black candles, as the custom is among you Jews."

"Hegemon," I answered, my mind reeling with the rapid back-and-forth transitions across some twenty centuries, "the black candles and the excommunication by oath on the Torah is a custom of later times, of these times which are dead for you and me. I have already sworn, and I repeat the oath, by the sacred vestments of the High Priest, by which all Jews swore—I mean swear—in *our* time, that whatever you disclose will remain between you and me in life and death. . . ."

"So be it, Jochanan!" he said darkly. "I am about to reveal to you that which no man has ever seen before, either in the present time or in the past."

Pan Viadomsky pushed back his chair and bent down to one of the drawers of his enormous desk. From a secret compartment at the back he drew forth a package wrapped in (of all things) Polish newspapers. When the outer covering was removed I saw a second wrapping, an Indian shawl or kerchief sewn up at the edges, and within this lay a bundle of ancient papyri which emitted a damp, mildewed smell. But these were not the treasure; they had to be peeled away, revealing a sheaf of half-decayed mummy linens. And only within these lay the documents themselves, close-written in the script known to us as the Samaritan. Moreover, the writing was not on scrolls, as was the case among Jews, but on sheets, in the manner of the Samaritans.

My heart was pounding with excitement. Pan Viadomsky's white face trembled not less than his hands as he laid the manuscript on the table. He turned his eyes on me and said:

"Do not seek, Jochanan, to discover how these documents came into my possession. That is a secret which will go down with me into the grave. You are looking now on the original records which Judah Ish-Kiriot buried in a tomb-cave outside the town of Sepphoris."

I drew closer, while Pan Viadomsky kept his hand on the manuscript as though he would not trust me to touch it. My eyes fell first on some elaborate Greek lettering, and one or two entire Greek sentences. It seemed that someone had begun to translate the original into Greek and had given up the attempt. I read: "The Gospel according to Judah Ish-Kiriot," and a few subheadings. The actual text began on the second sheet, and was clearly legible.

"Can you read this script?"

"Yes, I know the script. It is the ancient Jewish, which we call today the Samaritan, and which we still find, both on Jewish coins of the time of the Second Temple and on ancient documents of the period. I know the alphabet, but it will take me some time to acquire sufficient command of it to read fluently."

"Good. From now on you will come here every evening, and you will read and translate to me, word for word, faithfully and in the spirit of the original, what is written here, according to your oath."

"As you command, Hegemon. But before I go, let me put one question. Did you yourself, Hegemon, with your own hands, remove the writings of Judah Ish-Kiriot from the cave where he buried them?"

"I have told you: do not seek to discover that. My time is not yet come."

There the conversation ended that evening.

* * *

But certain fragments of information relating to the provenance of the document escaped Pan Viadomsky on subsequent evenings, and I have tried to piece them together, as will be seen shortly. Meanwhile I gave my attention to the text. I perceived at once that what I had before me was a fragment, albeit a large one. Some of the sheets were palimpsests, superimpositions of scripts of various periods. There were Greek sentences difficult to decipher because they were transliterated into Hebrew and again Hebrew sentences transliterated into Greek. I gathered that a large part of the text was missing at the end. I was left with the impression that in the actual redaction there had been at least two opposing parties, each of which had sought to insert its views and interpretations.

The historic sources relating to Bible research are far from exhausted. On the contrary, it is precisely in our period that important discoveries have been made by the excavation of *genizot* or collections of documents in ancient synagogues. These are sources of enormous significance, which have confirmed certain statements which were until recently considered entirely speculative. Again, there have been unearthed, between the linen wrappings of Egyptian mummies of human beings and of crocodiles, papyri with fragments of biblical texts, recognizable as such, and other fragments, in Syriac or in Ethiopian, not to be found in the known books but obviously relating to them. The dry clime and soil of Egypt have preserved them in excellent condition. Documents which far-off generations entrusted to the dead, or concealed in caves and the secret repositories of synagogues, are now coming to the light, to unravel riddles which we once believed would remain unanswered forever.

And now as to the provenance of the document in so far as it related to Pan Viadomsky: concerning this I have nothing to offer but a hopeless confusion of suggestions and imitations. On one occasion, long before I made his acquaintance, Pan Viadomsky had spoken openly of an ancient New Testament which he had discovered in a monastery on Mount Sinai, with the help, it later appeared, of a notorious forger. Later he had declared that he had discovered in an antiquarian's shop in Warsaw an unknown Gospel, which he was keeping to himself until he had prepared it for publication. If we discount the second story as an invention, we are thrown back on the first as being the only clew to the origin of the manuscript, and the clew is strengthened by certain allusions which Pan Viadomsky made, in his abrupt, irresponsible way, to the man who had helped him. But now the discovery was shifted both in time and place, and called up a long-forgotten incident in the life of Pan Viadomsky. The scene was Damascus, the time the close of the last century.

In the period following the abandonment of his regular studies, Pan Viadomsky had often been seen in Egypt and the neighboring countries in the company of a professional forger of antiques. The latter was widely known in the academic world both for his unparalleled erudition and his dishonesty. It appears that the two men, one of them already illustrious and notorious, the other still a youngster, came together in a monastery on Sinai. Together they entered the employ of a group of Levantine merchants engaged in illegal excavations, and operated in Egypt, Palestine and Syria. At that time—that is, long before Pan Viadomsky launched his first story—there were rumors that the two men, or the older scholar alone, had found in a cave near Sepphoris in Galilee an ancient document of amazing importance, the original, in fact, of a new Gospel by one of the apostles! But nothing followed the rumor! Shortly afterwards the older man was found dead in a room of a little hotel in Damascus. The Sultan's police sought his companion, known to be his accomplice in the illegal sale of antiquities. But the man had disappeared. The document was never heard of again. The Levantine dealers did not dare to pursue the case, for fear of being implicated in secret excavations, a serious criminal offense. By various means they helped to spread the rumor that the professor had been killed by the curse of the ancient Egyptian priests. In time the whole incident was forgotten; and I, who had read of it, would never have called it to mind if the confused and inconsistent statements which escaped Pan Viadomsky at irregular intervals in connection with the provenance of his manuscript had not made me ransack my memory.

I need hardly say that it is not my intention to attribute to Pan Viadomsky the slightest connection with the tragedy which took place so many years ago in the obscure little *khan* in Damascus; though, to be frank, the most commonplace scholar, confronted with a discovery of such magnitude and uniqueness, would have been sorely tempted, in the name of science—and Pan Viadomsky was no ordinary scholar, but a passionate, one may say a frantic, devotee. I too must confess that whenever I put my hand on the manuscript, in the course of my translation of it, a shudder passed through my body, and a voice proclaimed within me: "Do you know what lies before you? This is the record and the original script left by Judah Ish-Kiriot in the tomb-cave of Sepphoris, in Galilee." It was not a comfortable feeling.

How, then, did the treasure come into Pan Viadomsky's possession, and what became of the missing parts? I know nothing beyond what I have related. The full secret will go down with Pan Viadomsky to the grave, to be uncovered when he must give an accounting of himself before the eternal judge. In any case, it has no bearing on the matter before us, and we will say with the wisest of all men: "That which is far off and exceeding deep, who can find it out?"

It is time now to let the manuscript speak for itself.

CHAPTER TWO

I

IT is written: Thou shalt inquire and seek out and ask diligently. It followeth, therefore, that of the true prophet thou shalt also inquire and seek out and ask diligently. And this I do likewise, your companion in thought, Judah the man of Kiriot. . . . I follow in the footsteps of my Rabbi, and I sit at his feet, and I measure every word, and I seek out closely all his acts, and I have found no evil in him, but his heart is at peace with his God and whatsoever he thinketh and sayeth is in God's ways. As it is written: Ye shall follow the Lord, your God, ye shall fear him and obey his commandments, ye shall hearken unto his voice and cleave to him. . . .

And as I have in part related unto you, our Rabbi called together a great multitude of people on a hill that is outside the city, and declared unto them the laws and commandments which they shall follow that they might be called the children of God and have their portion in the kingdom of heaven. Many scribes and learned men came likewise to hear the words of my Rabbi. They came from Migdal and from the great city of Sepphoris and even from the city of Naim, which hath a great name because of its scholars, and there came thence Simon the Pharisee and many other Pharisees, also

Hananiah the potter and Hanan the tanner and Rabbi Jonah the tent weaver and the disciples of Jochanan, whom they call the Baptist, with all the learned men and scribes of K'far Nahum, and a great multitude was gathered at the hill. And my Rabbi, Yeshua ben Joseph, who is of Nazareth, interpreted the law for them and brought their hearts nigher unto their father in heaven. The Rabbis and the learned men were greatly comforted by his words and they were cleansed of all the doubts which they had carried in their hearts concerning our Rabbi. They perceived that he walketh in God's ways and whatsoever he doeth is for the sake of God.

And ye shall know that in many things my Rabbi followeth after the house of Shamai, that he maketh heavier the law and doeth after the manner of the Rabbis who build one fence behind another about the heavenly garden. This he doeth in all things pertaining to man and wife, and maketh the law exceedingly severe. For he hath even set at naught the writing of divorcement, saying that this was given unto us by Moses only because of the hardness of our hearts; and in this matter the Rabbis were not of one mind. But they considered it thus, that this was the custom of the Hasideans with whom my Rabbi sojourned what time he learned the word of God from Rabbi Jochanan the Baptist. For it is known that some of them are so exact in the laws of purity that they have destroyed the commandment to be fruitful and multiply and do not take or give in marriage, for which reason they have been called "crazed Hasideans" by our sages. But the doubt which the Rabbis had in their hearts because of this matter was altogether removed by his great uprightness and simplicity and because of the exceeding faith which he hath in our father in heaven. For his faith in the Lord of the world is beyond all knowing, as King David, peace be upon him, hath said: The Lord is my Rock. Yea, though I walk in the valley of the shadow of death, I fear no evil, for thou art with me. And even as Moses our teacher hath commanded us, even so he bids us be "children of our father in heaven," and we shall cling to the deeds of God, and as he is compassionate and gracious and sendeth his sun to shine on the good and the wicked, and letteth his rain fall on the just and the unjust, so shall we too love our enemies, bless those that curse us and pray for those that persecute us. Who hath heard such righteousness heretofore? He hath bidden us be like the angels of heaven and like the children of this earth. And even when he touched the honor of the Pharisees, saying, "If your righteousness be not greater than the righteousness of the scribes and Pharisees, ye shall surely not enter the kingdom of heaven," they all forgave him, for he did speak but of the false Pharisees, whose deeds are like those of Zimri and who demand payment like Phineas and who make a great show of their piety. For he standeth, like the Pharisees, on the law, and hath oft repeated, "till the heavens and the earth shall pass away there shall not be destroyed one jot or tittle of the law." And in many things he lighteneth the law, as in others he maketh it heavier, but the chiefest thing with him is goodness of heart. And he teacheth the whole law according to the sage Hillel, that it is between a man and his neighbor: "That which thou wouldst not have another do unto thee, that thou shalt not do unto him." For that is the chief thing. As to that which concerneth a man and God, it shall be done modestly and in secret and observed of no one. "When thou fastest, anoint thy head and wash thy face, that men may not mark that thou fastest, but thy father in heaven, who seeth it secretly shall reward thee openly."

Happy is the mouth that has spoken these words, happy are the ears that have heard them. Happy is Israel that it possesseth a teacher and prophet who hath arisen in our day to lead us back to our father in heaven.

But I shall not dwell at length on his doctrine, for I have caused his words to be written down as he spoke them by Hananiah the scribe, whence ye shall see that the heart of my Rabbi is at peace with God. But this I would have you know, that in the midst of his speaking there came to him all the wise men and the learned men and the scribes to do him honor, according to the law concerning a great teacher, and to inquire of his peace. And we, his disciples, who sit at his feet and drink his words, were mightily exalted also with his greatness, and a portion of his honor fell upon us. And Rabbi Simon the Pharisee and all the scribes and sages of Naim which were with him entreated our Rabbi to go with them to the city of Naim and to teach there and spread the waters of his learning, and to come with them under one roof and break bread with them; and this our Rabbi promised to do. And they departed from our Rabbi with great love, for they are of one spirit with him! And Rabbi Simon the Pharisee and the learned men that were with him turned back to their own city.

And it came to pass when our Rabbi came down from the hill where he had preached the word of God and was preparing to return to the city that a great multitude surrounded him and went with him to the house of Simon the fisher, where he lived. And there were many sick and such as were possessed with evil spirits. And there were sundry other sick persons waiting for him at the house of Simon, having heard of his miracles, and they stretched out their arms to him, crying: "Hosannah, help us!" And the number of the sick and the possessed increased, and he could not go forward, for they surrounded him like a sea which cast up its waves at his feet. For there were very many poor people, and many afflicted with sorrows, who had come to K'far Nahum, having heard of his wonderful deeds. And his heart was filled with pity for the pain of so many people, and many of them he healed, and he comforted many of them, so that he grew weak with much speaking; and he could not, because of the multitude of the people, go apart to rest or to pray in silence or even to eat his bread in peace, for they would not leave him. Then Simon the fisher bore him away from the people and brought him to the shore of Genesaret where his boat lay.

We, his disciples, were with him on the ship, and he said the evening prayer with us and ate the evening meal with us. Then Simon laid him on the floor of the boat and covered him with his cloak from the coolness of the night. And our Rabbi rested that night like a day laborer after the day's labor, and we his disciples sat about him and guarded his breath in the deepness of the night.

Then when the morning star showed itself our Rabbi arose from sleep, and Simon conducted us to a field of olive trees which they called "the field of the King" because it was of the government; and it was on the shore of the lake. And we did the morning ablution in the lake Genesaret and we said the morning prayer, and the disciples took out their bread from their bundles, and after they had prayed they ate the morning meal.

And the way of our Rabbi is on this wise: he is not like other learned men who stay within the four ells of their commandments and preach the law in the study houses to their disciples who sit at their feet; but he is like a brimming well which standeth at the wayside so that all who pass may come and draw of its living waters. My Rabbi goeth about among the common people and guideth them into the right path. In the weekdays he goeth out to the port, where the fishers bring in the nets with the fish and the porters carry their burdens to the ships. Many folk are assembled there, for they come hither to sell the merchants the labor of their hands. And our Rabbi standeth there among the folk and teacheth them of the kingdom of heaven through beautiful parables, and this one he comforteth with a word and the other he healeth of a sickness. On the Sabbath he cometh to the synagogue and sometimes he preacheth on a text from the Torah, and sometimes he doth not so. But the Rabbi spreadeth his doctrine not only in the city of K'far Nahum, but he leadeth us through the towns and villages round about, and he showeth us how the modest people live and biddeth us take their example. Ofttimes it chanceth that as we come to a city the eventide encountereth us and the sky encloseth the earth in faith, and from the houses goeth up smoke where the bread is a-baking which labor hath earned. Then the man cometh home from the field or from his work to the house, and the goodwife waiteth at the door with the lamp in her hand, on the threshold of the house. And when the Rabbi cometh to the city, he goeth not to the house of study to the learned, but he turneth aside to the houses of the poor, and he stationeth himself at a door till that they bid him enter. He bringeth peace with him, he blesseth the house and sitteth with the folk to eat the bread of the poor, and saith a benediction thereon and praiseth the goodwife to the husband. And when they have eaten he calleth the children to him and inquireth of them concerning their lessons, and every child telleth him his text. Then he blesseth the children and saith: "May your like multiply in Israel," and the mothers sit on the thresholds of the doors, and when they hear that the Rabbi praiseth the fruit of their womb and maketh them beloved of their husbands, so they say to each other, It cannot be but that this is a man of God, for he bringeth peace with him into the house. Then he sitteth late into the night with the men, and questioneth them concerning their business. He knoweth that which causeth them concern, and their needs are nigh to him, and for one he healeth the body with a remedy and the other he giveth a good word for his soul. And he comforteth them all and declareth unto them that salvation is nigh. The gates of the kingdom of heaven are open to give entrance to all that are ready. And he maketh his speech fair with parables and beautiful words. And we lodge in the night with these folk, in one bed, upon one mattress, not as the learned do, which consider the bed of the man-of-the-earth unclean. And in the morning he betaketh himself with the people to the field, and sometimes he helpeth them at their work and sometimes he thanketh them only with a blessing for the bread and lodging. And when we come a second time unto this place, then the folk come of themselves to welcome us, and the women stand on the thresholds of their houses and they call unto the Rabbi, "Let the Rabbi stay with me, let him lay his head under my roof and let my house be blessed for his sake." And the children likewise run forth to greet him, and they make a circle about him and they seize his robe and they tell him the texts which they have learned that day in the school. And when we the disciples do sometimes speak angrily to the children and bid them begone from molesting the Rabbi, he will not have it so, but saith unto us: "Suffer the little ones to come unto me, for theirs is the kingdom of heaven." And thus he goeth into the town with the children all about him, and the men come forth to greet him and they call unto him:

"Come, thou blessed of God."

And when eventide cometh he calleth them together in the house or the yard of one of them, and they come bearing their lamps. And the Rabbi sitteth with them, and breaketh bread, and telleth them of the kingdom of heaven, and the people turn back to God. And the name of the Rabbi spreadeth like an ointment through the land.

II

And in K'far Nahum my Rabbi dwelt in the house of Simon bar Jonah's mother-in-law, in the booth which was on the roof. And in the day he goeth to the port of the city, and he teacheth after the manner which I have told you.

Now in the port of K'far Nahum there standeth the booth of the custom at the bridge which leadeth to the water, and in the booth sitteth Levi at the receipt of custom, and whosoever bringeth the fruit of his land into the port, or would send it from the port, he must pass by this bridge. And the collector of the custom putteth forth his head and his hand from the booth, and the badge of government is on his breast, that he is in authority to collect the tax. His bag hangeth at his girdle, and each one payeth him the custom and then he openeth the gate and letteth the man pass with his merchandise, and if the man payeth not so he letteth him not pass.

And the collectors of tax and custom are accounted as sinners in Israel.

But the tax gatherer Levi is not like the other tax gatherers, and when our Rabbi passeth by his bridge in order to enter the port and speak unto the people, so Levi doth rise and bow before him, and his face beareth witness that he repenteth of his sins and that he hath it in his heart to turn back and walk once more in the path of the Jews. For as often as my Rabbi spoke to the people within the port, so the tax collector sat in his booth, and his head was in one hand, while the other pulled the hair of his beard, and he thought many thoughts. And once when my Rabbi passed by the booth, so Levi stood up and looked at my Rabbi, and his eyes were full of repentance and longing, and he said:

"I know that the great and terrible day cometh, which thou proclaimest, and I shall remain outside as a sheep that is thrust out of the fold. . ."

And my Rabbi placed his hand on him and said:

"It is written: 'God is near to the humble of heart.' And I perceive by thy countenance that thou repentest thee of thy deeds. Rise and come with me."

And the tax collector left his booth and followed after our Rabbi.

And the Rabbi asked Levi, the collector of taxes:

"Are there many like thee in Israel?"

And he answered the Rabbi and said:

"There be many in the city which have been thrust out from

Israel even as I was, for they are accounted sinners. I entreat thee, come and I will lead thee to them, that they may be comforted of thee as I have been comforted."

And the Rabbi said:

"Bring me to them."

Then when it was the evening of that day Levi the tax collector made a feast for the Rabbi, and he gathered many tax collectors and sinners into his house, such as come not into the congregation of Israel. For there were among them such as doubted of God in their hearts, and others that are not received in marriage because of suspicion of bastardy; there were likewise among them robbers by the wayside, and dove catchers, who may not be called as witnesses in the courts, and those who betray Jews to the government and who should be torn like a fish, also women of ill repute, harlots that lead men from the right path. And the Rabbi sat down with them at one table, and he bade us also sit down with them and be friendly with them. And this was a hard thing, yea, as hard as the splitting of the Red Sea; and we that were scholars did feel then as if we were serving the golden calf. But the hand of the Rabbi was heavy upon us, and we broke bread, and ate, without that we had washed, and the Rabbi only said a prayer and uttered the blessing over the bread. Simon bar Jonah did stand and serve them, likewise the brothers Zebedee. For them it was not a hard thing.

And the Rabbi did speak to each one separately and comforted them and turned their hearts toward goodness and told them what to do if they wished to win eternal life. And they listened to his words and said: "We will obey and hearken!"

And the people said one to the other: "Who hath ever spoken to us such words of comfort? The learned thrust us away from them, and they thrust us out of the congregation as a sick sheep is thrust out of the fold. And see how this one cometh and taketh us to his heart, as a father taketh to his heart his beloved son."

And the Rabbi took Levi, the tax collector, and placed him in our midst, and put his hands upon him and said unto us: "From this day forth he shall be a brother unto you and a son to Abraham."

And this thing was hard for us. Should we be a brother unto a tax collector? And should we consort with harlots? For until now this hath not been heard in Israel, that a sinner shall be a disciple unto a Rabbi.

And when the Rabbi saw that we were greatly astonished he said unto us:

"Why say ye unto me Lord, Lord, and ye will not obey my words? The disciple shall not be higher than his master, he shall be content to be as his Rabbi. Why seest thou the mote in thy brother's eye and seest not the beam in thine own? These people are nigh unto God. He hath seen their broken hearts and he hath drawn them nigh unto himself, and ye shall not thrust off afar that which God draweth nigh." And he told them a beautiful parable: "To what may the kingdom of heaven be likened? The kingdom of heaven may be likened unto a man that soweth seed in the earth," and he told us other parables until he had taken over our spirits and made them obedient unto him. For we perceived that God was with him.

But on the morrow when we came to the synagogue to pray we were surrounded by the learned men, the Pharisees and the disciples of Jochanan the Baptist, and they said unto us:

"What are these things that are told concerning your Rabbi? And what paths hath he chosen to walk in? Is there lack of that which needeth mending in Israel that he must go to tax collectors and sinners? Who hath heard of such a thing that a Rabbi shall sit at one table with them and eat bread with unwashed hands? Who hath ever heard that a Rabbi shall consort with harlots? For the breath of their mouths maketh impure, and the look of their eyes is full of sin. And the voice of a woman is uncleanliness and the touch of her hand is whoredom. The bread of the man-of-the-earth is unclean and forbidden, for he taketh not tribute from the dough and delivereth not to God his heave offering and tithe; and his bed is unclean, and a *chaver* may not lie in it, for they know not how to guard themselves in what pertaineth to purity. And their table shall be contemned, for it is covered with pots, and their food is like the flesh of corpses. And tax collectors may not bear witness in the courts and they are not accounted of the congregation of Israel. And with such your Rabbi consorteth, and he eateth and swilleth with them. Hath not the harp of Israel sung: 'Blessed is the man that walketh not in the counsel of the ungodly, nor standeth in the way of sinners, nor sitteth in the seat of the scornful'? And your Rabbi doeth contrariwise."

We brought the words of these people to the ears of our Rabbi, and we said:

"The wise men murmur that we sit at one table with tax gatherers, and we know not what to answer them."

Then the Rabbi gathered us about him that same evening in the booth which was on the roof, and we pressed close about him and he spoke to us by the light of the lamp and declared the matter unto us:

"Who of you, if he possesseth a hundred sheep and loseth one of them, will not leave the ninety-nine sheep and go in search of the lost sheep until he find it? And will he not bear it on his shoulders, and rejoice therewith, and call together his neighbors and friends and say unto them: 'Rejoice with me, for the sheep which I have lost is found.' And I say unto you: so shall your rejoicing over one sinner that repenteth be greater than for ninety-nine just that have no need of repentance."

And he told us further a beautiful parable of a man who had two sons. . . . And it came to pass that when he told this parable Simon bar Jonah stood and his face was shining with joy, and the tears ran down his shining cheeks into his beard. And he said: "Whatsoever he biddeth me do, that will I do, though it be to sit with tax gatherers and to serve them. For all that he doth is for the sake of heaven." And these words the twelve disciples all said. And the women that stood by the door and listened to the words of the Rabbi cracked their fingers and puffed their cheeks and swallowed his words and cried out with joy that filled their breast as the wine filleth a grape when it is ripe. And we thanked God and praised him that he had been gracious and brought us nigh to this man of God.

And the moment came upon our Rabbi and he was moved of the spirit and he taught us in what manner to serve our father in heaven and how to comport ourselves that we might be worthy to enter into the kingdom of heaven. And he told us many parables that evening, which no ear had heard since the beginning of the world, and they made our hearts draw near to our father in heaven. But that evening he performed no miracles and he healed not the sick, for he had bidden us strictly to let none other draw near, for that he would be alone with us, his chosen ones.

And exceeding great was our rejoicing then, and we rejoiced in our Rabbi and he in us that evening.

And when the second day came I hastened to the synagogue and there I found Zadok the potter sitting with the chief men, and they were teaching the little ones to read and remember the sacred scriptures. And I said to them:

"Be not suspicious of the pure, for ye have sinned in murmuring against my Rabbi. Know ye all that whatsoever he doeth is for the sake of heaven." And I repeated to them the words of our Rabbi which he had spoken concerning the great commandment to bring back sinners to the ways of righteousness.

And Zadok the potter answered me and said:

"These things be indeed good, and our sages too have taught that in the high place where the penitent standeth even the true saint cannot stand. They said, furthermore: 'He that restoreth one soul to Israel, it is as though he had restored the whole world.' But he hath not the right to remit sins. For we do not know and we have not heard that one of flesh and blood can forgive the sin of another—that is, not the sin between a man and his neighbor, but the sin against God—but only the Lord, blessed be he, can do so, as he hath indicated in the laws and commandments handed down by Moses our teacher, together with what a man shall do in order that he may win forgiveness."

And the other wise men of the synagogue were of one mind with him, but they said naught because my Rabbi had done it for the sake of heaven and there be many ways of serving God.

And we were then twelve disciples who had left our own, wife and child, house and field; we had forsaken all that was ours and we had followed after him. For he persuaded us and we hearkened unto him, and we became his possession, the souls which he had made. And we were in his hand as the clay in the hand of the potter, and he could do with us as he willed, for we believed in his words.

And it came to pass on a certain day that we were on the way with our Rabbi and it was the oncoming of night, and we reached a certain inn and we entered there. And we encountered therein a company of scorners, and the chief among them was a dissolute old man; and they drank beer mixed with honey and they laughed and mocked and spoke much folly. And the slave that served them was a scholar and a man of learning who had been sold into slavery for debt. And it came to pass that when the company of scorners grew merry, they threw what was left of their drinks in the face of him that served them, and they broke the vessels on his head, and the slave stood and endured the shame that they did unto him and answered not a word. And the dissolute old man laughed loudly so that his cheeks became red and the white locks of his beard shook, and he said:

"Tell me thy text, thou son of an ass."

And the learned man that was the slave answered and said: "The days of man are like the grass, he is like the blossom of the field." And when the old man heard these words he smote the slave with his fist and said:

"I have come out with my friends to rejoice and be merry, and thou comest and disturbest our joy. A bad servant art thou.

And when we saw this thing, then Jochanan, of the brothers Zebedee, spoke unto our Rabbi:

"Rabbi, why sufferest thou him to have dominion? Shall I make him silent?"

And our Rabbi answered: "I am not come to destroy a soul, but to build up." And he drew near the old man and said unto him:

"I will give thee such joy as none shall ever disturb, and none shall ever take it from thee."

And the old man answered:

"Thou speakest assuredly of wine. For it is written: 'Wine rejoiceth the heart of man.' "

And the Rabbi answered him and said:

"A joy whereof the end is sadness is not a joy. Come, I will give thee a joy which is like unto a well, which groweth ever stronger and it hath no end."

And the old man asked:

"What is that joy which hath no end?"

And the Rabbi answered him:

"It is the joy which a man hath of his father, the creator of the world. This is the joy that hath no end, and the joy of the kingdom of heaven none shall take from thee, for it is not outside of thee but within thee."

And the old man said:

"That joy is hidden from me, for the path to my father in heaven is cut off by many sins which I have committed in my life."

And the Rabbi said:

"Thou makest thyself great in that thou makest thyself little. The gates are ever open for those that would return."

And the old man said:

"Is there still hope for me? I in no wise knew it."

And he drew near to the slave and fell at his feet and begged forgiveness of him; and our Rabbi said unto us:

"Come and behold: with one word canst thou fling thy brother into the nethermost pit and with one word canst thou bring him under the wings of the glory. Therefore be not deceived by that which your eyes see, but see what is in the heart of a man." And to the servant he said: "When thy brother sinneth against thee, punish him, and when he repeneth, forgive him." And he made peace between them. And he said to the old man:

"Arise, thou art comforted."

And he sat down with them, and drank wine with them, and he changed the company of the scornful into a company of brothers, as it is written: Brothers dwelling together.

And there was in the city a disciple of Jochanan the Baptist, who tormented his body with mortifications and fasting and refrained from eating meat and from drinking wine, as was the manner of the disciples of Jochanan. And he was exceedingly devout and was among the first each day to betake himself to the synagogue and among the last to go thence. And it was so that when he fasted he put ashes on his head and wore sackcloth, and he went about among the people and reminded them that the kingdom of heaven was at hand, and they should repent. He went about the city and did not cease from reproaching the people and calling them to repentance. And when he saw that our Rabbi sat with sinners and ate meat with them and drank wine with them, he came unto my Rabbi and warned him: "Such was not the manner of Jochanan. Jochanan ate no meat and drank no wine, but he mortified his body; but thou eatest meat and swillest wine with tax gatherers and sinners."

And our Rabbi retorted upon him and said: "I am not come to put new patches on an old garment, and the ways I have chosen are my own. Hath not God said: Justice do I demand of you and not the blood of sacrifices? I am not come to call the righteous to repentance, but the sinners, and not alone by mortifications and fasting shall man serve the Lord. I say unto you that ye shall come nigh to him only in joy, for the good man, even like the good tree, giveth forth good and not evil. Have ye not been told of old: And ye shall guard your bodies? And I say unto you that your bodies are not yours but the Lord's." And he turned unto us and said: "Beware of overmuch righteousness; they that fast overmuch are sick more than the sick, for the sick man knoweth that he needeth the healer. There be some that gather treasures of money, and some that gather treasures of righteous deeds, but their treasures are consumed by rust and moths, for they gather these treasures not for their father in heaven but for themselves. Therefore guard yourselves from performing your good deeds in order that men may see them, for ye shall not await any reward from your father in heaven. When thou doest alms, blow not a trumpet before thee, as do the hypocrites in the streets and synagogues, that they may be seen and praised of men. I say unto you they have their reward. But when thou doest alms let not thy left hand know what thy right hand doeth, that thy alms may be in secret, and thy father who seeth in secret shall reward thee openly. And when thou prayest, do not as the hypocrites do, who love to pray standing in the synagogues and at the street corners, and who make a great noise like the gentiles, that they may be seen and praised of men. And when thou fastest, thou shalt not be, like the false hypocrites, of a sad countenance, who do thus that they may be seen of all men and praised; but when thou fastest comb thy hair and wash thy face and show thyself not before men that thou fastest, but only before thy father in heaven, and thy father in heaven, who seeth thee in secret, shall reward thee openly."

And it came to pass when I rehearsed the words of my Rabbi before the learned men of the synagogue that they said, concerning him: "It is a mouth which poureth forth pearls. Blessed are the ears that hear him. Likewise it was Antigonos, the man of Socho, he who received the tradition from Simon the Just, who also said: 'Ye shall not be like servants who serve their lord that they may receive reward.' And the doing of alms in secret is an exceeding great virtue, as our sages have taught. And surely the prayer that is offered up for thy brother's sake is accepted sooner than the prayer which thou offerest up for thyself. And surely to serve the Lord in joy is an exceeding great virtue, for joy is love, and the glory resteth only in the midst of joy. These be assuredly words of God which thy Rabbi speaketh. But the fear of God is the beginning of wisdom, as it is written: The first wisdom is the fear of God. Therefore the words that are spoken and the deeds that are done in the fear of God shall endure, and without the fear of God there be no wise words and good deeds, for they be an empty babbling."

And about that time our Rabbi led us into the fields and showed us the wonders of God and bade us learn the lesson of his creation. And he taught us the way and the commandment to be observed between a man and his brother. And he said: "Judge not, that ye be not judged, for with that judgment wherewith ye judge others ye shall yourselves be judged, and the measure which ye mete out to others shall be meted out to you." And he said further: "If thy brother hath sinned against thee, let thy punishment be between thee and him privily. And if it be that he hearkeneth, then wilt thou have found a brother, and if he hearkeneth not then take with thee two or three witnesses, for all matters shall be ratified by two or three witnesses. And if he will not hearken, then let it be known to the congregation, and if he will not hearken to the congregation he shall be unto you as a gentile or a tax collector. But let not offense stay overnight in your hearts, but drive it thence. Be children of your father in heaven, and as he forgiveth you your sins so shall ye forgive them that sin against you."

And then Simon asked him:

"How many times shall I forgive my brother? Seven times?"

And the Rabbi answered and said:

"Not seven times, but seventy times seven. For as ye deal with one another on earth, so shall your father which is in heaven deal with you." And he told us a parable, for he did not speak but by parables. And when I came into the synagogue, and I saw the wise men sitting there, and their pupils made a circle about them like a wreath of olive, then I told them the words of my Rabbi, and the wise men did drink of his wisdom like those who thirst, and they said:

"Truly we do not understand thy Rabbi, for he speaketh like one of the disciples of the venerable Hillel, who came to spread peace on earth, and yet he doeth deeds which stir up the hearts of the learned men, for they are against the Torah which hath been delivered unto us through the sages and the wise old men from Moses our teacher who brought it down on Mount Sinai. Shall we cover our eyes with our hands, that we may not see his deeds, and listen only to the words of his mouth?"

And another said: "If their words and deeds be for the sake of heaven, they shall endure, but if not, they shall pass away."

And they waited to see how the thing would be.

And the wise men became daily further and further removed from us, for they did not understand the ways of my Rabbi. And the people of the city, they likewise began to murmur against us, and we were separated from them, for they would not take us into their houses and no one bade us sit at his table. But we were alone with our Rabbi and he led us through the fields. And it chanced one day that it was the Sabbath, and we found ears of corn standing in a field, and the harvest time was near, and the ears of corn were bent to the earth with the weight of the seed, and they were a temptation to the eyes with their ripeness like unto gold when the sun shineth thereon. And the disciples were hungry, and they plucked the ripened ears and ate of them. And the Rabbi saw them and said nothing.

And it was told in the city that the disciples of the Rabbi desecrated the Sabbath and that the Rabbi had seen the desecration and had not prevented it. And the murmuring of the wise men became exceeding loud, and they and the chief men of the city said:

"We do not understand the man and his words. He speaketh one thing with his mouth, and he doeth otherwise with his hands. It must be that he hath come to destroy the Torah and the laws and commandments which Moses gave unto us."

And thus it was, when my Rabbi came into the synagogue to preach and would have mounted the pulpit, they would not let him, and they said:

"See, thy disciples do that which is forbidden on the Sabbath."

And they thought that he would repent, and would answer softly, but he replied thus:

"They were hungry. And have ye not read how in the old time David and his men that were with him, when they were hungry, did enter God's house and eat the shew-bread, which might not be eaten, neither by him nor by the Levites that were with him, but only by the Priests? Or have ye not read in the Torah that in the sacrifices the Priests desecrate the Sabbath? And if one may desecrate the Sabbath to bring a sacrifice, how much more may one desecrate it for the sake of one that is hungry? For it hath been said by the prophet: God desireth kindness and not sacrifices."

Now the head of the congregation, who was his friend, heard these words and rejoiced, and he said to the chief men of the city:

"It is clear that the Rabbis have found permission for this thing. For the Rabbi appealeth to the Torah and interpreteth the law according to the tradition."

And the chief men of the city, and the wise men, meditated on the matter, and they came to our Rabbi and said to him, with much love:

"Teach us, Rabbi, in which house of learning was the permission founded for this thing, and the alteration made, that danger of life suppresseth the Sabbath? Hath the law so been amended by the sages, and so been approved, or is it but the opinion of one man? For the matter is of great importance, and it is meet for us to know whereon the Rabbi leaneth."

And the Rabbi answered:

"Man is also the lord of the Sabbath."

And when he uttered these words all those that were assembled with him were stricken with terror, and there was silence in the synagogue, and one man looked at the other in astonishment, and they asked: "What meaneth the Rabbi with these words? Who is lord over God's Torah, save he that gave it, the Holy One, or his messenger whom he will send to liberate us, if we should be worthy of it?" And they turned to our Rabbi, and they asked him out of the fear of their hearts: "Tell us, what manner of man art thou that thou darest to utter such words?"

But the Rabbi answered not, and he left the synagogue. And the assembly wondered greatly, for such words had never been heard in Israel.

III

And on the next day our Rabbi said to us: "Come, let us arise and go to the city of Naim."

And the city of Naim was three days' journey from the place where we sojourned. Then Simon and his brother Andrew took us in their ship and we came to Migdal, but we did not descend from the boat, likewise we avoided the city of Tiberias, for our teacher told us that the city is impure and forbidden, meaning thereby the government of Herod, which is in the city. And then we went on by boat until the middle of the day, and we came to a place and landed there, and from there we climbed up the mount of Tabor. And from the summit of Tabor the whole land lieth before thee as spread on a man's hand, all the level of the Sea of Genesaret, and the green Valley of Jezreel, with all the towns and villages which are in the midst of the fields of grain and the vineyards, the palm trees and the olive trees. And my Rabbi saw the tents of Israel, how they were at peace, and he was filled with a great compassion for them. And he lifted up his hands over the whole valley and he said: "How goodly are thy tents, O Jacob, thy tabernacles, O Israel." And he said further: "The harvest is plenteous, but the laborers are few," and we did not then understand his words, but understood them only later.

And it was the will of our Rabbi that we should sleep in that place, under the sky. And in the morning, after the first morning prayer, we went down from the mount and we came into the city of En Dor, which is as a Sabbath walk from the foot of the mount. But the place is unclean, for the Baal Peor still reigneth there, as in the days of the witch, in the time when Saul came to her and bade her bring up the soul of Samuel the Prophet.

And from that place it was not far to the city of Naim. And as the name of the city is, Naim, or pleasant, so is the city. And thus it is written: "And Issachar saw that the land was pleasant"... for the portion of Issachar is like the garden of God before Adam sinned with the tree of knowledge of good and evil. The land was as one garden, and the fields bore wheat and oats and fruit trees and flowers. And we saw many people working in the fields. And some of them were reaping with song that which they had sown in tears, and the Rabbi blessed the work of the day laborers and told us many parables and wise similitudes. And when our Rabbi saw the fields, how they were sown by the labor of men, and the vine stalks were heavy-laden and the trees blossomed, he lifted up his voice and said:

"The heavens, the heavens are for the Lord, and the earth he hath given to the sons of man. And as the heavens declare the glory of God, so the fields declare the labor of man. Verily I say unto you, the men of the army are not so numbered by their commander, as the grass of the field is numbered by the creator, and for every blade of grass he hath appointed an angel which shall guard it. By the harvest on the threshing floor shall ye know the work of the husbandman, and by the harvest of good deeds which ye shall cut in the field and gather on God's threshing floor shall ye be judged. There shall be no other measure and no other weight and no other numbering, but according to the good deeds which ye have created. For the field is not yours, it is only leased unto you, therefore let your plow bring forth the more grain, for ye know not when the field will be taken from you."

And he told us other parables as we went through the fields which lead to Naim, concerning the plow and the plowman, and concerning the gardens and the gardeners whom we met by the wayside; and since the wisest of all men, King Solomon, and likewise since the time of ben Sira, the like hath not been heard in the land. And all his words did have but one purpose, to plant in our hearts the fear and love of our father who is in heaven, that we might be bound to him.

Blessed are the ears which heard him. I did engrave his words in my memory that I might write them down later for the edification of generations to come.

And when the sun had fallen to the edge of the sky, and it poured light on the garment of our Rabbi, we came to the gate of the city.

And there was a great press of people at the gate, for many folk returned then from the fields, and they had with them donkeys laden with grain; likewise there were caravans of camels laden with cruses of oil and honey and flaxen and woolen clothes and all manner of merchandise. For the city of Naim was rich with possessions and the rich men were not content with the produce of their land, but imported much merchandise from afar. But for all that, there were some in that press of men and animals who remarked that a Rabbi had come to the city with his disciples (for we had surrounded him, that his robe might not be soiled) and they called to one another, "Make a way." And when it was toward darkness, there was one at last—he was a boy leading his donkey—who looked upon us and called out: "See, the man of wonders of the city of K'far Nahum is coming unto us."

Thereupon we were surrounded by many people, for the good name of my Rabbi goeth through the land like the odor of ointment. Then craftsmen left their desks, the merchants left their shops, and they came out on the thresholds of their houses with their lamps, that they might light the way for us, and they called out:

"Blessed be ye that come in the name of the Lord."

But we hastened to the synagogue of the city, for the evening had fallen and the time had come for the evening prayer.

And in the city of Naim there was a devout man whom they called Simon the Pharisee. And the man had been in K'far Nahum and he had heard the sermon which my Rabbi had preached on the hill, and the words had pleased him. Therefore some of the disciples were decided that our Rabbi should lodge in the house of Simon the Pharisee, for it was a house of assembly for the learned, and wise men and scribes came to it. And I was preparing to seek out the house of Simon the Pharisee and to impart to him the coming of our Rabbi. And the disciple Levi, who had been a tax gatherer, had a friend in the city who was likewise a tax gatherer, and his name was Jochanan, and he was a rich man. And therefore some of the disciples, to wit Simon the fisher and the brothers Zebedee, were decided that the Rabbi should lodge in the house of the tax gatherer, for he would meet there the common people and those that had been thrust out and were condemned and who had great need of the help and consolation of our Rabbi. But our Rabbi said to us: "We will go to the synagogue where all the people assemble, and we will stand there, and whosoever shall ask us to go into his house and lodge under his roof, to him shall we go, for the words of God have been sent to all Jews, and none shall be excluded." And we did according to the words of our Rabbi.

And when we entered the synagogue many people came with us, for it was noised abroad that the man who performeth wonders had arrived in Naim. And Simon the Pharisee heard that our Rabbi was in Naim, and he put on fine raiment and he gathered the scribes and Pharisees, and they too put on fine raiment, and they came to the synagogue to receive our Rabbi with honor. And Simon the Pharisee lifted up his voice and said to our Rabbi:

"The sages of our city have come to receive thee honorably, according to the law and custom, and I entreat thee to turn aside to my house and to sit at my table and eat with us, that I may fulfill the commandment of the welcoming of travelers."

And my Rabbi answered:

"Simon, is it solely to fulfill the commandment of the welcoming of travelers that thou art come to entreat me to thy house?"

"In order that we may sit at one table and eat and converse of the lore of God, according to the law," answered Simon.

For it had come to Simon's ears concerning the strange deeds of our Rabbi, which were not after the manner of the learned men, and which had stirred up the chief men of the city of K'far Nahum; and therefore Simon was desirous of making inquiry of our Rabbi, that he might know how the matter was and what he was to do. And for this reason he had entreated our Rabbi to his house and called the wise men of Naim to him.

And our Rabbi knew of this thing, but he said naught, and he consented to go to the house of Simon and to sit with the learned men.

And Simon and the learned men conducted him to the house, and a great multitude followed, for it was known that the Rabbi Yeshua ben Joseph was in the city and that he would sit with the wise men in the house of Simon the Pharisee and they would make inquiry of his teachings.

And when we came to the house, we found at the gate a press of people, and they sought to enter with us to hear the word of God. But the servants of Simon stood before the house and would not permit them to enter, and drove them hence with staves and whips, and they admitted only the learned men and such as were called *chaver*, or colleague. And when my Rabbi saw that the servants drove away the people from before the gate, he said to Simon:

"Why will not thy servants and thy slaves permit the people to enter thy house?"

And Simon answered:

"The people of the land are ignorant, the ritual is not strong in their hands and they know not the laws of purity and impurity, therefore we are afraid that they may contaminate the house, the vessels or the bread."

And the Rabbi looked with compassion on the people and he said:

"The people is like an abandoned flock of sheep which have no shepherd."

Notwithstanding, he went into the house of Simon, and took us with him. But Simon bar Jonah and the brothers Zebedee stayed without in the midst of the people and waited for the Rabbi.

Now Simon the Pharisee was a wealthy man, and his house was large and filled with many precious vessels of silver and gold and ivory, and tended by many servants. And the servants brought salvers of silver and jars of water, and sheets, and they washed the hands of Simon and of the learned men that were with him. But they did not wash the hands and feet of our Rabbi or of his disciples. For it had already been told them that our Rabbi had rejected the commandment of the washing of hands and that he ate bread with tax collectors, not having washed.

And the Rabbi beheld all this, and was silent. And I thought in my heart: Who knoweth what will come of this thing? For it could be seen of all that Simon had invited the Rabbi into his house, to sit with the learned men, in order that he might prove him.

And it was thus afterwards, that the servants handed our Rabbi the bread, and it was wrapped in a cloth, that it might not be defiled, and he took it and said his prayer, and broke the bread and distributed the pieces among us, his disciples, and we ate, not having washed.

And the learned men wondered greatly, for they had indeed meant to prove the Rabbi, whether he eateth bread without the washing of hands, and therefore the servants had been commanded by their master not to wash the Rabbi's hands. Then one of the learned rose and inquired of our Rabbi:

"The sages of Israel have decreed a great decree by tradition from of old, and now we see that a Rabbi who spreadeth his doctrine in Israel eateth bread without the washing of hands; therefore we ask the Rabbi: Teach us that we may know, are the words which thou utterest and the deeds which thou doest, the tradition which thou hast received from thy Rabbis, or from the ancient Hasideans? For thou utterest words and thou doest deeds and thou findest not support for them in a text of the Holy Writ, and thou sayest not whence thou hast received these things."

And our Rabbi answered:

"That which the son of man doeth, and that which the son of man saith, he hath received from his father in heaven."

Then the learned men were greatly astounded and they looked upon each other and upon the master of the house, upon Simon the Pharisee, for he was the greatest among them in learning and wealth.

Then Simon the Pharisee took his long black beard in his hand, and he frowned and said:

"From the words of the Rabbi three things may be deduced, whereof two are clear to me, but the third is doubtful. Now the first of these things is this, that the Rabbi believeth himself to have been sent of God. For it is written in the text: 'And God said unto me, son of man, I send thee to the house of Israel.' Therefore it followeth that if the Rabbi speaketh of himself as the son of man, he believeth himself to have been sent of God. And the second is this, that every son of Israel hath the right to call God his father, for it is written: 'Sons are ye of the Lord your God.' But whence can we learn that what the Rabbi saith he hath received from the source of all strength?"

And my Rabbi answered:

"The birds on the branches say it."

"We accept no proof from the birds on the branches," said Simon the Pharisee.

"The stones in the streets say it."

"We accept no proof from the stones in the street."

"The dead, the leprous, the possessed, bear witness thereto."

"The possessed and the sinners, the leprous and the dead, are not acceptable as witnesses."

"If it be so, then let the subject of the dispute appear in person to confirm."

And as the learned men thus sat together, and I in my heart applied to them the text "How good and how pleasant it is for brethren to dwell together in unity," we heard a great commotion in the vestibule before the entrance, and before we were aware of what had taken place, a woman rushed in with great force to where the learned men reclined at the banquet. Then the servants pursued her and sought to restrain her, but the master of the house made a sign that they leave her be. And the woman was draped in delicate stuffs of Zidon, many-colored, in the manner of women of ill fame; and her hair was not, after the manner of Jewish women, concealed, but it fell over her neck and her bosom; and likewise there hung on her body by a golden chain an alabaster vial with refined and delicate ointment, the scent whereof was spread abroad in all the house; for this is the manner of rich women, who wear such vials on their necks, but this woman was barefoot, and she stretched forth her hands and asked:

"Who among ye is that wonderful man who hath called to all and sundry: 'Come unto me ye that are heavy-laden and I will give you rest'?"

And when there came no answers from any one of them, she looked among the learned men and the Pharisees who reclined at the banquet, and she sought with thirsting eyes until she perceived our Rabbi. Then she drew near and fell at his feet and wept bitterly, and the tears which ran from her eyes fell on our Rabbi's feet and washed them. And when she saw that her tears had wet the feet of the Rabbi, she took her hair and she dried them, and she kissed them with the lips of her mouth. Then she took the vial of alabaster which hung at her throat, and wherein was contained the costly oil of myrrh, and she poured the oil on the feet of our Rabbi and anointed them.

And when the scribes and the learned men that sat about the table saw this they smiled and they said to each other: "If he were a prophet he would know what manner of woman this is . . ." for the woman was a sinner, and she was known in the town and thereabouts, and she came from the city of Migdal. And the learned men thought that she had come into the city to spread her net for the rich men of Naim. And they thought moreover that she anointed the feet of the Rabbi with the ointments wherewith she awakened the lust of her lovers that they might lust after her. And they said: "If he were a prophet, he would know who the woman is. . . ." But the learned men knew not that the woman had repented, and that she had come with blind Bar Talmai, who had brought her hither in the footsteps of the Rabbi after they had sought him in K'far Nahum and he was gone. And the precious raiment which she had put on was not put on that she might increase her beauty, but to do honor to our Rabbi, and so it was with the precious ointment. But beneath the silk raiment her heart was filled with repentance.

But all this was known to our Rabbi, and he said:

"Simon, I will ask a question of thee: there was a creditor who had two debtors; one of them owed him five hundred dinars and the other owed him fifty dinars. And when they were unable to pay, he made a gift to both of them of their debt to him. Now tell me, which of the debtors will thank him and love him more?"

And Simon answered:

"Assuredly he whose remitted debt was the greater."

Thereupon my Rabbi spoke and answered:

"Thou hast judged rightly, Simon. And now mark: I came into thy house, and thou didst not give me water to wash my feet; but this woman washed my feet with her tears and wiped them with the hair of her head. Thou gavest me no kiss, but since she entered she hath not ceased to kiss my feet. Thou didst not anoint my head with oil, but she hath anointed my feet with costly oil. Therefore I say unto thee: her sins shall be forgiven her, for she hath loved much." And to the woman he said: "Thy sins are forgiven thee, thy faith hath helped thee. Go in peace."

And when the Pharisees and the learned men heard this, there was much commotion among them. And they stood up from the feast where they had reclined, and they asked of each other: "Now who is this that can forgive sins? How is this thing? Because the woman kissed his feet and anointed them with her sinful oil, therefore shall her sins be forgiven her?" And others asked: "What, is he a prophet sent of God that he can remit sins?"

And my Rabbi answered them naught, but he turned to Simon the Pharisee, who had remained reclining on his couch of ivory, and he had been so moved that his face was pale and his black beard trembled and his eyes sparkled:

"Simon, hast thou seen, how the party to the dispute came and delivered the treasure into my hand?"

But Simon answered him:

"Thou canst not cite the sinful in proof. Sinners are not admitted to testimony."

And my Rabbi answered:

"They that are whole have no need of a physician, but the sick have need of a physician, and I say unto you that the sick are more whole than the whole; for he that is whole knoweth not that he is sick, but the sick man knoweth it."

And he turned to the Pharisees and the learned, and he said:

"The broken heart is nigh unto God. And did not Isaiah say: 'I that dwell in the high and holy place dwell with him who hath been thrust away and is lowly, in order that I may comfort the spirit of the lowly and lift up the heart of those that are thrust away.' What have ye done that these words might be brought about? Woe unto you, ye Pharisees, for ye love the high places in the synagogue and to be greeted in the streets. Woe unto you, ye scribes, ye hypocrites, for you are like whited sepulchers."

And when the learned heard these words, they became pale of countenance and they arose in their places and they asked: "Who is this man, who taketh unto himself the right to speak such words?" And one of them turned to our Rabbi and said: "Rabbi, an thou sayest these things, thou offerest us offense."

And the Rabbi answered:

"Woe unto you, ye learned men, for ye do place burdens on the people which are heavy to bear, and you will not touch the burden so much as with your finger!"

But the learned men answered:

"That is not true, for we observe the laws and commandments."

"You do observe them, like a trade which hath been learned, in order that you may boast yourselves of it. You come early to the houses of prayer and stay there long that men may point their fingers at you. You pour ashes on your heads and tear your clothes, so that it may be seen that ye fast. But you will not open a place at your tables for the people, you drive them from your houses that they may not make unclean your vessels. You cleanse the platter and the cup without, but within it is full of filth, therefore your houses and your vessels are unclean, and the eating at your tables is the eating of carrion, the sacrifices of the dead, for ye have driven the people away. And of him that sitteth with you it hath been written: 'He shall sit in the seat of the scornful. . . .' "

And when he had spoken these words our Rabbi arose and went forth from the house of the Pharisee and the table of the learned, concerning which I had thought it was written: "How good and how pleasant it is for brothers to dwell together," and which had been turned into a stone of contention.

IV

My knees tremble, my loins yield, my heart panteth and all my limbs are seized with shaking and trembling, as though I had been seized by the hair of my head and borne aloft. I know not who standeth before me, who goeth before me and whose footsteps I follow.

My Rabbi is more than a Rabbi; he is that which I do not understand. I know not from what sources he draweth his strength, and what permission he hath received. Who is he? Do I stand nigh unto the holy one of Israel? Woe is me, I am a man of unclean lips and evil heart.

When my Rabbi went forth from the house of Simon the Pharisee, and from the presence of the learned men who sat there, I and the other disciples went with him. And when we had passed by the many guards and servants and reached the gate, we beheld a great assembly of people, and they held in their hands kindled oil lamps, and Simon bar Jonah, the disciple, was with them, and likewise Jacob and Jochanan, the Zebedees, and the three of them were of one mind. They had conspired among themselves to conceal from the other disciples a certain thing, and Simon bar Jonah drew near to the Rabbi, and the people lifted up their lamps that they might shine on the face of the Rabbi and on his white garment in the night, and they cried to him: "Rabbi, Hosannah, help us," and Simon bar Jonah said:

"Teacher, have compassion on the people of this city, Naim; they have come forth to thee with kindled lamps and they long to see thy countenance and to rejoice in thee, to drink the waters of thy source and to be healed by thee."

And Jacob of the Zebedees and his brother Jochanan implored with Simon, for they were all of one mind, and Jacob said:

"Rabbi, the learned men believe not in thee, and they seek speech with thee concerning the Torah only that they may make a show of their learning; but the people love thee and believe in thee. And hast thou not said: 'Blessed are the humble'? And they come to thee, humble in spirit, and they bring thee the love of their hearts. Go with them, for thy place is among them."

And his brother Jochanan also spoke with persuasion to the Rabbi and said:

"Thou drawest unto thyself those of a broken heart. Come with us, Rabbi, to the house of Jochanan the tax collector; he hath cleansed his house to receive thee, and he would assemble the people under one roof, that they may rejoice in thee."

But I inclined myself to the ear of my Rabbi and said:

"Now, when the learned will see that thou didst forsake their house and art gone unto the sinners, and hast changed the table of the learned for the table of a tax collector, they will be greatly offended and they will bring thy evil report before the elders of Israel."

And my Rabbi answered:

"Judah, men do not light a candle and hide it under a bushel, but they place it on high that all may see it. . . ."

And the tax collector, being there, bowed himself before the Rabbi and said:

"Come, thou blessed of God, under my roof that it may be blessed for thy sake."

And he lit the way for my Rabbi with his lamp. And Simon bar Jonah was near him, and Jacob and Jochanan, and the people with lamps and torches in their hands conducted our Rabbi through the streets of the city Naim to the house of the tax collector.

Now Jochanan the tax collector was a rich man, and his house was large and could receive many people; and many were assembled there, both rich and poor; and Kuza, the officer of Herod, was also there with his wife Jochanah, and with a certain woman whose name was Susannah, and they were of the rich women of the city. And the woman whose name was Miriam of Migdal, and who had washed and anointed the feet of the Rabbi in the house of the Pharisee, had followed after the Rabbi.

And as the Rabbi entered the house of the tax collector, the people encircled him and obstructed his steps. For the sick threw themselves down before him, and there were blind folk who felt with their hands and sought to touch his garment; and those that were possessed with spirits called to him for help, and the sinners bowed their heads before him and sank to the ground, and others concealed their faces in their hands for shame; for they were afraid to look into his face lest he know the sins which were written on their foreheads and corrupted in them the image of God. And many stretched out their hands to him in great longing, and they cried: "Rabbi, help us."

And when our Rabbi saw so much faith about him, then he was filled with might, and his face became like a burning fire, and his hands also.

And it was as though we beheld the sparks that issued from his face and his beard, and his eyes sparkled like amber, as if the heavens had opened in them and we beheld the depths of the heavenly light. And his garment, which was white, gave out blinding rays, as if it were all of fire.

And when the people saw the light which beat from the Rabbi's face and his skin and his hair, and the light of his garment, they were seized with a great trembling, and they drew back for fear and they made a circle about him and he stood in the midst of the circle like a burning light.

But there was one woman who dared to come forth from the press and enter the circle. Her limbs gave way under her and her face was pale and her eyes as though they were blind and she bent to the earth and touched the hem of his robe.

And the Rabbi trembled, as though fire had touched fire. And he looked around and asked: "Who hath touched my garment, for I felt that power went out of her?" And when he beheld the woman who lay with her face to the earth before him and trembled like the last leaf on the tree in the days of rain, he raised her up and said:

"Go, thy faith hath saved thee."

And after her there were others that dared come into the fiery circle of the Rabbi. And one blind man came, and with hands stretched out before him entered the fire and knew not whither he went. And when the blind man felt the Rabbi's hand, he leaped as if he had touched a burning fire, and he cried out:

"A fire hath burned me; surely I must have touched the Rabbi's hand."

And the woman that came from Migdal stretched herself at his feet in all her length. Like the strings that are stretched upon a harp she lay stretched on the floor. And for a while she lay still. But soon the spirits that were in her belly began to stir and they flung her about as the wind flingeth about the sea, and she threw herself hither and thither, as though the spirits would go forth from her body and could not. Then the spirits seized her and lifted her up and she began to turn with her hands and her hair as the wind maketh the cypress in the field to turn, and she sought herself. And the foam came upon her lips, and her eyes were large and like flames and her hair was like fiery tongues which darted about her. And voices and lamentings began to issue from her. And at first it was like the crying of a child, which singeth and entreateth without words. But the voices changed into a wailing, and she stretched forth her hands as if she saw someone before her, and she began to sing from the Song of Songs, which is Solomon's: "Who is this that cometh up from the wilderness?" And she went as if to encounter one, with dancing steps and a purified countenance, as if she beheld him that was destined unto her. And then she became afraid, and she trembled and fluttered in all her body, and bent herself in three. And she began to weep, saying that her sins had suckled evil spirits in her belly, and now they bind her with ropes and say that she belongeth to them and they will not let her approach him. And like one that falleth into the nethermost pit, and is surrounded by snakes and scorpions which torment his soul, so she implored the Rabbi and stretched forth her hands to him:

"Save me, thou chosen one, from the torments which dwell in my body, thou art my only help."

And she fell and concealed her face in her hands and wept long and bitterly. And the Rabbi placed his hands on her head, saying:

"Clean, clean, clean art thou."

And he commanded the demons and spirits to leave her, for her sins had been forgiven. And he took her by the hand and lifted her up from her place and said to us: "She is our sister," and sat her down at his feet. But she stretched herself out on the floor in all her length and she covered the Rabbi's feet with her face and hair and she lay still, like a newborn child, at his feet.

And when the people saw the miracles which our Rabbi wrought with the sick and the heavy-laden, they stretched forth their hands to him and entreated:

"Rabbi, teach us what we shall do that we may be saved and inherit the kingdom of heaven."

And our Rabbi stretched out his hands to them and said:

"Ye shall attain to the kingdom of heaven only with the yoke which ye take upon you. For the time is near, salvation knocketh at the gate, and those that are prepared they shall enter by the gate, but the others will remain outside."

"But what shall we do, Rabbi?"

"Give up the earthly riches which ye have gathered, for only they that entrust themselves to their father in heaven, and not to the superfluity of bread which they have concealed in hidden places, can inherit the kingdom of heaven. If one of you have two loaves he shall give one to his brother, and if one of you have two garments, he shall give one to his brother. For narrow is the gate into the kingdom of heaven and only the naked and hungry can enter thereby. Ye cannot serve God and Mammon, and he that would follow me, he shall first throw off himself his earthly riches, and put his faith in his father in heaven and not in his money."

And there was long silence among the people and no one dared to utter a word. Many stood with their heads sunk to the ground, for the rich were among them, and they would not tear themselves away from their wealth which they had gathered. But there came from the outer circle a woman, and she thrust herself through the press, and she approached the Rabbi; and she took off the golden circlet from her neck, and her nose ring and her hand rings, and she put them at the Rabbi's feet. And she took off likewise her mantle of rich weave, and her alabaster vial of sweet-smelling ointment, and these she placed at the Rabbi's feet. And she was left only with a linen tunic to cover her shame, and she said:

"Teacher, take me as I come to thee."

And she was Jochanah, the wife of Kuza, the officer of Herod.

And our Rabbi said:

"Jochanah, thou art our sister in the kingdom of heaven. Go, take thy station behind me."

And after her he lifted up another woman, who did like the first, and her name was Susannah, and she was of the daughters of the place.

And the woman whom he had purified of her sins, and whose name was Miriam, said unto him:

"Rabbi, I have no more to bring thee, save my soul which thou hast purified. All which I possessed I gave away as an atonement for my sins, and I bring only my soul to lay at thy feet."

And my Rabbi answered:

"Thou too art our sister in the kingdom of heaven; go, take thy station behind me."

And some of the tax collectors that were there came before him and said:

"We have nothing in hands but our office, and our office is a sinful one. What shall we do to be saved?"

"Take no more from your debtors than that which is your due under the law, and do not oppress the poor; and for the rest ye shall be rewarded according to your deeds, for God looketh into the heart of man and judgeth him according to his thoughts."

And so they came before him, the tax collectors, one after the other, and they confessed their sins before him and he said to them: "Serve your father in heaven as you serve your king."

And the Rabbi instructed me to take the gold and silver and the ornaments and the rich apparel which the women had laid at his feet, and to sell them and distribute the money among the poor. But there was not overmuch beyond what the women had laid down, for the rich men that stood there said: "He increaseth the yoke of the kingdom of heaven upon us even more than the Pharisees. For the Pharisees bid us give only the tithe or tenth, but he would have us give away the substance. And if we give away the substance, wherewith shall we be left?" So they left the house of the tax collector and went away. And the Rabbi said concerning them:

"Come and behold! It is easier for a camel to pass through the eye of a needle than for a rich man to enter the kingdom of heaven."

And the Rabbi took the poor people that were there, and the sinful tax collectors and the sick women that had been healed, and he sat with them at the one table and ate bread with them. And when our Rabbi saw that the simple people did not wash their hands because the law was not strong with them and they did not know how to follow it, so he too did not wash his hands in order that he might not shame them; but he only said his prayer which he saith before eating. He blessed the bread, which was brought to him broken, and he distributed it to those at the table. Then he asked for wine, and he pressed the people to eat and drink and rejoice that their sins had been forgiven them and they were ready to receive the kingdom of heaven. And he strengthened them with comforting words, and he bade them have no care and not to be sad because they knew not the law. For God desireth not the law by rote, but the pure heart and meekness of spirit are the most acceptable sacrifices unto him. And Moses our teacher said in his Torah: "This law which I give thee is not in heaven, nor is it under the sea, but it is thy heart." Not the laws which were engraved on the tablets did Moses bring unto the Jews from Sinai, but the ten commandments engraved in the heart of man. And as the prophet hath said: "I will put up the Temple in the heart."

And when they saw that the Rabbi was willing, and the moment was come to him, they rejoiced greatly with him that he was with them, and the rejoicing in the company was without ending, so that they saw throughout the city the lights which burned in the house of Jochanan the tax collector and they heard the songs which issued therefrom.

Then when Simon bar Jonah, the disciple, saw that our Rabbi was in spirit, and that the moment was come to him, he took up an oil lamp and went into the street, where darkness reigneth and the children of the night are, and he said to them:

"In the house of Jochanan the tax collector now sitteth the man to whom the power hath been given to remit your sins and to receive you into the kingdom of heaven."

And there came into the house of Jochanan the tax collector people of the night, such as enter not into the congregation of Israel, and whereof the faces bear witness that their souls are sick and corrupted, people that are heavy-laden with sin. There were among them such as were in tatters, and their nakedness showed through their decayed rags, and all manner of sores on their skins, sickness and leprosy, even as on their souls. And there were others who were painted and adorned, but their souls were foul and unclean, for many harlots were in their midst, who wander in the streets of nights and spread their nets for passers-by. Some there were likewise who had fled from the fear of the judgment or concealed themselves from the government. And all of these Simon the disciple brought into the house of Jochanan the tax collector. And when the Rabbi perceived them and the stench of their bodies came to our nostrils, he stretched out his arms and cried:

"Come, all ye that are heavy-laden, come to me." And he rose before them and gathered them to the table and made them sit by him and said: "All ye that are forsaken and thrust out, to what shall I compare you? I will compare you to the garden of Isaiah the prophet, but not to the garden which was planted and tended, but contrariwise. No one hath plowed and seeded your garden, no one hath watered it in time, the fences have been cast down, and everyone could enter and tread upon the young plants, so that the garden might have given forth none but sour grapes; and behold, it hath given forth sweet and good grapes."

And our Rabbi took the bread which lay near him, and he broke it and shared it with them and said:

"Come, eat with me, my brothers and sisters in the kingdom of heaven: For our father in heaven hath seen the torment of your souls and he hath forgiven you your sins."

And part of them began to weep and they said: "Who art thou, thou blessed man? Who hath sent unto us the consolation of heaven?"

And there were at the table such as rose and said: "We be indeed ignorant people, and we are not close-bound to the law, but our hearts are at peace with our God and we would go in his ways. And though we be poor folk, yet we earn our little bread with the sweat of our brows, and it is not fitting and becoming for us that we sit at one table with thieves and harlots," and they left the table of the Rabbi.

And our Rabbi called to them and said:

"For the Pharisees and the learned ye be sinners and fallen ones, and for you these be the sinners and fallen ones; and I say unto you, the more a man hath been flung down the stronger he is, and the more fallen the higher he is in God. And was it not King David, peace be upon him, who said: 'Out of the deeps I cry unto thee, O God.' And who lieth so deep as these? And I say unto you that they are nearer unto God than you and those others, and he that doeth good unto them doeth good to my father in heaven, and he who removeth himself from them removeth himself from my father in heaven."

And I inclined myself to my Rabbi and I spoke into his ear and asked:

"Rabbi, where is the border to which mercy goeth and where the judgment begins?"

And the Rabbi answered me and said:

"There is no border. Go with thy brother to the edge of the pit and beyond."

And I dared to remind my Rabbi, and to say:

"Is it not written: 'The Lord is a just judge'? and is it not written further: 'The Lord shall deal justly in all his ways'?"

But my Rabbi looked at me and answered, saying:

"Judah, Judah, am I come to put new patches on old garments? I am the last door, and if this door too be closed to them, where shall they knock?"

And I understood him and was silent.

V

Then Simon went forth and sought, and he found a resting place for the night for our Rabbi, for our Rabbi often lodgeth not under a roof but under the heavens. He that sleepeth without hath the heavens for roof and he is at home with his father. He that sleepeth under a roof confineth himself within four ells and hath only himself for guard. And he lodged that night in the booth of a watchman in a vineyard which was of the possessions of Jochanah, the wife of the rich officer of Herod.

And when it was the morning of the second day, and our Rabbi had said the "Hear, O Israel," he commanded Simon, his disciple, to open the bundle of bread that we might eat before we began the labor of the day. For on that day the Rabbi had much for us to do, and he said: "There is much work and little time, the harvests are plenteous but the harvesters are few." And when Simon had placed bread before us our Rabbi saw the watchman of the vineyard, who stood off afar and watched what we did, for he was of the men-of-the-earth, who draw not near to Rabbis lest they defile them. But my Rabbi said to the watchman of the vineyard:

"Why standest thou afar off? Approach and sit with us and eat of our bread."

And the watchman answered:

"How shall I approach and eat of your bread if you are learned and I am of the men-of-the-earth?"

And our Rabbi said:

"It is written: 'Ye are all children of your father in heaven.' "

And the watchman answered:

"Yea, but I am not of the learned, the law is not strong in my hand and I know not how to observe the commandments of clean and unclean, and my hands will defile the bread."

But the Rabbi looked at the heavens and said:

"Behold and see, O my father in heaven, how they have divided thy children into clean and unclean, pure and impure." And he said unto the watchman: "Come, Mattathias, sit thee down by us and eat our bread; not the learning which is outward lifteth man and maketh him clean, but the learning which is in the heart. Mattathias, thou fulfillest all the law...."

And the watchman of the vineyard did even so, but with great fear, and when he took in his hand the bread which the Rabbi gave him, his eyes were full of tears and the tears fell on the bread; and he said:

"Woe is me, Rabbi, I know that I shall fall into the nethermost pit because I have not observed the law, and I know not that which one may do, and that which one may not do."

But the Rabbi wiped the tears from his eyes and said:

"I say unto thee, Mattathias, that not thou, but they who complain against thee to our father in heaven, and speak evil of thee unto him, shall suffer the fires of hell. Thou hast brought thy heart before God, and a humble heart and lowliness of spirit are the most acceptable sacrifices unto him." And he turned unto the city and lifted up his hands and he said: "Woe unto ye, scribes and Pharisees, who travel over land and sea to win one soul and when ye have it ye make it a child of hell."

And the Rabbi said unto Mattathias the watchman: "Lead me abroad in thy garden, for I would delight my eyes with the sight of God's creation."

And as the Rabbi sat in the vineyard of Jochanah, the wife of Herod's officer, he looked on the green that blossomed from the earth and the fresh blossoming which was in the buds. For it was the time of the uttermost beauty in the land, which is the spring. And God had sent forth his sun, his love, and his graciousness over the earth. And the night dew was still on the branches, and the sun gave forth warmth and took away the coldness of the night. And the birds in the branches awakened and were much busied, and they brought food into the nests which were built in the trees. And the garden was filled with life and creation, and it was as though the trees and birds rejoiced to fulfill the commandment of God, to live and have fullness of life, and the joy of peace was poured out on the land, for God had sent peace.

And when our Rabbi perceived the joy and peace which God poured down from heaven, his heart was filled with love toward the earth, toward men and toward all creatures; and he loved and blessed all that created and built. And he took the spade from the hand of Mattathias the watchman, and he helped him in his work. And his heart was filled with gladness that his father in heaven cared for all his creatures, and he lifted up his voice and taught us in this wise:

"The Lord is my shepherd, I shall not want." And he said further: "Therefore have no care of your lives, what ye shall eat, or of your bodies, wherein ye shall clothe them. For the life is more precious than food and the body more precious than raiment. Behold the swallows and learn of them. They sow not neither do they reap nor gather into barns, and God nourisheth them. And how much more precious are ye than the birds of the air. Who of you can by taking thought add one day unto his life? And if ye cannot create so small a thing, why take ye thought for the rest? Behold the rose, which neither spinneth nor weaveth, and I say unto ye that Solomon in all his glory was not so arrayed. If God so clothe the grass of the field, which is today, and tomorrow is cast into the oven, how shall He not clothe you, oh ye of little faith? Be not so sunk in care what ye shall eat and drink, and be not proud, when ye are clothed and fed, for thus do the heathen. Your father in heaven knoweth your needs."

And there came from the road the messengers of the court. And there was among them one whose body was covered with the skin of a camel, and he was lean and withered from fasting and mortifications, so that we beheld the bones of his body; and his hands were like staves for leanness and his hair was wild and unkempt. And this man was one of the disciples of Jochanan the Baptist, and his name was Zadok. He was a very devout man and the people believed in him. And they that were with him were the messengers of the court of Naim. And they came nigh to us, and turned unto the disciples and not unto the Rabbi, and they said:

"Disciples of Rabbi Yeshua, ye are commanded by the court of justice to appear before it and to testify concerning the deeds and words of your Rabbi, for evil reports have come to the ears of the devout and learned concerning the doctrine and teaching of your Rabbi; and ye are responsible even as he is."

Then the Rabbi said unto us, his disciples:

"Go and appear before the court of justice of Naim and testify concerning all that ye have seen and heard. See, I have placed my cause in your hands."

Then said Simon bar Jonah, who was affrighted by the words of the messengers:

"Rabbi, I am not learned, and the scriptures are not in my mouth. How shall I dispute with the learned and the scribes?"

"Thou too, Simon bar Jonah, shalt go and testify. And that which God, my father in heaven, shall put into thy mouth, that shalt thou say, for I place my cause in thy hands."

And Simon bar Jonah came with us, and only the brothers Zebedee remained with my Rabbi, for he said that they were choleric, and the words of the learned must needs be listened to in calmness.

And the court of the city of Naim was already assembled, and the head of the court and the chief men and the learned and the interpreters, and with them also many of the disciples of Jochanan the Baptist.

And when we, the disciples of Rabbi Yeshua, came before the court, then Simon the Pharisee said unto us:

"Disciples of the Rabbi, ye are called before the court of justice that ye may testify concerning your Rabbi, what is the doctrine which he preacheth, and the deeds which he performeth. For his deeds are not understandable unto us. He remitteth the sins of the wicked. But it is not known to any of us that flesh and blood can forgive the sins of flesh and blood, and only our father in heaven can forgive. As it is written: 'And he shall pray unto the Lord and He shall forgive him.' Perchance it be known unto you, scribes, whether there were such among the past generations of the sages and saints as remitted the sins of other men in their own name, and upon what authority they leaned."

And Jochanan, the eldest of the scribes, who was learned in the scriptures and a master in the tradition, pulled down the eyebrows which guarded his eyes and answered:

"It is not known to us, and it hath not been heard, from all the generations of the past, that one man shall remit the sins of another man, which only our father in heaven can do. And the prophets did no more than call upon the people to repent before the Lord, as it is written: 'Return, O Israel, unto the Lord thy God.' And the Torah giveth reckoning concerning all the sins which a man committeth, whether of set purpose or unwittingly, that he shall bring this and this sacrifice and confess himself before the Lord. But no man hath the right to forgive the sins of another, save they be the sins which were committed against him."

And the head of the court turned unto the disciples of Jochanan the Baptist and asked:

"Was it thus with your Rabbi, that he forgave you your sins when ye went unto him to be baptized, in the wilderness of Judaea?"

"Jochanan the Baptist called us to repent before our father in heaven, and to purify our bodies with fasts and mortifications and to do prayer with our bodies, by baptism, for the kingdom of heaven was at hand."

And Simon the Pharisee lifted up his voice and said:

"And when we inquired of your Rabbi by what authority he remitteth their sins, which none of flesh and blood may do, and was not done even by Moses and the prophets, nor by the oldest of the Hasideans nor yet by Jochanan the Baptist, then he spoke with harsh words to the learned and the scribes who were assembled there, and he left our company and went unto the house of Jochanan the tax collector, into which no Jew may enter, for the house of the wicked is unclean. And he exchanged the table of the learned and the scribes for the table of tax collectors, sinful women and men-of-the-earth, whose hands are unclean, for they know not how to act according to the law; and he showed miracles unto them, he exorcized evil spirits and remitted sins, and he spoke with authority as if the law had been delivered into his hands and he could do therewith as pleased him. The words of your Rabbi are not understandable to us, and we have called you before the court of justice: you, the disciples, are responsible for your Rabbi, as he is for you. And now declare unto us explicitly: Who is he that is your Rabbi? Upon what authority doth he lean for his words? And with what power doth he perform wonders? And thus we may know how to deal with him."

Then rose Zadok, who was the disciple of Jochanan the Baptist, and his voice was thin and weak, for his body was withered with much fasting and mortification, and he said:

"Jochanan the Baptist called us into the wilderness, and he bade us mortify our bodies with hunger and thirst, that our souls might be strengthened, for the Kingdom of God is at hand. And our bodies were sanctified by baptism and became worthy dwelling places for the lodgment of our souls. But who is he that eateth and drinketh with sinners? We hear his words and we behold his deeds, but they are not to be understood. For he goeth not in the footsteps of Jochanan."

And we, the disciples of our Rabbi, looked, each man in the other's face, and we waited that one of us might lift up his voice and testify for our Rabbi. But we were all silent. And when I perceived that there was no man, then I, Judah Ish-Kiriot, the least of his disciples, rose to testify for my Rabbi and spoke thus:

"Most just court, hear the words of the least of his disciples. I am a man of Judah, and all the days of my life I sat in the courts of the Temple and searched into the words of God. The Rabbi Nicodemon was my Rabbi. Joseph of Arimathea and Simon Cyrene are my comrades. And we sat and conversed among ourselves: which is the way of God? And in what paths shall we tread? That which we heard from the Rabbis concerned solely the matter of law; the Torah was cut into commandments of commission and omission, and through this wall we could not see the wholeness which compriseth everything. And there came to us a man of Galilee and reported concerning a Rabbi who had appeared there and preached the doctrine of the venerable Hillel. And we thought evil in our hearts and made this Rabbi to naught, for he came from Galilee, and who hath heard that aught good shall come from Galilee? But there came further to our ears the reports of the signs and wonders which he performed, and of the holy law which he propagateth among the people. And then Nicodemon the Rabbi said: 'It is a matter worth inquiry,' and they sent me to Galilee that I might see with my own eyes and hear with my own ears. And I came to inquire, and I will say now with Saul: 'I came to seek asses and I found a kingdom.' He stood in the synagogue of K'far Nahum, a pale young man of the Jews, and he was draped in his prayer shawl and he preached to the people at the hour of the reading of the Torah: 'There is not anything that can stand up against faith,' and 'Give, and it shall be given unto you,' and 'The measure which ye mete out shall be measured unto you,' and 'Why seest thou the mote in thy brother's eye and seest not the beam in thine own?' and 'Judge not lest ye be judged,' and other sayings of this kind. And I thought at first that the venerable Hillel had from his grave sent a favorite pupil that he might renew his doctrine in the land. But when I searched and inquired diligently I perceived it was otherwise. My heart melteth with fear and my knees tremble and the terror of God is on me because of the deeds which my Rabbi hath performed and the words he hath spoken with his mouth. Most just court, standeth not the house of Jacob abandoned and shamed in the eyes of the gentiles? Edom hath made his nest on the holy hill of Zion. His feet tread insolently in God's house, his yoke hath fallen on our neck and his whip falleth on our back. The word hath been cut off from us, there hath not arisen unto us a prophet and no sign hath appeared. Are we not as worthy as were our parents? Why hath God turned His countenance from us? We hold in our breath and listen intently, whether there already be footsteps, and we look, whether the light showeth upon the hill, and if voices are lifted in the wilderness, according to the promise that the anointed of God will come and justify us of our waiting and breathe upon our suffering and make true the words of our prophets. And I came and saw. What did I see? The words were fulfilled which the prophet foretold: 'The deaf hear and the blind receive their sight.' With the breath of his mouth he commandeth evil spirits, his words are like sharp knives, he gathereth the people as the reaper gathereth the ears, and he garnereth them for God. Who hath brought so many hearts nigh to our father in heaven? Who hath awakened such a trembling of hope among the poor and forlorn? Who hath returned to heaven so many wandering and rejected souls? Who knoweth his ways? Who comprehendeth his purposes? Touch not the plant which God hath planted! Let us with trembling hearts and with prayer upon our lips wait, and let us observe well the light which hath been kindled in Israel for Israel's salvation."

And after me rose Simon the Zealot and began to speak:

"Most just court, I went with the Zealots, and took with them to the hills, for I could not bear to see the feet of Edom on the neck of Jacob. We would not bow the knee to any man of flesh and blood, and no lord would we acknowledge but the Lord of the world. We fell upon armies, thinking God would help us to break the yoke of Edom, but we were deceived in our hopes. I hid me in the caves like a wild beast, I fell upon travelers, I made the roads uncertain, and I believed it would be thus for ever. Our hearts were filled with doubt and on our lips there was the complaint: 'What, then, if our parents have sinned? How long shall Edom triumph over us? Are the gentiles better than we? And do we seek salvation for ourselves alone? Is not the glory of God referred to us? Where is the promise which was given unto our parents? Why waiteth it so long? No help, no call, no sign, as though, God forbid, the words of our prophets had been sown on the wind.' Like a jackal in the desert I lamented in my bitterness, I fell into evil ways and I destroyed men as if I were a wild beast. And I would have fallen into the nethermost pit if God had not helped me and guided my steps to my Rabbi. I encountered him in the port of K'far Nahum, where the fishers keep their boats. He called unto the poor: 'Come unto me, all ye that are heavy-laden,' and I saw how the folk went unto him. They came first to mock and deride, then they were thoughtful and became earnest; then joy entered their faces, and their backs were straightened, and their spirits were strengthened. And I was filled with wonder, and I drew near and asked: 'Rabbi, when will God redeem us from Edom's hand?' And he answered: 'Only they are free who take upon themselves with love the yoke of the kingdom of heaven; only they are redeemed who loose themselves from the bonds of sin; and then freedom is in thy hand and none can take it from thee.' And I was filled with wonder by his words and I did not understand them. But I followed in his steps, and day by day I watched his deeds and hearkened to his words and a light fell on my eyes and I saw that while I had sought freedom I had sold my soul like a Canaanite slave into the hands of Satan. And I went to my Rabbi and said: 'Rabbi, save me!' And my Rabbi took me and bound me as one binds a calf and brought me under the yoke of our father in heaven, and I found the true and eternal freedom which no man of flesh and blood can take away from me, for I am the servant of God."

And after him rose Simon bar Jonah and testified:

"I am a simple man, a fisher of K'far Nahum, not learned in the law, but my heart yearneth toward my father the creator, and without Him I am like a leaf fallen from the tree and like a sheep lost from the fold. My heart longed to be bound unto God, but the ways were twisted and many-branching whereby the learned men would have led me to the creator of the world. Who shall master them? Ye have divided God's law into a thousand parts; who shall gather them up and hold them in his hand, save the learned who are occupied therewith day and night? For us, the unlettered and heavy-laden, God's word is closed with many seals. We know not that which is permitted and that which is not permitted. We wander lost in darkness, we beat our bodies like blind men against the walls without number which ye have put up about our father in heaven. And we hear from you only the warning words, 'Ye unclean hands, come not nigh to touch us.' But our hearts, too, search the thread which leadeth to God, our souls long to be bound to him, to find the way to the throne of his glory after death; and we have worn out our eyes looking for him that will come, that will free our souls and bind us to the eternal glory, that we may have a share in the eternal life and not fall into the pit and into endless night to which you have consigned us. Thirsty and a-hungered we sat on the thresholds of your synagogues and houses of study, and picked up the crumbs of learning which fell from your tables, at which you would not have us sit. Until he came, and stretched forth his hands to us, the blind. In K'far Nahum, in the fishing port, I beheld him from my boat, as he stood among the poor folk, and I heard him as he called: 'Come unto me, all ye that are heavy-laden.' And the people gathered about him, as the chicks gather under the wings of their mother on the day of storm. So he took them under his wing, and he came likewise to me in my boat and he said: 'Simon bar Jonah, come with me and I will make thee a fisher of men,' and since that time I have followed him. And I behold his deeds all day long, and I hear his words. And I know not who he is. But he is the light in our darkness, the word for us that are dumb, the guide for us forlorn and abandoned ones. He showeth us the nearest and simplest way to our father in heaven. He teacheth us how to pray to him, and he showeth us how to have faith in him. And from that day on when he revealed himself unto us, it is as though there is a roof over our heads, we are part of the people of Israel, children of Abraham, Isaac and Jacob. God is our father, from him we came and unto him we return. He keepeth guard over us in this world, and in the world to come no evil shall befall us."

When Simon bar Jonah had made an end of speaking there was a great quietness among the Rabbis and the learned men, until the head of the court lifted up his voice and said:

"Are there others of the disciples of Yeshua who would come before the court and testify concerning their Rabbi?"

Then rose Jochanan the tax collector and would have testified, but they said: "He is not an acceptable witness, for he is a tax collector," and then the court meditated, and one said to the other:

"I see no sin in the Rabbi."

And the other said:

"According to the testimony of his disciples he bringeth the hearts of men near to God, therefore may his hands be blessed."

And Zadok, who was the disciple of Jochanan the Baptist, said:

"Who knoweth? It may be that God hath had compassion on His people; let us wait with this matter and see. If it is of God, then none of flesh and blood can destroy it, but if it be not of God, it shall fail of itself. As it is written: 'If God buildeth not the house, the builders labor in vain.' "

And thus the matter ended.

VI

It is written: "Cast thy bread upon the waters and it shall return to thee after many days." Therefore we forsook our homes, and left our possessions behind us, and we went with our Rabbi in an unknown land, as the text sayeth: "With the kindness of thy youth thou wentest after me in the wilderness, in a land that was not sown." And we believed in God and our hope was not deceived.

And our Rabbi said unto us:

"Let us arise and go to Nazareth, the city of my home, for we are near unto the place."

And we took our sacks with bread, our provision for the way, and one or two garments in honor of our Rabbi. And before our Rabbi left the city he blessed the watchman of the vineyard, saying:

"Woe unto those who declare unclean that which God hath purified. Mattathias, thou are our brother in Israel, be comforted. The law is not strong in thy hand, but the law of God is in thy heart and in thy meekness of spirit."

And he left the place and went forth before us, and we his disciples followed after him. And the peace of God was poured out on the fields wherethrough we passed.

And as our Rabbi perceived that the peace of God lay on the world, he became joyous, and the glory rested upon him, for the glory cometh to rest only where there is joy. And he told us many parables, and many good words, which tied our hearts to our father in heaven. Many of them the disciples learned by heart that they might remember them for future generations, that they too might hear and learn the moral thereof, but many of them were lost.

And in the warmth of the day we came to the edge of the valley, whence the road ascendeth by the hills. And when we came upon the hill we encountered shepherds which pastured their flocks there. And the shepherds knew our Rabbi, for he had often come out to them what time he still dwelt in the city of Nazareth. And the sheep surrounded him and licked his feet with their tongues, for they knew him again.

And there came up in the sky a little black cloud no bigger than a man's hand; and the hand opened and enclosed the heavens and the heavens were laden with clouds which concealed the light of the sun. And shadows passed over the face of the earth and spread darkness around. And one of the disciples said:

"Let us hide ourselves in a cave or take shelter under yonder stone, for a storm of rain is about to pass."

For it was the time of the latter rain, and the latter rain cometh always with wind and storm. But our Rabbi said:

"Where wilt thou hide thyself from God? In the heart of the stone He will find thee, and in the cave He will seek thee out, and the most secure place is under God's heavens. Consider the sheep and learn from them; they seek not a cave nor do they take shelter under a stone, but they deliver their bodies to the compassion of God. Behold how in the time of storm they do not hide one from the other, but they come together, and they put their heads near each other; so deliver your bodies to the compassion of God and put your trust in your shepherd that he will come at the right time and save you."

And as he spoke the storm-wind came and seized upon the four pillars of the earth, and there went past a great noise and shouting, with thunder and lightning; and the wind combed with combs all the grasses and growths of the fields, and bent their crowns to the earth, once this way and once that way; and the wind came among the branches and thought to break them. And then the storm was released in a downpour and we sought shelter each one where he could, and the shepherds did likewise. And the flock of sheep made a circle about our Rabbi and pressed to his feet, as if they sought shelter in him, for their shepherd had forsaken them. And as they stood thus on the slope of the hill, the storm-wind returned and it seized on one or two of the lambs that were on the edge of the fold, and the lambs were lifted up in the teeth of the wind as it were in the teeth of a wild beast, and they clung with their feet to clefts of the rock. But the teeth of the storm-wind were stronger than the feet of the lambs, and the wind lifted them in anger and flung them down the slope of the hill into the abyss. And it was so, that when the lambs were carried toward the abyss they called to the shepherd with the cry of animals. But the shepherd heard not the cry of the falling lambs, for he had hidden himself from the anger of the wind in a stone cave.

And when the rain ceased we sought our Rabbi and we could not find him. For each one of us had found himself a hiding place from the storm-wind under the shelter of a stone or in a cave, and we had not seen that our Rabbi was gone down into the abyss after the fallen lambs. And we sought him here and there and found him not. We called, "Rabbi, Rabbi!" and he did not answer us. Then when a while had passed we saw our Rabbi coming up out of the abyss, and his garment was steeped in rain, and the water ran over his feet, and his hair and his face were wet. His feet were bare, and they bled from having been dashed against the stones, and he carried a lamb on his shoulders and he returned it to the flock. And when we beheld him, how he came up from the abyss with the lamb on his shoulders, we became ashamed before him, and we remembered our forefathers who had also been shepherds, all of them, and I learned by meditation on my Rabbi now, what the sages had learned of Moses. "And Moses was a shepherd," which meaneth that God first taught and tested Moses through sheep, so our sages say. When Moses was pasturing the flock of Jethro in the wilderness, one sheep fled from the flock, and Moses followed after it, and the sheep fled until it came to a place of shelter. And when it came into this place of shelter God sent a spring of water, and the sheep stood there and drank thereof. And when Moses came near to the sheep he thought in his heart: "I knew that thou fleddest from the flock because thou wert thirsty. But now, belike, thou art tired too," and he took the sheep on his shoulders and went back with it. And God said unto Moses, "Thou hast compassion enough to feed the sheep, I swear unto thee thou shalt feed the sheep of Israel."

And now God sent the sun forth from his hiding place, and the clouds fled before the sun. And we sat down on the stones of the hill and we took off our clothes to dry them. And as our Rabbi sat upon the stone drying his garment the sheep came to him and lay down at his feet.

And we were a Sabbath walk distant from the city of Cana where our Rabbi had shown his first miracle, having changed the water into wine at the wedding of some poor folk. Notwithstanding, we went not into the city, for it was the fifth day and our Rabbi had said that he would come to his city, which is Nazareth, to celebrate the Sabbath there, and to fulfill the commandment to do honor unto his mother; and his father was then not alive.

And we rose and we went along the road, and as the sun was setting we came to the gate of the city. Now this city resteth, even as it were a child on the back of a camel, between two hills, and the name of it is Nazareth, and it lies on the road which goeth from the coast of the Great Sea to Damascus. And the inhabitants of the city sustain themselves with the labor of the field and with carpentry, for the roads go through the city to Damascus. And our Rabbi too was a carpenter, and the son of a carpenter, but there are no sages and learned men in Nazareth, save for the head of the synagogues and the chief men thereof, who are likewise the judges of the court.

Now when we came nigh to the gate of the city, the sun had set, and it was the time of the evening prayer. Therefore we stood in the middle of the field, and in the silence of evening, when the stars had begun to shine over the hills and valleys, and our Rabbi said the "Hear, O Israel," and he said unto us:

"It is not good that we should all enter together into the city, for the place is small and its inhabitants are of the simple people, and when they will see a Rabbi with his disciples they will be affrighted. Therefore let each one go his own way and find his night's lodgment and when it is morning let us meet in the house of my mother, that we may there sanctify the Sabbath and fulfill the commandment of honor to mothers."

And the Rabbi took with him only Simon bar Jonah and the sons of Zebedee, Jacob and Jochanan, who were his most beloved disciples, and Miriam, the woman that had followed after us. For the other souls which he had made in Naim, to wit Jochanan and Susannah, had remained there, that they might go to K'far Nahum, to the mother-in-law of Simon, where the Rabbi abode.

And when I saw that the Rabbi was leaving us, I strengthened myself and stood before him and entreated:

"It is written: 'Thine eyes shall behold the king in his beauty'; and who is a greater king than the Rabbi? Now let us come with thee to the house of thy mother, that we may see how thou fulfillest the commandment of honor to thy mother, and learn therefrom."

And the Rabbi consented thereto.

And the house of my Rabbi's mother stood by the way as thou comest out of the city, where the wayfarers pass and the wagons travel, so that she might be the first to fulfill the commandment of receiving travelers, when a stranger came into the city. For my Rabbi's mother was a God-fearing woman.

And when we had passed through the narrow streets we came into the open field beyond, and near the foot of the hill we beheld a light shining through the opening of a door, and the Rabbi said unto us:

"That is the house of my mother."

And the Rabbi took two of us, Simon bar Jonah and myself, who am the least of his disciples, and sent us forward to his mother's house to announce the tidings of his coming. For it is not well to come with suddenness and surprise, but to send forward news thereof. And we came into the house and his mother sat with her sons and daughters at the table and they ate the honest bread of the laborer. For it was the hour when the worker eateth his evening meal. And we bowed ourselves and said:

"Peace be unto ye."

And the people looked upon us in astonishment and they asked whence we came. And we said:

"We are sent unto you by your son and brother. He sendeth through us the tidings of his coming, and he standeth without at your door."

And at first they sat thus at their bread and knew not what to answer for surprise. Then one of his brothers-in-law spoke and said: "Wherefore is he come? To blacken our faces again in the eyes of the people of the city?"

But the mother rose and stretched forth her arms and said:

"Where is my beloved child, that I may embrace him?"

And she took up the oil lamp from the table and she stood on the threshold of the door and she called into the night:

"*Tinoki, tinoki,* my little one, my little one!"

And the Rabbi answered, "*Imi, Imi,*" which signifieth, "My mother, my mother," and he came before her, and he bowed himself and said: "Mother, crown of my head, peace be unto thee."

And she answered him:

"My first-born, peace be to thy homecoming."

And he embraced his mother and kissed her, and he went into the house and we, his disciples, with him.

And the house of his mother was not large, and there was not much space therein, for the work bench of carpentry stood there. (Now when the Rabbi had forsaken the house that he might do the work of God, his brother Jacob had taken over the carpentry, that he might give sustenance to the household, as it is written: "Great is work, it honoreth him that is occupied therein.")

And Jacob rose before his brother and bowed himself and said:

"Greeting to thee in thy homecoming, my Rabbi and my oldest brother. Is peace with thee?"

And our Rabbi answered:

"Peace is with me; my father in heaven was with me all the time. Is peace with you, my brothers?"

And Jacob and the others answered: "Peace."

But the brothers-in-law, the husbands of the sisters, rose and went from the house, for they were angered against him.

And the mother said to her sons:

"Go, bring water and wash the hands and feet of the guests. And I will go prepare the best that is in the house, a meal for thee and for the guests that came with thee. For ye must surely be hungry and thirsty from the way."

And my Rabbi answered:

"I pray thee, do not thou go, but remain with me that my eyes may sate themselves with thy countenance, for it is long that I have not seen it. Let my brothers prepare the evening meal, and they that came with me shall help them, for they are my disciples and it is good that disciples shall serve their Rabbi, and they are skilled therein."

And his mother said:

"Let all the oil lamps be lit, for today it is Sabbath with me. I have set aside and kept, in the store, a gourd flask with some good oil, against the time of my son's return. Go now, bring the cruse of honey, and go into the stall and milk the sheep, and let there be prepared a meal of beans and green stuff, and let cakes be placed on the table, for it is a great festival with me now, my son hath come home."

And we went to carry out the commandments of the mother, and we made a fire in the oven which was in the yard, and we prepared the cooking of the meal. And the brothers rose and left their mother alone with her eldest son. For many days had passed since he had left his mother's house, and they longed to be alone and to converse with each other.

But I stood by the door and looked in through an opening, and I saw in the light of the lamp the face of the mother shining with joy, but her eyes were sad and wet with tears and she looked on her son sorrowingly. The skin of her face was wrinkled like a leaf in autumn with the lines of care, and her countenance was like unto the book of Job, save that her eyes were like the Song of Songs, and her lips trembled, and the veins that were on her thin neck; and she said:

"My son, I was with thee in every need."

And he held her right hand, which had known much labor, and he said:

"My mother, I knew it."

And she said further:

"My heart is for ever restless for thee. There came people from K'far Nahum and from other places, and they told me wondrous things concerning thee. My heart trembled between hope and fear: thou wert oft in great need, my son."

And he answered:

"God my father was with me."

Then his mother said:

"Dangerous is the path which thou treadest, my son. My heart is heavy in me. Ofttimes thou disappearest from me and I see not whither thou goest. God's compassion be with thee, and may He ever be with thy footsteps."

And my Rabbi held his mother's right hand in his and said:

"Be calm, my mother, all is for the sake of God and for the sake of His glory."

"My child, I know that the grace of God resteth upon thee, and guardeth thee night and day, and it is my strength and comfort."

Then said my Rabbi:

"But tell me how is it with thee, my mother? How is it with thee in thy house?"

"I am an old woman. Thy father is dead, thy brother Jacob hath taken over the labor and he nourisheth the house meagerly and in poverty. But the children are young and they need over them a brother's hand to guide their footsteps in righteousness, and thou art the eldest and shouldst be their guide in the way of Jewishness, and thou hast forsaken the house, my son."

And my Rabbi answered her and said:

"My earthly father is dead, but my heavenly father liveth, and he hath called me to make good his work and to lead his children in the ways of righteousness. Jacob can be in my stead in the house, for he is a devout Jew."

"My son, when I hear thee speak thus, my heart melteth with fear. Who art thou, then, my child? I myself know thee not."

And my Rabbi held his mother's right hand in his and said:

"Be calm, my mother. And let thy heart be filled with joy, as a grape is filled with wine in the autumn. The peoples of the earth shall bless themselves in thee, thou shalt be likened to Rachel, and to Sarah and Rebeccah, the holy mothers, and thy portion shall be with them. . . ."

And the mother wiped the tears from her eyes with the hem of her robe and she said:

"May God so comfort thee as thou hast comforted thy mother. Now let me go, my child, for they need my help in the room and by the fire. Behold the vessels, wash thy hands and feet and let those that are with thee wash their hands and feet and seat them at the table."

And when she said these words she left her son and went into the room where the meal was being prepared. But on the way, in the joyousness of her spirit, she loosed a sandal from her foot. And when my Rabbi perceived this, he hastened to her and bent himself to the earth and spread his hands upon the floor and said:

"Mother, I pray thee, tread upon my hands that thy naked feet may not touch the floor."

But his mother said unto him:

"My child, I would not have thee so lower thine honor before me."

And my Rabbi answered her:

"My mother, let me fulfill the commandment of honor to mothers even as Damiah ben Nathainah of Askelon did for his mother."

And he meant thereby a certain Kushite of the city of Askelon, whose name was Damiah ben Nathainah, who was mighty in the fulfillment of the commandment of honor to mothers, and the sages of the city could not emulate him in his degree and they were envious of him. And his honoring of his mother was of this degree: it chanced that he sat once at a feast with the great men of his city and his mother appeared before them and she spoke to him and reproached him vilely, and she took off her sandal and smote him therewith, for she was sick in her mind. But her son would not put his mother to shame before the chief men of the city, and he received her blows and said: "My mother, is my punishment sufficient?" And when the sandal wherewith she was beating her son fell out of her hand, then Damiah ben Nathainah bent him down and lifted up the sandal and gave it to her, that she might not have need of bending to the earth.

And when I beheld the honor which my Rabbi paid unto his mother, then I was filled with rejoicing in his fulfillment of the commandment, and in that he had surpassed the virtue of the Kushite Damiah ben Nathainah of Askelon.

VII

We had washed our hands and we sat about the table. And in the house of my Rabbi's mother the table, which is like unto the altar of God, was tended with great cleanness and set according to all the commandments. And they of the house sat about the table in the order of their years; the mother at the head of the table, and her eldest son by her and the brothers according to their years. And we too, the guests, were dealt with honorably, and were seated by the mother on the other side from her eldest son. And the Rabbi blessed the bread and broke it and dipped the piece in salt. And we all did likewise and dipped our bread in salt, as the commandment biddeth: the eldest first and the others in the order of their years. And thus it was with the dish; the eldest first dipped his hand in the dish that stood upon the table, and the others after him in the order of their years. And after we had eaten, and washed our hands with water, we blessed the Lord who had sated us so that we still had food left.

And then the mother prepared for the Rabbi a bed in the booth that was on the roof, wherein he abode what time he was in the home. And the Rabbi lifted up the night lamp, and said Peace unto his mother and his brothers and ourselves, his disciples, and he went up to the booth on the roof, for he was weary with the wandering and work of the day. And we were left in the room with the mother and the brothers.

And when we were alone with the mother and brothers, then we two, Simon bar Jonah and myself, drew near to the mother and bowed before her, and said:

"Thou blessed of women, blessed be the womb which hath brought forth the light of Israel. Our mother, too, art thou, for the mother of the Rabbi is the mother of his disciples. As it is written: 'He that teacheth the Torah unto one, is as if he had begotten him.' Now tell us, we pray thee, of the life and acts of thy son until this day, that we may know who our Rabbi is."

And the mother sat upon the threshold of the house and by the light of the stars she recounted unto us:

"What shall I tell you and what shall I recount, disciples of my son? Blessed be the Lord that I have been deemed worthy of him. We come of poor people, and our dwelling is with the common folk, and our being springeth from the workers. And it was thus when I was big with my son, that joy filled my breasts, and I knew that the Lord had sent something great unto me, and I prayed to our father in heaven and I said: 'When it shall be Thy will that Thy maidservant bringeth forth a son, I shall make him Thine, as Hannah made her son Samuel.' And when my time came near, then my husband took me, his wife, and the small burden of his household, and took us unto Bethlehem in Ephrath, which is in Judah, for we came thence. And when there was the census in the land, each of us was commanded to appear in his place. And the city of Bethlehem was overfull with people, for all those that were of the city had been commanded to appear there. And there was none that could admit us into a house, and we lodged with others of the poor in the yard of an inn, and my husband fared forth and found work with a carpenter that he might earn our daily bread. And when it was time for me to be brought upon the midwife's stool, then my husband spoke with the shepherds which kept their flocks outside the city, that they might give me leave to bear the child in the stable where they kept their young sheep. For it was winter in the land, and it was exceeding cold, and we were in the street and there was no roof over our heads. And the shepherd folk were filled with compassion, and they were men of kindness and God-fearing. And they made a corner for me in the stable in the midst of the sheep, and they spread out hay and straw to keep me warm. Now may ye know in what spirit I poured forth my sad heart before the Lord, saying: 'Look thou upon my shame, that I bring forth my first-born amid the sheep, like a beast.' And my husband sat by me and comforted me, saying: 'Be not downcast, wife, for in a stable shall be born he that is to help Israel. And was not our king and father, David, a shepherd of this city, and did not God take him from among the sheep to be a king in Israel? Who knoweth, my wife, but that our son shall likewise be a king—for he is of the seed of David.' And other words of comfort like these my good husband spoke to me. And when it was time for me to go on the midwife's stool, there was none near to help me save my husband. But God looked upon my need and came to my help to lift up my spirit, and He lit the moon and stars above me, and they looked in through the open roof and it was as though they comforted me. And there was stillness about me, and my heart trembled, and fear came upon me. For I am but a sinful woman, and unlearned in the law of God, but it seemed to me that the heavens had covered themselves with glory, and peace and goodwill descended to all men with the coming forth of the child. And I called to my husband and said: 'I know not how it is with me, but meseemeth that I see a great light, and singing reacheth my ears, and sweet odors like those of Eden surround me.' And my husband answered: 'It is because thy heart was heavy, and God looked upon our shame and comforted thee, for thou hast borne a son.' And I asked him: 'But whence cometh this light, for it seemeth to me that the moon and stars have entered the stable to give me greeting.' And he, helping me, said: 'It is a good sign, my wife, that thou seest much light for it signifieth that a light hath been born in Israel.' And he laid my new-born in my hands and he covered me with a mantle of hair. And the young sheep and the cattle pressed about my resting place and they licked me with their tongues, and they crouched by us as to keep us warm. For it was cold in the stable. And my husband said: 'See, my wife, even the cattle come to rejoice with thee.' And he comforted me, saying: 'Our forefathers too were shepherds, and God called Moses from the midst of pasturing his sheep that he might lead Israel out of Egypt. Therefore my wife be not fallen in spirit that thy son was born among sheep.' Thus my husband spoke to me at that time.

"And the good shepherd folk, likewise, came from their flocks in the fields, and they greeted me and comforted me, and they brought a cruse of milk and bread and put them before me. And they said: 'Peace unto thee, mother in Israel, God meaneth well with thee, for it is a night of great brightness, such as we have not seen before. The stars are big and the moon in the fullness of light is above, and the peaks of snow look down from the hills. It must be that a light hath ascended in Israel.'

"And I said to them:

" 'Thanks be unto ye, good shepherds, for your words.'

"And they covered my feet with sheepskins, for it was cold, and the hour of my need became the hour of my happiness.

"And we abode there with the shepherd folk until the time came that I should bring my son into the covenant of Abraham, and we called his name in Israel Yeshua, which signifieth a help unto Israel. And my husband took me, and his first-born son, and all that he had, and we went up to Jerusalem, the holy city, on our way home; for the time had come for me to bring my sacrifice of purification, and to put my son before the Priest, that he might give redemption and release to my first-born.

"And I brought the offering and sacrifice of the poor upon the altar, two doves, and my husband took my son in one hand, and in the other five silver shekels of the weight of Zidon, and he stood before the Priest, and the Priest asked him: 'What wouldst thou rather render unto the Lord, thy son, or the five shekels of silver to redeem thy first-born, who belongeth to God as Moses taught us?' And when my husband gave the five shekels of silver to the Priest, the Priest took them; but there stood near by a devout man, and his name was Simon, and it was known in all Jerusalem that he was a just man and the spirit of God rested upon him. And he took my son out of the arms of his father and lifted him up on high, and said: 'It may be that this is the Messiah. I thank thee, O Lord, that I have seen the helper of Israel.' And it came about later, when I told this to the mothers that were assembled in the court of the women, having come likewise for the redeeming of their first-born, that they said: 'He hath done this with our first-born likewise. For this man waiteth for the redeemer of Israel, and he hath prayed God that he shall not see death before he hath seen the Messiah of the Jews. And he waiteth the whole day by the Priest, and every first-born son that is brought to be redeemed, he lifteth up in his hands and saith: "Perchance this is the Messiah." For it may be the portion of any Jewish mother to bring forth the Messiah, the redeemer of Israel.'

"And my husband brought me and his son and his household to our home.

"And my child grew in God, and when he had already begun to stammer I taught him to say the 'Hear, O Israel,' so that what had been written might be fulfilled: 'Out of the mouths of babes and sucklings cometh thy praise, O Lord.' And when he was still at my breast I put before his eyes the holy writ, so that what had been written might be fulfilled: 'With the milk at the breast. . . .' And the child grew in God's grace, and the mothers of the city blessed themselves in him, for he was beauteous to behold, and God rested upon him, and he found favor in the eyes of God and men.

"And when my son was six years old his father wrapped him round in a prayer shawl and carried him to the synagogue, that he might there learn the Torah together with the other children of the city. And the child came home each day with his text. And it was thus, that when we sat down to eat each day, the father said: 'Tell me thy text, my son, which thou didst learn in the synagogue this day.' And he said his text: 'The fear of God is the beginning of wisdom.' And his father taught him in the evenings, that he might fulfill what is written: 'And ye shall teach this to your children.' And he could read in holy writ and knew many texts and verses by rote. And it was always thus, that when one encountered him in the street, he would say to him, 'Boy, tell me thy text,' and he would answer with the text which he had learned that day.

"There was once a drought in the land, and the grain in the fields withered with dryness, and man and beast panted for water, for the wells had dried up. The elders of the city went to seek out a sage who dwelt in the fields, and the sage was famed for his devoutness, and they said that his word had much weight with God. And on a certain evening when the sage returned to his house from his labors in the field, the elders of the city followed him and entreated: 'Pray for rain, for our grain withereth and when the winter cometh there will be nothing to gather into our barns; likewise our beasts faint in the fields for thirst.' But the sage answereth them, saying: 'For your sins this punishment hath come upon you, for ye have left the path of righteousness.' And he would not pray for them, lest they should not repent. Then my boy drew near, having just returned from the synagogue, and he thought in his heart—for thus he told me later—: 'Is it not written: "When need is nigh I will cry unto the Lord"? And is it not written further: "As a father hath pity on his children, so God hath pity on those that fear him"? Now if he will not pray, then I will do so.' And he stationed himself and prayed to God, and God heard the prayer of the boy, and the heavens were covered with clouds, and the rain came. And when my son saw that the Lord had hearkened to his prayer, he was greatly afraid of the thing and he came home and told me of it. And I approached him, saying: 'Wherefore dost thou take such foolishness into thy mind? God hath done this for the sake of the poor and not for the sake of thy prayer.' But I kept the matter in my heart.

"And it came to pass that when my eldest son was twelve years old, they said to me that it was time that he went up with us during the festivals to Jerusalem, that his eyes might behold the glory of Israel, which is the Temple of the Lord, as it is written in holy writ. And we took a sheep from our poor flock and we placed upon it a wreath of olive leaves, and we went with our countrymen for the Passover to Jerusalem. And on the road we made one company with countrymen of other cities, and we went singing with them through the valleys in the time of the spring. And we said words of praise from the Psalms, and other devout songs, and my husband and I rejoiced that the boy was with us, and that our eyes would soon behold the sanctuary. And we came to the city of Jerusalem through the hills that are about it and our eyes looked on the glory of Israel. And the Temple glittereth like the sun above the Mount of the Temple, and the boy rejoiced exceedingly, and it was as if he had received wings and would fly thither. And he knew every corner and alley of the courts of the Temple, as if he had been one of the blossoms of the Priesthood and the Temple had been his home. And he knew all the retreats where the sages sit and judge the people, and where the Priests withdraw that they may rest, and where the stores of oil are kept and the robes of the Priesthood, and all the side paths and the arches and the attics under the roofs. And he lingered likewise between the pillars under the Temple, where many pilgrims are gathered at the time of the festivals. And he came to every company from every part of the land, and sat with every family, to listen to that which the people said. And his ear was open unto every cry of pain, and every sigh, and his heart received every woe which the people suffered in Jerusalem. And it was then a hard time in Israel. For the hand of Rome was on Israel and the people murmured against the new High Priest who had been appointed by Rome, for that he helped Rome to make heavier the weight of taxes upon Israel. And there was talk about that time concerning the days of the Messiah, that the footsteps of the deliverer had been heard, for the waters had come up unto the soul of the people. And the people could no longer carry the yoke which Rome and the High Priest had placed upon them, and a great bitterness went from mouth to mouth. And there was a great crowd before the Beautiful Gate. And the Roman soldiers that were between the pillars in the Court of the Gentiles, threw themselves upon the people, saying that they were rebelling against the High Priest, who was a friend of Rome. And the Romans drew their swords and pursued the people across the bridge into the city. And many died that day by the sword, and many more were killed in the press, also many fell from the bridge into the valley. And my heart was as water for fear, and my little son ran in the multitude, and who knew what might happen with him. And in my heart I prayed: 'Into Thy hands I give him, and be Thou his guard.' But soon my son came to the family place which was in the cellars, and we were assembled there with all those that had come from Nazareth, and I looked on my son and he was as another in my eyes, for his face was pale and his eyes were as flames. And I remember even now the words that were on his lips: 'O Lord, strangers have come up into Thy sanctuary!' And he said this again and again. And I asked of him, 'My son, what ails thee?' And he answered: 'Wherefore tarrieth the Messiah and cometh not?' And I said: 'Be at peace, my child, he cometh and his footsteps are heard, for our tribulations are counted and our tears are gathered up, and soon the count will be completed.' And he asked: 'And when shall we be deemed worthy?' 'Perhaps he is here with us now and waiteth till we be worthy, and until we return to God with all our hearts, so that we may be delivered.' 'And where is he, where is the redeemer, mother?' 'Perhaps thou art he, my child. Who knoweth? For the deliverance may come from every Jew.'

"And both of us were afraid of the words which had issued from my mouth.

"And when the festival was ended and we turned homeward, then my son was lost to us on the way. And I thought that he was with other people of our city, as was his way, to mingle with all people. And thus we went a while. And in the evening I sought him among friends and found him not. And we left the company and returned to Jerusalem to seek our lost son. And we found him at last in the hall of the polished stones, where the learned and the scholars were assembled. And he sat in the midst of them and was attentive to their learned talk. And he sat at the feet of an old man and asked questions of him, and the old man answered him, as was the custom, that is, to reply to every child that asketh questions concerning the text. And the old man rejoiced exceedingly with the wisdom of my son and he said: 'May such as thou multiply in Israel!' And when I saw my son at the feet of the learned, I called to him and said: 'What is this that thou has done unto us? Thou hast made heavy the hearts of thy father and mother for thy sake.' And he answered: 'Mother, it were best that thou leave me here in the house of God. For didst thou not dedicate me unto the Lord from my birth, as thou hast told me, and sanctify me unto the Torah?'

"And when we had returned home, he longed always for Jerusalem, to learn there the word of God at the feet of the wise men. But we being of the common people, my husband, peace be upon him, said that the Torah is good only if thou hast a trade in thy hand, so that thou makest not of the Torah, as certain of the learned do, a spade to dig with. And he that teacheth not his son a trade teacheth him, as the proverb sayeth, to be a thief. And when my son was thirteen years old, and his father taught him the commandment of the putting on of phylacteries, then he led him also to the carpenter's bench to teach him the craft of his forefathers, as the custom is, father to son. Now God had blessed my womb and I had borne my husband four sons and daughters, and the family was large, and the earning of bread for such a family is, for the poor man, as great a task as the splitting of the Red Sea; and we all worked during the day, and, as the custom was, we said at our work verses from the Psalms. And in the evening my husband taught my son whatever he had in the way of learning. By the light of the stars he passed on to him the texts which he knew by rote. And there is also in the possession of the family a scroll, which is the most precious possession which my husband inherited from his forefathers, and it hath passed from generation to generation through the eldest son. And it was guarded with utmost care of cleanliness in our house, and it was draped in cloth that our hands might not defile it; and on the festivals, and perchance on nights of the moon, they unrolled the scroll and studied therein, as it is written: 'And thou shalt meditate thereon by night and by day.' And my husband could transmit to my son only the written law, for of the oral law he knew but little, that is, of the tradition; only that which he had brought with him from Jerusalem, only here and there a law and an interpretation which he had heard from the lips of the sages in the Temple; these were handed down to us as from the venerable Hillel and other men of old. And at times there cometh also into Nazareth a Rabbi, from the city of Naim, to be here on the Sabbath for the reading of the law in the synagogue. But my son longed to know much, as it is written: 'As a hart panteth for the streams, so my soul longeth for God.' And he sat in the synagogue and learned what he could from the chief men and the cantor and the head of the congregation. And when there came a Rabbi into the town, so he sat at his feet and took into himself the word of God. Likewise he would assemble the little ones that learned in the school and lead them to the synagogue and teach them to say, in the right places, the words 'Amen' and 'Let the Name be exalted'; and the head of the congregation praised him. And the boy was much beloved, for he went in the ways of the Lord and was devout in his behavior. And when he prayed it was as if angels stood by him to carry his words to the assembly that is in heaven. Nor do I say this because he is my child, but the people of the city testify thereunto. And he was acquainted in the holy writ like one of the wise men. And when they called him on the Sabbath day to the reading of the Torah in the synagogue, he stood and preached, and the people opened mouth and ear, for they had never heard the like from a youth. And they asked each other in astonishment: 'Whence cometh this wisdom to him? Is he not the son of Joseph the carpenter? Where hath he learned this?' But the Lord had placed his hand upon him and he found favor in the eyes of the people; and when he prayed it was visible unto all that his prayer was accepted. And it chanced once that he saw a sick old man seated on the threshold of the synagogue, and he could not go further for his legs were palsied. And my son looked at him with compassion. And when the old man saw that my son looked on him with compassion, he lifted up his voice and said: 'Why lookest thou on me with such eyes as if thou wouldst heal me?' And my son answered: 'If thou believest that I can heal thee, then I will indeed heal thee.' And the man said: 'I behold in thine eyes the great power of compassion. I believe with perfect faith that if the Lord so willeth I shall be healed through thee.' Then my son answered: 'Thou hast said! In the name of the Lord I command thee to rise upon thy feet, thou art healed.' And the man rose upon his feet. And know ye that the man had been palsied many years. And the thing was told in the city and it was said concerning my son that he possessed a secret power which the Lord had given him. And folk began to seek out my son with their sicknesses and cares. And when we, his parents, saw how far this thing had gone, we were afraid, and we spoke thus among ourselves: 'Who knoweth what God intendeth with our son, for the grace of the Lord resteth upon him?'

"And he came to us and asked: 'Is it indeed the truth that we are of the seed of David?' for there was a tradition in our family that we came of the house of David, because we were people of Bethlehem. And it is written in the book of the genealogies of the families of Israel. But when Herod the king began to persecute all those that came of the house of David, so the book disappeared; but the tradition remained in the family of my husband and was guarded by it. And when my husband heard these words from my son, he rose and said in a loud voice: 'Wouldst thou be like Joseph the dreamer and lift thyself above thy brothers? God loveth only those of an humble spirit.' But we kept this thing in our hearts.

"And about that time there came a great change in the manner of my son. We knew him no more. His deeds were not as of yesterday and the day before. For he went out of our sight for many days, and he stayed in the woods, and rested there in the nights, and returned in the morning, with the dew of the night on his head. Else he would go into the fields and help the laborers on the land, and would teach them holy writ, repeating verses of the Psalms and comforting them in their need. And he was seen only in the company of the oppressed and the rejected, the abandoned of God and men, in the fields or by the door of the synagogue. And he sought out and visited the sick, and wherever he was, there was want and pain. And he would help all bear their burden of sadness. And I heard him often uttering bitter words against the rich and the learned who oppress the poor and take not up the cause of the fatherless. And the heart of my child was tormented by the evils which the rich and learned commit against the poor and the common folk. Now our city lieth in the open fields, and most of the inhabitants thereof are workers on the land, unlearned in writ, and among them are likewise such as doubt of their Jewishness, and the rich have made a band against them to oppress them. And they put upon the poor many taxes and tributes for the Caesar, and for the Temple, and for the Priests and Levites; and the officers and the tax collectors are strong-handed. And it is thus in our sinfulness, that they take away from us our possessions, our asses and our fields, which is against the word of the holy writ, which saith thou shalt not leave the poor man without his cloak in the night. And they likewise cast the poor man into prison, or he is made into a slave and worketh for another in the field that was his own. Many cruel things are done against the people of the country, and the hatred waxeth between the learned men and the men-of-the-earth. And my son seeth these injustices and crieth for the justice of God. 'Woe to the generation which hath such leaders,' he crieth, 'for they are like shepherds that shear the sheep in the time of rain and winter, that they may warm themselves in the skin of the poor. The wrath of God shall be poured forth upon them.'

"And it came about then that he was no longer at peace with the head of the congregation and the chief men of the synagogue, for that they let such things be in the city, and they sunder themselves from the simple folk and hold themselves great in their learning and piety. For in our sinfulness our learned ones have made a great division between themselves and the common man, and they call him unclean and despise him. And my son could not bear the injustices which were committed against the common man, and there was much quarreling between him and the men of the city, and he spoke harsh words against them. And it chanced once that when he was called up in the synagogue to the reading of the Torah, he took up the Book of Isaiah and read therefrom: 'They join border unto border.' And he preached against the rich men of the city and said: 'Woe unto you, ye rich, that ye oppress the poor man,' and other bitter words. And there was murmuring in the synagogue and they asked: 'Who is this that cometh to teach us and reproach us? Is it not he that was the son of Joseph the carpenter?' And they took him and led him out of the city and smote him, and they would have thrown him from a rock into the abyss, as they did once with the prophet Zachariah. But God saved him from their hands and they let him go.

"And the spirit of my son was heavier from day to day, and he sought the justice of God among men and found it not. And I perceived that with each injustice he loseth the blood of his heart, as the thorn pierceth the heart of the rose. And the time was hard for him, and I feared, God forbid, that it would be too much for him. For he sought perpetually, and we knew not what he sought. Till there came a man unto the city, one of the Nazarites, such as dwell in the wilderness and seek the word of God. And he stood up in the market place and called unto the people to repent, for the kingdom of God was at hand and the footsteps of the Messiah had been heard. And my son clove to the Nazarite; and he came to us for leave that he might go with the Nazarite into the wilderness there to search out the word of God. And he said: 'I have taken a vow upon myself to go into the wilderness and inquire into the ways of God, for my soul longeth to know God.' And my husband said: 'If his soul longeth to know God let him go in the name of God, and dwell with the Nazarites in the wilderness, for he hath taken a vow and he beareth responsibility for himself.' And I parted from my son with a heavy heart. For though the Lord had blessed me with sons and daughters, he was my first-born, and he was unto me and my husband as Joseph was unto Jacob, the most beloved. And I gave him bread and a dried cheese and a shirt and I sent him into the wilderness in the name of God.

"And there went by days and years and I heard not how he fared. But my heart ceased not from longing for him, for my soul was bound unto his. And when a time had passed, the Lord took away from me the crown of my head, my husband, and he slept with his fathers, and I was left a widow and my children orphans, and I knew not any more what might be; for I had not a redeemer in the city, and my children were young and of tender years, and there was none to nourish them or to speak comfortingly unto us. And it came to pass that on a certain day there came a man to my door, and his hair was long, and he was barefoot, and he was clad in a leopard skin. He was lean of body and countenance, and burned by the sun of the wilderness. He came to my door, and when I opened I beheld my son before me, and he said: 'It hath been told me that thy husband now sleepeth with his fathers, and thou art left alone, thou and thy children, and I have come to be thy help in the time of thy need.' And he took up the work of his father at the carpenter's bench, and by his work he nourished us, and he gave instruction to his brothers and brought them up in the faith of Israel. But I knew not any more the ways of my son. For he made his nights into the day, and in the winter nights he sat in his room by the light of the oil lamp, or by the light of the moon and stars in the nights of summer, and he meditated on his thoughts and in the holy books which he had brought back with him. And at his work too he spoke verses and texts to himself, and they were verses and texts which were not yet known. And he told me from the Book of Enoch concerning the giants which had fallen from the heavens and had mingled with the daughters of earth, and concerning the evil generations which came from them, and concerning the dark times wherein we lived. And he said that help and redemption were at hand, and a son would arise in Israel to shine upon the world. And he told me, in text and in parables, of the defeat which awaited the wicked, and of the light which awaited the just, and of the help which would come to the poor, and the disaster which would come upon the rich, whereof all would be brought to pass by the son of David. And he kept himself sundered from all, and did ever purify his body, touching nothing that was unclean and abstaining from the eating of flesh and the drinking of wine but nourishing himself with green things, save that upon the Sabbath he took some honey upon his bread. And I spoke to my son, saying: 'Behold the time hath come for thee to go to a wise man and a sage, that he might release thee from thy vow, for the time is here that I should find comfort and joy of thee. For have not the sages said: "At eighteen it is the time for the bridal canopy"?' And such things I spoke to him, as a mother might speak to her son. But he answered me: 'Didst thou not relinquish me to the Lord even before thou broughtest me forth, hast thou not told me this thyself?' And I was filled with compassion for my child, and I said unto him: 'My son, I did not mean it thus.' But he answered me: 'My vow abideth and standeth, mother.' And he would not speak more thereof. And he went his way, and his way was not what it had been till then: he did not visit punishment upon the rich and he did not resist evil, for he said: 'Evil too is from the Lord, even like the good. Even as it is written that he created light and created darkness, he maketh peace and createth evil, for He is the Lord and doeth all things, so the evil is here that we might become better thereby; and we shall not resist it, for it cometh of

God, and we shall take suffering upon ourselves in love and submission. Man is not created to resist evil but to do good.' And he visited the sick and healed them with herbs and grasses which he had found in the wilderness. He dwelt among the poor and comforted them, saying that in the kingdom of God they would be among the first. And he avoided the company of the rich and the learned, and when he went to the synagogue he stood by the door, among the shamed and rejected ones. And in his booth on the roof, which I had prepared for him, I often saw a great light in the nights, and I heard the speaking of voices, as if strangers had come to him. And it seemed me that he spoke to them with verses and texts, and there came answers in strange voices. And I was affrighted and I trembled for the things that were coming to pass in the booth on the roof, and I said to my son: 'My son, it seemeth me that I know thee no more, and I know not who thou art, and the deeds which thou doest.' And he answered me and said: 'Be comforted, my mother, for all that which is said and done is for the sake of my father in heaven.'

"And it chanced that one night I lay in the darkness and I meditated on the fate of my child, and there came a storm-wind and seized upon the four corners of the house, and made the house to shake, so that I feared that the walls would fall upon me. And as I lay and trembled thus, behold my son came to me and asked: 'Mother, didst thou call me?' and I said, 'Nay, I did not call thee.' And thus it was three times. And on the third time my son said: 'It must indeed be that my time is come,' and I knew not what he meant, and I asked him: 'What intendest thou, my son?' And he answered: 'I must go forth now with the message and tidings, whithersoever my father sendeth me.' And I was astonished by his words and I cried to him: 'Now with whom wilt thou leave me here?' And he said: 'Behold, my brother Jacob is now grown, and he shall take my place at the carpenter's bench, and he shall bring up the children in the ways of Israel. And as for me, I must go whithersoever I am sent.' And he forsook me and went forth into the night. And I cried after him: '*Tinoki,* my little one, let God go with thee,' and he answered from the night, 'Be comforted, my mother,' and he was swallowed up in the darkness of the night.

And the days went by, and the years, and I had no word of him, nor did my eyes see him; till there came to me certain people of K'far Nahum and they told me concerning the wonders which he wrought by the shore of the Sea of Genesaret. And there came to me likewise people from other cities and told me concerning the doctrine which he spreadeth in Israel. And I know not what the Lord hath done with me, for my heart fluttereth between hope and fright. Great things indeed hath the Lord done with him, and yet I know not why my heart fluttereth so; I know not his ways, for I am but a simple woman. And now declare it unto me, ye, his disciples, who my child is."

And I rose and bowed myself before the mother of my Rabbi and I said:

"Blessed art thou, happy among women, for the peoples of the world shall bless themselves in thee. Blessed be thy womb from which issued this saint."

And afterwards in the night, I said to Simon bar Jonah:

"Simon bar Jonah, happy are we that we have been found worthy of this; great things doeth the Lord with us."

And Simon bar Jonah knew not what my speech intended and he answered:

"Behold, I am not learned in the writ, and tell me plainly what thou meanest?"

And I said:

"Simon bar Jonah, the mother testifieth for him, that he was born in Bethlehem of Judah, and that he is of the house of David."

And I explained the thing no further, but I guarded it in my heart.

And we stood thus in the night and we looked upon the house wherein reposed the holy one of Israel. And the house, which was covered thickly with shadows, began to shine, and the light of the moon and stars poured strong upon it, and it rested securely in the protection of God.

VIII

Great is the Sabbath; it hath been likened to the Messiah of God; and as the Messiah was with the Lord in heaven before the world was created, even so was the Sabbath. Which meaneth that there was repose before there was movement, and there was redemption before there was slavery.

Now the next day was the sixth day, which is the eve of the Sabbath; and my Rabbi bestirred himself at an early hour, and before he began the preparations of the Sabbath he looked to it that his brothers be occupied at their labors as was proper; for such order had been wont in his father's day, and in his own what time he abode in the house, and the family was famed for this order from generation to generation.

He called unto his brother Jacob, who had taken over the labor from his hands, that he might nourish the family, and he went with him into the carpentry shop, and there he proved and tested him, and looked to the wood wherefrom the wains were to be made, whether it were not too fresh and therefore easily broken, nor too dry and withered; and he looked to the wheels that they be strong and well-fitted and the spokes firm and well-fastened and that the reins be loose enough that they close not perforce the mouth of the ass, or of the ox when it treadeth the grain, that it might be able to eat thereof, as the Torah commandeth. And when he saw that his brothers did their work fittingly and well, according to the reputation of their family, he praised them therefor.

Then he took his brother Simon and went with him into the garden which was in the field, for his brother Simon was the one that had charge of the little portion which was the inheritance of the family, and Simon worked in the garden and in the field that were about the house. And our Rabbi saw to it that his brothers observed in their labor all the commandments touching the work of the field, as they are written in the Torah; that they left the corners of the field for the poor of the city to garner, and for strangers. And he inquired likewise whether his brother set aside the tithe or tenth of the harvest for the Priest, according to the commandment. He inquired further whether his brother left the second aftergrowth of the grapes in their little vineyard for the poor of the city, and gathered them not into his cellar; also whether he left in the field that which fell under the scythe, which is not to be gathered with the sheaf but left where it lieth, according to the commandment. And it was the time of the spring, and the wheat stood up in the field, but it was green and hairy, and it bowed devoutly before the wind, and my Rabbi blessed it.

And he took his brother and went with him into the small garden about the house, and he saw to it that on every tree every fig that showed first to be ripe was marked with a bent twig around it, that it might be sanctified for the first fruits and brought in the right season to the Temple in Jerusalem. And the garden was in blossom, and the mother stood in the midst of the green, and digged onions and carrots from the ground to prepare for the Sabbath meal. And my Rabbi said unto her:

"Mother, do not thou labor, but leave the work for my disciples, for they will come shortly from the city and they will prepare the Sabbath feast for their Rabbi, for such is the commandment concerning disciples and their Rabbi."

And his mother answered:

"The commandment and good deed of Sabbath preparation is very great, and the more one laboreth therein, the greater is the fulfillment. And my custom is still as it was in thy father's days, and the fruits which are ripest, and the vegetables, I put aside in the week, and mark them, and gather them on the sixth day for the Sabbath."

And he took his youngest brother Judah and went with him into the stable. Now the youngest had been but a child what time his father had died, and the Rabbi loved him beyond all his brothers, for he had been left an orphan in young years, and my Rabbi had been as his father; and he called to him, saying:

"Judah, *tinoki,*" which signifieth, Judah, my little one, "come, lead me to the flock."

For the youngest had been charged with the care of the little family flock. And the mother drew from her flock the milk and cheese for the house, likewise woolen garments for the winter nights, and she spun and wove the garments with her own hands. And the flock was small, having but a few sheep and a few goats. And when we came to the flock, the sheep made a close circle about my Rabbi, as if they would know him, and they licked his hands and his feet. And he asked concerning the well-being of the sheep and inquired closely of his brother whether he listened when he heard the dumb crying of the beasts for water. And his brother answered:

"The work is well done and with skill, for have not our forefathers been shepherds from the days of Abraham our father on?"

And my Rabbi said: "Thou hast answered well, my son."

And as they spoke thus, the disciples returned from the city, and there was with them the woman who had followed after our Rabbi from Naim, to wit, Miriam. And when the mother saw the disciples (for they had not all been in the house the night before) she said:

"Who are these?"

And my Rabbi answered:

"All these are the souls which I created; and there be not many, but their name shall be legion in the time to come."

And the Rabbi took the hand of the woman that had come with the disciples and he led her to his mother and said:

"I deliver her unto thee and thy grace; take her unto thee, for till this day she hath been rejected; and do thou teach her all the commandments which pertain to a daughter of our people."

And the woman bowed before the mother and touched the hem of her garment and said:

"I am not worthy to touch with my hands the hem of thy garment, for I am unclean."

But the mother raised her from the ground and said:

"Arise, my daughter; that is no more unclean which my son hath cleansed." And she said further: "It is a great day with me, for not only hath the Lord granted it to me to see the face of my son, but he hath brought before me his disciples which he hath raised and the souls which he hath made. Is there a mother in Israel as fortunate as I? Now let them go into the stable, and take a sheep, and slaughter it according to the commandments, and prepare it for the Sabbath which approacheth. And thou, my daughter, shalt come with me and bake the bread and prepare the lamps."

And she took the woman with her into the room, and they took white meal and kneaded it with oil which she poured forth from a gourd flask. And she took of the dough and cast it into the fire, sanctifying it thereby unto the Lord; and she began to bake the breads.

And the disciples went with Judah into the stall, and took a beast, and slaughtered it according to the ritual and the commandments. And Jacob and Jochanan, the sons of Zebedee, digged a hole in the ground, and lit a fire with straw and wood, and they roasted the beast over the glow of the wood, on a spit. For the good deed is of double virtue if each of the disciples shareth in the labor of preparation of the meal for the Rabbi, and each is occupied with the work for the Sabbath. And so the brothers Zebedee turned the sheep over on the fire. And Philip betook himself to the greens and rubbed the beets. And one brought oil from the market, and dipped fish therein, and rolled them in dough and baked them over the fire. And Timothy and Jacob ben Halfi washed the outer garments of the disciples, which they had taken off at their labor, that they might not serve their Rabbi at table in the clothes wherein they worked and wherein they had cooked the meal for him. And the clothes dried in the sun that they might put on fresh garments for the Sabbath. And I worked with the lamps, and prepared the wicks, drawing them fine that they might not smoke and give forth bad odor. And Andrew worked in the preparation of the wine. For Andrew and I had received learning and we knew the laws which pertain to the preparation of wines and lamps and oils, and the laws which pertain to the Sabbath. And Simon the Zealot drew water from the well. But Simon bar Jonah occupied himself with the Rabbi, and prepared the Sabbath bath for him, heating the water and pouring it into the large jar which stood in a corner of the yard, surrounded and screened off with palm leaves as is becoming. And he took my Rabbi thither and washed his body and anointed it and put his robes on him, and the outer garment with the fringes which are the *zizit*, and shod him in sandals, and laid him down upon a couch, that our Rabbi might look like an angel of the Lord who had come down to bless the Sabbath.

And when my Rabbi lay on his couch and took delight in the beauty of the world, which was covered with sunlight, and when he beheld his disciples busying themselves with the preparation of the Sabbath, and was filled with joy thereby, there came many townsfolk. And there were among them also such as had great possessions, and they came out of eagerness to see a new thing; and there were among them the poor that came for gifts, for they had heard that our Rabbi distributed to the poor the money which he received from the rich. And there came also the blind and lame, but not to be healed by him, for they believed not; but they came, too, out of eagerness to see a new thing. But no learned men were among them all, for there were no learned in the city save for the chief elder of the synagogue and the Rabbis and the overseers of the Temple tribute, which were also the members of the little court. And the people stood about and some of them mocked. And they said to each other: "Behold, he hath brought disciples with him." And the lame led the blind, and they stood about us, and spoke mockingly. And the blind asked: "Now tell us, hath he not brought with him many camels, laden with cruses of oil?" And the lame answered, "Nay, we see no camels laden with oil." And the blind asked again: "Perhaps he hath brought with him bags of dinars." And the lame answered: "Nay, we see no bags of dinars, which he hath brought with him." And the blind said: "Now look well." And the others answered: "We see only poor folk, like himself, which he hath brought with him, and they are his disciples, and there is also a woman among them." Then the blind inquired further: "But perhaps he hath transported the king's palace hither by magic, for his mother to dwell in." And the lame answered: "Nay, we see but the broken house of the family, where it hath always dwelt." Then the blind said, further: "But mayhap there is a golden table laden with all manner of good things, sent down from heaven for the celebration of the Sabbath." And the others answered: "Nay, no golden table, and no manner of good things, but the disciples roast small fish in oil, as do all the poor, for the Sabbath feast." And still the blind asked: "Now tell us, hath he not adorned his mother in royal robes, and with many precious stones?" "Nay, his mother weareth still the sackcloth clothing of the poor man's wife."

And Simon bar Jonah called to them and said: "Ye blind ones, why stand ye there and make mock? It were better for you to fall to the ground and stretch out your hands to him and entreat him to take away your blindness. For salvation lieth in his hands, and he may yet help you as he hath helped many others that were blind." And the blind answered: "Oh, we be not fools, like the folk of other cities. For if he could indeed help, he would help himself first. What, do we not dwell in this city among his brethren, and see we not how they labor in the field and at the bench, and are as poor as ourselves? Why loadeth he not them with gold? Why bringeth he not to them great treasuries by magic?" And the blind and lame mocked the more and laughed loudly, and they called to my Rabbi: "Physician, heal thyself!" And one of the blind went forth from the circle and felt with his hands and sought the Rabbi, saying: "Where is the man that performeth such wonders, and why doth he not show himself unto us as he hath done to others?" And thus speaking he came near to my Rabbi, and the others cried out with laughter: "Oh, thou blind one, flee now, for he hath sent a serpent against thee, and a hole openeth in the ground before thee." And the blind man stood affrighted and cried: "Where? Where?"

And when the brothers Zebedee saw all this they left their work of the preparation of the meal, and they said to our Rabbi:

"Rabbi, shall we drive them hence? Why lettest thou these people make mock?"

And the Rabbi answered:

"I am not come to destroy lives, but to build."

And he rose from his place and went to the blind man who stood in confusion and took him by the hand. And we thought of a surety that he would change him into a heap of ash. But the Rabbi did naught, saying, only:

"What shall it avail if thou art made seeing with thy eyes and thy heart remaineth blind?" And he led him to the circle of the blind, saying: "Thou blind one, stay among the blind."

And he took money from his bag and he gave it to the poor, and he put his hands upon this one and that one, and said: "God grant that ye find faith, for he that hath faith shall never be poor."

Now before long we heard the calling of the ram's horn from the roof of the synagogue, to signify that the Sabbath was nigh and no more work could be done. Then the people left the place and hastened to the city. And the disciples likewise gave over from their work, and the brothers of the Rabbi left their labors, and they covered the instruments, that the Sabbath might not be troubled with the sight of instruments of labor. And the disciples washed their hands and their faces and their feet in the jars of water in the yard, and put on their new-washed and dried garments. And the brothers of the Rabbi did likewise. And his sisters came with their husbands and their children from the city to greet their mother on the Sabbath. And the disciples prepared the tables, and laid boards on the floor and covered them with a sheet. And the mother of the Rabbi, and the women, washed their faces and combed their hair and put on their Sabbath garments and prepared the lamps, as many lamps as were in the house, for it is a good deed to light the Sabbath with all the lamps that are in the house. And when they heard the second blowing of the ram's horn from the roof of the synagogue, they lit the lamps. And then the mother took flowers and leaves of the olive tree and adorned the house and the table, and she hastened to her room and brought forth the bottle of date wine and placed it on the table, where the Sabbath loaves were.

And when the sun went down we heard the blowing of the ram's horn for the third time. Then the Rabbi took his disciples and stationed himself with them in the yard to receive the Sabbath. And when the first stars showed he said the "Hear, O Israel" of the evening, and all answered, "Amen."

And we came then into the house, which was lit with many lamps and adorned with flowers and wreaths of olive. And my Rabbi in his white robe shone amid the lamps and flowers like an angel of the Lord. And when he had greeted the angels which had entered the house with the coming of the Sabbath, he took his mother's hand and bade her sit by him, and all his brothers he seated in the order of their years. And thus it was with the disciples, and the sisters and their husbands. Then he rose and lifted his beaker of wine and sanctified the Sabbath and drank the wine, and he gave the children to drink thereof, and they all answered, "Amen." And we drank after the children from the beaker of the Rabbi. Then he washed his hands and we did likewise. And he said the prayer which entreateth the Lord for our daily bread, as was his custom at all meals. And he shared the food, first to the children, then to his mother, then to his disciples and his brothers and sisters.

And we, the disciples, rose, and each one in turn served the Rabbi, for great is the virtue of service to the Rabbi, even greater than service to one's father and mother. And the Rabbi served his mother. And we lifted the dishes that were on the table, and first we let the children dip their hands therein, for it is the custom that the little ones shall be fed before the grown ones. Then the Rabbi took with his fingers, and each one of us in turn, in the order of his years.

And we sang verses from the Psalms between one dish and the next, and our Rabbi explained the words of the text to us, and there was great joy at the table. Blessed is the eye that hath looked thereon. And when I beheld how the mother sitteth among her children, and the lamps burn, and the light of the Sabbath shineth, and the house is cleaned and adorned, and the spirit of God resteth on the table, for that they spoke of holy things, then I thought concerning her of the verse: "As the mother rejoiceth with her children, Halleluiah!"

And that night we, the disciples, lodged in the yard of the Rabbi's house, each finding what place he could, for we would all be with our Rabbi in the morning, and go with him to the synagogue. For thus it is written: "In the multitude of the people is the majesty of the king," and a Rabbi is likened unto a king, and it honoreth the Rabbi that his disciples accompany him on the way.

And when the morning came we bestirred ourselves and fared forth to the synagogue. And the people came forth from all the houses and went upward on the slope to the synagogue, which stood in a high place and was seen from all parts of the city. And the synagogue was already full, for they knew that the Rabbi would come to the prayers with his disciples, and they waited to see if he would perform a miracle as he had done in other cities. In the high place by the eastern wall, toward the ark where standeth the holy scroll, they sat—the head of the congregation and the chief men of the city. And the head of the congregation was an old man, and his beard was long and white, and it shone above his white Sabbath garment. And on one side of him sat the prayer-leader, who was the teacher of the little ones, a man in the strength of his years; he was of the Priesthood, of the sons of Aaron, and he was hairy, and his beard was combed and knotted in the fashion of the Priests.

And on the other side was the chief assistant of the head of the synagogue, and he was a young man. And by them sat the elders, in their Sabbath garments, and their prayer shawls with the fringes. And the people were stationed in the synagogue, all according to their rank, the rich and important in the first places by the pulpit and the poor by the door. As it is written: "Like a poor man at the door." And the women went in to the women's part, which was to one side of the synagogue, and divided from the men's part by a double row of pillars, that they might hear the prayer of the men and not see them. And our Rabbi took his place, as the custom was with him, at the door, and we, his disciples, behind him. And when the synagogue could contain no more people, the head of the synagogue rose and said:

"Is there come unto the city a visitor of importance, whom it is fitting we shall call to the reading of the Torah?"

And some of the worshipers answered:

"There is returned to the city Reb Yeshua ben Joseph, who hath been found worthy to become a Rabbi in Israel, and he is returned to fulfill the commandment of honor to mothers. He is now in the synagogue with his disciples."

Thereupon the head of the synagogue said:

"Let Rabbi Yeshua ben Joseph be the mouthpiece of this congregation for this Sabbath."

And it was a custom in Israel that when a man was entreated to be the mouthpiece and messenger of the congregation in prayer, he refused the honor three times, as asserting of himself that he was unworthy, and to demonstrate his modesty, and only upon the fourth offer did he follow the bidding of the head of the synagogue. But our Rabbi did not thus. And when the head of the synagogue requested of him to be the mouthpiece of the congregation in prayer, he came forward straightway and went to the pulpit. And he wrapped himself in a prayer shawl and began the prayer in a loud voice:

"Blessed art Thou, O Lord, king of the universe, creator of light and of darkness, bringer of peace, creator of all things."

And the people fell upon their knees and covered their faces with their prayer shawls.

And when he came to the passage wherein the messenger of the congregation blesseth the Sabbath, then our Rabbi uttered the words with great strength:

"Bring down upon Thy people a great and everlasting peace, for Thou art the prince and king of peace."

And here the Rabbi broke off the set prayer, and as the custom was with great Rabbis, he said his own prayer. And when the people in the synagogue heard his prayer, behold, it was the prayer of the poor man, that which the Rabbi said at every meal. And they said, one to the other, "It is the prayer of the poor man, and it is good." And they repeated it after him.

And the mother of the Rabbi stood among the women in the women's part, and when she heard the voice of her son raised in great strength to pray for the congregation, she was filled with happiness and pride, and the women said to her: "Blessed be thy womb, which hath brought forth this fruit, thou blessed among women."

And then the Rabbi, accompanied by the chief men, mounted the steps where the sacred ark is built into the wall, and he drew forth the scroll of the Torah, and when he stood thus, wrapped in his prayer shawl, and lifted the scroll above the heads of the assembly, he was in appearance like Moses our teacher upon Sinai, and the people bowed and sang the song of degrees which they sing mounting toward the Court of the Temple.

Then he and the head of the synagogue and the prayer leader brought the scroll upon the pulpit and they unrolled it to be open at the place of the week's portion, and they called up to the honor of the reading the important men of the city. And each of them read forth his passage to the assembly, and the translator translated it to the people.

And when the time came for our Rabbi to be called to the reading of the Torah, and his portion was the addition to the weekly portion, then he read with great strength; and when he had ended, the chief assistant rolled the scroll to the section of the Prophets, and he showed our Rabbi the portion of the Prophets to be read for that Sabbath.

But our Rabbi took the scroll and changed the portion and turned to the Book of Isaiah, to that section wherein the prophet speaketh of the tidings of the Messiah. And wrapped in his prayer shawl he lifted the scroll on high, and read forth mightily: "The spirit of God resteth upon me, for he hath anointed me to bring tidings to the poor. He hath sent me to heal the hearts that are broken, to set the prisoners free. . . ."

But when the head of the synagogue heard these words, he trembled in all his body and went to my Rabbi and said:

"Not this is the prophet which is prescribed for reading today as additional portion." But our Rabbi gave over the scroll into the hands of the chief assistant, and he continued to speak the words of the prophet Isaiah by heart:

"He hath sent me to free the bound, to proclaim a year of will toward God. The people which walketh in darkness have seen a great light."

And the head of the synagogue and the prayer leader and the old men were pale and affrighted, and they pressed about my Rabbi and they said:

"What are these words which thou utterest, and whom dost thou mean? Art thou not the son of Joseph and Miriam, and do not thy brothers and sisters dwell with us? At whom dost thou point those words, and what meanest thou with them?"

But he listened not to them, and he cried out in a mighty voice:

"The Lord God hath given me the tongue of the learned, to speak a word unto the weary. The Lord God hath opened my ear and I have not rebelled or withdrawn. I have given my back to the smiters and my cheeks to those that tear out the beard, and I have not withdrawn my face from shame and from being spat upon. Therefore I have not been shamed; therefore have I made my face like to a strong stone and I know that I shall not be shamed."

And the chief of the synagogue called to the people in a great voice:

"Draw him forth from this place, for he blasphemeth against God!"

And the people stood astonished and frightened, and fear was on all faces. For the face of our Rabbi was white, and it shone like the sun, and his voice was like the voice which issueth from the thunder when it falleth from the hills, and his words were filled with grace and beauty. And the people said in wonder, one to the other: "But this is the son of Joseph; who hath taught him to read thus from the holy writ?"

And Simon bar Jonah came between them and said:

"Have ye not heard, then, that which he did among the people of K'far Nahum, that he healed the sick, and gave the blind their sight? And have ye not heard that which he did in Naim? And have ye not heard what the people say, that he is a holy one in Israel? But your hearts are stopped up. Go now to him, and stretch forth your arms to him, for your help lieth in his hands."

And some, looking upon the face of our Rabbi and hearing his voice, fell at his feet and stretched forth their arms and called: "Rabbi, help us! Show now the miracles which thou didst show in K'far Nahum." But he answered them: "But did ye not point at me the parable: 'Physician, heal thyself'? Verily I say unto you, there is no prophet that hath honor in his own land. Many widows there were in the days of Elijah, when he held up the clouds for three years and six months and there was hunger in the land, and Elijah was not sent but to one of them, to Zerifin, which is in Zidon, to the widow woman. And many lepers there were in the days of Elishah, and he cleansed none but Naaman the Syrian."

And when they heard this there was a great tumult, and they were seized with anger at these words and they would have smitten and insulted him. But we, his disciples, surrounded him and would let them do no harm to him. And we went forth with him from the synagogue and the worshipers were mightily perturbed.

And it came to pass afterwards that when he returned to the home of his mother, his sisters quarreled with their husbands concerning him. And the men said: "How shall we lift our eyes here in the city? Moreover, they will take away our bread because of the words thou hast spoken." And even some of the brothers of Yeshua were dark of countenance, and they said, one to the other: "The people of the city will take vengeance on us." But the mother sat in a corner of the house with her son, and though her heart was sad she would not let it appear, for it was the Sabbath. But she said to her son:

"It regretteth me for thee, my son. God be thy guardian!"

And when evening came and the stars appeared, the Rabbi gathered his disciples and said:

"Now I no longer have aught to do with them. Let us arise and go to K'far Nahum."

And there were some who asked:

"Wilt thou not lodge this night in the city?"

And he answered:

"A city which destroyeth her children is worse than a wild beast. Let us shake the dust of this place off our feet."

And when he came to his mother, to beg leave that he might go, then she caught her dress to her face and she wept, saying:

"My child, I will not let thee go. Now I see how dangerous is the path thou hast chosen to walk, and I fear for thy life."

But he said:

"The path hath been laid before me by our father in heaven, and my footsteps are already upon it. But thou shalt not look again upon the face of thy son until he hath reached his goal."

And he left his mother as she wept, and forsook the house of his parents, and we went with him. And when we were without, in the stillness of the night, we heard his mother's voice calling after him, "*Tinoki, tinoki,* my child, my child," and he answered her: "*Imi, imi,* my mother, my mother."

And when we were gone a distance from the city, there came up footsteps behind us. And when we looked around it was Jacob, the brother of the Rabbi. And the Rabbi asked him:

"Jacob, my brother, what doest thou here?"

And Jacob answered:

"I will go in thy footsteps."

And the Rabbi answered:

"Jacob, return: thy hour is not yet come."

And the two brothers fell upon each other's necks and they kissed each other. And Jacob returned home, and we went further upon our way.

IX

And we went through the night, and with the early morning we came to Migdal, which is the city of the dyers. And we stayed our steps at a house which Miriam, she of Migdal, pointed out to us. And the city of Migdal was rich, and well filled with people, for hereabouts they find in the water the mussel fish, which they call *hiluzon,* whereof they take the gall and distill therefrom the purple dye. Likewise the people here breed doves for sacrifices in the Temple—and therefore the city was stained with the dye of purple and flecked with the shadows of doves. And the Rabbi sat with us in the study house, there where the scholars sit, and he taught his doctrine to us, his disciples. And many of the city people and the scholars also came to listen, and they spread abroad his fame, and said concerning him that pearls poured from his mouth. And it pleased my Rabbi to sojourn in this place, for the people paid us much honor. And my Rabbi performed no more miracles in this city.

And when some days were gone our Rabbi bade us take ship and pass over from Migdal to K'far Nahum. And Simon the fisher brought the Rabbi into the house of his mother-in-law, and she had prepared for him his booth upon the roof.

And there came to K'far Nahum the women of Naim, to wit, Jochanah, the wife of the officer of Herod, and Susannah. And Jochanah was the wife of a rich man, and she possessed many fields and she brought her money and gave it into our treasury; and we bought bread to feed the poor who assembled about our Rabbi. And Susannah clove to the mother-in-law of Simon and to other devout women that were about the Rabbi and they tended the needs of the Rabbi and his disciples. And they tended likewise to the feasts which the Rabbi gave for the poor who came to seek salvation from him. Only Miriam, the woman of Migdal, was not with the other women, and she did not labor in the household, but she gave herself to the duty of attendance upon our Rabbi. And it was thus in the evenings; when the Rabbi went into his booth to rest him from the holy labor of the day, and it was evening and the hour of grace, she would fall at his feet in submission of spirit, and foam would be on her lips and a holy spirit would descend on her, and she would be filled with the exaltation of prophecy. But we of the disciples that were learned in the writ liked not this matter, that Miriam had separated herself from the other women, and we murmured against her ways, also that she brought our Rabbi into the company of sinners.

And we saw that the countenance of our Rabbi unto sundry of his disciples was not as yesterday and the day before. Me, the least of his disciples, likewise Andrew and Simon the Zealot, he held off from him, and day by day he drew nearer to him Simon bar Jonah, the brother of Andrew, and Jacob and Jochanan, the brothers Zebedee; and they went in and came out more than we. And our Rabbi oft closeted himself with them and said things to them which we heard not and knew not of. And the other disciples were envious and quarreled.

Now Simon bar Jonah was among the great of faith, and he was like one that is in love. And he stood before the closed door of the Rabbi's room, and he believed that he heard many voices within when the Rabbi was alone. And he and the brothers Zebedee believed that salvation would come only through the ignorant and the simple. For it is faith and not wisdom which carrieth the key to the kingdom of heaven. Now the brothers Zebedee were men of might and wealth. They had many ships of their mother, and they had left their ships to go after the Rabbi. And Jacob, the older of the brothers, was the beloved pupil of the Rabbi, for Jacob was great in faith, even like Simon, and perchance more than he. And we came once to the shore of Genesaret and were desirous of passing to the other side and there was no ship nigh, and Jacob said to the Rabbi:

"Rabbi and teacher, when thou so willest, thou canst split the sea even as Moses did in his time when the Jews came out of Egypt, and we shall pass through the dry land."

And the Rabbi answered:

"Were I with thee alone I would do it, for there is nothing beyond the power of faith, but the littleness of faith of the others preventeth me."

And this he meant, I know, because he saw that I believed not this thing. And Jacob sat at the Rabbi's feet, and served him as Simon did. And Jochanan his brother was taller and broader of shoulder than all the others, he was a giant, and his voice was the voice of a giant, and he was intimate with the common people, for he was of them. And the Rabbi made signs for his three disciples, thus: of Simon he said: "This is the rock upon which I stand, and Jacob is the staff on which I lean, and Jochanan is the trumpet through which I call."

And as we returned to K'far Nahum, Jochanan went down to the shore where the fishers are, and to the market place, and he sat him down at the gate of the doves which is the entrance to the city, and he called to the simple folk: "The wonder-man is again in the city; come hither all ye that thirst for help."

And when the people heard that the Rabbi was returned to the city, they began once more to assemble in multitudes at the narrow entrance to the house of Simon, and they would have entered, all. And they stretched forth their hands and cried: "Rabbi, help us!" And when the Rabbi saw the thirsting multitude, his strength was renewed and the Holy Spirit descended upon him, and he became like a brimming well which poured forth salvation and consolation for Israel.

And he put on his white robe and the fringed garment, and he went forth with his disciples. And when the multitude saw him thus, white-clad and surrounded by his disciples, they fell at his feet, calling: "Holy one in Israel, help us!" and the Rabbi said:

"Compassion cometh not down from heaven till it hath been called down from the earth."

And he entered into the midst of the multitude and comforted the broken and healed the sick and remitted sins.

Now in the city of K'far Nahum there was a man of dignity, learned, and held in esteem, for he was the head of the synagogue where the Rabbi preached to the congregation, and he believed in the Rabbi. And he came before the Rabbi and fell at his feet and entreated him that he might come to his house, for that his only daughter, a child of twelve, was about to die. But there was such a press, and the people about the Rabbi made such a wall, that he could not go forth from among them. And while the man still entreated, there came one running and he said to the head of the synagogue:

"Thy daughter is dead, thou needest not trouble the Rabbi any more."

But when the Rabbi heard this, he said:

"Fear not, but be strong of faith, and thy faith shall help thee."

And they went forth, and came to the house of the head of the synagogue, and the Rabbi gave leave to none to enter with him, save the three disciples Simon and Jacob and Jochanan, and he said to the father and mother of the child:

"Weep not, for the child is not dead, but sleepeth." And he took the child by the hand and said, "Little one, arise," and the little one rose and was like unto one of us. And we, the disciples that were not there when the thing happened, murmured among ourselves: "Why were we not deemed worthy to be present when our Rabbi performed this miracle?" And we were angered, and envious of Simon and the brothers Zebedee, whom the Rabbi had drawn close to him.

And the manner of our Rabbi was thus: he went forth in a boat which was rowed by his two beloved disciples, Simon and Jacob, and he came to the shore of a city by Genesaret, and the people assembled on the shore and our Rabbi spoke to them from the boat; and he said many wise things and uttered parables, to teach the people to come under the yoke of the kingdom of heaven. And he said: "The kingdom of God is likened to a man that soweth seed. And he sleepeth in the night, and awaketh in the morning, and the seed springeth and he knoweth not thereof. For the earth draweth forth from herself her fruits and grasses." And other similitudes he told them, and he that was wise understood in a deeper way, and he that was simple was drawn to the beauty of the parable. And he spoke not without parables. For it was known that Herod Antipater had heard of our Rabbi and feared him, and would see him and speak with him; for the people believed that our Rabbi was Jochanan the Baptist, whom Herod had beheaded in his fortress. And Herod was afraid in his heart, and asked: "How can he have returned to life, whom I beheaded?" And the wise men, too, were discontented with our Rabbi, in that he did not comport himself as was becoming to a scholar; and even the disciples of Jochanan the Baptist were of an unfriendly spirit, for that he did not tread the path of Jochanan, who had bidden the people to fast and mortify their flesh. Likewise there were many householders and men of wealth that disliked the thing, for they said that he wasted the time of the day laborers.

And when the police of the city would approach the shore where my Rabbi spoke, then Simon and Jacob would ply the oars mightily, and they would take the boat into the midst of the sea, whither they could not follow him. And they would do thus, also: they would take the many boats of their mother, and load them with people and take them into the sea to follow our Rabbi. And we would prepare bread and other food in the boats, with the money given us by Jochanah and Susannah and other devout women. And the Rabbi and the multitude would pass in their boats to another shore of Genesaret, perchance by Bet Zeida, or some other spot that was empty of people, and we would descend there and spread ourselves upon the green field. And there were times when we went among ruins and hid ourselves among the vineyards which are upon the shore. And the Rabbi sat in the midst of the people, and broke bread with them, and taught them the ways of God, and proclaimed the coming of the kingdom of heaven. And he taught them what they were to do that they might inherit the world to come, and be worthy of a portion in the kingdom of heaven. And sometimes he would heal a sick man with herbs, and sometimes only by the laying on of his hands. And he brought calmness to the stormy of spirit and comforted the fallen and remitted the sins of sinners. And the people clung to him, and he was as one body and one soul with them.

And the faith of Simon bar Jonah in our Rabbi grew stronger from day to day. And he came to believe that our Rabbi could do those things which no man of flesh and blood had ever done before, and that the power had been given to him not only over men, but over the spirits and the forces of the world and the elements thereof; and that angels stood ready to do his bidding. And Simon saw visions and heard voices which none other saw or heard. And the following thing came to pass: We had left our Rabbi alone by the edge of the sea, for he had told us that he would pray alone. And we went off a distance into the sea on our boats, and we were to return later for him. And in the meantime the night came and there was a mist as of dew on the water, and the mist hid the lights of heaven, and it seemed to us that earth and heaven had become molten together and were as one body. And the darkness was thick, so that we could not see the prow of the boat, and our rowers felt their way in the darkness. And the sons of Zebedee, who were the rowers, said: "Come, let us return to the shore where we have left our teacher, for it is late." And Simon bar Jonah and the other disciples were in our boat and we were uneasy in spirit for our Rabbi, for the sea had changed her face. Then of a sudden we heard the cry of Simon bar Jonah, who called in affright: "Look! Behold!" and we looked into the night, but the darkness hid everything from us, as if a net were hung before our eyes, and we saw nothing save the thickness around us. And we asked in terror: "Simon bar Jonah, what seest thou? Say!" And Simon bar Jonah pointed into the thickness of the cloud which covered the world, and he cried: "I see my Rabbi, and he filleth the space of the world, and his head is lifted unto the stars, and he walketh with naked feet on the waves, and the waves lie at his feet like sheep and let him tread upon them." And we strained our gaze into the darkness, but the darkness lay like a buckler of steel upon the water, and we no longer saw each other, but heard only the voice of Simon bar Jonah, which ceased not from calling: "Behold, he walketh, he goeth before us!" And we believed the words, for the terror of the Lord had come upon us. . . .

And on a certain day our Rabbi went out with some of his disciples and a great multitude upon the sea, and they came to a shore, and landed there, as his custom was, to break bread. And some of the disciples, I, Judah, among them, remained at home, in charge of the vessels. And the night came, and the Rabbi and the other disciples and the multitude returned not, and we went down to the shore to await them. And a storm arose on the waters, and it smote the waves in anger, so that they reared up like hills. And we, standing on the shore, heard the evil roaring of the waves, which threw themselves, one upon the other, like unto leviathan, which smiteth with his tail. And our hearts were like water, with fear for the fate of our Rabbi and the other disciples. And the women came out with lamps and we waited on the shore. Then of a sudden we heard the voices of men from the night, and a crying: "Hosannah!

Save us!" and there was silence, as if a great sword had cut off the heads of the waves and made them to lie down. And from the night there cometh forth all calmly a ship, and our Rabbi steppeth in his white garments upon the land, and there follow him Simon bar Jonah and the brothers Zebedee, and their garments are torn upon their bodies by the arrows of the storm, and their hair is wild, their beards are blown about, and they are drenched in water from head to foot. And Simon, with hands stretched forth and eyes burning, crieth unto us, and we hear in his voice the beating of his heart: "Hear now and see what God hath done with us: we were upon the sea in our boats, and when we were in the midst of the water, a storm came. It came on a sudden, so that or ever we knew it we were encircled by high waves as by the wild beasts of the field, and demons and evil spirits rode upon them as in a fever. And the waves opened their mouths and thought to swallow us. And we looked to our Rabbi, that he might save us from destruction, and we saw that our Rabbi slept on the deck of the ship. For he was weary with his holy work, and had leaned his head against the ship and he slept. And his head was upon his right hand, his body was covered with his garment; and we watched him as he breathed. Then there came a mighty wave and smote us. And the ship stood on end, and the rudder was broken, and the boards of the ship groaned under the blows of the waves. And we cried: 'Rabbi, Rabbi, hearest thou not this tumult, seest thou not our terror? Have compassion on thy people which followed thy footsteps even into the midst of the stormy sea.' And he awoke and looked on us with awakening eyes and said: 'O, ye of little faith!' And like unto a lord, who reproveth his dogs that they molest his beloved guests, so he reproved the waves, and they were submissive and bowed their heads at his feet and lay there. And we passed on, as the Jews passed on through the Red Sea."

And when we heard what Simon bar Jonah had told us, we lifted our hands to heaven and praised our father that dwelleth there for the kindness he had shown unto us, and the terror of our Rabbi fell upon us all. And those of us that had been of little faith melted for fear. And we came before our Rabbi in trembling and awe, and we scattered ashes on our head, and took off our shoes, and fell at his feet and cried: "Thou holy one in Israel, woe unto us that we have sinned against thee in our hearts! Forgive us and thrust us not away from thy countenance!"

And he placed his hands upon us and said:

"Arise and be comforted, your sins are forgiven, for nothing shall stand up against faith."

And we were comforted and our hearts were filled with certainty and we said, one to the other:

"Salvation standeth at the door. Blessed is he that hath lived to see it."

And among those that begged forgiveness of our Rabbi was I, Judah Ish-Kiriot.

X

In those days arrived the messengers sent from Jerusalem by Hanan, the eldest of the High Priests, to inquire into the ways and teachings and deeds of our Rabbi. For the report of our Rabbi had reached the Sanhedrin in Jerusalem, and they had heard concerning the acts of Rabbi Yeshua ben Joseph, and the strange doctrine which he spread, likewise his miracles, and all this was not in the spirit of the accepted tradition; and the Sanhedrin sent men to search out whether the reports be so or not.

And the number of the messengers or deputies was seven, all of them learned in the writ, such as counted and weighed and interpreted every word.

And there was among them one whom I knew well from Jerusalem, Nicodemon by name. He had been my Rabbi and associate, a man of one mind with me, devout and just, who waited for the anointed one of God to come and redeem Israel. And I, the servant of his lord, bestirred myself and went to Nicodemon and spoke thus:

"Touch not the holy one in Israel."

And I told him concerning the wonders which my Rabbi had shown until that day, and concerning the doctrine which he taught. And I told him, moreover, that which the mother of the Rabbi had said in Nazareth, to wit, that he was born in Bethlehem of Judah, concerning which city the prophets had prophesied.

And when Nicodemon had heard all this, he said:

"There is surely something in this matter."

And there came also the disciples of Jochanan, who after the death of their Rabbi whom Herod had beheaded, were scattered like sheep without a shepherd, and they awaited him of whom Jochanan had prophesied the coming.

And I went to them and told them of the wonderful deeds of my Rabbi; and Nicodemon and the disciples of Jochanan came secretly at night to the house of Simon, and they appeared before our Rabbi. And Nicodemon said:

"Now tell us who thou art, and give us a sign and a proof. Art thou he for whom we wait, or art thou not?"

And the disciples of Jochanan spoke in their turn and said:

"When our Rabbi still lived he sent us unto thee and we asked thee in his name: 'Art thou he or shall we wait for another?' And thou didst say to us: 'Go back and tell Jochanan that which ye have heard. And blessed be the man that cometh to me, for he shall not fall.' And we returned, and behold, our Rabbi was already dead, beheaded by Herod, according to the incitement of his wife. And we stand here now like forlorn sheep, for thy ways are different from the ways of Jochanan wherein we followed him. For our Rabbi taught us to keep the body pure, and thou sittest with tax collectors and sinners and transgressors. Now art thou he on whom the prophets prophesied? If thou be he, we shall blow the great trumpets and spread the tidings in Israel." And they stretched out their hands to him. "Have compassion on thy servants, and torment us no more with uncertainty."

But our Rabbi answered neither Yea nor Nay. He spoke to them in parables, saying:

"Now to whom shall I liken the men of this generation, and with whom shall I place them? They are like children in the market place, who call to one another: 'We piped for you, and ye did not dance; we lamented for you and ye did not weep.' Now Jochanan came to you, eating no meat and drinking no wine, and you said: 'He is a spirit.' And the son of man cometh to you and he eateth and drinketh, and you say: 'This man is a glutton and a winebibber, the companion of tax collectors and sinners.' But wisdom shall be justified of her children."

And more he said not. So they went forth from before him as ignorant of the matter as when they came, and Nicodemon said:

"Now nothing more remaineth for us but the law, which is in our hands. This is the thread by which we hold. For it hath been given to us by God, and we will follow it. And let God do that which is just in His eyes."

And the next morning the deputies of the Sanhedrin sat them down, and they called our Rabbi to judgment, that he might come and declare himself on the ways of his disciples. For the Rabbi beareth responsibility for the disciples, as they for him.

And the deputies of the Sanhedrin sat in the judgment chamber which is part of the synagogue of K'far Nahum. Now among them there was Eliezer the son of Judah, who was of the party of the High Priests, and Nicodemon the son of Nicodemon, who was of the disciples of Hillel and who guarded strongly the tradition. And Nathan the son of Ishmael, who was strong in the writ, and was of the disciples of Shammai. And they had called to themselves Simon the Pharisee of the city of Naim, who had been host unto our Rabbi and had the first dispute with him in the matter of the remission of sins. And Rabbi Judah, the son of Hanan, was the chief elder of the court, for he was of the place. And the chief assistant and the prayer leader of the synagogue sat with them, and the people came and bore witness concerning the words and deeds of our Rabbi. And they said: "We saw the Rabbi, Yeshua ben Joseph, sitting at one table with sinners; we saw him consorting with tax collectors, who are likened unto robbers; and there were about him women of ill repute." And having heard this, the court sent question to our Rabbi: "Yeshua ben Joseph, why consortest thou with sinners and tax collectors and women of ill repute?" And our Rabbi sent answer: "The physician healeth not those that are whole, but those that are sick." And the court accepted his answer. And there came others and testified: "We saw how the Rabbi went with his disciples on a Sabbath in a field of growing corn, and some of his disciples tore off the ears of corn on the

Sabbath, and ate, and their Rabbi said naught to them concerning the matter." And the court sent for our Rabbi, and when he had appeared, said: "Yeshua, son of Joseph, knowest thou not it is written: 'And the Sabbath shall be a sign between me, the Lord, and the children of Israel, for ever'? And now, if thy disciples desecrate the Sabbath, thou bearest the responsibility, for the Rabbi shall take upon himself the sins of his disciples." And our Rabbi answered, saying: "Ye have read that which David did when his men were hungry? How he came into God's house and did eat of the shew-bread, which no man is permitted to eat of, save they of the Priesthood alone. And ye have read in the Torah, that the Priests do desecrate the Sabbath in the Temple, and it is not accounted to them for a sin. And I say unto you that there is a thing which is greater than the Temple. Know ye not it is written: 'I desire mercy, not the blood of sacrifices'? And ye shall not accuse the pure, for the son of man is the lord of the Sabbath."

Now when the court heard these words, it became silent, and after a time Eliezer the son of Judah asked: "Whom meaneth he thereby, the son of man?" And Nathan the son of Ishmael called out: "He meaneth thereby the Messiah, as it is written in the Book of Daniel." Then rose Simon the Pharisee and said: "Now have our sages accepted the doctrine that danger of life taketh precedence of the Sabbath?" And Nicodemon the son of Nicodemon answered: "Yea, that we have by tradition from the venerable Hillel. And the sages have deduced the same from the Torah, for it is written: 'And it shall be holy unto you,' and that signifieth that the Sabbath hath been given unto you, and not you unto the Sabbath." And Nathan the son of Ishmael ratified this with the words of the prophet, for it was said by Isaiah: "And ye shall call the Sabbath a delight," which meaneth that the Sabbath is a delight and not a burden. And the head of the court said: "Now the Rabbi Yeshua ben Joseph hath cited King David, therefore he standeth upon the foundation of the Torah, and his answer is accepted!"

And there came others and testified: "Now we have seen the Rabbi sitting at one table, he and his disciples, with tax collectors and sinners and men-of-the-earth, and he broke bread with them and they did not wash their hands before, as the commandment prescribeth, neither he nor his disciples nor the people." And the court was greatly angered, and they sent again for our Rabbi to appear before it; for this last transgression outweighed all the transgressions whereof they accused him heretofore.

And our Rabbi put on a black mantle, according to the law, and came and stood before the court. And when it was known that our Rabbi had now come to answer this charge, then the people assembled to the court, and the worker left his bench, the fisher his boat and the field laborer his plow. And the judgment chamber of the synagogue was too small to contain the multitude, and the people stood without and looked into the court room through the door and windows. For the court sat with open door and windows, that all the people might see that its sentence was just. And the head of the court said:

"Yeshua ben Joseph, an evil report hath been brought concerning thee before this court, and we have sent that thou appear before us, to answer in person whether this thing be false, to wit, that thou, Yeshua ben Joseph, who art strong in the observance of the law, didst sit with sinners and men-of-the-earth, and break bread with them, not washing thy hands before, as the law prescribeth, nor didst thou call upon thy disciples and all the people that they fulfill this law."

But now, instead of answering in modesty and quietness, strengthening his words with the authority of the Torah, as is the way of the learned, our Rabbi answered in anger, saying:

"And why do ye desecrate the law when it pertaineth to your tradition? God hath commanded thus: 'Honor thy father and thy mother, and he that curseth his father and mother shall be put to death.' And ye say: 'He that taketh a vow before his father and mother, and sayeth: "Let that be a sacrifice which is your pleasure in me," he needeth not to honor his father and mother.' Do ye not thereby destroy God's word for the sake of your tradition, ye hypocrites? Well did Isaiah the prophet prophesy regarding you: 'The people is near to me with its mouth, its lips honor me, but its heart is far from me. Vain is the honor ye do unto me, for that is a thing learned of men.' " And therewith he turned to the people that were in the court, and to them that stood in the street, and said: "Hear and understand! Not that which cometh into the mouth maketh men unclean, but that which cometh out of the mouth." And he left the court room and went away.

And when this had come to pass, I did not follow after my Rabbi as the other disciples did, but I stayed there to hear the sentence which the court would pronounce and what they would say.

And Eliezer the son of Judah, who was of the party and family of the High Priest, said:

"We are all witnesses and we have heard the words of this man. He meriteth punishment not for his deeds but for his words, for he hath blasphemed against the tradition which is not written in the Torah, and we know not what the punishment is therefor. But in that he hath diminished the honor of the sages and trodden upon the good name of those that study the law; it is as if he had spoken shamefully of all the Torah. As our sages have taught: 'The honor of a sage is greater than the honor of an angel.' Therefore I would know what this most just court shall lay as punishment upon the man that hath shamed the sages."

Then rose Simon the Pharisee and spoke thus:

"The honor of the sages resteth in its place, and God be our witness that not the matter of our honor or of the honor of our fathers' houses concerneth us here, but the honor of God, the Only One, and of His just Torah. We cannot punish the Rabbi for having said that to the sages which he said, for it is a virtue to tell the truth to a man's face, the more so in a court which sitteth in judgment; and it is a virtue to say 'hypocrites' to sages who do not that which they preach, and make a show of their devoutness before the world; for certain of our sages have done likewise, and it is written: 'Ye shall burn out the evil in your midst,' which meaneth also the sages and scholars. Now for this there cometh no punishment to the Rabbi, for he said that which he desired to say. But this thing I would know: what sentence will this most just court pronounce against him for the deeds he hath done? Most just court: it is known and accepted that Moses received the law on Sinai, and he handed it on to Joshua, and Joshua handed it on to the ancients, and the ancients handed it on to the prophets, and the prophets to the men of the great congregation; and from the hands of the men of the great congregation it came into the hands of the sages, till the days of Shemaya and Abtalion. And Hillel served Shemaya and Abtalion, and learned the Torah from them, and from the venerable Hillel the tradition cometh down that the washing of hands is deduced and prescribed from Moses and Sinai, and this is one of the eighteen prescriptions on which the houses of Hillel and Shammai were agreed. And all this passed from our parents unto us. And we observe the commandment of the washing of hands with utter devotion, and we have made one fence after another about us, we have sought to counter the danger of impurity in our vessels, and in our food, and in our garments; even a scroll in the sanctuary is subject to the danger of impurity, and we must wash our hands before we touch it. And wherefore do we carry with such devotion the yoke of the kingdom of heaven? And wherefore have we thus circumscribed our lives, and made heavy our burden, and drawn fence after fence about us? Hath it been for our pleasure? Hath it been for our honor or the honor of our fathers? Nay. We have done all this that we might be sundered from the gentiles, that we might remain a holy people and sustain the light of God. We are a small island in a sea of impurity, evil and idol-worshiping. Observe now the peoples of the world, they that rule over us; they worship sticks and stones and call to gods that hear not and see not. They say unto the beast: Thou art my father who hast begotten me, and to the animal: Thou art my god who canst shield me from evil. And they sacrifice their children unto them, and their wives play the whore in their temples, and their men practice all manner of indecency, and the justice of God reigneth not among them, they know not God's laws, they oppress the widow and sell the fatherless, and they enslave their people in everlasting slavery for the pleasure of their rulers. And they fill the world with a sea of sin and whoredom, so that the cry of the earth mounteth to heaven. And it is well for them, for they rule the world; and we, the guardians of the light, are in submission to them and we are trodden underfoot. Thus we may perhaps look with a corrupted eye upon the follies of the world and think in our hearts: Mayhap, God forbid, the truth is with them, and we will imitate their deeds. And thus, God forbid, God's justice will vanish from the earth, as happened in the days of our parents, who were driven forth because of their sins, and for whose sins the Temple was destroyed. But there arose prophets unto our parents, and the prophets punished them and reminded them of the one and living God; and they would not let our parents mingle with the peoples of the world, that the light of God's word might not vanish from the earth. But in these days we have no prophets, and because of our sins the spirit of the prophets hath departed from us, but there be in their place the words of our sages and learned men, and according to the words of their mouth do we live. And they have sundered us with many fences from the people about us, and they have put up a great dividing wall between clean and unclean, and they have laid upon us the yoke of the washing of hands, so that in every moment of our lives we may remember and know that we be Jews, that we be a sanctified people of God, chosen to fulfill his commandments, to guard His Torah and uphold His name. Even until the Messiah cometh, who will fill the earth with justice and all men will acknowledge the one living God, as the prophet hath prophesied: 'And it shall come to pass in the last days.' Then, in the last days, all the nations will accept the God of Israel. As the prophet sayeth: 'And the peoples shall stream unto Him, and many nations shall say, Come, let us go up the house of God.' In that day the division that is between us and the nations shall be removed. But until that day cometh, we shall be sundered from them, for we have been dedicated to guard the light of God, as it is written: 'And ye shall be holy unto me.' Therefore our sages have put up these fences, and he that cometh to break one of the fences, it is as if he breaketh all the laws of the Torah. And for this reason our sages have put more weight on the tradition than on the written law: the tradition is dearer unto us for we have ourselves and of our own will made the burden heavy, and we bear it with love for His name's sake without having been bidden. Shall we then let each one that so chooseth enter into our garden and tread upon the beds and go unpunished? Who is he that cometh to destroy the wall between us and them? He calleth himself 'Son of Man.' Now 'Son of Man' meaneth the prophet, as it is written in Ezekiel. And

'Son of Man' meaneth likewise the Messiah. Is he Messiah? Then where are the signs? As hath been promised: 'Behold, I send unto you Elijah the Prophet before the coming of the great and terrible day of the Lord.' "

And there were voices heard from the people: "He performeth wonders, the blind receive their sight and the sick rise from their beds." And others called: "With one word he healed my father of leprosy." And still another called: "He comforted my sister and forgave her her sins."

And Simon the Pharisee answered these voices, saying:

"We regard not miracles, for miracles are not a proof of the Messiah. There be also black forces, forces of impurity, which God hath created to prove mankind, as the prophet hath said: 'He created light and made the darkness, he maketh peace and createth evil,' which things the gentiles worship from the ancient serpent onward, which brought upon us the sin of Adam, even unto the abomination of Beelzebub, the god of flies, which they of Ekron serve. They have their false prophets, and with their powers the false prophets perform miracles."

But the people called out: "What then is the proof of the Messiah? Tell us, for what shall we wait? We are weary of straining our eyes after him, our parents went down dishonorably to their graves in the hope that Messiah would come. Now the everlasting pit covereth them, and we perish in need and oppression, and Messiah showeth himself not. Now tell us, for what thing shall we wait, and what is the sign and proof of the Messiah?"

And Simon the Pharisee answered:

"It is written in the Torah: 'There will arise among you a prophet or a dreamer of dreams, and he will give you a sign and will perform wonders, and the sign will be fulfilled, and he will say unto you: "Come, let us follow other gods, such gods as we know not, and let us serve them" '; then ye shall in no wise listen to the words of this prophet or dreamer of dreams!"

And they called: "He biddeth us not serve other gods, but the one living God of Israel."

"But he biddeth you not to obey the commandments which are in the Torah, which the one living God gave to Moses for his people Israel. And he biddeth you not to have regard to the tradition of the sages, into whose hands was given the power to interpret the Torah. He that destroyeth the Torah destroyeth the covenant between God and Israel. He that denieth the Torah denieth the God of Israel. Only he may do that who proveth unto us that he is Messiah, sent of God; only he hath the authority and no man of flesh and blood. If he be the Messiah, why appeareth not Elijah the prophet to proclaim his coming? Why gathereth he not the host of heaven to destroy the rule of Edom, why bringeth he not the peoples upon the holy mount, as the prophet hath prophesied? Why declareth he not this unto us? Hath he not been sent for us and unto us?"

But Nicodemon the son of Nicodemon said:

"Who sayeth that the Rabbi Yeshua ben Joseph is the Messiah? We have not heard it from his lips, nor have his disciples ever affirmed it."

Then demanded Simon the Pharisee:

"But again, if he be not the Messiah and the messenger of God, why cometh he to remove the law and the division between us and the gentiles, he that is flesh and blood? I therefore ask of this most just court that it pronounce strict sentence against the Rabbi Yeshua ben Joseph, who destroyeth the tradition which hath been transmitted to us by our parents."

But Nicodemon the son of Nicodemon answered:

"There hath not been put into our hands the power to punish. For this court hath been appointed only to search and inquire and not to pronounce sentence."

And the chief elder of the court and all the judges were in agreement with the words of Nicodemon ben Nicodemon, and they said:

"The Sanhedrin of Jerusalem gave us not the power to judge the Rabbi Yeshua ben Joseph, but only to search and inquire."

But Simon the Pharisee returned to the argument and said:

"Then I ask not of this most just court that it pronounce sentence against the Rabbi Yeshua ben Joseph, or that it lay punishment upon him, which power hath not been conferred upon it. But I ask that this just court, having heard the depositions concerning the deeds and words of the Rabbi, and having heard with its own ears that he speaketh with contempt of the tradition of the washing of hands, which is unto us as a law of Moses received on Sinai, I ask that this just court issue a warning to the people against the Rabbi Yeshua ben Joseph, that he performeth not his miracles, and healeth not the sick, with the pure power of the Torah, but that he performeth his miracles and healeth the sick with the impure power of Beelzebub."

And again the court was divided in its opinion. For some held that a warning to the people constituted pronouncement of sentence, whereto the court possessed not the power. And others held that inasmuch as the court laid no punishment upon Yeshua ben Joseph, but limited itself to a warning, this was not a sentence, but a ruling of note, which the people needed that they might not be led astray; and for this the court had power, because there was a danger.

And the court inclined toward that side which would issue the ruling to the people, and it was so done.

XI

Now the matter fell out thus on the day when the court uttered its opinion. I, Judah Ish-Kiriot, having alone remained of the disciples, returned toward evening to the house of Simon bar Jonah; and it was the hour of the late afternoon prayer, when the Priests in the Temple bring the evening sacrifice and the laborer returneth from the field to his wife. And my Rabbi had ascended to his booth on the roof of the house, and the disciples were gathered in the yard; and they talked of the events of that day. Their hearts were heavy and consumed with care; for they had no understanding of the words which the Rabbi had uttered in the court chamber, and they knew not any more what was clean and what was unclean. And when they heard from my lips the sentence uttered by the court, to wit, that the Rabbi performeth his miracles with the power of Satan and Beelzebub, their hearts became like water, and they knew not what would be with them. As we stood thus, one saying this thing and a second saying another thing, the Rabbi appeared before us suddenly, and none had marked his coming. Like a light fallen from heaven he stood before us, and before one had told him of the judgment of the court, he called:

"Now how can Beelzebub drive out Beelzebub? A kingdom that is divided against itself shall not stand, and if Satan riseth against himself and is divided, then surely his end cometh. Shall a man enter into the house of a giant, and steal what is therein, before he hath conquered and bound the giant? Surely he shall conquer and bind him first, and afterwards carry thence his possessions. . . ."

But the disciples remained without a word, and their heads were inclined toward the ground. Then Simon bar Jonah confronted the Rabbi, and bowed before him, and put our speech before him, saying:

"Now teach us, Rabbi, that which thou didst mean when thou spokest before the court. For thy words are beyond our understanding. Our parents taught us of things that are clean and of things that are unclean. But now, after thy words, we know not any longer what is clean and what is unclean."

And our Rabbi answered, saying:

"Are ye too without understanding? See ye not that that which cometh into a man from without cannot make him unclean? For it cometh not into his heart but into his belly, and passeth out. But that which cometh out of the man, that maketh him unclean. For from within the man come all evil thoughts: lechery, wantonness, murder, theft, lusts, wickedness, concupiscence, the evil inclination, a wicked eye, blasphemy, pride, folly—all these come out of the man and make him impure."

Now those disciples whose faith in the Rabbi was strong were greatly contented by this reply. But those of the disciples that were learned in the writ were tormented still more by doubt, and they stood with broken hearts and locked lips. Thus too stood Simon bar Jonah.

And the Rabbi, seeing the show of our countenance, said:

"Have I not said unto you that men do not put a new patch on an old garment, for then the patch will tear and the hole in the garment will be wider. Neither do men pour new wine into old bottles, lest the bottles break and the wine be spilled; but they pour new wine into new bottles."

But hearing this, we were more dumb than before. And Simon bar Jonah said:

"Now, when the scribes and Pharisees hear these things, they will be greatly angered, and their rage will grow against thee, and against us thy disciples."

Whereto our Rabbi answered thus: "Men do not light a candle and place it under a bushel or a bed; but they light it that it may shine through the house and that all may see it." And he said further: "He that loveth his father and mother more than me, he is not worthy of me. And thus be it with each one of you: he that leaveth not all that he hath cannot be my disciple. Salt is good, but if the salt hath lost its flavor, wherewith shall it be salted? For it is then without worth, and shall be cast away. He that hath ears, let him hear."

Therewith he left us and returned to his room on the roof, for the night had fallen and covered the earth with darkness.

And I, Judah Ish-Kiriot, the man of heavy spirit, lay in the night, my mantle wrapped about me. And my heart was oppressed by doubt as if the mountains of Gilead lay upon it. It was as though I had been driven from one house, and could enter no other, and the street was my home. And it was also as though I had fallen from heaven but had not lighted upon the earth, and I hung between heaven and earth. And there was none to spread out a net beneath me, and I was falling into the pit of hell; for I had passed from under protection of one authority and had not entered under protection of another.

Then I asked myself again, and still again a thousand times: Who is he in whose paths I follow, whom I know and I know not, though I see him with my eyes each day? I behold his deeds, yet know not who he is. His voice hath power over the storms of the sea, and over wild spirits, and he commandeth Samael and bindeth Asmodeus, and maketh them to lie in submission at his feet; who is he? He that comforteth the poor with his word, and wipeth away the tears of the wretched and the oppressed—who is he? And I bethought myself of all the deeds he had done in the time I had been with him, and all the words he had spoken and I had heard, and I was seized with trembling. I said in my heart: Now surely there must be in this man that which speaketh with the force of prophecy; there worketh in him that which hath permission and authority from heaven. He leaneth not on the Torah or the tradition or the ancients, but acteth as if the word had come to him from heaven, direct. He lifteth it up as Jacob lifted the stone from the well, with his own strength. Now can this be he for whom our eyes look—he that will remove the last barrier betwixt ourselves and God? He of whom the prophets prophesied, the hope of Israel?

And thus thinking I was wrapped in wind and flame, as when the storm lifteth the dust of the earth. And I said within myself: "Judah, Judah! What thoughts are these that come into thy heart? And what words are these that come upon thy lips? Thou art a man of unclean lips and impure heart."

And by me lay the man of bitterness and zeal, and like me he waited that help might come from the Lord as the lightning cometh from the sky, to wit, Simon. His father had been quartered by Herod the Edomite, because he had removed from the Temple the abomination of the Roman Eagles wherewith Herod had defiled the sanctuary. His brothers had been crucified by the man of sin, Varus, when he leveled the city of Sepphoris with the dust. He alone, Simon, had fled, and like a beast of the field, like a jackal of the wilderness, he had dwelt in caves. Snakes and scorpions were his brothers, the wild honey-hive was his vineyard. He had sought the word of God in the wilderness among the disciples of Jochanan, and he had found no comfort until he had found our Rabbi. And having found him, he clung to him. For like us he believed that a cleft had now appeared in the rock of our prison: who knoweth, the door may open, and salvation enter.

And he lay by me in the darkness of the night. And God had concealed his face behind heavens of steel, and had flung the earth into the pit of ignorance and doubt. And Simon lay like a plant that is uprooted by the wind and cast beyond the hills. And I called to him and said:

"Simon, thou zealous one: hast thou heard the words of our Rabbi and Lord? Hast thou seen the hand which he lifteth like an ax to cut at the roots which bind Israel to the navel of his father? Hast thou heard and understood? Now tell me, what words hast thou, and what are the thoughts thou harborest?"

And he answered me, saying:

"I am the slave of God. And the slave hath not the right to question the ways and deeds of his Lord; he hath but to obey and to hearken to the will of the Lord, which our Rabbi bringeth to us."

"But who is this that bringeth to us the will of the Lord of the world? Is the will of the Lord that old will, which the sages taught, or is it the new will, which we have heard from the lips of our Rabbi?"

And Simon, the zealous one, was affrighted and rose on a sudden from his place where he slept. And as though a snake had bitten him he seized my hand with piercing fingers and cried:

"Judah Ish-Kiriot, God forbid that there be an old and a new! There is only that which is everlasting from beginning to end."

But I put my lips to his ear and said: "Simon, thou Zealot, this day we have heard something new from the lips of our Rabbi, that which the ancients taught not."

Now we both stood, and he clung to my hand, for he was like to fall. And he said, trembling: "Now, Judah Ish-Kiriot, whither wouldst thou lead me and what is thy meaning? I understand not." And I answered: "Hast thou not heard the words of the Rabbi?" And Simon the Zealot was silent.

There slept near us Simon the son of Jonah, a man whose heart was whole with God, and he was filled with faith as the ripe grape is filled with wine. And he was sleeping the sleep of the just. And I awoke him and said: "Simon bar Jonah, how canst thou sleep when the disciples shake like the leaves in the storm because of the words which they have heard this day from the mouth of our Rabbi?" And Simon answered: "My heart is still, and my spirit is at peace, for I have faith that he will not deny the holy one of Israel."

But I asked him: "Tell me, Simon bar Jonah, who speaketh the will of God, and to what shall we listen, the old or the new?"

And Simon bar Jonah answered: "Far be it from us to believe that there be either old or new; there is but the whole from beginning to end. As it is said: Both these and these be the words of the living God. Hath not David proclaimed: 'By the way of faith I know how to guard thy laws.' And it is also written: 'The just man liveth in his faith.'"

But I would not leave go of him, and I pressed him to tell me that in which I should believe: the laws and commandments which our sages have taught us, and which they received from Moses our teacher through the prophets and then through Ezra the Scribe and through the ancients, those same laws and commandments which had come to our Rabbis, the teachers of our own day; or the laws and commandments which we had heard from the mouth of our Rabbi. For if our Rabbi spoke as he spoke, it must be that he had authority over the law. And if that were so, who could tell how far this thing might carry?

And when the disciples that were awake heard these words, there rose a great tumult in the darkness. And one voice called: "Now tell me what is toward here? Do we tread in the ways of our fathers, or have we, God forbid, entered upon new ways? And if we be upon new ways, what do we here with this man?"

Then Simon bar Jonah called out: "Disciples of my Rabbi—what are these words? Surely the hope of Israel shall not be deceived!"

And there was the noise of many voices as the disciples assembled about Simon bar Jonah. And one said to him: "Thou, Simon bar Jonah, go and bring our doubts to the ear of our Rabbi, for thou art nearest to him, and he will not hide the thing from thee."

Then Simon bar Jonah answered: "I will not go alone, but send with me two of the disciples who are learned in the scriptures, and let us ascend to the room of our Rabbi, and let us throw ourselves at his feet and say: 'Rabbi, thus and thus is it with us'—and God will be our help and make all clear to us. For everything which our Rabbi doeth is for the sake of heaven."

Then Simon bar Jonah took Simon the Zealot, and me, the smallest and unworthiest of the disciples, and we mounted by the ladder and came to the door of the upper room; and we beheld through a crack that the room was filled with light, as if the light of heaven were with him. And silence and fear came out of the booth unto us, so that out hearts melted, for the terror of God had fallen upon us.

And Simon Bar Jonah called to him through the crack of the door: "Rabbi, Rabbi, have mercy upon us!"

And we heard the voice of our Rabbi: "Simon!"

And Simon came before him, and we behind Simon; and Simon threw himself down, so that his beard touched the naked feet of our Rabbi, and Simon cried:

"My lord and Rabbi! Thou hast dealt graciously with thy servants. Thou hast gathered us from the street, and it hath been granted to us to sit at thy feet and to drink the words of thy mouth. Our lord and Rabbi! We know that the Lord intendeth greatly with thee. We behold the zeal of God burning in thee like a fire, and thy soul is consumed with thirst for salvation and redemption. We see thy deeds and are filled with amazement, for God hath put power into thy hand, to bind and to loose. Thou hast dominion over the spirits and demons, thou liftest thy voice and they hearken. Our hearts run over with joy and hope because we see that redemption ripeneth in thee, as the child ripeneth in the mother's womb. But thou hast placed upon us burdens of care, and clouds descend upon our eyes. We behold deeds and cannot interpret them, we hear words and cannot understand them. We stand before the well like thirsting sheep, the stone is rolled away, but the water floweth not into the trough to slake our thirst. Lord and Rabbi, hide not thyself from us. Thrust us not away, but take us unto thy heart; comfort us with thy word, and bring calmness to our disturbed spirit."

And the Rabbi spoke gently, saying: "What is it that oppresseth thy heart?"

"The words which thou spakest today before the court, Rabbi; we have not heard their like before. Is this the old, that which cometh to us from Sinai, or leadest thou us in new paths which our forefathers have not trodden? This thy disciples would know."

Then the Rabbi said:

"Oh, ye of little faith, how oft have I not said it unto you, that I am not come to destroy the Torah, nor am I come to destroy the words of the prophets, but to fulfill. For I say this unto you: heaven and earth shall pass away before there shall be changed one jot or tittle of the Torah, and before all that is written therein shall be fulfilled."

And Simon stretched out his hands to him and called out in joy: "Lord and Rabbi, thou art our comfort and our support." And tears filled the eyes of Simon, and fell upon the folds of his face. And rising, he turned to us and said: "Have I not said it to you, that the holy one in Israel will not deceive our hope?"

And Rabbi said to Simon:

"Be comforted, Simon. Go now and light the lamps, and tell the women to prepare whatsoever there be in the house, for I would break bread with my disciples, and I shall say unto you that which ye are to do."

And the women did as they were bidden, and we assembled in the house of Simon's mother-in-law. And the bread was placed upon the table, and the disciples were about him, and the women stood in the door.

And the Rabbi said his prayer and broke the bread and distributed it among us.

And even as he divided the bread he spoke to us words which our ears received but our hearts understood not. Yet they fell like fire upon our inner parts, and they melted us all and drew us together into one family. And these were his words:

"Know now that great trials approach for the son of man.

"Father in heaven. Open the eyes of those that believe in Thee that they may see Thy light. For it is revealed and known unto Thee that not for my honor and not for the honor of my father's house have I done the things I have done, and spoken the words I have spoken, but only for the honor of Thy beloved name, that Thy faith may be spread in the hearts of men, who are sheep without their shepherd and know not what is about them. . . ."

And we sat in silence, and the Rabbi called to us and said:

"Know ye, that not the happiness of this earth is the sign of God's grace, and not him whom the Lord loveth doth He exalt with happiness and good fortune. The possessions of this earth are not the prizes which God distributeth among His chosen. The possessions of this earth He giveth to the wicked for the little merit that is in them. Often He maketh His chosen one the target of arrows; His beloved ones He rewardeth with sorrows; He filleth the way of the righteous toward Him with thorns, for the sorrows of man bring him nearer to God.

"Did not God bid Abraham bring his only son as a sacrifice upon the altar? And did He not hold His children four hundred years in bondage in Egypt? Look around and behold: wickedness triumpheth, men of evil lift up their voices, they tread impudently upon the heads of the just. The measure of the world is not the measure of eternity; God measureth with another measure, nor shall the son of man flee from that which is destined him, but he shall pay the full price."

And here the Rabbi ceased from speaking.

And we were filled with fear and knew not what he meant.

And Simon bar Jonah said: "Lord and Rabbi, declare unto us the meaning of thy words."

And the Rabbi answered:

"Simon bar Jonah, also he that goeth with me must be prepared to pay the full price."

And Simon said:

"Rabbi, but have we not left all behind us and followed after thee?"

And the Rabbi lifted his eyes and said:

"Blessed are ye, the poor, for yours is the kingdom of God; blessed are ye that weep now, for ye shall rejoice hereafter; well is it with ye that men do hate you, and withdraw from you, and say all manner of shameful things of you for the sake of the son of man. Rejoice in that day and spring for joy, for behold, your reward is as great as heaven. For thus also did their forefathers to the prophets. And it sufficeth that the disciple shall be as the Rabbi and the slave as his lord. And if they called the master Beelzebub, how much more shall they put this name upon his household? Therefore fear ye not them. That which I say unto you in the darkness, that shall ye proclaim in the light, and that which is said into your ears, that shall ye proclaim from the housetops.

"Even as God said unto the prophet: 'And see, I have made thee this day a fortified city and an iron pillar, and walls of brass against the whole land, against the kings of Judah, against her princes, and against her priests and against the people of the land.' Therefore I say unto you: Fear not those that destroy the body but who cannot bring the soul into hell. Are not two sparrows sold for a farthing? And not one of them falleth from heaven without your father's knowledge. Even the hairs of your heads are counted. Therefore fear not."

And our Rabbi placed his hands upon our heads, each one in turn, and dedicated us.

And we were twelve in number. And the Rabbi gave us power to drive out evil spirits and to heal the sick and the suffering, and he said: "Go not in the way of the gentiles, and come not in the cities of the Samaritans, but go unto the lost sheep of the house of Israel, and as ye go ye shall call: 'The kingdom of heaven draweth nigh.' Ye shall take neither gold nor silver nor copper in your sacks, nor shall ye take food for the way, nor shall ye have two shirts, nor shoes, nor a staff, for the laborer earneth his hire. He that would go with me must deny himself. He must take upon him the yoke of God and follow me. For he that seeketh to save his life shall lose it, and he that loseth his life for my sake and for the sake of my tidings, he shall win it. For what shall it avail a man if he win the whole world and lose his soul; and what shall a man give in redemption of his soul?"

And the night of darkness was changed into a great light, and the hour of mourning into rejoicing. And in that night the Rabbi bound us close together and made us into one family. We were as men that had died in that night and had been born again.

XII

After this, when it became known in the city and the region round about what sentence had been uttered against our Rabbi by the messengers and deputies of the Sanhedrin, then many of those who had followed after our Rabbi withdrew from him; and many souls which he had made in Gederah and Bet Zeida and Migdal and other cities fell away from him. And many rich women who had contributed to our treasury ceased to do so and returned to their homes; and only such were left as had not whither to go, and clung to him.

And when I, Judah Ish-Kiriot, beheld the poor folk that were left in the house and yard of Simon bar Jonah, my heart failed within me. For I, Judah Ish-Kiriot, was entrusted with the belt of the monies of the treasury; and when the wealthy had withdrawn from the Rabbi, the treasury began to empty, and I thought in my heart, What will be now? Who will now feed these poor? For until now it had been thus with the feeding of the poor: Jochanah, the wife of Kuzah, the rich officer of Herod, and Susannah, the young woman, the two souls which the Rabbi had made in Naim, came of wealthy homes and had many possessions. And they sold of their possessions one by one and added the money to the treasury of the poor, as the Rabbi had commanded them. And thus did others of the wealthy that came to the Rabbi. For otherwise the Rabbi would not take them into his congregation of souls.

With these monies we bought bread and other food, and we fed the poor which were always assembled about the Rabbi. But now, having heard of the sentence uttered by the court, there came the husband of Jochanah, and would have compelled her to return home; there came likewise Zadok, the rich father of Susannah. And these two women refusing to leave the Rabbi, they were disinherited. And with the woman Miriam of Migdal the matter was thus:

Save on the one day when she appeared first before our Rabbi, in the city of Naim, she had been wont to wear sackcloth. Bar Talmai, the blind oil mixer, who had been of the disciples of Jochanan the Baptist, had taught her to walk in his ways, and to practice fastings and mortifications of the flesh for the sins she had committed, that she might repent and be cleansed. But our Rabbi had taught her that she need not mortify her body, nor wear sackcloth, in order to repent and be purified; for, he said, God looketh into the heart of man and not upon his clothes; also the glory of God descended not save through joy; and the true repentants wear the sackcloth upon their flesh, but above that they put on silk and purple, and anoint themselves with sweet-smelling oils, that it may not be known of men that they fast and mortify themselves. And it came about that Miriam of Migdal changed her clothing before long, and she anointed her body once more with oils, and wore silken clothes of many colors, and likewise many ornaments, whenever she appeared before the Rabbi. And she, rather than the other women, tended the Rabbi, washing his raiment and sewing for him shirts of fine linen to which she gave a sweet odor with costly perfumes; these she had brought with her, and they hung about her neck in precious vials. Now all the other women had given their possessions into our treasury, some having even cut off their hair and sold it to the wig makers and beard braiders, that they might bring contributions to the treasury. But she did not thus, though many poor could have been fed from the sale of her possessions;

moreover, the other women labored in house and court, at the spinning wheel and the washing, to minister to the needs of the many poor, and of the disciples. But Miriam of the city of Migdal bestowed care upon her hands, that they might not become unsightly, and that she might think them fitting to tend the Rabbi. For she said that she had dedicated her soul and her body as a pure offering to the Rabbi, and inasmuch as her hands were deemed worthy to touch the feet of her lord, it were wrong that they be made coarse with heavy labor. Thus she worked not about the house like the other women, save that she ministered in the booth of the Rabbi on the roof of the house, and kept it with great cleanliness, and adorned it with many flowers of the field and with sweet-smelling herbs, which she knew how to find. And she brought into his couch sweet-smelling spices and oils from the Phoenician vials whereof she had many.

Now when the Rabbi returned daily from his holy work, it was as though he had taken upon himself all the sicknesses and fears, the pains and sorrows of those that he had healed, and he was weary. And his body seemed like to break under the burden, and his face was pale with sorrow. And then Miriam of Migdal would enter into his room and she would wash his feet and anoint them and dry them with her hair. And the Rabbi suffered her to do so. And sometimes the spirit would descend upon her and she would fall to the earth, and she would have foam upon her lips, and she would deliver herself of messages and tidings, and prophecy spoke from her, out of her love and devotion to the Rabbi.

And the other women envied her for her nearness to the Rabbi, and there was quarreling among them that she did no labor about the house, but dedicated herself to the Rabbi and clad herself in colored raiment and ornaments. And there were women who had contributed to the treasury but had withdrawn, saying: "Now let Miriam sell her precious oils and feed the poor." And for this reason too our treasury became smaller and our congregation lost in number.

Now the house of Simon's mother-in-law was filled with such of the poor as had no homes, and with the sick that could not betake themselves elsewhere, and with the heavy-laden of sin. And they lay in the court, like to heaps of refuse which are thrown out of the house; and some of them wandered about the city and begged bread. And the people of the city murmured against our Rabbi, saying: "He hath called the people unto himself, and he cannot help them any more; surely his power hath departed from him." Likewise the poor said: "Where are the paths whereof ye told us. Why helpeth he us not? Are our hopes deceived again?"

For now it came about that the Rabbi closed himself in his booth on the roof, and concealed himself, and would see no one. Then Simon entered to him and said:

"The poor are assembled in the courtyard below and they wait for thy salvation. What shall I do with them?"

And the Rabbi answered:

"I would be alone with you for a little space. Come, let us go from here, for I am weary of them. There is a ruin in the neighborhood of the city of Bet Zeida. Let us go there and hide ourselves from the multitude, which crieth ever, 'Give! Give!' And we will prepare our hearts for our father in heaven."

And I, Judah Ish-Kiriot, went forth, and bought provision out of the little that was left in the treasury, five loaves and two fishes, and we entered into a boat, and we went to Bet Zeida, which is on the shore of Genesaret. But when the multitude that was in the house saw us depart, so they fled after us, those that could move. And some of them got themselves into boats, and others went on foot along the shore of the lake. And when the people of the city saw our Rabbi going hence, they laughed, saying: "Behold, Beelzebub getteth him forth, and the demons with him."

And we came to the shore in the neighborhood of Bet Zeida, and we entered a ruin which stood there and we hid ourselves from the multitude, for our Rabbi was weary and would have been alone with us.

But the poor and the sick hastened after us; and many wandered over the fields, and inquired closely, and found us.

Likewise it was told in the city of Bet Zeida that we were in the ruin in the fields, and their sick came out likewise to seek us. And the sick and the hale surrounded us, and the blind and the sinners, and they cried: "Rabbi, Rabbi, come out to us, and why hidest thou thy countenance from us?"

And when our Rabbi heard the cry of the multitude, his heart was filled with pity, and the fire of God came into his countenance, and he went out with stretched-forth arms to the people and cried:

"Come, all ye that are abandoned and thrust out, unto me!"

And the spirit returned unto him and he was filled with grace; and the people rejoiced in him and drank in his words. The blind felt their way to him to touch his garment, and the sick that could not walk crawled on the ground toward him; and soon the Rabbi was walled in like the cornerstone of a building, by the sick and the poor that surrounded him.

And one he touched with his hand, and to another he inclined his head, and to a third he uttered comforting words. And the multitude was happy to be by him and to listen to his comforting words. And the time thus passing, I saw the sun preparing to set, and I asked in my heart what was to be done with so many poor? And in my basket there were but five loaves and two fishes, and these had been prepared for the disciples.

Therefore I spoke to the disciples, saying:

"Now what shall we do with this multitude of the poor? For the treasury is all but empty and there is scarcely wherewith to buy bread for them. Let us speak to the Rabbi that he send them home."

And we, the twelve disciples, made our way to the Rabbi among the bodies of the poor that surrounded him; and we all spoke, that it might not seem that any were of less faith than others, and we said:

"The end of the day approacheth, and this place is empty and abandoned, and the people have no bread; now do thou send them home, and let them spread themselves in the villages, and go into yards, that they may obtain food and lodgment for the night."

But our Rabbi said:

"And shall ye not feed them?"

Now when I heard these words my heart melted for fear, and I asked:

"Shall I go forth and buy bread for two hundred dinars?" But I told him not that the girdle was empty of money.

But the Rabbi asked, as in astonishment:

"Have ye not prepared food? Now go ye and arrange the people, row by row, so that none shall be missed in the feast. And place before me the baskets with bread which ye have prepared, that I may make a blessing over them to our father in heaven and thank him for the food."

And hearing the Rabbi speak thus, I felt my heart beating with fear, and I was filled with dread that my Rabbi be not put to shame before the whole multitude and I thought in my heart: "What will be now?" And I went to Simon and said:

"Simon bar Jonah, I must go into the city, and buy bread. But there is no money in our treasury, and we have but two ornaments. It may be that I shall be able to exchange them against bread. For there is a great multitude and in my basket we have but five loaves and two fishes. And the Rabbi hath summoned all of them to the feast." And Simon said to me: "Go!"

And I hastened with swift steps to the city, and I came to Bet Zeida. And God was gracious unto me. For I exchanged an ornament for money, and I entered into the house of a baker, and behold, there were four baskets of loaves which he had baked for the city, and I bought them of him. And I found likewise, without delay, a man who hired me two donkeys, and he came with me, and we hastened back to the ruin, with the baskets of loaves, for I would not let it come to pass that my Rabbi be shamed.

And now the night had fallen and the stars came out; and we drove the donkeys with all speed. And when we came nigh to the place where I had left my Rabbi with the multitude I heard from the distance a great noise of rejoicing voices, and the field was illumined with many fires which they had lit thereon. And when I came to them, with my donkeys laden with bread, I saw the Rabbi seated in his white mantle, and a circle of children was about him, and the glory was upon him.

And all the multitude, men and women and children, the hale and the sick, were filled with joy, and some of them danced, and they clapped their hands, and they cried aloud: "Hosannah! Hosannah! He hath fed us!"

And I stood as one astonished, and knew not what this meant. And it came to pass that when I showed myself with the laden donkeys, that a great laughter rose, and the people pointed to the crusts of bread which lay like fallen snow on the field and could have filled many, many baskets. And they said: "Thou wentest forth to bring us bread, but one that was much nearer fed us, and we ate and were satisfied, and we have left much." But I asked in amazement: "Now what hath been here? The place is empty and remote from a dwelling place. Where got ye this bread?"

And Simon bar Jonah said: "He lifted his eyes to heaven what time he made the benediction; then he broke the bread and divided it, and there was enough for all, and much was left." And I looked at the earth, and the donkeys stood by me, and I was ashamed of my little faith.

And the multitude ceased not from rejoicing and singing and crying, late into the night. And they danced about our Rabbi and rejoiced in him. And the woman Miriam, that was with us, fell at his feet, and her eyes were covered, and there was foam on her lips; and she rose, and bent herself, and circled like the whirlwind, and she cried out in a singing voice: "Behold, he is like the bridegroom on the day of his marriage, illumined with the light of redemption. See, the clouds stoop down to the earth, and they spread themselves under his feet. Thence he commandeth the spirits to do his will. Like Moses he bringeth the manna down to us. He came with all his glory in the hour of our need. . . . He bleedeth more than we with our wounds, he hungereth with all the hungry, and is thirsty with them that thirst. He goeth with the blind through the holes of the night, and he carrieth before them the light of their eyes. He leadeth the sinners through the darkness and beareth upon his shoulders the torment of their sins."

And the voices ceased not to grow louder, and the crying rose like flames toward heaven. And the people called, one to the other: "Now why should he not be king over us?" And one man was there, who had been blind of one eye, and his body covered with running sores, and the Rabbi had healed him. And the man cried: "Bring the crown of David, and let us crown him king over us. He that feedeth us shall be king over us. Who is so fitting as he to be king of the poor?"

And when the women who were there heard the word king, many of them fell to the earth in such case that foam was upon their lips.

And they began to prophesy, and even children were visited of the Holy Ghost, and they turned in the madness of prophecy and they screamed forth verses of holy writ which they had learned of their teachers; and they likened the wisdom of our Rabbi unto Daniel's, and his miracles unto those of Elijah. And some said that this was Jochanan the Baptist who had returned to earth.

And I looked around and sought the disciples of my Rabbi, and I found Simon bar Jonah. He stood off, saying nothing; he danced not, neither did he shout, but in the midst of his hair and beard, which the days of his years had touched, his eyes shone like stars, and they were turned steadfastly upon the Rabbi, who sat in his white garment in the midst of the garland of children, and the tears flowed from Simon's eyes.

Then with the lateness of the night, the multitude dispersed, for our Rabbi was weary with his service of the day and bade them depart; and many of them scattered in the villages, and others went to Bet Zeida, for that was their home. And the waters of Genesaret, which had slept under the kindness of the stars, were awakened by many boats leading the multitude back to K'far Nahum and other places whence they had assembled. There remained the Rabbi, and we, his disciples.

Then the Rabbi said unto us: "Go now, take shelter in the ruin, and I will go up on yonder hill to pray alone; then I will come to you." And Simon asked him: "Shall I not accompany thee, Rabbi?" And the Rabbi said: "Nay, go thou with the others."

And the disciples came into the ruin and laid themselves on the ground, and covered themselves with their cloaks, and a deep sleep fell upon them, for they were awearied with the labor of the day. But sleep came not to visit mine eyelids, and I found not rest.

And many cares were in my heart, and I asked of myself: "Now how cometh it that among all the disciples of the Rabbi God hath chosen me alone to cover mine eyes with a covering, that I shall not see the wonders of my Rabbi, but that I should only hear of them? And I alone of the disciples stand without and knock at the door and it is not opened unto me. Wherefore is it not opened unto me? A buckler of sin surroundeth my soul, and is it therefore that the light falleth not upon me, and I must stand without? And if this be so, what have I to do here?" And my heart wept in me. And I said: "It was taught of old: 'All things are given from heaven, save the fear of heaven.' Whence it followeth that a man must acquire faith through his own efforts, even as he acquireth the food and clothing of his body." Then I prayed to my father in heaven: "Open my eyes and give understanding to my heart, that I may see and feel like the others." And I strengthened myself and said: "Is it not written that the Torah is not in heaven, but hath been given to man? And is not that which my Rabbi preacheth and doeth the continuation of the Torah? Therefore it pertaineth to me not less than to the others of the house of Israel."

And I went forth in the night and I perceived that my Rabbi stood alone on the hill, and the whiteness of his garment was covered with light, and his arms were uplifted as he prayed alone. And it was with me as if the shadow had fallen from mine eyes, and I saw my Rabbi as if he were an angel of heaven, and I fell at the foot of the hill, and lifted my hands to him and cried: "Rabbi! Rabbi! Help me!" And my Rabbi said to me: "Judah, come to me up the hill; it is for thee that I send my prayers to heaven." And I arose to ascend the hill. But the ascent of the hill was filled with bushes and thorns, and there were many hindrances. And I wandered this way and that and could not come to my Rabbi. He was lost from before mine eyes, and I remained alone in the night in a wood of thorns, and the thorns stretched out their spears to me, and hands that would seize me. And I called: "Rabbi, where art thou?" And I heard his voice, but him I saw not. But when a time had passed he appeared before me and took my hand and ascended with me, and I stood near my Rabbi and the heavens above were spread out wide and covered with light. And the Rabbi said unto me:

"Judah, thy heart is restless; it is like a lost ship in a stormy sea. Why canst thou not find rest, like my other disciples?"

And I answered, saying:

"Rabbi, perform now one of thy wonders and strengthen my faith in thee." And my Rabbi answered: "Even for this did I pray now, Judah, for thou couldst have been my most beloved disciple."

And he took my hand and led me down to the ruin, and we entered and saw the disciples of the Rabbi sleeping in a corner, their heads resting upon the stones, their bodies covered with their mantles; and the light of the stars fell upon their faces and beards and poured out its mercy upon them, and they slept the sleep of the just, even as Jacob our forefather slept in Beth El.

And the Rabbi said: "I thank thee, O father in heaven, that thou hast hidden the thing from the wise and understanding, and hast unveiled it to children and the innocent." But I found daring in my heart and said: "They who hold in their hands the thread which was given to us by our fathers cannot sleep; they are not at peace with themselves, for they fear to let the thread drop from their hands. For if they lose it, what shall they do? They will not find another to hold to, and then will they not wander lost in the night of their lives?"

Thereupon my Rabbi answered:

"Thou art left but one which holdeth the treasure in his hand, but not they that hold the treasure have it; only they that think they have lost it and continue to search. . . ."

"Rabbi, I understand thee not."

Thereupon he answered: "He that seeketh to save his soul from me shall lose it. But he that loseth his soul for me shall find it."

And I bowed myself before him and said:

"It is a great thing thou askest of me. Behold, I will not leave thee till thou tellest me who thou art."

But my Rabbi answered, saying:

"Judah, I am only he who sitteth in thy heart. I am faith. I dwell in each heart in that measure in which the heart can hold me."

But I threw myself at his feet and cried:

"Rabbi, I know who thou art. Only he can speak thus who hath been given the power thereto." But my Rabbi lifted me up, and pointed to the sleeping disciples and said: "Go, Judah, and lay thee down among them, let thy heart find peace."

And I lay down among the others, and I slept with them in the ruin by Bet Zeida.

XIII

Now on the morrow, when the inhabitants of K'far Nahum and the cities round about learned of the wonders which the Rabbi had performed for the hungry in the fields, their hearts were moved with astonishment and unease; and there were some that said: "It must surely be that God intendeth great things with him," and others that said: "His power cometh from Satan. He will bring great misfortune on us."

And when they heard further that they whom the Rabbi had fed would have proclaimed him king and demanded for him the crown of David, a great fear fell upon them. And the people of the city said: "Now when the government will hear that the Jews would have proclaimed another king the guilt will fall upon all of us; and we shall bear responsibility for the foolish speech of the poor, and we shall pay for it."

And certain of them came before our Rabbi and said: "Arise, and get thee gone from our city, for the government hath heard of thy deeds, how thou wouldst be king over the Jews, and they follow after thee to take thee captive. And it will come to pass, if we do not deliver thee into their hands, that they will say we have sworn an oath to proclaim a new king over the Jews, and calamity will come upon us because of thee."

Then the Rabbi called us to him and said: "Come, let us be gone from this place. We will go up to Tyre and Zidon. For did not God say unto Elijah the Tishbite: 'Arise, and go to Zarephath in Zidon'? Why should we be otherwise than Elijah, for the people of this day are not better than the people of his day, and even as Ahab had his false prophets, so they have their false prophets likewise."

And my heart melted with fear when I saw that our Rabbi was minded to leave the cities of the land of Israel, whereon the spirit of holiness resteth, and to be gone to the base cities of the idolators, which are given over to impurity. But we dared say no word to him, for his might was upon us as the might of the lord over the slave, and his burden was upon us like the yoke on the beast of the field; and we bowed our heads in silence and we followed after him.

And it was as if the Rabbi knew my thoughts. For I was meditating on food, and on what we should eat in the land of impurity, and he said: "O thou of little faith! For did not God feed Elijah through the ravens and the wild bees?"

And we took with us our coverings of sackcloth to cover ourselves therewith in the night, and it was morning when we set forth. And the women folk, and our friends, went with us part of the way out of the city. Then they returned, and the women abode in the house of Simon's mother-in-law, there to guard the vessels. For the Rabbi said that he went not now to preach the word of God, but to rest himself from the tumult of the people, and to search in his heart for the way which God would have him follow.

And ere we left the shores of Genesaret, we bathed in the waters thereof, and we said the "Hear, O Israel," and we ate the bread which we had taken as provision for the way. Then we went up among the hills which lie between the land of Israel and the land of Tyre and Zidon. And though the hills were thick with settlements as a pomegranate is thick with seeds, we came under no roof, for it was the will of our Rabbi to lodge at night in the shadow of the branches of the great cedars. And we went two days, until we came to a place which is called Cheder Bayarim, and we rested outside the city.

And when the sun rose on the morning of the third day, his light lay upon the levels of land which pour themselves into the Great Sea; and we saw the western shore which was sown with multitudinous cities set in green gardens and girdled with meadows. Now the cities were not spread upon the land alone, but thrust out into the sea with their many-peopled harbors. And from the heights we perceived how the sea was thick-sown with ships, and we were amazed by the mightiness of this kingdom. Their houses were not like unto ours, for they dwelt in mighty places of brick and stone, and they hid themselves from the sun in the shadows of columned halls. But when we approached the border of Zidon we understood the reason for their great wealth, in that we saw, on the first fields whereon we trod, that they use not the ox and the ass for their plows, but put the yoke upon men.

The earth of Zidon is fattened with the blood and limbs of fallen slaves. The cry of need goeth up like a cloud above Tyre and melteth in the air and descendeth again in a rain of tears and terror. And in the first field our Rabbi encountered a man who plowed his field, and he had yoked two men to his plow, one old and one young. For it is the custom with them to yoke an old and marrowless man with a young and strong one, so that the old man might sweat after the young one. Naked the two men were. And when the old man could not pull the iron colter through the sandy earth with the speed and strength of the young man, and his feet stumbled in the holes, then the leaden riders in the whip of the plowman came upon his old, withered body. And when our Rabbi saw this, he would have stopped the wicked man, and he called out: "Why smitest thou thy brother? For thou seest he is old and weak and cannot do the same work as the younger man." But he that held the plow answered: "Callest thou him my brother? He is my slave, which I bought with my good money. Fifty silver drachmas by Tyrian weight I gave for him in the slave harbor when our ships brought a cargo of slaves from the lands of Gaul. Scarce two years hath he served me, and behold what he hath become. I give him bread according to his work, but no matter how little bread I give him, the use I have of him is less than the cost. But who art thou that comest to disturb the laws of our land? According to thy dress and the sound of thy voice I know that thou art a stranger, and a Hebrew to boot. Thou hast not yet shaken the dust from thy shoes and already thou wouldst be a judge over us."

Then the sons of Zebedee called out: "Rabbi, what murmureth this wicked man? Shall we make him silent?" And the Rabbi answered: "I am not come to destroy the lives of men, but to heal." And we answered him not and went upon our way. And the nearer we came to the city, the more we encountered of the work of slaves. For whereas we in our land labor with beasts which rest, even as we do, on the Sabbath, they labor with men. We saw many water wheels, such as in our land are pulled by the ass and the camel, and they were pulled in this land by slaves, and their eyes had been pierced, for among them a man costeth less than the beast of the field.

Yet all this was as nothing by the side of that which our eyes beheld when we came within the city. The sandy level which spreadeth out by the shore of the Great Sea was covered with mighty houses, which hid the waters and crowded upon the peninsula which cutteth into the sea. And the deeper we went into the city the more we beheld of the sinfulness of the slavery of Zidon.

And with every step we beheld more and more of the slave laborers. We came first into the streets of the weaving looms which are gathered to one side of the city. For in Zidon it is not as with us; the woman weaveth not clothes for the house in hours of rest, by the light of the fire of the house, surrounded by her household and the sound of devout singing. It is far otherwise with them. Their kerchiefs and their clothes, their coverings and their shawls, are woven by slaves which they purchase in the slave markets. They weave not at the loom that which each one needeth for himself, but they weave to send out their linens to all the lands of the world. Therefore they assemble their slave weavers in large places, and the slave weavers are fastened to the looms as the ass is fastened to the plow. And an overseer sitteth above them with a rod in his hand and counteth out, and as he counteth, the slaves send the shuttle through the loom. And there are other overseers with whips, and the slave that keepeth not pace with the counting taketh the lash on his body.

They were numberless, the looms which filled the large places covered over with branches. Numberless were the slaves, like spiders woven into their own webs. For the greatest part they were old, their marrow dried up in them, men and women such as had no strength for heavy labor; and the young and strong had been taken as oil treaders and workers in the dye houses. And the women that threaded the spools lay like trampled worms at the feet of the weavers, like the forlorn of God, like the grass which is thrown out. And the greater number of the spinners were children; their eyes were covered with sores, their hair had fallen out; and there were such as were covered with boils, and the matter ran from their ears. For those children that are strong and well-favored they use as servants or for their lusts to sin with them, and the ugly and sick are sent to the weaving places.

And we encountered there men and women chained together who knew not each other's tongue. And it is thus with them: when a slave groweth old and serveth no more for labor, they take him not into the family as is the custom in the lands of Edom, nor do they after the manner of the Greeks, who build quarters for the slave, and there the slave may live until the day of his death. For they use not the slaves, as do the peoples of Edom and Greece, to serve them and their own needs; they of Tyre and Zidon keep their slaves to make the varieties of merchandise which they load upon their ships for many markets; therefore, when a slave becometh sick or weak and can work no more, so they throw him out of the slave quarter and give him no more food. Therefore we encountered about the weaving booths such as lay in heaps and with their last strength begged for a little bread, or the hand of death; but there was none to pity them. They know not here the meaning of compassion, which is the quality of the Lord of the world, which he imparted to our forefather Abraham. There is no end to the work, and no man or woman prayeth for the coming of the night to find rest therein. We saw likewise lines of young, strong slaves harnessed to wagons and bringing without cease the loads of colored thread from the dye houses which are by the sea. Thus they feed the wild beast of enslavement, and as a river poureth forever, so poureth the slavery day and night in bitterness and rage.

And when our Rabbi saw the slavery of the weavers he uttered no word, but the show of his countenance bore witness to that which was in his heart. And his countenance changed, being cut as with pain; and his lips being twisted with anguish hid in his beard and his eyes were turned to heaven. And I heard the groaning that came from within him, and the cry that broke forth with it: "Lord of the world, have compassion on thy creatures."

And we arose from this place and turned back from the city; and we followed after the slave wagoners which brought the colored thread from the dye houses which are on the seashore.

Greater than the pouring of the Great Sea is the pouring out of injustice on the shores of Tyre. We could not gaze in adoration on the aspect of the mighty waters which God hath made, for our eyes were darkened by the aspect of the leprosy which was spread upon Zidon's shore.

All the shore of Tyre and Zidon is but one chain of slavery, and the edge of the land is filthy with the sweat of men and their tears. The waters of the Zidonian sea have not their own foam, but the foam of human decay. We saw the fisher slaves bring to the shore boats laden with the water snail which carrieth their purple. All night long the slaves lowered their baskets into the sea and brought up the snails, and all night long they heaped them on the shore. And there, among the heaps of sea creatures, stood men mighty of stature, chained to great stones; and the eyes of the men were bound or pierced, that they might not see what they did. And they pulled the stones forever about the mills, under the whips of the overseers, and they ground the snails which other slaves threw with spades upon the stones. And the violet marrow which is in the liver of the sea creatures spirited upon the naked bodies of the slaves and dyed them. The heaps of ground snails grew at their feet, and their bodies were drowned in the foul masses of crushed intestines which mingled with the ground snails and became a stinking mud. The air was filled with a thick stinking, and men trod as in dung. There walked chains of bound slaves bearing on their shoulders the bales of white wool, coming from Damascus, and from our ports of Caesarea and Joppa; likewise bundles of flax coming from Egypt; and they threw this into great troughs of thick purple, whereinto the dye ran from between the millstones.

Young women and maidens trod the wool and flax in the troughs; others drew them forth and laid them upon the seashore to dry. And the whole seashore was inhabited by naked men and women who had upon them nought but the purple of the dyes, which was as a second skin and took away from them the likeness of human things, so that they looked like spotted beasts. And in the manner of beasts they were treated.

And here likewise, even as by the weaving booths, old slaves lay among the heaps of the crushed snails, the day of their work being gone. They were eaten by the diseases which the poison of the dyes bringeth upon the body. Their limbs were broken and their eyes were burned out, and they rolled about in the filth and none heeded them. They ate the filth which fell from the crushed snails thrown out by the mills; and their bodies swelled up therewith.

And the cry of their pain was stilled by their weakness, till they rolled in their pain to the edge of the sea and the waves took them and washed them out of life. And we left this place and went further; but whithersoever we went we could not flee from the sea of slavery.

Wherever our eyes fell, we saw the nakedness of flesh harnessed to labor. Without number, likewise, were the ships upon the sea, with the colored sails of the nations, of Egypt and the Greek Islands, of Spain and Persia and Italy and Africa. There were slaves that carried the cargoes into the ships, silks and woolens and glassware and all manner of vessels and instruments; and other slaves carried down from the ships the merchandise of the world, the silks of Persia, the wines of Cyprus, bronze and silver of Spain. Like diligent ants the people labored on the shore, and like ants they were for number; and the chains of the slaves drew endlessly from the ships to the dye houses, to the forges and the workshops, so that the city of Tyre was woven about as with a girdle of sin and pain.

And our Rabbi stood at every work place and looked upon the people. All things he would know and see; and as if he would empty the cup of injustice to the dregs, he went from one vale of tears to the other, from the weavers to the dyers and from the dyers to the sewing women.

Now even as they used the men for the heavy labor, so they had enslaved the women to the work of sewing the garments which went forth from Zidon. And they that did the sewing were likewise slave women, but they were also put to uses of pleasure, therefore they were given light labor that their bodies might be unspoiled.

And we came after that to the crippled children in the metal workshops; and there were young ones upon whose lips the milk of their mothers was scarce dried, boys and girls that sat with hammers in their hands and fashioned into vessels the copper and bronze and silver drawn from the furnace. And these children had upon their bodies the burned-in marks of their slavery, even like their parents, and the decree was upon their flesh to use up their strength in slavery till they fell among the heaps of dung, even as their parents did. And some of them were nigh to blindness and some had had their faces burned by fire, for that they were not skilled enough. And the flesh of others was torn by the whips of their overseers. For they that sat by the furnaces were unfit any more for the lusts of the Zidonians, therefore their bodies received no care. Nor were they good to be sold in the slave markets, therefore they were gathered together in the forges that they might end their young lives in this labor.

Then we saw how young hands touched fire as if they were not flesh but iron pincers; we saw children with bellies swollen high from much drinking of water against the great heat; and the water which they drank was the unclean standing water which they used for the cooling of the wheels.

And we went forth from this place to the place of the great furnaces. There we saw the slaves bring in woven baskets the loads of lead earth which the ships had brought from Britain. And the furnaces stood upon the seashore, filled with the fires of hell. And they cleansed the lead earth, and mixed it with iron and silver from the mines of Tarshish. And others nourished the flames of the ovens with loads of wood which they brought in wagons from the Carmel. And about the fires which beat from the furnaces danced naked men half concealed in the clouds of thick smoke which poured from the ovens and darkened the light of the sun. And in the midst of the heat and smoke the naked were like sinners in hell; and they moved about and with long shovels they poured the molten lead into the molds; and they drew these forth, and felt them with their hands. And it came to pass that the boiling metal spurted from the molds and fell upon their bodies and burned them.

And we saw there cripples with burned-off limbs and half-faces; and when they would turn from the work they were driven with whips into the smoke and flames by the overseers that stood about them. And when the spurting metal took out the eyes of the slave, he was taken away and put to work on the dye mills. And when a slave could no longer labor at the dye mills, then they found other work for him; and there was no ceasing and no flight from work, until death took pity on them, as it was with our forefathers in Egypt.

And we went forth and came to the place of the glassblowers, and here too great fires burned in ovens and their flames went up to heaven. And these fires likewise were fed with loads of wood which the slaves brought down from the Carmel and Lebanon. And here, likewise, slaves dragged heavy baskets of glass sand, as our parents dragged loads in Egypt; and the glass sand, which is found here on the shore, is poured into the furnaces and becometh a glassy fluid. But in this place there worked not strong men, but women, and children even more; such as were young of breast, and that had much breath in them to blow through pipes into the hot glass-stuff.

And there were children fleshless to the bone from the great heat of the ovens, and charred limbs, as among the metal workers. And they pulled forth blazing glass from the caldrons, on their pipes, and their lips were fast to the pipes and they blow into the fiery stuff, and the breath of their breasts hollowed out the glass vessels. And while the fire was in the stuff they formed it with their naked fingers into the beaks and necks and ornaments of the vessels. And it was so, that the sun burned their bodies from without and the hotness of the stuff burned their inward parts. And it came to pass that here and there a child fell under the burden of the fiery work; and being carried away from the ovens, he came under the eye of an overseer. And if there was still life in the child, the overseer awakened him with the lash; and if there was no more life in him he was thrown upon the dungheaps by the sea, and became the prey of the sea birds.

And it chanced that as we stood by the glass furnaces they carried forth a child that had fallen from the heat, and they laid it upon a heap of glass sand under the sun, and one of the overseers looked at the child, then let fall upon it the rain of leaden riders of his whip. And when, after a while, the child did not waken under the whip, then the overseer let it lie there, for the soul had departed from the child and there was no more worth in it. And there was none there to take the part of the child. And our Rabbi stood there, and looked upon the thing, and we thought in our hearts that now he would lift up his hand, and he would change the overseer, as Lot's wife had been changed, into a pillar of salt; or he would do as Moses had done when he smote the Egyptian and buried his body in the sand.

For we beheld the face of the Rabbi when he gazed upon the child, and it was as if a fire had come into it, and he trembled as if a storm had passed through him. But he said naught to the slayer of the child, and his lips were locked and the line of his mouth was twisted in pain. So we too were silent. And Jochanan, the son of Zebedee, smote with his fist upon his own heart, wherein his rage burned.

And the other disciples too were seized with anger against the slayer, and we longed that the Rabbi might utter a word and make the slayer sink into the sands, even as he had made the child to sink into death. But our Rabbi was still silent, and we understood there was a reason for his silence, and we contained our anger.

But when the slayer had left the child, then the Rabbi drew near to the dead body, and we with him. And he looked down upon the dead child, and it was a boy, in his ninth or tenth year, and his body was withered with the heat, so that there was no flesh upon it, but it was wholly bones with skin thereon, and the skin was covered with sores and boils. And one leg was lame, and he had but one eye, for which reason they had put him to the ovens. But he bore in his right ear the sign of his mother's love, the ear-ring which she put in his ear when he was born. And his hair was black, and his face was not the face of a child, but hard and extinguished like that of an old man, and full of wrinkles. And we waited, thinking that the Rabbi would have compassion on the little one and awaken him from the sleep of his death. But he did not so. And we understood that there was a reason for this, and we asked not. And our Rabbi was silent, but I marked that the tears ran from his eyes and fell upon the body of the child.

And we went from the valley of the pain of children and we came to the place where they keep their slaves when they are brought from the ships which come from all the lands of the world. And this was a hedged place upon the shore, covered with palm leaves; and there we beheld the men and women and children, the old and the young, of all the races of the earth, and there were mothers with children at the breast. And the Zidonians get not their slaves by the conquest of the sword, as other nations do, but by traffic in souls. They follow after the captains and commanders and buy their prisoners, and they go wherever the sword of Rome reacheth, to the isles of Britain, and to the lands which are beyond the deserts of Africa, and Armenia and the Caucasus; and they buy also the slaves of the lands which neighbor on their own. And they put the slaves in groups and classes. Some they send to the mines in the far-off lands of Spain and Britain, whence they bring silver, lead and iron. These be the slaves which are condemned to look no more on the light of the sun, for they are held forever in the mines and are not released from their living graves; and these are for the most part the strongest men, in the best years of their life. And there were such now upon the shore, and they kneeled in chains, hard by one another, and their eyes were fixed upon the sun as knowing what would be their lot and seeking to take with them into the everlasting darkness as much of the sun as they might now gather. And there were other slaves who would pass their lives upon ships. And still others there were whose lot was fixed according to the trades which they had known in their homes. And yet again there were some, young and fresh of body, to be sold upon the markets of Zidon, and to be taken to markets beyond the seas, to serve the lusts of their buyers. And they were all sorted and set apart and treated according to their worth upon the markets, and so their food was. Those that were strong of body and enduring, were set aside for coarse labors, and they were fed with raw foods, with carcasses and stinking fats, and they were placed under the lash. But those that were destined for house use and for lusts were treated gently; they were kept under shelter and their food was tender, and the overseers guarded them from harm, lest their worth be diminished. And we saw an owner of slaves cry out in rage against an overseer for that he had lifted his whip against goodly young slaves, and diminished the worth of the merchandise. And such slaves they anoint with oils, that they shall awaken desire and their price be higher.

And our Rabbi stood there a long time and looked upon the lines of slaves, for he would hear and see all. And that day he ate no bread, but he was as if sated with the pain of those he looked upon. And we knew that something was toward in his heart. And again I heard him groan as if a storm had gone through him, and he was seized by a great anger. I had not seen him thus in all the days I had been with him, for fire went out of his eyes and his body was like a red flame, and he called out: "Thrice unclean art thou, Tyre; thy flesh is the flesh of corpses and thy water is poured out blood."

And he went from there, and we came into the heart of the city, and we sat down in an open place, for our Rabbi would not enter into a house, the roofs of Zidon being unclean as if death dwelt under them. And he would not eat their bread, for "the bread of Zidon is the flesh of corpses and the water thereof is as poured out blood." He would only endure the night there and return to the borders of the land of Israel, for their manners and customs were strange to us, and we were as lost in the midst of the tumult of their pain and sin.

And the city, girdled with the sin of the torture of men, was in appearance like a harlot colored and raddled. Their gold was pressed from the blood of men and their wealth from the sweat of the young. Their houses were strong-built, with columns and broad steps and ornamented roofs like unto temples. And in every open place they had temples for the abominations of their idols, and we saw the passing of many people, and they were clad in many-colored clothes. And the more important the man, the more were the colors of his dress, ornamented and many-hued like unto the plumage of wild birds, and with golden circlets upon their heads. And their wives too were adorned in multi-colored raiment, and they went accompanied by slaves who were naked, with their shame exposed, and the city was filled with song and play. And we encountered time without number bands of celebrants proceeding to or from their sinful gatherings, accompanied by the music of flutes; and the men like the women were prinked and rouged, and naked slaves went with them so that Tyre uncovered her shame to the light of heaven.

And our Rabbi with his disciples, garbed in black, were gathered together and sat in a heap in the corner of a palace, beneath a palm tree, and we closed our eyes that we might not see their indignity. And they remarked by our clothes, which differed from theirs, that we were strangers; yet not one of them drew near to us to entreat us to his home, as is the custom in the blessed land of Israel, where the fear of God lieth upon us. And though there was peace since our fathers' times between Tyre and us, and there was commerce between the two lands, nevertheless none looked round upon us.

Here, in the city of Tyre, we the disciples perceived how far the gentiles be from us. And we approached none of them for that they would not have comprehended our ways and they would have mocked us. Here, in this strange place, we perceived at last how holy is Israel, and how well it is with us that God hath made his spirit to rest upon us, and that instead of being the slaves of men of flesh and blood we were elected to be the children of the Lord of the world. And we longed to be among our brothers in the bosom of the Jewish law of the Torah, whereunder we are warmed as under the wings of our father who keepeth watch over us.

And as we sat thus lost in the alien city of the gentiles, there approached us a man, and his garb was black and simple, like ours, and he asketh us in our tongue:

"Brothers, surely you are children of Israel, that you pass the night in the street and enter not into the houses of the heathen."

And we answered:

"So it is; we are brothers in Israel."

And the stranger called to us and said:

"Blessed be the God of Israel that he hath sent my brothers unto me. Now be ye gracious unto me and enter under my roof. Blessed will be the threshold of my house that you cross it. I have bread in my house, also wine, which is ritually pure according to the laws of Israel. And my wife, the keeper of my house, rejoiceth already, and my household likewise, that such important guests be come."

And he rejoiced with us, and kissed us each one on the cheek, as is the custom in Israel, and we with great rejoicing accompanied him to his home.

XIV

Blessed art thou, O father in heaven, that thou hast chosen our portion that we may serve thee, and that thou hast not made us as the peoples of the world into idolaters which bow down and worship the work of their hands. Have compassion, father in heaven, on thy creatures and open their eyes, so that all of them may see that thou alone art king of all the worlds, and that there is none beside thee.

Joshua ben Kalman received us in his house; and when he learned that they that were come under his roof were a Rabbi and his disciples, he held it a great honor, and he took it upon himself to serve our Rabbi. Now we did not impart to him who this man was that had crossed his threshold, for our Rabbi had bidden us strictly to tell no man his name or of his deeds, for he would not be known in this strange place. And even though he that had taken us under his roof perceived from the manner of our acts that we were of the sect of the Pharisees, natheless we forgot all divisions among ourselves, and all felt that we were but children of the one living God.

Now when the man had brought water in earthen ewers, and he and his children had helped us to wash our hands and feet, then we sat down about the table. And his wife had hastened into the kitchen and had prepared food for us, for we were a-hungered from the long way, and no food had come into our mouths that day. And the woman put upon the table bread, likewise butter and cheese, all prepared according to the ritual of the Jews; and there were also green things, but there was no meat, for that they dwelt among the gentiles which eat of the living blood of the beast, and they could not demean themselves to eat thereof; and only when they went up on the Passover pilgrimage to the Temple in Jerusalem did they eat meat, to wit, of the Passover sacrifice.

And the man told us of the manner of living of the Jewish congregation in the midst of the gentiles, where the witnesses of the living God had made a nest for themselves. And he said: "Praised be He, we dwell here in peace, and each one helpeth and strengtheneth the hand of the other. There be among us such as are learned in the writ, and we have here our little sacred synagogue, and we assemble on the Sabbath and some of us are called up to the reading of the Torah. And the elders and the prayer leader read forth for us every Sabbath the portion of that week, once in the Holy tongue and twice in the version, and the preacher preacheth. And those that have been on pilgrimage to Jerusalem then deliver the greetings of God's house. And he that heard there a tradition unknown to us, or a new word from a Rabbi, telleth of it. And oft there is a good deed to be done, such as the ransoming of a slave, for they that deal in human souls bring at times a Jew in the midst of their merchandise, he having been captured upon the sea or upon dry land and sold into slavery. And it is so, that whenever a new ship cometh into harbor, so the chief of our synagogue, to whom this hath been entrusted, goeth to the harbor and searcheth and enquireth lest there be, God forbid, a Jew among the slaves. And we have our treasury therefor and we redeem him. And in past years, in the great unrest under Archelaus, many Jewish slaves were brought from Galilee, the which Varus, the wicked one, had sold to the sons of Tyre; and God sent punishment upon him therefor later. In those days of the war with Varus our congregation did great things, with the help of the Temple and the funds sent us by the High Priest, and we ransomed many slaves; and some returned home when the troublous times had become quiet. But many of them remained here and added to the number of our congregation. Likewise we have here many that have dwelt long years in the land; they came here of old in the days of the Hasmoneans. And we comport ourselves here among the gentiles as though we dwelt in the holy congregation of Israel. We make our pilgrimages to Jerusalem, on each festival another group, and we bring back strength and firmness for our faith. Likewise we renew our faith every Sabbath. And when it chanceth that a learned man passeth this way, and he preacheth of the Torah on the Sabbath day, so the whole assembly gathereth to hear the word of God. And if it pleaseth your Rabbi to sojourn with us until the Sabbath and to preach to us, then I will go straightway and apprise the elders."

And the man would have gone straightway to bring word to the elders of the synagogue, that they come to honor the Rabbi in his house; for he said that it was not fitting that he alone should have this honor; and when they would learn on the next day that a Rabbi and his disciples had been in the city and they had not been bidden to the feast they would have hard thoughts against him. But our Rabbi forbade this thing strictly, for that he would remain unknown in the city.

And as we sat as brothers together, and thanked God that he had been gracious unto us and brought us under a Jewish roof, that we might not pass the night in the street among the gentiles, there was heard on a sudden the approaching of a noise like the waves of the sea, a whistling and a playing of flutes and a beating of drums and a tumult of men, so that the voices filled the night and mounted to heaven. And when we were filled with wonder thereat, then the master of the house declared it unto us, that these were preparations, and on the morrow the inhabitants of the city would offer a sacrifice, the first-born son of a family of honor, to their idol

Moloch. For whensoever there cometh a disaster on the city, so they offer their god the sacrifice of a human being. And there had come evil tidings to the city, that ten of their ships laden with merchandise had been overtaken by storm on the sea by Tarshish and swallowed by the waves. And the tumult in the streets signified the preparations for the dissolute sacrifice, and eight days the city delivereth itself unto abominations: for they unman themselves openly and in public, and they throw the severed parts into houses, and they in the house throw out in return the garments of women, wherein they deck themselves and take part in the whoredoms which are practiced in the temple of Ashtarot.

And when we heard this the terror of the night fell upon us, and we thought to flee from the city and get us gone as quickly as might be from this unclean land. And I looked upon my Rabbi and knew him not, for his countenance was as black as earth, and his eyes were buried deep and clouded, and it was as if the pain of the world weighed upon his shoulders and bore them down. But his lips were sealed and he spoke not.

And later in the night I heard the praying of our Rabbi, and though it was the fifth night that sleep had not come to his eyelids, and though we had lain in the open upon the hills and were now under a roof, and were weary, natheless sleep came not to him and he stood among his disciples that were stretched out upon the terrace of the house which the master thereof had given us for lodgment. And I beheld the hands which he stretched up to heaven, and I heard the voice which went forth from him, a groaning and suffering, but words I heard not, and it was as if his heart had been extinguished.

And on the morrow we thought again to leave the city with hasty footsteps, and to return to the land of Israel which we had lost like sheep which hear no more the flute of the shepherd. But our Rabbi said unto us that he would remain until he had seen all the abomination which was done in the city, by its inhabitants, before their idols. And he entreated the master of the house to lead him that day to the place of the idols. And we were filled with wonder thereat, but we followed him. And when we came into the city, lo, the city was like unto a drunken harlot. And the streets were filled with folk in holiday attire, and they were clad in garments and shawls and sheets of the colors of lilies, and violet striped and streaked with blue and red. And as their garments were colored, even so were their faces, and their lips were crimson as if they had but just drunk of the blood of slaughtered beasts. And there were such of their menfolk as were garbed in the attire of women, and as they walked they imitated the manner of women; and they wore nose-rings and ear-rings and chains that carried perfume vials upon their bosoms which they bared in the manner of women. And there were such women as wore the attire of men, and they had fastened to their faces braided beards, and they had upon their heads the wigs of men. And these were the holy and sanctified ones, the priests and the priestesses of their idol Ashtarot. And they went in processions, and carried the teraphim of their idols; likewise they carried trees which they cut from their gardens; and musicians went before them and played upon instruments, and there was a dancing of naked men and women.

And there followed other processions of their great idol Bel; and in this procession they wore high headgears and colored girdles upon white raiment, and the flute players blew before them and the sistrum players beat upon their sistra, and a great host followed after the priests.

And there walked among the priests a mother that led her child by the hand; and the child was a boy, in his ninth or tenth year, without blemish and fair to look upon. And the boy, even like the priests, was clad in a white garb girdled with red, and he wore a golden circlet upon his head. And the boy wept and was loath to go, as knowing that he was destined for the sacrifice. And the woman spoke gently to the child, and would win it with sweetmeats; and the multitude paid great honor to the mother and her child, and more to the mother than the child, for that the mother must be of strong spirit, to show no weakness, but to bring her child willingly to the god, lest the god Moloch find not the child acceptable and turn not his wrath away from the city. And it is thus, that the mother must be of the honored families, for only from among these may the sacrifice be brought.

And we went with the processions till we saw that they came to the court of the temple of the god Moloch. And the court was filled with the most honorable people of the city. And in the court there were trees, which they of the city had cut from their gardens and brought thither to plant in pots; and among these trees they erected their gods. And the idol Moloch was in the likeness of a sitting man, and his head was in the likeness of a steer, save that he had the twisted horns of a he-goat. And on either side of him there stood two he-goats. And his hands were held forward and turned up, that he might receive the sacrifice. And all of him was poured of iron mixed with copper, and he was hollow within, like unto an oven. And by him they had placed their other idol, to wit, Melkart, which meaneth *Melech Kiriot*, or the king of the city. And he was in the likeness of a man in the fell of a lion; his face too was in the likeness of a lion, with a curled beard, and upon his head he had horns like unto a he-goat, and in his hands he held a kid, rent in twain, this being the sign of his strength. And on the further side of their god Bel stood the image of their goddess Ashtarot in the likeness of a naked female, and she pressed a dove to her bosom, this being the sign of her fruitfulness; and after their god Moloch she was the most beloved among them. And about Ashtarot were gathered the sacred men and women, those that we had seen in the processions in the city. And there stood other idols there, which the priests drew forth from the temples and brought forth on the day of the great festival of Moloch. And about each god stood his priests and priestesses.

And when the mother came with her son, surrounded by priests, into the court, then rose the High Priest, who was the elder of their city, and approached the god Moloch, and offered up prayer to him, and with a torch he lit the heap of wood which was heaped up in the hollow belly of the idol. And the priests of the other gods lifted their voices in song and praise, and the High Priest and his servants threw wood into the belly of the god that his iron image might glow with heat.

And in the time while the fire was being prepared in the belly of the god, the mother stood apart and held her child by the hand, and she looked upon the fire that was to receive her child, and there was no change upon her countenance, neither was there any groaning from her lips, neither were there any tears in her eyes, but she comforted the child and calmed it with sweetmeats. For the child wept and would have fled, but the priests that encircled the place would not let him, and the mother held him fast. And we know not if the mother did this out of love for her god or out of cruelty of heart.

Then, when the iron body of the idol had grown red with the heat of the fire, the High Priest approached mother and child; and he lifted the child in his two strong arms and showed him to the people. And a great cry burst out from the people, so that the boy was affrighted, and ceased to weep, and knew no more what was happening with him. And the boy stretched out his hands to his mother, to seek her protection; but the mother, standing off from the child, still made as to quieten and comfort him, pointing with eye and finger at the High Priest. And the High Priest took the child, and carried it to the blazing idol and placed it upon the fiery arms.

And there was heard a great screaming from the child, and the white garments upon the child burned straightway; and the cry of the child, in pain and fear, split the hearts of the people, but there arose a shout of voices and a clashing of sistra and a shrilling of flutes; and the people were caught up in the rejoicing of the instruments, and the weeping of the child was heard no more.

And the mother stood apart, and she looked, and she beheld how the flames did eat into the flesh of her child, and how the fat of his body did pour into the flames with a crackling; for the sacrifice had been well prepared and given much food to eat before he was brought to the flames, so that he might be found acceptable by their god. And the hair of the child burned off straightway and the head sank down and lay against the fiery breast of the idol. And there was no groan from the mother's lips, nor were there tears in her eyes; but she smiled and laughed as though it were a joy of the spirit to her; all this that the idol might find the sacrifice acceptable, for that it is well in the eyes of their god that the mother shall show no pity on her own flesh and blood.

And Simon bar Jonah, who stood with the Rabbi by the entrance to the temple court, lifted up his voice and said:

"Now let the children of Israel behold and learn from these idolaters to serve the one living God."

And our Rabbi answered not. But I saw a great anger upon his face, which was white as with fire; but his eyes were filled with fear. And it seemed to us that with one breath of his mouth he would utterly destroy all the abomination that was before us, even as our forefather Abraham utterly destroyed the idols of Terah his father, when he took a hammer and smote them; or that he would lift his hand and they would be swallowed even as Korah and his congregation were swallowed of old. Or there would come lightning from heaven and utterly consume them, for the stink of their abomination reached into the heavens. But our Rabbi did none of these things, but was silent.

And while the child burned in the arms of the god the people danced about the gods, and they sang and threw flowers and wreaths of olive and branches of palm; and they mingled with the priests and the priestesses; and they whored with them, kind with kind, under the trees which had been raised in the court of the temple.

But our Rabbi spoke no word, and his mouth was locked; and he was swallowed up in meditation; but the show of his countenance bore witness to that which was in his heart. And he made his farewells to the man that had brought us thither, though it was a late hour in the day; but the Rabbi desired no more to enter under any roof in this city, nor eat within its walls; and he made a sign to us that we leave the city in great haste, and shake the dust of it from off our sandals.

And a Canaanite woman that had been in the throng about the idols (now the Canaanites are slaves among the Zidonians) withdrew therefrom, and as we hastened from the place followed after us.

And when we had passed the gate of the city, the woman did not turn back, but she followed us still. And she ran and cried aloud to our Rabbi: "Have pity on me, my lord, for my daughter is tortured of an evil spirit," but the Rabbi answered her not.

But still the woman pursued us, and she stretched out her hands to our Rabbi and ceased not from crying: "My lord, thou son of David."

And we wondered greatly at this thing, that she knew our Rabbi and that she called him "son of David." And we asked in our hearts if it had happened with her as with Balaam's ass, which had perceived with its eyes the angel of the Lord.

And the disciples said to the Rabbi: "Send her away, for she crieth after us." And some of them said: "Help her; sanctify the God of Israel."

And the Rabbi answered: "I have not been sent but to the lost children of Israel," and we justified the thing in our hearts, but the woman came before our Rabbi and bowed herself before him, and cried: "Lord, help me." And our Rabbi answered: "It is not good to take bread from children and cast it before young dogs." And he went on. And we justified this thing in our hearts, for that which we had seen in the city had embittered our hearts against the gentiles and made them as dogs in our eyes.

But the Canaanite woman cried after our Rabbi: "Yea, my lord, but even the young dogs eat of the crumbs which fall from their master's table."

And as she uttered these words, behold our Rabbi stood still, and a light came into his face, and a holy fire shone in his eyes, as if the spirit had renewed him. And he became filled with strength and bade us call the woman and bring her before him.

And when she was bowed before him he put his hands upon her head, saying: "Woman, great is thy faith, thy entreaty shall be answered."

And from that moment on a great change came over our Rabbi, and the darkness of spirit left him, his strength was renewed, and he was filled with joy. But this was an amazing thing in our eyes, and the secret of it he declared to us but later.

XV

God of Israel, purify my heart and open mine eyes, so that my heart shall feel and mine eyes perceive that which happeneth about me. For I am as one that is blind and feeleth in the darkness. The sun shineth and I see it not. I hear voices and understand them not. Father in heaven, have compassion, for great and dreadful days draw near.

Now when we went forth from Zidon our Rabbi led us not to the cities of Israel, but to those cities which lie beyond the Sea of Genesaret, which Pompey the wicked took away from us, settling many heathens therein, so that the cities are half pure and half impure. Therefore our Rabbi would not lead us into the cities, but we wandered about in the fields and lurked about the cities like thieves. And in the place where we spent the night we spent not the day. In the day the sun ate us, and in the night the cold. We ascended the heights and we went down into the valleys. And in the day we were with the shepherds of the field, and in the night we lit fires upon the hills. And we put herbs and roots in the fire and we sustained our hearts with the honey which the wild bees left in the hidden places of the rocks. So we wandered from place to place among the hills. And we pointed at ourselves the verse of the psalms: "The birds of heaven have their home and the fox hath its hole," but we the disciples had no place where to lay our heads. Scorpions and locusts became our food. Yet we left not our Rabbi. For we had left all things behind us and we trod in his footsteps, which were illumined with the light of our faith. For even as the wind scattereth the chaff of the thresher and leaveth but the grain, so we, the disciples, were left alone of all those that had followed our Rabbi.

And we came to the city of Caesarea Philippi, which lieth beyond Genesaret and pertaineth to the kingdom of the Herod Philip. However, we entered not the city, but we rested upon the mount which is called Pamias and which is nigh to the city. And at the foot of the mount there is a cave, whence issueth a spring, which is the spring of the Jordan. And the place is pleasant to look upon, for there are many springs, and the earth is fat and fruitful, and broad meadows lie on every hand; and here the shepherds feed their flocks. Likewise there are many gardens, and the vines are fat, even so are their figs. Natheless the place is unclean, for in the cavern whence the Jordan issueth they have built a temple to their goddess Diana. And her image standeth there, and all day long they come to her from the city, bringing sacrifices of doves, and offerings of meal and oil, and adornments of flowers. Likewise the women cut off their hair and bring it as an offering to the goddess. The shepherds gather about the cavern and play upon their flutes, and all manner of abomination is practiced under the pleasant trees which grow about the cave.

And I marked how my Rabbi stood upon the mount and watched

the inhabitants of the city coming forth to sacrifice to the goddess. And I marked likewise how the countenance of my Rabbi changed, and he talked with himself like one that is possessed by a spirit.

And on that day our Rabbi was not at peace, and all day long he kept himself apart from us. And it seemed to us that he prepared an important matter, for he was as a man that contendeth with himself, even as Jacob our father contended with an angel of heaven. And once or twice he made as to approach us, to impart aught to us, but bethought himself, and only gazed upon us and withdrew, leaving us in ignorance. And our hearts beat mightily with fear and hope.

And when evening came, there fell a quiet on the place, as if the glory of God had descended and spread itself upon the earth. And the stars covered the heavens, and we saw Mount Hermon thrust into the clouds, and his base was hidden, but his head was as torn from the foundations and swimming among the stars which fell upon him. And we said unto each other: "How fearful is this place!"

And the Rabbi called unto us, saying:

"Tarry a while, for I would go up on yonder hill to pray."

And the Rabbi stood apart from us upon a little mount, and he prayed in solitude. And what with the darkness, we saw him not, but only his white garment, and the sleeves thereof stretched out to the heavens. And fear came upon us, for our Rabbi was in the night like a shining angel of the Lord. And when a while had passed he came toward us, and in the whiteness of the night it was as though his feet touched not the earth, but he swam toward us in his starry garment. And he stood before us, and his face was not as heretofore, neither as yesterday, nor as the day before, but he shone with a new pale holiness. And the dew of the night dripped from his hair and earlocks and fell upon his beard, and he trembled in all his body with a holy fever. And our hearts melted with terror, and he looked upon us a long time in silence. And we awaited a great thing.

And he called out to us and said:

"Now who do the people say is the son of man?"

And we were silent in our fear, then one among us answered: "Some there be that say he is Jochanan the Baptist, and others that say he is Elijah the prophet. And still others there be that say he is Jeremiah, or another of the prophets."

Now I, Judah the man of Kiriot, knew that his time had come and he would be revealed as to who he was. And I would have opened my mouth to utter the word, and to call out the name upon which we had so long waited. But my tongue clove to the roof of my mouth, and in the extremity of my fear I could not bring the word out of myself.

And our Rabbi turned to us and said:

"But who say you I am?" and again a great silence fell upon us. And I felt that the eyes of the Rabbi rested on me, and the holy and dreadful word was upon my lips; and now my tongue no longer clove to the roof of my mouth, and yet I said not the word, because of the fear that was upon me. But Simon bar Jonah threw himself before the Rabbi and stretched his hands to him, and he took the word out of my mouth and cried in a loud voice: "Thou art our Lord Messiah, concerning whom the prophets prophesied."

And when we heard that dread word issue from the lips of Simon bar Jonah, it was as though the thunder had fallen upon us from heaven. And we threw ourselves down, and dared not look, because of the terror of God. But the Rabbi lifted Simon bar Jonah from the earth and said: "Happy art thou, Simon bar Jonah, for flesh and blood hath not revealed this unto thee, but our father in heaven."

And we, the other disciples, hearing these words, pressed our faces still closer into the earth, and did not dare to look, forasmuch as there stood before us the Hope of Israel. But we stretched out our hands to him and we called out after Simon bar Jonah: "Thou art our Lord Messiah, concerning whom the prophets prophesied."

And our lord called to us, saying: "Now reveal this thing to no man as yet, but conceal it in your hearts."

And the silence of night became deeper about us, and the lights of heaven fell upon us. And we were as those that dream, and it seemed to us that the heavenly hosts were assembled on high and looked down from the stars. And it seemed likely that the patriarchs, yea, and the prophets, were about to show themselves. For we heard as it were footsteps that approached, and there was in our ears a rushing of wings, and the place upon which we stood was filled with souls, even as was the place about Sinai when our forefathers received the Torah from the hands of Moses. Even so we believed that the angel Messiah was with us. And we wondered that we were here alone, and that all Israel was not gathered with us on the mount, even as all Israel was gathered at Sinai. And our hearts overflowed with joy, and we would have sung, and we would have shouted salvation into the night, but that for joy and terror we could not open our lips.

And we heard a sound of weeping which was filled with joy, and the voice entreated: "Bring me before the holy one of Israel. I will fall upon my face before him, I will bow me down to him."

And the voice was the voice of Bar Talmai, who was blind, and who stood at a side. And there arose one of us and brought Bar Talmai by the hand before our Rabbi, saying: "Lo, here standeth the holy one of Israel."

And when Bar Talmai came before the Rabbi, he threw himself upon his face and a great cry went out of him: "I see! I see!" And when we asked him: "What seest thou, Bar Talmai?" he answered: "An angel of heaven standeth before me, clad in a robe of fire."

And Bar Talmai lay before the Rabbi looking through closed eyes. And his lips uttered prophecy: "I see the holy one of Israel. He strideth over the hills, the trumpets blow before him, the joy of God walketh behind him. Jerusalem, put on thy lovely raiment, rise upon the heights, see, thy children, from east and west, from north and south, they come, gay of spirit. God gathereth them from the far islands of the sea, the high mountains are leveled before them, the valleys are straightened, the forests make shadow on their path, sweet-smelling herbs spring under their feet. O Jerusalem, put on thy fine raiment, open wide thy gates, the holy one of Israel strideth in through them!"

And the words of Bar Talmai loosed our bound tongues, and the joy that was in our hearts poured forth in the words of dream and prophecy. For we were as those that dream in the night, and we sang to him the songs of the bearer of glad tidings. And we clapped our hands, and Simon the Zealot came before him, and applied to him this verse:

"The messenger is upon the hills, the bearer of peace: Celebrate thy festivals, O Jerusalem, thy vow hath been fulfilled. Thou shalt be enslaved no more by every base villain."

And we danced about him and clapped our hands. And we sang the songs of David, his father. And Simon bar Jonah came before him and applied to him this verse:

"He is my servant, upon whom I lean. My soul loveth him, I have let my spirit rest upon him, that he may utter judgment upon the nations."

And I, the least of his disciples, came before him, and threw myself upon my face, and applied to him this verse:

"I shall send my messenger to make free the way before him. Suddenly shall he come in his sanctuary, the lord whom ye seek, and the angel of the covenant whom ye desire. He cometh, saith the Lord of heaven."

And thus each one came before the Rabbi and applied his verse to him.

And the Rabbi stood among us, and it was our thought that now he would lift up his hand, and the heavens would divide and legions of angels would descend in fiery chariots with the winged cherubs harnessed to them; and they would pass through the world in thunder; and the kings of the earth would lie at his feet like bound sheep, that he might judge them, even as the prophets had prophesied.

And behold, as we still danced about him, and rejoiced in the salvation which had come upon us, "as the dew of God falleth in drops upon the grass, when no man hath hoped, and the children of men have ceased to look for it"—we looked up and we saw that sadness had come into his countenance. And there was that in his look which is upon the father's face when he rejoiceth over his ignorant children, but his eyes are veiled. And the lips of our Rabbi were twisted, and he lifted his hand, and we became silent. And he said:

"Know that much suffering awaiteth the son of man."

And when we heard these words our voices were fast in our throats, and our cries of jubilation were made dumb, and we looked one upon the other in fear, for we understood not his speech; yet it burned in our bodies like a living fire. And Simon bar Jonah trembled, and threw himself before the Rabbi, and clung to his feet, saying:

"Nay, Rabbi, God forbid this thing, it shall not be!"

And the Rabbi spoke unto him harshly:

"Get thee gone from me, Satan. Thy heart thinketh of the things of men, and not of the things of God." And he said unto us: "He that would follow me must deny himself. He that seeketh to save his soul shall lose it. And he that shall lose his life for me and for the message which I bring, he shall be saved."

And as we stood thus, even like those that have been flung from the heavenly heights into the nethermost pit, yea, like those that have been stripped of their royal raiment and thrust out naked and uncovered, the Rabbi called unto us, and his face was filled again with the holy light of joy, and words of comfort came from his lips:

"I say unto you, there stand among you those that shall not taste the cup of death before they shall see the coming of the kingdom of God in all strength."

And having said these words he withdrew from us once more and returned to pray alone upon the mount.

And when the disciples were left alone, they were silent a long time. And each of them thought in his heart concerning the words of the Rabbi, and sought to interpret them aright. And those of us that were learned in writ sought among the utterances of the prophets, that we might find there an intimation; and those that were not learned in the writ inquired of the others. And Simon the Zealot said in the bitterness of his spirit: "We have borne insult and mockery that he might shine in his glory. We have bent to the yoke of Edom in order that he might come to joy. And shall he too fall under the shadow of the rod? What meaneth he with those words? Shall we have ground dust in our mills? Shall he that will judge the world be brought to judgment? O seek well, find in the writ a proof, an intimation that he meaneth otherwise with his words."

And the disciples sought and meditated; for many of us had not heard that the Messiah would pass through much suffering; and for such of us as had not heard, this was a new thing.

And the disciples looked toward me, for I was strong in the writ; and they looked toward Bar Talmai, and toward Andrew, who was strongest of all therein, and who was of the disciples of Jochanan; and from us they looked to Philip. And we that knew the writ sat down together and we awakened our memories and we called up the verses we had learned even in our childhood; and we found an intimation in the Book of Isaiah. For it is written there: "And God opened my ears, and I rebelled not and turned not back. I gave my back to the smiters and my cheeks to them that plucked off the hair, and I hid not my face from shame and spitting." And the ending of the verse we could not remember, and we said this to the disciples. And they asked: "But what meaneth it?" And I answered: "It concerneth the travail of the Messiah." And they would have known, what be the travails of the Messiah. Who was he that could interpret the words? Had not one of us heard from the Rabbi at whose feet he had sat concerning this thing? Could not such a one declare it unto them? And behold, I remembered on a sudden a discourse which I had heard, and I spoke of it to the disciples:

I sojourned once in the court of the Temple and I saw an old man seated on the steps in the shadow of a booth, and he spoke to his disciples concerning the travails of the Messiah. And I sat me down and listened with the others. For his words had the authority of the tradition which his Rabbis had brought with them from Babylonia to Jerusalem. And his Rabbis had received the tradition from their Rabbis, and the legend came out of Babylon. And as I began thus to speak unto the disciples, they were filled with eagerness and they said: "Now let us hear what this old man told concerning the travails of the Messiah, for we must know it."

And I repeated the discourse which I had heard from the lips of the old man in the shadow of the booth in the court of the Temple.

"The Holy One, blessed be He, made this condition with the king Messiah, saying: 'They for whose sins thou wouldst suffer shall put thee under an iron yoke. They shall make thee like the calf whose eyes are darkened. Because of their sins it hath been decreed that thy tongue shall cleave to the roof of thy mouth. Wouldst thou this?' And the Messiah answered: 'Lord of the world, with the light of my soul and the joy of my heart I take this upon myself. But with this condition, that there shall not be lost one soul out of Israel. And not only shall the living be helped in my days, but even all they that have died since the time of Adam, the first man, until now. If this be granted I agree and take upon myself all these sufferings.' "

And I, Judah Ish-Kiriot, continued thus the discourse concerning the travails of the Messiah:

"Our Rabbis have taught: the week of the coming of the Messiah ben David, they will bring iron bars and place them upon his neck, until his body shall break and he will cry out and weep. And when his voice shall come to heaven, crying: 'Lord of the world, how much can my strength endure, how much my spirit and my limbs? Am I not flesh and blood?'—then in that hour the Holy One, blessed be He, shall answer: 'Ephraim, my just Messiah, thus have I decreed for thee from the six days of the creation. Now let thy pain be like unto my pain. For from that day when Nebuchadnezzar the wicked destroyed my house, and burned my sanctuary, and drove my children among the peoples of the earth, since that day I have not sat upon my throne. And if thou believest me not, behold the dew upon my head.' And in that hour the Messiah shall say unto God: 'Lord of the world, now am I comforted. For it is enough that the servant shall be as the master.'

"The Rabbis have taught this: our patriarchs will come before the Messiah and they will say, 'Ephraim, our great Messiah, we are older than thou, but thou art greater. Thou hast suffered for the sins of our children, and great torment hath been sent against thee, such as neither the first nor last among men have suffered. Thou didst become the mockery of the peoples of the world for the sake of Israel; thou sattest in thick darkness, thine eyes saw no light; the skin shrank upon thy bones; thy body became dried like withered wood, and thy teeth fell out with fasting. All this hast thou taken upon thyself for the sake of the sins of our children.'

"And in that hour the Holy One, blessed be He, will lift up the Messiah into the highest heavens, and he shall spread his glory over him. And the nations shall come, and they shall lick the dust from under the feet of the Messiah.

"And it is written: 'Like a bridegroom that shineth in beauty.' Therefrom it followeth that the Holy One, blessed be He, shall lothe the Messiah in a raiment the light of which shall shine from nd to end of the world, and Israel shall rejoice in that light, aying:

" 'Blessed be the hour wherein he was born.
Blessed be the womb whence he issued:
Blessed be the generation which beholdeth him.
Blessed be the eye which hath gazed after him.
The breath of his mouth bringeth benediction and peace.' "

And when I had finished telling the legend, then Andrew, the brother of Simon, said: "And now I remember the ending of the verse! 'God shall help me and I shall not be shamed.' Which meaneth that Messiah shall come forth strengthened from his sorrows."

And when the disciples heard these words, they said: "Now we know the meaning of the travail of Messiah." And they were restored, and joy returned to them. But Simon bar Jonah sat alone, draped in the mantle of sorrow, as though he sucked at the breasts of pain; and he was silent a long time. Then he called unto us:

"Natheless, I shall not let him ascend to Jerusalem. Must the Messiah come only from Jerusalem?"

And I answered him:

"Simon bar Jonah, sin not with thy speech. Thou canst not take from his shoulders the yoke that was meant for him. And they know that the path to salvation lieth through Jerusalem, and without Jerusalem there is no Messiah."

And then we, the disciples, sought out places to sleep that night, beneath the shelter of stones, and each one drew his mantle over his head. And they lay there where they lay. But two were awake through the night, and a third watched them. The Rabbi stood upon the summit of the mount, and prayed alone. And Simon bar Jonah sat at the foot of the mount, covered in the shadow of the night. And when the other disciples slept, I beheld how Simon bar Jonah crept up like a thief toward the Rabbi on the mount. And I saw, by the light of the stars, how Simon bar Jonah did spread out his hands, as one that entreated, and the Rabbi drove him from the mount with a cry: "Get thee gone from me, Satan!"

XVI

And we, sleeping or awake in the night, hoped in our hearts that ere the morning a voice would go forth to proclaim the tidings of the Messiah over the hills and valleys; and rising at sunrise we would behold the children of Israel gathered hither from all the ends of the world and encamped about the foot of the mount. But there went forth no voice from heaven, neither did Elijah come leaping over the hills, and there was no bearer of tidings, and the day that followed was like unto all the other days, and the world was as yesterday and the day before.

And when we arose that morning, we, the disciples, were a-hungered, for the last of the bread was gone from our sacks. And the summer had come, and the land withered and there came none to refresh the Messiah.

And we were upon the mount Pamias, above the city of Caesarea of the kingdom of the Herod Philip. And the Herod Philip was a just king, and left us in peace. And daily we looked down from the mount, to see the women come to the cave whence issueth the spring of the Jordan, and where the goddess hath her grove. And the women brought their offerings of white meal, and cruses of oil, and jars of wine, and doves and incense and flowers; and on the mount was the Messiah of God, and he was a-hungered and thirsty, and had not where to lay his head.

Then we arose from that place and went further. But the Rabbi brought us not into the blessed cities of Israel, upon which the sanctity resteth. But we hoped that when he would reveal himself to the people, then his holy reign would begin. But he led us further among the cities of the gentiles which are beyond Genesaret. And it was thus when we came into one of the cities; we closed our eyes and stopped our ears that we might not see the abominations of the gentiles, nor hear their songs and laughter; but we sought out the tents of Jacob. And we came among our brothers in each place, and into Jewish homes, and rested under Jewish roofs, and ate Jewish bread; and they took us for a Rabbi and his disciples. For our Rabbi's command was strictly upon us to conceal the thing from men. And the people know not that Messiah was among them. And there was a division between us and our Rabbi, as though a curtain of fire had descended from heaven. For behold, he was still our Rabbi, as we had known him, to whose words we had listened yesterday and the day before, and in whose presence we were blessed to be, and who broke bread with us and was gracious unto us; yet he was likewise another, as if the light of God had fallen upon him, to hide him from us; one hand's breadth revealed and two hands' breadths concealed; and we saw him and saw him not.

And in those days we came to Gederah, on the further side of Genesaret. And the city was filled with gentiles, and it contained many open places and gardens, likewise many temples with their idols, and the greatest among them was the temple of their abomination Zeus, whom the people of the city chiefly worshiped. Natheless they worshiped also other idols, their own and alien. And every vain idol had its temple in the city, which was mighty and opulent; there were temples for the god Re, the sun god of the Egyptians, and for Astra, the goddess of the Zidonians. And every temple had its priests and priestesses, and the sacred men and sacred women who follow them. And the markets and the shops were filled with harlots. And when we came to the city it was the festival of their chief god, Zeus, and the men and women of the city were garbed in festive garments of many colors, some in costly purple and some in tender violet and others in pale lily, such as the Zidonians make cunningly. And they went out in bands to their temples, and the players on instruments went before every band. There marched at the head the trumpeters; after them came the flute players, and those that made the cymbals clash; and to the sound of this music they led the sacrifices to the gods. The horns of the animals were adorned, some with wreaths of gold, others with olive wreaths; and the oxen were behung with costly ornaments; and maidens and youths, their heads adorned with roses, danced about the sacrifices. And the priestesses followed, and their bodies were wreathed in costly coverings of thin stuffs, and the folds thereof were cunningly disposed, both concealing and revealing the nakedness of their bodies, that they might awaken the more the lust of the beholders. And after them came the hero of the day, a youth in the flower of his years, who had that day obtained first place in their races. And he was wholly naked, save that he wore upon his head the wreath of victory, which was of olive leaf. And to him, the hero of their races, they accorded greater honor than to all the priests and priestesses; and they delighted in the nakedness of his body and the strength of his muscles, and they praised the depth of his breast and the straightness of the lines of his hips. And the men and women admired the might of his arms and his legs and his manhood, and they threw flowers before him, and they stretched out their hands and cried to him as to a god: "Adonis! Adonis!" which meaneth, "Thou beautiful one!" And then, after him, came the people, men and women mingled, bearing fruits and flowers; and their demeanor was base and abominable, such as would not be tolerated in Israel.

And we were thrust aside by the multitude and pressed to a wall; and among us was the anointed one of God, and none recognized him and none knew of him.

And I looked upon my Rabbi's countenance, and it was pale, even as it had been on that day in Tyre, amid the rejoicings and the abominations about the idol of Moloch, and his lips trembled and his eyes burned with the fire of God. And we thought now, of a surety, he that possesseth so the power of God would from this point on begin his reign. And we waited for the miracle, and for the cry which would issue from his lips, where it lay ready. But he did but murmur to himself. And I, inclining mine ear, heard him utter the words which God's finger had written on the wall in Babylon: *"Mene, Mene, Tekel, Upharsin."* And I understood him and contained myself in patience.

And it was thus with us, that we began now to perceive the deeds of our Rabbi in another light, and we began to understand.

Sayeth Judah: "It is known to the lord of the world, not for my honor and not for the honor of my Rabbi do I relate these wonders, but for the honor of God, blessed be He, in order to strengthen the faith in the hearts of his creatures."

And we arose out of this place, which was unclean with idols, and we left the city and went down to the shore of Genesaret; and it was a long way, for the city stood upon a hill. And even though the shore of the sea was part of the city, natheless we rejoiced greatly to be near our beloved Genesaret; for beyond, on the farther side of the water, we could see the land of the holy cities of Israel, covered with the gracious light of the sun, and we cried out: "How goodly are thy tents, O Jacob, thy tabernacles, O Israel." But before we came to the water's edge we came upon a steep hill, the head of which hung straight above the water. And the place was empty and forlorn and without inhabitants, and it had not the aspect of a habitation of men. And wild stones were sown upon the hill, one behind the other, like unto a stairway hanging falsely above an abyss. And a damp green moss grew upon the stones, and herbs such as are not seen in inhabited places, thick and thorny and grasping like the claws of beasts at our garments and tearing them, and at our flesh, making it to bleed. And even like these herbs were the overhanging trees, withered and crooked, and like lame pigmies; as though they belonged not to our creation. Their heads were bald as if the demons in the nethermost pit had smitten them with fiery whips. And all things that grew upon this hill were of like character, having not the appearance of the green things which men plant or are accustomed to see, but being wild of aspect, with horns and fiery tongues. And it was as if there had been war among the growths on that hill, plant clawing at plant and smiting it, and sucking each other as beasts do, and piercing each other, so that the softness ran out of the wounds.

And we beheld ourselves enclosed and encircled among the spear-like growths upon the hanging steps, and great terror fell upon us as though we had been set beyond the bounds of God's grace. For the place was such as seemed in no wise to pertain to the creation of the Lord. And though it be forbidden to think such a thought, that there can be a place beyond the bounds of grace, for it is written: "the earth is filled with his glory," yet it was as if it lay within the bounds of the Evil One, and drew its being from the founts of uncleanliness and abomination. And as we stood there it seemed to us that the forbidden thought was confirmed. For there arose soon a mighty cloud of dust which veiled the light of the sun; and in the darkness there was a tumult, and the tumult was not of the storm, but as of the oncoming of evil hosts. And in the tumult there was a yelling, but not as of beasts but as of tormented spirits. And the dust and yelling came from hordes of wild swine, which like demons descended upon the place from unknown heights among the stones; and many of them fell among the holes and pits which were concealed beneath the grasses, and others fell upon sharp rocks, and they were pierced; likewise the wild growths pierced them. And the rest fell down from the heights into the sea. And then, after them, there came running the swineherds; and they cried in fear, for they were pursued by a wild man, a giant for size, with limbs the like of which no man hath seen, and all naked and covered with growth like a beast of the field. And he had not a face in human likeness, but in that of a beast, and his eyes shed fire, and his nose was like a mighty, twisted trumpet, and from his mouth, which was as the gateway of hell, looked forth his teeth like unto spears. And he pursued the swineherds as though the storm-wind carried him. But when he beheld us, then he ceased from pursuing the swineherds and turned his path toward us. But ere he reached us he perceived the white robe of the Rabbi, who stood among the wild growths with arms outstretched as though to receive him. And the wild man paused in his flight and looked upon our Rabbi. And it was as though he was afeared of the white dress, for he would have turned again, but our Rabbi stretched out his hands and cried: "Come to me, thou lost son!"

And we saw the wild man start, and flee toward our Rabbi, at first as it seemed to us in fury, and as if to fall upon him. But when he came close he halted, as if the look of our Rabbi had calmed him, as the look of the trainer calmeth a wild horse. And they two stood over against each other, the wild man and our Rabbi with outstretched arms. And behold, it was like the wrestling of Jacob with the angel; even so our Rabbi wrestled with the evil one, but not with his hands, only through his eyes. And our Rabbi spoke to him with much compassion:

"Calm thyself, my son. I know thy father's house, and I know whence thou comest. Return, for thy father awaiteth thee."

And when the wild one heard this, he lifted up a mad voice and cried:

"And how shall I return to my father's house, seeing that my ather's house is clean and I am unclean? Demons have made their nest in my flesh, and they smite me continually with a thousand sicknesses. Legions dwell within me and my name is legion."

And he threw himself to the earth and yelled with a thousand voices, as though armies of wild cats were within him and coursing through his body, seeking a way out and finding it not. And he shook and trembled in all his limbs.

And my Rabbi laid his hands upon him and bade the demons depart from the man, and torment him no more; but that they should enter into the swine, which rolled upon the stones and fell into the sea. And my Rabbi said unto him:

"Legion is no more thy name, but Israel, as thy father hath called thee. And no more a wild man art thou, but a child of thy father, a lost son that returneth home."

And our Rabbi lifted him from the earth and commanded one of us to go down, and bring up water from the lake, and wash the man, and cover his nakedness with a garment. And the Rabbi made him sit down by him and he spoke unto him:

"The demons have left thee and entered into the swine which have fallen into the sea. Now art thou whole."

And the man sat at the Rabbi's feet like unto one of us.

And the Rabbi opened the sack of bread and gave the man to eat, and the man ate like unto one of us.

And our Rabbi said unto him: "Now thou art purified and healed. Return now to thy father who awaiteth thee with outstretched arms."

And the man replied, in a voice like one of ours: "How shall I return to my father's house? I have taken his money, and I have squandered it with harlots and evil men, so that I became like unto the swine, and I housed with them."

And our Rabbi comforted him and said:

"Thy father hath sent messengers to seek thee."

But the man trembled and said:

"I fear my elder brother, who is angry against me."

But our Rabbi calmed him, saying:

"Thy father waiteth with open arms to receive thee. Go home, and tell of the wondrous thing that God hath done with thee."

And we looked into this matter closely, and we understood the deeds of our Rabbi; for not with the wild man alone did our Rabbi wrestle, but with all the gods of Tyre and Zidon; and it was not the demons which he banished into the swine, but Moloch and Ashtarot and Zeus and Aphrodite, and all the abominations of the gentiles; yea, these he had sent into the swine and drowned in the sea, so that he had healed thereby the wild one and sent him home to his father.

And we perceived on a sudden the greatness of our Rabbi. For he had contended with the gods of Tyre and Zidon and conquered them, and he cleansed man and prepared him to receive the kingdom of heaven.

And we praised God therefor.

XVII

Behold, God hath declared through the prophets: "I will send Elijah the prophet before the great and fearful day. Prepare ye the way!"

Now wherefore is my heart restless again? The nigher we draw unto the cities of Israel, the greater is my unrest of heart, and the greater seemeth my fear of that which is to happen.

We left the cities of the gentiles and we came to the borders of Israel, where the sanctity is. And every day my hope grew more sure that soon my Rabbi would reveal himself. And there would appear Elijah the prophet and would bring the tidings and bear witness to our Rabbi. But meanwhile our Rabbi went by the cities, and sojourned with the shepherds in the fields. Till we came to a mount and the Rabbi said: "Here we shall lodge this night"; for the night had fallen on the place. And the light of heaven was poured down upon the hill, as though the spirit of God brooded upon it; and a stillness came upon the world, not like unto that stillness which is before a storm, but the stillness of everlasting rest, which cometh when all living things do become one with their creator, and they fulfill themselves as was decreed in the moment of their conceiving. We heard the song of night; and what is the song of the night? The song of the night is silence; and it sang into our hearts all terror and desire and love of the creator.

And the Rabbi said: "Here shall I pray." And he enfolded himself in a *tallit*, and he took with him Simon and the sons of Zebedee and ascended with them to the summit of the mount to pray, for the hour was auspicious. And the other disciples remained at the foot of the mount.

And we took the stones of the place and laid them beneath our heads, and we covered ourselves with our mantles, and sleep came soon to us, for we were wearied with the walking of the whole day. And when half the night had passed and the second watch was gone, and we were deep sunken in sleep, we wakened, hearing a mighty voice from the mount. And when we opened our eyes, we were astonished by the whiteness of the night, for the land was steeped in light, and the mount whereon our Rabbi had gone to pray was covered with a cloud, which was like the wing of an angel; and it was as if the snows of Hermon had come hither to cover the mount.

And Simon came out of the cloud and his face was pale, and his hair disarrayed by the wind, and his eyes were large, and wide open with fear, and he trembled with a great trembling. And after him came the brothers Zebedee, Jochanan first with swift and certain steps, his arms outstretched, and his brother Jacob after him. And they likewise were terrified and distraught, even like Simon bar Jonah. And we, the other disciples, arose and went to meet them, for we said unto ourselves that a thing of great import had come to pass. And we said to them: "Now tell us what hath chanced that ye be so shaken as if the storm had passed through you." And Simon called: "We have seen Elijah the prophet, him that we sought so long." And the brothers Zebedee testified likewise. And we asked Simon further: "When? And where?" And he answered: "There, on the mount, whither the Rabbi went to pray. Elijah the prophet standeth there even now with the Rabbi, and Moses a third with them." And we were filled with astonishment by these words and we said: "Simon, tell us how this thing was, for it importeth greatly in our lives." And Simon related:

"Behold, we were upon the mount, and the Rabbi said unto us: 'Tarry here awhile, I will go to yonder place to pray alone.' And he drew off from us a space, and stood where we saw the light of heaven falling upon his *tallit*. And his arms were stretched out to his father on high, and he prayed. And as we stood thus and beheld him in the light of heaven, there fell upon us the terror of God. For his raiment ceased not from growing whiter and whiter, and there was a flickering about him as of the amber wings of the cherubs standing between him and us. And we heard the noise of footsteps that approached but we beheld no man. And it was as though a wind were driving upon us. And then on a sudden we beheld two old men in white raiment, and they stood with the Rabbi and held converse with him. And in yet a little while they all vanished in a white cloud, as though the snow had fallen on the three. And out of the cloud there came a voice, which testified concerning our Rabbi in the words of the prophets. And then the white cloud disappeared, and our Rabbi stood there alone, and we asked him: 'Who were they that were with thee?' And the Rabbi answered: 'The first of these was Elijah the prophet, whom ye seek, and the other was Moses our teacher.' And I called out to my Rabbi: 'My lord, it is good to tarry upon this hill. And if it seemeth well to thee, let us put up three booths, one for thee, and one for Moses and one for Elijah the prophet. For I would not that the Rabbi go up to Jerusalem, because of that which awaiteth us there.' "

And Jacob and Jochanan testified according to the words of Simon.

And as we stood there in great astonishment, we saw the Rabbi coming down the mount, and his raiment was whiter than the hand of man could wash it; and the glory of God was upon his face, and his feet were naked and it was as if he trod not upon the earth in his going. And there was a cloud about him, and we trembled.

And the Rabbi drew close and touched us with his hands and said: "Arise, and fear not." And he bade us reveal this thing to no one, until the time came.

And we asked: "Rabbi, is this the significance thereof, that Elijah the prophet shall come before the Messiah, as the scribes say?" And Rabbi Yeshua answered: "Elijah came first, but they knew him not, and they did with him according to their will. And thus shall they also do with the son of man, as is written concerning him."

And we gazed upon the ground and thought hard on the words, for we knew that the Rabbi spoke of Jochanan the Baptist. But Simon cried out: "That can never be."

On the second day we rested by the shore of the Sea of Genesaret, and took shelter from the heat of the sun. And the land was pleasant to behold, for the wheat was like a sea which covered the levels of the land, and the clusters of grapes as they hung from the stalks were like the full udders of dreaming sheep, and the fig tree sent out its savor; and man went out into the fields, and the song of the reaper was within him, as it is written, "Those who sow in tears shall reap in joy," for it was the time of the gathering of the ears in the field.

And our Rabbi called to us:

"Go after the reapers and gather the ears which fall from under the scythes, and rejoice in the bread which God has set aside for the poor."

And we were filled with wonder and we asked each other: "But is not the whole earth his? Hath not God made him to govern over us, as the harp of Israel hath sung, even David, his father: Ask of me, and I will give thee the peoples to be thy inheritance, and thy portion shall be the borders of the earth"?

But the Rabbi understood our thoughts and spoke thus:

"The richest shall be the poorest."

Then the Rabbi commanded us to take the ears and grind them between the stones and make meal and bake cakes, and put them on the fire. And this we did.

And it was the evening, after the saying of the "Hear, O Israel," when the worker sits at his meal. And the Rabbi gathered us around the fire. And his face was exceeding sad, and he was utterly filled with the holy spirit. And he sat near us at the meal which we had prepared over the fire in the night, and he was silent a long while. And we too were silent.

Then the Rabbi took one of the cakes and made a benediction over it. And before he took any in his mouth, he broke it into pieces and said:

"I am the living bread which is come down from heaven. He that will eat this bread, he shall have everlasting life. And the bread which I will give you is my flesh, which I sacrifice for the life of the world."

The Simon called out:

"These are hard words. Who can give ear to them?"

But the Rabbi took the pieces of bread and shared them out among us, the disciples, and commanded us to eat.

And we stared at each other in great amazement, for we had never before heard such words from him.

From that time on the Rabbi spoke to us of the bread of life, and to others likewise.

And we did not understand the meaning of it.

And we arose from this place and we went to K'far Nahum. And envy of Simon bar Jonah and the brothers Zebedee grew stronger in our hearts, and we asked of each other in sorrow and bitterness: "Wherefore maketh the Rabbi a distinction among his disciples? Wherein have these three merited that they be drawn into the secret of the Rabbi and that they be witnesses of great things that come to pass with him, while we stand without?"

And the brothers Zebedee held themselves proudly against us, and they spoke among themselves as if they were the foremost after the Rabbi in the kingdom of heaven, and they would sit upon his right and left hand, and the government of the world would be given to them.

And Jochanan said: "Now was I not with the Rabbi upon the mount? And was I not a witness of the great things which came to pass up there?"

And the Rabbi heard the speech of his disciples and answered not. But when we came into K'far Nahum, we chanced upon children that played at the entrance to the city. And the child that was biggest was the king, and the others his servants. But after a while the king arose and left his throne and said: "Now let him that is smallest among us be the king, and we his servants." And the Rabbi went to the boy and said: "Now tell me the verse thou didst learn in school today." And the boy said: " 'From the dust thou raisest the poor man.' And the Rabbis preach: 'The Holy One, blessed be He, sayeth unto Israel, "What do I desire of you? Only that ye shall love one another. And this I fulfill even now." ' " Then the Rabbi said unto us: "What was your quarrel by the way?" And we told him. And the Rabbi said: "Now verily, verily, unless ye become like children ye shall in no wise enter the kingdom of heaven. For the kingdom of heaven is like the kingdom of the child; and after the kingdom of heaven the kingdom of the child is the only one that abideth and cannot be taken from him. He that would be the first among you, let him be the last, and serve you. He that can lower himself even as a child, he shall be greatest in the kingdom of heaven."

But the children of Zebedee were not content with their portion in the Rabbi, and they meditated on how they should be the greatest of the disciples. And Jochanan of Zebedee left us and went up to Bet Zeida, for the matter stood thus: The brothers Zebedee had left the rich ships of their mother to follow after our Rabbi. And their mother was angered against them, and quarreled with them, for that they had given up the sure fishing of fish for the fishing of men. And she said unto them: "That business will bring you nought, and ye waste your mother's labor, and the nets lie idle and dry, and become torn." But Jochanan came to her and said: "The time draweth nigh now for the coming of the kingdom of heaven, and thy two sons will be great lords therein, for we are nearest unto him and he prefereth us before the other disciples and he hath entrusted his secret to us. Now shall thy reward be great; it will be thy portion to see thy sons great lords in the land, for the whole earth belongeth to the lord, even as the prophets have prophesied. Therefore be strong, mother, and go to the Rabbi, and ask his grace upon us, that he may seat us upon his right and left hands."

And the mother saddled an ass and loaded thereon a sack of white meal and a basket of fresh figs and two cheeses and two cruses of honey, which she put in the saddle pack, for the woman was rich; and her name was Susannah.

And she came before the Rabbi and she bowed herself and said: "If thy maidservant hath found grace in thine eyes, let me speak unto thee. My two sons left their father's house and abandoned the calling of their father. They were fishers and thou hast made them fishers of men; and thou hast torn them from their work and they have followed after thee. And now that the kingdom of heaven cometh, and all the riches of the world shall be in thy hand, and thou shalt command kings and princes, I beg thee that thou recompense them for their labor, and let my two sons, Jacob and Jochanan, sit upon thy right and thy left hands."

And the Rabbi became sad because of the words of his disciples, and he was silent a while. Then he answered the woman, saying: "Are they prepared to drink the beaker which I shall have to drink?"

And to the sons of Zebedee he said: "Are ye able to take the baptism which I shall take?" and they answered: "Yes, Rabbi." But the Rabbi said to them: "Even so ye cannot be the greatest. For the son of man, too, is not come that he may be served, but he shall serve others, and he shall give his life as a sacrifice for others."

XVIII

Now when we came to the gate of K'far Nahum, there was none to greet us either with candles or palm branches. No man played for us on the psaltery or the flute or the drum. They of the city had forgotten that which he had done for them, the bread which he had made to appear for them in the wilderness, and all the wonders which he had performed for them and they had witnessed day by day.

And we mounted to the house of Simon's mother-in-law; and there greeted us but a handful of the poorest, whom the Rabbi had nourished with the monies given to him by the wealthy. Howbeit, when the poor had seen that the wealthy turned from our Rabbi, the most of them abandoned him. And they said: "There is nothing more to seek here." And we were left, we, the disciples, and the women that were with us. And some of us went forth to labor that we might earn our daily bread; and the brothers Zebedee went unto their mother, and got them two boats, and they and Simon bar Jonah went forth and cast their nets; and in this wise we nourished ourselves and the little handful of the poor that clove to us.

And the important people of the city murmured, saying: "Wherefore hath he returned to the city? The messengers of Herod seek him. And when they will find him in our midst they will cast the guilt upon us. It were better he go from here." But they whom he had healed, and for whom he had performed miracles, said: "Nay, let us wait and see how the thing falleth out. For if the messengers of the government come, he will destroy them, and let us not stretch forth a hand against this man, for he is holy." And among the latter there was the chief of the synagogue whose daughter our Rabbi had healed, likewise the centurion of K'far Nahum, of the hosts of Herod; and the centurion hid the presence of our Rabbi from the authorities, and would not lift his hand against him, for in his heart he believed in the might of the Rabbi.

And even as the day surely followeth with firm footsteps upon the night, and driveth it hence, even so our Rabbi began to build up again his congregation, and he was clothed again in strength. And it was felt that the authority was in his hand. Yea, there were many that scorned and laughed, but he regarded them not, and he built his nest again within the web of the government of the wicked. He gathered again to him the sick and the poor and the abandoned and the rejected, and there was none too low to be received into his congregation. And with the authority given him from on high he went in the open day to the harbor of K'far Nahum, and spoke as of old to the porters and the fishers. And though he revealed not the great things that had happened with him, natheless by hints and nods he bade them understand that the reward was approaching for their labor and sufferings, and that redemption stood at the gate and the kingdom of heaven was nigh. And the people believed him again and awaited the event. But there were others that said: "Nay, with this Yeshua nought more will happen." For the people were divided concerning him.

And on the Sabbath he gathered us, his disciples, about him, and went up to the synagogue. And some said: "This is he that doeth miracles with the power of Satan." And others said: "This is he that healed our sicknesses." And when our Rabbi went up upon the pulpit to preach after the reading of the Torah, then some said that he be permitted to preach, and others said nay. And when there was silence, our Rabbi said: "I am the living bread which hath come down from heaven. He that eateth of this bread shall live eternally. And the bread which I shall give you shall be my flesh which I sacrifice for the life of the world."

And there arose a great tumult in the synagogue. And the head of the congregation called out: "Who can comprehend his speech? How can he give us his flesh to eat?"

And the worshipers began to murmur: "Is he not Yeshua, the son of Joseph? How shall he give us his flesh to eat thereof?"

But our Rabbi called out, saying: "Verily I say unto you, he that will not eat of the flesh of the son of man, and drink of his blood, for him there shall be no life. And he that eateth of my flesh and drinketh of my blood, he liveth in me and I am in him."

And when the worshipers heard him say this again, there was a great laughter in the synagogue; and they said that surely an evil spirit had entered into him. Natheless they did him no harm, save that they laughed him to scorn.

And the rumor spread through the region that an evil spirit had entered into the Rabbi. And when he appeared in the harbor among the fishers, then the people came not to him as had been their wont. And some were ashamed and said: "Behold, there goeth the man that drave Satan from others, and Satan hath now taken up his dwelling-place in him." And the children called after him, "Go up, go up, thou possessed one." And others yet said: "No man knoweth; surely something must come of this man."

And only they that were strong in their faith clove to him. And among these were many of the poor, bitter of heart, who had nothing more to lose. And there were also among them such as could not be received in the congregation of Israel, and such as were unclean, and he spoke to them of the kingdom of heaven with hints and signs. And some he even made unto disciples, and conferred upon them the power and authority to drive forth evil spirits; and he sent them into near-by cities. For he said: "The harvest is plenteous, but the reapers are few. Therefore he that hath command over the reapers must send them forth to work." And again there began to come to him people from the villages, for they had heard the tidings from his disciples. Some brought their sick with them, and others came but to look upon him, and to ask nothing for themselves, but only to hear and learn of the hope and of the kingdom of heaven whereof his disciples spoke. And the Rabbi received all these people, even to the sinners among them. And some there were of the children of Ammon and Moab, and could not be received into the congregation of Israel; nevertheless he made no distinction among them, and they sat about him even like the others. And though the danger waxed daily that the messengers of the government would fall upon him, he regarded it not. And when there was no bread for them, for my girdle was empty, and the wealthy of the city came no more to help us, he fed them with the holy bread of the kingdom of heaven. And though he revealed not unto them the great things which were at hand with him, and though it was hard for us, his disciples, to keep silent concerning them, yet the poor clung to him. For the Rabbi drew their hearts near to himself and we were all like one family.

And when they of the city perceived that once more he gathered into K'far Nahum the poor and the sick of the surrounding villages, then they came to him and said: "Thou bringest misfortune upon our head. The messengers of the government are behind thee. And when they will see the multitudes gathered about thee, their anger will be hot upon us." But the Rabbi answered them: "Go and tell the old fox: my hour is not yet come."

And the word going about that our Rabbi had returned from the land of the gentiles and that he abode in K'far Nahum, the talk and rumor concerning him increased mightily. And the noise thereof came to the ears of his mother who was in Nazareth. And she gathered her children, and she came with them to K'far Nahum, in order that they might persuade the Rabbi to return to the house of his mother, for she feared for his life. And it came to pass that the Rabbi sat in the house of Simon's mother-in-law, and they that followed him were gathered with him. And his mother came to the door and she looked upon him; and there was compassion in her face and her eyes were red with weeping. And tears fell upon her face and clung in the folds thereof. And she stretched out her arms to him and said: "My child, what misfortune bringest thou upon thy head? For that which I feared hath come to pass. In the nights I sleep not, because of thee. The sword of the government hangeth over thee, and the people quarrel because of thee. Return now to thy mother's house; thy father's work waiteth for thee, and thou shalt find rest in the bosom of thy family. For this is a dangerous thing which thou hast taken upon thyself." And she spoke more in this wise, even as a mother speaketh to her son that goeth in bad ways.

And the Rabbi sat among us and heard not the words of his mother. For she could not approach him through the press of the people. And one called to the Rabbi, saying: "Behold, thy mother standeth at the door." But the Rabbi answered: "Who is my mother? Who are my brothers? They that do the will of our father in heaven, they are my brothers and my mother." And when her children heard these words, they led her forth with a great weeping.

And I, Judah Ish-Kiriot, say this:

All my life I have dwelt among the sages and the wise, and I have not yet seen such a thing. I see lightning, and I hear thunder, and the rain cometh not. I behold the deeds of my Rabbi here in K'far Nahum, and I know him no more. His deportment is not as it was. And his doctrine is otherwise, and the paths upon which he treadeth are not the same. And I am as a lost man, and know not what happeneth here.

And there was a trembling in my limbs, and I was lifted up by doubt and cast down again by it. And I knew not what to do, till there came to me, as I slept in the night on my couch, the likeness of the Rabbi, Nicodemon of Jerusalem. And I said within myself: Thou alone, Judah, man of Kiriot, wilt not penetrate to the truth concerning the Rabbi Yeshua, and all those things that are upon the summit of the world. How canst thou take it upon thyself?

And I wondered greatly that it had not come to me before, even on the day when we returned once more to the gates of K'far Nahum.

And when the morning came I sought me out a messenger and I said to him: "Go thou up to Jerusalem, and seek out the Rabbi Nicodemon, and bid him set aside all things and descend straightway to K'far Nahum, for great things are toward. And say to him that his disciple hath no more the power to understand, and knoweth not whether he standeth within the authority of heaven, or, God forbid, without it. Therefore let him hasten hither, for it pertaineth to things that touch the roots of Israel."

And I bade the messenger say no word of this to any man, for the message was only for the ear of the Rabbi Nicodemon.

XIX

And Rabbi Nicodemon hastened and descended to K'far Nahum and sought me out in secret; and he inquired closely of me concerning the entire matter. And I recounted all that had happened, both in the city and without, on the roads which we had followed; I told him of the words and deeds of our Rabbi. And I said: "Likewise have Moses and Elijah come down from heaven, to bear testimony to him."

And when Rabbi Nicodemon heard this, he became pale with fear, and trembling came into his hands. But great joy was in his eyes, and he cried: "Surely the Lord meaneth well with us. Surely these things have not happened in vain. And for that which he doeth and for that which he teacheth, he surely hath received authority; and without that authority in his hand he could not so have done and spoken. And wherefore should we doubt it? Now do thou lead me to thy Rabbi, that it may be confirmed by him."

And in that hour our Rabbi was in the booth on the roof of the house, as was his wont.

And we took with us Simon the Zealot, among the disciples, for that he was of one mind with us.

And we went to our Rabbi in the secret night, and the other disciples knew nought thereof.

And Nicodemon bowed himself before our Rabbi and said:

"We hear voices and understand them not, we see signs and know not how to interpret them aright. Now tell us, art thou he that hath been promised to us, or shall we wait for another? And if thou be the one that thou art, hide it not from us, for we have no more strength to wait. But give us a sign that God hath sent thee unto us, and we will throw ourselves at thy feet and acknowledge thee the anointed one of Israel, and carry out thy commands, even as thou shalt utter them."

But our Rabbi answered him concealed wise:

"When evening cometh ye say: The day will be good, for the

heavens are red. In the morning ye say: Today the rain will fall, for the heavens are gray and heavy. The signs of the skies ye know to interpret, but those of the earth you know not. An evil and adulterous generation desireth a sign, and there shall be no signs given."

But Rabbi Nicodemon bowed himself again and said:

"How shall we believe that thou art he, and follow thee without a sign? Behold, we are bound by the laws and commandments which Moses our teacher gave to us; and he hath shown us how to demean ourselves when a prophet appeareth among us."

But the Rabbi answered:

"He that believeth in me shall possess the world and life eternal, for I am the bread and the life."

But Nicodemon became astonished, and he was pale, and he meditated. Then he bowed again and spoke:

"Moses too came to us. And he did not bid us believe in himself, but only in God, who had sent him, and in the laws and commandments of God. Likewise the prophets came to us, and they did not bid us believe in them, but in God who had sent them that they might help us. Art thou greater than Abraham our forefather, and greater than Moses, and all the prophets, who bade us believe in God and not in themselves?"

And the Rabbi answered:

"You hold potsherds in your hand, but I am the whole vessel, a new vessel, which the Lord hath created."

"But how shall we understand thy words, Rabbi?"

And the Rabbi answered:

"Have I not said unto you, One putteth not new patches on an old garment, and one poureth not new wine into old bottles?"

And Rabbi Nicodemon answered him:

"But it is even because of thee that we ask a sign of thee, for thou leanest not upon the men of old time, but wouldst bring forth something new, which the generations of the past have not taught unto us. Therefore there must be surety in our hands, that thou art indeed the new and whole vessel, which hath been promised, and that thou hast heavenly authority."

But the Rabbi was angered and answered:

"Woe unto you, scribes, who win souls above the graves of the prophets which your parents slew. If these wonders had been done in Tyre and Zidon. . . ."

But Rabbi Nicodemon answered him thus:

"But neither law nor commandments were given to Tyre and Zidon, and they are not bound to the Torah of Moses. But unto us the Torah hath been given, and we have said: 'We will hearken and obey.' How shall we now do aught against the Torah?"

And when I saw that these things were going too far, I asked of my Rabbi:

"Rabbi, I pray thee tell me: how far goeth faith? Where is the border where faith pauseth?"

And the Rabbi answered:

"There is no border to faith. Faith is the thread that man holdeth in his hand even when he descendeth into hell beneath. It goeth with him to the edge of the grave, and even beyond. Hath not King David said: 'Yea, though I walk in the valley of the shadow of death, I fear no evil, for thou art with me'? If ye believe in me, then I am even that which I am. Have I not taught you, Judah, that if ye had even as much faith as a mustard seed, ye would say to the fig tree: Take thy roots from the earth and plant them in the sea,—and it would be so?"

And we gazed upon each other, Rabbi Nicodemon and I, and we were afraid of him, for there was power in his speech.

And Rabbi Nicodemon bowed himself again and said:

"Many words have we heard from thee which have filled our hearts with hope. But we stand before a wall and see not our way. Hide it not from us, for we are they that have waited for thee. Teach us, Rabbi: When shall we expect thee, when wilt thou come and redeem us from the bonds of Edom?"

And the Rabbi answered:

"Nicodemon, the kingdom of God is not here, and it is not there, and it is not perceived of the eye; but it is in your hearts. And I have come, not to redeem you from the bonds of Edom, but from the bonds of sin which are wound about you like serpents. I am come to bring a redemption which knoweth not the limits of land or sea, but covereth the whole earth like the spirit of God, and none of flesh and blood can take it from you, for it is within you."

But Nicodemon answered:

"Happy are the ears which receive those words. And the prophet too hath prophesied: 'And I will make you a covenant unto the nations, and a light unto the gentiles, to open the eyes of the blind, and to take the prisoner forth from bondage, those that dwell in darkness.' But hast thou not, Rabbi, thy trumpeter, thy messenger, who shall call thee forth in Israel? We have closed our hearts to the joys of the world, in order that we might be given over entirely to God. Our enemies have devoured with a thousand mouths all the joys of life; their lips have run over with the sweetness of might and victory, while ours are sealed with the bitterness of the despised. We sat upon the breaking branch and ceased not to hope. Behold, our sufferings have conjured forth the redemption. And now, when the redemption standeth at the door, shall it not spread its skirts abroad in Israel? We are they that have paid the full price for this guerdon. And it is ours."

But the Rabbi said to Nicodemon:

"Nicodemon, Nicodemon, woe to those that measure God with the measure of man. The guerdon is not bought, it is given; it is given for nothing, and it is received for nothing, a gift from the father in heaven to the chosen one among his creatures, which is man. Before the earth was created, before it was fashioned and sent into space, that guerdon was with him in the heavens. For the sake of this guerdon he created the world, and for the sake of it hath he sent the son of man into the world. No price could obtain it, only the grace of God, for the guerdon is beyond price, and it is higher than the law, hence it is higher than the Torah. No scales can weigh it, and no measure measure it. It is the grace of God, which he hath conferred upon man."

And Nicodemon said:

"Edom maintaineth dominion with chariots, horses and swords, and he cannot be made to bow with the spirit, but only with thunders and lightnings. He that cometh to him with other weapons is a son of death."

But the Rabbi answered:

"Nicodemon, the son of man is likewise the lord of death."

And we knew not then what the words meant, but when we heard them we were silent. And the words of the Rabbi were among us three, and we told not the other disciples concerning them.

And after these words which he spoke to Nicodemon, our Rabbi called together his disciples and said to them:

"My time is come to go up to Jerusalem; therefore prepare yourselves. And ye shall know, that there shall be fulfilled on the son of man all the prophecies of the prophets."

And he further revealed unto us all that would be with him in Jerusalem.

And when we, the disciples, heard that the end was drawing nigh, our hearts became as water for terror, and our knees trembled, and we knew not what to say. Only Simon bar Jonah fell at his feet and stretched out his arms to him and cried: "Go thou not up to Jerusalem, but stay here with us, and we will build three booths for thee on that hill, one for thee, and one for Moses, and one for Elijah"—and Simon bar Jonah knew not what to say out of fear. But the Rabbi answered: "If ye so will, ye may leave me, as the others did." And Simon stretched out his hands to him and said: "Rabbi, what have we, save thee? We have left everything, and we will follow thee even to Jerusalem."

And before we departed from K'far Nahum, to cross the Jordan and the borders of Judah, we, to wit Simon the Zealot and I, Judah, the man of Kiriot, went to Rabbi Nicodemon to take farewell of him. And we told him that which the Rabbi had revealed concerning the going up to Jerusalem, and how the Rabbi would go nathless. And Rabbi Nicodemon said to Simon the Zealot: "And thou followest him?" And Simon answered: "Yea, I am the eternal slave of God." "And thou, Judah, goest thou up to Jerusalem?" "Yea, Nicodemon, for I believe with perfect faith that the guerdon is in his hand."

And when the people of K'far Nahum heard that our Rabbi was departing to Jerusalem, some of them followed him, for they thought that perchance our Rabbi would perform great wonders there, and take away the wealth of the rich and distribute it to the poor, and they would have a portion therein. And one of them came before the Rabbi and said: "My lord, I will follow thee whithersoever thou goest." And Yeshua said unto him: "The foxes have their holes, and the fowl of heaven their nests, but the son of man hath not where to lay his head."

And when the people heard these words of our Rabbi, they were frightened, and turned back from the road and returned to their homes. But the Rabbi called to one of them, saying: "Come, follow me." And the man answered: "Rabbi, let me first go home and bury my father." And the Rabbi said to him: "Let the dead bury their dead, but go thou and proclaim the kingdom of heaven." And a third said to him: "Yea, I will go with thee, but give me first thy permission to say my farewells to my household." And the Rabbi answered: "He that hath put his hand to the plow and then returneth, he is not worthy of the kingdom of heaven." And he left them all and continued on his way.

And none followed him to Jerusalem, save we, his disciples, and we made our portion with him. And though our hearts feared that which stood before us, yet we followed him; we, his disciples, and Miriam, the woman that guarded the ointments, and that led the blind Bar Talmai.

Note of the transcriber:

Here the manuscript put into my hands by Pan Viadomsky came to a close. The last page was torn; the raw edge of the papyrus bore silent witness to the brutal hand which had ripped it.

PART THREE

CHAPTER ONE

ONCE more a change entered into my relations with Pan Viadomsky. I was finding it increasingly difficult to maintain contact with him. He had plunged suddenly into a new activity, and was surrounded by a group of persons whose character and identity were for some time a complete mystery to me. I would come to him on one of my regular visits only to find him locked in his room, in consultation. I would wait for him by the hour in the long, narrow corridor; and invariably, when my patience gave out and I was about to go, he would come rushing from his room unkempt, distraught, possessed, a pen stuck behind his ear—as if a strange instinct had warned him of my intended departure—and apologize hastily and incoherently, while begging me to return to him later in the day.

I discovered before long the nature of Pan Viadomsky's new preoccupation. He was collaborating with a priest on nothing more nor less than a treatise designed to prove that Jews made use of Christian blood for the preparation of *matzot* for the Passover! In connection with his "researches" he spent whole days in the company of scholars of dubious reputation. One of them, I established, was a theologian who had a smattering of Hebrew and knew all the "dangerous" passages in the Talmud, as well as those which dealt with *"goyim," "necharim," "minim"*—words which may be translated approximately as "non-Jews," "strangers" and "heretics," but the exact meaning of which is no longer known—and similar matters. The special task of this theologian was to gather the "theoretical" material of the slanderous attack made by the anti-Semitic Roman writer Felix on the primitive Christians, to the effect that they employed the blood of children in their secret nocturnal feasts. (Later on the Christians turned the identical slander against the Jews.) Another collaborator, a "historian," was assigned to the collecting of historical data, consisting of the records of trials for the crime of ritual murder, of confessions obtained or purported to have been obtained by the Inquisition, under torture, and of sentences passed by secular and ecclesiastical courts. For himself Pan Viadomsky reserved the high task of welding the hodgepodge into a coherent whole, indicating the transference of these "habits" and "customs" into the contemporaneous life of Jewry, and adding a running commentary of his own in which was to be reflected the "protest" and "indignation" of the Christian masses. I had no means of knowing whether this distinguished production was intended for home consumption or for export abroad; nor did I know whether it was planned actually to launch a blood-ritual accusation against certain Jews, or merely to begin a general anti-Jewish agitation. Whatever the purpose, the business consumed all of Pan Viadomsky's time and energies. It need hardly be mentioned that as I became aware of his new enterprise, my calls became rarer and rarer; finally I suspended them altogether and our work suffered a long interruption.

Once again I made up my mind to regard my connections with Pan Viadomsky as irrevocably terminated, and I did my best to forget him. But I should have known—in fact, I did know—from previous experience that the resolution was futile, and that the connections would be resumed as soon as he chose to honor my poor garret with his high presence. I should have known that there was no escape from the curious dual roles which Pan Viadomsky and I were apparently destined to play opposite each other. And I must confess that in spite of the disgust awakened in me by his latest enterprise, the old, queer attraction was still there, as if I had been cast under a spell. It was really as though I could no longer do without the man. Let me be frank: I missed him, I longed for our regular nightly meetings, I remembered with nostalgia those winter evenings which we had spent summoning out of the past that once-forgotten life which we had in common. Now that our connections were cut off, my modest life had lost—so it seemed to me—whatever had served to make it interesting and significant. For me too those fantastic incidents, born of fever and imagination, which Pan Viadomsky had woven about both of us had become a simple necessity. My "actual" life, the present, had turned into something gray, pitiful, trivial, shot through with vanity and hatreds; I was asphyxiated by it. My spirit was fixed hungrily on the great events and passions which had filled that far-off time. I could not forget the streets of Jerusalem, the tumult of the Temple courts, the winds that blew across the hills and valleys of Judaea—from all of which I had suddenly been carried off, irrevocably, it seemed, by the break in my relationship with the Pan. For months now I had lived in that world and breathed its air. One consistent consolation worked at the back of my mind: the forest would keep on calling to the wolf—Pan Viadomsky would succumb to the pull of the ancient, multicolored world, and forget the driveling rancors of the contemporaneous world which now occupied his attention. He would remember suddenly the catastrophic drama in which he had been playing a part, and return to resume his role.

Exactly this was what happened.

The weather changed. The mild gusts of wind which herald the spring and Passover began to blow across the country, and Pan Viadomsky shook off his awareness of the surrounding life like an animal which shakes off its winter covering; he sloughed from about him the Pan of the twentieth century and emerged once more as the Cornelius of eternity.

There ensued an odd inversion of the situation. Around the time of the Jewish and Christian religious festivals Pan Viadomsky began to act even more queerly than before. He would have had me believe that he had dropped his interest in the "historic" work. Instead of hiding from his colleagues his relationship with me, he tried to hide from me his relationship with them! He paid me frequent visits in my wretched garret; he spent whole days wandering in my company through the poorest Jewish sections. With my help he hunted up former acquaintances of his in the old city; he unearthed the tailors and shoemakers he had known years before. We crept down lightless and airless cellars; we astonished and terrified Jewish housewives occupied, at that season, with the cleansing of home and utensils in preparation for the Passover.

"I don't know what it is," he confided to me, "but when the Passover days come I simply have to feel myself surrounded by Jews. I—well, I just can't do without them. They bring back the pre-festival days in Jerusalem. There too the time which ushered in the Passover was full of bustle and preparation. They came streaming toward the city from every corner of the land, they, their families and their sheep, bringing the Passover sacrifice. The streets were filled with farmers and peasants and pilgrims. Jerusalem became so gay and lively that when this season of the year comes round, I feel downright homesick, and I have to go back to my Jews, I have to feel them about me, I have to peep into their homes. They put me back, once more, into Jerusalem. It's enough to look into their faces: I seem to see again the swarming alleys about the Temple area."

He spoke dreamily, his half-closed eyes focused on remote, invisible scenes. On his yellow, wrinkled, parchment-like features lay the fresh light of the spring sun which shone on the dirty, noisy streets of Warsaw. The few solitary hairs which adorned his skull stood up as if to take the light. There was vain longing in his voice as he declaimed the words of an unknown poet:

"Oh, Jerusalem, the spring entereth thy gates, accompanied by the footsteps of death."

"What do you mean?" I asked, astonished.

"Oh, nothing. Just a mood of mine. Spring, you understand.... When the spring approaches I sicken for Jerusalem. If I cannot pass through her gates, I must at least haunt the dwelling places of her children. Would you like to see Judah, the man of Kiriot, Judah Ish-Kiriot? Come with me, we'll visit him. Oh, yes, when the Passover comes, I look up my old friends. I quite forgot to tell you that my friend Ish-Kiriot lives in Warsaw."

I had thought that Pan Viadomsky could never surprise me again; but this was quite new.

I asked him to repeat. "What? Judah Ish-Kiriot in Warsaw, too?"

"Why, certainly! I knew him the moment I saw him. I recognized his face among ten thousand. And not only he. Simon is here—him whom they also called Peter; I came across him in the Jewish streets of Warsaw. So many of them are here, the men I knew in the alleys of Jerusalem, in the Temple courts, and in the Lower City. It is extraordinary. Whenever I come into a crowd of Jews,

I seem to know all of them. It's as though I'd had dealings with each one personally. I know their manners, their gestures, their customs, their proud, stiff bearing, their obstinacy, their unbreakable will. I stare at them in the midst of their huckstering and chaffering, here in the Old Market; and it seems to me that any moment they'll throw off their long gaberdines, and stand before me in their white robes—lean, fiery children of the desert, with dark faces, blazing eyes, long hair, thronging about me as they did in the Temple alleys on festival days. Often I feel that it's some blunder of destiny which transported them here into these cold streets, with their shops and stands, with muddy snow underfoot and chilly winds blowing through them. It was thus that I encountered my old friend Judah Ish-Kiriot."

"Judah Ish-Kiriot?" I mumbled, incredulously.

"You can meet him, if you like. He has his place on the Old Market."

Then one day, just before we set out from his house, Pan Viadomsky drew from a corner an extraordinary possession which I had not seen before: a long black cape, with the hood of a Capuchin monk atop. I had not suspected that Pan Viadomsky had hidden anything from me.

"But what do you want that for?" I stammered. "It isn't cold today."

"Hush!" he answered. "I don't want all Jerusalem to know that the Hegemon is visiting Judah Ish-Kiriot. Such matters are done in secret."

Pan Viadomsky drew the hood over his head, and we ventured forth; and I need hardly remark that this odd garb only served to draw the attention of the passers-by. He led me to the Old Market and paused before an ancient, dilapidated house, which was obviously on the point of collapse and would no doubt have collapsed long ago except that the pressure of its equally ancient neighbors maintained it in a precarious erectness; the walls had once been painted red, the shutters green. Pan Viadomsky looked cautiously right and left, to note if he was being observed; then he took me by the hand and conducted me down the narrow, crumbling steps into the cellar.

The interior seemed to be occupied by an antiquarian's shop. Since it happened to be the pre-Passover week, the owner of the shop had just had the walls covered with a new layer of whitewash; the contents therefore lay about in the wildest disorder; there were bronze lamps of all shapes and sizes and tottering piles of trays and plates which trembled and tinkled at the lightest touch; there were ranks of pictures, framed and unframed, chairs, loose bundles of precious stuffs, glassware, figurines of marble, metal and plaster. At the center of this Babylonian disorder stood a Jew in a long capote apparently engaged in the task of restoring order to the pre-Passover chaos. We had hardly entered when the Pan brushed against a candelabrum which stood jammed in among masses of silver and glassware; the pyramid gave forth a warning ringing sound, and the Jew came scampering toward us, terrified.

"Help! You'll smash everything!" he shrieked. He put his hand out to the swaying heap, balanced it, caught his breath, and turned his face toward us, trying to force on to it a smile of courteous welcome.

"Aha, Judah! You weren't expecting me! Your booth is not prepared for a visit from the Hegemon!"

"Sarah! Sarah!" the Jew called into an adjoining cellar, in hearty Warsaw Yiddish. "That old gentile's here again!" And turning to me he continued in the same language. "Every passover eve he comes to visit me. Once upon a time he used to buy things; but during these last few years I haven't earned anything from him. But he comes just the same, stares hard at me, and changes my name to Judah! May this festival be turned to mourning if I have the slightest idea what the old heathen's driving at."

"Ah, Judah, Judah!" said Pan Viadomsky, shaking his head reprovingly, "you never did keep things in order—neither there nor here."

"May I be paralyzed if I know what Judah he's talking about. Though come to think of it, my grandfather's name was Judah; but what's that got to do with it? My name happens to be Mordecai. Not that I care what name he calls me by, if he'd only spend a little money here before the festivals."

"I knew him at once!" Pan Viadomsky turned to me, triumphantly. "That face! There's no mistaking it. I happened to wander into this place one winter's night. I saw him sitting under a small petroleum lamp. He was shivering with the cold, his face was blue, his earlocks trembled in the wind, so did his long, pointed beard as it hung over his gaberdine. I looked once into his face, and knew him! I asked him: 'Judah! What are you doing here?' At first he refused to recognize me—just as he did that time in K'far Nahum. But later on he did recognize me." He turned again to the Jew. "Well, Judah, you did recognize your Hegemon, didn't you? Do you feel like walking with me up the Mount of Olives, to Gat Shemen? This evening?"

The antiquarian fixed his puzzled eyes on me. "Maybe you know what he's talking about. He drops in here every Passover eve, when I'm cleaning out the leaven. He babbles about Jerusalem and the Mount of Olives. Seems to be a learned sort of heathen, too; always wants to know if I have any Hebrew books for sale. What does a heathen want with Hebrew books? Once he found a tattered old manuscript here, and you should have seen the fuss he made about it! He paid well for it, too. What can he be using it for? Does he want to cure somebody? Every time he sees an old manuscript he's beside himself with curiosity and joy. He used to have money, and spend it. But it's all gone now. I don't see him from one year's end to the other. Only on Passovers, when I'm up to the ears in preparations. I suppose he's nothing but a penniless old man. Sick, too, poor old loony!" And the Jew pointed significantly to his forehead.

"He says," I addressed the shopkeeper, "that he knew you once in Jerusalem, in the days when the Second Temple was standing. Your name at that time, he says, was Judah Ish-Kiriot. You were the man who sold Yeshua of Nazareth for thirty pieces of silver."

"What's that? What's that? What did I sell? Thirty pieces of silver. Listen, Pan! Tell him I could do with thirty pieces of silver, to prepare for the festival, and if there's anything here—"

"Yeshua of Nazareth," I explained. "That's Jesus Christ. You sold Jesus Christ for thirty pieces of silver to the High Priest and the Roman officials."

The Jew suddenly turned white as chalk. The ashen pallor flooded downward, it crept in under his beard, so that his face took on a resemblance to a death mask. His eyes became glassy with terror. They rolled from side to side, as if he had been smitten with a sudden sickness. In a voice that trembled with horror he said:

"If the Pan wants to make fun of a Jew, tell him to find someone else. Sarah! Sarah!" he yelled. "Come here at once!"

"What's he shouting about?" Pan Viadomsky asked me impatiently. "He's recognized me, ha? Did you see how frightened he got? That's just how he used to look. The same pale face, with the hair standing up. He knows me! He knows his Hegemon. No, no, Judah, don't be scared like that. I won't give you away." The Pan even held out his hand. "We've got a pact between us, you and I. There's a bond between us."

The woman had now come into the shop. When her eyes fell on Pan Viadomsky she burst into a torrent of abuse. "May ten thousand black curses carry him off!" she shrilled. Her tattered wig danced on her head. Her sleeves were rolled up; her ragged apron was wet. "What does he want with his thirty pieces of silver? We see him every Passover. If we only knew—"

"I know what he wants," her husband answered, excitedly. "It's one of those plots. Against me. That's all I need these days."

"What plots?" his wife gasped. "What are you trying to scare me for?"

"Plots about their God," the Jew babbled. "He says I sold him for thirty pieces of silver."

"May the Evil Spirit descend on him! Does he want his thirty pieces of silver back? Does he think we've got them? Let him search the whole house, and see if we've got thirty pieces of silver. All he'll find is thirty curses."

I whispered in Pan Viadomsky's ear: "We're frightening these poor people. Let us go." And taking his hand I tried to pull him from the cellar. He resisted at first, then yielded reluctantly.

"Ah, Judah, Judah," he called back, at the trembling Jew. "You've forgotten everything."

I would have taken the Pan home with me, but he would not consent. He dug his bony fingers into my arm, and said, urgently:

"Come with me. Let's go in search of Israel! I want to see the children of Israel."

He pulled me deeper into the Jewish section. We pushed our way into arcades thronged with buyers and sellers, Jews and Jewesses laying in their stocks for the festival. We found ourselves in the midst of an indescribable tumult. Women carrying baskets and pails slung over their arms stood by the tubs of the fishermen, by the butchers' blocks, and bargained furiously. Hens clucked and fluttered about in their coops. Women stood by barrels of pickled cucumbers, looking as sour and wrinkled as their wares. Pan Viadomsky had to be everywhere, see everything, penetrate into every corner. He pushed his way through a press of women purchasing new plates and cups and pots in a hardware shop; he insisted on examining a linen and haberdashery store. He displayed the curiosity and gaiety of a child. And he kept on muttering delightedly:

"Absolutely unchanged! Absolutely the same! Just as in those days!"

He paused in front of a small *matzot* dealer's stand. A group of poverty-stricken Jews in tattered festival coats and long boots were laying in, at the last moment (undoubtedly they had not been able to obtain the money till now), their pitiful store of unleavened bread for the Passover. The Pan hopped from one foot to the other n feverish excitement.

"Matzot!" he sang. *"Matzot!* As I live! The unleavened bread which they brought with them out of Egypt. Three, four thousand ears ago! Whenever I see those *matzot* I have to think back. An old eople! A tried and tormented people! *Matzot!* The bread of liberaion!"

Then suddenly he whipped round toward me.

"Tell me, you—I know that men like you are too intelligent, too ssimilated, too rotten with the decadent, slimy humanistic culture f the times to pay attention to this; you and your like want to prouce men of a single mold—rows and rows of baked or half-baked ttle loaves, out of a single oven. You don't believe in these things; ou find them mad, fantastic, fanatical, revolting; you'd like to ipe it all out. Just the same—listen to me!—just the same there must be among you obscure sects, secret, conspiratorial, mystical groups, religious plotters, you understand, who practice dark and fearful rituals without a name. . . . You follow me? You understand what I'm alluding to. . . ."

"No, Pan Viadomsky, I don't know what you're alluding to, and I don't understand what you mean."

"Well, of course you aren't likely to reveal it to me. Your lips are sealed with the seal of the great ban. And it's not wholly impossible that you yourself are not privy to those secrets. Unfortunately the religious motif has declined a great deal among your people, yet I don't doubt that there are deep levels where the ancient tradition survives unspoiled, where the thousand-year-old national ritual is still observed by sects which have remained for ever unrevealed. Tell me now, in all honesty; do you not believe that there are sects among you which still cling to that ritual?"

"But what ritual?" I asked.

"Well—if you must have it—the ritual of using at least one little drop of Christian blood for the baking of your *matzot*."

"And you actually believe that?" I turned on him.

"Certainly. Why not? An ancient people . . . a culture which goes back thousands of years . . . Moses . . . Jehovah . . . the God of Vengeance. . . . A stiff-necked people, not belonging to our contemporaneous, characterless, flabby Christian world, the final product of the religion imposed upon us by your countryman. You have remained uncorrupted, surely, a hot-blooded desert tribe, bursting with passion, with eternal hatred and eternal loyalty. . . . Why not? If I were a Jew, I would certainly belong to one of those sects which cling to the ancient and bloody ritual, yes, even though it might be attended by the most frightful dangers; even if I had to pay for it with my life. Such a people would be worthy of the name! That is what I would call a race, a religion, a nation! But individuals like you, moderns, feeble descendants of a fiery ancestry, tremble at the very words. Your race, too, is degenerating. . . ."

"And you would really cling to some such horrible ritual?" I asked him, curiously.

"Of course! Why shouldn't I? To feel the blood of my enemy

on my lips, even if it be only a drop, a touch, a taste: a symbol at least. The call of race, the call to eternal hatred! Look!" he cried suddenly, and his wide-open eyes radiated a wild light. "Look at the women grabbing at those onions! I like Jews who eat onions, I like Jews who send out blasts of garlic, like a hot desert wind, through their bushy beards. The stench of onions and garlic is woven into the texture of their skin. Powerful, authentic men! Ho, ho! Your women know what their husbands like! Onions and garlic! The reek of the true male. . . . Not like us degenerate, disintegrating, modernizing Europeans. . . ."

Suddenly Pan Viadomsky became rigid and motionless. The blood left his face, his eyes expanded with astonishment and fear, while his nostrils began to quiver. His fingers closed convulsively on my arm.

"Look! See who stands there! I know that face. I've seen it before. Look!"

And before I could recover from my astonishment, Pan Viadomsky left my side and dashed toward a squat, powerful looking, heavily molded Jew, who stood by a tubful of fish.

"Simon! Simon bar Jonah! What are you doing here?"

But my astonishment increased when the fish dealer turned his face on Pan Viadomsky, for it was indeed the face of the Apostle Simon bar Jonah, as tradition has fixed it among the classic painters. A square hard skull, covered with a tough, wrinkled skin; big, black, brilliant eyes withdrawn in profound sockets under the mighty arch of the forehead. The eyes blazed in their depths above the thick tangles of the gray beard, which surrounded with its heavy border the thick-veined cheeks. The short, flat nose, terminating in wide wings, surmounted a pair of fleshy lips. The Jew, apparently as astonished as I, stretched out a powerful, sinewy hand which resembled the uncovered root of an olive tree, exposed to the weather and the hoofs of passing animals, and stared at the Pan.

"That Pan knows me?" he asked.

"Of course I do. And don't you recognize the Hegemon of Jerusalem, Simon?"

"The what?"

"Why, man, I'm your Hegemon."

The Jew wrinkled his brow, and turned to the bystanders. "Hegemon? And what may that be? What does he want? What's he talking about?" And ignoring Pan Viadomsky he took up his huckster's cry: "Fish! Fresh fish! Good, fresh pike for Passover! Buy, good women, buy!"

"Simon! Simon! Don't you know me? Where have you left your Rabbi?"

"Rabbi? What Rabbi? And what has a gentile to do with a Rabbi? What is he babbling about? I've no time for nonsense now. Fish, good housewives, fresh fish! Two *gulden* a pound!"

"Think of it!" gasped the Pan, turning to me. "This is the man who once drew a sword against me! The only Jew who ever dared to stand up to me! He actually sliced the ear off one of my most faithful men. Look what's become of him! Simon, what have you done with your sword?"

"What sword?" asked the fish dealer, angrily. "Someone take this gentile away, or there'll be trouble."

"Come, Pan," I begged him. "You're feverish. You're not well. We'll go home. You're frightening these good people."

It was with difficulty that I managed to drag Pan Viadomsky away from the tumultuous market place.

"Oh, Israel, Israel, what has become of thee!"

"Come, Pan."

"And I love them so!" he croaked, mournfully, half to himself.

I was taken aback. "Whom, Pan?"

"Why, you, my little Jews, my Hebrews." A dark cloud settled on his face. His hands and lips trembled, his nose quivered as the breath passed through it. He repeated, miserably: "Israel, Israel, what have you done to yourself?"

"Come, Pan Viadomsky, we'll take a carriage."

But Pan Viadomsky did not hear me.

"Shoemakers, peddlers, hucksters, dealers in old clothes and rusty iron, that's what's become of you! You sit in the gutters of an alien, barbarous city, steeped in mud and snow. The Jochanans, the Simons, the Judahs, the Jacobs, the Josephs. . . . And over there the trumpets of rams' horns peal out to the watchers about the Temple towers, the sun rises and flashes back from the gilded gates, the Priests come forth to their morning services, the streets and alleys about the Temple are already thronged with the first pilgrims bringing their sacrifices. And they sit here, cobblers, tailors, what-not, hidden in their miserable cellars, while I, their Hegemon, am with them, steeped in the same muddy time and place. I breathe the same air, and they do not recognize me, they do not know who I am. Do they not see their own faces? Do they not hear their own voices? Israel, what art thou become? Behold, thou preparest thy Passover far, far from the house of thy father! And I, thy Hegemon, am in exile even as thou art."

He almost burst into tears for wretchedness of spirit. People stared at us as we passed, and a small crowd even began to follow us. There was a spring freshness in the air which awakened a spirit of eagerness and curiosity in human minds and hearts. I was beginning to worry that Pan Viadomsky's queer babblings about another life, about the Jews and their decline, would be overheard; and that would have been equally uncomfortable for him and for those that caught the words. I hailed the first carriage that came our way and practically forced my companion into it.

Night had fallen when we arrived at his home, and the interior was solid darkness. I would have lighted the lamp, but this Pan Viadomsky categorically forbade. I drew the curtains and opened the window. I laid the old man down on his bed, and let the mild spring wind blow over him. Instead of soothing him, it only increased his restlessness. Moonlight poured down through the grated window, and laid a pattern of bars on his drawn, yellow-white face. The incredibly thin, hawklike nose stood out below the fantastic, demonic eyes. Then a sort of rigidity seized him, and he began to speak, more to himself than to me:

"Just as of old. . . ."

"Try to forget, Pan Viadomsky."

"No, I will not forget, I do not want to forget. I want to be with them . . . I am with them . . . now . . . ."

He sat up suddenly on the bed. He stared unseeingly before him, his eyes tranquil, his face composed, and spoke.

CHAPTER TWO

"THAT winter in Jerusalem was unusually severe. Once we even had a snowfall which covered all the surrounding hills, including the Scopus. True, it did not lie there long, for the sun came out and wiped it away; but the sight of Jerusalem in the morning, a beleaguered city surrounded by white strongholds, left an unforgettable picture in my mind. The Jerusalemites, unaccustomed to such extremes of weather, suffered greatly. Theirs was mostly an outdoor life; and they went about, during that season, wrapped from head to foot, the rich in mantles of felt, the poor in sackcloth and rags. Crowds took refuge in the prayer houses. The Rabbis and teachers who frequented the Temple area found shelter in the basilica of Herod; they sat with their pupils crouching over braziers brought to them by pious women. The Priests in their linen trousers and light white tunics shivered as they went barefoot in procession toward the sanctuary to fulfill their holy office. That winter Jerusalem was fairly quiet. During the long interval between their Feast of Booths and their Passover, an interval without sacred holidays, few pilgrims appeared in the city. The public squares and the Temple area were haunted only by the regular crowds, official beggars, loiterers, escaped slaves and revolutionary trouble-makers. Most of the rich people, the aristocracy of the city and the high Priestly families, fled to the warmth and sunlight of the eternally blooming, palm tree-shaded area of Jericho. If there was any influx from outside, it consisted mostly of pupils who came to sit at the feet of the Jerusalem Rabbis. These were not drawn entirely from the poor classes; there were well-to-do families of Judaea, and of countries beyond the seas and deserts, who sent their sons to be educated in Jerusalem. Young neophytes came also to the Priestly and Levitic schools, and they mingled with the throngs which attended the Rabbis about the burning braziers.

"There was very little to interest or occupy me that winter in Jerusalem, and I was rarely in the city. I spent a good deal of time with Pilate in Caesarea, discussing an important project on which he had set his heart. Pilate had long dreamed of finding a method which would give him access to the immense treasures of the Temple, and the project which he now revolved in his mind had a double purpose. Jerusalem has always suffered from a shortage of water. The pools which King Solomon had dug on the Hebron road and from which he had laid pipes into the city had been neglected through the ages; the pipes leaked; between this loss and the increase in the population of Jerusalem, the supply was wholly insufficient. There were, of course, the waters of Siloah and a few wells. There were the cisterns, too; but they did not come near meeting the needs of the Jerusalemites. Now, besides hungering for the Temple treasury, Pilate was moved by that common ambition of Roman proconsuls; he wanted to leave behind him, for the future generations of the province which he administered, a memorial of his governorship. What could have been more striking or honorable than the creation of a vast aqueduct, which should bring water to the ever-thirsty city from a great distance? The enterprise was not a simple one, for Jerusalem lay in the hills, with descending slopes on three sides; but Pilate was determined to make the attempt. To this end he would need the fabulous treasures accumulated in the Temple vaults, the deposits of votaries, the possessions of widows and orphans. His fingers itched to be at the money, as his mind itched to acquire fame. But if the erection of an aqueduct across such natural obstacles was difficult, not less difficult was the task of winning over to his plans the heads of the Jewish people. There would, of course, be a tremendous outcry from the plebeian masses, and against this we had to prepare carefully. I spent many hours in Caesarea with Pilate, discussing methods of breaking through this resistance. I paid frequent visits to the High Priest and the most important Priestly families, in Jericho, to sound them out. Thus, between the pleasant, warm city of Caesarea, on the coast, and the palm groves of Jericho, I passed very little time that winter in Jerusalem, all of which I counted to the good.

"On one of my infrequent sojourns in the capital, while staying at the Antonia, I happened to set out for a stroll, and without any purpose in mind made my way toward the sheep market. Passing through this, I came to the miserable little quarters lying about the spring which the Jews call Bet Zeida—the gathering place of the halt, the blind, the diseased, the crippled, who wait there until the spring sends forth a spurt of water, and throw themselves into the muddy hollow in the belief that they will be cured.

"I had seen that in the summer. It did not occur to me that in the winter days, when a covering of melted snow hid the earth, hardening sometimes into a rigid mass, there would be any visitors to the spring. To my amazement, however, I came upon a vast crowd, in a state of wild agitation. There was a panic abroad, and yet it differed entirely from the kind of panic which I had witnessed before. I distinguished cries of joy, a sound of hosannahs. My curiosity was stronger than my disgust. I suspected something, and when I drew near my suspicion was verified. A Rabbi had appeared among the sick and had healed one of them with a miracle. Not that this was anything new in Judaea. Miracles of this kind were more or less of a commonplace among the Jews. What astonished me, however, was the impression which this particular miracle seemed to have made on this concourse of the sick. I was by now familiar with the ecstasies of Jewish masses; I had seen their outbursts of fervor in the Temple; I knew something of their religious frenzies; but such a spectacle as I now beheld was new to me. The sick and the half-dead who lay in the chilly mud of the spring, the hale who had come as attendants on the sick, screamed exultantly as a white-robed figure, of which I barely caught a glimpse, disappeared from their midst. Then followed complete silence; countless hands were stretched out in the direction taken by the Rabbi.

" 'Who was that?' I asked of a cripple who came limping toward me, leaning on a stick and dragging after him a withered limb.

" 'He uttered one word, and it came to pass!' the cripple sang. 'Do you see that old wreck of a man there? He's been lying on his bed for years, the flesh rotting on his bones. He begged us to bring him to the spring, but no one paid any attention to his groans. Who could have thought that anything would help him? All of us had given him up for dead, or as good as dead. Then suddenly a Rabbi appeared in our midst. The sick man lifted up his hands and murmured something. The Rabbi looked at him, and said, in a voice of command: "Arise, take thy bed, and walk." And the man did as the Rabbi commanded. No! He didn't even tell him to sit down in the pool. He did it with a word of his mouth. And it happened like a flash of lightning. Oh, if he had but done it for me!'

"An amazing people, yours. Other nations, too, have their magicians, thaumaturges, enthusiasts and wonder workers who have the power to exorcise evil spirits, drive out sicknesses and tranquilize madmen. They too can restore the crippled to wholeness with a glance. I've seen not a little of all that among the Chaldaeans and Egyptians. Alexandria, Antioch, Askelon and Tyre are full of miracle men, but none of them look upon this practice as a special grace from God, or hail it as a divine attribute. Magic among them is simply a profession, like that of the barber, or the bath attendant, or the scribe who prepares amulets on parchment to keep demons at a distance. It's only among you Jews that these commonplace occurrences are regarded as a suspension of the laws of nature, a sign from the gods, who for such occasions leave their regular occupations, turn aside from their eternal tasks, to confer a special favor on some obscure wretch who wants his hump straightened out or his limbs healed. You are definitely not what might be called a modest people, you Jews.

"For some reason or other I suspected at once that the wonder-worker in white had been none other than the Rabbi of K'far Nahum. And I was not mistaken. Very soon after, I was passing through one of the alleys leading to the Temple and I caught more than a glimpse of him. It was he! It was my old acquaintance, in his white robe; but how changed! He had become longer, bonier, more emaciated; a skeleton! His head towered skyward. He stood in the midst of a crowd of fanatics, engaged in earnest conversation with them. I took up my station under an overhanging arch of the outer wall and watched him. This group by the Temple was composed of the same kind of people who had frequented his company up there in K'far Nahum; plain folk all of them; water carriers with their skins balanced on their shoulders, artisans with their tools in their hands, and the like. There were likewise among them types which I recognized as *kanaim,* Galilean enthusiasts who hung about Jerusalem from one festival to the next. Jerusalem swarmed with these dangerous idlers, men who supplied recruits for every revolt and riot. I recognized them by their bearing and their clothes, that is, whatever they had of the latter; for they were known as 'the naked men of Galilee.' Even in winter they wore nothing more than sackcloth tatters, with a girdle to cover their shame. They were indifferent to cold and rain; their bodies were hardened against both. They stood there, a cluster of fierce, tangled locks, about the Rabbi. From where I stood I could hear his words. He was not teaching, as other Rabbis did; he was not uttering texts and interpreting them; he was telling them something, recounting and expounding; and what he said created such excitement, called forth such divisions of opinion, that I expected a fight to break out at any moment.

"Not all the listeners, however, belonged to the simple folk. I marked one man who joined the group though he was obviously not of the kind which listens to wandering Rabbis. At first he remained at a distance. He was quite clearly a member of the higher class, probably one of the Sadducean aristocracy. He was dressed in a woolen mantle held together by a many-colored girdle which went down as far as his knees, hemming his footsteps. At the bottom hung a rich fringe which further impeded his walk. His hair was twisted into countless little ringlets, in the Chaldaean style, and his beard was treated in the same fashion. Even from afar I could catch the heavy perfumes of the oils which anointed his body. Suddenly, becoming interested in the recital of the Rabbi, he issued a command to the two slaves accompanying him, and they thrust a way for him among the half-naked beggars and workmen who surrounded the speaker. The richly clad Sadducee came forward and confronted the Rabbi; then he lifted up a hand covered with rings and asked a question. There must have been something very comical in his words, for the two slaves at once burst into sycophantic laughter, and some of the bystanders joined them. The Rabbi, ignoring the laughter, answered gravely, but the Sadducee did not even listen to him; instead, he turned away with a look of mocking triumph and marched off.

"I remained at my post. After a time I observed, standing toward the rear of the Rabbi, an extraordinary creature whose appearance continued to haunt me for a long time afterwards. It was an apparition from among the dead, clad from head to foot in sackcloth: a skeleton. True, the skull was covered with a sort of skin, but the color of it was neither human nor animal; it was like the fell of a wild beast which has been dried and burned with fire: ashen, bluish and lifeless. In the deep sockets of the skull two eyes, as lifeless as the skin, as inhuman and deadly, peered out. To the top of the vast skull, which resembled a fragment of pottery, clung one or two tangled locks, hanging down over the naked, bony throat and neck, on which the head managed to maintain its balance as on a thin wire. But the most remarkable feature about this apparition was that in its motions it suggested death even more than in immobility. The man—I supposed he was one—stood to the rear of the Rabbi, and as the latter moved forward, or stepped back, imitated him. But every gesture, every step, called forth the feeling that the motion was not voluntary at all; the man himself was incapable of performing it; something from the beyond animated the mechanism, without imparting life to it. There was always a slight interval between any motion which the Rabbi made and which the figure repeated, and this served, in a horrible way, to accentuate the impression that it was not a living thing, but a structure of limbs and muscles controlled from without. I stared at the extraordinary object, till it was gradually borne in on me that there was something familiar about it. I approached a man on the outskirts of the crowd and asked:

" 'Who or what is that thing, there?'

" 'Don't you know?' he answered. 'That's Eliezer, the brother of Martha and Miriam.'

" 'Eliezer, the brother of Martha and Miriam? But of course I know him. What has happened to him? He looks like a dead man.'

" 'But he is a dead man! The Rabbi awakened him from death!'

" 'Awakened him from death?'

"Yes, I remembered the young man. I had seen him in Gat Shemen, in the house of Miriam of Migdal, when I visited the place with Hanan. And I remembered also that even then the young man, with his slow movements and his wooden, inexpressive face, had made upon us a strange, slightly terrifying impression. We had observed even then, as we remarked his wide-open, childlike eyes, which resembled those of a calf, or of some other dumb animal which expresses itself through its eyes, that he was not entirely normal. He had suggested something not of this world. Why, yes, yes, I thought now; all sorts of things can happen with such a creature. He is like clay in the hands of these mystics, and especially of such a mystic as the famous Rabbi of K'far Nahum. Who knows? I went on thinking; it is not at all impossible that these Rabbis possess strange sources of magic, brought down, in the utmost secrecy, from their remotest forefathers, who are said to have been 'the friends of God.' Or they may have brought with them, out of the desert, or out of their slavery in Egypt, recipes and devices which can awaken the dead and bring them forth from their graves. Indeed, looking at him whom they called Eliezer, I was quite ready to believe this; for the miracle was written in the bearing of the apparition, and could not be denied. Then I remembered that the case had been mentioned in some of the more cultured and educated homes in Jerusalem, even among the aristocrats. I started back. No, no! This was too much. A man who can recall the dead is a danger to any government; particularly so in a country so prone to unrest and rebellion as Judaea.

"One evening shortly after this encounter I was in the company of the oldest High Priest and his sons. I was there on my regular mission—which was to further the project of the aqueduct. It was—as we knew from the beginning—a very difficult mission. It would need much skill and patience to wring from the High Priest the permission to lay hands on the Temple treasury. But we had not expected such resistance as we actually encountered. They were united in their opposition; they were of a single opinion. 'The Temple treasure is sanctuary, and sanctuary may not be touched!' Even my friend Theophilus concurred in this judgment. What surprised me most, however, was the attitude of the youngest son, Hanan. I had expected a more intelligent and enlightened outlook on his part; he understood and admired our Roman civilization, he honored our institutions, and he had—as I supposed—the outlook of a statesman. But there came no help from him. 'The national Temple treasury? Touch that, and you undermine the faith of the people in the Temple itself. The Jews of all lands will be outraged if we lay a finger on the possession of widows and orphans! The Temple will cease to be the one unchallenged center and unifying sanctity of the Jewish people. No, no—such a step may well undermine the foundations of our state and people. We don't deny that your aqueduct is an important enterprise, but the money would have to be raised through new taxation. It will be necessary for the Proconsul at Antioch to approach the imperial government; but the Temple treasury must remain untouched!' I had reason to suspect that it was something other than the so-called sanctity of the treasury or the sentiments of Jewry within and without Judaea which produced this unity of opposition among the various parties; the Temple moneys were being collected for the ultimate rebellion against Rome! We Romans are not easily deceived in such matters. We know the strategy of the nations. Gold is might. Gold buys arms, armies and allies. And thus, listening to the High Priest and his family, I decided to drop a hint, to touch on something they would find uncomfortable. I brought up the subject of the Galilean Rabbi.

" 'You remember,' I said to the High Priest, 'the man of whom I spoke to you, the man of Galilee who has been assembling about him a group of dangerous followers? I saw him only the other day in the Temple area. He was carrying on the same agitation, quite openly, in Jerusalem. There was no one about to stop him. And those that were gathered about him were of exactly the same element as flocked to him in Galilee, the restless trouble-makers and rebels. He probably brought them along with him. I find it altogether extraordinary that the overseer of the Temple area should tolerate it—altogether extraordinary.'

" 'Oh, Hegemon, do you mean the Rabbi of K'far Nahum?' asked the oldest of the High Priests, and laughed so heartily that the tears started to his eyes. 'You don't take *him* for a dangerous figure, do you? Why he's—' and he made a little circular motion with his finger near his forehead.

" 'He's what?'

" 'Mad. Out of his wits. He drives evil spirits from others, and he himself is possessed by one. What do you think he says of himself? That he is nothing more nor less than "the living bread of heaven." And all his followers must eat his flesh and drink his blood before they can enter the gates of the heavenly kingdom.'

"There was a burst of laughter in the great hall.

" 'You see,' said the old High Priest, wearily, 'all sorts of visionaries assemble in the Temple courts; prophets, messengers of the

Lord. Thus we are afflicted with all sorts of foolish visionaries. As long as they remain within the limits of the law and confine themselves to religious or ethical sermons, strengthening the faith and exhorting the people to piety and good deeds, they can have all the visions they want. We don't interfere. Naturally, we keep watch on them, and see that they observe the provisions I have mentioned. If they are not a danger to the existing order, as long as they don't create a tumult in the Temple, they can babble all they want. And let me say that perhaps the worst thing you can do is to persecute one of these enthusiasts prematurely. Trust me, Hegemon, there are among them such as would only be too eager to achieve the status of martyrs. That is their first big step! It is then that they become really dangerous. As for this Galilean of whom you speak, Hegemon: I should not be at all surprised if he too were waiting for just this windfall—to be dragged off, tried and persecuted. Perhaps even put to death. I understand that he has hinted as much in his utterances. We know these men. But we are not going to play their game. No doubt he thought that the moment he appeared in the Temple courts with his followers, the boors and peasants of Galilee, we would send the Temple watch after him, and have him haled before the Sanhedrin. But as soon as we learned that his talk was harmless, that it was not directed against Rome or the Temple, but had to do only with dreams of resurrection and the kingdom of heaven—he is going to parcel the latter out among his followers—we ignored him. And now you see to what fantastic absurdities he has gone: he talks of having his followers eat his flesh and drink his blood.'

"I would not let this pass off so easily. I addressed myself to the High Priest: 'But the man's power is growing over the people. He has magic powers which awaken faith. He has but to say a word to the lame, and they rise and walk; such is the strength of his spirit over the sick. I myself have witnessed him exercise it in Galilee. And in the Temple court they pointed out to me the man he had brought back from the dead. Let me say that this resurrected creature does indeed look as though he had been among the dead. I insist that one who has this skill in suggestion is not the harmless dreamer you would make him out to be. You cannot know what he will command his followers to do; only one thing is sure—they will obey him blindly.'

" 'Time enough for that, Hegemon, when it happens. Trust us; we won't have much difficulty with him. We have overcome much more dangerous rebels. I am against hasty, ill-advised, and premature measures. Until now the man has not shown himself to be dangerous. And on the whole, it appears that the moral content of his sermons is not at all disturbing; on the contrary, if we ignore the nonsense about eating his flesh and blood, we could even support much of his doctrine, which has to do with repentance and preparation for what he calls the kingdom of heaven. What exactly he means by his kingdom of heaven I do not know, but whatever it is, he exhorts the people to do good, to love each other, eschew oppression of each other, and so on. It's perhaps a little lofty and exaggerated, but that's to be expected of one who thinks he brings a message direct from the divinity. As a matter of fact, I believe him to be much more of a danger to the Pharisees than to us! He's a hard nut for them to crack. They too believe in those follies, in the resurrection, angels and demons and what-not. Let them look to it. He is no danger to us; at least, not yet. Then again, we rely on the healthy instincts of the masses.'

" 'But it appears that the masses follow him.'

" 'The masses follow anyone who promises them a little happiness, either in this world or in what they call the world to come. But my friend: the masses are easily won—and as easily lost. Besides—' here the High Priest changed his tone—'we did have in mind, some time ago, the idea of bringing the man to trial before the Sanhedrin; not for crimes against Rome, but for possible crimes against our faith. We were about to issue orders to the Temple watch for his arrest. But the matter became known when certain quite important persons intervened. I was, I must admit, quite astonished at the quality of those who were ready to defend him. There was, for instance, Joseph Arimathea, a member of the Sanhedrin. There was also Simon Cyrene. What astonished me most, however, was that even Nicodemon, the Pharisee, a pious and learned man, came to his defense; for I hear that there's a good deal of quarreling between the Pharisees and the Rabbi of Galilee. I am told that he is forever denouncing and insulting them. But for all that, this same Nicodemon came to us in the greatest haste, to assure us that the Rabbi hadn't intended any offense to the faith. It was only a way he had of speaking, with parables and stories. Nicodemon went further than that; he launched into quite a panegyric on the Rabbi, exalted his virtues, and advised us strongly to let the matter rest, and see what would come out of it. It appears, if you like, that they have ideas concerning this Rabbi; they think that—'

"But at this point I observed that the sons of the former High Priest, and particularly Eliezer, the oldest of them, were making frantic signs at their father. Suddenly old Hanan interrupted his long narrative, shrugged his shoulders, and changed the theme.

" 'Yes, he appears to be a very pious sort of person; indeed, a little too far gone in his conception of piety. He is obviously of the party of the Pharisees, even if he does have his differences with them. No, no, Hegemon, there's no danger in the man. Were it otherwise, such people of standing would never have intervened for him.'

" 'But what is it exactly that they think of him?' I asked sharply, turning back the conversation to the point where the old High Priest had broken it off. 'What do they expect of him?'

" 'Oh, that? They expect him to bring the masses back onto the path of righteousness. Unfortunately it cannot be denied that faith has grown weak among the masses, and such preachers and leaders may increase the faith, and with it the gifts and sacrifices for the Temple.'

"Very obviously this was not what old Hanan had almost let slip when his sons interrupted him. The father High Priest had let his tongue run away with him. If Joseph Arimathea, whom I knew quite well, and who was a man of high culture, had intervened for the Rabbi of Galilee, the case was not so trivial as they would have me believe. The same was true regarding their Rabbi Nicodemon, an opponent of the Sadducees, a man held in great honor and beloved of the masses. It was very odd indeed that a teacher of such standing should come to the defense of a Galilean Rabbi whose following consisted of ignorant 'boors'—as the learned and pious Pharisees called them contemptuously. I smelled conspiracy. They expected of the man of Galilee something other than vague ethical instruction. What was it, then, that men like Joseph Arimathea, Nicodemon and Simon saw in him? I never found out; not even later, when his own followers abandoned him, at the time of his death, while these remained faithful to him. No, that was an eternal mystery. But you, Jochanan, surely you can tell me something about that."

And suddenly Pan Viadomsky came to; his eyes lost their remote dreamy look and focused brilliantly on me.

"Can *you* tell me what their expectations were concerning this man? Can you tell me what the father High Priest was about to say when his sons interrupted him? If you have the secret, you may disclose it now, when everything is over, when none of us is among the living, when all of us have become shadows and memories."

"What, I?" The question startled me almost out of my wits.

"Yes, you, Jochanan. Were you not of the pupils of Nicodemon? Did I not see you often enough in the band of comrades which formed round the sons of Simon Cyrene, Alexander and Rufus? Don't I remember how you tried to break through the ranks of our legionaries when we were leading the man of Galilee to the cross on Golgotha? And how often have I not seen you following Nicodemon, or following the man of Nazareth? And on that special occasion, too, in the garden of Gat Shemen. Think back, Jochanan, remember."

Something extraordinary was happening within me.

CHAPTER THREE

HOW this thing came to pass I do not know. I do not understand the inner processes which accompanied it. I had long observed, of course, that when Pan Viadomsky recounted the incidents of what he called his former life in Jerusalem, there was a vivid evocation of the ancient world. But side by side with this there was something else, infinitely more mysterious; namely, an actual touching off of personal memories within me, a stirring of contacts, so that I was gradually drawn out of my present identity, which became weaker and weaker, until it abandoned me altogether, and another took its place, occupied my brain and body and nerves, and transformed me into a contemporary of his world of narrative.

Aware of this fantastic transformation even while it proceeded, I tried to resist. I struggled; I held onto my senses, my immediate surroundings, my foothold in what I have always known as my life. I fought off the arms which pulled me out of myself into a remote and vanished age. For a long time I was successful in the struggle. My living self stood by me like a faithful guardian. Yet I was aware of a perceptible weakening. For it often happened that when Pan Viadomsky was giving his version of a certain event, a personal memory of it arose in me; and it was so vivid, so intimately my own, that I became feverish with the desire to correct him. There were inaccuracies of fact; there were errors of interpretation which stung me; there were details of which he was ignorant and which I wanted to supply in order to fill out the picture and restore the true balance. There was a certain dangerous sweetness in this impulse; and I would not yield. But on this occasion, when the narrator suddenly confronted me with a question so close to me, the last resistance within me dissolved. It was as though the solid earth had melted under me, leaving me the victim of whatever forces were impressed on me. Why did this crucial surrender occur just when it did? Had the long, exciting day wearied me? Was it the softness and seduction of the spring air which broke all my defenses? The faithful guardian of my living self was no longer at my side; he had been put to sleep; he too had fallen into the world which Pan Viadomsky had evoked. There was joy in my surrender; there was fulfillment of an ancient desire to plunge headlong, without restraint or reserve, into the past.

What swam out first, most clearly, from the dimness of the dead world, was the face of my Rabbi, Nicodemon. And from within me there swam out, to meet it, the old feeling of love, enthusiasm and boundless admiration which that face had always awakened. Alternating waves of warmth and terror rushed through my heart, as when one beholds, after long separation, the face of one beloved. For my heart had been given to my Rabbi in utter love. I saw once more, then, that round, full, radiant countenance, dark-red, smooth, like a pomegranate, or like a sunset star set in the deep blue spring heavens of Judaea. It was a countenance that shone with goodness. No cloud of care, pain, despair or ill will was ever permitted to cast its shadow thereon. Never had I seen him yield to sorrow; no matter what difficulties arose or what evil filled the times and laid its cruel hand on his heart, there was never an outward sign. That strong, manly face was always bright with faith and certainty. The skin of it was dark and lustrous, and always tended with the finest oils. He was a young man in those days, one in the prime of life, around the age of forty, and the might of his spirit no less than the might of his body sang in him. It sang from the broad, full figure, which might perhaps have been considered a little too short in view of its fullness. The locks of his hair hung down like bells over his powerful neck and his high, round throat. But the power of him streamed strongest from the great, black, fiery eyes, which were like lakes set in the fastness of the sockets which protected and overshadowed them. No matter what pain or sorrow or distress tore at your spirit, it was enough to look into his eyes, and tranquillity returned. These were eyes which poured forth a sunlight of faith, confidence and love. They were a source of strength to the hands of the weak. They bound me to him, as they bound all his pupils, as a calf is bound; they made our will identical with his. This is the face which shines now, and will shine forever, in my memory of him. No wonder, then, that when the ancient world became part of me once more, or when I once again became a part of it, the face of my Rabbi should rise like a portent before me.

Concerning the inner spirit of my Rabbi, perhaps this circumstance will serve best to introduce a description. He refused to make of his learning a spade to dig with, that is, a means of earning his daily bread; it was rather a brimming spring, whose waters flowed fresh and free for all that thirsted. In order that he might not exact a fee, however small, for tuition, he earned his livelihood by other means than the Torah. Joseph Arimathea, a man of great wealth, was his friend; he came often to the house of learning where my Rabbi taught and sat down among the pupils, to take in with them the words of God flowing from the lips of our Rabbi. This same Joseph Arimathea wanted to take upon his own shoulders all the worldly worries of the Rabbi, and support him in great style. The Rabbi would have none of it. He was fond of repeating the proverb: "You may purchase a friend, but you must *make* a teacher for yourself." He meant thereby that friendship may be bought with presents, but a Rabbi and teacher could be acquired only by faith and by following, without offering in exchange any part of one's worldly goods. However, Joseph Arimathea did support out of his wealth the school and a number of the students. The Rabbi himself earned his daily bread at a little sandal booth in the lower part of the city. There came to him many distinguished women of the city to place orders with him; they had to have the measure of their feet taken by the Rabbi. Some of them were pure in their motives, for they knew that the Rabbi in his modesty paid no attention to their persons when he made the measurements; others came because they wanted to gaze upon the beauty of the Rabbi whether or not he paid attention to them; and they came when they were pregnant in the belief that with such a model before their eyes, they would bear beautiful and gifted children. But the Rabbi did not spend much time at his manual labor, for he gave most of the day to us, his pupils. His needs were few and easily satisfied. He was without children, and this circumstance was a reproach in the eyes of the other sages, who held that the Rabbi was neglecting the commandment concerning fruitfulness. But his reply was: "A sage and teacher must not hang a millstone round his own neck," whereby he meant, of course, the upkeep of a family. He believed that a sage and teacher must be free to give all his strength to the Torah. When he was asked why he had not taken a wife unto himself, he answered: "My bride is the Torah." He was not altogether singular, in this respect, among the sages of Jerusalem. There were others, too, who looked down upon woman as a temptation and snare. They remained unmarried, both for the sake of purity and in order to devote themselves without distraction to the Torah: this they called "eternal betrothal to the holy maid."

I was the third pupil of Rabbi Nicodemon. The first two were

Alexander and Rufus, the sons of Simon Cyrene, who, like Joseph Arimathea, was a friend of the Rabbi. Like Joseph, again, Simon was in the habit of visiting the house of learning and taking his place among the regular pupils. Other pupils were Hillel the water carrier and Judah Ish-Kiriot, who came with other grown-up men to sit on what was called the "footstool of Messiah," to hear the lectures and discourses of the Rabbi. They constituted a regular band or company, which was held together by its belief in the imminence of the coming of the Messiah. Because of my contact with them, I was a witness of and a participant in the great events which came to pass during that Passover in Jerusalem.

But before I proceed to a recital of those events, I must first make known certain matters concerning myself; I must reveal who I was, from what manner of house I came, and how it was that my destiny was linked with this company and this Rabbi.

The place of my birth was the plain of Sharon. Our village lies at the foot of the hills of Ephraim. From the particular hill which overshadowed our village, the plain stretched level as far as the sands of the Great Sea. In the evenings a heavy dew would fall from the heights and veil in mist the surrounding country. The bronze-colored earth absorbed the richness of the dew and sprouted a thick grass much beloved of our flocks. Thus the rich dew nourished a breed of sheep whose heavy wool was greatly sought after by the dyers and weavers; for it was of the finest thread, as soft and as delicate as silk. Indeed, we felt the effects of this dew even on the locks of our own heads. The greenness of the grass persisted throughout the whole year, but he who has not seen our spring, when the forest-covered hills were adorned with a heavy, delicately woven carpet, has never known what real greenness is. The rich cucumber-green of the heights and meadows lay like a glowing shadow upon the neighborhood; and in the midst of this shadow shone, side by side with myriads of anemones, the famous roses of Sharon. Every thorny bush, with its clusters and chains of crimson and cream-white roses, was like a bridegroom adorned for the day of his nuptials. Bands of flowers lurked in beds of green moss and peeped out from under the shelter of the rocks; they seemed to send forth, as they danced in the mild winds, a delicate ringing *sound* of color. Where the plow had passed, the good, fruitful earth looked forth, cinnamon-tinted. In this tapestry of color our fields lay, sprinkled with colored rocks, dazzling in the adornment of nuptial roses, stretching away until they were lost in the dreamy shadows cast by the forests of Carmel, the boundaries of this part of the country. Westward the meadows and woods melted into the sand dunes which were the approach to the sea.

The soil of our valley is not only rich in itself; it is abundantly provided with wells. The natural fruitfulness of the earth, which brings forth a juicy and nourishing vegetable growth, is enhanced by the science of our sages, who have laid down rules and laws of sowing and harvesting. The sheep and cattle which feed hereabouts are desired above all others in the land; equally famous, and in equal demand, are our wines, which, because of their fig flavor, do not yield even to the wines of Jericho and Cyprus, for they are to be found as frequently as these on the tables of the rich, both within Judaea and in countries beyond the sea. God has blessed our valley with the blessing of milk and honey. There were legends concerning the fatness of our soil and the richness of our milk and of our flocks and herds. In the poverty-stricken hills of Judaea it was believed that the sheep of the valley of Sharon pastured on ripe grapes; honey dripped from the mouths of our cattle, and milk ran without pressure from their overfull udders. Even until this day I am homesick for that generous soil which fed us with such a prodigal hand. I am homesick for the sunlit afternoons, when the shepherds and the workers in the fields were wont to lie down in the shadow of the grape vines. I long for the quiet, tranquil evenings, wrapped in the dewy mantle fallen from the sky. Shadowy wings were spread then over the great valley; and from the thresholds of the little houses, where the evening lamps shone, came the sound of flutes piping the song of rest.

But the beauty and kindness of this region was also marred by unhappiness; for there was much trouble with these little houses of our industrious workers, especially such as were close to the shore. The sea cast up sand dunes which crept up like thieves upon the houses. The earth is shifty there, and often the foundations of the houses yielded and melted and sank. We were not sure where and when such things would happen. There would suddenly appear, in what had seemed to be solid earth, a rift or cleft; a vast mouth would open and swallow up whole houses, as happened of old with the wicked Korah and his congregation. For this reason we do not build large houses, but little ones, like booths, and this is true for the rich not less than for the poor. And though the roofs are very light, they nevertheless come tumbling down upon us. For this reason the High Priest has a special prayer on our behalf, when he enters, once in the year, the Holy of Holies: a prayer that our houses shall not become our graves! However, we, the Sharonites, are very proud that we alone are mentioned in a special prayer uttered by the High Priest in the Holy of Holies!

I grew up among flocks of sheep. How I loved the feel of their wool, how I loved to caress their soft, damp mantles when the dew was thick in them! I would thrust my fingers into the massy tangles, and I would be dragged along when the shepherds drove the sheep to the well, to water them; so that often I had to be rescued from their midst. I loved the flutes of the shepherds; I would follow them out into the meadows; I would rest with them in their booths when they took shelter from the midday sun; I would run after a lost or wandering kid. When the time of the shearing came, the festival of the shepherds, I would linger about the pool where the sheep were washed. . . . One sheep would be roasting on an open fire, and the valley echoed with the singing of the shepherd boys. Those are the visions which come back with the dreams of my childhood, interwoven with the damp, dewy evenings which descended softly on the Sharon.

I remember my mother only out of my youngest years, when I was still under her loving care. She was always occupied with many tasks, and her hands were never idle. She worked with the shepherdesses, milking the sheep and pressing out cheeses which were laid upon the roof to dry; she worked with them likewise at the weaving of carpets, which were made of the broad leaves of the palm tree. It seemed to me that I always tasted the sweetness of figs in the cheese my mother made. But what occupied her most was the spinning of wool, in the company of the wives of our laborers; and in between she was busy at the washing of dishes. The labor of bringing forth and suckling many children wore her out, so that I see her still as a sickly woman, with a waxen face and lightless eyes. But from her I drew in, together with her milk, a God-fearing spirit. She was the first to tell me of the Temple, and of the city of Jerusalem; and she pointed out to me the stars, beyond which is the dwelling place of the Almighty. From her I learned my first verse of the Writ: "The fear of God is the beginning of wisdom"; and from her too I learned to utter the benedictions for every mouthful of food and every swallow of water.

But I was still young when they took me away from the women's quarter to that of the men. Here it was my father who dominated, and who pointed out the ways in which I was to tread; for he was like the pillar of fire which went before the Israelites in the wilderness.

My father was no longer young, even then, and I was the fifth child of his second wife. He was a short, powerful man, with a snow-white beard, with kind, friendly eyes above networks of tear sacs. His hands were like the roots of an ancient olive tree, bony, thick-veined, hard with much labor. For he was himself a diligent worker among his hired men; he plowed the field with them, threshed the grain, gathered the sheaves, trod the wine and pressed the olives, providing from his own labor all the needs of our household. But he was most diligent in his attention to the sheep. He was a great sheep-breeder, having inherited this profession from his father. He had manifold uses for his animals; he sold them for meat; he supplied the markets of Jerusalem for the sacrifices; he sent his sheep to K'far Saba and Ludd; and he drew from them supplies of milk. His largest income was derived from the sale of wool. After the sheep washing and shearing, the wool was cleaned, combed, and packed in great bales. Then it was loaded on camels and sent to one of the two ports, Joppa and Caesarea, to which came the merchants of Phoenicia, who sent them on to the spinners and dyers of their country. In the cosmopolitan harbor of Caesarea the wools of Sharon always commanded a higher price than in the Jewish harbor of Joppa. But my father did not like Caesarea; like most Jews he preferred Joppa, for nationalist reasons.

The trade of sheep breeding has been in our family for a long time; and it was said of my father that he knew every sheep in every one of his flocks. He had but to cast his eye over a flock to know what it lacked or what ailed it. He could tell whether the shepherd was observing the right hours for the watering of the sheep, whether he kept them exposed too long to the sun, whether he led them to the right pastures or whether he had made them clamber over stony ground. He knew all the sicknesses of sheep and all the herbs which could be made into unguents for the cure of diseases; all this had come down to him from his forbears. He could read the footprints of animals and identify any marauder which had approached the fold in the night. He could read signs in the heavens and foretell by the light of the sun or moon the onset of bad weather. He would start up in the night, when all were asleep, and with the energy of a young man run through the fields to his flocks; for even in his sleep he smelled the oncoming of a storm, and he wanted to be with his sheep when they needed him. In spite of his years, he would go in search of strayed sheep or kids, and would not take his rest till he had found them. It was indeed something to behold my father in the time when the animals were bringing forth their young. He would spend his nights in the field, along with the shepherds. He knew at a glance when a sheep was missing from a flock; not by counting, but by the mere sight of the flock. Night might fall while he was searching the fields for a strayed lamb, but he would not give up until the lost one had been found and restored to its mother.

This devotion to the flock was part of his faith. He believed that God had put the sheep in his care, and he was responsible for their well-being. It was as if the sheep did not belong to him but were the treasure of another man who had appointed him the guardian under the severest penalties. This was a tradition not only with my father, but with all shepherd folk.

He was likewise a God-fearing man, and though not learned in the Writ, he was always concerned with the thought whether he was doing God's will. He worried a great deal over the complicated laws and ritualistic regulations concerning his occupation. He once imported into our village a learned man of the city of Ludd, to give him full instructions concerning what was permitted and what was forbidden in planting and in the crossing of seeds, also what was prescribed with regard to the distances between the kinds of growth. He was more at ease when it came to the simple commandments of the firstlings of the flock, which had to be given to the priesthood, and the leaving of certain parts of the field, after the second harvest, for the use of the poor. This too was of the family tradition and had come down to us generation by generation. It was a great sight, too, when the Priest arrived from the city of Ludd; with what reverence and friendliness my father received him as he prepared for him the tithe and the first-born kids of the flock! This was, to him, the essence of sanctity. But he was often reduced to embarrassment, one might almost say despair, by the complicated laws of purity, the washing of the vessels, and the guarding of bread and wine from contact with non-Jews. There were, in our neighborhood, numbers of aliens, Canaanites, Greeks and the like, dwellers on the seacoast. Our daily business brought us into thousandfold contact with them. My father was in constant terror whether, in the course of these contacts, some impurity had not been imparted to his vessels, his bread or his wine. He was terrified lest he himself fall under the influence of these strangers and lest his cult suffer diminution of purity, or corruption, by the infiltration of alien practices. His greatest fear was for our women, who in turn could be corrupters of our men. For the Jewish women were easily seduced to the worship of Ashtarot, the goddess of fertility. Jewish women who were barren, or who conceived rarely and with difficulty, would often carry flowers and doves in secret to the altar of Ashtarot. Nor was it a rarity to discover images and figurines of the goddess, molded of clay, in the huts of our workers—hidden there by their wives. When the priest came from Ludd to collect the tithes, my father would go with him into the dwellings of the laborers, hunt out the images kept secretly by the women, and destroy them, stamping on them with his feet. Often there would ensue bitter family quarrels, and husbands whose wives had sinned in idolatry would drive them from their homes. But the women still hankered in secret after the cult of Ashtoreth. And my father trembled; he was haunted by the fear that he too might some day be tempted to the same transgression. Whenever he was in doubt concerning the interpretation of a commandment he would send a rider to Ludd. Was this or that pure? Could he use the wine which had been touched by a son of the uncircumcised? He had always envied any neighbor who had a son learned in the law, and it was his dream that a son of his own would prove worthy to be accepted in study and be given permission to interpret the law.

So great was his fear of being infected with the godless ways and customs of the heathen that, in addition to the regulations and prohibitions formulated by our sages, my father had invented a number of his own.

When I was a young boy, my father would take me along with him when he set out with a caravan of camels delivering wool to the harbor market of Caesarea. This city, though it lay within the borders of Israel and had been built by a Jewish king, who had populated it mostly with Jews, was considered by all of us an abode of the gentiles. And before we began the journey my father admonished me sternly in no circumstances to take into my mouth any food of the unbelievers—no, not so much as a piece of bread the size of an olive. I can still see the great harbor city. The houses of white marble rose into floods of light from amidst the surrounding gardens. I had seen only one great city before, to wit, Jerusalem. The effect which Caesarea produced on my spirit was of a quite different order. Jerusalem had uplifted me, exalted my soul in boundless reverence and worship; but Caesarea, with its wealth, its ordered streets, its pillars and marble halls, oppressed and infuriated me. I saw in all this insolence of possession an expression of hostility toward us. Instead of the sanctuary of our God, I beheld the gigantic temple of the Emperor Caesar Augustus, towering above all the other structures of the city. Very different, too, was this harbor from the harbor of Joppa; there the boats unloaded among the rocks, which was dangerous; here a wall, two hundred paces long, was driven into the sea, to break its waves and provide a shelter for the ships. And within this area, becalmed and protected, rode unnumbered boats with sails of all colors. From these colors, my father explained to me, one could tell the country whence the ships came. There were ships from Tyre and Zidon, from Egypt and the island of Cyprus; yes, there were ships from the Greek island of Rhodes, and even from remoter points on the borders of the Great

Sea. The approaches to the harbor were paved with marble, and here the merchants of many lands, in their strange costumes, assembled and chaffered round their unladen wares. We, too, were stationed among merchants, in the wool market, where we had unloaded the bales from our camels. The buyers from Tyre, in their multicolored mantles, drew near to us. They felt and tested the wool, and then began to bargain with my father. In payment for his wares, my father received from them little sacks of Tyrian drachmas; then slaves would lift up the bales of wool and carry them into the sailboats at the foot of the steps.

When these transactions were over, my father would leave his camels in the care of the drivers, take me by the hand, and lead me through the city. First we passed down a long arcade, which was made up of marble pillars and crossbeams of cedar, over which lay stretched great sheets of white woven stuff. A tumultuous crowd flowed back and forth, gathering about the booths, with their stores of dyed cloths, vessels, utensils and furnitures of cedar wood inlaid with ebony. There were also for sale images of the gods, figures of male and female divinities, poured in Corinthian bronze or sculptured in alabaster; there were statuettes of naked women, with their arms laid on their breasts or their stomachs. The buyers handled the wares, examined them, and chaffered over the price of a divinity as one chaffers over a skinful of wine or a basketful of sweet pomegranates. In the shadowy niches of the arcade lingered women who called or made signs to the male passers-by; there were also little booths, out of which came the drunken singing of sailors. My father drew me along and made me pass swiftly through this part of the city, in order that I might see as little as possible of the sinfulness and impurity of the heathen; and he did not slacken his pace until he had brought me into the Jewish quarter. We came to a khan or inn; the yard was shaded over with linen coverings, and here the Jewish drivers and herdsmen who had brought wares to the city took their rest. Here we also found neighbors of ours from the Sharon valley. The beasts of burden, freed of their loads, were brought into the yard to be watered. We untied the bundles we had brought with us from home, and ate in the company of the other Jews.

As we ate I said to my father:

"My lord and father, let me learn from you. The gentiles serve idols and other abominations; they do not observe the laws and commandments which we observe, but follow evil according to the lust of their eyes, as we have seen today; yet God does not punish them. He punishes only us, and He has made them masters over us."

"Why this is so, my little one," answered my father, "I do not know. It is not for us to question God's ways, but to accept them in love and say: it is all doubtless for the best. Thus my parents taught me. But the sages and the men of the Writ look deeply into these matters, they penetrate the mysteries and seek out the meanings of the ways of God. To them the reasons are unveiled. Would you, my son, like to be of their number?"

"Yes, my father. I too would look into the mysteries of God's ways."

My father answered: "All my life long I have dreamed of a son, of a man sprung from my loins, who would be sanctified to the study of the Torah, so that my latter years might be illumined by him, and that I might be assured of the fruits of the world to come even as I am assured of the fruits of this world. Your brothers have chosen this world as their portion, and have trained their hands to the work of their forefathers. They are breeders of sheep. But it may be God's will that my hope will be fulfilled by the youngest of my sons."

"What must I do, my father, to be worthy of the Torah?"

"I have heard a word of the sages, that the Torah can be purchased only at the highest price. He that would obtain the Torah must eat dry bread, drink water by measure and sleep on the hard earth. He must be the servant of his teacher, and stand before him as a slave stands before his lord and master. For your Rabbi shall be more to you than your father. Your father begot you, but your Rabbi will breathe a soul into you. That is the Torah. Are you prepared, my son, to pay this price for the Torah?"

"My father, I am prepared to pay this price, and every other that is needed, if only I may seek out the ways of God."

"So be it, then. I will send you first to a Rabbi of Ludd. And in the fullness of time I shall send you also to Jerusalem."

My father lifted his hands heavenward and said:

"I thank thee, Father, that Thou hast filled the heart of my son with the desire to seek out Thy Torah."

CHAPTER FOUR

WHEN I reached the age of thirteen my father pronounced the benediction: "I thank Thee, O Lord, that Thou hast rid me of this responsibility." For according to the Jewish law, I reached, with the beginning of my fourteenth year, the status of manhood, and was responsible for my deeds in the eyes of heaven. My father sent me to Ludd, where there were many synagogues. In one of them I became the pupil of a local Rabbi, and from him learned the written law, the codes and the histories which are part of the higher education of every Jew. I lived with the family of my father's brother, who was a saddlemaker, and from him I learned this trade. For although my father was well-to-do, and although he had destined me for a career of learning, it was proper that I learn a handicraft, according to the saying: "He that does not teach his son a trade brings him up to be a highway robber."

I will not dwell on the years I spent in the pleasant city of Ludd, where I made many friends. I will only say that my inclination was always to my studies, and that I learned much, both of the written law and of the oral tradition, which has come down to us from generation to generation. When I reached my sixteenth year I returned home, and my father asked me again:

"Is it your desire, my son, to consecrate yourself utterly to the Torah?"

"With all my heart and with all my soul," I answered.

"If this be so, you shall accompany me on the next festival pilgrimage to Jerusalem. As you know, I have a friend there whose two sons are pupils of the famous Rabbi Nicodemon. I will leave you in their company."

And thus the matter fell out. Shortly before the next festival we went up together, my father, two elder brothers of mine, and myself. There went with us a small flock of sheep, to be sold, and two donkeys; on one of them my father rode when he was tired; on the other he had loaded two jars of wine and a cruse of honey, a gift for his friend in Jerusalem, likewise our own provisions for the journey, dried cheeses, fruits and bread.

When we passed through Ludd we were joined by a whole caravan of pilgrims. At Jabneh we were so numerous that we filled the whole market place. Thence we began to mount the hills of Judaea toward Jerusalem, and the road echoed with the piping of our flutes.

This was not my first pilgrimage to Jerusalem, but it has remained more clearly in my mind than all the others. I can still hear the tinkling of the bells which hung from the ears of the camels and donkeys, and I can see the long procession of happy pilgrims winding up and down along the roads. I knew that this time I was going up to Jerusalem to remain there, and that henceforth my life would be irrevocably dedicated to the Torah. I was eager to set eyes on my new Rabbi, and I was filled with curiosity concerning my new life. I remember clearly the night time of that pilgrimage, when our group rested in a village, all of us gathered about a well. The men would not enter any houses in the village, since it was more fitting to pass the night of such a journey under the open sky. I, accounting myself a man, followed their example, and entered neither a house nor yet the tents of the women, but sat with the men about a fire which they built up near the well. The night was chilly here on the heights, and the older folk wrapped themselves in mantles of sheepskin, and lay down; we, the younger folk, stood about them in a respectful circle, and served them. But no one slept between nightfall and morning. It was the early part of the month, and a thin, pure crescent of a moon followed the sun into the blue depths of the western heavens. The stars sprang out, thick and brilliant. The old folk told stories of the great rebellion under the leadership of Judah the Galilean, in which some of them had taken an active part. They remembered how they had stolen away from their homes, their swords concealed under their mantles, to join the rebels. Fisherfolk went with them from the haven of Joppa. Hope ran high in those days; the rebels believed that salvation was at hand, that our people was about to be freed from the yoke of Edom. But the hope turned out to be a deception, and the sword of God was shattered by the heathen.

"God's sword is not shattered, for God's sword is His Torah," said a learned man of K'far Saba.

"Not the sword of the Torah is our need today, but a sword of steel," called out one who stood in the shadows. "The sword of the Torah must be sheathed awhile, till the sword of steel has conquered."

Heads were turned toward the last speaker: Who was it that dared to utter such words? Someone lifted up a blazing brand, and by its light we beheld a mighty figure of a man, with wild locks of hair and eyes that flashed back from the darkness.

"Bar Abba!" a murmur went up. "Bar Abba is among us!"

"Does God need iron, or chariots, to help Him? Has He not at His command the hosts which fill the heavens? Let the time only come, when He will send His anointed one."

"But why does He wait so long?"

"It is written: Though he delay, yet we must await him daily. Who knows but that we shall encounter him in Jerusalem when we arrive there?"

"Nay, Messiah will not come down from heaven until we have forged him ourselves on the white hot anvil, and until we have beaten out our swords thereon!"

"God does not desire a rabble of slaves as His people; God desires sons of freedom," called out one in support of Bar Abba.

A spirit of uneasiness, of terror, descended on the assembly. I behold even now the figure of Bar Abba, standing out now in the light of the campfire. He was a fisherman who worked in the harbor of Joppa, gigantic of stature, burned by the sun, dark like an Ethiopian, with muscles of steel. The locks of his head and of his beard were tossed in the wind. His teeth flashed out, milk-white, from between his lips. He lifted a hand toward the Rabbi who had rebuked him and said:

"The bitter gall of oppression is overfull in our bosoms. I say to you that if one could be found today in the mold of Judah the

Zealot, to gather the hosts about him, we would drive Edom and his hired fighters before us as the storm drives a ship."

"Bar Abba! Bar Abba! Those are the words of a sinner! Do you not see to what a pass we have come? Without God nothing can be accomplished. Such is the will of God, and we dare not question Him until He sends his Messiah to gather us up."

Another spoke up: "They say that in the wilderness of Judaea there is a man who calls the people to him to prepare by baptism for the coming of the Messiah."

"It is not by baptism of water that we shall prepare for the coming of the Messiah!"

"Woe to the ears which have heard such words. May your lips be stopped up, Bar Abba! Men who follow you only delay the redemption. It is God's will that we shall make our necks a footstool for our enemies. And we shall obey Him in love, and be silent; we shall not question His decision," the Rabbi cried.

I saw the white beard of the old man tremble, while his eyes turned a bluish red and seemed to protrude from their sockets as if they were about to fall out.

"But why?" cried other voices.

"Because we are sinners, all of us," the old man replied.

"And are the heathen better than we?"

"But He has not made a covenant with the heathen. He has made His covenant with us. That is the bond between Abraham and God, which imposes on us the duty of the Torah. Every one of us, even unborn, was there when the bond was confirmed, and every one of us must take on himself the burden of the Torah. And now, because we have thrown the burden from our shoulders, He punishes us. For He has chosen us to be His holy people, and to be a light to the world, a light to the gentiles, observing His laws and commandments until He sends His Messiah. And in that day all the nations shall bow themselves before God and accept His Torah. And until then we must carry the yoke and be silent: we must be silent." And the old man put his fingers to his lips.

In that night on the hills I became a man. I was confronted, for the first time, with the living forces which are in our people.

In Jerusalem I lived in the house of Simon Cyrene. His dye

works were situated by the waters of the Kidron, in the Lower City at the foot of the Mount of Olives, there where the tanners and other workers lived who could not reside in the city proper. Simon, too, is very clear before my eyes. He was an extraordinarily tall man, very thin. His head, set on a long, slender neck, drooped; his backbone was bent from constant stooping over the pails of dye. He was bald, for the stuff of the dyes had eaten away his hair. He had his own way of preparing colors from various plants, according to a recipe which he had brought with him from his country. His skin was mottled from the constant handling of the dyes. A few colored threads were drawn through holes bored in the lobes of his ears. Simon Cyrene was a quiet, smiling man. When we came to the city on this pilgrimage, he went out to meet us, and embraced my father, kissed him, and asked after the welfare of his family, then led us to his house.

It was a small, low house which he inhabited. It consisted of one long room, along the sides of which were ranged narrow couches of woven straw; some of these, covered with colored cloths, were for the use of the master and his guests, while the others were provided merely with sacking. Over part of the floor lay a bamboo mat, which served as the sleeping place for the children of the guest. The room was divided by a curtain, behind which the women had their couches. Outside, hard by the door, there was a low structure of stone, on which stood water cruses and other household vessels. The section of the house which was destined for the guests was newly whitewashed. If the house itself was small, the yard, surrounded by a living hedge of beanstalks, was roomy enough, for it stretched deep down into the valley. Here were storerooms for raw and finished wool. Three huge caldrons were set into holes dug in the earth, and about them stood innumerable pitchers and jars of coloring stuff. There was also a vast water cistern, hollowed out in the lower part of the yard and fenced about. The evidences of Simon's trade were everywhere. Vessels, hedges, stones were streaked and splashed with deep purple, violet and crimson. Even the solitary olive tree in the yard, and the awning which was stretched overhead to provide shelter from the midday sun, were plentifully besprinkled with color.

On our arrival we were received into the house of Simon Cyrene nembers of his own family. Our hands and feet were washed, ood was brought to us at once. Then we unloaded our supplies, ried cheeses, the honey and wine. The women of the household ated to a corner of the room, to talk of their little worries, the men discussed more important affairs. My older brothers out into the city to inquire about the condition of the market he latest prices for sheep and wool. I was left alone with my r and Simon, for Alexander and Rufus, who were of my age, ar it, were with their Rabbi.

ter their first interchange of news, my father and Simon went nto the yard, and took their seats on overturned pails, which dry because of the festival, and I sat down on the earth at their

was now the evening hour when the Priests of the Temple ght the *Minchah* sacrifices. Light still lay on the summits of the about Jerusalem, though shadows lay heavy on the Kidron y. My father and Simon discussed their eternal theme: Why hings go so ill with the House of Jacob, while Edom triumphed us? Why had the original blessing of Jacob been inverted, so he foot of Esau oppressed the pride of the sons of Israel?

uietly my father asked: "Has there been no sign of late? Has been no hint of good tidings? What do the sages say?"

ochanan has gone into the wilderness and calls the people to sm and repentance, in preparation for the Messiah."

This I have already heard as I came up to Jerusalem. There were r company such as had been in the wilderness and accepted sm from him."

Yes, there are many who go down to him from Jerusalem. n the festival is over I too will descend into the wilderness, to ochanan with my own eyes, and be baptized by him."

mon waited awhile in the silence of the evening, then continued low voice:

They say that the awaited end is close at hand, and the sages aver that the Messiah pangs have begun, for our trials and rings have increased beyond our endurance. Pilate the wicked in the place of power. His soldiers slay our pilgrims on the s. Taxes and extortions increase from day to day. The sons of

the High Priest whip us with scorpions, and the words of the ve
are being fulfilled: 'The land is given into the hands of the wicke
The waters have come up to our lips."

"And what is the meaning of our agony?" asked my fath
"What do the sages say?"

"These torments are a sign of God's love, the sages tell us. Th
are visited upon us for our good, so that our hearts may awaken
God's commands. We are the salt of the earth. God has chosen
from among all the sons of men. We must not oppose evil, we m
not rise against God's will, we must take these trials upon us in lo
For God cleanses us through suffering, he purifies our hearts so th
we shall not fall into baseness and corruption and give oursel
over to the delights of this world, as the heathen do. We shall,
stead, make stronger the bond between Him and us, until the d
when He will reveal himself to all the earth, and send down t
Messiah, who will destroy all wickedness with the lightning of
glance, and gather unto him the hosts of the righteous. In that d
the gentile peoples will behold and understand, and we too will p
ceive beyond all doubting that our suffering was a preparation f
the salvation of the world and the unfolding of God's glory. A
for all these reasons we must not yield to despair because of t
degradation which we suffer daily, without cessation; nay, we m
bear our suffering in pride. And even though God has made us in
a target for the arrows of the gentiles, we shall not falter in o
love when the arrows enter our flesh; we shall receive them in lo
as becomes faithful soldiers of a King who conducts a war
righteousness."

These comforting words, and others like them, Simon pour
into my father's ears. I marked how my father's eyes shone wi
joy and hope as he seized the hand of his friend and asked:

"Simon, tell me, I beg you, in which house of study these wor
were uttered, and from whose lips they issued. Blessed be the lips
which rest the message of God!"

Then Simon Cyrene lifted up his head, and he looked into t
distance, while the last glimmer of sunlight shone on the nakedne
of his skull, fringed with hair. "These words," he said, "I hea
from the mouth of my Rabbi, Nicodemon the son of Nicodemo

He speaks to us every Sabbath, after the reading of the Torah, in the synagogue of the Cyreneans, and this is the substance of his preaching."

"Where is he, this man of God? Take me to him; I too would drink now from this well of fresh waters."

"You shall see him this evening. I have asked him to grace with his presence the feast which I have prepared in honor of your son, here, whom you have brought to Jerusalem to learn the word of God. I have invited, likewise, other friends. Judah Ish-Kiriot will be there; he is a potter by trade, a God-fearing man, a seeker after God's wisdom, a Pharisee and the son of Pharisees, one who awaits the Messiah daily. There will come also Hillel the watercarrier, the humblest of men, a saint. I mention last, in greatest love, Nicodemon ben Nicodemon, the teacher of my children. I will bring you before him that he may accept your son among his pupils."

"May God reward you for the lovingkindness which you have shown to me and to my son," said my father, and bending down to me he added: "Rise, my son, and prepare yourself for your new father, the Rabbi who will be your instructor in God's ways."

"It is time for all of us to begin the preparations," said Simon Cyrene. "The women have lit the lamps in the house. I must be ready to receive my guests."

My father and Simon Cyrene washed themselves with the water in the wooden vessels which stood outside, then they anointed themselves and put on fresh garments, that they might greet their guests worthily, and not in workaday raiment. I too washed and anointed myself and put off the clothes of my journey. I drew from my bundle the *ketonet passim,* the coat of many colors which was my holiday garb; I rubbed unguents into my hair and earlocks, and while I did so I prayed in my heart: "May it be Thy will, Father in heaven, that I find grace in the eyes of my Rabbi, so that he shall draw me nigh to him and not hold me at a distance." When I was all prepared I took up my station on the threshold of the house, and waited with trembling heart.

The men of the household helped to arrange the mattresses and to set the little tables near the couches. The women made the last preparations; they brought in raw and cooked vegetables in colored earthen pots and plates; these Simon Cyrene must have brought with him from his own country, for I do not remember that such were in use in Judaea. The room had been swept clean, and fresh olive branches were placed as adornments on the tables. Simon's wife, wearing a violet-colored head covering, brought forth flat cakes wrapped in white cloth coverings. She also put, before the seats which were to be occupied by the Rabbi and my father, two wreaths of olive, such being the custom in their country when guests of honor were awaited. Cruses of olive oil and vessels of rich honey were ranged on the tables, and near them stood gourd flasks, into which my father poured the wine, and baskets of dried figs. On the stone structure outside the door were prepared bowls of fresh water and clean towels. The oil lamps hanging from the ceiling threw their quiet light on the friendly room. A white sheet was hung in the open doorway, as a sign that guests were awaited, and to proclaim that any that were hungry might enter the house and eat.

Soon the first guests arrived, two dyers clad in washed garments, with colored threads in the lobes of their ears. They were countrymen of Simon's and wore the costumes of Cyrene, tunics of violet and black, and high leather sandals; their heads, anointed with oil, were covered with olive wreaths. When they had been presented to the guests from Sharon, they were shown to their places at the tables. As others arrived, they were directed, according to their rank, their age and their learning, to the mattresses in the middle of the room or the couches ranged round the walls. Hillel the watercarrier entered, and was shown to a place of honor, at the head; the same distinction was accorded to Judah Ish-Kiriot, the Pharisee, who like Hillel was counted among the sages. Thus we waited for the coming of the Rabbi, who arrived when night had fallen. With him came his two foremost pupils, Alexander and Rufus, the sons of Simon. They walked across the yard carrying oil lamps in front of their Rabbi, to illumine his path.

The entry of the Rabbi was the signal for all of us to stand. We waited until he had washed his hands and taken his seat at the head place, which was indicated by the adornments of tapestry and woolen cloths which overhung it. Alexander and Rufus did not sit down with the rest of us, but stationed themselves by the Rabbi, to serve him. How I envied them, that evening, the honor which was theirs to be the servitors of the Rabbi! I looked forward to the day when I too might stand by the Rabbi's side and anticipate his wishes. I did not take my eyes off him for a single moment. I marked with the utmost attention every gesture he made; I learned from him there and then the proper way of breaking bread, of placing salt upon it before uttering the benediction, of dipping the pieces in vinegar or honey; I observed the manner in which he ate, quietly, attentively, as though he were preparing a sacrifice before the altar. Thus indeed it was, as he later instructed me; for the table at which men sit and eat should be likened to an altar, and those assembled about it must be pure and respectful, as in a sanctuary. Moreover, when men break bread together and do not converse of the Torah they may as well be eating the flesh of corpses or the sacrifice of idols. Indeed, soon after we had begun to eat the Rabbi lifted up his voice and told the assembly the reason for his lateness.

"This year, as you all know, the Passover will coincide with a Sabbath. Whenever it happens that the first day of the festival is a Sabbath, there arises again, between the sages and the Priests, an ancient division of opinion, and the problem is this: Shall the Passover sacrifice be considered as having priority over the Sabbath, or shall it be delayed until after the passing of the Sabbath? Again, as sundry of you know, there is an old regulation which has settled this question; it was promulgated by the Venerable Hillel, who acquired great fame thereby, and it ruled that the Passover sacrifice takes precedence over the Sabbath. The Venerable Hillel referred his decision to the teaching of Shemaya and Abtalion, the sages from whom he learned the law. But even until this day the Priests, of the Sadducean party, raise the whole question anew, and challenge the ruling of Hillel. And they do this because the triumph of Hillel's interpretation has given great standing to the Pharisees, and has opened the way for them to introduce others of their laws in the Temple service, which the Priests regard as an infringement on their prerogatives."

Thus, chiefly for the benefit of those who were not learned in the details of the law, Rabbi Nicodemon explained the nature of the discussions which had kept him till a late hour in the Sanhedrin.

"Observe, all of you, the greatness of the Venerable Hillel," the Rabbi continued. "The regulation which he handed down to us teaches us much more than the simple fact that the Passover sacrifice takes precedence over the Sabbath. It teaches us that we must perform the will of God in love and in freedom of spirit; and we must likewise bring to bear our understanding upon the manner of our obedience. We must apply, in His service, all the gifts and faculties with which He has blessed us. We are not blind slaves to Him, as the Sadducees teach, carrying out His Commands without desire. We are His children, as the verse says: 'Ye are sons unto the Lord your God.' Sons of freedom! We have not been given unto the Torah, it is the Torah that has been given unto us; and having received it, we shall study it closely and learn its meanings. Thus it is with the rules and commandments also! Ye shall live in them! Such is the Sabbath, too; for the Sabbath is not a taskmaster; it is not like a beast that has been sent upon us to destroy us. We have not been delivered unto the Sabbath, but the Sabbath hath been delivered unto us, to be our delight."

The guests swallowed eagerly the words of the Rabbi. Their eyes were fastened on him as he swayed back and forth, drew gently at his beard, and continued to preach:

"Our sages have ruled that we shall repeat twice daily the prayer: 'And thou shalt serve the Lord thy God with all thy heart and with all thy soul.' To what may this be likened? It may be likened unto a master who addresses himself thus to his slave: 'Thou shalt serve me not for the sake of thy pay, but in love.' But how shall the master know which of his slaves serve him for pay, and which in love? Those slaves that return to him after liberation, and cleave to him, are the ones that serve him in love. God has given unto man freedom of will, that he may choose between good and evil. For God desires that man shall come to him of his own choice, not like a slave that serves for hire, but like a son who serves his father in love."

These were the first words of the Torah which I heard from my Rabbi, and they have never departed from my mind. I stood, as I remember, behind my father, and looked breathlessly at Rabbi Nicodemon. Not the words alone entered into my heart, but the gestures, the utterance and the accentuation. My soul was bound to his from that first evening on, and my love for him was stronger than the first love of a youth for the maiden of his choice.

Later that evening my father took me by the hand and approached the Rabbi respectfully, saying:

"Rabbi, this is my son, whom I have brought to deliver into your hands. If he has found grace in your eyes, be his father henceforth; be as he that gave him life in that you give him the Torah."

My heart hammered so loudly in my breast, that I was sure everyone could hear it. My hands trembled, and my whole body shook with happiness and fear. The Rabbi took my hand in his, and calmed me. I remember also that he passed his hand over my hair, and it was as though the fingers of a beloved one had been lifted over me in a caress.

"My child," said the Rabbi, "tell me thy verse."

This was the custom among us. Every child was given a verse of the Holy Writ, and this was his verse, which was to accompany him in life.

I answered, stammering:

"*L'hakshiv l'chochma hozneicha*... incline thine ear unto wisdom, and turn thy heart toward wisdom."

"And for what reason dost thou seek wisdom, my son?" the Rabbi asked.

"In order that I may serve God with an open heart, like a son of freedom, and not with a blind and unseeing heart, like a slave," I answered, "even as you, our Rabbi, have taught us this night."

Rabbi Nicodemon placed both hands upon my head and uttered this benediction:

"May those who are like you multiply in Israel, and may it be the will of God that you shall grow in worthiness as a son of Abraham."

With that he charged his other pupils to receive me in their midst, saying:

"Henceforth he is your brother. Receive him as such and let him be a third with you."

That same night I said farewell to my father. When the feast was over I gathered my clothes in a bundle and followed him who had begotten me in the Torah.

CHAPTER FIVE

RUFUS, the younger of the sons of Simon Cyrene, became my closest comrade. We had known each other before, but on the day when I became his fellow student our souls leaped together and remained united in an eternal bond. He was comely to look on, with his locks of deepest black poured down over his high, round throat and strong neck. His eyes were a lustrous gray; they shone with freedom and happiness, but they likewise gazed deep into you, and awakened within you the noblest and tenderest dreams. In build he was tall and slender, like a young palm tree, and wherever he passed he drew all hearts after him. He was beloved by all, for he was as swift as a hart to obey the will of the sages. He and I ate together, took our lessons together, and chanted in unison the verses of the law and the tradition which we received from our Rabbi. We wandered together through the streets of Jerusalem. Young, filled with the gaiety of our years, we went hand in hand, or with arms entwined round each other's shoulders. We explored the alleys of the city, we lingered in the Temple courts, we listened to the preachers in the Temple alley of the gentiles. Jerusalem was a tumultuous city, and wherever anything exciting occurred, wherever a crowd gathered, there Rufus and I were to be found. We picked our way through the market place between the wine jars and the cruses of oil. We stumbled among the baskets of fruit and vegetables, we bumped against the tables laden with dyed woolens, we gave ear to the cry of the perfume sellers, the dealers in stuffs, the silversmiths and goldsmiths, whose voices were loudest and most insistent, and toward whom the women were drawn as if by magic. We ventured into the most dangerous places, down by the Dung Gate, or round by the inns of the camel drivers near the ancient walls. We had our boyish secrets, too, and we often lingered in the city gardens where the daughters of Jerusalem walked in the evenings with veils over their hair.

Our first duty every morning, after we had washed our hands and said the first "Hear, O Israel," was to wait upon our Rabbi in the synagogue of the Cyreneans. The entire building consisted of two rooms. The larger was the House of Prayer, and here were found the ark containing the Scroll of the Law, from which there were ritual readings on the Sabbath, as well as on the second and fifth days of the week, and also the pulpit for the prayer leader. The smaller room was the house of learning. Here classes were conducted for the children of the Cyreneans of Jerusalem. There was an elementary Rabbi for the little ones; among the older children those of superior promise were chosen to continue their studies under the guidance of Rabbi Nicodemon. In the courtyard of the synagogue there were several huts; and in these the Rabbi and his pupils passed the nights; all ate at a common table which was prepared in the house of learning by the younger pupils. It was a strict rule that every Rabbi, and necessarily every pupil, also had to learn a trade or craft. My own Rabbi was, as I have already said, a sandal maker. In later years, however, the rule was relaxed, in Rabbi Nicodemon's case, to the extent that he visited his work booth only occasionally. He was taken up almost completely with his duties in the Sanhedrin and the school. He lived in common with us, shared the food which was provided for us by the Cyrenean community and the contributions of Joseph Arimathea, and slept in one of the huts in the yard of the synagogue. It must not be forgotten that the Rabbi was not only teacher to the youth, and counselor in the Sanhedrin, but the spiritual leader of the Cyrenean community of Jerusalem. The members of the synagogue came to him for advice on every problem which rose in their daily lives, whether it was of a religious or a secular character. The inner community, or Companionship, was limited to a small number of the Cyrenean Jews who attended the synagogue. They were chosen by the Rabbi, and he conferred on them the official title of *Chaver*, which signifies Comrade or Colleague or Member of the Companionship. The Rabbi was attended or served by his immediate pupils, of whom one was assigned to him daily, in rotation. We cooked his food, laid the table for him, washed his garments, carried the vessels for him to the bath, prepared his couch at night. We were five in number, those pupils whom he had chosen to prepare in the Torah: the two sons of

Simon Cyrene; Zadoc, the son of Hillel the watercarrier, who lived down by the Dung Gate but was one of the most distinguished members of the Companionship; Shemaya, a Babylonian, whom his father had brought to Jerusalem during a pilgrimage, and left there; then myself, the youngest.

During the hours of instruction we sat on little stools or on a bamboo mattress at the feet of our Rabbi, who took his place on the raised seat called the Seat of Moses; the posture which we thus assumed was symbolic: we literally looked up to our Rabbi, with the awe and reverence with which we looked up to heaven. The instruction was free; but for the use of the buildings we, the pupils, had to pay a certain small fee, which we either earned with the labor of our hands or received from home. Occasionally, however, such payment was made for pupils by pious women of Jerusalem who had taken it upon themselves to support poor students of the Torah. In our case there was no need for such contribution, since Joseph Arimathea, a man of wealth, was always prepared to make up any difference.

Sitting at the feet of our Rabbi we chanted verses of the Torah, the Prophets and the Hagiographia, which we had learned by heart. We counted the words and letters in each verse. We repeated the laws and regulations governing the religious and secular life of the Jewish people, as these had come down in the tradition from the days—as we were told—of Moses himself: the rules of the washing of hands, of the putting on of the phylacteries, the laws of the tithes and offerings, the laws of sacrifice, the laws of purity and impurity. These were definite and accepted instructions formulated by the sages of old and sanctified by tradition. With regard to these, there was no challenge possible, and no questioning; they were the code which had to do with a man's relationship to God. But, as distinguished from these, there arose questions having to do with a man's relationship with his fellow men. Such problems, emerging from the infinite variety of human contacts, could not be fitted at once into the laws; the latter had to be interpreted and adapted. Traditions and laws certainly existed from of old, but not every shading of application had been anticipated. Here, then, we had to apply our commonsense and our understanding of human responsibility, using at the same time the rules which the Venerable Hillel had formulated for the interpretation of the Torah. Now this latter part of our studies occupied much time, for it covered the whole range of life; it included the method of measuring fields and the study of human anatomy and of the rules of hygiene, which entered into matters concerning purity and impurity; it went into ordinary legal procedure, into civic disputes and criminal law, reaching to cases of robbery and murder. A large section of our studies was devoted to botany and zoölogy, of which the former was of special importance. We were required to become experts in grasses, herbs and fruits, to be able to classify the entire flora of our land, according to species and family; for there were laws which forbade the crossing of types and the production of hybrids, and as sages and advisers we would at some time in our lives be called upon to give advice in such matters. It would also be incumbent upon us to protect from hybridization the rich varieties of pasture. Astronomy took up a considerable part of our studies; we were required to know the stars and the other heavenly bodies, the time of their appearance, their rising and setting, and their use as demarcations of the seasons and sacred festivals. In brief, the preparation of the *Talmid Chacham* or sage, by way of what was called the study of the Torah, actually included every reach of knowledge.

Part of our studies, as I have indicated, was conducted through the channel of the oral tradition; part of it was fastened down in documents, parchments and papyri which were transmitted from Rabbis to pupils with the utmost care. In the pursuit of our botanical studies our teacher would lead us into the fields outside the city. Often we spent the night in the shelter of vineyards, or even in the open fields. Our Rabbi pointed out to us each species of grass, and taught us to distinguish between the various groups and families. He would conduct us also to farms and acquaint us with the labor of the soil, the plowing, sowing, and reaping, the fertilization of the fields and methods of irrigation. He led us likewise into the vineyards and the olive groves; we learned how the ordinary oils are pressed in large stone mills worked by donkeys, and how the more precious oils, which are destined for religious or cosmetic or medicinal uses, are pounded out carefully in polished stone hand mills. Nor was this all. Not a single trade or handicraft could be omitted.

We went, in the course of our studies, to the spinners, the weavers, the tanners, the dyers, and the potters. The most unpleasant of our contacts was with the workers at the looms, for the weavers—and for that matter all workers whose products were intended in the first line for women—did not enjoy a good reputation. We were bidden to be extremely cautious in our dealings with such as had commerce with women. Among the learned and their pupils a proverb was current: "It is better and safer to pursue a wild lion than a woman." Thus it came about that the ranks of those workers who dealt with women were recruited from the lowest ranks of the population, from among the coarsest and most vulgar young men, the turbulent, the ignorant and the uncontrollable. But since we could not omit a single handicraft from our studies, we went even to the wigmakers, for we had to be prepared, as sages, to give judgment in matters pertaining to every kind of occupation.

We submitted to other than moral dangers, too; in the study of diseases we went down into the foulness of the valley of Hinnom, where the lepers lived behind their fences. It was our business to understand not only the varieties of herbs, but their uses in the healing of sickness. We were taught how to gather the herbs, how to grind them and prepare them into unguents. For we would be called upon not only to answer ritualistic questions, and settle disputes at law, but likewise to exorcise evil spirits, ward off the evil eye, cure melancholia and even practice magic.

Now all the foregoing branches of knowledge came under the heading of *Halachah*, or law, regulation or ruling. They constituted but one half of our education. To the other half our Rabbi devoted an equal measure of time and attention; and this was known as the *Agada*, and had to do with all such tradition as contributed to the moral, spiritual and cultural ennoblement of man. The task for which we were being trained did not confine itself to the transformation of man into an intelligent animal; there was a higher purpose, too, namely, the bringing of man ever closer to the divine spirit, the planting in him of virtuous impulses, so that he might become a vessel of God. To this end we learned from our Rabbi innumerable stories, incidents and legends which had come down from the immemorial past illustrating the eternal striving of humanity toward the higher spheres, away from the earthiness of the flesh and its needs. Compassion, the love of man for man, reverence for God, the pursuit of the good, the anticipation of the purity of the heavenly life—these were the themes of the lore of the *Agada*. But above all, it was inculcated in us to regard man as a creature that waited in trembling expectation of the coming of the Deliverer. He, the Messiah, would be sent down not only to restore the oppressed to equality with all others, to reward the just and punish the guilty, to destroy Edom and the House of Hanan, like all other wicked governments but, much more, to unite all the peoples of the earth, introduce a universal bond with God, and to exalt all life to a higher, mystic level, upon which only goodness would reign in a kingdom of heaven, even as the prophets had foretold. In this spirit our Rabbi recited the stories of the past, interpreted the verses of the Writ and explained the prophetic utterances. This type of teaching, however, was not only for his pupils. Every Sabbath and every festival would be the occasion for sermons which the Rabbi addressed to the congregation at large. And in the winter evenings he gathered about him for secret and intimate instruction the Companionship, consisting of the choice spirits he had admitted to the circle; with them he studied the esoteric lore of the coming of the Messiah.

The members of this inner circle were drawn from all levels of society, without distinction of wealth or standing. Once they had been admitted, they became equals. They made up a single family, under the fatherly guidance of the Rabbi. I knew well four members of the Companionship, and of them I will tell. One was the rich and distinguished Joseph Arimathea, another was the watercarrier, Hillel, a third was the man whom we called Judah Ish-Kiriot, and the fourth was Simon Cyrene, the father of my closest friend. I do not mention in this connection my father, who was also among them. But before I describe these men, I must describe what manner of person my Rabbi was; and such a description would be impossible without mention of the teachers from whom he drew the lore which he translated to us, his pupils.

The teacher of my Rabbi was the Venerable Hillel. But this only in a manner of speaking; Nicodemon the son of Nicodemon was a pupil of Hillel in that he had been brought up in the spirit of that mighty teacher in Israel, as, indeed, had all the scholars and Rabbis of the Pharisees. But my Rabbi had developed to an unusual degree his love and admiration of the founder of the Pharisaic interpretation of the Torah. He had collected with the utmost care all the regulations which the great Hillel had issued during his life, all his interpretations of the Writ and all his methods of study; and he never failed to mention humbly and in utter reverence the name of the ancient sage, whenever he transmitted to us one of his illuminations. Even in that day the land was filled with legends concerning the beloved old scholar. And our Rabbi repeated these legends, in order that he might fill our hearts with the same longing for the ways of Hillel as moved him. Sweetness issued from his lips, and his eyes shone with exaltation, during such recitals. He told us of the marvelous virtues of Hillel, of his infinite patience with human beings, and of the trials which men put upon him in the deliberate effort to break down his gentleness and forbearance. Rabbi Nicodemon never grew weary of describing Hillel's piety and humility. When he wished to strengthen in us the longing for learning, he would place before us the image of Hillel, and dwell upon the privations and sufferings through which the great one had passed, in all patience and sweetness, in order that he might acquire the word of God. He told us more than once of that incident of Hillel's youth which best described the inexhaustible will of the seeker after knowledge. During a certain period in his youth Hillel was so poor that he had not the copper coin to offer in payment at the door of the house of learning; thereupon he crept up on the roof and listened through a hole to the discourses of Shemaya and Abtalion. He continued this practice until one day there was a heavy snowfall, and he was found, half dead, frozen to the roof.

It is true that Rabbi Nicodemon went beyond all others in his reverence for Hillel; but there were others, too, who exalted the memory of the sage. It sufficed to indicate that a certain rule or interpretation could be traced to the words of Hillel and all disputation came to an end. So great was the name that many scholars revolved in their minds a plan to found a dynastic school of Hillel, which should serve as a counterpoise to the rule of the High Priests; and

ıis, being known to the ruling Priestly caste, occasioned much un-
asiness. As it was, the learning of the Pharisaic leaders had long
een a thorn in the side of the Priests; and they were perturbed by
ıe thought that a school might emerge round which the opposition
ɔ them could be organized. For the Pharisees exceeded the Priests
ot only in general learning, but likewise in their knowledge of the
ıws of the Temple service. In the plan to create a dynastic Rabbinic
chool stemming from Hillel, the High Priests rightly saw a danger
ɔ their own dynasty. But no practical steps had as yet been taken
ɔward the realization of the project. True, they paid honors that
ere almost royal to the grandson of Hillel, namely Raban Gamaliel;
o assembly of sages, however distinguished, failed to rise to its feet
hen he entered, or to give him the place of honor. However, the
ctual authority to say the last word on the Hillelite interpretation of
ıe law had been vested in the pupil of Hillel, Jochanan ben Zakkai,
pon whom they had likewise conferred the high title of Raban. He
as considered the spiritual guardian of the Hillelite tradition. And
ıch was the power of the name of Hillel that it imparted to
ochanan ben Zakkai a luster almost equal to its own.

Jochanan ben Zakkai was, for one who occupied so high a place,
ɔmparatively young. He was, in actual fact, middle-aged, whence it
as clear that he must have been received as a pupil by the great
acher while he was practically a child; and this enhanced his repu-
ıtion, so that although there were in Jerusalem many distinguished
cholars much older than he, none could compare with him in the
ıatter of reputation. Indeed, the older men, even when they were
ɔnsidered superior in breadth of learning, looked upon Jochanan
en Zakkai as their spiritual leader and proclaimed that the words
hich he uttered came as it were direct from the lips of that man of
od whom Jochanan in his youth had served. Such was his standing
ıat even the Sanhedrin, dominated by the Sadducees, could not
gnore his utterances, even when they related to their own special
eld of authority, the Temple service.

I often saw Jochanan ben Zakkai, surrounded by pupils and fol-
ɔwers, on his way to the sessions of the Sanhedrin. It was his cus-
ɔm, too, to preach under the open sky in the Temple courts, though
ot, of course, for the purpose of interpreting the regulations of the

service. But such sermons he did preach, as the inheritance come down from his master, to countless pupils in the Great Synagogue. I heard him preach in various other synagogues and schools, particularly on festival days, when the pilgrims filled the city; I heard him also under the covered arcades of the courts, where a great sea of heads surrounded him.

On many occasions his sermons and utterances roused the anger of the officials of the Temple; but more than once they were equally distasteful to the Zealots, those who were for rebellion against Rome. The followers of Bar Abba were incensed against him. They were almost prepared to proclaim him a traitor; and had it not been for the glory which rested on him because of his teacher, they would undoubtedly have driven him from the Temple courts. For in all of his sermons Jochanan ben Zakkai expressed himself in opposition to the political passions which the followers of Bar Abba sought to spread among the masses.

I remember clearly one such sermon. I was then in the Temple court together with my Rabbi and my fellow pupils, for Nicodemon made it a practice to take his school to hear Jochanan ben Zakkai. I have two reasons for remembering the occasion: one is the astonishment which the words of Rabbi Jochanan ben Zakkai awakened in me; the other is the disturbance which ensued at the gathering. Among the unruly elements there were some who shrieked that the Rabbi was desecrating the Temple area by such utterances. I recall that one or two half-naked fellows, Bar Abba-ites, actually tried to address the gathering in competition with Rabbi Jochanan and would have incited the people to riot had it not been for the opposition of the Rabbi's pupils.

On that occasion Jochanan ben Zakkai preached not standing, but seated on the upper steps of a gate. A mighty, gray-flecked beard descended on his chest, a broad white cloth, the sign of his rank, covered his head. His pupils were seated on the ground before him. He was such a majestic figure that he would not have needed to be seated on an upper step in order to tower over all of them. The theme of his sermon that day was one of his sayings: "It is not the place that exalts and glorifies the man; it is the man who glorifies and exalts the place." He gave it this interpretation: the whole earth is the footstool of God, and therefore neither this corner nor that corner of it may be called its center. The life of the Jewish people, therefore, was not dependent on any particular place, and was not bound up with time. It is able to live itself out in all places, in all times, amidst any circumstances. For, he went on, this peculiar life is not fastened with material possession, as is the case with other peoples, but is pure spirit. The Jewish homeland is not contained within the rigid borders of a defined area, so that if the people is torn from the framework it perishes, as is the case with other peoples. The Jewish homeland is boundless, that is, without boundaries, for it does not rest upon the earth, but is of heaven.

But cries went up from the outer rim of his auditors: "We want to be like all other peoples. We do not want a fatherland in heaven, but here, on earth. Is it not written: 'The heavens are unto the Lord, and the earth hath been given to the sons of man'?"

One cried, more loudly than the others: "These are words that pierce my eyes with thorns, and penetrate mine ears like serpents. Who can listen to him? God promised us a land flowing with milk and honey, here on earth, and not in heaven."

"Silence, sinner! Who dares to offend heaven by interrupting the Rabbi?"

"The Rabbi is right! The Compassionate One desires the heart of man!"

By their numbers, by the weight of their voices, the pupils of the Rabbi silenced the "sinners." Quiet was restored, and the Rabbi continued.

"There are two Jerusalems, a Great Jerusalem and a Little Jerusalem. Little Jerusalem consists of houses and vineyards, and in these the wealthy live while the poor lie in the street. Only the few have their portion in the Little Jerusalem; but in Jerusalem the Great all have their portion. For Great Jerusalem does not consist of houses and vineyards and fields and olive trees; it consists of the word and wisdom of God. They that cling to the ways of the Lord are of that fatherland. But they that despise God's word, let them even live in the heart of Jerusalem, they are not of the fatherland of the faith. Thence we may see that there is no need for us to rise in resistance against the might of the stranger who has overwhelmed us. For our true fatherland, which is the lore of the Lord, the stranger cannot take away from us. And as long as the stranger does not prevent us from living in our fatherland of the spirit, in the Jewish faith, we need not oppose him or try to throw the yoke from off our shoulders; we must not try our strength with him, but wait patiently until God will fulfill His promise and send His deliverer. Until that day comes we must carry the yoke in patience, love and humility."

But this was more than the Zealots on the fringe of the audience could bear. Eyes deep sunk under wild and tangled brows shot arrows of hatred at the Rabbi; faces burned by the desert twitched with resentment. The time, as I remember, was the Feast of Booths, a season which awakened high moods of liberty in the masses, recalling to their minds the glory of the Maccabees. The Zealots who listened on that day to Jochanan ben Zakkai had come up from the desert to stir the Jerusalemites to action. It was the gayest, most tumultuous time of the year; the city throngs were sated with fruits, drunk with joy not less than with wine, exalted by the beauty of Jerusalem. The strict rules of decorum which the sages imposed on the people were relaxed, and the severity of the division between the sexes was mitigated for the time. Every home in Jerusalem was packed with visitors. All drank from one cup, slept on one mattress. It was a period, in brief, when desperate undertakings could be launched—and the followers of Bar Abba would have used the occasion to stimulate a rebellion. But the Roman forces were prepared against any such contingency. The watch in the streets had been doubled; Askelonite and Syrian auxiliaries were mingled with Roman legionaries; the district from the Herod palace to the Antonia was roped off. The alleys leading to the Temple were lined with troops. This sermon of ben Zakkai's, then, had not only a general purpose. It was designed to calm the public, and there was no doubt that he had chosen this theme in consultation with the other sages of Jerusalem.

In spite of the efforts of the Zealots, the day passed off quietly.

Yet I have heard Jochanan ben Zakkai in more extreme utterances than those which enraged the Zealots that day of the Feast of Booths. I have heard him deny not only the sanctity of the land, but even—in a sense—that of the Temple, which he displaced from the center of our life, denying to it the title of the footstool of God. But then he would come back upon his words. "Assuredly the land of Israel is holy," he said, "but why is it so? Only because the holiness of the Law rests in it while Jews live there and observe the law. This is not the idolatrous sanctity which other peoples bestow upon mere soil, on earth and stones, which they come to regard as the essential of their existence, and for the sake of which they will commit murder and destroy nations. With that sort of sanctity the land of Israel has no commerce. And these truths belong to the Temple not less than to the land. Surely that place is holy whereon Abraham laid his son Isaac as a sacrifice, and whereon the Lord of the world permitted His glory to rest. But the glory of the *Shekhinah* rests likewise on any assembly of ten Jews which calls upon His name. Bethink ye that if the sun, which is only one of God's creations, shines on all lands and on all beings, then God shall surely be in His glory in all places. There are no heights above, no caverns below, where He is not. Our wits cannot conceive of an area so small that it can be excluded from the eternal Presence. He is everywhere; as it is written: 'And in whatsoever place thou shalt remember my name, I will come to bless thee.' "

My Rabbi, Nicodemon, who was a passionate admirer of Jochanan ben Zakkai because he had been the pupil of the great Hillel, admired equally the lore which he brought to his generation. There was no disagreement in their outlook on the world and on the problems of the times. Nicodemon ben Nicodemon considered himself a follower or pupil of Jochanan ben Zakkai; whereby he did not mean that he had literally acquired his learning at the feet of Jochanan. For there was not so much difference in their ages; nor was there any at all in the degrees of their learning. For all that, my Rabbi would come and sit at the feet of Jochanan when the latter preached, and conducted himself as though he were literally a pupil. And inasmuch as our Rabbi called himself "pupil of Jochanan ben Zakkai," we did likewise, for whatever the Rabbi is, that his pupils are too.

CHAPTER SIX

IN THE study house of Rabbi Nicodemon there was a stone bench worked into one of the walls. This was called "the bench of the Messiah." The name was given to it because it was upon this bench that the Rabbi sat when he preached of the Messiah.

Among the most eager listeners was Joseph Arimathea. Those who were aware of this fact wondered greatly that a man of such wealth, one, moreover, who had long been steeped in Hellenistic culture, and who frequented the company of Roman officials and the circles of the Greek philosophers, should enter a Companionship which centered on a Pharisaic Rabbi, and should submit to the severe ritualistic discipline which such a Companionship demanded.

Yet the simple truth was that under his semi-pagan exterior Joseph Arimathea had long been a God-seeker. Before the days when he was admitted to the Companionship, he would come, a stranger, and take a seat near the door of the synagogue, among the poor, and listen to the sermons of Nicodemon ben Nicodemon. He was drawn slowly into the group of the Messianists, and in the end became an open and ardent follower of my Rabbi. Finally he was admitted to the Companionship and was the chief supporter of the school. He would come and sit among us while the Rabbi taught, and on occasion we, together with the Rabbi, would go to his house, for all the laws of purity, of purity and impurity, were strictly observed there, so that the most pious Jew might cross his threshold without fear. The house of Joseph Arimathea had become, in the phrase of the sages, a gathering place or council chamber of the wise and learned. But Greek and Roman were as frequent there as Jewish aristocrat and Pharisaic Rabbi, and thus the Jews were able to make contact with the wisdom of Javan. There were other possibilities of contact; for Greek philosophers were no rarity in Jerusalem. Some of them were minor officials; others had been slaves, and on their release had taken service in aristocratic Jewish homes. It had been established as a custom in the days of the Great Herod for Jews to purchase learned Greek slaves on the markets of Zidon and Askelon, and to entrust to them the education of the young. In the majority of instances, the Jewish owners would liberate the slaves, so as not to be subject to the severe Jewish laws concerning alien slaves. But the Greeks remained, as freedmen, or freedmen of a sort, in the employ of their purchasers.

These former slaves were those who set the intellectual tone in the Jewish aristocratic homes of Jerusalem. Together with the Roman officials and the Sadducean elements, they constituted a sufficiently large group to support the Hellenistic institutions which Herod had founded, such as the theater, the races and the occasional games. But the bitter hostility of the Rabbis to this heathen culture world kept it off the streets of Jerusalem. It was confined to the homes of the rich, but there it struck deep roots; and this was true not only of the Sadducees and the Priestly families, but of sundry wealthy Pharisees too. It need hardly be said that the Romans were enthusiastic supporters of this Hellenizing movement. In Greece proper the ancient hatred still subsisted against the conqueror; but everywhere else there was an alliance; the Greeks regarded the Romans as the protectors of their culture, and the Romans made use of the attractions of that culture to win over to themselves the races which they ruled. Thus Greek and Roman went hand in hand. And it was a powerful alliance. All the measures taken by our Rabbis to halt the advance of this demoralization were vain; the poison spread through a thousand secret channels into the heart of Jewish life. It affected the daily conduct of the Jews; it was manifest in the meals they prepared, their clothing, their headdress, and their choice of ornaments. But there was something deeper: a change in the attitude toward the body. This was, among many Jews, no longer regarded primarily as the vessel of the soul, but as an intrinsic treasure, a gift of God to man. The influence of the Greeks crept into our language, too, and the Aramaic dialect of Jerusalem began to sprout Greek words.

But it must not be thought that this influence was wholly one-sided. Many Greeks, observing at close range the pious modesty of Jewish life at its best, learning for the first time the nature of the Jewish faith, with its central concept of the single and living God, were deeply affected in turn. They were moved by the lyric expression of the desire for a life beyond death, and they meditated on the universal hope which was embodied in the Messianic idea. The Greek mood of fatality was disturbed, the Greek mind set in motion among unaccustomed thoughts by the measureless devotion of the Jew to his God, by the voluntary acceptance of a strong discipline, by the tragic struggle against the temporal and the destructive, springing from deep faith in the divine and the timeless. It was as though a cold Greek statue had ceased to stand in moveless indifference, but had been touched with spirit, so that the lines trembled and the original harmony was disrupted. There was something extraordinary in the juxtaposition of Greek and Jew; two hostile worlds felt an inner longing for each other. They were like the complementary halves of a single being which had long regarded each other as enemies, and which now, brought into intimate contact on the soil of Judaea, were beginning to discover in the midst of warfare a unifying principle.

The song of that contact between the two worlds was heard in its most harmonious form in the house of Joseph Arimathea.

The original home of this man, as his name indicates, was the village of Ramat in Gilead. His family was ancient and distinguished. Antigonos Arimathea, the father of Joseph, had been a contemporary of Herod. The Hellenization of the family began with him, as a matter of policy rather than personal inclination. For in order to save his estates and possessions from confiscation by the rapacious king, he gave himself out as a great supporter of his policies, and outdid him in his worship of the alien culture. Tradition could not be so far flouted as to keep his son completely ignorant of Jewish matters; but in addition to the Rabbi, there was a Greek tutor in the house, Philippus of Gederah. Joseph traveled in the company of his Greek tutor to Alexandria, Gederah, Damascus and even the remote Greek provinces. He spent some time in Rome. Antigonos was anxious that his son should be on friendlier terms with the royal house than even himself; he paved the way for him by costly gifts, as well as by the education of Joseph. In Rome, where the sons of Herod were being educated, Joseph was perpetually in their company; he raced with them in the circus, and wrestled with them in the gymnasium. But this part of old Arimathea's plans went awry. The social successes in Rome of Herod's sons aroused their father's envy, and Antigonos was shrewd enough to withdraw his son in time from the danger zone. He called him back to Ramat, so that he might not be in the path of the storm which was about to break on the younger generation of the Herods. Joseph remained for a time in his native village; there he married the daughter of a rich Jewish family of Alexandria, and occupied himself with the administration of his father's estates.

When old Herod died, Joseph was sorely tempted to plunge into political life in Jerusalem and to make a personal career of it. He resisted, though he possessed all the equipment which could insure success: tact, a balanced temper, and above all that profound inner calm without which it would have been impossible to steer the right course in the struggle which the Pharisees conducted against the heir of Herod, Archelaus, until the day when the Romans took over the Judaean province. Joseph's Hellenic training, his high cultural gifts, his wealth and his generosity gave him easy access to the house of the Procurator. But by that time he was already caught up once more in the Jewish faith; he observed all the minutiae of the Pharisaic ritual, he frequented the company of the scholars of Jerusalem, he supported their schools and synagogues. But above all, he resisted political temptation in that he refused to ally himself with the plans of the House of Hanan, which the Pharisaic leaders regarded as the inheritor of all that had been worst and most brutal in the rule of Herod. This abstention of Joseph's awoke the special love and gratitude of the Rabbis.

His friendly relations with the two opposing forces inevitably raised him to the position of the unofficial but recognized mediator between the Pharisees and the Romans. The former were particularly happy to use his services whenever they had to approach the government, so that they might not be beholden to their enemies, the Priests, who were the official representatives of the Jews. There were also instances when Joseph Arimathea obtained for the Pharisees privileges and concessions which old Hanan might have been unable or unwilling to demand. The very severest among the Pharisees—those who actually considered it sinful to enter the house of a Greek or Roman—were prepared to ignore Joseph's laxity in this respect. In any case, he himself conceded the sinfulness of such acts, and purified himself by sacrifices in the Temple. Certainly they were prepared to forget the early years when Joseph had belonged to the court of the hated Herod; and though he was no scholar in Jewish matters, he was admitted by the Pharisees to the Great Sanhedrin.

The unhappy struggle between the Greek and Jewish worlds found its echo in Joseph's heart. His strict adherence to the tradition of his people had by no means killed in him the inclination toward the brilliant world of the gentiles. He carried on a perpetual if secret war within himself; he dreamed of finding reconciliation with the temptations of Hellenism without at the same time destroying the barriers which the Jewish sages had put up against its spiritual barrenness.

The childhood of Joseph had been passed in a world steeped in the Hellenic culture. The little town of Ramat, in Gilead, was surrounded by Greek settlements. Almost within walking distance lay the Decapolis, the cluster of ten Greek towns, a spearhead of paganism thrust at the very heart of the Jewish people. There, within sight and hearing of the Jews, reigned the spirit of eternal youth, of gaiety, of infectious enthusiasm, disarming and—in the eyes of the Jewish leaders—spiritually fatal. Its magic appeal of earthy, sublunar happiness never ceased to disturb the gravity of Jewish life. Within the same distance, but in a more southerly direction, lay the city of Bet Shan, with its race courses, its gymnasia and its temples of Ashtarot. On the shores of Genesaret, twinkling down from the summit of Gederah, the temple of Zeus dominated the countryside. The tumultuous loveliness of Gederah, too, besieged Jewish life from the other side. It was not Decapolis alone, then, which threatened to send the Hellenistic flood over the dykes erected for the perpetuation of the Jewish faith by its leaders. In Joseph's case, however, the danger consisted less in the superficial appeal of the Greeks than in the pagan philosophers of Gederah. Gederah was a city filled with gaiety and gamesomeness, with laughter and sin; but it possessed also its coteries of earnest thinkers. Whether he went of his own accord, or was led thither by his tutor Philippus, Joseph Arimathea always found his way to the forum where, among the pillars of the temples, the schools of Philodemus the Epicurean and Theodorus the rhetorician—this was the home of the latter before he went to Rome to become the teacher of Tiberius—argued with each other and with the followers of Meniphrus, the biting satirist. Most deadly for the young man, from the Jewish point of view, was the Greek tutor whom his father had chosen for him, and from whom he did not part as long as he lived. In later years Joseph Arimathea, following the general usage of the times, converted his tutor into the administrator of the family estates.

I was a frequent visitor in the house of Joseph Arimathea. My Rabbi held to the belief that his pupils should listen to his discussions with the Greek philosophers, in order that they might be prepared in later years against their wiles. Occasionally the entire Companionship would gather in Joseph's house, and sometimes the young pupils were admitted to the sessions.

The house stood in the new quarters which were being extended on the side of the Antonia in Bet Zeida. The area had been appropriated by the Jerusalem aristocracy, for here they were able to lay out gardens and swimming basins within reasonable distance of the city. The style of the house was Greek, in keeping with the fashion which had become almost universal among the wealthy since the time of Herod. Instead of the old, heavy walls, severe, massive and repellent, which characterized the ancient structures, such as, for instance, the palace which Herod had inherited, these new homes were light, and seemed to swim upon their columns; such too was the style which Herod had adopted when he built his own forum in Nablus. The "Herod architecture," as it was called, was characterized by the use of slender, pointed towers, which rose above the flat roofs, of upper-terrace balconies which gave a wider appearance to the façades of the houses, and of double rows of Ionic columns which cast a shadow over the entrances. But one of the unforeseen results of the style was that the walls of the rich houses were forever beleaguered by passers-by and by beggars, who sought shelter there from the heat of the sun. In the festival seasons, moreover, the stretches under the double rows of columns became regular camping grounds, and pilgrims slept there through the nights. It was impossible to keep those spaces clear; nor did the owners of the houses want to incur the odium of chasing from their place of shelter either beggars or pilgrims who were trying to escape from the heat of the day in a city where a shady spot was a rarity. Like all the Greek houses, Joseph's had two stories. On the lower were the common rooms and the library; the bedrooms were on the upper story. A peristyle surrounded the garden, affording retreat from the sun. In every respect the garden itself, with its flower beds and cypresses, resembled the garden of a heathen Greek, except that there were lacking statues and images of the gods.

The discussions which I attended took place, during the day, under the shadows of the peristyle, and in the evenings by the light of oil lamps in the banqueting hall or the library. The disputants lay stretched on couches, and made an enjoyable ceremony of the occasion.

When I came to know Joseph Arimathea he was no longer young, for he had passed his fiftieth year. But his body had retained all the manliness and vigor of its prime. His limbs were firm and muscular; his body was erect and square, as if cut out of a giant cedar. But the whole was light and elastic in movement, as became a man who had frequented the gymnasium in his youth. Even his head was still youthful, despite the streaks of gray in his curly hair and trimmed beard: and I noted that, in the matter of his beard, he did not encourage the full growth, as the pietists did, nor, of course, did he permit a razor to touch his face. He compromised, and the result was the Roman style. It was strange that he should make this impression of unspoiled pristine vigor, for his face was a mask of care and thoughtfulness. Only the straight Roman nose and the long jaws had been rescued from the network of wrinkles. In the company of the philosophers Joseph was all ears; he took their discussions perhaps more seriously than they; his eyes were drawn down in the intensity of his concentration, and he sat on his raised stool like a picture of spiritual concern. One would have said that he was not listening to an analysis of distant themes, but rather to a debate which had a practical life-and-death significance for him; and the conclusion of the discussion would have for him the validity of a juridical pronouncement on his own fate. In a sense this was comprehensible; for the struggle still went on within him, and the argumentation which moved back and forth dragged his soul now to this side, now to that; it was a battle for the possession of his inmost self. Yet it was more than this: for he conceived that the dispute over his individual soul was parallel with that over the possession of the soul of his people; indeed, the soul of the world. My Rabbi was like a seraph armed with a fiery sword, bursting into the harmonious earthly paradise which the Greek philosopher Philippus had created for Joseph. Beauty, and the grace which flows from it, was for the latter the highest conceivable good; the soul of man was but a note in the wholeness of the harmony of the gods. But the soul was not entrusted to all men; it was the privilege of those who were blessed with a superior intelligence. The soul introduced balance into the passions of man, calmed the fiery outbursts of lust and imparted to his bearing the grace of the gods. Therefore the wise man followed the golden mean, having refined his desires and impulses according to the nobility of the soul.

It was an extraordinary circumstance that this spokesman of beauty, this man who saw in earthly loveliness the essence of divinity, should have been treated with brutal stepmotherliness by the powers which he adored. Philippus of Gederah was, in fact, a cripple; his back rose into a hump behind, his chest into a hump in front. These two humps lifted the short Greek shirt which he wore, so that his crooked, hairy legs were made visible. He might perhaps have concealed the deformity of his body by the skillful disposition of the folds of a toga; but as if to make sure that he would be a walking contradiction of his life's philosophy, his gods had given a sharp sideward and downward twist to his head; so that his natural posture compelled him to look forever in the dust rather than at the heights which harbored his divinities.

I do not know whether he was born to this shocking array of defects or whether they were an unhappy acquisition during the course of his life. I was inclined to the latter view, for I could hardly conceive how such a monstrosity should have been chosen to be the tutor of a child. On the other hand, he compensated for his appearance by a liveliness of spirit, by a swiftness of mind, which often put to shame those who could more easily than he keep their eyes on the heavens. Perhaps again, it was the sufferings of his body which had impelled him to concentrate on the worship of the god of wholeness and completeness; and he did this with a strength and brilliance which made it easy to forget his physical repulsiveness.

There are men, as I know, who are whole enough in the flesh, but who are so crippled spiritually that the image of the inner sickness is projected upon their physical appearance. There are others who belong to the opposite extreme—whose flesh has been cruelly mishandled by fate, but whose inner harmony and wholeness casts an illusion of physical balance on their exterior. It may even happen that the intensity of their spiritual harmony may convert the defect into a positive acquisition. The body of Philippus was a living contradiction to his pagan philosophy. I see before me the withered, bony body—a child's body—the thin, hairy legs and the humps lifted, instead of the head, toward the heaven. But I see also his swiftness and, strange as it may sound, the rhythm and harmony of his movements, which spread tranquillity about him; when he lifted his face and looked about him, there radiated from it spiritual peace which had an immediate effect on those who beheld it. His eyes were dark and beautiful, and the light in them was soft, gentle, almost apologetic. His skull was naked on top, but the fringe of hair around its base made one think of a wreath; it was as if nature had thus symbolized the magnificent victory which he had won over the infirmities of his flesh.

I used to ask myself concerning Philippus: "What is the inner characteristic, the specific possession, which imparts nobility to his person?" And I came to the conclusion that it was the light touch of sadness which lay on his features and irradiated his body. This was an element which affected all who came in contact with him; and its power resided in the curious paradox of its origin. For he was not afflicted with the sadness of his personal lot and of the privations laid upon him. It was, instead, the sadness which is born of insight and wisdom. Or let me say, born of *his* wisdom, for it was not of the fiery kind which blazed on the countenance of my Rabbi; it was a wisdom of despair and ultimate bewilderment. These were eyes that had seen everything, penetrated everywhere, and found only darkness and emptiness.

Widely divergent as were the paths followed by the two men,

Philippus the Greek and Nicodemon ben Nicodemon the Jew, they were one in their hunger for knowledge. Daylong, nightlong, with the same insistance as my Rabbi, Philippus studied and meditated, still seeking the answer to the ultimate secret of life; but there was this difference—and it could not have been greater: in his ceaseless search my Rabbi found his way illumined by the light of faith, while Philippus wandered blindly in darkness, not upon land, but upon the sea, like a ship driven by tempests under a starless sky. He could not choose a course or steer the vessel, he could not even be certain that there was a shore to be reached. Here, again, was the source of his sorrow. And there was a curious resemblance, in the practice of their lives, between the two men. Philippus had brought himself, a pure sacrifice, to be laid upon the altar of knowledge. There was in him no desire other than for the ways of wisdom. He had abandoned the pursuit of earthly pleasure, had made his body subservient to his spirit, and hated whatever might have diverted him from his eternal quest or bound him to earthly responsibility: woman, for instance. He had refused to marry, though Joseph Arimathea would gladly have given him one of his slave women, by whom Philippus might have had children. But the latter avoided life, its entanglements and uncleanness; his soul was given in eternal virginity to wisdom, to the pursuit of truth. What could have resembled more closely the life impulse of my own Rabbi? What wonder that though their conclusions were as far from each other as the eastern and western horizons, they felt themselves held together by bonds of brotherhood and ever sought each other's company? It might sometimes come to pass that they forgot the first rule of wisdom: that truth is sought in calmness of spirit; their words might become heated; but they could not live without each other.

What was the substance of their conversations and discussions? The answer is simple: Everything. My Rabbi was always prepared to obtain from Philippus whatever knowledge the Greeks had gathered concerning the laws of nature, and to compare it with or add it to that which was accumulated in the lore of the Jews. "To gather knowledge," my Rabbi said, "is to draw nearer to God. And the nearer we draw to God, the more we love and revere Him, for the more we understand His boundlessness. And how shall we know

God save through His deeds? As it is written: 'The work of Thy hands declares Thy glory.' " This last quotation would burst spontaneously from his lips when the Greek acquainted him with some new law of nature, or inducted him into some new mathematical process. On the other hand, the Greek was forever eager to learn from my Rabbi the foundation of the Jewish faith; he desired to know what constituted the power of our belief, what were the commandments and laws which had been laid upon us by the Almighty and Invisible One. He desired also to be given the proofs of the existence of the Eye which saw everything and the Hand that guided everything on earth.

All the treasuries of knowledge were accessible to the Greek, for the keys had been given him by his teachers; but there was one citadel which remained closed to him: and this was the citadel of faith. Because he had no key to it, he remained, in the midst of the treasuries to which he had access, forlorn and helpless. Without faith, he might go on forever accumulating fragments of information; they were like heaps of stones which he could not erect into a comprehensible structure. He lacked the plan which the citadel of faith held concealed. There the heaps of stones lay—they did not afford shelter. Faith would transform them into a dwelling place and a refuge; but faith was precisely that which all the wisdom of the world, and even the wisdom which reached up into the pantheon of their gods, could not provide. And as against this impotence of wisdom and knowledge, a simple man without knowledge, without the resources of philosophy and science, could penetrate to the inmost mystery of the citadel and find the plan of life.

There the philosopher stood, locked out. And the greatness of the man Philippus consisted in this, that he *knew* he stood without (there are many who do not even know this much). His desire to enter was all-consuming, even according to the verse: "And my soul was inclined to the Lord." And our sages have declared that if a non-Jew seeks God, he is greater therein than the High Priest himself, and his desire may bring him into the shelter of the wings of God's glory.

My Rabbi knew of the spark that burned in the soul of the other; he felt his desire for the truth, and he was therefore drawn greatly to the man. It was a saying of my Rabbi that every soul is part of the universal divinity, and every soul is capable of creating its own contact with the Heavenly Father. And even though this soul was not present—as all the unborn Jewish souls were—at Sinai, to receive upon itself the yoke of the kingdom of heaven, it could nevertheless, by the spark within, lift itself through all the stages achieved by the Jewish soul in the course of many generations and with a single bound reach the universal Fount. Therewith it reaches as high a level as the Jewish soul, and perhaps a higher one, for it acquired its position by its own will power, and the souls of all the Jewish patriarchs and sages and prophets are added to it. But if, in addition, this soul of a non-Jew belongs to a sage, how much the more is it apt to approach the Fount? Therefore Rabbi Nicodemon was eager to help the soul of the non-Jewish sage, wandering tormented in darkness, and to free it from the sins of idol worship which kept it in bondage. He did not frighten Philippus by stressing the burdensomeness of the Torah, as the pupils of Shamai were wont to do, but was gentle and encouraging after the manner of Hillel.

I often heard discussions between Philippus and Nicodemon on the subject of worldly laws. But I was also present on one occasion when they disputed over the concept of the eternal nature of the human soul.

The conversation began on this related subject: What is more desirable, the primacy which God has conferred on man over the beasts of the field, so that he may seek out God, or the blindness of the beasts. The Greek philosopher argued as follows:

"There is, as a matter of fact, no proof that we are indeed different from the beasts of the field, and we have no right to accept your proud conclusion. Our intellect? Every beast, every worm, has been provided by nature with the means to secure its own existence and to propagate its own kind. We, instead of claws and fangs, make use of a certain cunning which we call the intellect, and with this cunning we have conquered the strongest beasts. But in truth we are but worms, to whom a few days have been allotted with a niggardly hand; we issue from our mothers' wombs and are flung naked upon the rocks of life. Or, if you will, we are flung into a pit of snakes, where the strong devour the weak, and where strong and weak alike are destined to perish utterly, to be ground into nothingness like a tiny acorn between mighty stones. What proof is there that we are better than the worms, when the law of the fang reigns in our midst?"

To which the Rabbi made answer:

"Come and behold the greatness of the Creator, for by His creations He shall be known. He has made man a worm, and man would be higher than the angels! If He has made us worms, wherefore has He planted in us the hunger and thirst after knowledge of Him? Why are we not content with the fate of worms, and of beasts? Why do we not devour our daily meat contentedly, and why do we not submit without question to being devoured by the stronger? Does the dust know, and complain, that the winds scatter it over the face of the earth? The animal rejoices in every tuft of grass which the Creator grants it; the worm rejoices in the little wingless insect that falls into its jaws. Why has the Creator made us different from them? In the thirsting after God there is God. Go forth and behold the peoples of the world, who make idols with their own hands and bow down to them. Why have they done this? Because they seek God, and long for Him. Through their idols they worship the one living Creator. True, their eyes are blinded, they have set their feet on false paths, but their hearts yearn for God. And where there is thirst, there is the means to quench it, for had there never been the quenching of thirst, there could never have been thirst, either. This is the graciousness which the God of Israel has performed with man, giving him the primacy among creatures."

"We do not know," answered the Greek, "whether we owe thanks to the gods for having instilled this thirst in us. Perhaps it was no graciousness, but an act of malevolence. We do not know whose fate is better, man's for having been endowed with intelligence to analyze, or the beast's, with no such endowment. It seems to me that the intellect of man is more a defect than a virtue, and we would do well to dismantle it, so that we may become like the beasts. What avails our intellect if it does not enable us to break through the wall which keeps us enclosed, as it keeps all other beasts enclosed. No, we shall not come to the ultimate truth."

"Without God, why should one seek the truth at all?" asked my Rabbi.

"But is not truth worth seeking for its own sake, without regard whether it lead us toward the gods or away from them?"

"Without God there is no truth. But without him there are many truths. Truth is One, like God."

"Then forgive me for saying that the verdict of intelligence turns such a view into a darker form of idol worship than any practiced by the barbarians. Those, at least, have some idea as to the appearance of their gods, in whose name they commit their crimes. They have their limited truth. But you do not even know what form your God has taken. This is not, in truth, a worship of the One God, but a baffled cry into the darkness. You do not even know if someone is there, in the darkness, to receive your cry."

"Not into the darkness," my Rabbi corrected him, "but into the infinite. And we believe that there, within the infinite, is an Ear which listens, an Eye which sees."

"But that is blind acceptance."

"Yes, not only blind acceptance, but blind love."

"But how can you love that which you know not?"

"We apprehend Him according to His attributes. And we love His attributes. Though we do not know Who He is, and we cannot imagine a form for Him, to contain or limit Him. Yet our love of Him does not depend upon this or that attribute, as is the case with your love of your gods. Our love is unconditioned and absolute. Therefore it is the only love, the true love, for it is as boundless as the Eternal."

"But this is the worship of a mouldwarp, not of a man; of a mouldwarp which has never seen the light of day, but crawls about in the subterranean channel it has dug for itself, and takes it for all the universe. So do you seek your God, with closed eyes and intelligence asleep. But the gods have conferred upon man the power to behold the sun, the forms of the earth, the stars and the flowers, the fields and the clouds, and all the treasuries of color. To you these enjoyments are forbidden by your God. We whom the gods have given a feeling for line, so that we may rejoice in the rhythm of dance and in the delicate changes of movement; we who can be filled with the harmony of completeness, and know the loveliness of song, not only as it strikes upon the ear but as it issues from the grace of a body in its nakedness; we, whom the gods ordained to bring order into the chaos of the world, making us equal with themselves—shall we willingly deny our role, strip ourselves of the glory which was made to illumine us? We worship our gods with the supreme attributes which they themselves distilled into us, with eyes, ears, feelings, emotions, senses, with the highest and noblest that man possesses—with art! Not like you! For your worship of the Highest is a worship of earthworms!"

My Rabbi was silent for a space. His face, which so rarely lost the radiance which was the outer expression of inner peace, darkened for a moment—but only for a moment. The sadness disappeared, the whites of his eyes flashed out, and he smiled under his dense beard. He answered:

"Each one of us serves his divinity with those attributes which he reads into his divinity. Your concept of the gods consists of idealized human virtues and gifts, and with these you would construct your worship: beauty, strength and harmony. We however ascribe to our divinity not human gifts and virtues, but heavenly attributes: infinity, indivisibility, timelessness, incorruptibility. Therefore our glorification and service cannot consist of earthly virtues, which are finite and changeable. We seek out in ourselves that part of us which is not mortal, but which is divinity in ourselves, our souls, and these we direct to the Eternal. We do not know what lines He occupies, in what color He shines, how the folds of His garment fall, and what motions His body makes. Therefore we address ourselves to Him in the language of the soul. The eyes of the soul perceive God, and the senses of the soul exalt Him. Our conception of God is divine, being itself part of the divinity. Yes, we have closed our eyes upon the beauty of the world, in order that we may perceive the beauty of the heaven. We have closed our senses upon the harmonious completeness of *this* world, that we may grasp the eternal wholeness of the *other* world."

"But what sort of self-delusion is this, that you alone possess the secret and virtue of the soul? We too believe in the immortality of the soul, but the soul cannot be a void and empty echo in an unconscious infinity. The soul can only be the sum and structure of all beauty, loftiness, power, love and friendship: that is, of all those ideals which we exalt in man, the creature. The soul is the measure, the touchstone of harmony; it produces within us the balance of our faculties. The soul is the wholeness of our being."

"That is acceptable only if one believes that somewhere there exists a separate angel or genius of harmony, or a separate well, from which harmony issues. If I believe that there is such a source of all the good, I can be persuaded that within me there is a drop therefrom, possessing all its attributes. But if I do not believe, if I refuse the premise that somewhere a core exists, a focus, the only and the eternal, the unchallengeable truth, which contains all good within itself, and from which my soul draws all its attributes—if I turn from this, I repeat, how shall I know that the soul I boast of merits being made the guardian of my being? Even if I grant that the soul possesses harmony, how shall I know that that harmony is of the right kind, which I must follow because it leads to completeness? Suppose it is the contrary! Suppose it is not the soul that should be followed, obeyed and regarded, but the lusts of the body! If there is no ultimate reference and judgment seat, how shall we decide?"

The Greek sage lifted his head with an effort, and from his eyes beamed the softness of the all-knowing smile which disarmed his opponents. He gazed with compassion on my Rabbi, who had become quite heated in the course of his argument, as one gazes on an excited child.

"The gods were niggardly," he said. "In the deep darkness which is about us, they provided us with a single little light hung about our necks, and that is the light of reason. Therewith we can dispel the gloom for a tiny area about us. Reason casts its light the distance of a few footsteps, but beyond that the darkness still reigns. Rabbi, you would leap forward into the abyss of endless darkness; you would break, or seem to break, through the walls, and returning, declare: 'At the end of the night there is eternal day.' But I know that the rays of my little lamp are flung back by the close thickness of the dark. How shall I know what lies there, in the night, if I have never penetrated, either with my eyes or with my other senses?

And wherewith shall I seek to penetrate, be it only the tiniest distance, if not with the reason which the gods have given me?"

"There is only one faculty which pierces the wall, the faculty of faith. These are the words of the singer of Israel: 'The righteous one shall live by his faith.'"

"But what is faith, Rabbi? Where does one find it? What gifts of ours can lift us to the level of faith?"

"The way to faith is pointed by faith itself. The hunger for God is the apprehension of God. He reveals Himself to all that seek Him. Desire Him, thirst after Him—and you will apprehend Him."

The Greek fell into silence. His head sank earthward again, his eyes closed, and he seemed to have locked himself in a citadel of peace, far withdrawn from us. After a long pause he lifted his head again, as if against the pressure of a heavy, invisible hand. His eyes sought out, once again, my Rabbi's face; the light of wisdom no longer shone in them, and the gentle compassionate smile had disappeared from his lips. There was fear in his look, touched by a ray of hope, when he answered:

"Perhaps that is indeed the way. Perhaps the truth is hidden from knowledge, and the secret can be reached only by a leap in the dark, such as you have taken, Rabbi."

Throughout the length of this discussion between my Rabbi and Philippus of Gederah, Joseph Arimathea remained wordless. His eyes moved steadily between the disputants, and his heavy lips were dry, as if they thirsted for knowledge just as they might thirst for water. A deep, gentle concern was poured over his features, as moonlight is poured over the waves of a lake. When the discussion was ended, he rose from his seat—but not before the sages had risen—and went forth with the company to the terrace of the library. The night was mild, and the heavens brightly lit. Far off the wastes of the hills of Moab glimmered under the stars, rising like massive walls which shut in the world of our being. Joseph stood silent among the pillars of the terrace; his gaze was fixed on the ramparts of the hills, but his inward eye went far beyond, seeking the spaces denied to the senses of the flesh.

He was silent. The heavy double shadow of his body was laid upon the mosaic floor and broke against a white pillar of marble, so that it rose again, behind him. There, on the white background, it loomed more mighty than he; and like him it seemed to be gazing out beyond the mountains of Moab, seeking out the mystery which was concealed beyond.

CHAPTER SEVEN

AND Philippus of Gederah, who all his life had not dared to step into the darkness further than the little space illumined by the lamp suspended from his neck, became, day by day, more inclined to take the bold leap—that is, to accept the unknown God whom the Jews preached. He was increasingly captivated by the glory which the Rabbis found in that which to him was nothing but universal night. The central point in that glory was their expectation of the Messiah, a messenger direct from the heavens, who should resolve all human problems and bring all human races into the kingdom of eternal goodness. This, more than anything else, inclined him to the great resolve.

Philippus of Gederah had grown up in a world alien to the concept of compassion. From childhood on he had seen human beings flung to the beasts for the delectation of masses; and that not only in the arenas, but in the streets of the cities. He too had been flung under the feet of beasts; in the sack of the city of Gederah he had been dragged from his home and sold in the slave market of Tyre. And he had grown up in the tacit belief that things could not be otherwise. It was under the influence of my Rabbi that he began to examine the deeds of men in a special light, weighing justice and injustice and acquiring a new faculty of sensitivity which revolted from cruelty and outrage. He became jealous for the righteousness of God. He moved ever more deeply into the mysteries of Jewish lore. The Aramaic dialect which was the daily language of the Jews was familiar to him; it served as an introduction to the study of Hebrew, which he soon mastered. Guided by Nicodemon ben Nicodemon, he delved deep into the Torah of Moses and the utterances of the Prophets.

My Rabbi devoted much time to his Greek pupil. He taught him the laws and commandments, gave him the interpretations of the difficult passages, inducted him into the ways of God as one would induct a child. There was a time our Rabbi even neglected us in order to help Philippus. His patience was extraordinary. He would forget sleep, ignore the nights, return again and again to the problems raised by the stranger, in the hope of filling his heart with the light of God and bringing him into the covenant of Abraham.

Sometimes we were astonished that the Rabbi should indicate preference for the stranger, so that we suffered in our studies. We would not have dared to complain, and we did our best to conceal our feelings. But our Rabbi suspected them, and he directed toward our unuttered distress a parable he had received from his teachers:

"Hear me, my pupils. Thus our Rabbis taught: King David has sung: 'Lord, keep guard over the stranger!' To what may this be likened? It may be likened to a king who had many flocks. Every morning the king's shepherds led the sheep and goats out to pasture, and every evening the shepherds brought them back to the stalls. But once a little hart came out of the field, and played with one of the kids. In the evening, when the shepherds drove the flocks home, the hart went with the sheep and goats under the roof of the king's stalls. Then in the morning it went out to pasture together with them. So it was every day. Then the king noticed the little hart and he was moved to love it. He would go out into the fields to see the hart feeding with his flocks. And he charged one of the shepherd lads to look to it that no harm came to the hart. Once, when the hart returned with the sheep to the fold, the king, standing by, said to the shepherd: 'Go now, and water the hart before watering the sheep.' The shepherds were filled with wonder and asked: 'Lord, thou hast so many flocks and herds, sheep and goats and cattle, yet hast thou never said unto one of us: "Do thus or thus for them," but for the sake of one little hart thou chargest us concerning its comfort.' Thereupon the king answered: 'It is a habit with sheep to go out in the morning to the meadows and to return evenings to sleep under a roof. But it is the habit of harts to spend their nights under the skies. It is not a habit with them to come under the roofs of men. Think, then, how the hart left the open fields, its brother and sister beasts, and came to us of its own free will. Shall we not consider it with more affection than one more sheep added to our flocks?' " And the Rabbi ended, smiling: "If a stranger, a non-Jew, come to us and leave behind him his former world, his flesh and blood, we must accept him with especial love, surpassing that which we show each other."

When the great resolve was taken, and Philippus of Gederah entered the covenant, he received the name of Abraham ben Abraham. From that day on he devoted himself to the Messianic idea more than his new brothers in the faith. He reached, indeed, the stage of hallucinations; he read everywhere signs of the immediate coming of the deliverance. He saw this as answer both to the needs of the world and the inmost needs of his own heart. He who had once maintained a calm balance and control of the senses now had visions, and heard voices. He no longer spoke the language of philosophy; reason had lost its ancient significance for him; and the Messianic hope was not simply a dream and desire: it was a palpable reality.

He was a strange sight, this Greek sage, squat, deformed, his two humps, back and front, supporting the ritualistic fringes which he now wore; it was strange to watch him hurrying through the streets of Jerusalem to the Temple, to make his offering. He was particularly careful in regard to the laws of purity and purification; indeed, he might have been called pedantic, even for a Jew. He paid strict attention to the minor laws having to do with the conduct of the house—such laws as generally fall to a woman to observe, and in all respects comported himself like a Pharisee of the Pharisees. So eager was he to keep himself in constant readiness for the reception of the Messiah.

There was one man in our Companionship who contributed greatly to keeping alive in the heart of the Greek the feeling of the imminence of the Messiah. This was Judah Ish-Kiriot, a dreamer and enthusiast, who was convinced somehow that he had already caught glimpses of the Messiah in the streets of Jerusalem. After the conversion of Philippus, Judah fastened himself to the former philosopher and helped not a little in destroying the last remnants of that ancient Stoic discipline which had characterized his previous life. If it went so far that Philippus began to see visions and hear voices, Judah Ish-Kiriot was finally responsible. Judah was passionately certain that the Messiah was already in our midst but that we failed to recognize him. He would come running into the synagogue, his jaws open, his eyes lustrous, exclaiming that he had seen him! He was practically certain he had seen him! He had caught a glimpse of him! The effect of such incidents on Philippus was extraordinary. He would accompany Judah in a search of the streets. Perhaps they would catch sight of the Messiah. Or, if not the Messiah, then of Elijah the prophet. They went up to the summit of the hills surrounding Jerusalem, and gazed about them, ready to behold Elijah come leaping over the heights, the messenger of the Messiah. They became so confused that they even took the beacons which were set off on the hilltops at night, to apprise the country of the first day of the month, for signals of the forerunner. In all this they felt that they were forcing the deliverance, anticipating the time, compelling the Messiah to declare himself.

When I came up to the school of Rabbi Nicodemon in Jerusalem, Judah Ish-Kiriot had already been a member of the Companionship for many years. A scholar, he followed the custom in sustaining himself by the work of his hands and spent one-half of each day at his trade of potter. Like the Rabbi, he was without a wife. He desired neither a family nor even a home of his own. His mind and heart were fixed on one impending event: the deliverance. Most of the time he walked about in a condition of ecstasy. Often he would sit alone in a corner of the synagogue, his eyes closed, apparently asleep. But when I drew close to him I would observe that his lips were moving. Sometimes he would laugh to himself, sometimes dissolve in tears. On several occasions he had fallen to the earth, in the middle of the Temple court; a foam had settled on his lips, and he had begun to prophesy. He would also rush eagerly among the crowds, peeping, staring, scrutinizing the faces of strangers. Then he would return to the synagogue always with the old cry: he had caught a glimpse of him.

Among the throngs which filled the Temple courts and the alleys round about them, there were always to be found visionaries, pilgrims from the provinces and abroad, possessed or half-possessed men who never ceased to speak of the Messiah and his imminence.

Not a few managed to persuade themselves that they were, in fact, the Messiah himself. Others, finding themselves in the Holy City, were so eager to behold wonders and to be the first witnesses of the arrival that they expected momently the lowering of a fiery cloud from the heavens which would discharge the Messiah. The Temple overseers, the watch, the servants, the cleaners, the singers—all the sons of those stepchildren among the tribes, the exploited Levites, as well as the lower ranks among the Priests—feeling themselves equally the victims of the evil times, contributed to the mood of restlessness and expectancy. The higher authorities were confronted almost daily with conditions that bordered on riot: this or that wild dreamer had risen momentarily above his fellows to precipitate about him a crowd of feverish admirers. Much skill and firmness was needed to dissolve the assemblies without invoking the assistance of the Roman guards, who, whenever they were called in, did not fail to take advantage of the situation in order to satisfy their natural ferocity and their hatred of the Jews.

I see Judah Ish-Kiriot before me now. He was dark, tall, lean, half-starved. His beard was gray. But this gray had come not with the years, but with pain and care, for his eyes were young, fiery, restless, and searching. His huge ears, of a flaming color, stood away from his head. His hands were never motionless. When he walked he waved them before; his gait was wild, so that the ritual fringes, thrown over his sackcloth covering, danced about and became tangled in his legs. He moved as if carried by a tempest, or as if he were himself a tempest. His covering, hanging loose, flew behind him like a crippled wing.

What was most astounding about this man, however, was the contradiction which he embodied: his visionary enthusiasms were accompanied by a profound skepticism. My Rabbi said of him: "Judah Ish-Kiriot is like a mother who eats her own young." He would come rushing into the school or synagogue, his eyes blazing, the hair of his head erect, his hands in violent motion; the laces of his sandals trailed in the dust.

"I have seen him! He is here! He is among us! He is standing in the Temple court, preaching to the multitude. It is he!" he babbled before he had crossed the threshold.

Then he caught up the Rabbi's fringes, and gasped: "Come with me, Nicodemon, son of Nicodemon! The Messiah is here!"

But he lost each Messiah as soon as he found him. The same day he would return to the synagogue, his head hanging, his eyes extinguished, silent, ashamed, as if he were returning from service in a heathen temple. He did not mention his loss. And if one was cruel enough to ask him: "What of the Messiah?" he would fetch a sigh which seemed to shatter his body, and mutter: "I was mistaken again."

In respect of his Messianic hallucinations he was, of course, wholly unlike a sage and scholar, and in utter contrast to Rabbi Nicodemon. The latter was scrupulous in the use of words, and uttered no opinion which he had not tested and examined. He was as careful in the expression of his views as a miser in the expenditure of money. He had this saying: "A word which comes from the mouth is a deed which leaves an imprint. No power in the world can wipe it out." He would also say: "The Lord of the Universe conferred upon man the power to create and destroy worlds with the words of his mouth. Therefore be guarded in your speech." Certainly my Rabbi was displeased with the recklessness of speech which his follower Judah permitted himself. Whenever the latter came panting with new revelations, my Rabbi would admonish him: "Judah, Judah, have you forgotten the command of the sages: 'Wise men, keep close watch on your words!' "

But Judah could hardly live through a single day without his Messiah, and without someone to whom he could pour out his ecstasy. My Rabbi also had this saying concerning him: "Judah needs a special hook on which to hang his faith; the Lord is not enough for him." But if a day passed wherein Judah had not caught a glimpse of the Messiah, he would be found sitting on the threshold of the synagogue, his head sunk between his bony shoulders, like the head of a wounded bird drooping between the wings, his eyes dead. His lips would be muttering: "When cometh he? When cometh he?" My Rabbi would comfort him, yet mock him gently. He reminded him of the folk sayings current in those days: "The Son of David will not come till the last copper coin is gone from thy purse." Or: "The Son of David will not come until the generation is wholly pure or wholly covered with sin." Then my Rabbi would advise Judah: "Go out into the street, take away the people's money; make all the world of men into saints, or into unregenerate sinners. Then the Son of David will come."

During a certain period Judah was a follower of Bar Abba, the fisherman of Joppa who dreamed of becoming a second Judah the Zealot. If the masses were eager for a heavenly Messiah, they were not less eager for an earthly deliverer, who would smash the yokes of the two oppressors, the Priestly and the Roman. Bar Abba found followers among the disinherited and dispossessed who came up to the city from the provinces. His watchword had been taken from the Venerable Hillel: "*Im lo achshav, eimatai?* If not now, when?" His plan was not to lead a rebellion direct against Rome, for he knew this would end in disaster; he hoped to break one oppressor at least, the house of Hanan, old Hanan and his son-in-law Kaifa.

This was the path of his thoughts: by directing himself against the Priests he would win over to his side the scholars and the Pharisees, who were always preaching submission to Rome, for they were convinced that liberation from the might of the Empire could not be achieved by earthly means. Undoubtedly his ultimate hope was the breaking of the yoke of Rome. But whether he intended to achieve one objective at a time, or foresaw a conflagration which would—whatever the announcement—sweep Rome before it not less than the House of Hanan, I cannot say.

Bar Abba was himself a child of the masses, whose faces were ground to the earth. He had been robbed of the boat which he had once oared through the stormy breakers of Joppa; that the robbery went under the name of taxation made the infliction harder to bear. He bore in mind that the taxation had been double, that imposed by Rome and that imposed by sons of his own people. Since that time he had lived with one thought—rebellion. But he was no hare-brained, irresponsible troublemaker, however hot-blooded he might be. He was aware of the changed mood of the people; physical rebellion would not come as easily as in the days of Judah the Zealot. The masses remembered Judah—but they also remembered the crosses, with their burdens of agonizing Jews, sown thickly through the land by Varus the Wicked. As regards Rome, Bar Abba preached only passive resistance, the refusal of payment of taxes. But he declared open war on the House of Hanan. The hatred among the masses against the Priesthood could be compared, in those days, with the hatred awakened against the High Priest in the time of Mattathias the Maccabee. And perhaps it was not so much the savagery of their direct exactions from the people, as their desecration of the Sanctuary by the manners and morals of the market place, which infuriated the Jews of Jerusalem and Judaea.

There had alas grown up among our people a sort of cult of the dead. The living, it seemed, could not bring themselves to be parted from those whom death had taken. There were mothers who carried around bones which were relics of children they had lost. This dreadful cult had been taken over from our heathen neighbors, and our Rabbis fought against it. There were ancient laws and commandments to support them. It was written that anyone who had touched part of a dead body was thereby rendered unclean; and to cleanse himself he had to be sprinkled in water in which were contained ashes of the red heifer. But ashes of a red heifer were costly. Very rare indeed were the animals found suitable for this ritual; for if a red heifer had even two white hairs on any part of its skin, it was unfit. Any farmer lucky enough to have bred, among his cattle, a beast perfect for the ritual, would ask a fantastic price for it. Messengers of the Temple were for ever scouring not only Judaea and Galilee, but Tyre and Zidon likewise, in the hope of finding such a specimen. Only once in so many years were they successful. Therefore the ashes of the red heifer were an immense treasure to the Temple; they were transmitted carefully through the generations. Now until the coming of the House of Hanan to the High Priesthood, these ashes were used in purification sacrifices without respect of the wealth or poverty of the suppliant. For this was a national possession, to which every Jew had equal access. But the Sons of Hanan introduced a high price for the use of the ashes, so that a poor man could by no means obtain it. Thus only the wealthy and powerful could touch the dead and be cleansed afterwards.

In thus using the embitterment of the masses, Bar Abba was assisted by rumors current in Jerusalem that there were other

Priestly houses, jealous of the House of Hanan, prepared to help in a revolution. There must have been some truth behind these rumors, otherwise he could not have remained so long at liberty, strengthening his influence over the masses.

Bar Abba was a man without any learning whatsoever. He was bitter, courageous, insolent, quite unable—wherein he was thoroughly Jewish—to submit to the slavery of speechlessness. He flung his harsh words among the masses, stirring to fury their accumulated bitterness. It need hardly be said that he could not carry on openly, in the Temple courts or the alleys. That part of the city was closely watched by the spies and agents of the Priesthood. Any assembly that threatened to become riotous was dispersed by the watchmen who were armed with lead-loaded whips. Bar Abba worked in the Lower City, in the marshy area about the Kidron valley, by the Dung Gate, among the poorest of the poor. He would appear, suddenly and unannounced, near the stalls of the laborers, the booths of the bakers and oil sellers. He would stand up on a millstone or an oil press or a dyer's block and call the masses to rise again the Sons of Hanan, to refuse taxes to Rome. He would enumerate the crimes of the House of Hanan: they had raised the price of doves for sacrifice and the price of meal for an offering. And when he mentioned the ashes of the red heifer, made inaccessible to these, the poor, by the greed of the Priests, he roused them to such fury that he could at any time have led a mob against the booths and stores of the Priesthood.

I saw Bar Abba often. Our school, attached to the synagogue of the Cyreneans, stood in the Street of the Spices, at the entrance to the old market. I witnessed more than once what looked like the beginning of an uprising. The sound of a tumult in the street would break in on our studies. When we came forth we would perceive Bar Abba, a wild figure towering above the crowd. Words came tumbling out of his huge mouth, words that recalled the shame of Jewish suffering, the humiliations, the burdens, the agonies of slavery; simple, coarse, heavy words, as rude as the street in which they were uttered, as rude as the poverty of the listeners. And the crowd of listeners, their eyes bulging, their sick faces aflame, their tortured bodies only half covered by sackcloth shirts, over which hung unwashed ritual fringes, a picture of disease and hunger—the crowd listened and roared back at the thunderous language of the orator. His words fell on them heavily, like hammer blows:

"Your wives," he bellowed, "go round unclean, not washed of the blood of the children they have just brought forth. They are forbidden to you, because they cannot bring the purification sacrifice. The High Priest has raised the price of the doves for purification offerings. Tell me, has anybody here, among you, ever been privileged to have sprinkled on him the ashes of the red heifer? All of you are unclean! Unclean! You dare not even approach the Temple, no, nor even draw near the outer wall. You have been pushed away, thrust out of the sight of God, where His eyes cannot reach you. You are locked out of the hosts of God, and the key is in the hands of the House of Hanan. It is a golden key, and only gold can buy the use of it. Is it not enough that you must hunger in these streets, and cover your bodies with the rags of slaves? Must you also live in filthiness of soul? The House of Hanan has made you all into stinking corpses, into putrefying beasts, into lepers!"

There was rude power in his words. The eyes of the listeners flickered with inner fire. Fists were lifted into the air. Here and there women broke into slobbering lamentation, their voices high-pitched and nasal, as in the keening for the dead. The multitude is caught up in a single passion and carried away. Then suddenly the watchmen appear. There rises into the air the harsh calling of the rams' horns, the signal to the Temple guards. If the crowd of excited listeners is unusually large, the Temple guards may come on the run accompanied by a squad of Roman auxiliaries in their short corselets, broadswords in hand. Occasionally German horsemen issue from Herod's palace and force their way down the narrow alleys. And then the whips, their lashes loaded with leaden riders, begin to fly. Here and there resistance is attempted; but always the multitude dissolves, leaving bodies here and there, bloodied, ripped, rolling among smashed pots and scattered stalls. And Bar Abba? He is gone! No one has seen him! He disappears into an alley, clambers up a wall, leaps from roof to roof, and is swallowed up in the labyrinth.

Disappears—but not for long. He has been known to show himself in the Temple court. There is a stir, an excited group has formed, words are flung into the air—Bar Abba is gone! And that same day he may be heard from again! He has broken his way past the watchmen round a rich man's house; he has torn aside the curtains of the banqueting hall, he has launched his curse at the luxury-loving diners—he has disappeared again.

For a time, as I say, Judah Ish-Kiriot was a follower of Bar Abba. In his characteristic fashion Judah came bursting one day into the synagogue school, ran up to Rabbi Nicodemon and cried out:

"I have found him! I have found him! The Messiah is outside, gathering his hosts!"

Nicodemon ben Nicodemon did not have to listen to more than one sermon of Bar Abba's, or to be the witness of more than one of these futile half-rebellions in the market place, to turn his back on the agitator and all his works. And to Judah he said:

"From this meal no bread will ever be baked, for the dough is swollen not with the leaven of God, but with the leaven of Satan. Ever since the day when God withdrew the gift of prophecy from the men of Israel and put it in the mouths of children, He has compensated us by pouring the strength of His spirit into the sages, so that they may make up by wisdom what has been lost in prophecy. Judah, Judah, where is your portion of the spirit? Do not your nostrils take in the stench of death which proceeds from the mouth of Bar Abba? Remember the verse, Judah: 'The Guardian of my soul keep me far from these!' "

But Judah's devotion and enthusiasm did not last long and he admitted that our Rabbi had been in the right. Bar Abba did not content himself with words; he passed to action. He organized a band which terrorized the roads leading into Jerusalem, attacked the rich merchants leading their wealth toward the capital, and robbed them. It was reported that in this he followed the example of Judah the Zealot, taking from the rich to give to the poor. But the decree went out against him not only from the Priesthood, but from the Sanhedrin, too.

Even before I heard mention of him on the night of my last pilgrimage to Jerusalem, I knew that one of the Essenes had gone down to a spring in the wilderness of Judaea and applied to himself the verse of Isaiah: "The voice that calls from the wilderness: prepare the way!" I knew also that many people, learned and unlearned, had gone to Jochanan, to be baptized by him in the Jordan, at a place not far from the city of palm trees, Jericho. He dipped their bodies in the water, after they had purified their souls, not to cleanse the flesh but to prepare it for the advent of the Messiah. At first the mission of Jochanan the Baptist did not make a great stir among us, the Pharisees, though some were impressed. The Pharisees held off from the Essenes because the latter had sundered themselves from the ways of life; they practiced frequent baptism, withdrew from the taking of wives, from participation in communal affairs, and isolated themselves in their own bands. The Pharisaic sages called them *Chassidim shotim*, foolish pietists, declaring that God desires man to *live* in His commandments, not to die in them. For so it is actually written: "Live in them!" Still it was known to us that Jochanan was a God-fearing man and one learned in the Torah. Likewise that which he preached, to wit, the coming of the Messiah, was close to us. Nevertheless the manner of the preparation, by withdrawal from the world, was not pleasing to many. Afterwards, however, we learned how Jochanan had dared to appear before the Tetrarch of Galilee, to curse and denounce him for having taken away his brother's wife for himself; then the name of Jochanan took a great upward leap. His words acquired new weight, for it was considered that he had displayed the virtues of a prophet. To this was added before long the intimation of approaching martyrdom, for Jochanan was imprisoned in the cellar of the Tetrarch's palace. His messengers, passing back and forth between the prison and Jerusalem, brought into the Temple courts the words of comfort and encouragement which he entrusted to them: he bade his followers, and all the Jews, not to despair, not to go under the sea of wickedness which rose about them, but to gather their strength and to endure until the coming of the kingdom, which was now close at hand; all this increased the expectation of those who awaited at least the announcement of Elijah the prophet, the forerunner of the Messiah.

Their numbers grew. There were thousands that woke up every

morning and asked: "Has he come in the night?" And receiving a negative answer, said: "Then he will surely come today." But the day drawing to an end without a sign, they still said: "He will come in the night." Hope did not diminish, but became more tense and feverish. Men walked about with their eyes fixed on the heavens, that they might not miss the first signal. One night a new star appeared over the Temple, and shone over the gate called The Beautiful. Multitudes ran through the streets shouting: "The Messiah is here!" There was a great panic in the city. The crowds about the Temple walls called on the guards to open the gates, which is strictly forbidden in the nights. The multitude was dispersed by force.

It was, of course, Judah Ish-Kiriot who first took up the rumors and stories of a wonderful man who had appeared in Galilee. He was always mingling with pilgrims from the provinces, asking whether they had not heard of a sign, in their localities, that the Messiah was approaching. Thus there came to his ears the reports of the Galileans concerning a Rabbi of Nazareth, who preached a great doctrine and performed miracles. I remember well that when Judah began to rehearse, with growing excitement, the tales from the north, we shrugged our shoulders and said: "A Rabbi of Nazareth! Can salvation come from Galilee?" But every day Judah brought to Rabbi Nicodemon new witnesses, pilgrims from K'far Nahum, and all of them testified to the wonders being done in their town. They told how the Rabbi of Nazareth healed the sick, lifted the fallen and drove out evil spirits. They recounted, moreover, that he came into the huts of the poor and lowly, ate at the tables of the ignorant, the men-of-the-earth, and even admitted to his company sinners and tax collectors, that he might teach them the ways of righteousness; he also surrounded himself with children, and blessed them. Yet what moved us most were certain verses of his doctrine which were repeated by the pilgrims, and which came near to our hearts. One such verse was: "Judge not, lest ye be judged." We likewise heard of certain parables which had come from his lips. My Rabbi at once recognized the Rabbi of Nazareth as a follower of Hillel. But soon afterwards other sayings of his were transmitted to us, and we were greatly perturbed. But Judah pressed my Rabbi to let him go to Galilee. "Send me to him," he insisted, "and I will find out who he is."

In the end, yielding to importunities, my Rabbi called together the Companionship. There were present Joseph Arimathea, Simon Cyrene, Hillel the watercarrier, and Abraham ben Abraham, the convert. It was decided that Judah be sent to investigate. And my Rabbi gave him this last admonition:

"Seek out the man and look into his deeds; give ear to his doctrine and find out all his ways. But bear always in mind the words of that wisest of all men, King Solomon, who warned the daughters of Jerusalem with these words: 'I charge ye that ye awaken not my love until he desires.' 'My love' means here the Messiah. Do you understand, Judah?"

"Yes, yes, Rabbi," answered Judah, eagerly.

"Then go, in the name of God. It may be that now the Lord has taken pity on His people, for the waters have come up to our lips."

Then Judah made up his sack and slung it over his shoulders, took up his staff, and set out for K'far Nahum. Only Rabbi Nicodemon accompanied him part of the way, for the Companionship kept the mission a secret, and no one outside the circle was to hear of their close interest in the matter.

CHAPTER EIGHT

IT was no surprise to the members of the Companionship that the enthusiast should once again have fallen under the influence of a teacher and visionary and that the investigator should have become, overnight, the advocate. It was the duration of the spell that astonished them. For letters continued to arrive from Judah, long and ardent letters, written and transmitted in secret, proclaiming that *now*, at last, assuredly, without error, he had found what he sought. The thirst so long endured was being slaked by streams of living waters, the hunger was being stilled, the bitterness dispelled. He wrote of the marvels which his new Rabbi performed daily, of the doctrine which he preached, of the glory which attended him. When these letters arrived, Rabbi Nicodemon called the Companionship into session, seated himself on the bench of the Messiah, and read forth to them. We, the excluded pupils, lingered near the door, applied our ears to the cracks, and caught what we could of the conversation.

But even if we had not eavesdropped, we would have become aware of important events impending. Our Rabbi kept his lips sealed, but the change that came over him could not be hidden. A new light came into his eyes; an unwonted restlessness, altogether alien to his manner, appeared in his bearing—even a degree of impatience. He taught us not as heretofore, with close attention to all the details and twists of interpretation which could be attached to every letter of the text, but more broadly. He directed us less to the laws and commandments, to the *Halachah*, and more to the *Agada*, the things told, the morals and stories. Likewise there was something mysterious in the hints which crept into his recitals and lessons; he quoted more than before the words of the Prophets, stressing but not clarifying their hidden significance. But all this was as nothing compared with the storm that broke in from the outside. Whether others than we, the pupils, had become aware of the secret letters of Judah to our Companionship, or whether the connection with the teacher of Galilee had been revealed from K'far Nahum, I do not know. Nor am I even certain that such a connection was actually established. I only know that when the Sanhedrin and the High Priests learned of the Rabbi of Galilee, or at least began to pay attention to him, my Rabbi was somehow involved. Then suddenly my Rabbi himself disappeared—we soon discovered that he had set out for K'far Nahum—on a mission to which he had been appointed by the Sanhedrin. What amazed us most was that he took none of us with him; for it was a universal custom that a Rabbi should be accompanied everywhere by his pupils. He would not even let us accompany him part of the way, as our duty commanded. Against this we protested, for we would not be deprived of the virtue of serving our Rabbi. Indeed, such a virtue cannot be relinquished even when the Rabbi is willing to dispense with it. Rabbi Nicodemon was compelled to exert his authority to the utmost and to make his refusal in the form of a decree, forbidding us to enjoy this pleasure. He went further: he forbade us to make mention to anyone that he had gone forth from Jerusalem.

Of the impatence with which we awaited his return I will not speak. We were oppressed not only by anxiety but a feeling of homelessness. We met daily and repeated the lessons he had taught before leaving, we rehearsed the laws and the *Agadot,* we tried to recall the hints which had accompanied the texts. But there was no happiness in these studies; we were like men who sit in a darkened room and tell each other of the wonders of the sunlight. And when our Rabbi returned, after an absence of two weeks, we hardly knew him. The joy had vanished from his countenance. He who had always been so open with his pupils, and indeed with all the world, was now like a book closed with seven seals. He who had always looked upon sorrow, upon "darkness of spirit," as a device of Satan, now sat apart by the hour, sunk in sadness. Yet we marked that this sadness was of a peculiar kind; it did not spring from despair, from surrender and failure. It was rather a strange state of suspense; a cloud covered his eyes, but in the shadow expectation lurked. Rabbi Nicodemon had become a man of dreams. He uttered words which were directed half to us, and half to something within him; for their meaning was obscure. In these moods he would start and tremble when the door opened or someone knocked. Something worse: we found out that he did not sleep in the nights; he rose from his couch and went wandering in the streets of Jerusalem. It was as though he sought someone in the shadows of the empty streets.

Then a messenger, a Jew of Galilee, appeared one day in the house of study. We knew whence he came by his attire, and by the accent with which he spoke when he asked after the Rabbi. But that was all we heard, for the Rabbi closed himself with the man in a separate room, and what went on there neither I nor any other of the pupils ever learned. But the Rabbi came forth in great agitation, his head erect, his face radiant, as though the glory of the *Shekhinah* had descended on him. That night there was a meeting of the Companionship, and the next morning, to our utter amazement, the Rabbi was gone from the city. It was not a long absence, such as we had feared. But on his second return, he displayed another profound change. It was our Rabbi Nicodemon who faced us again, the Rabbi we had known in the days before the letters began to arrive from Judah Ish-Kiriot. The dreaminess, the silence and sadness were gone; he was at peace with himself, as he had always been. The old tranquillity lay on his features; and his eyes shone with that quiet light which declared to the world that all was well. Faith and security, his ancient companions, attended him. He took up his lessons with us, and now he directed us again toward the laws, the regulations and the commandments, as the old teachers had transmitted them, from the days of Moses on. Thereupon we understood, without further explanation, that the time had not yet come for the abrogation of the law; likewise the judgment of Edom, which hung above us like a sword, was not yet to be removed.

Then came the unforgettable moment of our first meeting with the Rabbi of Nazareth.

It was an unexpected encounter, unheralded and unarranged. We were at services on the Sabbath morning in the synagogue of the Cyreneans, and we had arrived at the reading of the Torah when suddenly the white robe of the Nazarene appeared at the entrance, shining out from the midst of the disciples who accompanied him. All the worshipers were assembled. The dignitaries occupied the bench along the western wall—for the Temple lay westward of our synagogue. The *Ab ha-Kneset,* or Father of the Congregation, was Joseph Arimathea. He stood with my Rabbi, one to the right, the other to the left of the Torah. The *S'gan,* or Chief Officer of the Synagogue, was reading forth that week's set portion of the Pentateuch. Suddenly there was a quiet stirring among the worshipers, and a whispering arose: "The Rabbi of Nazareth. . . . The Nazarene!"

The presence of the Nazarene in Jerusalem was by this time widely known, and the miracle which he had wrought by the pool was the subject of much discussion and much division of opinion, especially among the scholars; for he had cured the sick man on a Sabbath. As the news of his presence among us spread, the whispering changed to a loud murmur of curiosity. A gesture from Rabbi Nicodemon restored order. He sent down one of the officers to bid the Nazarene approach and take his place on the semicircular stone bench by the western wall, among the dignitaries of the congregation. He might have gone himself, were it not that the Torah lay open before him on the reading desk, and to turn from it would have been an impiety. And the Rabbi of Nazareth came forward and sat down on the stone bench, leaving his disciples at the entrance.

This was my first glimpse of the man of wonders, whose name had gone before him. Rufus and I stood together, our hearts shaken. It seemed to us that showers of sparks issued from his dazzling white robe. His face was long and pallid, framed in a little, sparse beard, black and shot through with white hairs, and curled earlocks hung down on either side of his beard. A sorrowful smile trembled on the thin line of his lips as he sat listening with attentive devotion to the reading of the Torah. The children in the synagogue, attracted by the stranger and by his shining garment, excited also by the rumor of his name, which had reached even their ears, congregated near him and stared at him reverently. One of the officers of the synagogue rose, intending to drive them away, but the Rabbi of Nazareth lifted his eyes to him and the stern officer stopped and resumed his seat; then the Rabbi of Nazareth smiled gently at the children, inviting them to come closer. This they did, slowly and timidly at first, their faces reflecting awe, but under his caressing look their fear melted away; they came close and even touched his garment; and the Rabbi laid his hands on their little heads and his lips moved in silent benediction.

Then the *S'gan* called out the Rabbi's name, and with his pointer indicated the passage to be read: "Our teacher, Rabbi Yeshua ben Joseph, is invited to ascend to the Torah!" Then the Rabbi rose, put aside gently the children who clung to him, and ascended to the pulpit. The *S'gan* handed him a *tallit,* which the Rabbi wrapped about himself, closing his eyes and whispering the benediction. Then he made the benediction over the Torah, read his passage, made the closing benediction and stepped down from the pulpit, all according to the prescribed commandments.

Then, when the reading of the Torah was ended, my Rabbi approached Red Yeshua ben Joseph and invited him to ascend the pulpit again and to preach to the congregation, as the custom was when a Rabbi visited the Sabbath services. And the Rabbi of Nazareth consented.

Wrapped in his *tallit,* as during the reading, he ascended the pulpit again. His lips moved, but it was in silent prayer. Then he approached the officer who held the scroll of the Torah. He lifted it up, and seated himself on the "Chair of Messiah" which is built into the pulpit, and which is occupied by the head of the court at trials. And with the scroll of the Torah in his lap he began to preach.

The congregation had been deeply stirred by the mere presence in their midst of the man of wonders, concerning whom so many contradictory reports had reached their ears; but now they were thrown into the profoundest agitation by the manner in which he deported himself on this occasion. For he did not do as other Rabbis did, that is, stand before the congregation while he preached. But he sat down in the seat of judgment, holding the Torah in his lap, as if he were a king. Very clearly, then, he regarded himself as wholly different from other Rabbis, and he dared to do that which he knew would bring a trembling into Jewish hearts and fill them with the highest hopes.

Had it not been for the grave and pious expression on the face of my Rabbi, Nicodemon, who stood on the pulpit and by his very looks imposed silence on the congregation, the strange deportment of the Rabbi of Nazareth even before he began to speak would have called forth cries of protest. But the worshipers were constrained to silence, and in the silence the heartbeat of their expectation was audible. I saw Hillel the watercarrier, who usually occupied a humble place at the door of the synagogue, carried forward by his excitement almost up to the pulpit. Behind him stood Simon Cyrene and the convert Abraham ben Abraham, and the hunchback was a forlorn figure with the *tallit* draped over his deformity. The disciples, too, had made their way forward to the pulpit; Judah Ish-Kiriot held onto the uprights of the pulpit and swayed piously back and forth; on the other side was Simon bar Jonah, guarding the steps, and near him were the Zebedee sons.

At first the words of the Rabbi of Nazareth were gentle and soft. He spoke of the power of faith, of trust in the Almighty and of the power of prayer.

"Ask, and it will be given. Knock and it will be opened. For everyone that prays shall receive, and everyone that seeks shall find, and to everyone who knocks shall be opened."

His speech calmed the agitation which had been roused by his first actions. For he spoke with parables which imparted sweetness to his words. When he spoke of faith in God he bade his listeners regard the ravens, which neither sow nor gather harvest nor store in barns, and which God nourished nevertheless. "And how much more are you than the birds!" he said. "And who of you by taking thought can add a cubit to his height?"

Now the great majority of the worshipers in our synagogue were indeed poor workers, and mostly they were dyers, for the Cyreneans had brought with them, out of their country, the secret of dyeing woolen stuffs in various colors; there were also among them silversmiths and workers in bronze, likewise saddle makers and tent weavers. For these, the children of poverty, his words were like soft ointment on wounds. But the scholars who were present were likewise edified by his speech. They perceived the strength of his faith and of his trust in God; they praised his words in their hearts because he strengthened the hands of the weak and lifted up the lowly. At first they had been alarmed by his manner; and they had taken it amiss that he had not begun his sermon as was considered proper, that is, with verses of the Torah, or of the Prophets, or of the Psalms, or even of ben Sirah; nor did he make mention of the names of Rabbis and do honor to those that had been his teachers. He spoke on his own authority. Yet, as he continued, they were won by his sermon, and said to themselves that no doubt this was but his way of preaching, for the substance in no way differed from the utterances of our Rabbis and sages.

Nevertheless we began to perceive that there sat before us a Rabbi who was wholly different. Indeed, he was not a Rabbi; he was a thousand times higher than a Rabbi. Who could measure him? Were we, perhaps, in the presence of the highest Jewish hope? For now we heard words which had not been spoken even by Moses on Sinai. Who was this that sat before us, with the scroll of the Torah on his lap? Our hearts began to melt in terror, and our knees trembled. We looked at each other with terrified eyes. We knew not whether God was not about to lift us to the gates of heaven, and fling them open, that we might behold the shining of that power for which our hearts had so long hungered. Or were we about to be thrown into the abyss?

He began to speak of himself as if he were the carrier of the highest of all authority. He spoke of our eternal expectancy of help, he bade us stand momently with loins girt, awake at our posts. "Let your candles always be lit. It may come with the lightning of heaven, at every instant."

Voices were lifted:

"But when will the kingdom of heaven come?"

And he answered:

"The kingdom of heaven comes not out of words. You cannot say, it is here, or it is there; for behold, the kingdom of heaven is in you. Like the lightning which flashes from one end of the skies to the other, so will the Son of Man be in his day."

And indeed, it was as if a lightning flash had broken in our midst. For a terrified murmuring was heard in the congregation.

"But these words of his can mean only the Son, the Ancient of Days, who has been at the side of God since before the creation!"

"Oh, he can mean only the Son of Man who is to come to our salvation riding the clouds," an old Jew muttered, his body swaying

"It is 'the eagle which will rise from the sea,' it is the vision of Daniel."

And on every side was heard the question:

"Whom does he mean? Whom does he indicate?"

And the Rabbi's voice was lifted higher:

"Israel, are you not God's most beloved inheritance? The field which brings forth the first growth? The vine whose first-fruits are brought upon the Table of the Holy House? Who, then, has sown your furrows with stones, so that the plow breaks against them and is dulled?"

Impatience seized the worshipers. They cried:

"Tell us who you are!"

And the strange Rabbi opened his lips and said in a mighty voice:

"I am the bread of life. He that comes to me shall not hunger, and those that believe in me shall never thirst. I am the tree which God has planted; and those that are united with my roots shall blossom and prosper; but those that are not united with my roots shall wither. He that is thirsty, let him come to me and drink, for I am the spring of life. I am the bread which is come down from heaven. Truly, I say to you that he who believes in me shall have everlasting life."

If the heavens had opened above our heads and hosts of angels had descended to range themselves to left and right of the Rabbi of Nazareth, we could not have been more astounded and terrified. For a while we were utterly silent, as if we had been turned to stone. Then an ancient, one who sat on the stone bench by the Templeward wall, rose and asked:

"Is not this Yeshua, the son of Joseph? Do we not know his father and mother? How then does he say: 'I am come down from heaven'? What words are these?"

A second rose and said:

"There came to us Moses, telling us to believe in the Torah which he brought down from Sinai. There came to us the Prophets, telling us to believe in the living God. This one tells us to believe in him alone. Who is he? Is he greater than Moses? Greater than the Prophets?"

The murmuring increased among the worshipers, and they said to each other:

"If he speaks such words, is he not certainly a prophet?"

"No, if he were a prophet he would not utter such words; for such words can only be uttered by the Messiah."

"Messiah! Messiah! Who has dared to invoke that dread word? Earth and heaven! Has not the Writ declared that the Messiah will come of the seed of David and from the city of Bethlehem?"

And now hands were lifted and stretched forth to the Rabbi of Nazareth, terrified eyes were fastened on his white robe, lips trembled as the question was asked:

"Who are you?"

The Nazarene looked round at the congregation and answered:

"I am he whom I mentioned in the beginning. I have much to say to you and much judgment to pronounce. He that sent me to you is true. And that which I heard from him, I say to the world."

The ancient who had first risen from the stone bench turned with a question not to the Rabbi of Nazareth, but to my Rabbi, Nicodemon, saying:

"You who are a Rabbi in Israel, how can you stand by while he blasphemes the Holy One of Israel, and say nothing?"

"God forbid that I should hear blasphemy from his lips," answered Rabbi Nicodemon. "Every Jew has a right to speak in the name of the Holy One of Israel, if he has been sent with a message to us."

But here the Rabbi of Nazareth rose from the judgment seat; his *tallit* was about him, the scrolls of the Torah were in his hands. He cried:

"The voice has gone forth, who can withdraw it? The work has begun, who shall hold it back? I am the door; he that will enter through me will be saved. Truly I tell you that I am the door of the sheep. I am the good shepherd; the good shepherd lays his life down for his sheep. Even as I know the father and the father knows me, so I will lay my life down for my sheep."

As he uttered these words, the tumult increased.

"Whom does he call the father? Who is the father?"

"But do you not see that a demon sits in him? He is mad. Why do you listen to his babbling?"

"Does a demon speak thus? Can demons make the blind to see?"

"We must not and dare not hear such words," cried others, and in protest they went forth from the synagogue.

But the Nazarene stood on the pulpit, wrapped in his *tallit*, the scrolls in his hands, and he continued to preach:

"More than the young calf desires to suck, the mother desires to give her young one suck. More than you were hungry for the redeemer did my desire go out to you. Out of the clouds your Father in heaven saw your need, and he hastened to your help. And now, when salvation knocks at your door, will you keep it closed? Were you not always on the watch for the redeemer?"

But the worshipers still raised their shoulders and looked at one another and asked:

"Who is he that calls himself the salvation?"

And again hands were stretched out to him and voices called:

"Tell us who you are!"

But he continued to preach:

"The sheep know the voice of their shepherd. I am the good

shepherd and I know my sheep and my sheep know me. And as the father knows me and I know my father, so I lay down my life for my sheep. And I have other sheep, which are not of the flock, and yet I nourish them. And they will hear my voice, and there shall be but one flock and one shepherd."

But when he said this the tumult grew louder still, and there was discontent even among the poorest and simplest, who till then had listened with trusting faces. And voices called to him:

"Are we not the children of Abraham, to whom salvation has been promised? And has not God called us forth to be his peculiar people? And do we not for that reason bear upon our shoulders the yoke of the Torah?"

And others asked:

"What does he wish? To go to the gentiles? To the Greeks? Or is it to the children of Tyre and Zidon?"

And the Rabbi on the pulpit lifted his voice again:

"Listen to me! To what may this thing be likened? It may be likened to a father who had six sons, and they were born blind, but he had a seventh, and he was born seeing. And when the father was busy in the field or the barn he left the six sons in the keeping of the youngest, and he bade him lead them out to the field to work, and back to their father's table to eat. Now the blind ones hated the youngest son, with his seeing eyes, because they envied him. And when he told them of the sun which shines in the heavens by day, and of the moon and the stars which shine by night, and of the colors of the flowers, and the greenness of the field, they said that it was all lies, and the young one was a liar. They said: 'There is no light of sun or moon, and there are no colors on flowers and no greenness in fields. He has thought of these things in his mind, for there is only night over all.' Now it chanced once that a seer came to the city, and the father said to his youngest son: 'I leave your brothers in your hands while I go to the city and speak with the seer; it may be that he will restore sight to my other sons. But you take care of the light of your own eyes, for if you lose that and it is extinguished, I shall have brought a blind generation into the world.' So the father went to the city, and when he stayed there a long time the blind brothers said to each other: 'Come, let us strengthen ourselves against our youngest brother, and fall upon him and stab his eyes out, so that he shall no longer mock us. For he does nothing but mock us, in as much as there is no light, and God has covered the earth with darkness.' And they fell upon their younger brother, and they seized him and they felt his face with their hands and they touched his eyes. And they said: 'Tell us now, have you not mocked us? There is nothing but darkness in the world.' But the youngest brother cried: 'Take not away my light, the last light which is left to our generation. For if you close my eyes, too, there will be none left of our generation to see the light and to give it to the generations which shall come after us.' But the brothers answered: 'It is all lies. Confess now that you have seen no light, and that darkness reigns over the whole earth.' And when he would not listen to them, but still cried, 'I see God's light!' they tore his eyes out. But he guarded God's light in his heart and still continued to tell of the light of the sun and the moon and the stars, and the colors of the flowers and the greenness of the fields. And still he cried: 'I see! I see!' For he that has once seen the light has light within him forever, and no power can extinguish that light. And thus the youngest son guarded the memory of the light till the father returned from the city with the blessing of the seer. And when the father beheld that his youngest son, too, had become blind, he wept and lamented, saying: 'Now my old age will go down into the pit in darkness.' But the youngest son comforted him, saying: 'Father, in my darkness I see the light of God, for I have guarded the memory of it in my heart, and I have not let myself be carried away in the floods of darkness. And as often as my brothers cry Darkness! Darkness! I have answered, I see light! I see light!' And the father answered: 'My blessing be upon you. Great shall be your reward for having guarded the light throughout the darkness. Now your brothers too shall see, and they will know that God's light is upon the world. For I have brought with me the blessing of the seer. And it is better that they should have been blind till now than that they should have followed a false light; for the blind can be made to see, but woe to those that see and see falsely, for they shall be forever blind.' Then the father gave the blessing of the seer to his six sons, and their eyes were opened, and they saw the light of

God about the world. And they were ashamed of that which they had done in the darkness, and they said to their youngest brother: 'Brother, forgive us for that which we inflicted on you, and the pain and the bitterness. Happy are you who guarded the light of God.' Now is it a little thing to you, O Israel, that God has entrusted to you the light of the world for all your brothers? Great is your reward, O Israel. In your name shall the peoples of the world be blessed."

Now when the worshipers had heard this parable till the end, their spirits were calmed and they said to each other:

"Let us await the end of this thing. It may be that God has had mercy on us and has sent us a redeemer in our need. His words are good, and now we shall await his deeds."

CHAPTER NINE

NOW these words, which the Rabbi had spoken in our synagogue, soon spread throughout Jerusalem. There were some among the sages who were offended with our Rabbi that he had listened to the words of the Nazarene and had not prevented him from speaking to the end. But the common people, and those that had heard him in the synagogue, waited for the deeds which would follow the words. Meanwhile his name went before him. Wherever he went, multitudes assembled to him, not so much to listen to his words as in the expectation of miracles. And his name grew from day to day, and with it grew the expectation.

But a certain time having passed without any event of importance, the divisions of opinion concerning him became sharper. Some began to mock him and his disciples openly. When he entered into a dispute with the Sadducees on the matter of the resurrection, or told his parables to an assembly, voices would be raised, calling out the old folksaying about nothing good ever coming out of Nazareth. Unbelievers would also accost the disciples of the Rabbi, to ask, "Tell us now, when is your kingdom of heaven going to descend on us?" But others said: "You cannot know from the top of the sack what lies within. Take heed what you say of him." But the first wave of enthusiasm having passed, both they that believed and they that did not began to hold themselves at a little distance from him. Also a certain fear attached to him, because of the miracles ascribed to him; and many were afraid to touch his garment.

But the scholars were the ones most at a loss as to what to do. Often they accosted the Rabbi of Galilee, and put questions to him, to find out where he stood on the matter of the Torah. But his answers were both Yes and No. On one occasion it would appear that he was rooted in the Torah of Moses, and taught it in the accepted tradition; in which case he would be counted among the pupils of Hillel. But on another occasion it would appear that he had his own doctrine, and this was so new, so unusual, that the listeners were amazed. When they asked him whence he derived this doctrine, he answered with such authority that one could have believed he had received things from heaven, as none before him had received them excepting Moses on Sinai. More than once he intimated that such was indeed the case, and there broke out sharp disputes between him and the scholars and scribes. Often his language against these was harsh in the extreme. Therefore opinion was divided among the scholars even as among the simple people. Some said that he interpreted the law for the benefit of the unlearned, and that his parables drew men nearer to heaven, therefore his work was blessed. Others contended that he debased and cheapened the Torah, and they applied to him the old saying: "Give us neither of thy honey nor of thy sting."

Here is what I witnessed one day:

In the market place of the Lower City, where the wine and oil dealers have their great pots and jars standing in the open, a crowd had assembled. I came out of the study house with my friend Rufus, and we drew near to the crowd to find out what had happened. We perceived, at the center, the Rabbi of Nazareth, who was by now a familiar figure to us. He was easily known even at a distance by the pure white garment which he always wore. Near the Rabbi stood a battered man, whose ripped sheepskin covering indicated that he was not of Jerusalem. His face, and his body no less, bore the marks of recent violence, for the blood still dripped from him. It appeared that the disciples of the Rabbi had rescued this man, and were still defending him, for the wine and oil and honey dealers were trying to break through to him. They shouted continuously that the man had occasioned them immense loss. When we inquired of bystanders what this meant, we were told of one of those common incidents which were for ever bringing tumult into the market places of Jerusalem. A Galilean boor or man-of-the-earth—this man in the sheepskin—had come by, driving his flock before him. He was gnawing at his food, that food of the unlearned and unclean which is ritually impure, and even as he passed he had let fall a fragment of the food into one of the open jars. But then a dispute had arisen as to the jar into which he had thrown, accidentally or by design, the contaminating crumb, for which reason all the open jars on the market place could be declared corrupted and unfit for use. The Jerusalem merchants of wine, oil and honey are extremely pious, and particularly strict in the observance of the laws of purity. They accused the man of having committed the crime of set purpose; and the truth is that sometimes a "boor," hating the Jerusalemites for their knowledge of the law, and for the monopoly in trade which this knowledge conferred on them, would revenge themselves by contaminating their wares just as this man was reported to have done.

The Rabbi, passing that way with his disciples, had seen the merchants murderously beating a man. He had commanded his disciples to rescue the man from the hands of his assailants. Being told of the offense he had defended the man-of-the-earth instead of condemning him. And this surely was a new thing. A Rabbi in Israel had failed to take the part of the injured merchants; he had not called for the guard to take away the offender to the Small Court; he had rescued the man—who now stood trembling in the midst of the crowd, the blood running from his face, the hair standing in wild disorder on his head—and had comforted him, and had actually declared him to be in the right! This was something which not only roused the resentment of the merchants. Even the purchasers in the market place, and the passers-by, murmured angrily.

"Only yesterday," howled one potter, his words scarcely intelligible because of the rotting teeth which were in the way of hi tongue, "only yesterday one such unclean creature fouled ten of my pots. Everyone here knows me! I come from near by—the village of Madiah. Everyone will testify that I know the laws and commandments of purity, and my pots are ritually perfect according to all the prescriptions of the learned. While my back was turned there came a boor, a beast of a man, and squatted among my pots to eat his filthy food. It is enough that one crumb shall fly out of his mouth and touch one of my pots, to render it impure. Ten pots I had to break into fragments!" So the potter howled, and his spittle went out in a spray and fell on the bystanders.

"Ten measures of barley were lost to me in the same way but a week ago," another shouted. "All the good people here know me. I bring to this market only grain which has paid the tithe and offering, therefore the most pious may buy thereof. I too live near by, in Modiin, so that I am within the range of the permission of the Rabbis. There came a seller of grain from a place I do not know, and poured his barley among mine, and spoiled ten measures. And he did it of set purpose."

"And me!" cried a third. "The other day a boor flung a piece of meat into my oils. They all do it on purpose. Let this man be dragged to the judgment."

The man of Nazareth looked mournfully at the excited merchants. He stretched his hands in the direction of the Temple and called out:

"Woe unto you, Pharisees. Your laws are more precious to you than the will of God. You destroy with your rulings the word of our father in heaven."

The multitude, hearing these words, was astounded. Voices were lifted:

"What has it to do with the Pharisees, if men-of-the-earth come here and contaminate our vessels?"

"Not the mouse is the thief, but the hole in which it hides!" cried one of the Rabbi's disciples. And turning, I caught sight of Judah Ish-Kiriot, or rather of his wagging beard, for more of him I could not see.

The Rabbi addressed the multitude again:

"Hear me, all of you, and understand me. Nothing that comes

into the man from without can make him unclean. Only that which issues from within can make him unclean."

The listeners shrank back, their mouths wide open.

"What does he say? What does he mean?" Voices broke about me. "Are there no more laws of purity and impurity for us Jews? Shall we become like the heathen?"

"Lusts, lies, evil thoughts, which come forth from within you, these are the things that make you unclean. But not food which enters into you, food which God created for man!" Thus the disciples of the Rabbi interpreted his words.

But the interpretation was not acceptable. Someone shouted: "Here one comes and flings down all the Torah of Moses, and the sages of Jerusalem know it and are silent."

"No, he does not fling down the Torah of Moses. Do you not know who speaks there? It is the prophet of Galilee."

"What? He of whom they say—"

"Yes, it is he. But ask not for clear words. Only hints and intimations shall be given. And the Messiah ben David shall himself make all things clear." These words were uttered by Judah Ish-Kiriot.

"Messiah ben David." An uneasy whispering broke out in the multitude, like a wind among ears of grain. The people began to draw off from the figure of the Rabbi, as if he were untouchably sacred. The report of his miracles was like a visible light about him. The merchants and the bystanders said no more, though if they had heard such words as his from another, they would surely have stoned him.

When Rufus and I came running back to the house of study, and told Rabbi Nicodemon of what we had seen and heard, repeating accurately all that the Nazarene had said against the Torah, we were astonished by the calmness with which he received it. For instead of starting to the fiery defense of the law, he fell into meditative silence; and coming out of it, he calmed us with these words:

"Even the ordinary converse of a sage merits study. And if one hear, from the mouth of a sage or scholar, things which at first seem incomprehensible, and which seem, indeed, to stand in contradiction to the Torah, we must still withold our suspicions; better ascribe to ourselves lack of comprehension than unwisdom or worse to him. Now as regards the Rabbi of Nazareth, it is well known that he is a pious and observant Jew. It is also well known to all that he is careful of the honor of the Torah, for he has himself announced: 'The whole world shall pass away before a single jot or tittle of the Law of Moses.' Therefore we must believe that there is reason in the discourse you have just heard. And if we do not understand him, he will in good time furnish proof that his words are those of the living God."

Thus Rabbi Nicodemon spoke, to quieten our spirits and allay our fears.

It happened once that we, the pupils of the Rabbi, were carrying his vessels, utensils and preparations for him to the bath, as the custom is: the vial of oil for anointment, his shirt, and his change of apparel. We passed thus through one of the streets which leads into the market place for vegetables; here the farmers who live in the neighborhood of Jerusalem come to dispose of their wares. Near one of the booths a crowd was assembled, and in the midst of it stood the Rabbi of Nazareth, preaching loudly and in perturbation of spirit. About him were market women, camel drivers, porters, and idlers. Certain of the shopkeepers, too, had left their stalls to draw near. Much to our surprise, our own Rabbi Nicodemon turned aside and mingled with the crowd to listen to the words of the Galilean. But they were such words as we had never heard before. They were like whips, laden with lead, falling upon the heads of the sages, the scholars, the scribes and Pharisees.

"The scribes and Pharisees," he thundered, "sit upon the seat of Moses. Therefore that which they bid you observe, that you shall observe. But beware of doing according to their deeds, for that which they say they do not. They lay upon the shoulders of men burdens which they cannot bear, but they themselves will not touch the burden even with a finger. And whatever deeds they do perform are performed in the sight of all men. They make broad the straps of their phylacteries, they lengthen the fringes of their garments, they love the foremost places at the banquets, and they stand in the foremost places in the synagogues. They love to be greeted in the streets, the people calling to them: 'Rabbi! Rabbi!' But you shall not say 'Rabbi!' to them. For only one is your teacher, and he is the

Messiah, and all of you are brothers. You shall not call anyone father on earth, for only one is your father, and that is your Father in heaven."

I glanced in terror at my Rabbi, and I saw that the blood had withdrawn from his face, so that the skin was pale to the roots of his hair. He turned and left the assembly, we following him. We still heard behind us the thunder of the Nazarene, directed against the scribes and Pharisees, and we wondered that no one had opposed him or answered him. And even our Rabbi, who was known to the people, and for whom they made a path, had let pass in silence the challenge to the Rabbinic leadership of the Pharisees. And we were filled with wonder.

But when we were at a certain distance from the crowd, we suddenly beheld Judah Ish-Kiriot in our midst. He had seen us and followed, leaving his own Rabbi.

"What has happened, that he speaks thus?" our Rabbi asked.

"Peasants came in from the country, bringing their greens for sale. They sold at prices below those demanded by the farmers about Jerusalem. Then the overseers of the Rabbis came and declared the greens of the countrymen to be impure. Thereupon the villagers from the country demanded to know why the overseers did not investigate the vegetable growers of Jerusalem, to find out whether they observed the tithing of herbs. Thereupon the overseers answered: 'The farmers of Jerusalem, all those that are this side of Modiin, are within the permit, for it is considered that they know the law. But you come from the land, and you are ignorant as to the observance of the law.' Thereupon the farmers from the land raised a bitter outcry against the scholars and scribes and Pharisees. They said that the learned men favored certain of the people and discriminated against others. And then the women, who had bought the cheaper vegetables for their household use, had to return them, and buy the costlier kind, whereat many of them wept. The Rabbi of Galilee was passing at that moment, and his anger was roused. Then he mounted on the steps of a booth and began to speak against the Pharisees."

My Rabbi lowered his voice—but not so much that I could not hear him—and said to Judah:

"That is not what I am asking about, neither the cause of the tumult nor his speech against the Pharisees. Their good name rests where it always has rested. But did you hear, Judah, what he said about the one teacher, who is the Messiah? Is it his intention to be revealed in Jerusalem?"

"This was what he said in K'far Nahum."

"When will it happen?"

"I do not know. He has not yet spoken concerning the day."

When our Rabbi returned from the path, we summoned our courage and dared to ask him the following:

"Teach us, Rabbi. We beheld you the witness of insult aimed at the honor of the sages, the scribes, and the Pharisees; but you did not turn aside to defend them. How shall we understand that?"

Then the Rabbi answered:

"The wisest of all men, King Solomon, has said: 'The punishers are sweet, and the blessing of God shall be on them.' Thence we may deduce that if one punishes and rebukes his friend out of a true heart, in order that his friend may repent, then the punishment and rebuke are for the sake of heaven; and the punisher shall be blessed. Because of the sinfulness of our times, there are indeed many among the learned who use the Torah as a crown to glory in, but they do not wear the Torah as a yoke. They have made great their own name in order that they may rule over the people. Now those scholars who loudly sing the praises of the Lord in order that they may be rewarded like Phineas—they will be filled with hatred against him who spoke those words. But those who are moved by the true will of heaven will love him. As King Solomon has said: 'Punish the wise man, and he will love you for it.' Now surely the Rabbi of Galilee was filled with the will of heaven. For did he not say to the people: 'The scribes and Pharisees sit in the seat of Moses; that which they say, hasten to do.' He did not speak against the Torah and her true interpreters, but against the learned men of false spirit, who have woven of the Torah a garment with which to cover the shame of their nakedness."

But in spite of what my Rabbi said, I could not understand how it was that the Pharisaic scholars of Jerusalem did not make an attack on the Rabbi of Galilee. It seemed to me that any Rabbi who uttered such words as the Galilean had uttered, against the laws of purity and impurity, would have been haled before the Sanhedrin. Indeed, I thought at times that the Galilean Prophet (such was the name which began to cling to him) was intent on such a challenge. Far from fearing death, it was as though he was seeking out the Slaying Angel. His denunciations of the scribes and Pharisees were not confined to the streets and market places; he flung them to multitudes in the Temple courts. And still the Rabbis made no response. Was it that they held him of no account? For sometimes I marked how certain of the pupils of the House of Shammai would pass him, as he sat on the steps of a niche, surrounded by his followers, holding forth on the resurrection, on Eden and Hell; one or two would stop, listen for a while, then raise his shoulders, smile in mockery, and pass on. Yes, I heard some of them call him *shoteh*, which signifies madman or fool. Nevertheless, as I knew well, there were scholars a-plenty who nourished, in the secret places of their hearts, great hopes concerning this man of wonders. For it was not the rumor of his deeds alone which had given him his name; that might have sufficed for the unlearned masses. There was also that about him, in his demeanor and bearing, which could not be denied. Many of those that saw him standing in his white garb and in his *tallit*, preaching to the people of the holiest things in Israel, could not but be moved. One would say to another: "Who can tell? Perhaps he is the One."

Was it this that held the scholars back from denouncing him for his harsh words and accusations? Certain is it that his words often went home like arrows, and that among the zealots of the schools of Shammai there was deep resentment.

Now the Sadducees looked on the Rabbi of Galilee as one who had lost his wits. When they came into the Temple court, and chanced to see the Galilean, seated or standing, surrounded by crowds of the poor and preaching of the resurrection, they rebuked the guards and the Levites for permitting him to spread this nonsense among the rabble. They carried their complaint, too, to higher authorities, and there was some talk in upper circles of forbidding him to air these views within the Temple precincts. But this would have been regarded by the Pharisees as an infringement of general rights, for they asserted that he was within the law, and had the support of the Torah, in such matters. Likewise the Sadducean authorities took into account the throngs of the poor who were the principal auditors of the Rabbi. The poor, such as those of the Kidron valley, had so little of the happiness of this world, that they grasped at the consolation of the world to come which he pictured in such shining colors. The leaders of the Temple reflected that it might be worth while to let "the fool of Galilee" lull the masses in dreams of the future; for this would surely discourage them from participation in rebellions against the House of Hanan and the power of Rome, such as were fomented by Bar Abba. Therefore they let him continue preaching, and some of them were even glad to have him preach. They were inclined to take that which offended them with that which helped, and turned a deaf ear to those utterances which made him liable to judgment by the Sanhedrin.

When he spoke of the kingdom of heaven, the Galilean stormed the hearts of the listeners; he made it appear that this kingdom was his private domain, which he would distribute among all those who listened and obeyed. But he also filled some with terror, in that he seemed to identify himself with the Supreme Holiness of Israel. Therefore his followers, too, quarreled with each other. And if it chanced that others were present when such words were flung to the masses, the tumult was great. I was present when certain of the followers of the House of Shammai objected violently to his views, and my own Rabbi Nicodemon suffered insult because he was a defender of the Galilean.

It happened in the time of the rains. The Pharisaic scholars were preaching in the Basilica of Herod which is near the entrance to the Temple, and in sundry other places in the court itself; they sat by their braziers, their pupils gathered about them. My Rabbi came, in the company of his pupils, to hear the words of Jochanan ben Zakkai. Suddenly there was an interruption. One of the Shammaites, known as a great zealot, came running in our direction with the cry:

"I say that this is rebellion against heaven. The man should be taken before the judgment and condemned to the lash." And as he shouted his earlocks danced with the violence of his speech.

Then others came running, and added their protest to his:

"Who has ever heard the like before from the mouth of a Rabbi in Israel?"

We turned, and beheld at a little distance an assembly gathered about the Rabbi of Galilee, in one of the arcades along the rows of columns. Among the listeners, most of them the poor, were also young pupils of the Rabbinic schools, Levites, and neophytes of the Priesthood. The crowd was in an uproar. Some gesticulated wildly as they shouted, others were trying to calm them.

Now we, the Rabbi Nicodemon and his pupils, were passing that way, going toward the assembly of Jochanan ben Zakkai. My Rabbi would have avoided the tumult. But this was not in the streets of Jerusalem, but in the Temple courts. It was a long time since such a turmoil had arisen here, for this was not a festival time, when the area is crowded with pilgrims. We could not avoid the throng; so our Rabbi drew near, and we with him. The Rabbi of Galilee, continued his sermon; or, no, it was not a sermon, but a speech of denunciation. He towered like a prophet above the throng, and his words descended like thunderbolts. He was draped in his *tallit*, and on his head were the phylacteries. He lifted up his uncovered arms from under his robe, and his cry came forth from his distorted mouth, which even from a distance spoke of pain and sorrow:

"Exert yourselves, that you may enter through the narrow way. For I tell you that many will seek to come in, and will not be able, for the master of the house will rise and will lock the door. You will stand without and cry: 'Lord, Lord, let us enter.' And the master of the house will answer: 'I know you not. Whence are you?' Then you will say: 'We ate and drank with you, and you taught in our streets.' Still he will cry: 'I know you not. Who are you? Begone from me!' Then there will be wailing and gnashing of teeth among you, when you will see Abraham, Isaac, and Jacob and all the Prophets entering into the kingdom, while you remain without. Then men will come from east and west, from north and south, and they will enter into the kingdom, and the last shall be first and the first shall be last."

To this he added:

"I am the light of the world. He that follows me shall not walk in darkness, but shall be in the light of life."

But at this point the momentary silence was broken, and a tall man with earlocks that stood away from his cheeks shrieked in the face of the Rabbi:

"But what is this? You bear witness to yourself, and your testimony is false."

The Rabbi answered:

"Even if I bear witness to myself, my testimony is true. For I know whence I come, and whither I go. But you do not know whence I come and whither I go. You make judgment still according to the flesh, but I am not alone, for there are two, my Father and I, and my Father sent me. And it is written in the Torah: 'Two witnesses shall establish the truth of a thing.' Now I bear witness to myself, and likewise my Father, who sent me."

The assembly surged back and forth; faces flamed. A voice shouted:

"Where is your father?"

The Rabbi answered:

"You know me not. Neither do you know my Father. If you knew me, you would also know my Father."

Here the storm broke forth in full force. For not one voice, but many voices yelled:

"Who has ever heard such words from Jewish lips?"

"But if he is that which he says he is, then he can say all things, for he has the authority," screamed one old man, turning his almost sightless eyes to the crowd, and pointing backward with his finger to the preacher.

"But *who* is he? Who speaks thus?" came the stormy questions.

Then hundreds of arms were lifted toward the Rabbi; white, weary, frightened faces were bent on him in supplication, and the cry arose:

"Who are you? Tell us who you are!"

Silence fell again. But the Rabbi answered them, as was his wont, in hints:

"I am the same as I told you in the beginning. I have much to say and many to judge. He that sent me to you is the truth, and what you have heard from me, that he has entrusted to me."

"But don't you all see that the man is witless? His words are formless, without meaning!" yelled one.

"No! No! If he speaks thus, there is something in it, and he doubtless has authority for it."

"Drag him to the judgment! This is impudence in the face of heaven!"

"Did you hear him? He would exclude us from the kingdom of heaven. He has favorites of his own. He has his own sons of Abraham, for whom he reserves the kingdom. Did you not hear? 'They shall come from the east and west, and they shall sit down with Abraham, Isaac and Jacob.' Does it not mean that he would shut us out?"

"Drag him to the courts!"

"Are we not the descendants of Abraham, Isaac, and Jacob, we, whom you would leave without?"

There was a lull, and the Rabbi answered:

"If you were the descendants of Abraham, Isaac, and Jacob you would imitate the deeds of Abraham."

The lull broke. Storm broke again:

"We will not bear it! An evil spirit sits in him! He is mad!"

But one powerful voice was heard:

"These are not words which come from an evil spirit."

Then those that were nearest the Rabbi took up the supplication, and begged him, as in one voice:

"Why do you keep us in doubt? If you are the Messiah, say it openly."

"Who has uttered that word of dread?"

"May that tongue be silenced for ever!"

Still they continued to beg him:

"How long will you keep us in doubt? Tell us."

I do not know what the issue would have been if the disciples of the Rabbi, those that encircled him closest, had not been his guard. I saw one powerful man, whom I already knew as Simon, a fisherman of Galilee, open his arms before the Rabbi. Jochanan, of the sons of Zebedee, was also there, and with him Simon the Zealot and others. But likewise the poor, yes, and even the halt and the lame, lifted their fists. Fighting had already begun, clothes were torn from bodies, when our Rabbi forced his way through the throng, and called out:

"Is it part of our Torah that a man shall be judged before it is known what he has done?"

Without knowing yet who it was that spoke, the outer ring of the crowd yelled at Rabbi Nicodemon:

"He has excluded the children of Abraham from the kingdom of heaven. He would exchange strangers for the true descendants of Abraham."

Our Rabbi flung back:

"In the Torah it is written: 'Ye shall not let a stranger sleep without.' What does the word 'without' mean? Our sages taught: Let not a stranger be excluded from the Jewish fold. A stranger who acknowledges the one living God, who has turned to the God of Israel, is as one of the Jews, and is of the children of Abraham, even like us. For Abraham is the father not only of those that were born to the Jews; he is likewise the father of the converted stranger. Was it not the special virtue of Abraham that he took strangers into the fold?"

"But I have just heard him say: 'He that will listen to my words, he shall never die!' Is he, then, greater than Abraham? Abraham and the prophets have died, and he says that some shall never die."

"But he speaks of the eternal life," my Rabbi answered. "The life of the kingdom of heaven."

"But why does he torment us with hints, and unclear words? Why does he not tell us who he is, if he takes upon himself this authority?"

"Who is he?" a mocking voice was heard. "I will tell you. He is a Samaritan!"

This was the greatest insult that could be thrown in the face of a Jew. But my Rabbi answered:

"Even of a Samaritan is it written: 'And thou shalt love thy neighbor as thyself.'"

"You have spoken well, Rabbi!"

"He has made himself the judge and master here. He is the one who opens and shuts the door. Whence has he authority?"

"But you have heard. 'I do not for myself, I do it as my father taught me.' "

"Then he would say that he is God's son. For that power and authority indicate God!"

"Every man has the right to call himself God's son. It is written: 'Sons you are to the Lord your God,' " my Rabbi answered.

"But he speaks against the Temple, and against the altar and the sacrifices," cried a rich Sadducean on the outskirts of the crowd. (We knew him as such by his rich garment, and by the rings on his fingers.)

"But the Prophet too has said: 'I desire justice, not sacrifices.' And who of us is greater than Jeremiah? And did not Jeremiah call the Temple a den of murderers?" my Rabbi retorted.

"Jeremiah was a prophet."

"Every Jew can be a prophet!"

"But has it ever been heard that a prophet shall come from Galilee?"

"It is written: 'All the earth is filled with His glory.' His graciousness fills the land, and from any corner of it may arise a prophet, to whom God has entrusted His word."

"Who says this?" yelled one who did not know my Rabbi. "Are you perchance also a Galilean?"

But others answered him stormily: "Fool, that is the great Rabbi Nicodemon!"

Thereupon a murmur spread through the crowd, men began to withdraw, and the multitude melted away.

From this time on the gatherings about the Prophet of Galilee became more and more turbulent and the opinions concerning him more and more sharply divided. His followers grew more devoted, his opponents more bitter. Enthusiasts of the House of Shammai, jealous for the Torah and the Lord, lurked in wait, hoping that they would overhear him utter something which no amount of exegesis could cleanse of the charge of apostasy or blasphemy. But everything he said was indirect, even if daring, so that interpretation could always save him from the rigor of the law. He was never placed beyond the pale of the Torah. I myself once witnessed such a scene: zealots of the House of Shammai in a conspiracy to tempt the Rabbi of Galilee into a fatal utterance.

On this occasion the Rabbi was accompanied not only by sundry of his disciples, but also by a woman. She was veiled closely from head to foot, so that her head and hands were covered, as was considered proper for women entering the Temple court. As she went, she led by the hand one of the disciples, who was blind. Now on this occasion the Rabbi had not come forth to preach. He simply went along with others who were proceeding to the treasury of the Temple in order to make their payments, for it was the time of the collection of the Temple taxes. The woman who was with the disciples of the Rabbi had also brought her gift. Then suddenly a man who stood near by recognized the woman, by her figure, and by the manner of her walk—for he could not see her face. And he called out to the treasurers:

"Beware of taking a gift from this woman. It is the gift of a harlot, and the money is tainted."

There was then, as always at such seasons, a great throng about the office of the treasurers. When the words were heard, "gift of a harlot," a wave of agitation passed through the press, heads were lifted, necks were craned. The man pointed to the woman and cried:

"Do you not know who she is? She is Miriam of Migdal, the famous Miriam of Migdal."

No sooner was this heard, than it seemed as though the entire crowd in the Temple courts gathered to the place. For certainly the woman was famous, for her one-time wealth, her lovers, her perfumes and her beauty. Miriam of Migdal, or Miriam Magdala, was a byword in the city. I too was drawn in the direction of the Rabbi, and I managed to get a glimpse of the heavily veiled woman. And then suddenly two men had taken her by the hands, and had brought her face to face with the Rabbi of Galilee.

"Rabbi," said one of them, "the woman you see has been taken in adultery and has often sinned. Now Moses taught us that such a woman should be stoned. What have you to say, Rabbi?"

A deathly silence fell on the throng, and all eyes were fixed on the Rabbi, who had turned pale. Suddenly he started from the spot, rushed over to where the men were holding the woman by the hands, and freed her. Then, as he stood by her, he made a circle on the ground, about himself and her; and the crowd started back in fear.

They waited, breathless with expectancy, for what the Rabbi would do. But he did nothing. He stood within the invisible circle which his finger had outlined, and it was clear that thereby he indicated that he shared the fate of this woman, that he had taken upon himself her sin, that he and she were now one. The assembly understood, and said nothing. But one of the two men—they were pupils of the House of Shammai—cried out:

"Tell us, Rabbi, shall we stone her, according to the law of Moses?"

The Rabbi lifted his head, looked round at the multitude and answered:

"He that is without sin among you, let him throw the first stone."

The two Shammaites found no word for the moment. Other voices were raised:

"Let the woman remove her veil, that we may see if it is really Miriam of Migdal."

Then the Rabbi turned to the woman and said: "Miriam, take the veil from your head and face, that the people may know who you are."

When the woman had removed her veil, and the people saw her face, they drew back from her with a gasp, jaws dropped, and a murmur arose:

"What? Is this Miriam of Migdal?"

I was amazed. Was this indeed the Miriam of Migdal whose beauty was a proverb in Jerusalem? Her long face was worn and yellow, covered with folds and creases as if a stormy sea had washed over it. Her big eyes, still lustrous, were deep withdrawn in dark sockets, and under them were the sacs, which were like dark clouds from which an endless rain of tears had poured, to run down the ravines of her skin. Only her lips, thin, delicate, and curved in a mournful smile, the finely formed nose and the shape of her chin, bore witness to a beauty that once had been.

"This is not Miriam of Migdal, this is Naomi," a woman called out. "Miriam is like a rose in bloom, her breasts are full, her body is blessed. Look how she stands, fallen and broken, a woman who has lost all her grace."

"It is Miriam of Migdal! See what has become of her!" cried another.

"A Ruth went forth to him in Galilee, and there returned a Naomi," croaked a third, pityingly.

So it was; there stood at the Rabbi's side not the famous and sinful Miriam of Migdal, but a Naomi sated with sorrows.

The people let their eyes drop in shame, and turned from the scene.

CHAPTER TEN

THE Rabbi of Galilee was not always like the stormy sea of a winter day. He could be as tranquil as the midday sun of summer. For the proud and powerful his tongue became a flashing sword; for the poor and forlorn it was a well of comfort and hope.

The Rabbi of Galilee appeared in places which the foot of no other Rabbi in Israel had trodden. He sat at table with those whom the others regarded as wicked, and of whom they said: "Let my soul keep far from them."

All this was already known in Jerusalem; but that he should go into the hostelry of the camel drivers and donkey drivers, and sit down at their table to drink with them and with shepherds—this was beyond the expectation and belief of anyone.

But I myself once chanced upon him in this very hostelry.

At the northwest corner of the city, far down in the valley, was the Dung Gate. The wall in which this gate was set divided off the city from two valleys, that of the Kidron, and that of Hinnom. But there was another wall, ruined and decayed, "the old wall," which ran about the alley of the watercarriers by the river Siloah. This wall had been built in the days of David.

Between these two walls lived the poorest of Jerusalem's poor. In the winter, when the Siloah overflowed, the ravine became a sea of mud, and the filth of the Upper City was carried down into it by the rains. The damp had eaten into the miserable foundations of the houses, and the cellar caves were flooded. In the summer, when the mud was dried, a foul miasma still rose from the bed of the Siloah and mingled with the clouds of dust and the blasts of unbearable odors which issued from the houses. The mephitic vapor settled down in layers on men and houses; it ate into the eyes of the children; and it bred indescribable diseases.

The old, ruined wall of King David had many niches, hollows, fragments of steps and overhanging galleries which had been added to it in the course of the ages. There were also great holes which the mighty battering rams of ancient eastern kings had broken in the wall during the wars. The memorials of these far-off sieges invested the gray structure with something that hinted at the age and endurance of the Jewish people itself; and it was as if the poor clung to the place because it was the inheritance that had come down to them from their glorious forefathers. Little grave dwellings had been chiseled into the one-time fortress, huts leaned against it, bound to protruding stones with rope and covered with mattresses and sackcloth and woven twigs. Families had dwelt here for generations, each with its own rights come down from of old; and often there were fierce struggles as to the boundaries of such rights, which had become traditions, undefined but deep-rooted.

The press of inhabitants in the David wall was so great that it occasioned frequent disaster. Corridors and tunnels had been cut in and under the wall, and people dwelt in these like moles. Now and again overhanging masonry would topple down and crush houses or passers-by. In my time one such catastrophe, of unusual extent, occurred. Eighteen men, women and children were engulfed under a tower which collapsed when the understructure had become so fragile with digging that it could no longer support the vast weight.

Close to the David wall stood the hostelry of the camel and donkey drivers. It consisted of a large court, or rather of a labyrinth of courts, marked off by hedges of woven branches. The hostelry proper, or lodging house, was built into the wall. From it rose perpetually an offensive odor of cooking and broiling, while the smoke which poured through its door laid a black coat on the vast, time-worn stones towering over the building. Not only drivers were to be found in the hostelry. (Inasmuch as it stood outside the strict city limits, the Rabbis had ruled that those who brought provisions to Jerusalem from the provinces could pass the night there.) Shepherds who drove their flocks to the market also used this hostelry. Drivers and shepherds alike had an evil name, the latter more than the former. They were held to be a thievish lot. They robbed their employers; and it was forbidden to purchase wool, cheese, milk or any livestock from them direct, since in most cases these supplies had been stolen. The hostelry also harbored other suspected persons, runaway slaves, escaped criminals, and the worst of the Galilean "men-of-the-earth." There would likewise be found here an occasional Samaritan, a Greek, or a Moabite Arab from the rock-city of Petra, generally in Jerusalem for no good purpose. Political agitators also frequented the place, less to spread their ideas than to hire fighters or even murderers. Sometimes a couple of Roman legionaries or Askelonites came down, to drink wine mixed with honey, or to swill beer. There were quarrels and brawls; knives were drawn; and the cause was usually some black-skinned Arab harlot, or a soft Samaritan woman; for these too were among the visitors and guests.

I had occasion to come into the hostelry. Now and again my Rabbi would send me with a message to Hillel the watercarrier, who had business here. He was a remarkable man, this Hillel. My Rabbi pointed at him the verse of the Writ: "He sitteth alone, for he hath taken silence on himself." I saw him often among the Companionship, and in the synagogue. When he visited the latter he sat among the poor at the entrance, his head sunk between his high shoulders, listening to the discourse of my Rabbi and to the questions of the scholars. But he never asked a question or joined in the discussion. Those that saw him seated thus felt that his shoulders, which were lifted against the pressure of the many skins of water he had carried in his life, were laden with another burden—the burden of all the sorrows of the world. But he uttered no complaint; instead, he seemed to be asking forgiveness for taking up room. The house—if such it can be called—of this man was in the King David wall. He had a niche, like the cave-dwellers of Petra, to which the entrance was a narrow flight of steps. This was "an inheritance" from his forefathers. He was often in the hostelry, among the camels and donkeys. During the day he carried supplies of water in asses' skins, from the Siloah to the market place, and as he went through the streets he seemed to be dragging on his back and shoulders the swollen carcasses of animals. Returning from his day's labors, he would not take his rest until he had watered the animals in the court of the hostelry, for it often happened that the drivers themselves, arriving in the city, took to drinking and fell asleep without attending to their charges; and Hillel could not rest because of the thought of the thirsty beasts. He could hear their plaintive whimpering and neighing from his cave; and often enough he would also go out to them in the morning, before he began his work for the day. He would carry skinful after skinful of water from the river to the troughs in the court. Therefore the best place to visit, when he was needed, was the ill-famed gathering place of the donkey and camel drivers.

My Rabbi and Hillel were often together; oftener now than ever before. There seemed to be secret matters for them to discuss. After a time I discovered their nature. Hillel the watercarrier brought reports to my Rabbi concerning the words and deportment of the Rabbi of Galilee, whom he encountered now and again in the hostelry.

I cannot forget the strange impression produced on me when I first saw the Galilean Rabbi among the rabble of the hostelry. I had come, of course, in search of Hillel. The room in which I stood waiting was dark with steam and smoke. The little oil lamps could not pierce through the heavy-laden air; they shed their light only on the tables. The smoke went up in spirals from the three-legged brazier over which the innkeeper and his assistants were preparing food; they were roasting meat over the flames, and cooking meal and vegetables in large pots. The cloud that went up formed into a heavy, floating canopy; and all around the room, guessed at rather than seen, sat and lay the customers. There were also little scattered tables, at which were placed those that could pay for the luxury of a stool. I caught glimpses of rags, of half-naked bodies, wild heads of hair, hairy legs, and backs, innumerable backs. There was a tumult of voices, a yelling, an exchange of jests and insults. It appeared that a rich man had entered the hostelry that evening; he had taken a table and ordered a sumptuous meal, two roast sides of lamb—which the owner of the inn himself was now preparing for him. The man of wealth had also ordered a jar of costly wine, and olives of the city of Shefchani—no others would do for him. These were famous and expensive. Those that heard the command were filled with envy, and mouths watered. When the innkeeper served up the roasted meat, men rose from their tables, or from their places round the walls, and drew near.

"A poor man may be likened to a dead man," said one, licking his chops.

"Who is wealthy? He that rejoices in his portion," cried another, and added: "Bring me a pot of beans and a wheaten cake."

"I say, skin dead horses in the streets, but ask no charity. Even if he were to send a messenger to invite me to the feast, and with the messenger a wreath to crown my head, I would not eat at his table," a third cried haughtily, and wiped away the spittle that dropped from his jaws. "The wheaten cake which the poor man eats he has earned with the labor of his hands, and it is therefore sweeter than honey." Thereupon he thrust some dried peas into his mouth, and chewed mightily.

"Innkeeper, bring me another measure of wine, and see that you add the right proportion of honey and sycamore figs," cried the man of wealth, to provoke the envious bystanders.

Someone called out mockingly, imitating the fat voice of the feasting man: "And bring me a stuffed capon, filled with spices and served on a Zidonian platter; likewise a skin of Cypriot wine!"

"He that multiplies flesh increases the worms that shall eat it," came from a skeleton-lean man, who hovered over the table.

"Let me but enjoy this world, and I give the worms leave to feed on me in the next world," the big eater answered with a roar of laughter.

"It is true enough: bastard children are known for their cleverness," someone flung at him.

The arrow went home; the rich man glared round him furiously: "Who dares put suspicion on my mother's name?"

"Slaves have neither fathers nor mothers," said several.

"Innkeeper! Bring me a jug of Jericho date wine. And send out for a fluteplayer. I want music with my meal!" Thus the solitary banqueter mocked the bystanders.

"And send for a couple of keening women, too! The Angel of Death stands at his elbow."

"Easy money! He deals in unpaid taxes!" The speaker meant thereby a dealer in untithed and therefore illegal grain.

"Not he! He's a collector for the Sons of Hanan. He flays the skin off the poor. That's why he thinks nothing of his shekels."

"A tax gatherer!"

"A Samaritan!"

"A foul sinner!"

"Wait a while! Bar Abba will soon have his legions, and then we'll have our reckoning with the likes of you. Hew down the tree, the branches will fall of themselves."

"Who said that?" squealed the innkeeper, terrified. "We don't know of any Bar Abba round here."

"I'm not afraid to mention him. Does it matter what kills you, the sword of hunger or the sword of Edom?"

"Leave me out of this, and don't invite disaster on my house. We don't know Bar Abba and we've never seen him. We don't even know what he looks like," the innkeeper pleaded.

"Ho, ho! We know him well enough here. I'm not afraid to say it. And if you want to know, I'm one of his men. Wait till the Galileans come up this Passover, there'll be another exodus from Egypt."

"Good people, have pity on my house, the hounds of the sons of Hanan have their noses everywhere," the innkeeper implored.

"Now I know where I am," the banqueter declared, rising from the table. "This is a den of Bar Abba-ites. I won't eat with robbers and dagger men." He fled toward the door.

"Stop him! Stop him!" yelled the innkeeper. "My money! He's been eating and swilling this hour past." And leaving his brazier he pursued the man.

The bystanders only laughed loudly. "The boozer has his eye in his cup, the shopkeeper in his purse," roared one. The man was gone!

At first no one noticed who had entered, for the corner by the door was unillumined. We heard only a rustling sound, as if the wind had blown in. Then we saw him, white-clad, glimmering in the half-darkness. He was followed by several others: I recognized them after a while, Simon, Jochanan, Judah, and also Hillel the watercarrier, for whom I was waiting.

I had heard of it, and yet I could not believe my eyes. The Rabbi of Galilee among such people!

But as soon as they perceived him the uproar died down. It seemed that most of those present were by no means as surprised as I. But one man, still carried by the riotous mood of a moment past, let fall the jibe:

"What does a priest in a burial ground?"

But his neighbors silenced him, thrusting rough elbows into his ribs. Naked heads were lifted from the benches and mattresses around the walls, and their eyes followed the footsteps of the Rabbi, who advanced to the center of the room and sat down, his disciples doing likewise. The innkeeper pushed a small, empty table toward them, and placed oil lamps on it. To my astonishment he also brought forward a gourd flask and several earthen cups. Judah took his purse from his girdle and laid down some coins in payment. Simon poured out for his Rabbi.

Soon strange creatures began crawling from the dark walls and corners; they did not rise, but formed a circle on the floor around the Rabbi's table. They were the ordinary donkey and camel drivers, some of them still holding their whips in their hands. The Rabbi addressed them, some by name, asking after the peace of their families and their animals too. Then he commanded Judah to order more date wine and more cups.

I was petrified with astonishment. I had never seen the like: a *chaver*, a learned companion of the learned, and a Rabbi to boot, seating himself among miserable drivers, tax collectors, half-heathens, men-of-the-earth, who are accounted utterly impure. Here he was, not only conversing with them, but drinking with them, as though they were members of one companionship of the wise, the knowers of the law.

The Rabbi spoke with them of daily and familiar matters. He

touched first on their labor, and on their beasts. And as he spoke he marked in the hand of one listener an awl, such as drivers used on lazy animals; they would pierce the hide, leaving a wound which they would not let heal, so that whenever the beast of burden became obstinate, and would not move, they could thrust the awl again into the raw flesh. The Rabbi bent down, took the implement from the man's hand, then began to speak of the virtue of kindness to all living creatures. He told them that when they tormented their beasts of burden, these cried to God, and the Holy One would demand reckoning of the owners of the beasts, for all living things were His; when He delivered one of His creatures into the keeping of a man, He held the man to accountability. He went on to say that in the measure that we show pity to God's creatures, God would show pity to us. As he spoke thus, a rough, rebellious voice was lifted from the darkness:

"Will He that has no pity for the chosen of creation have pity on beasts? We know the good words of the wise. Their tongues drip honey, but they place the yoke of their laws about our necks."

Heads were turned in the direction of the daring speaker, and some called out:

"Shut your mouth! It is full of scorpions and crawling things."

But the mouth that was full of scorpions and crawling things refused to be shut. It thundered:

"Where is He, your God of goodness? Why does He look on while the wicked man places his foot on the neck of the just, and remain silent?"

"Come to me, all you that are crushed of spirit," the Rabbi said.

There rose out of the darkness a colossus, a Samson figure, but not blind; and as the man advanced he sent his voice before him. He came toward the light and we saw his open mouth, a black hole, foam-flecked and set with smashed and rotting teeth like the stumps of felled trees: a Samson with bloodshot, seeing eyes which blinked as he came within the circle of the lamps. His mighty body was covered with nothing but a shirt of sackcloth held together at the waist by a rawhide rope. The voice roared continuously:

"If there is any justice in heaven, I call it to trial even as Job did."

The Rabbi stretched out his hands and said:

"Come to me, and tell me what oppresses your heart. Who has thus shamed you?"

"Who has thus shamed me? All of those people, the Priests and the learned."

"Tell me, then, how this thing fell out?"

A place was made for the giant at the table. Simon poured out wine for him, and the man, taking his seat, began his recital.

"Joseph is my name in Israel, and I am of the family of the Ephrathites in Israel. My inheritance of land was in Jericho, a garden of date trees, twenty rows of them. My grandfather planted them, and my father already gathered their fruit. Twelve measures of dates I gave yearly to the Priests and the Levites, the big and the little tithe. I left the corners of the field for the poor, according to the law. My dates were fat, and the sweet juice spurted from them. I had a wife too, and she was desirable to look on. I wrote out the marriage contract with two hundred dinars, not counting the gifts of money and clothes which I gave to her father and brothers. I had a name in Israel. Now I have nothing. The raiment on my body is not my own. They sold me as a slave, they bound my eyes as they bind the eyes of a beast, that I might drag in a circle the stone of an oil mill. To this condition have they brought me."

"Who are *they*, my son?"

"All. The Priests, the wise men, the men of power."

"Tell me further, my son."

"My inheritance lay between the estates of two rich men, Sadducees, of high name. They made alliances by marriage with the House of Hanan. They have date forests which cover many miles, spreading through the fat valley of Jericho; vineyards they have, houses, bathing pools. They cast envious eyes on my little portion; they wanted to join the borders of their estates and thrust me out of my father's inheritance. They offered me a plot of land elsewhere, by Beersheba. But my heart was in the inheritance of my father; and I told them I would leave it to my sons, as he had left it to me. Then they sent against me the overseers of the Priests, who increased my tithes, the first and second, the great and the little; daily they found new taxes; they declared my dates impure, so that certain harvests I could not sell. But they did not decrease my taxes. I turned then to the scholars and wise men; and they could do nothing against the Sadducees, for these are of the aristocracy of Jericho, and care nothing for the words of the scholars. In Jericho they have their own laws. The High Priest, and all his family, are with them. They pressed me harder and harder. Before the fruit was ripe on the tree the Priests came to inspect it, and they set aside for themselves many times more than their tithe. But when they saw that I still held out and would not move from the place, then the youngest of them, Zadoc, cast his eyes on my wife. He it was who wanted to inherit my orchard and my wife. In secret he visited her, and urged her to give me a writ of divorce. He promised her that he would take her to him as his wife. Then my wife began to demand of me that I bring her gifts and that I double her portion. Day by day she demanded richer garments of me, Zidonian stuffs, costly wools and fringes. She pleaded that she would be more beautiful for me in Tyrian purple. If I had not the money for such gifts, there came moneylenders, sent by Zadoc. My debts increased, and in the bitterness of my heart I turned to the consolation of wine. Thus they united, the tithes and the taxes, the tax collectors and the moneylenders and the Priests, and they took away my inheritance. I was thrown out of my father's house, and I fell lower from day to day, till I became a thief. My wife took back her marriage contract, and divorced me. And I was sold as a slave."

The Rabbi listened till the recital was done, then he laid his hand on the speaker and said:

"I tell you truly, Joseph, not you are the slave, but they that sold you. They are enslaved to sin. And the ropes of their sin will bring them down to the grave." Then he lifted up his hand and called: "Woe to you, scribes and Pharisees, hypocrites! For you tithe mint and anise and cummin, but you leave out the weighty portion of the law, justice, mercy, and faith. For these things you should observe, nor neglect the others. But you, my son, be comforted. You have paid your due in full measure."

Then the Rabbi spoke to all those who had heard the tale of Joseph:

"Come to me, all you who are abandoned and oppressed. Blessed are the meek of spirit, for theirs is the kingdom of heaven. Blessed are those that mourn, for they shall be comforted. Blessed, blessed are you all, the tormented and shamed. Great is your reward in the world to come, when you will return from that day of heavy labor which was your life."

A great silence had fallen in the room, and others crept away from the walls and gathered ever closer about the Rabbi. Joseph the slave opened his mouth again to speak, but he closed it. The words of the Rabbi had softened him, as a wild animal is tamed. His eyes were turned in amazement and confusion on the Rabbi, as though he struggled inwardly with the bonds which the soft and gentle speech had laid on his rebellious spirit. Like one who thirsts for sleep he yielded slowly to the peace which flowed from the Rabbi's lips. And others in the room were overcome even as he.

Now they all lay at the Rabbi's feet, like sheep about a good shepherd, and the Rabbi took them to him, and lulled them into sweet sleep. Their faces were like the faces of children.

The thickset innkeeper had forgotten to pour out the last measure of wine which had been ordered; he had left his table, and vessel in hand he kneeled among the others, to hear the parable of the two sons which the Rabbi now told them:

"A father had two sons. The younger of them said to him: 'Father, give me my portion in our inheritance.' And the father divided the inheritance between the sons. After a few days the younger son gathered up all his possessions and went away to a far land. There he squandered everything in loose living. When he had nothing left, there came a famine on the land, and he was in bitter need. Thereupon he hired himself out to one of the inhabitants of the country, who sent him to guard swine in the fields. And he would have filled his belly with the acorns which the swine ate, but no one would give him any. And when he came to, he said to himself: 'How many servants my father has, and all of them have bread enough and to spare! But I am dying of hunger. I will rise and return to my father's house, and I will say to him: "Father, I have sinned against heaven and against you. I am not worthy any more to be your son. Make me as one of your servants." ' And he arose and came to his father. But while he was still far off, his father saw him, and was filled with pity, and ran out to him and fell on his neck, and kissed him. But the son said: 'Father, I have sinned, and I am not worthy to be your son.' But the father turned to his servants and said: 'Bring out the richest garment, and put it on him. And put shoes on his feet, and a ring on his finger. And bring out the fatted calf and slaughter it. For my son was dead, and is alive again; he was lost and is found again.' And they all rejoiced. Now the older brother was in the field, and as he returned to the house he heard the singing. So he called to one of his men and asked the meaning of it. The man replied: 'Your brother has come home, and your father has killed the fatted calf for him, for he found his youngest son again.' The older brother was angry to hear this, and would not enter the house. Then his father came out, and begged him to enter, but the older brother said: 'See, I have served you these four years, and I have never trespassed your commandment, and you have never given me so much as a young kid, that I might rejoice with my friends. But when your son returned, he who wasted your substance with harlots, you killed the fatted calf.' And his father answered: 'My son, you are always with me, and all that I have is yours. And now you should rejoice, for your brother was dead and is alive again, he was lost and has been found.'

"And thus it will be with you, Joseph," the Rabbi said, leaning over the embittered slave.

Joseph covered his face with his hands and wept.

Later, when the Rabbi and his disciples left the hostelry, I followed at a distance. At the entrance to the courtyard a crowd was gathered. The word had gone round among the cave homes in the wall that the Rabbi of Galilee was among the drivers. He was widely known now in Jerusalem, and many believed that he could confer happiness and good fortune with a touch of his hand or a word of his lips. The women came out, holding their young by the hand, or their sucklings in their arms. When the Rabbi came out, they lighted his way with lamps, and they also crowded about him, and lifted their children to him that he might bless them. The Rabbi placed his hands on each child, and uttered the Jewish blessing: "May it be your portion to grow up to the Torah, to marriage and to good deeds."

But in the crowd outside there happened to be one of the scholars of the city. When he saw the Rabbi issue from the yard of the hostelry, he called out in astonishment:

"Rabbi in Israel! Has not King David said: 'Blessed is the man that walketh not in the counsel of the wicked, and goeth not in the path of the sinners, and sitteth not in the seat of the scornful'?"

The Rabbi answered, not him, but those who had brought their children to him to be blessed:

"What shepherd, if he loses one of his flock, does not leave the ninety-nine sheep in the wilderness and turn back for the lost one, until he has found it? This is what I say to you: There is more rejoicing in heaven over one sinner who repents than over ninety-nine of the righteous who do not need to repent."

I returned to Rabbi Nicodemon, and told him of all that I had seen and heard in the hostelry. When I repeated what I had heard last, concerning the one sheep and the ninety-nine, my Rabbi asked, wondering:

"Did he really say that one leaves the ninety-nine to go in search of the one?"

"Yes, he said that, Rabbi. And he added that there is more rejoicing in heaven over one sinner who repents than over ninety-nine righteous who do not need to repent."

My Rabbi's face became very earnest, and he thought a long time. Seldom had I seen him so sunk in dark thoughts. His high forehead was drawn down intensely, and he kept passing his thumb again and again over his thick, short beard. Then at last he said to all of us:

"God be praised, he follows in the footsteps of our sages. For they have likewise said: 'He that loses one soul, it is as if he had lost the whole world. And he who rescues one soul, it is as if he had rescued the whole world.' Our sages had other sayings in this sense. 'One man,' they said, 'is the equivalent of all the act of Creation.' One man that is born in the image of God is in his singularity even like the Lord, his Creator. God enters into secret union with every man, through the soul which He breathes into him. This is the meaning of the verse: 'For Thine eyes watch closely all the ways of Man.' Man is one, singular and special, by virtue of an individual Providence."

It happened to be a day on which my turn had come to act as the servant of my Rabbi. I washed my hands and feet and anointed myself. I put on a fresh shirt and wrapped myself in a washed mantle, for it was not seemly to wait on the Rabbi in workaday attire. I laid the table for my Rabbi, I put before him the meal of lentils which Alexander and Rufus had cooked for him. Then, when I poured out the wine for my Rabbi, I gathered courage and asked him:

"Teach me, Rabbi. The words which I heard from you today are the same as those I heard from the Rabbi of Galilee; or they are a commentary on them. And this is true also of other things you have taught me, whether out of the *Halachah* or the *Agada*; and of things which I have heard from other sages. All come together in the words which are uttered by the Rabbi of Galilee, and one fills out the other. What, then, divides the sages from the Rabbi of Galilee, and what is the dispute between them? Why is it that when an encounter takes place between the Rabbi of Galilee and sundry scholars, there are hard words between them, which the ears shrink from?"

"The words of both the Rabbi of Galilee and of the sages are the words of the living God, my son. But the ways of the scholars and the learned are different from those of the Galilean. Now the ways of the scholars are familiar to us, having come down to us in the tradition, but those of the Rabbi of Galilee are unfamiliar to us. But know this, my son. Every dispute which arises in the name of heaven and of heavenly purposes must in the end be adjusted in peace."

After these words my Rabbi lifted his hands to heaven and uttered a short prayer.

"Lord of the world, Thou knowest that not for our glory and not for the glory of the house of our fathers do we conduct this dispute, but for Thy name's sake, and that we may do that which is acceptable in Thine eyes. Therefore bring our hearts nearer to Thee, for only in Thee shall we find peace. See, we have reposed our hopes in Thee. All that we have, we have received at Thy hands. There is nothing without Thee, Father in heaven."

CHAPTER ELEVEN

NO one knew where the Rabbi of Galilee lived. He would appear suddenly in the synagogues or market places or the Temple courts, surrounded by his disciples and by hordes of the poor. Just as suddenly he would disappear, sometimes for long stretches, perhaps for days, perhaps even for weeks. No one saw him. His disciples were scattered about the poorest sections of the Lower City, where the houses were like tombs of the living. Their walls were clay baked in the sun, and the lower parts were covered with filth. All the slopes of the Kidron were densely covered with such houses, and the narrow labyrinths of the streets swallowed up him who entered. Sometimes we had tried to follow one of his disciples to his home, but in the dense throngs which thrust back and forth through the choking alleys, he would escape our pursuit. Also the disciples were scattered, and walked separately when they were not with their Rabbi, as though they were evading observation.

But once Rufus and I followed hard on the trail of the Rabbi and some of his disciples as they came out of the Temple court. We shouldered and elbowed our way through the crowds, determined to keep the Rabbi in sight, as he descended toward the Lower City. They walked with hasty footsteps, the Rabbi in front, Simon bar Jonah, Jochanan and Jacob in the rear. The sons of Zebedee differed greatly in appearance. One had a mighty head, covered with a wild brush of upstanding black hair, like a forest on a slope. The other was also tall, but thin, pale, with a delicate face. We learned afterwards that these three were the most beloved of the Rabbi's disciples, who always accompanied him.

When they had cleared the crowds, they went swiftly along the quieter alleys downwards, into the poorest areas; then they turned from the wall, cut through the Dung Gate and sped—almost ran—up the slope of the Mount of Olives.

We found it by no means easy to keep pace with them, for they seemed to swallow the earth with their footsteps. We clambered after them from the Kidron valley upward. This further slope, outside the city, was still thick-sown with the dwellings of the poor; there were also stalls of leather dressers, dyers and weavers. Then, as we panted toward the heights, we came gradually on little patches of green, sown with vegetables, and separate houses fenced off by groves of cypress. We hastened past the shops of the Sons of Hanan, the storehouses and barns where the Priestly house assembled the produce to be sold to the poor. Then at last we came to the place known as Bet Paga, which lay at a good distance from the city walls; but everything hitherwards was still considered part of the circle of Jerusalem. There used to be a popular saying: "You will find me anywhere as far as the walls of Bet Paga"—which meant: "I am anywhere and everywhere in Jerusalem." However, the place itself was beyond those limits and had no walls of its own. As a memorial of its name, a few fig trees still sustained themselves wretchedly hereabouts. The hot winds from the desert of Judaea strike the unprotected slope, and trees shed their fruit prematurely: hence the name Bet Paga, "the house of the unripe figs." Now, in the winter time, the dead branches of the fig trees thrust their naked hands upward among the other trees, as if they implored pity.

In the village there was a house known as Bet Eini, and here lived a man who went by the strange name of Simon the Leper. Strange, because the man was not a leper, for in that case he could not have lived in the village; the name was given to him because he always gathered about him the most miserable and rejected of human beings. There was not a man so low, so broken and tattered, that Simon would not take him in, and share with him his table and even his bed. He would not shrink from lying down side by side with the most revolting cripples or from dipping his bread into the same bowl with them. "In the end," was his saying, "we shall all share one bed—the earth; why then should I now shrink from anyone?" Others called him Simon the Modest. But in Hebrew the word "modest," *zenua* differs by one letter from the word "leprous," *zerua;* and whether by error or deliberately, the names had been interchanged. It was hereabouts, we discovered, that the Rabbi of Galilee made his home.

In the house of Simon the Leper we found crowds of the poor and the sick. We, who knew Jerusalem, were accustomed to poverty, but we had not seen the like of this. It was as if the lowest pit of misery in the Kidron had spewed out its mud into the hut of Simon the Leper. These were not men, but half-men, fragments, with rotting limbs, men who possessed nothing, no, not even their own bodies. They possessed—or were possessed by—sickness only.

On the way we had already encountered beggars and cripples, clambering in this direction, the blind and the lame helping each other along, processions of wretchedness directed toward the house. Here we found them in heaps, sitting in the damp, dew-melted mud of the yard. And what joy burst out on their faces, what hands and voices were lifted, when they saw the Rabbi approach in his white robe, accompanied by his disciples. They dragged themselves over toward him, pressed close to him, a wave of sickness and decay. He bade them come into the house, and they followed, till the room overflowed with them, like wine overflowing in foam from a beaker. It was a chilly winter afternoon, yet none of them trembled with the cold. They did not even try to cover their limbs with the rags which dangled from them. For they were all warmed by an inner light, kindled when they came in contact with this man.

Now all Jerusalem knew of the wonders which he had performed in Galilee; how he had healed the sick with a touch; how he had pulled men back from the gates of death with a single word, how he had fed the hungry and driven evil spirits out of the possessed. We were sure now that we would be the witnesses of similar wonders and that he would heal the hordes of the sick with a word. We believed, indeed, that he would conjure down baskets of bread from heaven and sate all the hungry. But no such sign appeared. And it was as though the poor and the hungry did not even expect bodily help from him, but something quite different; for they all became still when he came among them.

Soon we heard his voice, and it was not the voice which we were accustomed to hearing in the market places and the Temple courts, when he reproached the mighty and spoke against the rich. For now it was as soft and gentle as music. It was as if he sang a deep-sorrowing melody into which he gathered them: a blind old man who had seized the hem of his robe and would not let go; another, covered with boils, to which his rags clung closely, so that he seemed to be covered with leprosy. Him the Rabbi lifted up and pressed to himself, his beard touching the man's naked head. Then he spoke, swaying to and fro:

"Suffering, my son, is the fount of love. Suffering is the grace, the great grace, which our Father in heaven pours down upon us. For suffering gives men submissive hearts. He that does not suffer thinks that he stands upon a mighty rock which he himself has raised. He does not see his brother; he sees only himself. He believes in no one; he believes only in his own strength. His heart becomes a swamp which swarms with reptiles: pride, obstinacy, and self-love. And when his footstool is rolled away from under him, he sinks, together with all the reptiles, into the depths of hell. But he to whom God has granted suffering shall find his pains like ropes which bind him to his Father in heaven. His heart is awake to feel the pains of his brother in need. He sends aictions upon you and makes you small on earth that you may be great in heaven."

The Rabbi lifted up his hands, and held them over the heads of the defeated and rejected, they that were spread out at his feet like a sea of bodily filth, and he cried:

"Blessed are you, the defeated and broken, that you pay for your sins on earth. But how bright will your portion be in the other world, in the life eternal. Woe to the rich, who snatch their brief joys on this earth! How dark will their portion be in the world to come! To what may this be likened? There was once a rich man who clothed himself in purple and fine linen, and made a feast every day. There was also a poor man, whose name was Eliezer, who lay at the door of the rich man, his body covered with boils. And he wanted to feed on nothing more than the crumbs and crusts which fell from the rich man's table, but he received nothing; only the dogs came out of the rich man's house and licked the sores of Eliezer. Then, when Eliezer died, the angels came and carried him to Abraham's bosom. The rich man died, too, and was buried. And when he found himself in hell, in the midst of his torments, he lifted up his eyes and he saw, afar off, Eliezer in Abraham's bosom. Then he cried out: 'My father, Abraham, have mercy on me. Send Eliezer, and let him dip his finger in water and cool my tongue therewith, for I wither in this flame.' But Abraham answered: 'Remember, my son, that in the life on earth you took your portion of that which was good, and Eliezer took his portion of that which was evil. Now he is comforted, and you are in pain. Furthermore, there is a great cleft set between us. Those that would pass from this place to yours, cannot; and those on your side cannot come to us.' Then the man that had been rich said: 'If this be so, send Eliezer to my father's house; for I have five brothers. Let him warn them, that they may not come to this place of sorrows.' But Abraham answered: 'Have they not the Torah of Moses and the words of the Prophets? They have not given heed to their words; will they give heed to one who has risen from the dead?' "

How changed were the faces of those that lay mingled at the Rabbi's feet! Under the magic of his words they were like the faces of princes. A light was kindled in their eyes. It was as though their broken limbs had been made whole again, as though their twisted backbones had been straightened, as though the blind had begun to see. It was as though they had suddenly become aware that they were not poor, but that they possessed something to which all the riches of the world could not compare. They were lifted up in joy.

A tiny cripple, holding on to the door post, cried out: "Rabbi, Rabbi! Will an angel of heaven carry me too into Abraham's bosom?"

"Why not, my son? Does not God regard you too as one of His children?"

"I have not fulfilled the commandments, I have done no good deeds, I have no learning, I am nothing."

The Rabbi stood up and made his way through the throng to the cripple at the door; a tiny figure it was, but the head was big and heavy with water.

"You are richer than the richest. In the world to come you will be envied by those that walk about on this earth, their bellies stuffed with the Torah; for not those possess who think they possess, but those that think they possess nothing. The lost ones are the found ones."

There was a woman who pressed toward him, but did not dare to come too close. She spoke to him from under the veil which covered her face and asked:

"And I too, will I be taken by an angel into Abraham's bosom?"

"You too, my daughter."

The woman began to weep. "I am full of sin."

And the Rabbi answered: "Happy are you, my daughter, that you know yourself to be full of sin."

Then he lifted up his voice and spoke to all of them:

"Has not King David said: 'Near to me are the broken of heart.' Happy are you, the brokenhearted; God is among you. There is a reward prepared for your labors. You have received your punishment with a full hand. You are the chosen of God, He has put His sign upon you, the sign of sorrow. Sweet is your burden, for you do the day's labor, and the table will be set for you when you return in the evening to the Master's house."

Later, when all was dark, the Rabbi, accompanied by his near disciples, left the house of Simon the Leper, for he was wearied by all the work he had done. It was as though he had poured out his own life. His face was deathly pale; the words had drawn the blood from it; his lips were thinner than ever, and the eyelids were heavy, as if he could not lift them. But it was not easy for him to leave, for the multitude would have him stay on and on. But Simon bar Jonah and the others sent them forth, and they dispersed, slowly and reluctantly. In their ears still sang the words of the Rabbi, and drunk, not with wine, but with the joy that filled their hearts, they went back to the city.

But Rufus and I remained there, though evening had fallen. We felt that something great and wonderful was happening before our eyes, and we wanted to learn more.

Not far from Bet Eini, where Simon the Leper lived, was K'far Miriam and the house of Miriam and Martha. Thither the Rabbi now went, with the three disciples. Simon almost bore him in his arms, so weary was he with his labor. Not all of the poor had dispersed; some had lingered in the darkness, and they came with us. We came into a room which had been prepared for the evening meal; the table was spread, and stools were ranged about it. Martha, together with other women, had been at work in the yard outside the house, in spite of the cold; they had done the cooking over the oven, and had made ready the meal. Within the house Miriam, Martha's sister, had lit the oil lamps and set the dishes. Then, when the Rabbi and his disciples were seated, she and her brother Eliezer took up their places behind the Rabbi, to serve him.

Suddenly, as I looked upon those two, standing behind the Rabbi, to right and left of him, a great light was kindled in me. It seemed to me that I saw not only the sister whom he had saved from sin, and the brother whom he had awakened from death, but far, far more.

In the glimmer of the oil lamp Miriam's face was not so old and withered, her eyes were not so extinguished as they had been on that day when she had lifted her veil in the Temple court. Here, in the peace of the house, in the quiet, in the earnestness of sanctity, Miriam's face was transfigured; it was like the face of a child which had wept and had been comforted: the tears still hung in her eyes, but they were tears not of pain but of joy. Her eyes shone with a strange, spiritualized luster which was shed upon her dark-skinned face. All the clefts which regret, pain and love had cut there were now filled and smoothed out. Yes, that light which was poured from her eyes awakened again the youthful, brimming olive tints of her skin, and the freshness of her girlhood was on her cheeks. Even her hair gave back the dark glint of its former radiance. She was as one liberated from deadly terror, one whose limbs have been loosened from the cramps of death. She was again Miriam of Migdal, but her beauty was now like a quiet, tender song, and everyone that looked on her was filled with emotions of happiness, was lifted to joy not in restlessness and thirst, as men had been lifted by her in the past, but by a singing peace which issued from a delivered soul. And I was aware that it was not she alone who stood there by the Rabbi; that transfigured smile hovered on the face of all those that he had delivered from sin; not Miriam of Migdal alone, but all who had been freed from under the shadow of Satan and returned to their Father in heaven.

Thus it was with her brother Eliezer, too.

Of course I had heard of the miracle which the Rabbi of Galilee had performed on her brother. And of course it was also passed around from ear to ear that Eliezer had not been dead at all but had fallen into a long faint. Nevertheless the story was still told how he lay dead, how the wailing women had lamented for him, how he had been carried away to burial, and how the Rabbi had brought him back to life; and, whatever the actuality, ever since then Eliezer had been looked on with a kind of dark respect in which was more than a touch of fear. For most he was a man that had been dead. Men were uncomfortable in his vicinity, started back from him, trembled lest they touch him. It was even suspected that whosoever came in physical contact with him was defiled as by contact with a corpse. For he might be alive and yet dead, he might be a corpse set in motion. Such indeed was the impression he made on many, of a thing that was animated not by a will of its own. Moreover, alive or dead, or both, the long, shriveled body reeked of the grave, and those that saw him in the Temple court, standing behind his Rabbi, would mutter: "There goes the Rabbi with the *golem* which he has fashioned!"

But on that evening, as he stood behind the Rabbi and to his right, serving him with slow gestures, with hands that seemed in fact to be fashioned of wood, the face that towered high up was informed by a smile of gladness. The huge calf's eyes which were set like full moons in the naked sockets were instinct with life; they did not spread terror, nor did they, in horrible fashion, beg forgiveness for not being closed in death; they were happy. The smile on his crooked lips was not that of an idiot, or one that lacked wit and will; it was rather the wise, gentle smile of one who had penetrated all secrets and had come through to peace, the smile of one who had looked into the face of Death, and conquered him, of one who solved the ultimate mysteries and had reached the certain decision that beyond the end waited eternal life. But it was the smile of *all* the defeated, the shamed and humiliated, the sick and the fallen, who had ever stood on the edge of the grave and had glimpsed the pit beneath with their own eyes—and returned to life.

Here, in the house of Miriam and Martha, seated at table with his disciples and with those he had healed and comforted, he was no longer the Rabbi of the word of thunder; he was not the stormy center of endless disputes; he was the Rabbi of forgiveness and reconciliation, of peace and rest. After he had washed his hands, he blessed the bread and said over it his prayer to our Father in heaven, then he added the prescribed prayer, dipped the bread in salt, tasted it, broke it, and distributed the pieces round the table. Later he preached to them, and how sweet his words were! I could only regret that the sages of Jerusalem were not present, that my Rabbi Nicodemon did not hear him then. It seemed to me that I had been exalted to the privilege of sitting at the table of the Venerable Hillel, and of hearing him teach, in the manner described by my Rabbi and others. He preached on the subject of prayer: he told them that prayer was the one thread which bound us to our Father in heaven. Then he spoke of the greatness of the man who makes his own will as nought before the will of his brother: "If two of you," he said, "become as one on earth, then everything you pray for will be granted by our Father in heaven. And if your brother sin against you, rebuke him, and if he repent, forgive him. And if he sin against you seven times in one day, and come to you seven times and say, 'I repent,' then you shall forgive him seven times." Then he told them to be not as servants that wait on their master for the sake of reward, but such as wait on their master without expectation of reward. He told them also a parable of a lord and his servants. He said: "When you stand and pray, forgive all those who have done you evil, and your Father in heaven will likewise forgive you your misdeeds. But if you do not forgive others, then your Father in heaven will not forgive you your misdeeds."

When Rufus and I left Bet Paga full darkness had fallen. The shadows had risen up from the vale of Jericho, and only the faintest glimmer of the sunken sun touched the sky where it stretched away toward the Great Sea. We hastened back to the city of Jerusalem, which was poured out over the hills and valleys. From innumerable houses shone the modest and hospitable oil lamps. They testified that the laborer had finished the toil of the day, and sat now with his household at the evening meal. On Mount Moriah the House which God had chosen, as His dwelling place among men, towered into the starry skies. The glimmering torches of the Temple watchmen made a living ring about the walls and turrets and terraces of the Temple, which was sunk in night but sent out a dim shaft of radiance into the heavens. Peace hung over Jerusalem.

CHAPTER TWELVE

DURING that season I was often in Bet Eini. It was an exceptionally damp winter. The rains fell continuously, and the earth was soaked through. Runlets appeared in the earth, as though many plows had passed over it. The few fig trees on the roads were naked. More than once, throughout the winter, they tried to put forth the green buttons of their shoots before the leaves appeared, but these, as soon as they issued, faded again.

The poor and sick continued to gather in the house of Simon the Leper. Some of them stayed there for long stretches of time. They had their home in the stalls about the yard, they lay on the rotting straw in the barns. The healthier among them made themselves useful about Simon's house or in K'far Miriam, where there was a yard, a garden of herbs and an olive wood. They weeded, they cleaned the trees and dug the earth. Others beat and ground the herbs and leaves in mortars, to obtain their essences and oils so as to sell them in the city. I often came across blind Bar Talmai, one of the disciples, who taught the workers how to prepare the spices. All the poor who had gathered about the Rabbi sat at one table with him and shared everything that belonged to the company.

In the house of the sisters Miriam and Martha were lodged other women who had come with the Rabbi from Galilee. One of them was Sulamith, the mother of Jochanan and Jacob. Once she had been a rich woman. It was told of her that at first she had opposed her sons when they decided to leave the many fishing boats which their father had left them on the Sea of Genesaret, and to follow the Rabbi. Afterwards she came to the Rabbi and begged him to give her two sons the right- and left-hand seats next to him in the kingdom of heaven. But when she had once seen the Rabbi, she remained with him. She sold her boats and accompanied her sons to Jerusalem. She gave the money into the common treasury, and she lived now in Miriam's and Martha's house. At first she helped in the management, but before long she took the management entirely into her hands. For until she did that the house was like a ship without a rudder. Whosoever wished came, and ate and drank; and hordes of the poor were forever pillaging and emptying the place. But when Sulamith took charge she made those that were capable of it render service in return. She was always busy about the house, issuing orders. She wore a thick, woolen dress, a heavy felt covering and hose of felt, with sandals over them, for she was not at home in the raw, damp winter of Jerusalem after the sunlit shores of Genesaret. Her severe voice was for ever lifted to rebuke and command:

"You there, lazybones! Do you think that because the kingdom of heaven is coming tomorrow you don't have to clean the field today? Time enough, when the kingdom has arrived, to pluck the ready loaves from the stalks. Meanwhile you must work the fields, and plow them with your nose, if need be. And you! Will you lie around all day, doing nothing? Go out and gather fallen leaves and twigs, and dry them; and pick up the dung of the animals and dry that, too, for fuel. How else shall we heat the oven?" She would turn from some elderly beggar to a young woman. "You too, pretty one, do you think that because the kingdom of heaven is coming we must sit in the dark? Go, polish the lamps, and spin wicks for them. Have you not heard how wise brides keep their lamps ready, that they may go out to meet their bridegrooms?"

She even lifted her voice against Miriam of Migdal, whom she looked on as the spoiled child of the company; she told her not to spend so much time pouring oils and perfumes from one vial into another, and sewing and washing garments for the Rabbi, but rather to turn her hand to the rougher work of the household. "When the kingdom of heaven will come," she said, sharply, "we shall all be favorites. I will be the mother of two princes. But until then all of us must work."

For the truth was this: they who had attached themselves to the Rabbi were overcome by stagnation and a kind of divine laziness. Everyone felt that the kingdom of heaven was immediately at hand, would descend any moment: what point was there, then, in making preparations for the next day, and for that matter even for the next meal? Had not the Rabbi himself said: "Turn over all your cares to your Father in heaven," and, "Ask not, what shall we eat on the morrow," and "He knows what your needs are"? But meanwhile one had to eat; garments were needed to cover one's nakedness, and a roof to take shelter under, not only for those who were nearest the Rabbi, but for all the poor that came to him, and remained.

In the house of the two sisters there was another woman by the name of Miriam, and to distinguish her from Miriam of Migdal they called her "the mother of Jacob and Joseph." She must have been a close kin of the Rabbi. She came from Galilee, and there were some who even whispered that she was the Rabbi's mother, but no one was certain. But it was seen of all that the Rabbi held her in great honor, seating her near him at the table; and therefore all the others respected her too. She was a woman of lofty stature. A dark veil covered her face when she came among people, and this testified to her nobility. She, like the other Miriam, did not concern herself with the coarser housework, but assisted her namesake in tending to the Rabbi's raiment and preparing his meals. On this the two Miriams looked as on a sacred service. Every garment which the Rabbi wore was in their eyes a sanctity, like the robes of the High Priest. The Rabbi was always clad in white, as the Writ says: "Let thy raiment be always white and let not thy head lack ointment." The Miriams did more than weave and wash his raiment; they also sewed his sandals for him. They prepared his meals in religious exaltation, as one prepares the sacrifice on the altar. For the Rabbi put great weight on his clothes, and conducted the meals as if they were indeed a sacrificial rite. He loved the odor of incense about him, and the grace of ointments on his body. The table at which he sat was spread with beautiful linens. He even dried his hands, after washing, in delicate linens. To all this the two Miriams ministered with holy devotion. They went about their work as in a dream, and they whispered like priestesses in a temple when they sat together over his garments.

Thus the heavy housework, and the work in field and garden, the feeding of the poor, fell on the other two women, Martha and Sulamith. There was only one man belonging to the household, namely, Eliezer. But he went about sunk in dreams even more than the two Miriams, for though he had been brought back from the dead, he was more of the other world than of this. Sometimes he was heard to speak to spirits which he beheld with the eyes of his dreams. He was therefore of little use about the house.

The disciples, too, were seldom at hand. Throughout the day they remained in the city. Many of them went out to work in order that they might give their earnings to the common treasury. Others spent their time in the poor sections of the city spreading the gospel of their Rabbi; but Simon, and the two brothers Zebedee, the Rabbi always kept by his side.

Martha was the very embodiment of work. I can still see her standing in the yard, in the cool damp of a winter's day, washing clothes in a pail, or stooping over the open oven baking flat cakes, or else boiling lentils and greens in a great earthen pot: her squat, thick body wrapped in a sackcloth dress, her legs, red and swollen, showing below the skirt, which was too short. Her face and arms were also raw and red, hardened by the cold, eaten by the smoke; her hair was thick and tangled, and covered with the dust which the wind carried. In the house stands her sister Miriam; she is clad in silk, her feet are shod in Laodicean sandals, her head is veiled in a hair net which falls over her face; her fingers tremble as she prepares the incense which is to burn in the house for the Rabbi's coming. Or she makes ready his food, asparagus or spinach, fried over a flame which is fed by the most delicate oils. There was not a moment of idleness for Martha. If she was not cooking, she was scouring vessels; if she was not washing clothes, she was in the garden tearing out weeds. Meanwhile her sister Miriam would be sitting with her namesake, recounting her dreams and visions of the Rabbi's kingdom and the kingdom of heaven. And certainly Martha's spirit had often rebelled. It was said that she had even lodged complaint with the Rabbi against her sister, who would not take up her share of labor. But it was also said that the Rabbi answered thus: "Your sister has taken the better portion." Since that time she complained no more; silently, submissively, she accepted the portion which had fallen to her to shoulder.

* * *

During the day the Rabbi of Galilee preached in the streets and market places of Jerusalem, and in the Temple court under the arcades. Evenings he went up to Bet Eini. There are two ways of reaching Bet Eini from the Temple: the shorter and quieter descends by a flight of stairs steep as a waterfall direct from the walls to the Kidron valley; the other is longer, and winds through the Lower City past the Dung Gate. The Rabbi always took the longer way, hastening with his disciples through the narrow, crooked streets. He was thus certain of throwing off those that sought to follow, for he kept secret the place of his abode in Jerusalem. His disciples, too, were careful to conceal it. Even after he had been several months in the city, and was widely known, the scholars, the sages and the Priests could not discover where he passed his nights. Even my Rabbi did not know it, until I disclosed the place, and told him of the sick and the poor there assembled. Then my Rabbi bade me keep the secret to myself, for if the Rabbi of Galilee did not want it known that he was performing these acts of charity and kindliness there was undoubtedly a good reason.

All through the winter months the Rabbi preached in the synagogues and the Temple courts concerning the coming of the kingdom of heaven. No one molested him. The city became accustomed to the tenor of his sermons, and it was generally accepted that his allusions to the kingdom of heaven were symbolic. The sages even learned to forgive him his sharp utterances against them: custom overbore their first resentment. It was widely known that the Rabbi of Galilee fulfilled all the commandments of the Torah, including the smallest and those which had come down in the tradition. And even though he spoke harshly of the Pharisees, nevertheless he told his auditors to obey that which the Pharisees preached, for, he said, they sat in the seat of Moses. His piety, his observance of the law and his acts of charity, his prayers and his defense of the poor and degraded, were known. And though he did not perform any miracles in Jerusalem, except that he healed one or two sick people, and comported himself like any other Rabbi, there were still many who awaited the day of the fulfillment of that which he preached in hint and symbol. Even some of those that laughed at him longed secretly for the time when he would reveal himself, and hoped for its swift coming. For the days were ripening toward great events.

Among those that now awaited daily the revealing of the mission of the Galilean was my own Rabbi, Nicodemon. I had marked that the appearance of the Galilean in the streets of Jerusalem had once again brought a deep change over my Rabbi. He had returned from his last visit to Galilee restored to his ancient tranquillity; but a sacred fever and restlessness, mounting from day to day, laid hold on him with the coming of the Galilean. As time passed his interest grew till it became an obsession; he took to following the Galilean, that he might hear more and more. And he himself resumed his Messianic sermons, and held frequent assemblies of the Companionship.

Then once Hillel brought about a meeting between my Rabbi and the Rabbi of Galilee. It was not done by Judah Ish-Kiriot or by any other of the disciples, but by the watercarrier. The encounter was secret, and it came to our knowledge, Rufus's and mine, by accident. We were struck, one evening, when the Rabbi asked us to give him his most formal attire, the broad, long, black *itztla* or mantle which he put on when visiting only the most exalted personages. We were overjoyed when he asked us to accompany him and carry the lamps before him. Hillel the watercarrier was with us, and he conducted us to his dwelling in the ancient wall. When we reached the narrow steps which led down to the cave, the Rabbi bade us wait outside; even Hillel was forbidden to enter. But at once Rufus and I were aware that within waited the Rabbi of Galilee. We had recognized one of the men who, like us, stood without; he was a companion of the Rabbi, but not one of his intimates, for even the beloved Simon was excluded from the secret of the meeting. A long time passed before our Rabbi came out. What they talked of I do not know. But our knowledge of the presence of the Galilean was confirmed when our Rabbi bade us mention to no one that he had gone that night to the dwelling of Hillel.

Not long thereafter Rufus and I went up on one of our visits to K'far Miriam, and were amazed to learn that the Rabbi of Galilee was no longer there. The disciples, too, were gone. Only the women remained and the assembly of the sick and poor, and the latter were as amazed as we. Nor would they wholly believe it when they were told that the Rabbi had withdrawn himself to some unknown place.

Judah Ish-Kiriot, who had of late been a frequent visitor to our Rabbi, had also disappeared.

The time was the end of the month of Adar, when the half-shekel tax became due to the Temple treasury. Winds of spring blew over Jerusalem. The evenings were lighter and gentler, and the sunlight lingered on the golden turrets of the Temple. Heavy smoke went up like a fiery pillar from the great altar into the red clouds which hung ever later in the heavens. In the homes of the Jerusalemites the women began to clean away the accumulations of the winter, and to prepare for the many pilgrims who would pour into the city for the Passover.

During this period the Rabbi of Galilee was nowhere to be seen.

CHAPTER THIRTEEN

WHOSE voice proclaimed that the Passover of this year would witness in Jerusalem a second exodus from slavery? It is true that something like this was said every Passover; but now the proclamation hung in the air like a divine utterance, and as though the heavens and the earth sent forth tidings. Never had the sun been so bright, never had God clad the season of the liberation in so radiant a garment. Great beakers of light were emptied into the streets, splashing back from the walls in cataracts of splendor. Even the motes in the sunbeams danced with unusual radiance; the terraces, the roofs, and the water cisterns on the roofs, the gates and towers of the palaces—all were sheathed in white fire.

And about the city the girdles of dark cypress and silver-shimmering olive suddenly became greener. Every empty span of earth was covered with green. From the yards of rich and poor alike floated the odor of opening buds on fig trees, and the air was filled with the incense of a virgin blossoming. The green covering, sown with fiery poppies, broke into the strongholds of poverty, into the valleys of Kidron and Hinnom, and from there mounted triumphantly into the Upper City. Round the waters of Siloah ancient, tattered oleanders began to bloom. Clusters of lavender lifted their heads even in the shadow of David's wall while beneath every hedge in the Old City lay circlets of sweet peas, and tiny torches of anemone and cyclamen were uplifted. The jasmine wandered down as far as the hostelry of the drivers, and bloomed under the very hoofs of the donkeys and camels. From myriads of opening buds a living exhalation issued, filling all men with vigor and will to activity, while the light which poured down on them touched off a restless expectancy.

Jerusalem put on a new garment and opened wide her gates for the children streaming to her from every corner of the world. The first to appear from remote places were the Babylonians. They were known at once by their thick, black, curled beards, by the locks which hung like bells over their shoulders. Their faces were dark and lustrous, as if anointed with oils; they wore sleeveless white mantles of woven camel's hair, which were fastened all the way up to the throat with golden hooks, and reached downward to cover their sandals. Nearly all of them were men of wealth; that could be seen at once in the rings which glistened on their fingers. They sojourned, during their stay, among wealthy relatives in the Upper City, as did many of the Tyrians and Zidonians, as well as the Cypriots and others who came from the Phoenician provinces. The Tyrians almost made a cult of their beards. All the ingenuities which the Syrian hairdressers had ever invented were displayed by the Phoenician Jews. Some of them wore their beards in tiny, curled rosettes, which surrounded their faces like wreaths. Others let their beards descend in broad beds over their breasts, like gardens. Others had woven their beards into successive waves, one falling over the other. Still others had twisted the strands into separate pendants which dangled over their bosoms. Not less than with their beards, the Phoenician Jews made great play with their dress. All the beasts of field and forest were embroidered on their mantles, tunics and girdles. The scholars of Jerusalem suspected that often the fabric of these garments consisted of a forbidden mixture of wool and linen. Likewise they protested against the display of woven likenesses of living things; but their protests were not heeded. The Tyrians and Zidonians were so accustomed to decorated raiment that they could not do without it.

In the same way, the Jews who came from the rock city of Petra imitated in their garb the customs and tastes of their heathen neighbors. Again the scholars of Jerusalem were incensed. They demanded of all such pilgrims that they bring a purification offering to the Temple and have themselves sprinkled with the water containing ashes of the red heifer, before they proceeded to their Passover sacrifices.

But these were the rich visitors from far places, who were housed among relatives or merchant friends, equally rich, in the Upper City or on the aristocratic heights of Mount Scopus. Below, in the houses and market places of the Lower City, were thousands of poor pilgrims, Jewesses from the valley of the Jordan, men from the hill country of Judaea, farmers of the Sharon, vine cultivators from the Shefelah, plowmen from Galilee and Bet Shemen, donkey and camel drivers from the country of Sodom which is beyond the Dead Sea, fishermen from Genesaret, sailors from Joppa and Akko; faces which the sun's rays had licked as with fiery tongues, faces beaten hard by fierce winds, and hollowed and pitted by need. The nakedness of their bodies was covered with camel skin or sheepskin, or with the fell of beasts of the desert. Others were imperfectly clad in sacking, their flesh exposed here and there to the sun. Their beards were not curled, or braided, or fashioned into waves and ringlets; they were combed by the wind, covered with dust and burrs. Their heads were not adorned with helmets hammered in silver and bronze; they were like wild treetops shaken by storm. Going through the streets these pilgrims of the Lower City did not spread about them a delicate odor of costly ointments. The smell of the fields and waters of Israel, the reek of flocks and herds, went with them. Their hands did not flash with rings; their fingers were hard, the veins stood on them in ridges, the sweat of labor had furrowed them. Their wives were not wrapped in silk of Persia and India; they were not adorned with golden girdles of Tarshish, and from their necks hung no chains bearing vials of perfumes. The upper part of their bodies was covered with the veil, woven into their hair, the lower part with the coarse weaves of sackcloth, in which the sole adornment was a colored thread. Their feet were not graced by Laodicean sandals; they were naked, worn and cut by the stones; they resembled the roots of olive trees thrust out from the ground. But they were the ones that filled the streets of Jerusalem. They burst through the gates of Jerusalem like the foaming waters of an overflowing river. Every corner was filled with them. They came in companies of all sizes, by families, by villages, by regions. They, too, for the most part, housed with relatives, friends and fellow villagers now settled in the city. There was not a house which did not take in as many as there was room for—and more. In this respect the Jerusalemites were extremely hospitable. Nevertheless many pilgrims had to make their home in the cellars under the arches which supported the great place of the Temple. Others yet—large numbers they were—camped in the streets. They were to be seen, groups of women and children, with their sheep and their cruses of oil, which they had brought as offerings, with their bundles of food and their other preparations for the journey. They spread out under every arcade, between open pillars, in the shadow of the public buildings and under the viaducts which connected the Upper City with the Temple area; they flowed up till their ranks broke against the stairways of the palaces and even till they reached the walls of the Herodian castle. Some of them actually crept in between the pillars of the theater and the hippodrome, where no pious Jew was ever seen at other times. And of course the slopes of the Kidron and Hinnom valleys were thick with them. Wherever they could, they made shelters for themselves out of olive and cypress branches. All the walls of Jerusalem were beleaguered by the visitors, and not a cave, not a hole under a rock, was left uninhabited.

And yet not a single one among them was heard to say: "There is no room for me, the place is too small." During the day they were bathed in floods of light; at night myriad clouds went up from the fires of their encampments. From the depths of the valleys which surrounded Jerusalem the oil lamps glimmered up, while from all the heights signal flames responded, like an interchange between the residents and the newcomers. It was like the fulfillment of the words of the Prophet: "And in that day the peoples of the world shall stream toward the Holy Mount."

But the densest crowd, the fullness of the invasion, was to be seen only in the Temple courts. The alleys which approached the area were so thick with pilgrims that a spear could not have found room between them. All were hastening, as well as they could, to prepare themselves for the great festival, to purify themselves, to pay their pledges and fulfill their vows, to bring their sacrifices and deliver their tax money. Before the office of the Temple treasury there was a furious press; the treasurers sat within, accepting the donations of gold and silver, of precious stones, of delicate silks and rare oils which pilgrims from remote places brought to the sanctuary. Here too were the tables of the moneychangers, and about them likewise was a great press of those who sought to exchange dinars, drachmas, tetradrachmas and all other manner of foreign coins, bearing on them the images of men and gods and beasts, as well as Jewish copper coins, in order to pay the Temple shekel. Others were assembled round the tables of the accountants of the Temple treasury: these accepted the money of widows and orphans which their guardians deposited for them. All sorts of funds were placed with the Temple treasury for safekeeping; and the sums so deposited were entered into registers of papyrus and parchment. In the basilica of Herod, which stood by the entrance to the Temple courts, the Sons of Hanan had set up special shops for the festival, bringing down the stores from the Mount of Olives, their usual place, the better to serve the throngs of pilgrims. In these shops could be purchased doves, oils, meal, incense leaves and spices such as were used for the purification offerings. Very often the women of the provinces waited with the purification which was obligatory after childbirth until they could unite this ritual with a festival pilgrimage. Again, there were many who could not offer the Passover sacrifice until they had purified themselves from the defilements they had accumulated throughout the year by contacts with forbidden objects. The demand for purification rites was so great, that a vast, fiery column of smoke rose from the altar all day long. The purification sacrifices could not be bought anywhere else than in the shops of the High Priest, which overflowed from the basilica into the courts. The sages and scholars of Jerusalem beheld with bitterness how the Sons of Hanan set up their booths under the arches and between the columns; in these places which all the year round echoed with the words of the Torah, nothing was heard now but the violent chaffering of merchants; there where the carriers of God's word had preached to God's people, stood the tables of the money-changers. But the sages could do nothing about it. The House of Hanan was mighty, the sages were weak; for behind the Hanans stood the Roman power, ever ready to defend them against attack.

That Roman power was visible enough in Jerusalem; and the evidences of it increased side by side with the sunlight and the pilgrims. The arms of Edom and his iron weapons held the House of God as in a vise. When the first waves of pilgrims were seen in the streets of Jerusalem, new cohorts of legionaries arrived from Jericho and Caesarea and Samaria and even from trans-Jordan. Askelonites, with bronzed faces, and yellow-haired German horsemen, were stationed everywhere in the Temple courts. They were like a spear thrust into the heart of Israel, and the blood flowed incessantly. The foot of Edom was in the Holy House; it trampled on every sanctity. The watches on the Antonia were doubled and trebled. They could be seen at every hour of the day, occupying the balconies and terraces of the tower. Their hostile eyes flashed down at us, their fists were clenched, their broadswords newly sharpened, their armor polished—and their hearts filled with hate and envy. All year round the Antonia kept its eye on the Temple area from afar; now its cohorts issued from the fortress and mingled with the throngs below. Strong watches were posted before the gates, those without, which gave on the area as a whole, and those within, which gave on the innermost courts. There was one even at the entrance to the Sanctuary. When the guards were changed there was a rhythmic tramping of feet, the metallic clashing of shields, a flashing of naked steel. At night the procession of their torches made a ring about the walls—the reminder of the ever-vigilant threat directed against the heart of Israel.

This year the Procurator took up his station in Jerusalem earlier than ever before. With him came a numerous staff; there was an unusual increase in the number of Romans circulating in the city. The fences about the Herod Palace were also provided with guards. No one was permitted to draw near the residence of the Procurator, or the other buildings of the Herod Palace, which were filled with soldiers, officials and the administrative staff. At night the blaze of torches reddened the crenelations and loopholes in the walls. Other palaces in Jerusalem, which nearly all the year remained gloomy and abandoned, were illumined at that season. The grim and ancient Palace of the Hasmoneans, wrapped in darkness from one year's end to the other, woke suddenly to life. The Herodian princes had come to Jerusalem, bringing their guards with them. Sometimes the populace caught a glimpse of Herod Antipater himself, newly arrived from Tiberias, walking to and fro behind pointed lattices in the company of his wife or concubine, Herodias. Popular demonstrations against them broke out now and again. Certain of the Priests, seeing the Edomite (as they called Herod) and his woman staring straight down into the Temple courts, had reported the desecration to Zealots in the city. Resentful crowds gathered, stones were hurled, the cry went up: "Edomite, begone from here!" The guards laid hold of the shrieking Zealots and turned them over to the Roman authorities; the latter released them, for there was bitter enmity between Herod and the Procurator.

Together with the staffs of Herod and the Procurator arrived hordes of Syrian cooks, Chaldaean hairdressers, Arabian harlots, oil masseurs, and perfume mixers. The Upper City reeked of them. The palace of the High Priest, too, was crowded with newcomers, for all branches of the family gathered to Jerusalem for the festival; and every one of them walked about in robes of office, for they all occupied some high position or other in the Temple hierarchy. Kaifa was the presiding High Priest; he was the son-in-law of old Hanan; and old Hanan himself, like his eldest son Eliezer, was a former High Priest, of equal rank with the presiding High Priest. But the highest administrative position, next to that of the presiding High Priest, belonged to Jochanan, Hanan's second son. He was in line for the High Priesthood, and was therefore the *S'gan* or Chief Assistant of the High Priest in actual office. The third son was Temple Treasurer. Still another son was overseer of the stores of oil and wood. And yet another was commander of the Temple guards. Kaifa's palace, in the Upper City, was the center of this tumult of officialdom which descended on Jerusalem with the approach of the Passover. Every evening there was a banquet; the mighty ones of the Priestly order feasted, drank, and made merry. The remainder of the aristocracy, returning to the city from the winter resorts, imitated the circles of the Priesthood. They too were accompanied by relatives and friends; they too passed the time feasting and banqueting. Every evening the sound of flutes floated from the windows of their residences. Innumerable lamps poured their light from the walls, the balconies, and terraces. Curtains of costly white stuffs hung over the entrances of the houses, to advise all passers-by that guests were being entertained within.

The Herodian hippodrome, in the Upper City, were always a hated sight in the eyes of the Jews of Jerusalem; but in the festival season it became especially loathsome to the scholars and sages because of the preparations for heathen spectacles. It was rumored that year that even the sons of Hanan had decided to participate in the masquerades, pantomimes and rhetorical contests, among the professional and amateur actors organized to amuse the visitors to the city. Pilate took charge of the hippodrome. Within its walls were many statues of Roman Caesars, erected by none other than old Herod, him whom they called Herod the Wicked. No wonder that this place was the focus of the hatred of pious Jerusalemites. Every Passover they dreamed of storming its walls, tearing them down stone by stone, till nothing was left but a heap of ruins. This Passover Pilate, seeming to believe that an attempt would be made to realize the dream, threw extra guards of Askelonite footmen and German horsemen about the pagan edifice. A dreadful rumor spread among the Jews that this season Pilate intended to hold gladiatorial shows and struggles between men and beasts, and that the latter had already been brought into the city in great cages. But this, the crowds muttered, would never come to pass in Jerusalem; no, not though thousands of Jews paid for it with their lives. The Bar Abba-ites, in particular, made use of the rumor concerning the wild beast shows, to stir up the populace. They poured bitter and inflaming words into the ears of arriving pilgrims. They intimated, further, that the storming of the hippodrome would be but the beginning of the tremendous events which were to unroll in Jerusalem this Passover. But what the nature of these events would be, no one knew.

Then suddenly, and unexpectedly, something happened.

I recall it all as if it had taken place this very day. It was early morning, about the time of the *shachrith* prayer, on the second day of the week after the Great Sabbath. We were still five days from the festival. My Rabbi, Nicodemon, was seated before us on his stool in the synagogue, and we, his pupils, sat at his feet; and while he discoursed there burst into the room Judah Ish-Kiriot. His eyes were inflamed with lack of sleep, and within them a wild light blazed; but they swam, too, in tears of fire. His figure had become leaner since we had last seen him, so lean that it seemed to float in the air. With mantle flying behind him he drew close to us, stretched out his thin, bony arms, and without a word of salutation either to us or the Rabbi, he cried, hoarsely:

"It has begun!"

We, the pupils, were turned to stone. But the Rabbi remained calm, and asked gently:

"What ails you, Judah? What has begun?"

"The Redemption!" cried Judah.

The blood withdrew from our faces. We stared at each other in terror. But still the Rabbi asked gently:

"Tell us what has happened, Judah. Where have you been all this time, Judah? And where is your Rabbi, Judah?"

"My Rabbi? The King-Messiah stands at the gates of Jerusalem.

He will come riding today, a poor humble man on an ass, just as the prophet has foretold, to take possession of the city."

And before there was time to put another question, Judah lifted up his hands, and his feet began to move in a dance. He clapped his hands together, and burst into song. "A star has risen over Jacob!" he chanted. "A child is born unto us! This day is the day of the Lord! And he will raise up the fallen abode of David!"

Still my Rabbi did not stir. He kept his eyes fixed on Judah, then he spoke again, not gently, but commandingly:

"Tell us, Judah, what has happened. This is not a time for chanting."

Judah suddenly revived. He began to pour out a breathless story, and this time our Rabbi did not bid us withdraw from the room. He felt, even as we did, that the time for secrecy and discretion was gone.

"Ten days ago," Judah gasped, "we left Jerusalem. The Rabbi gathered us and led us out to the wilderness of Judaea. There we came to the place where Jochanan had taught. The Rabbi told us to proceed in advance of him, to the Jordan, and there to wait for him. No one remained with him, not even his most beloved disciples, Simon, or Jacob or Jochanan; but he remained alone in the wilderness. Nor did we leave either bread or water with him. There was only the water which issued from a spring and is deep enough for a man to baptize himself in it. There the Rabbi remained alone three days and three nights. When he came to us out of the wilderness we fell down before him, for he was not the same. The terror of God was poured out over him; it was as if the cherubim had lifted him up and carried him through the ranks of the heavenly hosts. His face burned with white fire and his limbs trembled, as King David has said: 'All my bones shall declare the Lord.' Everything about was not as heretofore, and all of us were therefore aware that something great and strange was about to happen with him, but what that thing was we did not know. Nor did we know what the Rabbi had done all alone in the wilderness. He stayed with us three days by the Jordan. He baptized himself, as if in preparation. And we, the disciples, said to one another: 'Now the time has come!' Thus it was! For as we came up from the Jordan to Jericho, the people knew and recognized him, not only the seeing, but the blind, too.

"There sat by the roadside blind Bar Talmai, and when the Rabbi passed it was as if he saw him. For he stretched out his hands and cried: 'Son of David, have mercy on me!' When we heard this great and dreadful utterance from the lips of the blind man, we would have silenced him. But Simon cried: 'It is a good sign! It is a sign that the kingdom of heaven begins, for the blind see that which the seeing do not see!'

"Then the Rabbi called out to the blind man, saying: 'Your faith has healed you!' From that time on Bar Talmai, whom we have always known as blind, goes about; he follows the Rabbi crying: 'I see! I see! Yeshua ben David, have mercy on us!' But now no one tries to silence him. It was thus that we entered the city of Jericho. It was as though a heavenly voice had preceded us, to bring tidings of our coming. For the people streamed out of the houses and filled the streets and stretched out their arms to him. It was as if they felt the power which clothed him; and they blessed him. They asked nothing of him. The mothers brought their children, and lifted them in their arms toward him. The people disputed with each other as to who should be given the honor of sheltering him; for each one wanted the blessing of his presence on his house. But the Rabbi saw a little man who had climbed up on a fig tree, that he might be able to see the Rabbi. To him the Rabbi called: 'Come down, Zaccheus, for today I will stay in your house.' When the man heard this, he sprang down from the tree with the lightness of a lad, for sheer joy, and hastened to the Rabbi, and bowed down before him, then conducted him to the house. The people of Jericho were astounded; they murmured, saying: 'See, he enters as a guest the house of a sinful man.' For Zaccheus is the chief of the tax collectors.

"But Zaccheus stood up before the Rabbi and confessed, saying: 'See, Lord, I give the half of my possessions to the poor. And if I have robbed any man, I make fourfold restitution.' The Rabbi, Yeshua, comforted him and said: 'Today salvation has entered your house, for you are a son of Abraham.' And to the people who stood around, astonished that he should go to the house of a tax collector, the Rabbi said: 'For the Son of Man has come to seek out and to save that which has been lost.' And the Rabbi consented to stay in the man's house three days. He ate there, and slept and rested there. All of us were with him, for the house of the tax collector is big and rich. On the fourth day, when he was rested from the labors he had endured in the wilderness, the Rabbi, Yeshua, gathered us and ascended with us to Jerusalem. We knew now that this was the last ascent. We knew now that great events awaited us in Jerusalem.

"And thus it was. We came up to the borders of Jerusalem, to Bet Paga, on the Mount of Olives. There the Rabbi rested awhile in the house of Simon the Leper. Then he instructed two of his disciples: 'Go out into the village which is across the way. There you will find a young ass, on which no man has ever sat. Unbind it and bring it to me. And if anyone asks you, "Why do you unbind the ass?" your answer shall be: "The lord needs it!"' The two disciples were filled with wonder, and asked each other: 'Why does he need an ass? Would he enter Jerusalem riding on an ass? We believed that he would enter Jerusalem riding the clouds, even like Elijah the Prophet.' But I reminded them of the verse of the Holy Writ. I said: 'Did you not learn the Book of Zachariah in your childhood, and do you not remember what he prophesied concerning the manner of the coming of the Messiah into Jerusalem? These are the words of the Prophet: "Rejoice greatly, O daughter of Zion; shout, O daughter of Jerusalem: behold thy King cometh unto thee. He is just, and having salvation; lowly, and riding upon an ass, upon a colt, the foal of an ass."' When the disciples heard this, they were filled with joy, and they hastened out to seek the young ass. But I hastened into the city, to bring the good tidings to you that today the King Messiah will come riding into the streets of Jerusalem, to begin the kingdom of God according to the prophecy, to destroy the enemies of God, to break their proud necks with a firm hand and to bring their backs under the foot of the just. The hosts of heaven will march before him!"

Foam broke out on the lips of Judah when he ended his speech. His face was pale and his feet stumbled under him. His body shuddered with the holy fire which consumed him.

On us too fell the terror of God, hearing these words. We too trembled with the sacred fire. Only Rabbi Nicodemon remained seated, even though the blood had left his face so that the skin was white to the roots of his hair. He was still all calmness when he said to Judah:

"Judah! Was it your Rabbi who said that he was coming into Jerusalem to break the power of Edom, and to humble him at the feet of the just?"

"No, the Rabbi did not say that."

"Why, then, do you put into the mouth of your Rabbi words which he has not uttered? Have you forgotten the saying of old: 'Sages, be guarded in your words'?"

"But what I have said all follows! For what else will the son of David do in Jerusalem? Do we not all await him? Have we not the promise from of old?"

"Judah, it will not come to pass according to our will, but according to the will of God. And not as we imagine it, but as seems good in the eyes of heaven. It is a dangerous path which your Rabbi treads, but doubtless he has received authority for it. If the thing is from God, it will stand; and if it be not from God, then the builders labor in vain. Go, Judah, fulfill the command of your Rabbi. For us nothing remains but to wait and hope."

To us, the pupils, the Rabbi said:

"Go and see what is toward in the city, for great events are coming to pass in our day."

CHAPTER FOURTEEN

AN ARROW cannot fly faster from the bow than did Rufus and I down the steps descending to the Kidron valley. We took the short path which begins outside the Temple wall, passes by way of our synagogue, and leads into the welter of the Lower City. Everywhere tents, booths of twigs, shelters, bundles sprawled in the streets. We leaped like goats among the men and animals; we crawled under hedges, jumped over fences, ran twisting through crowds—and Judah Ish-Kiriot was behind us all the time. Then we began the upward race toward the summit of the Mount of Olives and Bet Eini, and encountered the procession. It was anything but a great procession, befitting the advent of a King-Messiah. A little ass led the way, guided by Simon bar Jonah, a gray, submissive ass with the head of a calf. It looked away in front, with simple, dumb animal eyes. And though it was young and untrained—for asses are mostly wild—it seemed to know whom it carried; it held its head low and planted its feet gravely and steadily on the stony road. Clothes and rags had been laid on its back—and on these sat the Rabbi of Galilee. His naked, skinny legs, sticking out from under his white raiment, reached almost to the ground, while his head and shoulders swam above the crowd which accompanied him. He looked strangely tall, far taller than I had ever observed him to be; he was lean—nothing but skin and bones—and his face, framed in its black, gray-flecked beard, was as white as his new-washed raiment. A profound expression of earnestness and sorrow rested on it. His lips moved, as if he were praying to himself: indeed, he made one think that he himself was an embodied prayer. The people who accompanied him behaved as though they were conducting a service before the Lord. They carried willow withes and twigs of olive which they had broken off the trees by the wayside, and they threw leaves and branches in the path of the ass. Now and again one among them would also take off part of his sackcloth raiment and spread it before the feet of the animal. It was not a large or imposing procession; it consisted only of his disciples and the poor whom I had seen in the house of Simon the Leper. Among them were some sick men, hobbling along on staves, or supported by friends, two blind men led by boys, and one or two tax collectors, who could be recognized by the badges of office on their clothes. There were a score or so of women, following the men; they too carried willow withes and field flowers. I observed among the women Miriam of Migdal. She was not leading by the hand blind old Bar Talmai—as she had always done in the past—but her namesake, the older Miriam, whose tall, dark-veiled figure rose above the other women. Behind them came Sulamith, the mother of the Zebedees; stout as she was, she panted, and found it hard to keep up with the others. Martha, younger and stronger than she, pulled her along. The strangest figure in the procession, a frightening apparition, was Eliezer, the brother of Martha and Miriam. He strode immediately behind the Rabbi. His yellow-ashen face stood out from among all the others, for it had the aspect of an empty skull above the covered leanness of a skeleton: his legs moved stiffly, like wooden supports, as he followed the ass.

When Rufus and I joined the procession its behavior was still restrained. True, there was a clapping of hands and a singing of verses from the Psalms; but this was no more than a form of prayer. But as they descended the hill and drew nearer the city, their exultation increased. The women lifted their voices higher, they broke into shrill jubilation, trilling and twisting the notes; and their delight infected the men. Miriam of Migdal suddenly detached herself from the group of women, ran in front of the procession, whipped the colored mantle of Persian silk from her shoulders, and laid it on the stony ground for the ass to tread on. She bowed repeatedly before the Rabbi, and we thought she was about to prostrate herself in the dust. She clapped her hands and called incessantly: "See, see, how he comes. The King comes in his glory!"

These words were like a sign to the others. Judah Ish-Kiriot was the first to make the dread announcement before the world. He passed over into such a frenzy of exaltation that he tore the clothes from his body, and clapping his hands wildly he cried:

"Blessed be he that comes in the name of the Lord God. Hosannah in the highest! Blessed be the kingdom of our father David, which comes in the name of the Lord. Hosannah in the highest!"

When the company heard these words issuing from Judah's lips their joy overflowed all bounds; it was as if the proclamation of "the kingdom of David" passed into them, and became a wild spirit. They ceased to intone verses from the Psalms and Prophets. They sprang from their ranks, they leapt about before their Rabbi, who was now coming to Jerusalem to assume the government of the kingdom of God. They waved their olive branches toward him. And Simon's voice added, above the singing and shouting:

"Blessed be the King who comes in the name of the Lord! Peace in heaven, glory in the highest!"

Then suddenly there was a change. The procession issued from behind the wall which hid the prospect of Jerusalem, and reached the foot of the Mount of Olives. The glorious panorama of the city unfolded before their eyes. Now Jerusalem has been likened to a hart which leaps from mountain top to mountain top. Its houses, its palaces, towers, citadels and walls were lifted on heights and lowered into valleys. The sight was most glorious now, for it was the first hour of noon; the heavens, illumined by the fresh spring sun, were unfolded above the innumerable buildings like the wings of a hen above her chicks. And one would have said that the city was built not of clay and stone, but of silver. On many of the roofs there were water cisterns; and those that were below the level of our eyes flung back the sunlight at us; they were like precious jewels in the walls which girdled Jerusalem. Yet the city had broken through the girdle; it poured out toward Mount Scopus; it stretched toward Bethlehem and reached out to Bet Paga. Out of the walls rose, like mighty breasts, the towers and watch turrets, with those of the Herodian palace dominating the rest. And all the city, houses, towers and walls, was spread like a conquered army at the foot of the flaming Mount of the House. The Temple, with its golden gates and balconies, was like an uplifted flame. From our place toward the foot of the Mount of Olives it seemed like something which no human hand had reared out of earthy substance; it was like a vision which had descended, perfect and glorious, from the heavens: flaming walls, flaming gates, flaming roofs. From the heart of the golden House rose a pillar of smoke. Below it was yellow flame, and above it was transparent gray cloud, which broke into floating rings. The appearance of the Temple was unearthly, strange, unbelievable. Only behind the vision of the Temple there rose a gray stone citadel, lofty, insolent, like a threatening spear held by a mighty fist.

The procession came to a halt, held fast by the panorama of Jerusalem. A full ripe pomegranate, the city grew upon the hills of Zion. Tears of joy sparkled in the eyes of the beholders. After a momentary hush, the women broke into a cry of praise: "O Jerusalem!" The Rabbi held in the ass on which he rode, and his countenance was fixed on Jerusalem and on the Temple. Silence fell again, and all held their breath. Two great tears were seen to well up in the Rabbi's eyes, and to roll down his cheeks. He knew in his heart that which all of us felt then. Our souls were liberated, and they mingled with his. It was as if those tears had molten us together and a single prayer was in all of us: "O God, have mercy on Jerusalem!"

The hush lasted no longer than a moment. Was not this the King riding into the gates of the city, to break the might of Edom like a staff, to loose the bond, to destroy all sin, to wipe away all evil, and to kindle a new light over the world? "Thine eyes behold the King in his beauty!" And again the hosannahs rose; again they shadowed the Rabbi with green leaves of willow and olive:

"Blessed be the King who comes in the name of the Lord God! Peace in heaven, glory in the highest! Hosannah!"

We entered the Kidron valley and encountered many strangers, who had made their shelters in the shadow of the walls. Many of those whom we had passed in our descent had not been Jerusalemites, but pilgrims from far provinces. They had not heard of the Rabbi of Galilee, and they did not know what this procession represented. Some joined us, out of curiosity, especially when they heard the Rabbi being greeted like an entering king. They did not know whether to take the words "Kingdom of the House of David" seriously or in jest. But such as had been in Jerusalem before, and had witnessed street riots and abortive rebellions, were not ignorant of the dangerous character of such demonstrations. They felt in their bones the staves of the guards, and the whips of the watchmen on their skin; they remembered the bloodshed, and the swords of the Roman legionaries. They were terrified by the words of the Rabbi's followers, and they therefore warned each other: "Keep away!"

"The guardian of my soul remove me from them!" cried one Babylonian, and began to run, his long black mantle flying behind him.

"I can smell death a mile off!" said a shocked Sharonite to his family, as the procession passed by his booth on the road. "We will have nothing to do with this!" And he laid hold of his sons, who wanted to join the procession.

All this took place before the procession marched in through the Dung Gate of the Lower City. There the crowds came out of the holes and caves in King David's wall; dyers and tanners and oil mixers came; the drivers poured out of the hostelry; a crowd of watercarriers joined us as we passed through their street—many of them even carrying their skins, empty or full. A coppersmith came out of his yard, holding in his hand the piece of metal he had just been hammering. He asked of the crowd:

"Tell me, good people, whom are they conducting thus to the Temple? Is it a Rabbi of theirs?"

"A Rabbi! Yes, a Rabbi, but no ordinary Rabbi. Do you not know him? This is the Prophet of Nazareth!"

"What? A Prophet of Nazareth? But who has ever heard that a prophet shall come out of Nazareth?"

"But this is the Galilean who came so often into our courtyards to bless our children."

"They are conducting the Prophet of Galilee to the Temple, to crown him with the Kingship!" a girl shouted up from the street to a hole in the upper wall, where her mother's face appeared.

The word spread within the labyrinths of the great wall, the labyrinths of the poor. The Prophet of Nazareth was being led now to the Temple, for the crowning! Women who had been busy preparing their miserable dwellings for the festival, came pouring into the street, their babies at their breasts, their children clinging to their robes. A dyer, who had been occupied at his trade, brought forth a roll of stuff, still damp with the fresh purple and crimson dyes, and spread it out in the street before the feet of the ass. He himself, besprinkled with color, fell in with the procession. An incense mixer emptied his mortar before the feet of the ass. Even the coppersmith flung down his piece of metal as an offering. It was as if all these people had been transformed by a magic word: "The Kingdom of the House of David." They were suddenly possessed by the idea that they would never have to return to their poverty and their daily occupations. Joseph the slave, he whom the Rabbi had once comforted in the hostelry of the camel drivers, came running from a distant courtyard. The word had reached him, too, and no doubt he had torn away from the bonds which kept him to the millstones; for fragments of rope were still in his hands, and the wooden yoke was still on his neck. It was as if the great seventh year had arrived, and he had been made a freedman. Storm in his eyes, his hair tumbled wildly, he came running toward us, flung himself into the procession, and shouted, "Hosannah! Hosannah in the highest!" while he waved a piece of rope as though it were a palm leaf.

Out of the narrow alley which led down to the waters of Siloah came Hillel the watercarrier, with others of his trade, all of them laden with filled skins. He too leaped into the procession, forgetting even to free himself of his burden. He dragged the heavy skins with him all the way.

The procession grew in numbers as it passed from street to street. The word flew ahead of us: "They are leading the Prophet of Nazareth to the Temple!" In the street of the weavers men simply left their looms or tore out the uncompleted stuffs to spread them on the ground; so that the ass seemed to tread here in a foaming sea of colors and fabrics. Sheets and tablecovers fluttered from the balconies, the doors and the window holes, banners of joy and poverty. Here and there a woman brought forth one good garment, perhaps the remnant of her far-off marriage day, and laid it on the street and on the ass: veils and nets, pieces of embroidery, colored kerchiefs were brought forth from their hiding places. And the ass, bedecked in finery, carried the Rabbi calmly; it trod without fear among the crowds, and on the sea of fabrics. And by now the multitude was jammed together in the narrow streets, one inextricable mass, men, women, children, the hale, the sick: they waved their olive and willow branches till the leaves dropped off, or they merely waved their hands: and all of them cried out in ecstasy. Thus the procession, like a broad stream forced between narrow banks, poured from street to street, and grew denser and denser, till the ass came to the sloping alleys mounting from the Lower City into the wide market place.

Here all the liveliness and tumult of a Jerusalem festival was concentrated. The merchants had brought out their wares and ranged them on tables. The entire area was jammed with pilgrims, with fathers of families and leaders of groups, all about to make their purchases for the festival. Others had come hither to sell their wares, brought into the city on camels. And still others were here for no other purpose than to gaze on the frenzy of chaffering, the wild confusion of colors and the strange variety of costumes. The greatest noise was before the tables of the goldsmiths, whither the women had brought their husbands to make them buy rings or chains or perfume vials or diadems or brooches. The weavers displayed their colored stuffs, the cobblers their sandals. The wine merchants had ranged their jars at the doors of their shops, and the perfume mixers had laid out their assortments of sweet-smelling ointments.

The procession, with the Rabbi mounted on his ass at the head, with the disciples about him, with the stream of the poor behind them, burst into the wide market place, and in an instant the whole area was filled with shouting, singing Messiah enthusiasts, waving branches and arms, crying: "Blessed be the King who comes in the name of the Lord!" The shopkeepers were thrown into a panic; the buying and selling ceased. Swiftly the wine and honey and oil merchants carried their jars and cruses into the interior of the shops. Some were too late, and jars were overthrown and trodden under foot, wine and oils flowed on the ground. The strangers in the market place—Babylonians, Phoenicians, Antiochans, Cyreneans—did not know what was happening. They turned in amazement to the Jerusalemites: "What is this? Whom do they lead thus to the Temple area, with song and praise?"

"Nothing at all!" a dealer in mantles answered, to calm them. "These are Galilean rebels conducting one of their Rabbis. We know them by their speech. We are accustomed to such things, here in Jerusalem. Every festival they lead another Messiah to the Temple. Their reward will be the staff, the rod, and the swords of Rome."

"Oh, yes, the guards are ready for them!"

There were also many Galileans in the market place, fishermen of Migdal and Bet Zeida and K'far Nahum, millers from Naim and other cities and harbors, where the Rabbi had appeared and performed miracles and comforted the people. When they heard that it was their own Rabbi, one of themselves, who was now being led to the Temple to be crowned king—Father in heaven!—they too flung their garments down before him, threw their girdles into the air, joined the procession, and cried:

"It is our prophet, our prophet of Nazareth, which is in our land of Galilee!"

They dragged along with them the people of Bet Shan and of the Valley of Yizreel. They called out to others, who stood aside, merely watching the spectacle:

"Come! Let us go up with them to the Mount of the House. With the breath of his mouth he will destroy Edom!"

"Yes, Edom! And with him the sons of the Herods, and the Sons of Hanan and all those that oppress the poor. He will make them sink into the earth, as Korah and his tribe sank into the earth of old!"

"How will he do that? With what hosts?"

"Hosts? The hosts of heaven stand ready to serve him. Has he not simply placed his hand on the sick and the halt, and made them whole? Did he not feed thousands with two loaves of bread, so that all were satisfied?" screamed a pilgrim from Bet Zeida.

"And did he not, with one word of command, drive out the evil spirits from our midst? Did he not heal seven that were mad, and five that were lepers? Did he not give sight to the blind?"

"And did he not, in our city, turn water into wine? Come north to our country, and they will tell you who the Prophet of Nazareth is! Yes, in Galilee too a prophet may arise!"

Another Galilean, a fisherman of Genesaret, beat his bosom in pride and excitement. Tongue-tied, he stammered praise of the Rabbi. "He—he's one of ours, f-rom K-K'far Nahum. He—he healed m-many people. Even *g-goyim* believe in him—a R-r-roman captain." He could not get another word out. Choked by his spittle, he relapsed into trembling silence.

"Oh, Father in heaven! The sword of Rome is sharpened on our festivals, too!" one skeptical voice flung at the dancing crowd of enthusiasts. "Judah the Galilean, too, wanted to bring the redemption prematurely. The roads were sown with crucified Jews."

"Rome's sword will become blunt! He will break it as one breaks a burned and blackened staff. Dust and ashes will the Romans be

—and all their friends. Come, let us go up to the Mount of the House and behold God's wonder with our own eyes."

The simple Galileans infected with their exaltation the Sharonites, the Hebronites, the Bethlehemites, those of the Valley of Jehosophat and those of the hills of Judaea. The stories of the miracles worked in the hearts of the listeners. By the time the procession poured out from the broad market place, by the viaducts and narrow alleys, into the paved aristocratic streets, it was no longer composed merely of the lame and sick and poor, followers and disciples of a Rabbi accompanying him to the Temple: it was the vast procession of a people hungry for salvation, a tormented people unable to wait any longer, rushing toward the Temple with their Prophet and Liberator, to be the witnesses of the great fulfillment.

Such too was the appearance of their Rabbi as, swathed in his *tallit*, his eyes uplifted in prayer, his hands outspread in benediction, he broke at the head of the ecstatic throng into the aristocratic streets. On this part of the city, too, the radiant spirit of the festival was shed: but not in throngs rioting joyously, as among the poor. Dark knolls of cypress trees swayed piously above the fences; well-tended palm trees adorned the entrances. Before every gate was gathered a group of slaves, drawn out by the tumult of the approaching multitude with the Rabbi riding at its head. Here and there on a balcony appeared the curled and oiled beard of a man, or the hair veil of a woman. Their faces were troubled as they looked down. What was happening? they seemed to ask. But when they beheld the man riding on an ass, they became calm, and laughed at the picture. On one terrace a group of young people mocked the procession as it drew by; they pointed at the marchers and shouted with merriment. At one gate guards appeared, to prevent the wild horde of Galileans from doing harm to the palm trees, which it was so difficult to cultivate on the cool heights of Jerusalem.

It seemed that the uprush of the multitude toward the Temple produced no great impression on the inhabitants of the Upper City. It was observed, if at all, with amusement or mockery or distaste. Here and there passers-by paused, murmured to each other their disgust that such wild scenes should be permitted in their part of the city, and continued on their way. But no one disturbed the marchers. Even the guard of slaves and Roman soldiers before the palace of Kaifa let them stream past without a hostile gesture. They only stood in firm ranks to prevent an overflow of the demonstration into the garden beds beyond the gates. And yet here, before the palace of the High Priest, the marchers lifted their voices still higher. As if to threaten the hated House of Hanan, they shouted:

"Blessed be he who comes in the name of the Lord God! Hosannah in the highest!"

I only observed that the captain of the priestly guard, gripping his leaden truncheon, muttered resentfully to himself. He had undoubtedly received specific orders not to disturb the demonstration; for no one lifted a finger against us, and many of us were astonished. Thus it was, too, when the procession poured by the stern, gloomy walls of the Hasmonean palace. It was known to all that "the old fox," as they called Herod Antipater, was within, for he had arrived with great pomp and accompanied by a numerous suite. Here too the guard was drawn up before the gate, headed by a Roman officer whom the Tetrarch had brought with him from Tiberias, and here too no effort was made to stop or disperse the throng. Only here and there a Syrian legionary laughed out contemptuously, and pointed at the Rabbi on his ass: "Look, they're leading the Jewish King to the Temple!" But his words were caught up seriously and triumphantly by the men and women who danced about the Rabbi, shaking their olive and palm branches in the air: "Blessed be the King who comes in the name of the Lord God!"

These words, echoing against the massive walls, cannot have penetrated to the inner chambers; those within undoubtedly saw and heard nothing of what was happening without. But high up on the terrace tower of the Hasmonean palace, the trophies and banners of the Tetrarch, which were always hung out when he was on visit to Jerusalem, flashed and fluttered in the sun; and among these suddenly appeared a head, peering down in astonishment on the riotous multitude passing by. It was Herod himself. He had been taking his ease among chosen friends on the sun terrace of the palace. He had heard the wild shouting of the demonstrants, and he had caught the words: "King of the House of

David!" For a moment his dynastic pride had been startled, but he gazed for a moment and no longer; clearly it was enough for him to perceive the man riding on the ass in order to realize that here was no genuine threat to his own royal claims.

Meanwhile the multitude grew. The report that the Rabbi of Nazareth, in Galilee, was about to induct the long-awaited kingdom of heaven, had reached down to the valley of the cheese makers, which is to the western side of Jerusalem. The narrow channels of the streets were thick with figures hurrying upward to the demonstration. From the sheep market, too, on the northern side, there where a vast traffic proclaimed the approach of the festival, shepherds and merchants, buyers and sellers, were drawn away. Many of them, being neither of Jerusalem nor of Galilee, did not know who the Rabbi of Nazareth was, whom they were conducting in such state to the Temple. Some were pulled into the ecstasy of the Galileans. But most of them were not infected with this spirit; they were attracted by curiosity and the expectation of some important event. They kept asking impatiently for miracles and signs. "When is he going to split open the heavens?" The enthusiasts reassured them that this would happen when the Rabbi reached the Temple courts. And thus a tremendous expectation was aroused in the masses who followed the Rabbi.

Meanwhile the man who rode on the ass, he who was the center of all this hope, comported himself not like an angel who had brought down from heaven the powers of both worlds, but like a simple Rabbi of the obscure and despised provincial town of Nazareth, who was proceeding to the Temple accompanied by his poor and ignorant fellow townsmen. Wrapped in his *tallit*, the fringes hanging down to where they touched the feet of the animal, he rode with closed eyes, and sank ever deeper into spiritual absorption as he drew closer to the Temple. His face became paler, and his lips did not cease to move in silent prayer. Withdrawn into himself, given over utterly to his thoughts, he did not see what was happening about him. They that were nearest to him, his disciples, were deeply moved; the sanctity of their Rabbi's thoughts passed into them, so that they felt themselves to be participants in a sacred service; they shook their olive branches as palms are shaken in the booths on the Festival of Tabernacles, and their voices trembled as they cried: "Hosannah in the highest!" It was as if they sought to strengthen the hands of their Rabbi for the great and dread event which was about to take place. From these, the disciples, the feeling of the vast sanctity of the moment spread to many who believed, in perfect faith, that the Rabbi was now bringing with him the heavenly deliverance. They too forgot their surroundings, and gave themselves up to inward, spiritual preparation, so that they might be one in will and thought with their Rabbi. They were pale, as if they felt this to be their last earthly journey before the heavenly life. I marked among the inner circle of marchers the convert, the Greek, now named Abraham ben Abraham. His head was bowed, as always, to the earth; but joy and expectation sat on his crooked shoulders. He walked hand in hand with Hillel the watercarrier, and like Hillel he was seized with a holy trembling. It was as if he had been a Jew from his mother's womb, so utterly was he caught up in the sanctity of the moment. With his free hand he waved a willow withe, and in his alien accent he cried, again and again, *"Hosannah b'marom,* Hosannah in the highest!" Then these two, Hillel and the convert, caught hold of Judah Ish-Kiriot, who was walking ecstatically before them, and the three of them danced before their Rabbi. The same impulse came upon the other disciples, Jochanan, Jacob and Bar Talmai who, with seeing eyes, walked like a blind man. Simon the Zealot clenched his fists and bit his lips; he was like one whose breast is filled with thunderbolts. Of like aspect was Jochanan, of the Zebedee brothers. Only Simon bar Jonah, who led the ass, did not dance and did not clap his hands and did not sing. He walked like a slave before his lord, like a pupil before his Rabbi. The joy and privilege of this indescribable moment had locked his lips but opened the springs of his eyes.

But in spite of the happiness, the love and the pride which was directed to him, as to a lord about to enter into possession of the Holy City, the Rabbi was sunk in boundless humility. Indeed he was "lowly, riding upon an ass." Twice, during his progress, he bade Simon hold in the ass, in order to give others the right of way. Once it was in the market place, when a bridal procession had issued from a side street; the parents of the young folk danced before the bride to the accompaniment of flutes, and sang: "Pleasant art thou, O bride; lovely art thou, O bride." When the singing and the clapping of hands and the clashing of the timbrels came to our ears, the Rabbi bade Simon stand still. They all passed before us, the bride, the dancing relatives, the musicians, and guests carrying lighted lamps in the middle of the day. Certain scholars who had joined the procession of the Rabbi, praised him greatly therefore, and said that he bore himself indeed like a Rabbi in Israel; for even a king must give the right of way to a bride.

The second interruption was less pleasant: the mailed fist of Edom broke a way through to the heart of the marchers. We were close to the viaduct which leads to the outer gates of the Temple, and our eyes were already fixed upon these, with longing and hope, when the unexpected happened. From one of the side streets which led to the Herodian fortress towers, now filled with the staff of the Procurator and with all the pride of the Roman officialdom, there issued a counter-procession of litters, which were being carried rapidly in the direction of the Herodian theater, where games were held daily for the Roman visitors and the Jewish aristocracy. Those that were within the litters must have been men of high importance —perhaps that father of abomination himself was there, the Procurator—for they were accompanied by a heavy guard. A mounted Hegemon headed the military procession, and behind marched a company of Roman legionaries with drawn swords. The litters, borne by black, half-naked slaves, were surrounded by German horsemen. However, the military train was preceded by the household suite. Two trumpeters were followed by a group of Roman slaves, under the guidance of a house marshal. The slaves carried metal-tipped bamboo staves, and with these they cleared a path for the soldiers and the litter carriers. When we first heard the trumpet peal which announced the approach of the train, our hearts stood still. We were faint with expectation of the great moment; we believed that it was almost upon us—that redemption for which so many tears had been shed. O how many generations had passed into the eternal sleep, taking with them into the unknown that one hope: that when the redemption came they would be awakened and called back to life by the trumpet peal of the announcement. It was here! It was upon us! God would arrest the passing of time in the instant when the two processions would come face to face. We already saw the glistering metal tips of Rome's insolent might. Now! They had but to come before the Rabbi, and he would lift up his hand: no, not even that; he would send forth a breath and turn them into dust and ashes. Then the Redemption would begin! But what is this that is happening? What do we see? No, no, it cannot be. The Rabbi gives the signal to Simon bar Jonah, and he pulls the ass to a side, he draws it into another street. And I see the metal tips of the might of Rome go swimming by. The road is clear! Make room there! Not for the bringer of salvation, who is mounting to the House of God, but for the insolent foot of Rome, which treads on Jacob's neck, for the Roman sword and fist, the tormentors of Israel. The marchers stood for an instant turned to stone, as if they could not believe their eyes, as if they would retain by force the hope which was slipping away from them. The Rabbi's withdrawal from the might of Rome was a bitter disappointment to the multitude. The exaltation of a moment ago still carried many of them, they continued to accompany the Rabbi, but the thread of faith and expectation which had held the mass bound to the prophet of Nazareth was now cut.

This was not all. Inasmuch as the side street into which the Rabbi had drawn was very narrow, it took some time for the procession to enter it, and so it fell out that the advance ranks of those who were clearing a path for the soldiers clashed with the last ranks of our procession. Without provocation, without call or need, but merely in answer to their lust for blood, the Roman slaves drove their tipped staves into the mass of the retreating Jews. And to the help of the slaves—who needed no help—came several German horsemen. In an instant men and women were rolling under the hoofs of the horses, their ecstatic cries still issuing from their lips, their willow withes still in their hands. Panic broke out in the rear section of our procession, though in front Simon still led the ass with the same exaltation, and the same holy ecstasy gripped those who were near him, just as if nothing had taken place. All this was as it should be, for it is said that the just man shall avoid the path of the wicked man. But many that had joined the procession out of mere curiosity left it now, with noisy expressions of contempt. Others shouted out that they wanted evidence of the Rabbi's power to perform miracles:

"Is this he of whom you have been singing: 'Blessed is the King who comes in the name of the Lord God'?"

"Has he not just seen how the foot of Edom was placed upon our neck? Why is he silent?"

"Why does he not break the might of Edom, as if it were a burned staff—according to your promise?"

Thus they demanded the fulfillment of the pledge from the disciples; but the disciples and the others who remained in the procession continued on their way; they still danced before the Rabbi, and they paid no attention to the mockers. It was as if they hoped, with their renewed ecstasy, to rouse up the multitude, even though it had just felt the heel of the Roman oppressor.

"Blessed be the kingdom of our father, David, which comes in the name of the Lord God!"

"Hosannah in the highest!"

But still others ran out of the procession, hastened before the Rabbi and called out to him:

"Rabbi! Rebuke your disciples! Let them not utter such words!"

The Rabbi answered:

"I say to you, that if they become silent, then the stones will shout!"

When the disciples heard the Rabbi's reply, their exaltation increased mightily, and they shouted out their words ever louder and louder, as if they wanted to force an answering cry of agreement from the walls and the stones. And others said: "Let us wait and see what the Rabbi will do when he enters the Temple courts."

How astounded, how bitterly disappointed they were when, the procession having reached the viaduct leading to the Temple gate, the Rabbi descended from his ass and like any ordinary Jew mingled with the great multitude of strangers which filled the court. Not a single miracle did he perform! The heavens were not split, no heavenly hosts descended; everything was as it had been yesterday and the day before!

The man to whom the ass belonged led back his property, together with the clothes and fabrics which the people had thrown over it. And those that saw the ass being led off said:

"The musicians played, the guests assembled, but wedding there was none!"

CHAPTER FIFTEEN

WHEN the great crowd which had followed the Rabbi as far as the Temple, in the hope of witnessing miracles, fell away from him and returned to the city, there was left with him only his disciples, the small group of his regular followers, and the women who did the daily work of the company. Within the Court of the Gentiles there was a furious press of people, for the pilgrims were all in by now. Among the latter the Rabbi of Galilee was quite unknown. Followed closely by his disciples, he wound his way through the masses, and none seemed to know that among them was he who but a moment ago had carried on his shoulders the hopes of Israel. A few did, indeed, note his white robes and the group of disciples; but they counted him among the many other Rabbis who had come up to Jerusalem on pilgrimage, together with his companionship. Their interest was slight and fleeting, for there was much else to observe in the courts and in the basilica of Herod. This vast edifice stood on the southern side of the Temple; during the winter and rainy season its arcades supported by pillars of cedar afforded shelter to the preaching scholars and their pupils. Now these spaces were crowded with the tables of the dove sellers placed there for the convenience of the pilgrims. Hard by the dove cages stood the tables of the moneychangers. Here the Rabbi of Galilee stopped, and jealousy for his God and for the purity of His dwelling-place, now desecrated by the booths of the Priesthood, burned in his face. But on this day he neither said nor did anything.

When the day was drawing to a close he left the Temple court, still accompanied by his disciples. He pressed through the crowded streets, and now no one recognized him. Thus, without interruption, he made his way into the Kidron valley, and began the ascent of the

Mount of Olives. I and my friend Rufus still went with them. When we had made part of the ascent, some of the company turned to look on Jerusalem, for it was a glorious sight. The last rays of the sun rested on the triple tower of the Sanctuary and on the high Golden Gate. The tower of the Antonia fortress was all dark; it stood like a mournful watchman over the glory of the House, and like one who prayed to God to have mercy on the Temple and to redeem it from the hands of the stranger. Then one of the disciples spoke:

"See, master, see, the Temple!"

But Yeshua answered:

"I tell you, truly, not one stone of the edifice will remain standing, there shall not be left a single stone which will not be thrown down."

The company of the disciples stood motionless, as if a thunderbolt had fallen in its midst. They looked into each other's faces, and their lips were drawn tightly. I turned toward Judah, and it seemed to me that he had grown smaller; his figure was contorted, as if his limbs were yielding under him. In a moment he would fall head-long to the ground. His yellowish face, which during the last months in Jerusalem had aged greatly, was a mass of folds and wrinkles, within which his eyes and lips were almost lost. He was trembling from head to foot, as if he were exposed to a mighty storm.

The disciples were silent the rest of the way.

The Rabbi walked in front with firm and rapid step, his robe shining white in the falling darkness. He avoided the friendly lights of Gat Shemen, which glimmered among its cypress groves in the last light of day, and entered the narrow pass between stone walls which lead to the summit of the Mount of Olives and the mournful little place which is Bet Paga. When we reached the yard of Simon the Leper in Bet Eini, which is near Bet Paga, full night was on us. The stars shone down through the coolness of the spring air, and a red half-moon hung so low overhead that it was like a lantern suspended above us. A wind blew from the wilderness of Judaea, a wind which was both warm and chill, and which brought in its wake terror and a feeling of asphyxiation. Far off, glimmering in the starlight, lay the Dead Sea, and the hills beyond seemed to be within reach of the hand, so clear was the night.

The house of Simon the Leper was in darkness, as if no one expected the Rabbi's return that night. Only a tiny earthen oil lamp glimmered before the door. The disciples stumbled about, seeking oil and vessels, and at last more lamps were lit. The Rabbi was tired. He lay down on a bed in the inner room, and the disciples sought in every corner for food to prepare a meal. In the poverty of that house they found but a sack of lentils. Then two of the disciples went into the garden, and by the light of the moon discovered a few salad leaves and a handful of carrots which had just sprouted. They also gathered thorns and dried dung, to make a fire in the oven; and thus they filled a pot with water, and cooked the meal for the Rabbi.

Then they laid the table, and brought water from the cistern. When the Rabbi had washed his hands he sat down with his disciples to the meager repast. The earthen pot with the lentil soup was set on the table, and after he had uttered a prayer the Rabbi dipped his hand into the pot, took out a few lentils and ate. After him, the disciples did likewise.

The Rabbi was silent all this while. He did not preach or quote verses of the Torah, but remained sunk in thought. And as they all sat thus at table, the door opened and Miriam of Migdal entered. Her face, uncovered, was shining with renewed youth, for the mood of ecstasy was on her. She carried in her hand a little alabaster cruse, and from it she poured ointment on the Rabbi's head, and the whole house was filled with the heavy perfume of spices. Then there was a stirring among the disciples, and some of them were heard to say: "That must be only the costliest nard." And indeed the ointment was of nard, which is used for the anointing of kings and of princes in their might, and the price of which is three hundred dinars for the smallest weight. No one had known that Miriam had held back so precious a possession from the common treasury for the poor.

Then some of the disciples were also heard to say: "Is it well to waste such a costly substance? The nard could have been sold, and the money given to the poor." Miriam stood there, shamed by these words. And the Rabbi said:

"Why do you sadden the woman? She has done a good deed for

me. The poor you will always have with you, but me you will not always have with you. For when she poured the ointment on me, she did it for my burial."

When the disciples heard this a heavy murmuring rose. They were amazed by the Rabbi's words. Simon bar Jonah cried out: "No, that will never be. Not for your burial, but for your crowning, has the woman anointed you."

But the Rabbi had turned his thoughts inward again, and he said, as to himself: "My soul is oppressed with sorrow now. What, then, shall I say? Father, help me past this hour! But I have nevertheless come to this hour." He addressed those about him, saying: "And I, when I shall be raised again from the earth, I shall draw all men to me thus."

Late that night the disciples prepared their Rabbi's bed in the house of Simon the Leper, but they themselves slept about the yard, every man where he could find a place to shelter himself from the cold which breathed in from the wilderness. Judah Ish-Kiriot and Simon the Zealot and others of the disciples crept into a barn to pass the night, and I went with them. It was too late for me to return to my Rabbi, for Bet Eini is more than an hour's distance from the city.

That night sleep would not visit me. I thought of all that the Rabbi of Nazareth had done that day, and the words he had uttered went through me again and again. But chiefly I thought of what he had said concerning the Temple, which should be destroyed, and his burial, which was nigh. I could understand nothing of all this, and I was oppressed. I thought: "Have we not learned from the Torah that the Messiah will remain forever? And *he* says that the Son of Man will be raised. Who is the Son of Man?"

The thoughts which tormented me must have tormented the others. I became aware that Judah Ish-Kiriot, lying near me covered by his sackcloth mantle, was groaning. On the other side lay Simon the Zealot, and he too was awake. He called to Judah:

"Judah, Judah, why do you groan, and why is your soul oppressed?"

"Did you not hear the master's words concerning the anointing for the burial, and his rising again from the earth?"

"I heard them, even as you did," said Simon. "They are the words which he once uttered in Caesarea Philippi, when he revealed himself to us as the Messiah. Now as then I cannot understand. We believed that the day of eternal joy was coming, the day of deliverance for which our parents and we have waited. But now, as it approaches, is it to be changed into a day of death and mourning? Declare to me what the Rabbi means."

Judah called back in the darkness:

"Simon, do you not remember what the disciples learned from the Rabbi's utterance in Caesarea Philippi, regarding the pangs of the Messiah, and the iron yoke which the anointed of God would carry, and the seven days of agony through which he would pass? Know that this week of agony is here, and the Messiah must pass through all the fountains of pain and sorrow, so that he may issue to salvation, for the highest joy lies cheek by cheek with the deepest pain, deliverance with slavery. For pain is the mother of joy. He has reached the goal of his striving, and he stands now before the splitting of the Red Sea. In their first deliverance the Jews had to pass through the Red Sea, but in this present deliverance the Messiah must pass alone through the Red Sea, for all of us."

"But, Judah, what is the meaning of these sorrows?"

"He is the Messiah. He bears in him the salvation of each separate soul. He brings deliverance for all of us. Before he can save one soul, he must feel the pangs of all souls. He must taste the depths of all sorrow down to the grave, and even deeper. In order that he may bring salvation, he must first pass through the depths of hell."

"Judah! What things are these you say?" And Simon began to weep in the darkness.

"Simon, do not weep. Rejoice, rather. He takes all sorrows on himself of his own will. It is within his choice to refuse to bear them, for all the power is in his hand. But he will not use it; he will bow his neck to the yoke, even as the Prophet has written of him. Did you not see how he turned aside to let the pride of Rome pass? He could have turned their hosts into dust with a breath of his mouth. Yet he did not do it. But riding in all lowliness on his ass he, the King-Messiah, the anointed of Israel, drew to a side before the slaves of Edom. That is the greatness of Messiah."

"But how long? How long?"

"Until he will have drained the cup of tears to the dregs, till his body will have suffered all the pangs of the flesh, till he shall have tasted all the agonies and sorrows that all men have known on earth, and God will say to him: 'It is enough, my Son. Thou hast received thy reward in double and treble measure.' Then God will stretch out His hand to him and say: 'Sit down at my right hand, till I make the earth a footstool before thee.' "

Then Simon called back in a voice which trembled, and in which I heard the beating of his heart:

"Will he also taste the taste of death?"

"God forbid!" cried Judah, in fright. "What are you saying? The Messiah and death? Never will the Messiah taste the taste of death. He is eternal. It will be as the Writ says: the Messiah knows that the Lord will not abandon or shame him."

"But why does he delay the moment? Why is he so mournful, as if, God forbid, as if he would avoid the destiny which is prepared for him? Did you not hear what he said concerning the hour which approaches?"

"In order that the Messiah may know all the pain of man, God created him of flesh and blood. He is as one of us. Nay, more: he feels all pain more deeply than any one of us. Know that God has taken the full and complete nature of man, and poured it into the King-Messiah; in order that the Son of Man may be able to lift up the son of man, he must first go down to the lowest depths; thus he will be able to lift him to the highest heights. He is the sum of all of us. All human creatures that were ever born in the image of God in all the generations, are poured into him. Know what the sages have taught: that the Lord of the World has filled the King-Messiah with the nature of every man, and has given him even the good inclination and the evil inclination: but in him the inclination is mightier than in the simple man of flesh and blood. And though he longs for the salvation, and strives toward it with all his Messiah-will, yet he is afraid and would put off the moment, because of the sea of pain through which he must first pass. For this sea is boundless, and the pains are beyond understanding. God wills that just as he, the Messiah, will attain to the highest joy through the redemption, so shall he descend into the nethermost abyss of pain. Already he sees the bars of hot iron which will be laid on him. He stands and waits for the moment when he will carry them. And yet he would delay it a moment or two, for his soul is in dread. But there is no other path to salvation, save through the pangs of the Messiah. Therefore we must help him to come to them."

"Judah! Judah! What do you mean?" I heard in Simon's voice all the tumult of his heart, and I caught in the darkness the strange flash of his eyes, like the flash of a sharp sword. "Judah! What is your meaning?"

"This! That we must help him to bring the end near."

"How?"

A darker image loomed in the darkness of the night. I recognized Judah Ish-Kiriot.

I rose from my place, I fled from the barn, out into the night. I ran with all my strength, by the light of the stars, toward the city. All along the stony downward slope the darker image within the darkness, the image of Judah Ish-Kiriot, pursued me.

CHAPTER SIXTEEN

THE strength gone out of me, I continued slowly on my way toward the house of Rabbi Nicodemon, toward the one man who could give me enlightenment, the one corner where I still looked for peace. My heart was heavy, and my soul wept over the words I had just heard from the lips of Judah, and I said to myself: "Father in heaven, Thou our protection and help, Thou who hast been gracious to the choice of Thy creation, man, and sendest him a saviour and liberator: why must he tread the path of blood and pain? Thou who art the fount of purest joy, the spring of love and everlasting happiness, why hast Thou made so hard the path of the redemption? Why canst Thou not shower joy upon us from Thy free and open hand? Why must we stand once more before the splitting of the Red Sea? Must I say in my soul—though my soul shrink from it—that there are two powers, a power for good and a power for evil, and that the power for evil can stand in the way of Thy power for good? Does the Angel of Edom make war on Thee above, even as Edom himself makes war on us, Thy creatures, below? No! No! No! What thoughts are these? Thou art the only power, the only ruler in all the heavens and in all worlds. Thou art He who made the covenant with our father Abraham, and Thy promise shall not fail. But why dost Thou make such harsh trial of us? Who are we that Thou shouldst put this high demand upon us, and make us pass through the torment of our souls unto Thee? Help us, Father, help us, let us not stand without!"

Such were my thoughts and such the words I spoke to myself as I approached Jerusalem from Bet Paga on the dawn of that day, the third of the week, the eleventh of the month, and the third before the beginning of the festival of the deliverance from Egypt. Now with every celebration of the Passover the liberation from Egypt is renewed for us. It was not only our bodies which went forth from slavery to freedom; much more was it our souls. And in this festival which was approaching God would liberate us again, but this time the liberation would be the true and eternal and changeless one. Thus I comforted myself as I walked in the half-darkness of the dawn. And I saw the morning star split the heavens like a blazing sword, and through the split light gushed and kindled all the sky. Underneath, on the earth, gardens and houses began to swim out of the covering of the darkness. And then suddenly Jerusalem lay before me, flooded by the first rays of the sun. One by one the torches in procession about the Temple were extinguished. The triangle of the great Sanctuary had the aspect of a flaming mountain, but above it towered the clenched fist of Rome, like the threat of a wicked man raised over a bound saint—the Antonia Tower.

I hastened through the awakening streets of Jerusalem to the synagogue of my Rabbi, for the hour had come for me to attend him.

I found my Rabbi in the *tallit* and *tefillin,* in the midst of the morning prayer. I waited till he had ended, and then I ran to him, and pressed myself to him, as a lost sheep runs and presses itself to its shepherd when it is found. I put my head on his breast and wept, and poured out all that was in my heart. I told him what I had seen and heard within the last day and night, in the Temple court and in the barn of Simon the Leper, the words of the Nazarene and the words of Judah Ish-Kiriot. All of this the Rabbi heard in peace, save when I came to that which Judah Ish-Kiriot had poured into the ear of Simon the Zealot. Then he flamed with anger, and cried:

"The true, great redemption will not come through anguish, but through rejoicing, for he that will be sent will be clad with the power of God. Thus it was that Prophets prophesied for him: 'I will conduct his wars and I will help his children.' For his anger against us is only momentary, while His compassion will endure forever."

For a while he was silent. Then he opened his lips again:

"Great things are taking place in our day, yet we do not know what is happening about us. Without the grace of God we are blind. Come, my son, let us pray together, that we may not fall into temptation, for nothing so illumines the heart of a man as prayer. Since prophecy was taken away from Israel, it can be attained to only through prayer; for prayer purifies and brings us nearer to our Father in heaven."

Then he prostrated himself on the earth, with his head toward the Temple, and I did likewise. In a low voice he uttered a prayer, which I repeated after him:

"Father in heaven, Creator of all things; see, all hands are stretched out to Thee, and all prayer directed toward Thee. Abandon us not in this hour of need. In the time of darkness, open Thou our eyes. Have compassion on us, cast us not away from Thee, for without Thee we are as thistledown which the wind carries without aim and purpose. Gather us about Thee, draw our hearts nigh to Thee, that we may unify our will with Thine, and serve Thee with all heart and soul. Form us in thy image, and fill us with Thy virtues. Spread the tabernacle of Thy peace over all the nations of the world, and open the eyes of all peoples that they may recognize Thee, that Thou art the beginning and the end of all hope and of all desire for Thy creatures. Amen."

The prayer of my Rabbi brought healing to my wounded soul, and I was comforted by it. The purity of cleansing filled me, and the veil of doubt was dissolved from before my eyes and heart, which had been covered by it because of the night in Bet Eini. I felt like a child which had just come in out of the cold night under its father's roof, and was now covered with its father's cloak.

When the Rabbi had taken a morning meal of bread and olives in the company of his pupils, he said to us:

"Come, we will go up to the Mount of the House, for there, among the pillars, Rabbi Jochanan ben Zakkai will preach today."

Carrying the vessels, we went with our Rabbi through the overcrowded streets toward the Upper City. When we came to the viaduct which leads through the gate to Herod's Basilica, the Rabbi bade us entrust our purses to one of the pupils, who should that day be treasurer for all of us. But he instructed the treasurer to remain without, for it is forbidden to enter the Temple court carrying a purseful of money; and the very pious also take off their sandals and leave them in the outer office even before they set foot in the Outer Court. In the winter, however, it is dangerous to a man's health to walk barefoot on the cold stones, and therefore the sages have ruled that it is permissible to enter the Outer Court wearing sandals, but not carrying staff or purse.

But we were greatly astonished when we entered the Basilica of Herod. We were greeted by the tumult of buying and selling, of chaffering and bargaining, all about the booths of the small sacrifices. Baskets and cages of doves were piled on each other. A mass of men and of veiled women pressed about the sellers. Levites in white headgear felt and scrutinized each bird before they handed it to the buyer, to be certain that it was free of all defects and therefore fitting for sacrifice. Now within the Basilica itself, which was frequented throughout the winter by the Rabbis and their pupils, we had never before seen a dove market. We therefore turned to our Rabbi, and one of us said:

"Teach us, Rabbi. But a moment ago you bade us put our purses in the hands of one pupil, who remained without, since it is forbidden to enter even the Outer Court carrying money; and here we see crowds before the dove cages, buying the small sacrifices. How can this be made to agree with the ruling of the Rabbis?"

"That which you see here has nothing to do with the Rabbis; it has to do only with the rulings of the High Priest and the Temple officials. But those that hearken to the words of the sages do not fill the House of God with the loud voice of commerce; for even before they enter the Outer Court, where the Sanctity does not rule, their hearts are filled with the dread of God. May benediction come on them."

But scarcely had the Rabbi ended speaking, scarcely had we approached the alley of columns where the pupils were assembled, when we heard a tumult behind us, a shouting and calling. We turned, our hearts filled with astonishment and terror. We beheld in the Basilica, which we had just left, a streaming of crowds. At first the Rabbi would have ignored the tumult and continued with us on our way, as his custom was; but it was borne upon us at once that something of vast import was taking place, for the people began to rush out from the inner courts. We hastened with them, back to the Basilica. There we beheld a strange and fearsome sight. It was the Rabbi of Nazareth, wrapped in his *tallit*, from which the fringes hung to the ground, holding in his hand a twisted rope such as they use to bind the wheat in the barn, or to yoke a beast to the cart: and he was wielding it about the heads of the buyers and sellers of doves, driving them before him right and left. Thus he broke through wildly to the dove cages, and opened them, and released the doves. The birds rose in the air; with a windy, rushing sound they circled above the arches of the Basilica, throwing the shadows of their wings on the people below. Cage after cage he opened thus. But what amazed us most was that no one hindered the Rabbi of Nazareth. Terror on their faces, buyers and sellers retreated from before him, leaving him to do as he willed with the doves. As if the dread of God had fallen on them, they fled from his path; and he, like a burning brand descended from heaven, like the sword of the Lord, whirled his twisted rope in the air and drove the people from the Basilica.

There the Levites stood huddled together, in their short trousers and white tunics, clinging to the wall. They were contorted with fear. The guards stood there, the Temple watchmen with the lead-loaded whips, and their beards trembled as if in a wind. Before a few minutes had passed the great Basilica was emptied of buyers and sellers. The empty cages and overturned tables rolled underfoot. Everyone fled before him as if he were the scourge of God, and he alone was the master in the Basilica.

Then he stepped forth on the threshold and gazed down on the twisted press of people who gazed up at him as at an apparition from heaven. Never had I seen the Rabbi of Galilee in this light: in his white robe, beneath which we saw his naked feet, in the *tallit* wrapped about him, he seemed taller than man. His face was as white as his robe. Even his beard, it seemed to us, was white: everything about him was white. But not herein lay his terrible aspect, neither in his robe, nor in his *tallit,* nor in his face, nor yet in his eyes which were filled with the jealous joy of the Lord; but in something beyond. It seemed to me that in the night which had just passed a mysterious and tremendous change had come over him, as if the twisted rope he now held in his hand was a sword entrusted to him by the Lord of the worlds to destroy evil from the earth and to bring the neck of the wicked under his heel. He had begun by clearing the Temple of the dove merchants, and he would go on. And all gazed on him in terror: What would he do now? The pilgrims who did not know him, and beheld him now for the first time, asked each other under their breath:

"Who is this man? Who is he?"

"Do you not see? It is a prophet of God. He has been sent to us."

"But that is the Prophet of Nazareth, which is in Galilee."

"It is Elijah the Prophet, sent by God to proclaim the glad tidings."

"It is Jochanan, who has risen from the tomb."

"Did you not see him yesterday, when he rode into Jerusalem on an ass?"

"This is he who has been sent to bring the redemption. Do you see the rope in his hand? It is the sword of the Lord, with which he will drive the wicked into the nethermost pit. Then the kingdom of heaven will begin. But what will he do now? Will he drive out with his sword the insolent Roman guards stationed before the gates of the inner courts?"

Then he stepped down, the Prophet, the sword of the Lord in his hand. And with the fury of God he strode toward us, rope in hand. The multitude divided, and made a path for him. He strode through to the tables of the moneychangers which were ranged before the Temple treasury—and in an instant the tables were overturned!

A ringing and clinking of coins was heard, of coins that rolled on the stones, of coins which none stooped to pick up. For no one could move, so dreadful was the sight. Only the moneychangers rose and fled, leaving their possessions behind them!

Afterwards, thinking again and again of this scene in the Temple, which I had beheld with my own eyes, I could not rightly understand what had happened. I could not understand how it was that they had permitted him to do these things, how not one man had dared to lift a hand against him, how, within a few minutes, he had become the sole master in all the Temple courts. The overseers, they who guarded their rights in the Temple as if they had received them direct from the hand of God, they who had regard for neither the old nor the young in the sternness of their administration, fell to pieces, fled into corners, and left the courts to him. Even the Roman guards, who waited with evil impatience for every pretext which might excuse the drawing of their broadswords, stood unmoving, surly, astounded, watching the tumult, and receiving no word of command from their officers, who were ashamed to reveal the terror which had seized them. It seemed as if the Rabbi of Galilee now had but to turn upon them, and they would flee from their posts. And in that moment our hearts were filled with tremulous hope, for we saw fear in the eyes of the Romans!

But by now the report of these events had penetrated to the innermost courts, and even to the altar, for the high officials of the Temple issued from within. Treasurers and scribes and singers rushed from the offices which they had been performing on this busy day. Among them were the Sons of Hanan: Eliezer, the oldest, in the purple robe which indicated that he had once been High Priest; Jochanan, the second son, also in a purple mantle, the symbol of the first officer after the High Priest, Joseph Kaifa: his beard, dressed in Syrian fashion, hung down like a bell over his robe, and a turreted white headgear sat on him like a crown. There came also his brothers, Theophilus, the Temple Treasurer, and Mattathias, the overseer of the chambers of clothes, vessels, wood, oils and utensils; likewise the youngest of the five brothers, Hanan ben Hanan, the administrator of the small sacrifices which we sold in the courts, and of other Priestly enterprises. All of them were in their robes of office, and about them were clustered the minor officials, and a host of Priestly neophytes, who held in their hands the vessels of the services, the fire shovels, the ash receivers, the incense lamps, which they had been using or cleansing in the preparations for the festival. They stood on the high steps which led into the inner offices, amazement written on their faces. They beheld the destruction which the Rabbi of Nazareth had wrought among the dove sellers and the moneychangers, the tumbled tables, the scattered coins; they beheld the center of this tumult, with the rope in his hand, and the enthusiastic, rejoicing multitude, which turned upon him their faces, hungry, expectant and delighted. The spirit which swayed the assembled mass infected the officials, and the beating of their hearts was visible in their faces; the terror of God was on them, too, as if they beheld something unnatural, and could not believe their eyes. Even through them there passed a strange, enthusiastic murmur, as of wonder at the daring of this man and his certainty in himself. Their pale, frightened faces, their shivering beards, showed that they were seized by uncertainty. Only one of them, the youngest of the High Priestly brothers, Hanan ben Hanan, bit his lips with rage and thrust himself forward. We saw how his face, set in the thick, black beard, which shone with ointment, was filling with blood; for this was an assault on his province, his special government, which the unknown Rabbi of the provinces had dared to carry out. All hearts ceased beating as these two powers confronted each other: the Rabbi of Nazareth, with nothing but the rope in his hand, looked up at the gathered Priesthood; and they, the highest officials of the Temple, in the robes of their religious and civil authority, surrounded by the hosts of their might, gazed back at him. This exchange lasted but an instant, yet it was an instant as long as eternity. The Rabbi pointed at the Priesthood with his rope, and in a voice of thunder, a voice which was like a hundred trumpets, cried:

"Is it not written: 'My House shall be a House of Prayer for all the nations'? And you have made of it a den of robbers!"

The youngest of the Priestly brothers had thrust his way to the front: his hand was lifted, to signal to the overseers with the lead-loaded whips to throw themselves on the Rabbi. A stern glance from his older brother, the Chief Officer Jochanan, arrested the order.

From the hearts of the multitude which encircled the Rabbi rose a great cry of jubilation, as if a mighty weight had been lifted from them. That which had oppressed them all, scholars and people, that which had gathered in every Jewish bosom, all the bitterness and resentment against the House of Hanan, had now become like a single stone which the Rabbi flung into the face of the oppressors:

"The House of Prayer for the peoples you have made into a den of robbers! You have turned the Temple into a slaughterhouse, into a boiling caldron of meats, into an open mouth which cries: 'Give! Give!' for it is never satisfied.

"The Sons of Hanan are the Sons of Eli, who snatch the meat from the altar with their forks!

"The House of Hanan and the House of Beitus: they have made their sons treasurers, their sons-in-law high officers and overseers, and they smite their slaves with clubs. Woe to you, Sons of Hanan!

"The House of God, which should be called a House of Prayer for the peoples, for all the peoples of the world, they have transformed into a market place. Upon the stone where Abraham bound Isaac for the sacrifice, they have opened their booths.

"A curse upon you, Sons of Eli!"

One by one they disappeared, the high officials and the overseers in their purple robes, with their oiled and curled beards; they withdrew behind the curtains of the Sanctuary court. The Rabbi of Nazareth remained alone, the sole master of the Temple courts on that day.

We thought that now, after he had scattered the sons of Eli by the power of the sanctity which streamed from him, after he had bound the Sons of Hanan, the rulers of the Temple, with the breath of his mouth—after he had done this, he would turn and destroy the greatest of all our enemies, the very source of evil, the fist which was laid on the neck of Israel: with the authority now vested in him, with the rope which he held in his hand, he would drive before him the earthly lordship of Edom. But it did not come to pass on that day. For he gathered his disciples about him and left the Temple court. He returned to the Mount of Olives. The people accompanied him as if he were a king; and all faces were radiant, all eyes shone, all hearts drew in joy. Now we saw clearly that deliverance knocked on the door; unto us, too, a protector had arisen. In that day the name of God was sanctified.

CHAPTER SEVENTEEN

IN THAT day all hearts turned to him. Jerusalem talked of nothing but what had taken place in the Temple courts: street and market place echoed with reports, descriptions and discussion. The common people were immeasurably proud of him, and most of all the Galileans, his countrymen; for these, always objects of ridicule because of their ignorance, and even because of the oddity and inaccuracy of their speech, were lifted to new heights. Out of Galilee a prophet had come; not merely a Judah the Galilean, but a true prophetic figure, a second Amos, who had dared to fling the truth in the teeth of the Sons of Hanan, they who had changed the House of God into a den of robbers; or, greater still, a second Jeremiah. Rope in hand, he had driven the Temple merchants before him, the slaves and servants of the Sons of Hanan; and the terror of God had fallen on the oppressors, so that they could not lift a finger against him. Who knew, now, what that rope was yet destined to do? A sword it was, not a rope—the sword of God. Nor was it only the common people who talked thus; pilgrims and strangers crowding the Temple courts, scholars and sages in the synagogues and houses of study, spoke of the provincial Rabbi, of him alone; and in their language there was awe and admiration.

I remember that after those incidents I attended, with my Rabbi, the study house of Jochanan ben Zakkai. The pupils of Jochanan came crowding about my Rabbi, knowing that he could tell them more than anyone else they knew about the mystic man of Nazareth; for it was known that they had met, at least in Galilee, and perhaps in Jerusalem. It was even rumored that Nicodemon ben Nicodemon was a secret follower of the Nazarene.

"Tell us about this unknown person of Nazareth," they said,

"about him who dared to go into the vineyard and drive out the black ravens which consumed the grapes."

"There is not much that I can tell you. His ways are veiled. Only his words and deeds are revealed. But even these do not help us to penetrate, for they uncover one hand's breadth and conceal nine."

"Who knows what such a one has power to perform, and what authority has been entrusted to him," said one pupil, and put one hand over his eyes.

"Power! Authority! An ordinary little Rabbi, I say. He has his moments of exaltation and takes himself for the Messiah. We have known others who behaved differently. The exaltation came upon them, and yet they did not utter insolence against the sages, much less against heaven. Were he that which he believes himself to be, he would not talk, but act; as the verse says: 'And his voice shall not be heard without.'"

"No, no, this is something else. If he speaks thus, no doubt he has authority for it. I saw with my own eyes the evidences of his authority. . . ."

"But what do you mean? Who is he?" The pupils pressed closer about my Rabbi. "You know him, and you have spoken with him. Whence does he draw his strength?"

"I do not know, I do not know," my Rabbi reiterated. "Sometimes I think. . . . No, I will not say it. I am afraid that my words will be a temptation and a stumbling block."

"But why should not the sages go to him, the scholars and the learned men, to ask him by what authority he does these things? See: if he is that which some suspect him to be, it is incumbent on us to know."

"Nay, we must know in any event," others added.

"Where does he live? In what synagogue does he preach? Where does he keep himself?"

Suddenly they became aware that no one knew where the Rabbi of Nazareth made his abode. He appeared in the streets and in the Temple courts, he shone like a heavenly light—and then he was gone!

"We must send messengers to him. We must inquire into him. We must know with whom we have to do."

"But whither shall we send?"

"He will come again into the courts."

"What? After that which took place, he will return?"

"If he is what we suspect, he will surely return, to finish that which he began. He will not conceal himself from anyone," my Rabbi answered resolutely.

"Good! If he returns, we shall know that authority has been given into his hand. That will be the sign. And until then we will hold off with our deputation," they agreed.

That afternoon I did not go up to Bet Paga, in the footsteps of the Nazarene, as I had intended, but went down instead to the house of Simon Cyrene, in the Kidron valley, to fulfill the duty of honoring my father, who had come up to Jerusalem for the Passover. He had before him the double commandment, to purify himself and to bring the Passover sacrifice. He likewise brought with him, as always, many gifts for the household of Simon Cyrene. For my Rabbi he had a jar of Sharon wine, pure according to all the laws of the ritual, a sheep for the sacrifice, and a measure of myrrh, mixed with the most delicate shamir oil, which my Rabbi liked greatly. My father was happy with my progress in the Torah, and prayed for the day when he might see me enthroned in the Rabbinate of Israel. On the evening of that day I put on for the first time the full-length mantle, as a sign that I had attained to the status of the learned man. After the evening "Hear, O Israel" had been intoned, the women of the house lit the oil lamps and the men washed their hands, after which they seated themselves on the floor about the low table to break bread together. But suddenly the door opened, and there came rushing in my friend Rufus, the younger of the sons of Simon Cyrene. He did homage to his parents, bowing before them and kissing them on the right cheek; then he greeted the guests. His father was astonished to see him and feared that something untoward had come to pass. But Rufus assured him that he had left his Rabbi's side only out of longing to see his parents, and to participate in the feast. He washed his hands and joined us.

At the table of Simon Cyrene the talk turned to the events which had occurred that day in the Temple courts, and to the hopes bound up with them. Simon Cyrene called out:

"These are great things that God prepares for us. We hear voices and behold signs which testify that the redemption is not far off, and the hand of God sustains us. How else shall we interpret that which took place in the courts? The sheep was in the jaws of the lion, and the lion did not dare to swallow it—out of sudden fear." Thus he alluded to the terror which had come upon the Sons of Hanan, when they seemed to have the Rabbi of Galilee in their power, and started back from his words of thunder and fled from before him.

"True! It is the beginning of the liberation," my father agreed.

Throughout all the talk concerning the Rabbi of Nazareth, the face of my friend Rufus glowed with joy, and his black eyes opened wider and wider, and shone ever more brightly, till it seemed that his face was nothing but a frame to his eyes. He stared at me, feverish with the impatient desire to impart something to me, and both of us waited for the moment when we could withdraw and be together, for I knew there was something which he was keeping for my ear only.

Scarcely had we finished the benediction after the meal when we both rose and went outside. The bright moon, somewhat beyond the half, sent down a flood of light.

I said to my friend: "You have something to tell me which you wanted to hide from our parents. What is it, Rufus?"

He answered with a long, hurried recital:

"I hastened after the Rabbi of Galilee when he left the courts which he had cleared of the merchants and moneychangers. I could not keep pace with him, but I knew that I should find him in the house of Simon the Leper in Bet Paga. And oh, wonderful things have come to pass this day!" My friend stopped for a breathless moment, and his eyes were brighter than the lights in heaven. "For when I came to the summit of the mount, and drew near to the house, I heard a great shouting, a sound of jubilation. I saw the disciples of the Rabbi gathered around a withered fig tree which stood on the road before the house. And they were crying to each other: 'Look! Look! See the wonder!' I asked them what had happened and they told me that that same morning the tree had been covered with opening buds. The Rabbi of Nazareth had gone out to it, to gather figs, for he was hungry. But when the tree had none to give him, for the buds were only just opening, and none of the figs was ripe, the Rabbi cursed the tree, that it might wither. And when they returned that afternoon from the city, they saw that the tree which the Rabbi had cursed, was withered, and all the opening buds had fallen."

"But Rufus," I said, "do you not know that the fig trees of Bet Paga wither early and lose their buds, because the place fronts the wilderness of Judaea; and the hot winds bring the desert dust and choke the air so that the bark of the fig tree is dried up? That is why they have named the place Bet Paga, the place where the figs never ripen."

"Surely I know this, and everyone knows it. The other trees, too, near the one which the Rabbi cursed, had also lost their buds in the heat of the long day. But with this tree it was different. For not only the leaves and buds had fallen, but the branches had shrunk, and hung down like the lifeless limbs of a man who is taken down from a cross. And the tree itself had the aspect of—of a *sh'ti v'erev.*"

"Of what?" I asked, frightened.

"A *sh'ti v'erev,* a cross, like those which the bloodthirsty Romans plant along the roads of Judaea, like those which stand on the summit of Golgotha, with living men nailed to them."

I had observed a change in the spirit of my friend ever since the time we had begun to visit the summit of the Mount of Olives. Rufus had always been a man of dreams. Whenever our Rabbi used to speak of the days of the Messiah, or recount the deeds and sayings of the generations of old as transmitted in the *Agada,* my friend sat with closed eyes, as if he had been carried to another world. But since we had begun to follow the Galilean this habit in Rufus had been intensified beyond all understanding. He brought to the acts and words of the Rabbi the will to see the most wonderful meanings and interpretations. His nights were filled with visions, so that he would speak in his sleep of the Messianic day; or he would start up and wake the rest of us, and tell us what had appeared to him.

I applied to my friend the verse of the Writ: "When the Lord returned the captivity of Zion, we were as in a dream." But this time I was seized by a strange fear, and I said:

"Rufus, tell me: did you alone mark that the tree which the Rabbi cursed had taken the form of a cross, or did others mark it, too?"

"I think that some of the others marked it, too. In any case, Judah Ish-Kiriot must have marked it, for while I saw the disciples dancing and rejoicing with clapping of hands and a crying of Hosannah, Judah stood aside, and trembled with fear, and his face was pale. It seemed to me, again, that Simon bar Jonah did not rejoice with the rest."

"And what did the Rabbi say?"

"The Rabbi did not speak of this thing. When the disciples pointed to the tree, and said, 'Rabbi, see, the thing you have cursed has withered and dried up!' he answered: 'Have faith in God. I say to you truly, if any one of you say to a mountain, "Lift yourself from this place and throw yourself into the sea," and if he say in full faith, having no doubt in his heart but believing that it will happen, then his words shall be fulfilled. Therefore I say to you: That which you ask in prayer, believe that it will be granted, then it will indeed be granted.' Then one of the disciples asked: 'Can everything be attained through prayer?' And he answered: 'Yes, if your prayer is for the sake of the heavenly will, and your hearts have been cleansed of every complaint against men. If you pray, first forgive everyone who has awakened your anger, and then your Father will forget all your sins.'"

"But what happened after that? Tell me; my soul thirsts to know."

"Philippus of Gederah came up to the mountain with a company of Greek Jews."

"Who? Philippus?"

"Yes, the Greek of Joseph Arimathea, Philippus the convert. He came up with the Greek Jews. His head was bowed down, more than ever, and he walked on a side; he looked like a ship broken by storm and barely making the harbor. But he talked eagerly and unceasingly to the people who accompanied him, and I wondered how he had learned where the Rabbi was to be found. When they had drawn near, they fell into a whispered conversation with one of the disciples, Philippus of Bet Zeida, who speaks their language, while Philippus of Gederah himself called aside Simon Andrew.

"Now the Rabbi was no longer there; he had gone into the house of Simon the Leper, to shelter himself from the cold wind which had begun to blow on the mountain, for the heavens had become dark and a chill had fallen. Then Andrew went into the house, and after a while the Rabbi appeared on the threshold. Philippus of Bet Zeida conducted the Greeks to the Rabbi, and Philippus of Gederah bowed down, so that what with his head which is always bowed to the earth, he looked like a little, dried-up worm. Behind him stood the Greeks, they too with bowed heads. The Rabbi called to them and said, with hidden meaning: 'The hour is come when the Son of Man shall be glorified. I say to you truly: If the seed fall not into the earth and die, it remains alone. But if it die, it shall bear fruit. He that lives out his life, shall lose it. But he who hates his life in this world, shall receive eternal life. He that would serve me, let him follow me. And there where I am, there my servant shall also be. And whosoever shall serve me, my Father in heaven shall do him honor.'

"He was silent then he spoke again: 'Now my soul is oppressed. And what shall I say? Father, help me through this hour; nevertheless, my hour has come. Father, glorified be Thy name.' And just as he said this, there was a thunder and lightning, and the heavens were split. But it was not thunder and lightning. Out of the rift in the heavens a fiery angel descended, and flew toward him."

"Rufus, Rufus, you are a dreamer," I called. In the city of Jerusalem everyone had observed thunder and lightning that day, and everyone had hoped that the latter rains would come to fill the half-empty cisterns. We had already begun to rejoice. But no rain had followed the thunder and lightning.

Still my friend Rufus clung to what he had said. The heavens had divided and a fiery angel had descended. True, there were many, during those days, who walked about in a world of dreams and beheld visions, their hearts beating high with hope and expectation.

During that same evening my friend and I walked about in the moonlit streets and alleys of the Kidron valley. Wherever we went we heard the happy voices of young men and young women, and the laughter of children. All hearts overflowed with joy. And no one paused to think or doubt, for everywhere the expectation of great events filled the air.

And as Rufus and I walked thus hand in hand through the gay, lively, rushing streets of the valley, we came into the alley of the coppersmiths and the ironworkers. The anvils of the smithies stood in half-caves; we saw how the fires flickered in the braziers, and we heard a ringing and clattering of iron on iron. We were astonished. We knew that the guards of Edom kept close watch on the smiths of Jerusalem. The servants of the High Priest, too, came on rounds of inspection, to make certain that the smiths were working on pots and pans and other household utensils and not forbidden implements of war. For the sake of the cleanliness of the city they were confined, together with weavers and dyers and tanners, to the lower slopes. Never had I witnessed such a stir of activity among the smiths as on this day, or observed such a spirit among them. We looked into smithy after smithy, and the faces of the men who stood at the anvils and braziers were filled with exultation and power. Mighty arms pulled at the bellows ropes or swung the hammers on the gleaming anvils; the flames shone on naked, hairy flesh, on wild beards and fiery eyes. Swords were being hammered, not pots and pans! And every time the hammer came down, there was a shout of triumph and revenge, of redemption and liberation. Skilled fingers tested the edges of the blades. Sword was added to sword. Men came, one by one, and carried them off. What was happening here?

But at one smithy Rufus and I stopped suddenly, as if paralyzed. We saw two men enter stealthily, both of them in sackcloth robes. One of them was elderly, short, but powerful of build, with the knotted limbs and body of a lion, and eyes that glared from under thick brows; the second was of lofty stature, broad-shouldered with vast limbs of steel. They too stretched out their hands to the swords, tested the blades, threw down their money, thrust the swords into their clothes and disappeared.

"Did you see? Did you not recognize them? Two of the disciples."

"Yes! Simon and Jochanan. Look! There they go!"

My friend and I stared dumbly into each other's eyes, and our hearts, not our lips, inquired: "What is the meaning of it?" Disturbed and restless we left the street of the smiths, and returned to the house of Simon Cyrene, I to pass the night near my father, Rufus to stay with me and his parents.

In the early morning we set forth for the house of study. I took with me the gifts for my Rabbi, the lamb and the jar of wine and the cruse of ointment. As soon as we entered the narrow streets we were amazed by the change which had come overnight. The joy of the approaching festival had disappeared utterly, and in its place were bitterness and mourning. Men walked about with dark faces and tightened lips. As we went further we encountered fluteplayers such as attend funerals, and women wept on the thresholds of the houses.

Then we asked what had come to pass in the night, and received a frightful answer. We understood then the meaning of what we had beheld, the activity in the smithies, the coming and going of men who bought swords. It was Bar Abba and his followers, they who were impatient with the promise of the Rabbis and the dream of the Messiah. The events of the previous day had awakened both the envy and the hope of the rebel. To him the reluctance of the High Priests to take captive the Rabbi of Galilee was a signal and a challenge. He believed his moment had come. He sent word to his men in the Lower City to arm themselves at once, and to gather in the hostelry of the camel drivers. But in the night the Roman legions swept down suddenly and stormed the place. Many had fallen in the fight. The streets leading into the hostelry were declared defiled, because of the corpses which lay there. The wounded had been left where they were struck down, and wallowed in their blood. Bar Abba himself had been taken alive by the Romans.

As we drew nearer the scene of the battle, the stillness yielded to a fierce murmuring. The bitterness of the inhabitants of the Lower City mounted higher and higher, and everywhere the word was: "Bar Abba!" In that one night he had become the universal hero. The story of his life passed from mouth to mouth. They spoke of his heroic temper, his goodness and his generosity: how he had stood up to the hated guards of the High Priest, how he had plundered the wealthy, on the highways and in their homes, taking away their gold, their utensils, even the preparations for their feasts, to distribute them, like another Elijah, to the poor and widowed; how he had brought costly ointments from the storerooms of the aristocracy to heal the friendless sick.

But as always in such cases, the talk of his fearlessness and of his love for the poor was greatly exaggerated. The robber of yesterday became the folk hero of today. They said everywhere that if he had not been betrayed by one of his own men, who told the authorities of the armed gathering in the hostelry, he would never have been taken. They remembered how he had been wont to appear suddenly in the streets and market places, and even in the Temple courts, to denounce the Sons of Hanan, and how he had disappeared as suddenly, to the bewilderment of the guards. And now everyone believed that he had laid tremendous plans; vast hosts had been waiting for the word of attack; he had been preparing to lead an assault on the Temple guards while the pilgrims were assembled there.

"No, no!" said others. "He would not begin the rebellion in the Temple. Bar Abba is a pious Jew. He would not have defiled the courts with corpses, before the Passover sacrifice. His plan was to attack the procuratorium, and to take Pilate himself captive."

"That was not the plan," others contradicted. "Not the procuratorium. He was going to surround the theater with a great host, just when the Romans and their friends were at their games. He was going to throw one vast net about Edom and Herod and the Sons of Hanan; he was going to capture them, lead them off into the wild caves of the Judaean wilderness and hold them as hostages."

"And if not for the traitor in the night, we might—God knows—have become free men this Passover."

This was the talk we heard among groups gathered at corners, and among the workers setting up their stalls in the Old City. But the Procurator and the High Priest had already taken stern measures. The guards had been doubled and trebled everywhere; not only in the Temple courts, but in the streets and market places, at the entrance to every alley, before the gates of the palaces: Romans, Askelonites and Syrians in full armor, their broadswords drawn. The German cavalry, too, had been brought out from the Antonia and stationed in the city. Great numbers of Priestly guards, the men with the hated lead-loaded whips, were on parade. Wherever they encountered a gathering, they attacked without warning, and sent men and women flying in all directions. Even Rufus and I, walking peaceably toward the house of study, carrying the presents to our Rabbi, were forced to take refuge more than once in houses or booths or courtyards. We were breathless and exhausted by the time we reached our destination.

We found Rabbi Nicodemon at morning prayer, and even while he prayed he sighed so deeply that his body seemed to break with the pain of it, and we who stood listening were shaken by terror and pity. Still he did not interrupt his devotions. We waited for him to end, and to hear what comfort he had for us. But when he had doffed the phylacteries and prayer shawl, he only said:

"May it be the will of Him to whom all the earth belongs, that the festival which approaches may pass in peace; may it be a Passover of redemption; not of liberation for our bodies, but of consolation for our souls."

For he had received a full account of what had happened in the night.

CHAPTER EIGHTEEN

IT WAS now the fourth day of the week, and two more days remained till the festival. We were seated at the feet of our Rabbi when a messenger came from the scribes and the Rabbis who were assembled in the Temple, bidding him proceed without delay to the Court, for a matter of great importance had arisen. My Rabbi did not lose a moment but put on his mantle and set out with Rufus and myself for the Upper City.

When we arrived at the Court, we learned that the Prophet of Nazareth had returned to the Temple courts. Ignoring what had happened in the night to Bar Abba and his men, ignoring what he himself had done in the courts the preceding day, and ignoring likewise the double and treble guard of Romans, whose officers were now on the alert for any pretext to proceed against the Jews, the Prophet of Nazareth had returned with his disciples, and he sat now before the Temple treasury, preaching to an assembly of the people. The scribes and the elders had therefore decided to send a deputation to him, to have him declare with his own lips by what right he did all these things; to explain, further, who he was and in whose name he acted. Many among them wondered if the time had not come, and God was ready to take mercy on his people; and the hope which had been kindled in the common people, and had spread among the scholars, was strengthened by the uncertainty among the Priests. For from among these, we were told, messengers had come to the Tribunal, asking that an investigation be made into the identity and authority of the man of Nazareth.

The Court had chosen a delegation in which were included some of the scribes, some of the elders, and even some members of the Priesthood; but the inclusion of these last was concealed, lest the Romans should become aware that the House of Hanan permitted itself to have dealings with the Nazarene. My Rabbi was added to the delegation, because it was known that he was favorably inclined toward the Nazarene, and was acquainted with him.

The messengers of the Court went forth and found the man of Nazareth seated in the midst of the people before the Temple treasury, teaching them, as was his wont, by way of hints and parables. They made obeisance before him and said:

"Teach us, Rabbi. With what power do you do all these things and utter these words, and whence have you the authority? Reveal to us who you are, for we are weary of wandering in darkness and doubt, and these are fearful days."

The Rabbi of Nazareth answered:

"I will ask you one thing, and you must answer it; then I will tell you by what authority I do these things."

"Ask, Rabbi," they said.

The Rabbi of Nazareth asked:

"Tell me, was the baptism of Jochanan from heaven or from man? Answer me."

But the sages looked at each other uneasily, for the scribes and Pharisees and elders had not yet decided among themselves whether the baptism of Jochanan was from heaven or from man. They replied:

"Rabbi, we do not know. Certainly Jochanan was a saint and a prophet and martyr, for he was slain for the sanctification of the Name. But we cannot say whether his baptism was from heaven or from man, for in such an important matter the scribes and scholars must accept the decision of the Council of Elders; and we have no authority to express ourselves without that decision."

Thereupon Yeshua answered: "Then I will not tell you by what power I do these things."

And while the messengers of the Court stood amazed and wordless Yeshua turned to the people and told them a parable of a vineyard:

"A man planted a vineyard, and he made a fence about it and dug a cellar and built a tower. And he hired out the vineyard to gardeners and went away on a journey. Then in the fullness of time he sent his servant to the gardeners, that he might take away the fruit of the vineyard. But the gardeners beat the servant and sent him back empty-handed. They did likewise with a second servant; they threw stones at him and wounded him and sent him away ashamed. The third servant they slew. Now the man had an only son, whom he loved greatly, and him he sent last. Then the gardeners said to each other: 'This is the heir; let us kill him and inherit the vineyard.' They fell upon him and slew him and threw the body out of the vineyard. Now what will the owner of the vineyard do? He will come and slay the gardeners and give the vineyard to others. For you have not believed the words of the Writ: 'The stone which the builders have despised has become the chief cornerstone.' This thing has happened from the Lord God, and it is wonderful for our eyes to behold."

When the scribes and the elders and the priests, the messengers of the Court, heard this, they became pale. They hid their eyes, their faces were overshadowed and their hearts trembled because they could not understand. At last the oldest of the members of the deputation said to the Rabbi of Nazareth:

"Far be it from us to despise and cast away the stone. None of us wishes to harm you. Tell us who you are and who sent you, and we will take the stone and build upon it the tabernacle of peace which has been promised us. Tell us, Rabbi, who among us sought to do you harm, and who among us would have rejected the stone? You ask of us that we accept you as the chief keeper of the garden, higher than Moses, and you give us no sign of him that sent you. It is well known to you how we are bound by laws and commandments, and how the Torah directs us clearly as to the manner in which we shall receive a prophet or a seer. And as a Rabbi in Israel you know likewise that we cannot reject a single law of the Torah without rejecting the whole."

Some of the scribes who stood there said:

"We have nothing more to do with this man. Have you not heard his parable? He has spoken blasphemously against the living God. It has been made clear to us how we shall proceed."

But my Rabbi called out: "One does not proceed on a parable."

Most of the scribes and Pharisees agreed with my Rabbi, but some of them withdrew in anger, because of the words which the man of Nazareth had spoken concerning himself without bringing a sign.

While the deputation and the man of Nazareth conversed thus, and the people stood bewildered, not knowing which side to take—for they did not understand what was being said—some of Bar Abba's men pushed their way forward. They were recognized by the marks on their faces and bodies, the half-dried wounds they had received in the night; and there were among them Pharisees, too, and even men that were of the circle of Herod Antipater. For the bitterness against Rome had united all, and among those that could be trusted with the secret it was known that Herod himself was gathering arms in his palace at Tiberias, in preparation for a revolt against Rome. And because the prophet of Nazareth had kindled the hopes of the people with acts and words, these men too gathered to him. One of them, whom they had chosen as spokesman, called out to the scribes and scholars:

"Is this a time for parables? The enemy batters at the gate without, and the people stumble about in the darkness within. Is this a time for dispute and discussion? It is a time for action!" With this he turned to the man of Nazareth and cried: "Rabbi, we know you to be a man of truth, and one that will not bow before the opinion of another. You seek no one's favor, but teach the ways of God and the truth. Tell us, then, freely and openly and without parables: Is it just that we, the people of God, shall pay taxes to the Caesar, or is it unjust? Shall we or shall we not give tribute to Edom?"

The multitude held its breath. They had not been able to discover a meaning in the exchange between the Rabbi and the deputation, and in the parable of the vineyard; therefore they had not known on whose side they were. But here was simple and straightforward speech, and they awaited a simple and straightforward answer. The Rabbi of Nazareth gazed long and earnestly at the man who had put the question. Then he said:

"Why do you try me thus? Bring me a dinar, and let me look at it."

And one of the men already held out a coin in the palm of his hand, a dinar with the unworthy image of Tiberius stamped on it—a thing which it was forbidden to bring into the Temple courts.

The Rabbi picked up the coin, looked at the image of Tiberius and at the lettering, then asked:

"Whose image and whose words are these?"

They answered:

"The Caesar's."

"Then render to Caesar what is Caesar's, and to God what is God's."

A murmur went through the crowd. Arms were opened in astonishment, beards wagged in disagreement, there was a bitter tightening of lips.

"What does he mean, 'Caesar's'? Is that dinar the Caesar's? Has the Caesar made a gift of it to us? Have we not sweated for it? Do we not pay for the foreign money which he forces upon us, with the labor of our bodies? Does not the Caesar take away from us oil and wine, corn and sheep and cattle, to give us in exchange his hateful image? What does he mean then, that we shall render to Caesar what is Caesar's?"

More clearly, voices were lifted: "No, never! We have paid enough to the stranger. We are God's children. We recognize only one Caesar!"

"To God alone belongs dominion!" The old cry of Judah the Galilean was heard.

But the sages and Pharisees sought to calm the crowd.

"The Rabbi of Galilee has answered in the spirit of our tradition," they said. "No less a prophet than Jeremiah bade us pray for the peace of those in whose dominions we dwell. And our scholars have taught: 'The law of the kingdom is law!' "

But the people would not listen to such words. They cried:

"There is nothing to hope for any more from the prophet of Galilee. Woe unto us! We have been deceived again!"

It was then that we first heard the shout. "Bar Abba! Give us Bar Abba!" Many of the people withdrew. Among those that remained were the Pharisees, my Rabbi in their midst. We waited to see what the end would be, for the Temple overseers began to disperse by force those that had shouted for Bar Abba.

Then there drew near to our circle some of the Sadducees, who had listened from a distance to the dispute between the Pharisees and the Rabbi of Nazareth. They were easily known by the richness of their garb, by their rings, and by their beards, which they dressed after the manner of the Phoenicians. Among them were also certain of their sages and scholars and interpreters of the law, these, again, being known by their lofty, pyramid-like headgear, and by the goosequills thrust behind their ears. They had listened from a distance, but taken no part in the discussion; only on their lips there was a smile of mockery for the Pharisaic sages who still seemed to hope for a deliverer risen from among their own.

Now they approached and asked the Rabbi of Galilee their eternally derisive questions concerning the resurrection, a matter on which the Rabbi of Galilee and the Pharisees were at one. "How will it be in the world to come, when seven brothers shall in succession have married the same woman, each one marrying her as the widow of a brother deceased, according to the law of Moses? To which of the seven brothers will she belong when they all rise from the dead?"

The Rabbi of Galilee answered:

"You do not know the Writ. When they rise from the dead they will neither marry nor give in marriage, but they will be like the angels in heaven. Have you not read in the Book of Moses how

God spoke to him from the burning bush: 'I am the God of Abraham, Isaac and Jacob.' God is not the God of the dead, but of the living; therefore you wander in error."

When the Pharisees heard this answer, they were won over completely. They forgot all that he had said against them.

"Rabbi, Rabbi," they cried, "you have spoken well! God strengthen your hands."

And one of the Pharisees added:

"Our ancient sages have taught the same. Whence do I know that the resurrection is given in the Torah? It is written: 'I shall confirm my covenant with them to give unto them the land of Canaan.' It is not written: 'Unto you,' meaning the Jews of this day, but 'unto them,' that is, unto Abraham, Isaac and Jacob. Thence it may be seen that the resurrection is promised in the Torah."

Still another scholar added:

"Why need you go so far afield? It has been stated explicitly by our sages: 'To every one of the people of Israel there is a portion in the world to come.' And not only to the sons of Israel, but to the righteous of all the people of the world. And in this world to come there will be neither eating nor drinking, nor marrying nor being given in marriage, nor begetting of children. But the saints will sit with crowns on their heads and will rejoice in the glorious rays of the *Shekhinah*."

The cries of the Pharisees were renewed: "Rabbi, Rabbi, you have spoken wonderfully. May God strengthen your hands. You have silenced the Sadducees." The common people, seeing the delight of the sages in the Rabbi of Galilee, felt their hearts grow lighter; they were comforted, and their hope was renewed.

Then one of the disciples of Jochanan ben Zakkai came before the Rabbi of Galilee and said:

"Rabbi, teach us. Which is the first commandment of all the commandments of the Torah?"

He answered: "The first commandment is: 'Hear, O Israel, the Lord thy God the Lord is One. And thou shalt love the Lord thy God with all thy heart and with all thy soul and with all thy mind and with all thy might.' That is the first commandment. And the second is equal to it: 'And thou shalt love thy neighbor as thyself.' There are no commandments which are greater than these."

When the scholars heard this, they were filled with joy. And the scribe who had put this question called out:

"You have spoken wonderfully. You have spoken truth. For there is only one Lord God and there is none beside Him. And to love Him with heart and soul and mind, and to love your neighbor, is more than all offerings and sacrifices."

Then my Rabbi Nicodemon spoke:

"Our sages taught: Whence do I know that when one of the sons of the other peoples fulfills the law he is as great as the High Priest? It is written: 'These are the laws which a man shall observe and he shall live in them.' It is not written: 'These are the laws which a Priest or a Levite or a son of Israel shall observe.' It is written: 'A man.' "

Another Rabbi took up the theme:

"Our sages have taught thus: It is written, 'Open, ye gates, and a righteous people shall enter, a keeper of the faith.' It is not written: 'Open, ye gates, and there shall enter a Priest or a Levite or a son of Israel.' It is written: 'A righteous people.' Thence we may deduce that when the son of another people is a keeper of the faith, he is as of the blood of Israel."

The Rabbi of Nazareth replied:

"You have spoken truth. You are not far from the kingdom of God." He turned to the people with these words: "And on those two commandments depend all the law and the prophets."

Again the Pharisees agreed with him. "You have spoken well, Rabbi. The Venerable Hillel taught thus, too: 'That which is not pleasing unto you, you shall not do to your neighbor. That is all the law, and the rest is commentary. Go forth and learn.' "

"He is of the disciples of Hillel! Happy is the woman that bore him," cried one of the disciples of Jochanan ben Zakkai, clapping his hands.

"I have taken the kernel and I have cast away the chaff. I take what is good in his speech, the rest I do not hear," said another.

But a third added: "If a sage has spoken of the Torah, and has said that which is in agreement with the tradition as accepted by the wise, then he shall be believed in the other things he has said."

Thus the assembled scholars rejoiced with the man of Nazareth, and they had no more questions to put to him, but accepted all that he said. The propitious hour had come, and all divisions between him and them were about to fall, and he was about to become the bearer of the hopes of the scholars and scribes. The hour was propitious for the union of all forces into one force, the force that was in the beginning, the force of the covenant which God made with Abraham and the other forefathers, the force of Moses and the Prophets: the force which should loosen the bonds of sin from men, that they might stand forever on the double foundation of love to God and love to man. Our hearts beat high with joy. The light of the *Shekhinah* was on the face of my Rabbi and on the faces of all the other sages, a light of pure joy. I beheld Judah standing by his Rabbi, clapping his hands and trembling with exaltation. He laid his hand on Simon and cried into his ear: "If the sages give their approval on earth, then approval is given in heaven." We thought that now the wonder which we had awaited would come to pass. But suddenly the Rabbi of Nazareth lifted up his voice to the assembled and said:

"How do the scribes say that the Messiah is the son of David? David himself has said: 'The Lord God says to my Lord: Sit at my right hand, and I will make your enemies a footstool at your feet.' If David calls him 'Lord' how is he His son?"

When the sages heard these words they were again confused, and they did not know what the Rabbi of Nazareth intended. One of them called back:

"Are the sons of David few? And yet not one of them has been proclaimed the King-Messiah. It does not suffice to be a son of David in order to be the Messiah. He must also be the chosen of God, and sent with the authority of heaven."

Then the sages turned to the people and said:

"It is known and acknowledged by Him that spoke and it came to pass, that not for our glory, nor for the glory of our fathers' houses, have we come to question the Rabbi of Galilee." And addressing themselves to him: "Therefore tell us, Rabbi, with what power do you do these things, and what authority have you therefor? Tell us, only that we may know how we shall bear ourselves. And we ask for a sign, not in order to try you, but to fulfill that which is written in the Torah by the hand of Moses concerning the time when there shall arise among us a prophet and a seer. But in place of a sign you have given us only parables and hints. But we cannot accept parables and hints, but must follow the commandments transmitted to us by Moses. And now we stand, and our hands are stretched out in darkness, just as when we came to you. Therefore we leave the thing in the hand of God, and let Him do that which is just in His eyes. We shall have no more to do with it."

But the Rabbi of Nazareth said to the people:

"Beware of the scribes, who love to walk about in long robes and to be greeted on the streets, who take the first places in the synagogues and sit at the head of the feast, and who eat up the houses of widows. They make a show of much prayer. They shall be judged with a more severe judgment."

To this the scribes did not answer. Only one of them said:

"This is what our sages have taught: 'They that are shamed, but do not shame in return, they that are disgraced and make no reply, they that do God's will in love, and rejoice in their sufferings, they shall merit the verse: "His lovers are like the going forth of the sun in his strength."'"

Then the scribes added:

"We have done that which it was incumbent on us to do. And there is nothing more for us here."

Thereupon they withdrew from the Rabbi of Galilee. With them went also my Rabbi, and many of the people. But part remained with the Rabbi of Nazareth, and continued to listen to his preaching.

CHAPTER NINETEEN

THAT evening we, the pupils of Rabbi Nicodemon, were occupied with the preparation of the food for the festival. My father had brought with him meal which had been guarded from all ritual contamination, and had not been touched by leaven. We had kneaded the dough and were preparing to bake the *matzot* of the Passover, when suddenly Judah Ish-Kiriot came flying into our midst, like a man pierced by a spear, and cried out wildly:

"I cannot! I cannot bear it any longer! He seizes me with the fury of the storm and casts me into the nethermost pit, from the heights of hope into the deep abyss. I can bear no longer the torment of doubt! Who is he? Has he come to comfort us, to bring healing and help, or has he come to increase our pangs, to bind us like calves and to lay us forever at the feet of Edom? Has he come to free the whole world, but to leave *us* in darkness? Why? Are we not blood of his blood? Have we not brought him forth in the sufferings of our bodies? Have we not borne upon our own shoulders the weight of the election of Jacob? Have we not been bowed to the earth under it, have we not let the blood stream from our wounds, while we carried the burden until the day of the redemption? And now, shall all the blessings be taken from us and given away to strangers? Why? Who is he, and what is he? Has he come to free us, or to enslave us deeper? Let him come now and fulfill his promise. Let him conjure down the hosts of heaven, let him destroy Edom with the fire of his mouth. I am weary of the doubt which crushes me. I can bear it no more."

Then, with all the strength gone from him, Judah fell on his knees.

Our Rabbi hastened toward him. We helped him to lift Judah from the stone floor, and to seat him on a bench. Then the Rabbi bade us bring him a cup of wine mixed with honey, which he made Judah drink slowly. A long time passed before Judah came to himself, and the Rabbi contained himself in patience. At last he asked:

"Judah, what has happened?"

"The Temple will be destroyed, and not one stone shall remain standing upon another. Jerusalem shall be leveled with the earth. Jerusalem shall be trodden under foot by the gentiles."

"Who has said these dreadful things?"

"My Rabbi, my Rabbi! He of whom I believed that he would bring salvation to Israel."

"What? You have heard him yourself?"

"Yes, Nicodemon."

Then Judah clasped his head with both hands, and swayed to and fro like one possessed:

"How I waited for the moment when my Rabbi would speak with the sages of our people, and they would find out that he is the bearer of our hopes, that he has come to fulfill the Torah, to give meaning to our commandments, that they might be a lifting up and a redemption for the whole world! My soul bathed in the light of joy when I beheld agreement between my Rabbi and the scribes and Pharisees. I said then in my heart: 'It cannot be otherwise but that God has wrought this, in order that we may rejoice.' And I thought that now his kingdom would begin, he would lift his hand, and our waiting and our hope shall not have been in vain. Therefore I even swallowed his utterance regarding that which must be rendered unto Caesar. I said to myself: 'I do not understand it, but if the sages concur with him, then surely there is a meaning in it. Tomorrow I shall see it.' I said to myself that those who believe in him blindly shall behold his work. All my hopes were laid on him."

"But Judah, Judah, what has happened? Do you mean the words which your Rabbi uttered against the scribes? The honor of the scribes and the Pharisees remains in its place. No one can take it from them. Is this all that your Rabbi said?"

"No, it is not all. No. When the scribes and the Rabbis had withdrawn, he led us to the door of the Temple treasury, and showed us a widow who had thrown into the treasury her last two copper coins. And he taught the people thus: 'She has given more than all the others, for they gave of their superfluity, and she—all that she possessed.' We rejoiced in these words, and made ready to leave the courts. Some of us went with him. It was about the middle of the day, and the full sun shone on the golden gates, and the Temple was like a fiery column which had descended from heaven; we rejoiced in its aspect, and delighted in the turrets of the Sanctuary. Then one of the disciples turned to the Rabbi and said: 'Rabbi, see what stones these are, and what an edifice this is!' And Yeshua answered: 'Do you see that mighty building? There shall not remain one stone upon another.'"

The face of my Rabbi twitched, as if a fiery needle had touched his flesh. His eyelids sank, and all his body shuddered. He was silent a while, then he asked:

"Did many hear the words which fell from the lips of the Rabbi of Nazareth?"

"Yes, all those that followed him."

"What did they say?"

"They tore their hair, as if disaster had befallen them. They could not look in each other's faces, for terror. Many of them fled from the Rabbi of Nazareth; only a small group of us remained with him. We went with him up the Mount of Olives, and when we had ascended halfway, he sat down on a stone by the wayside. We saw the threefold turrets of the Sanctuary, touched by the last rays of the sun, sinking into the breast of the night. The Rabbi sat apart with his three most beloved disciples, Simon, Jochanan and Jacob, and conversed with them of things he would not have us hear. Then he addressed himself to all of us and revealed that which would be at the end of things. He spoke also of the Messiah-pangs, which were approaching, and his speech was that of a man who prepares for a long journey, and says farewell; and we did not know where he was going. And he, he who should bring comfort and joy, foretold sorrow and gnashing of teeth and wars and terror: 'And one people shall rise against the other, and brother shall deliver brother unto death.' We too, his disciples, he said, would be delivered to the Sanhedrin. 'And then, only then, when the sun will be darkened and the moon will give no more light, shall they see the Son of Man come in the clouds, in great power and great glory.' And he bade all of us wait for him and be alert, lest, he said, he come suddenly and find us sleeping in the night.

"I heard these words of my Rabbi, and did not understand them. But then suddenly a great terror fell on me, for doubt had begun to pinch my heart with cold fingers, and it was as if death was darkening the light before me. I fled suddenly from this terror, and I have come to you, who were my teacher. Help me, make clear the ways of my Rabbi. I am like one who hangs in air, and cannot move. He has torn me from the earth, but he has not brought me into heaven. I cannot live thus!" And Judah wept and covered his face.

My Rabbi thought a while, then asked: "Judah, have you lost your faith in him?"

"God forbid! But where are the boundaries of faith?" asked Judah, in an extremity of pain.

"Would you empty the sea with a thimble, Judah? Even so can you measure the depth of faith. Faith is not merchandise, to be bought today, sold tomorrow. The decisions of God are not for us to understand, not for you, not for me. They are concealed from us by the bounds of our days, and they shine in their meaning a day after our death. Why do you hasten so, Judah? Wait, and it will be revealed." So my Rabbi counseled him.

"But is there no boundary to waiting, either? How long, how long, how long?" cried Judah. "Why does he not bring the redemption? The authority has been given him, the power and the might. Why does he delay? He sees the feet of Edom trampling the beauty of Israel, and he hears the heathen make mock of God's name. He sees the hand of Edom lifted against the Holy One of Israel—and he is silent. Why does he pour forth his wrath on the scribes and scholars, while he bids us pay tribute to Edom? Let him call down his hosts from heaven, let him lift up his fiery sword against Edom; then the Rabbis and the scribes and the High Priests and all the great in Israel will come and bow before him and cry: 'You are the King-Messiah.' He wishes to break the might of the Rabbis with words. Let him prove himself with deeds against Edom, and all Israel will be at his feet. No, no, the worm of doubt has reached the roots of my faith."

"Have you ever heard coming from the lips of your Rabbi, the words: 'I shall come and break the might of Edom'?"

Judah thought a while, as if seeking to remember. "No, I have not heard those words issue from the lips of my Rabbi."

"Why, then, Judah, do you ascribe to your Rabbi words he never uttered? Do you not know that if a disciple fails to transmit with utter faithfulness the words of his Rabbi, he helps destroy the justice which rules the world?"

Judah let his head sink and spoke as if to himself: "If this be so, who is he? What hopes does he bring?"

"Judah, for a long time I could not understand your Rabbi, and he was a sealed secret to me. When you sent for me, and I came to K'far Nahum, I stood before your Rabbi and implored him: 'Give us a sign, show us that you are he for whom we wait.' But he was obstinate in his refusal. And I could not answer the riddle in my heart: Who is he? Certainly I could not say that he had forsaken the Lord, and now persuaded others to do likewise; for I saw that all his deeds were done for the sake of heaven. But one moment it would seem that he was with us, and the next moment that he was against us. One moment he bids us observe every part of the Torah, without diminution or change, saying that he is not come to destroy but to fulfill—and he conducts himself like a pious Jew, according to the traditions of the ancients and the scribes; and the next moment he says: 'You cannot pour new wine into old bottles.' And this can only mean that both the wine and the bottle are new which he brings us. I stood before a riddle. I sought, I inquired diligently and looked for the truth, to know who he was: but I could not find out. My thoughts then were like your thoughts now, Judah, I asked myself: 'If the power and the authority have been given him, why does he delay the redemption, and what is he waiting for?' And when I had no answer, doubt began to work at the foundations of the house which I had built about the Rabbi. Till suddenly a light rose upon me, and I saw him all differently, all differently."

"What happened, Nicodemon?"

"You know, do you not, that one night Hillel the watercarrier conducted me to the Rabbi of Nazareth. At the time we kept the visit secret. I went to inquire once more, seek once more, for perhaps I might yet learn what God intended with us. And I said to him: 'Rabbi, we know that you are a teacher sent to us by God, for no one could perform the wonders you have performed, save he had God with him.' Do you know what he answered?"

"You have never spoken of this before. How shall I know?"

"Your Rabbi said: 'I say truly, he that will not be born again shall not see the kingdom of God.' "

"But what did he mean, 'born again'?" asked Judah, starting in fear.

"This I asked him: 'How can a man be born when he has grown old? Can he enter again into his mother's body and be born a second time?' Then the Rabbi answered: 'He that is born of the flesh, is flesh. But he that is born of the spirit, is spirit.' This is indeed so. But I asked, 'Are we born of the flesh alone? Is not the Torah our mother, and are not Abraham, Isaac and Jacob our fathers?' And I said to myself, Judah: 'This Rabbi's doctrine is good and great for those that are born without the spirit, or for such as would deny the spirit. But we that are born in the spirit and of the covenant which God made with Abraham—how shall *we* be born again without denying the spirit?' And in that day I withdrew from your Rabbi."

"What does this mean?" cried Judah loudly. "That between us and him lies death?"

"God forbid," answered my Rabbi. "Not death, but life. The rebirth of all those that are born without the spirit. And a light broke upon me. Judah, is it not possible that your Rabbi has come for the gentiles?"

"For the gentiles!" cried Judah, in despair.

"For the peoples of the world, for those that are born only in the flesh, and not in the spirit. He has been sent to bring them close to our Father in heaven. And now I understand certain words which he once uttered: 'I am a shepherd of many sheep.' And has not your Rabbi also said: 'In my father's house there are many mansions'? Yes, from that time on, since the light broke on me, I have warmed in my heart a nest of hope. I follow his footsteps with longing. My mind and heart are open, and there is goodwill in me for the interpretation of his acts and words. For I say to myself: He has been appointed the prophet to the nations, according to the prophecies of former times, that he may open their eyes to the great light of the One God. And all the nations will make a covenant to serve God with all their hearts, and to love one another. These will be the two pillars of the world, according to the words which he uttered this morning in the Temple, and which the sages found acceptable. I bow my head in reverence before him, and I wait with a trembling heart for the fulfillment of his mission. But not unto us has he been sent; unto them! Leave him, Judah!"

Judah listened, and he held his hands in his mouth, and bit on them. He swayed this way and that, he twisted his body, like the sea turtle when it withdraws in his shell. And when my Rabbi was done, he asked:

"What? I—leave—my Rabbi? Leave him that is pain of our pain, hope of our hope, our countenance and our inward parts? Leave him? Throw out mother and child together? Cut down the branch to which I cling? Fall into the pit of ruin and corruption? Leave him, the fruit for which the tree was planted? Leave the last hope, close the last door?"

"The last hope, the last door—that is our Father in heaven, Judah."

Judah stood up now. His faith had returned to him, and he seemed taller than before. He was liberated. He called out:

"He is the King-Messiah!"

"Judah! You take a great responsibility on yourself concerning your Rabbi."

But Judah, erect, restored, spoke as in a dream:

"I believe with perfect faith that he has come to bring the redemption. Like Abraham, he will shatter the temples of the idols. The mighty shall lie like carcasses at his feet. He will trample on the glory of Edom, and he will pass through his ranks like a fiery storm. He will gather the peoples of the world as the reaper gathers the ears, and he will bring them into the house of God."

"If that is so, Judah, why your impatience? Why your restlessness and your tottering?"

"It is because I cannot wait longer. I cannot. The waters have come to my soul, the cup is full. Suffering has ripened the time and Israel waits in anguish."

And now Judah listened no more. He began to walk about the room, like a man lost and confused. His eyes protruded, he seemed to see that which was hidden from us. His body had loosed itself from the knots. He was so tall now that he seemed to touch the ceiling with his head. He spoke to himself, like a man possessed by a spirit; or rather it seemed to be the spirit which shrieked out of him:

"The fruit is ripe! Why does Israel wait? The heavenly hosts are assembled. The patriarchs are gathered about him. Everything waits. There is silence in heaven, there is silence on earth. A voice is heard, the voice of a woman, Rachel weeping for her children. Moses is there, Jeremiah is there. What are they waiting for? The might and the authority have not yet been granted. The Evil One interferes and indicts us. The angel of Edom has claims. Israel is sinful. The powers struggle with each other. The cups of the scales rise and fall. The angel of Edom gathers strength. The King-Messiah does not bind on his sword of vengeance! Nay, God forbid! God forbid! The angel of Edom still gathers strength. Pangs of the Messiah! Blood, blood, God forbid! Oh, the deliverance! Gabriel and Michael stand with him, one on each side. The might and the authority are given to him. Fire spurts from his mouth. The hosts of heaven come hastening to him. With the breath of his nostrils he destroys the angel of Edom. He treads on the mighty as one treads on a worm. The earth splits. Evil sinks down. The heavens draw near to the earth, the earth draws near to the heavens. One light! Salvation! Salvation!"

And Judah fell into my Rabbi's arms.

When he had come to, my Rabbi sat down next to him and said:

"Judah! Surely you are the son of an impatient people. How often have I not told you: 'Thou shalt not awaken nor stir up my love until he please'?"

"My soul is famished for the redemption."

"Judah, redemption is fire. Those that carry it can either illumine the house or set fire to it."

"Then let one of the two happen! Let the name of God be glorified, now, even today! I am utterly weary of waiting."

"Go, Judah, lie down and rest. Let sleep come to your eyelids and peace to your heart. Remember the word of the sages: 'It is not incumbent upon thee to complete the task.' "

Then my Rabbi led Judah into one of the rooms where the pupils slept, and he laid him down on the bench and covered him with his mantle against the cold of the night.

* * *

In the night I was awakened by a lamentation. But it was not the weeping which comes with the tears of the eyes, but rather the weeping which comes with the tears of the heart. The voice was like the mourning of a jackal in the wilderness. I started up, and I saw Judah seated on his bench. His body mingled with the shadows of the night, but his eyes shone forth from the darkness, and he wept, and spoke to himself:

"Father in heaven, why hast Thou chosen me alone from among all to be the accursed one? Torment me no more, but take away the restlessness which thou hast awakened in my body. Why hast Thou lit in me the fire which is the thirst for salvation? Why dost Thou smite me with the whips of desire for redemption, then drive me out into the night? Bring peace into my heart and tranquillity into my spirit. Send down repose on my tormented soul, and let me take leave of this life in the tent of faith, singing the song of Thy promise. For is not Thy promise enough to give strength and firmness and repose? Why must I see the promise fulfilled? Get Thee gone from me, O God—or Satan! I long for quiet and rest, I long to pass into the shadowy waves of the night. But who is it that tears and rips my heart? Can there be thirst without Thee, Father in heaven! Thou hast poured it like a fire into my veins. Thou hast put Thy sign upon me, Thou hast chosen me as the stone from which to strike the spark and kindle the light of the world. Thou sendest me—and I will go! Like the scapegoat I shall be shattered on the rocks, but these will be the everlasting rocks of the unborn generations. Yet will I do it for the sake of the redemption. I am a part of that redemption. Without me it cannot come. And if this be so, it is my pain too, and my suffering. I, more than all others, will suffer every pang with him. More than all others I will bleed with every bloody wound of his. I will drink into myself the drops of sweat that will pour from his body, and they shall come into my inward parts like molten lead. I will fling my body under the lashes of the wicked, even as they fall upon him. I shall groan with every groan of his, and I shall cry out with his cry when the redemption comes! The redemption is mine, too! Rabbi, Rabbi, see, I go down into the nethermost pit, in order that you may rise in the highest to God!"

Then I saw Judah lie down and cover his face with his robe. He became silent.

CHAPTER TWENTY

THE next day was the fifth of the week and the second before the Passover. When dawn came up Judah left us and returned to his Rabbi, for it had been ruled that the Passover sacrifice would begin in the afternoon of this, the day preceding the fourteenth of the month. The High Priests had ignored the ancient decision of the Venerable Hillel, accepted by the Pharisees, that the greatness of the Passover sacrifice took precedence over the Sabbath, and that therefore the sacrifice ceremony could be continued until the evening of the sixth day, which is already the Sabbath. They, the High Priests, asserted that the Passover sacrifice was a *korban yachid*, that is, an individual and personal offering, therefore had not the power to override the Sabbath. The Pharisees were filled with bitterness against the Priesthood because of this contempt for the law as laid down by Hillel; but they had to consume their bitterness inwardly, being helpless against the Sons of Hanan.

We, the circle of Rabbi Nicodemon, began the preparations early in the day. The *matzot* had been baked the day before. We measured off the wine and ground and mixed the herbs for the *seder* or Passover feasting ceremony: all this even though my Rabbi did not intend to offer sacrifice on the fifth of the week (which was the thirteenth of the month) but on the sixth, the eve of Sabbath, according to the Hillelite interpretation. Now the Rabbi of Galilee, notwithstanding, made ready to slaughter the sacrifice on this, the fifth day. The Galileans were distinguished by their scrupulous observance of the Passover. Among them it was the custom to regard the entire day on which the *seder*, or Passover evening feasting ceremony, falls, as a holiday, and they did no work therein. And early that day Judah, being the treasurer of the group, went with Simon to the sheep market, to buy a kid for the Passover sacrifice.

Later in the day there came to us Hillel the watercarrier and imparted to us the news that the Rabbi of Nazareth would eat the sacrifice with his disciples within the city, according to the law deduced from the Writ: "Within thy gates, Jerusalem!" For the

Nazarene was careful in the fulfillment of all the prescriptions handed down to us. But as he had no home in Jerusalem, he would celebrate the *seder* ceremony on the terrace above Hillel's poor dwelling, which was in the ancient wall. Therefore Hillel had come to Rabbi Nicodemon to beg his help in making the arrangements and preparations. But the whole matter was to be kept secret.

My Rabbi was filled with joy at the opportunity to perform this act of piety. He took the jar of wine which my father had brought him as a present and sent it by Hillel to the Rabbi of Nazareth, for the making of the benediction; he also provided Hillel with *matzot* and herbs. Rufus and me he bade go to Joseph Arimathea and ask for the loan of vessels and fine coverings and woven things, and out of his small store of spices—the only store of possessions which my Rabbi permitted himself—he set aside a quantity of precious *d'ror* for the Nazarene.

We brought our Rabbi's request, written in a letter, to Joseph Arimathea, and the latter instructed the overseer of his house to take two servants and to send them to the house of Hillel the watercarrier with lamps and jars and bowls for the washing of hands, a cruse of choice wine, supplies of greens and fruits, a couch for the Rabbi and sheets and silk tapestries. These were for the ceremony, but as a special festival present for the Rabbi, Joseph Arimathea sent a sweat kerchief of delicate weave. All these things the servants and we, that is Rufus and I, brought to the house of Hillel the watercarrier, and there we also helped in the preparations.

This house, of one room, was a kind of cave cut in the vast, ancient wall of Jerusalem, and access to the room was by a small ladder. In shape the room was long and low, and its sides consisted of the mighty square-hewn stones of the fortress wall itself. A small window had been cut through and looked out toward the Water Gate by the Kidron. In this cave stood a bed, a table and a three-legged stove. At one end a narrow flight of steps led to a terrace, which was surrounded by a fence; over part of the terrace Hillel had woven a roof of thin bamboo rushes, and on the open side he had hung tapestries of dried palm leaves as a shelter against the sun. From this terrace in the wall a man might look upon the four corners of Jerusalem and himself remain unseen. It was here, then, that we made the preparations for the *seder*. We hung the costly silk curtains and tapestries over the fence; we made a canopy at one end of the terrace and placed beneath it the couch for the Rabbi; we spread matting of rushes on the floor for the disciples to sit on. Then we brought planks of wood and laid them on small carriers to make a table, and on the table put the fine coverings, the vessels, the jars, the cups; for the disciples the cups were of earthenware, and for the Rabbi Joseph Arimathea had sent an alabaster vessel. We distributed the *matzot* and the greens, the herbs, and the fruit; we arranged the bowls of water for the ceremonial washing of hands. We sprinkled light spices on the towels and kerchiefs, and we poured the incense into a pan, and kindled it, and placed it near the Rabbi's couch. We filled the lamps with precious oil, cut and pointed the wicks, and disposed the lamps in their places. Further, Rufus and I begged to be permitted to serve the Rabbi of Nazareth, but Hillel told us that it was the Rabbi's desire to be alone with his disciples that evening and to celebrate the *seder* only in their company. Thereupon we returned to Rabbi Nicodemon and reported to him:

"We have fulfilled your command, and we have made fitting *seder* preparations for the Rabbi of Nazareth."

"Strength be in your hands!" our Rabbi answered. But then he bethought himself and asked: "Who of the disciples were there, and which of them helped you to prepare the terrace? And who among the neighbors knows who will be celebrating the *seder* in the house of Hillel the watercarrier?"

We said: "Not one of the disciples of Yeshua was there, and not one of them helped us. We together with the servants of Joseph Arimathea, did the work, and no one among the neighbors knows who will celebrate the *seder* in that house."

"The matter must be utterly secret," the Rabbi warned us again. Then he added: "My heart is heavy. I am filled with fear for this Passover. May God grant that the festival pass in peace. Tell me, have you marked anything more concerning Judah?"

I told my Rabbi what I had heard Judah say to himself in the night; and when he heard the words of Judah, my Rabbi became paler than the earthen vessel which he held in his hand and in which he was grinding the bitter herbs for the *seder*. He said:

"I am afraid for Judah! Who knows what thoughts he carries about with him? May God be compassionate with him."

Having thought a while, the Rabbi said:

"Go forth, and follow in the footsteps of the Galilean. Keep watch from afar and see what happens to him and his disciples and bring me report. And if you chance on Judah, say to him: 'Our Rabbi's heart is heavy for you; you stand in need of heaven's help.' "

It was now afternoon, and the sun was setting toward the Great Sea. We heard the blowing of the silver trumpets from the Temple courts, and the Jews who were obeying the Priestly ordinance concerning the sacrifice, streamed with their sheep and young goats toward the Upper City, that they might sacrifice on this, the fifth day of the week, toward evening. Among them Rufus and I encountered some of the disciples. Simon bar Jonah carried a kid in his arms, and with him were Jochanan and Jacob; a little distance behind were Judah and other disciples, but the Rabbi of Galilee was not there.

We followed them and came into the courts, which were filled with Israelites and with their sacrifices. Most of those present were Galileans, hastening to fulfill the commandment betimes. We went as far as the fifteen steps which lead up to the Nicanor gate, and the bronze doors which guard the court of the Israelites were now open. At the top of the steps stood Priests, and in their hands were silver trumpets, which they still blew, to proclaim to the city that the Passover sacrifice was now being slaughtered. Behind the Priests stood rows of Levites. Permission was given to the pilgrims and the bringers of sacrifice to mount the steps, by twos only, two from each family or company; and these two went down on the other side, by the court of the women, to perform the sacrifice. From the court of the women all could look up and see what happened on the steps, for the Nicanor gate was open, and we could see the great fire burning on the altar, in the court of the Priests, before the Sanctuary. There were two long rows of Priests, in white garments, from the altar to the court of Israel; they held in their hands golden beakers, broad at the mouth, narrow at the stem;

the beakers were passed from hand to hand till they reached the Priest who stood by the sacrificing Israelite. The latter laid his young goat on the block; in the block was a hole through which the blood ran into the canals below the Temple. The Priest held the beaker under the sacrifice and caught one drop of blood; then the beaker was passed down the long row, till it came into the hand of the Priest who stood at the altar; he sprinkled the blood on the altar and handed the beaker again to the Priest on his other side to pass down the row to the place of sacrifice. On the three steps which led from the court of Israel to the court of the Priests, stood the Levites, holding in their hands harps and timbrels and flutes; and as the Priests sprinkled the blood on the altar, they played on their instruments and accompanied themselves with words of praise to the Almighty.

Of the Rabbi's disciples but two ascended the steps, Simon bar Jonah, who carried the kid, and Jochanan of the Zebedee brothers, who held in his hand the blade for the slaughtering. The others remained among the people in the great court of the women. But when they heard the singing of the Levites they, with all the others, bowed themselves and sang: "*Hallelujah,* praise ye the Lord, praise Him, His servants, praise the name of the Lord." And the others responded: "Praised be the name of the Lord from this day for ever and ever."

Soon Simon and Jochanan went down from the court, and Jochanan was carrying the slaughtered kid, wrapped in a sheet and slung on his shoulders, and Simon followed him. They joined the other disciples and left the Temple courts, Simon and Jochanan leading, the disciples following, and Rufus and I behind them, at a distance. Simon and Jochanan led the way down to the market place, and we could mark from the manner of their walking that they did not know the way, and that their footsteps were hesitant, as if they were waiting for someone. Thus they walked awhile, uncertain, then found their way to the narrow steps which led to the Lower City. There, at the end of the steps, and by the wall, they found him they were seeking, to wit, Hillel the watercarrier. He, as soon as he perceived them, made a sign, and they followed him; but they did not walk together, but scattered, that they might not be observed. Hillel brought them to the entrance of his house in the wall of David. Rufus and I, standing without, soon saw the smoke go up from the terrace, and we knew that the disciples were roasting the sacrifice on the three-footed stove we had seen there.

The day was now ending; the sun had sunk lower toward the Great Sea, and only its last rays were caught by the summits of the mountains of Judaea which look down into the valley of the Dead Sea. The shadows became heavier, and it was the twilight hour when day contends with night. And now we saw the Rabbi of Galilee approaching, in the company of one disciple, Jacob of the brothers Zebedee. This time his raiment was not merely white; it sent forth rays of whiteness about him. He stood motionless for a moment, and I saw him with the red mountain tops of Moab behind him, a white light in the midst of redness. His face was pallid but serene, as though all the tormenting questions in his heart had been answered. And this peace was veiled in a quiet sadness, which was not the sadness of suffering or pain, but that of wholeness, which is a sort of joy. The Rabbi of Galilee made me feel in that instant that he was utterly at peace, all prepared for the sacred service which lay before him. The hair of his head was dressed, and divided on his brow, and water dripped from his locks as though he had but just come from the baptism. And the drops ran down his curled earlocks, and wove together the locks of his hair and his earlocks and his short, graying beard into a modest frame about his sad, peaceful face. His garment was long, like the garment of the scholars, and it covered his feet. The fringes of his ritual garment hung out. When Rufus and I saw him step forward, against the flaming background of the hill, a trembling came upon us, as though a ray of his white garb had illumined us. Fear woke in our hearts, and we pressed ourselves against the wall. We could not utter a word. We watched, silent, while Hillel the watercarrier came forth from the house, bowed himself before the Rabbi and said:

"Blessed are you who come in the name of the Lord."

And the Rabbi answered: "Blessed be you in the name of the Lord."

Then Hillel helped him on the ladder which led into his house, but Hillel himself did not enter, but remained standing without. For the Rabbi had told him that he wanted to celebrate the *seder* with his disciples and with no one else; and none but the Rabbi and his disciples entered the house of Hillel. At the moment when the Rabbi went in, in order to begin the celebration of the *seder*, the silver trumpets of the Priests sounded from the Temple, proclaiming that the first watch of the night had begun. It was only then, after the Rabbi had disappeared into the dwelling, that Rufus and I found our speech again. Rufus said:

"I tell you, it is none other than an angel of heaven come down to attend service. Such he seemed when he drew near."

I answered:

"You are right, my friend. This day it was our privilege to stand face to face with an angel of the Lord. Let us remain here, and let us keep guard, as our Rabbi has commanded us. Perhaps it will also be granted us to witness great things which God intends for this night."

Rufus asked me:

"What great things?"

"It may be that Judah is right! Perhaps this night the heavens will break open and the hosts of heaven will pour down, they and the patriarchs, the mothers, the Prophets and Moses and Jeremiah—all of them!"

"Jochanan! Jochanan! Look!" cried Rufus suddenly.

I saw him trembling with fear.

"Rufus, my brother! What is it?"

"Do you see that light in heaven? It is the light of the creation, the light which God has kept concealed in heaven from the beginning. Look, it shines on us now!"

And it was indeed as if a new light, which no one had beheld until that hour, had burst open in the heavens. The moon swam out, now at the full, and her glory and radiance dimmed the stars. She issued alone from the midst of a coil of dark blue, smoky clouds rimmed with white. All the sky was one bright blueness. It was as though the firmament were blazing with suns hidden behind the living garment of the heavens, but breaking through to illumine the world with a light never known before. The glory fell upon the ancient stones of the Davidic and Solomonic wall, which was now clad in a silver garb, as if the royal raiment of the great kings had been laid upon it; and from the folds of the raiment faces peered out, white, patriarchal beards, and eyes that sent forth their own luster. And Rufus cried in terror:

"I see faces! The forefathers, in silver mantles, come riding on camels! Costly stuffs glitter on the camels. I see beards . . . I see . . . I see. . . ."

"Where?" I clasped Rufus's hand. It glowed with a strange warmth.

"There! Beyond the ancient walls. Do you not see their raiment fluttering in the night?"

"It is the light of the moon, falling on the old stones. It is the face of the fortress wall bathed in the moon's radiance."

"No, it is the patriarchs, come up out of the double cave by Hebron; they ride on camels. It is the Prophets, the kings, all the generations of the past, which went their way and have waited for the resurrection. Now they are assembling and returning."

"Rufus! Rufus! This is a dream of yours. Wake, Rufus. It is night, and the moon is shining."

In that moment we heard a voice. It came down to us from the terrace, where the lamps were burning. The voice was strong and clear, and it was poured out in devotion, uttering the benediction of the festival.

"The Rabbi makes benediction over a beaker of wine!" It was Hillel who approached us, breaking in on the dream of my friend.

"Yes, it is the Rabbi dedicating the festival." And we answered the closing of the benediction with "Amen!"

I do not know what passed that night on the terrace between the Rabbi and his disciples. None of the following, save they alone, had been admitted, none of the poor, none of the women. But later there were sundry reports. Some of the disciples were said to have reported that this night they received from their Rabbi grants of the highest powers and authority, and that he had linked them to him in a New Covenant. Further, the confirmation of the Covenant was through the flesh and blood of the Rabbi: this I heard much later from my friend Rufus, when he joined the Messianists. Again, the

Rabbi is said to have revealed to his disciples, that night, certain things regarding the coming days which I have not the right and authority to repeat, not being of their Covenant. But meanwhile, standing in the shadow, together with Hillel, we ourselves heard only the benediction of the festival. And later there came down the singing of Psalms, as is proper when the *seder* is celebrated. Still later, when we had kept our posts a long time, we beheld Judah come creeping out, a huddled, knotted figure; and he was speaking fiercely with himself, as possessed by an evil spirit. He came close to us, and looked at us out of red, swollen eyes, but it was as if he had never seen us before. For he cried out:

"Ha! Who are you?"

We answered, frightened: "We are pupils of Rabbi Nicodemon. He sent us to look for you, and to tell you, from him, that he is afraid for you, and that your soul needs the help of heaven."

But Judah still stared at us, as if he had not heard our answer or, having heard, had not understood the words. He still spoke to himself, repeating again and again:

"That which you have to do, do swiftly . . . that which you have to do, do swiftly. . . ."

Then Judah lifted up the edge of his robe, and covered his head, down to the eyes, and strode away from us. We saw a great shadow detach itself from the wall and accompany him; and like Judah the shadow had drawn the mantle backward over its head, to cover itself to the eyes; like Judah, again, the shadow was bent double, and as it ran it muttered with him:

"That which you have to do, do swiftly."

And Judah and his shadow vanished together into a narrow alley way.

CHAPTER TWENTY-ONE

WHEN a little while had passed the Rabbi and his disciples issued into the street. The Rabbi was garbed in white, and he held in his hand the kerchief which Joseph Arimathea had sent him as a festival present; and now and again he wiped the sweat from his face. For the hours he had spent with his disciples had taken the strength from him, and the peace which I had read on him before was touched now with darkness and weariness. He was no longer like a pillar of light, as when we had seen him approach the house, but walked with head sunk and leaning on his disciple Jacob. It was clear to us that he had poured himself out utterly in the service of the *seder*.

The disciples followed, and they were somewhat heavy with meat and wine. Sleep was casting its shadow on them, and as they walked they hummed fragments of verses from the Psalms. The Rabbi was lonely and apart; he did not sing, but sighed heavily. Rufus and I, accompanying them at a little distance, were filled with wonder, and did not know why the Rabbi was thus divided off in loneliness from his disciples, or what had happened at the *seder*. In many houses the celebrations still continued, for most of the people had, like the Rabbi, chosen this day for the sacrificing; the lights shone from windows and open doors, the sound of the Psalms floated into the street. Here and there the Rabbi paused, glanced into the houses and became for an instant lighter of spirit, hearing the music of the happy celebrants. The darkness was lifted from his face as he raised his hands and blessed the tables and those that sat at them. All throughout the Kidron valley the lamps twinkled from houses and booths. It was as though Israel had returned to his God, was gathered from the ends of the world to the mount of Zion. Blessing them, the Rabbi called out:

"How goodly are thy tents, O Jacob, thy tabernacles, O Israel."

And he blessed the tents of the poor.

Then he encountered a group of children who had come out with laughter and singing from the booths, for here and there the services were over, and the streets were filling with people. He went in among the children, and rejoiced in them; one he caressed on the cheek, a second he lifted to his heart, on a third he laid his hands and blessed him. Thus he scattered benediction as he walked among the poor; and the disciples thought that the spirit was upon him, and they rejoiced in him.

When we came on the heights of the Mount of Olives the Rabbi did not enter the narrow passageway between the rocks leading to Bet Paga, as was his wont, but turned aside toward the right, in the direction of the fruitful part of the Mount. He passed by the cypress groves which peered out of the gardens of the rich people. The trees stood up, quiet in the moonlight, and their green crowns nodded with modest and pious motion. And as before in the valley, the Rabbi paused before the houses, and looked into the gardens through the open fences. He placed his hands upon the trees, and his lips moved as if in benediction.

Among the disciples Simon bar Jonah alone seemed to know what was in the heart of his Rabbi, for he drew near, and touched his robe lovingly, as if to strengthen him. They were, at this moment, passing by the house of the Sons of Hanan, and the overseers sat before the doors. The Rabbi turned and said to Simon:

"All of you shall be tempted in me, and shall fail, this night. As it is written: 'I shall smite the shepherd and scatter the sheep.'"

Simon, hearing these words, cried out—and I saw his great head uplifted in the night:

"Though all will fail you, I shall not do so. I am ready to go with you into the dungeon, and even into death." And the disciples, having heard the cry, came running to their Rabbi, one by one, and said:

"I too, Rabbi."

But the Rabbi, his lips smiling sadly, answered Simon:

"Simon, I say amen. But this night, before the cock will have crowed three times, you shall have denied me three times."

Simon beat himself on the heart with clenched fist, and cried again and again:

"Though I know I must pay for it with my life, I shall not deny you." And the others repeated his words.

With slow footsteps, as if he were drawing near the sacred service in the Temple, locked within himself and sunk in sorrow and earnestness, the Rabbi entered the narrow path leading to the garden of the oil pressers. Along each side of the path there was a row of cypress trees, their dark, heavy heads rustling. The Rabbi trod among the thick blue shadows which the moon cast upon the narrow way. Behind him, a close-pressed glimmering group, came the disciples, whispering among themselves. The alley of cypresses led to a close fence of olive trees which surrounded the garden of the oil pressers. In the bluish light of the moon the olive trees took on a strange and unfamiliar silvery color woven mystically about the entrance of the garden, and out of the mournful web the branches were thrust upward toward heaven, like hands in prayer.

When the Rabbi entered the garden of Gat Shemen, we heard from afar the dying echo of the trumpet peal which issued from the Temple to announce the beginning of the second watch and the changing of the guard.

But as against the stillness without, the garden of Gat Shemen was a tumult of life within. It was as though the torrents of moonlight descending from the heavens whipped into new fruitfulness the green-growing masses, and we were as witnesses to the secret of creation. An odorous heaviness, like that of a poured wine, penetrated us, flesh and bone and blood, and pressed down our eyelids. When the disciples felt the soft grass under their feet, when they drew in the sweet incense of the blossoming garden, their senses became dim, and they laid themselves down and fell into a deep sleep. Thus it was with those that lingered outside, on the rim of the garden, and thus too with Simon, Jochanan and Jacob, who had entered and would have kept watch with their Rabbi. They fought against sleep, for here in the garden everything was the opposite of death, the opposite of that fear and restlessness which had oppressed the heart of their Rabbi. And if there was restlessness at all, it was that of creation and the movement of life. A murmuring of insects, which had been awakened by the light and had betaken themselves eagerly to the flowers, rose in the air; there was a weaving of colors and lights between the moon's rays and the dark-green thickness of the bushes and blossoms, a shuttling upon looms of branches, accompanied by an outpouring of odors and a singing of creation.

Out of that song of creation the voice of the Rabbi was lifted; he called to Simon and Jacob and Jochanan, and the sound of his voice was filled with terror and pain:

"My soul is oppressed unto death! Stay here, and wait."

He left them, and entered into the thickets of the garden. There, in the heart of the secret of creation, the Rabbi of Nazareth knelt down. We saw him bow his head among the plants and grasses. He touched them with his lips. He stretched out his arms in their white sleeves, and it was as if he would have embraced the world, as if he would have pressed the creation to his breast; and it was also as if he were clinging with all his might to life. Thus he remained a while.

My comrade, Rufus, who dared to steal close to him with careful steps, heard the words of his prayer: "Father in heaven, have mercy on Thy creation, and gather it into Thy compassion. How lovely is Thy world, how great are Thy deeds! See, God, the blossoming of things and their eagerness in life. But shall I go into the shadow of death? If it be possible, let this hour pass from me. All is possible to Thee, Father."

Then he rose, and approached Simon and Jacob and Jochanan, and found them sleeping. He said:

"Simon, are you sleeping? Could you not wake this hour? Waken and pray that you be not tempted and fail. The spirit is willing but the flesh is weak."

He withdrew from them again, and fell to the earth and prayed:

"Father, Father, they are the field in which I have sown my seed. They are the furrows which bear my grain. If the field be destroyed, what will be the purpose of my plowing? My seed will be lost. Father, Father, this is all that I have. In them have I planted my word. Guard Thou my plant. See, Father in heaven; let not my life have been in vain, and let not my labor be lost."

He arose a second time and returned to Simon and Jochanan and Jacob. He beheld how Simon had laid his head on Jochanan's mighty breast, and how Jacob had his head in Jochanan's lap, and the three of them were deep in slumber, made drunken by the odors which were spread abroad by the blossoms.

Yeshua called to them:

"Simon, Simon, I have prayed for you that your faith shall not be destroyed. When you will repent, strengthen your brothers."

Simon answered, his eyes still lapped in sleep:

"Rabbi, Rabbi, though I have to go with you into the dungeon, or into death"—and he fell back into slumber.

Again the Rabbi withdrew from them, and again he threw himself to earth. A long time we heard the whisper of his prayer. Then his voice was lifted clearly as he repeated sorrowfully the verses of the Psalms:

"I was surrounded by the agonies of death. The narrowness of the pit came on me, sorrows and sadness. I call upon the name of God. I implore Thee, God: Save my soul! Father, Father, take away the cup from my lips. But not as I wish it, but as Thou wishest." And after a short silence he cried, in a loud voice: "Yea, though I walk in the valley of the shadow of death, I fear no evil, for Thou art with me."

Then he rose and came a third time to Simon, Jochanan and Jacob, and still they were asleep; their eyelids were fastened. He said to them:

"Sleep on, and rest. It is enough. The hour has come."

And Rufus and I looked at him, and we beheld not the angel of the Lord who had come to the *seder*, but a man of flesh and blood. The terror of death stared out of his eyes. In the moonlight his face was ashen blue. He trembled from head to foot, and great drops of sweat, like gouts of blood, ran down from his hair, his beard, his body, and fell upon the ground.

We stood thus awhile, at a distance; then Rufus fell on my breast. Tears glimmered in his eyes, and he asked, in a broken whisper:

"Is this the angel of heaven which we saw approaching for the feast? Is this the Prophet of Nazareth, with whom the redemption is to come? See, he trembles, and terror is poured out on him."

I replied in a whisper:

"Not long ago, in Bet Eini, I heard Judah impart to Simon the Zealot the secret of the Son of Man: in order that the Son of Man may understand and know all those whom he comes to save, he has received from God the nature of mankind, in flesh and blood. He desires life, he knows the meaning of sorrow, and the terror of death falls on him with a heavier hand than on every other man of flesh and blood."

"But why is he so afraid? He knows that God is with him. The power and the authority are with him, and he will triumph."

"Yes, but when the pangs of terror assail him, he is like every child of the flesh."

"But what is it that he fears?"

"I do not know. He sees something which we cannot see, something that is to happen."

"But what will happen? What, tell me, tell me."

"I do not know. Listen! Listen!"

From a distance came the echo of marching feet, drawing closer. First it was like the sound of rushing water on far-off hills; then it became a rhythm, heavy, interspersed with the ringing of arms and armor. It came closer and closer, and we stood breathless, awaiting the issue.

"The hour has come. The Son of Man will be delivered. Arise, let us go. He is near us now, he who betrays me," the Rabbi called out.

Then Simon started to his feet and with a strong motion shook off his sleep; and Jochanan and Jacob awoke also. They encircled the Rabbi, and in Simon's hand a sword flashed.

The disciples that had been sleeping at the entrance to the garden came running toward the Rabbi. Their eyes still wrestled with sleep. They must have been awakened by the approach of the strangers, for close on their footsteps came the flicker of torches, and by their light we beheld faces, bearded and unbearded. Steel armor threw back the red flames, swords rang. And at the head approached Judah. He limped on one foot, but he walked swiftly, he hastened, he looked with seeking eyes among the disciples, his head was flung from side to side; the black mantle was dragged after him. Finally he beheld the Rabbi, and came toward him with outstretched arms:

"Rabbi! Rabbi!"

And he fell into Yeshua's arms, and kissed him.

But the group which accompanied him stood at a distance, swords and clubs in hand, armor glittering in the light of torches and lamps. They stood at a distance as if the fear of God had fallen on them, and they dared not draw near the Rabbi. In vain did Judah turn round after he had kissed the Rabbi, and in vain direct his eyes at those he had brought with him. They held off, motionless, their hands fallen, as if the power to lift them had been taken from them. In that moment I beheld in Judah's eyes a great flush of triumph.

Thus it was too with the other disciples, whose faces shone. Hearts began to beat tumultuously with expectation, rising from the depths of terror to highest hope, and lips formed the unspoken words: "They do not dare!"

Then the Rabbi called out in a loud voice—all his strength returned:

"Whom do you seek?"

"Yeshua of Nazareth!"

"I am he," the Rabbi answered.

Our hearts stood still, in expectation. What will happen now? Will they dare to lay hands on him? No! They do not dare. For a stronger hand, the hand of God, has been laid on them; and fiery bonds are about them, to hold in their strength; the wind of God has blown upon them, and they start back.

The shout of triumph struggled to issue from our throats; but we could not open our lips. One minute more, and the heavens would be split. Already we could hear the wheels of the hosts drawing near.

"Whom do you seek?" the Rabbi asked again.

"Yeshua of Nazareth." This time it was a weaker voice that came from among the armed men.

"I have told you, I am he."

Then one of them dared to draw near, and in that instant a sword flashed; there was a cry of pain and again the group of armed men shrank back.

"A servant of the High Priest has been wounded!"

"Simon, put up your sword in its sheath. They that take up the sword shall perish by the sword," said the Rabbi.

Then the Rabbi went up to the wounded man, and bound up his ear in the kerchief which Joseph Arimathea had sent him: he tore the kerchief into strips, and tied them about the man's head. And while he was thus occupied, the commander of the troops, a Roman Tribune, drew near. It seemed that until now he had waited for the servants of the High Priest to take the Rabbi prisoner. But when he saw that the Jews were afraid of the Rabbi, and dared not approach him, he came forward. I saw him clearly; the moonlight was poured upon him; I saw the hard face, the long eagle nose, the gray, cold, cruel eyes. In one hand he held his drawn broadsword, and laying a powerful, naked arm on the Rabbi's shoulder, he said:

"What are you all afraid of?" And, addressing the Rabbi: "You are my prisoner."

We were certain, then, that the Tribune's arm was about to wither in a fierce flame. We were certain that the man would be consumed and transformed into ash and dust. This was the belief, likewise, of the men who accompanied the Romans. On the lips of all of us trembled the ultimate cry of salvation and joy. But moments passed, and the Tribune did not burn. The earth did not open beneath him and swallow him: instead, his grip tightened on the Rabbi, and his men surrounded him with their swords and clubs.

"Woe!"

But the Rabbi lifted up his voice:

"Why have you come forth as if against a robber, with your swords and clubs, to take me? I was with you daily in the Temple, and taught there; and you did not take me. Therefore you have only come because the Writ must be fulfilled."

They did not let him speak longer. They only said:

"All this you may complain of before the High Priest."

And already the rope was thrown round the Rabbi's hands.

"Woe is us!"

Within one instant all those that were with the Rabbi, every single one of them, the disciples, the nearer ones and the remoter ones, fled, each one to save his own life. They were gone! Simon bar Jonah and Jochanan and Jacob and Simon the Zealot and Andrew and Philip. They scattered, they sped away, and left the Rabbi in the hands of his enemies.

He stood there, and let them do with him as they would. They drew his hands behind him, and tied them; and he said nothing. Only for one instant did he pull down his lips in pain; but the next instant he had tightened them. He lifted his eyes and gazed in deep pity at those that were taking him prisoner. It was not easy to know whether the pity was for himself or for them.

Soon we saw them leading him off. He walked in their midst, his head bowed. His white robe shone out among the Roman soldiers, all bathed in moonlight; and the mournful tranquillity which was on his face also rested on his robe.

Then I marked how Simon bar Jonah crawled out from the field where he had concealed himself and followed at a distance the officers and soldiers who were leading his Rabbi to the High Priest.

Rufus and I ran to the city to report these events to our Rabbi.

CHAPTER TWENTY-TWO

A VOICE called:

"Jochanan! Do you not recognize the Hegemon?"

I started violently, I looked, and I beheld before me the face which I had seen that night: the same finely chiseled eagle's nose, the same shape, save that now the face was old and sunken and wrinkled. Veiled in mist, the eyes looked back at me. Instead of the mighty throat which had risen naked out of the steely corselet, I saw a network of shriveled flesh, the uncovered skin of a gander from which the feathers have been plucked. I felt like one who has been hurled out of the clouds onto the earth; for I was suddenly back in Warsaw, in the dark, melancholy apartment of Pan Viadomsky.

It is now in place for me to record that when Pan Viadomsky conjured back for me, through the wizardry of his own memory, the remote past of another life, we agreed between us that I should set down in writing my recollections of that world event, so that we might compare and complement our experiences. We decided further to publish this common fund of memories in a single book, so that our contemporaries might obtain a clear picture of the tragedy of which we had been witnesses. During the day I would sit at home, transferring to paper everything I could remember; evenings I would come to Pan Viadomsky, to find him divested of all affairs and interests of his actual life, ready to listen to the script. Until this point in the narrative he had listened without a single interruption, and had offered no observations. But when I came to the incident in the garden of Gat Shemen he broke in suddenly with the question which heads this chapter.

Yes, I recognized him: the same face, the same man, except that now the quivering mass of wrinkles in his flesh spoke of the passions and experiences of a score of generations—bitterness and joy and revenge. The weight of thousands of years lay on that countenance.

"Yes, I know you now, Hegemon. You are he, then, who first laid hands on the Rabbi of Nazareth, on that moonlit night in the garden of Gat Shemen?"

"I am he, the man who laid the first hand on your Rabbi, when your frightened little servants of the High Priest thought that if they but touched him they would be consumed by the fire of his mouth."

"And it was you who conducted him to the courtyard of the High Priest, when the rest of us ran away?"

"Yes, when all of you fled, I conducted him to the High Priest."

"I was present only later, at the sitting of the Sanhedrin in the house of the High Priest Kaifa, in Jerusalem, together with my Rabbi," I told him. "Will you not tell me what happened at the first examination, in the courtyard of the Hanans? Two more questions I have for you, and I beg you, Hegemon, to be as clear as you can in your replies, because they deal with what is a riddle to the whole world. First, as to the words which the Rabbi of Nazareth addressed to you when you arrested him: How is it that you permitted him to preach in the Temple courts and did not dare once to molest him? Why did you wait so long before seizing him? And in what manner was it that the disciple of the Rabbi came to you—Judah Ish-Kiriot?"

"I can easily answer these questions. The fact is that your frightened little Jews did not dare to place a hand on the Rabbi. I have good grounds for believing that even your foxy old Hanan was infected by the terror; he took your Rabbi for a fiery angel direct from heaven. They were frightened out of their wits before I brought the man to them, a prisoner; and even afterwards, in the very court of Hanan, they shied away from him. The fact is that the High Priests gave me a great deal of trouble in connection with your Rabbi, particularly after you proclaimed him the Jewish King and brought him in procession to Jerusalem. Your behavior, on that occasion, was insolent and provocative in the extreme. My suggestion to the High Priest was to have the man of Nazareth arrested there and then. You have mentioned the clash between your procession and ours on that day. Here is what happened. The Procurator was anxious to attend the games in the amphitheater, to witness a contest between the Sons of Hanan and certain visitors from Phoenicia. He sent for me and asked whether the streets of Jerusalem were quiet, and whether he could pass through them, together with his wife Claudia, in litters. I took the responsibility on myself, and answered, Yes.

"I myself conducted Pilate and his lady that day. When we came out of the Herod street, by the Herod towers, we saw your procession advancing toward us; and there was such a shouting and singing and clapping of hands and waving of olive and palm branches that we became uneasy. Pilate sent for me, thrust his head out of his litter and asked me what was happening. I told him it was nothing of importance; there was no danger; it was just a group of Jews conducting their Rabbi to the Temple. However, to play safe, I ordered the advance guards to drive your procession into the narrow Sictus street. But your Rabbi anticipated me. I may as well tell you now that if he had not, your dancing and singing would have turned into funeral lamentations, for our men had drawn their swords. Pilate and Claudia both looked out of their litters, and saw your Rabbi riding away on the little ass. I have seldom seen anyone laugh as he did. Only Claudia seemed to be frightened. Why this was so I shall tell you later. But of course all the attendants chimed in. It became an uproar. Pilate went into spasms, so that the veins stood out on his neck. It was your good fortune that the procession struck us simply as a farce. Later, when I learned what you had been chanting, what phrases you had dared to utter, I took a much more serious view of the business. Your Rabbi of Nazareth, as I perceived, was not the innocent little lamb you would make him out to be. I told myself that there was more in the affair than met the eye. I did not bother Pilate with my views. But I went that same evening to the High Priest's house and demanded the arrest of the Galilean insurrectionist. I spoke plainly:

" 'Words like those spell revolt. You have heard them; they shouted them loud enough. They called him the anointed of God. They hailed him as the King, of the Davidian line.'

"Kaifa pretended to be very phlegmatic. 'Why,' he said, 'every year our Jews proclaim a new King-Messiah, and no harm is done; the Roman Government still stands where it did, and Herod's authority is not diminished by a hair. Let them have their little joke.'

" 'Jokes like these,' I insisted, 'in these turbulent times, and especially when the town is filled with unruly Galileans, may turn out to be very dangerous. I demand that your Chief Officer of the Temple administration instruct the guards to arrest him the moment he shows up in the courts. In any case, commonsense dictates that we hold him a prisoner over the festival; just as a precautionary measure.'

" 'Exactly as a precautionary measure we ought to leave him untouched over the festival. The man is too popular among the poor masses in the Lower City. And the Galileans are very proud of their fellow-countryman. To arrest him in the courts would probably provoke a serious riot. After the festival, when the pilgrims will have left the city, we can make our reckoning with him.' Thus spoke the youngest of the Sons of Hanan.

"Then the oldest son, Eliezer, added his views. 'The man is not dangerous at all,' he said. 'On the contrary, he is extremely useful. He soothes the masses with his beautiful stories, and he pleads with them to do no evil. **In fact,** he tells them specifically to return good for evil and to carry the burden of life with loving patience. The only reward he offers them is a claim on the world to come, a portion in the kingdom of God, and assurance of the resurrection. We, for our part, don't recognize the claim. We did not issue the promise. When they come to collect, it will be at his hand, and if he cannot pay, so much the worse for him. Meanwhile he keeps them peacefully in harness. The real danger, as far as we are concerned, is Bar Abba; that big mouth of his is ever opened to preach rebellion against us, the High Priesthood, and against the Government. That's the man to arrest.'

" 'I agree wholly with my brother,' said the Chief Temple Administrator for that year, and played with his beard.

"Here the old man himself came in, and we all rose to our feet. When he heard what was being discussed, and what my demand was, he burst out laughing, just as Pilate had done earlier in the day when he saw the Rabbi riding on his ass. He repeated what his youngest son had said:

" 'Every year, without fail, we have a Messiah who comes riding into Jerusalem on an ass. If you want to make a real Messiah of him, arrest him. But as long as you let those people alone, they can't become Messiahs, even if they shout till their lungs burst and promise their followers the sun and the moon and the stars. And by the way: we have our own sources of information concerning this man. Far from being dangerous for us, he serves our purpose. It's Bar Abba we must be rid of, before he has time to make the first uprising. My men are right at his heels.'

"Thus they went on, making the Nazarene out to be utterly unimportant, and I let myself be talked over once more.

"It was a very different story the next day, when the Rabbi played havoc with their booths in the Temple courts, drove out the merchants, and overturned the tables of the moneychangers. It was not the money loss alone, but much more the blow to their prestige. The daring of it! The words he flung at them! 'Nest of robbers,' and what not! And how the people, the mob, and even the Pharisees, had howled with delight! No, this time they blazed up into fury. Once the man had started on this path, where would he stop? They felt the foundations of their institution trembling under their feet. And so they took counsel. But the remarkable fact was that by this act the man of Nazareth gained enormously in their eyes. He ceased to be the innocent and slightly ridiculous lamb; the joking and the sneering died abruptly away. Instead, there was sudden and profound respect and, in even greater measure, fear. Yes, genuine fear. I simply cannot understand what there was in the spirit of the man to awaken fear. I tell you that even amongst the greatest and highest of them, among the leaders of the Priesthood, they spoke of him thenceforth with lowered voices; their faces were earnest and thoughtful, not as if they were dealing with some obscure and insignificant provincial, but as though they were confronted by a gigantic and mystical power. I have grounds for believing that they were more afraid of him than of our Roman authority. The only explanation I can think of is that their Asiatic spirit—it existed even among the driest and coolest of them—had somehow been touched off; their fantasy was at work. I have known the strongest men among them to be seized with fits of remorse, to be plagued by conscience, lashed and tormented by it, and to excite themselves into states of frenzy which made every supernatural possibility a reality to them—experiences thoroughly alien to us Romans. They actually came to believe that what this man did and said had the direction and authority of a higher power; that behind him stood legions of demons which he could conjure down from heaven. Were it otherwise, they argued, did he not have the authority direct from his God, he would never have dared to act as he did in the Temple.

"How else am I to interpret the events of that extraordinary day, and their subsequent behavior? Nor must you think that they themselves brought us the report. By no means. They would have been glad, it appears, to pass over the riot in silence. Pilate sent me that day to the High Priest, directing him to hand over to us both rebels, Bar Abba and the Rabbi of Galilee. We suspected that the two men were co-operating in a conspiracy, and we decided to act swiftly and energetically. As far as Bar Abba was concerned, our task was straightforward. The spies of the High Priest informed us of the gathering called for that night in the hostelry of the camel drivers, down in the Lower City. (They knew everything—if they only wanted to.) It was another matter with the Rabbi of Nazareth. When we asked the Priests for him, they turned livid. And the old High Priest himself, who was present at the conference in the house of Kaifa, refused to define his attitude toward the man. He told us, to begin with, that they had no idea where the man was, where he lived in Jerusalem, though this would have been the easiest thing to find out, since he was to be seen almost daily in the Temple courts. Then old Hanan demanded that we avoid any sort of clash with the man within the Temple itself. He said they were afraid of riots; the masses idolized the Rabbi of Nazareth; the masses believed in him, and so on and so on. He insisted again and again that we wait until the passing of the festival and the withdrawal of the pilgrims before we arrested him.

" 'And meanwhile,' I said, 'with the door open, we'll find an empty cage.'

" 'What do you mean, Hegemon?'

" 'Your prophet will be gone. He will run away from Jerusalem.'

" 'Messiahs do not run away. Messiahs fulfill their mission, or else they die,' the High Priest answered, and his eyes twinkled at me equivocally.

" 'And what sort of mission is this Messiah of yours expected to fulfill?' I asked the High Priest, and stared straight back at him.

"But there was no answer to this question. They only looked at each other dumbly, fear written on their faces. Then the High Priest said, uneasily:

" 'That which happened in the Temple courts was an internal religious affair. It had to do with the administration of the Temple, and was in no way related to the government. And if we find the man guilty, we will deliver him to the Roman authorities. In any event, it is not within our jurisdiction to carry out the death penalty.'

" 'What happened in the Temple court,' I replied, firmly, 'was not directed solely against the Temple administration. It was an assault on the whole system of laws and a threat against all order in the Province of Judaea. Considering the harm which the man did to your prestige, we cannot but wonder that you extend your protection to him. How can we help suspecting that you have your own reasons? We have neither the time nor the means to untangle all the details of your mystical, complicated religious affairs, which so easily take on the aspect of rebellion. Our straightforward Roman commonsense tells us that if the supreme religious authority extends its protection to a man who has delivered such a blow against its prestige, then this same highest religious authority must find it to its interest to make common cause with a rebel and a disturber of the peace. That interest cannot be in consonance with the well-being of the constituted order.'

" 'Hegemon, do you dare to doubt our loyalty to Rome?'

" 'It is not a question of doubting or of not doubting. Can such an attitude on the part of the High Priesthood seem otherwise than suspicious to the legate and the Procurator?'

"The High Priest looked at his father-in-law and at his brothers-in-law; they looked back at him. Every drop of blood had withdrawn from his yellow-freckled face. For a moment it seemed to me that even his beard, which he had so carefully dressed and oiled and curled for the festival, had lost its color and turned white. At last he said:

" 'What is it you demand of me, Hegemon?'

" 'The Procurator demands that you, the supreme religious authority, responsible for the observance of law and order in the Temple, arrest the man who created a disturbance in the Temple and undermined the prestige of the Temple authority.'

" 'But we assure you that we do not know where the man is; and we promise we shall take immediate steps to discover his whereabouts. The moment we ourselves know, we shall transmit the information to you.'

"This time I was halfway satisfied with the assurances of the High Priest.

"Concerning the raid on the Bar Abba-ites you already know. We surrounded the hostelry in the night, and it was just as well for us that we surprised them when they were mostly asleep. As it was, they put up a stiff resistance. I never knew how many were killed on their side, and I do not remember how many on ours, but we did manage to take Bar Abba alive. The arsenal which we uncovered in the hostelry was evidence of the seriousness of conditions in Jerusalem.

"There now remained the second fomenter of rebellion, the man whom we considered the more dangerous of the two; I personally was convinced that he was the heart and spirit of the movement and that even the High Priest had somehow fallen under his demonic influence.

"We—that is, the Roman officials—were utterly astounded to learn, on the day following, that not only had the Rabbi of Nazareth appeared again in the Temple courts, and preached there, and not only had the High Priest failed to take him captive, but that the Priests—some of them, at any rate—had actually joined a deputation to the Rabbi. Their purpose? To find out by what authority he did what he did! Our spies informed us that messengers of the High Priest, concealing their identity, joined in the discussions with the scholars who interrogated the Rabbi. They did not come to an agreement. There was something in their mystical writings, signs, and portents and interpretations which the Rabbi of Nazareth did not seem to satisfy. From which we, the Roman officials, at once deduced that if he *had* satisfied the conditions, they would have proclaimed him king on the spot.

"When I brought Pilate my report on Bar Abba, on the quantity of arms we had found in the hostelry, on the resistance we had encountered and, finally, on the second rebel, whom the Priesthood was in some way sheltering, he flew into a rage. I can still see the Procurator, and the manner in which he received the information that the Priests had let the man of Nazareth slip through their hands—or rather, had sent secret emissaries to negotiate with him. When I came in to him, at the Procuratorium, he was seated behind a massive bronze desk, which hid the lower part of his body, but the upper part, rising behind it, gave the impression of being poured of the same ponderous metallic material as the desk: a gigantic, square-shaped head, bald as a desert rock, a wide, fleshy face, equally hairless, and a powerful breast, with rolling muscles. There was not a single break anywhere from the flashing head down to the thick, shining folds of the neck and the swell of his chest—it was all poured and hammered of a single piece. And this enormous figure suddenly exploded into a frenzy. He reminded me of one of those idols popular among your Asiatic neighbors, a Moloch, in whose iron belly a white-hot fire has been lit. A tide of blood washed right through the successive folds of his neck. His big ears stood out. His eyebrows, the only hairy spots on his face and skull, bristled, and his cold, gray eyes flamed. He stood up, almost toppling the desk over, and roared like a lion.

" 'Command the High Priest to deliver the rebel to me at once!'

"I did not wait for a second command. I hastened without delay to the house of Kaifa, and I found assembled there not only the High Priest, old Hanan and Kaifa himself, sons and brothers and brothers-in-law, but a group of their scholars and interpreters of the law.

I must have interrupted some special session of theirs, but it was no time for ceremonies. I observed their frightened, uneasy looks, and I said, abruptly:

" 'The lion has roared!'

"They understood me at once. Their faces paled, they started back with a single motion. But they remained silent and stared at each other helplessly. Finally the High Priest spoke out: the old excuse:

" 'We don't know where he is.'

" 'You had him in your hands. He was in the Temple. You sent messengers to negotiate with him.'

" 'We cannot take him in the Temple. He is too dangerous.'

" 'We have troops enough stationed in Jerusalem to take care of any situation. In times of danger the High Priest knows to whom to turn.'

" 'But that is what we want to avoid—a second massacre like that of a year ago, when the blood of the Galileans was poured out together with the blood of their sacrifices. The same danger confronts us this year, if we act too hastily.'

" 'You err. The danger this year is greater. It is not only the blood of the Galileans which may mingle with the blood of the sacrifices; but the blood of other Jews, from the highest to the lowest. "Tomorrow I shall sit in trial on him—or on them!" Those are the words of Pilate.'

"They stood before me as if turned to stone, yes, even the courageous High Priest himself. Finally a frightened murmuring arose.

" 'All for the sake of one man! Our fields will be taken away! Our lives!'

"Old Hanan spoke up.

" 'We quarrel about the fox before we've trapped him. It isn't just a question of taking him. We would have done it before now if we had been able to catch him outside the Temple gates and spirit him away quietly. And to do this we must first find out where he stays. And in the second place we must make sure that it is the right man we seize. I want to assure the Hegemon that I have put some of my most skillful men on his trail, and despite the high price we have set on it, we still have not been able to obtain the right information.

The masses believe in the man and shelter him from us. It is not only a question of discovering his hiding place; we must be absolutely certain of taking the Rabbi of Galilee and not another. He has among his pupils and disciples those who are ready to defend him to the death. They would let themselves be arrested in his place. And for this reason we have been trying to get at one of his followers and to bribe him, with money or some other reward, not only to indicate where his Rabbi lives, but to point out the right man to us. So far we have not made the contact, but I give my most solemn promise to the Hegemon that as soon as the opportunity offers itself, we shall take the Rabbi prisoner and deliver him to the authorities.'

"I returned to Pilate and rendered my report. I added that in my opinion the High Priests themselves had certain secret reasons for concealing the rebel from us.

" 'What kind of reasons?' asked Pilate.

" 'They ascribe a mystic power to him. They believe him to be the Messiah.'

" 'The what?'

" 'The King of the Jews, for whom they have long been waiting to liberate them from our rule.'

" 'The King of the Jews! There you have it! And I tell you this King of the Jews must be delivered to us before tomorrow morning. I will not give them a moment longer. And I shall hold the High Priest personally responsible.'

"From this time on Pilate had only one name for the Galilean: The King of the Jews.

"This time I applied to old Hanan. He had good news for me.

" 'I believe,' he said, 'we have an indication as to the Rabbi's hiding place. The man we've been looking for has turned up.'

" 'How did you get him?'

" 'He came to us of his own accord. We don't know the reasons which have moved him to betray his Rabbi, nor what is behind it all. I do not believe that he is doing it for the bribe, for the thirty pieces of silver. The man is one of the leading disciples, the keeper of their common treasury. If it were only a matter of money he could make more by clinging to his Rabbi than by betraying him. There are most assuredly other motives behind his action. We have not been able to ferret them out yet. My sons are interrogating him in the guardroom. The whole thing may be a kind of trap, and we must act with great caution.'

"I went at once to the guardroom, which was within the wall of the inner courtyard. And whom did I find there? Judah! His eyes were red and flooded, as if he had not slept for a long time. And yet the look which he turned upon the sons of the High Priest was one of insolent challenge, and his voice wavered between a sobbing helplessness and a hoarse defiance:

" 'Yes, yes! For thirty silver pieces! If you are ready to give me the money, I am ready to show you where my Rabbi is. If not, let me go. For then I will know that you are afraid of him, that you dare not set foot in his vicinity. He will destroy you with the breath of his mouth. You are afraid of him!' And here Judah broke into a sickly cynical laughter which issued from his bare gums. 'You tremble when you think of him.'

" 'Thirty silver pieces,' the son of the High Priest said, penetratingly. 'Could you not have taken thirty silver pieces from your treasury, with no one knowing about it? For thirty silver pieces you will deliver your Rabbi? There is something behind it.'

" 'That is my business. I want your money, and I have my reasons. I have fallen away from my Rabbi, and I want to go to a harlot. Isn't that enough for you? You will not deal with me? Well and good! I know *your* reasons. You are afraid to lay a hand on my Rabbi.' And he made a gesture as if to go.

"Here I called out:

" 'Wait, Judah! If they will not give you the price, we will. If the High Priest has secret reasons for suppressing the affair, and for letting the Galilean steal away from Jerusalem, he will have to answer for it to the Procurator. The Galilean has risen not only against the Temple administration, but against Rome. The Procurator demands the man. This night he must be delivered to the Roman guard, to be tried by Pilate. Judah: I will speak of you to the Procurator. You will have deserved well of Rome. You will have delivered to us one of the most dangerous disturbers of the peace. You want to be of service to us, and these men reject your offer. We shall find out why!"

"The sons of the High Priest trembled. Here old Hanan intervened:

" 'We must be certain that Judah indicates the right man.'

" 'I will point him out to you.'

" 'How?'

" 'The man whom I will kiss, and call "Rabbi! Rabbi!" is the one you seek.'

" 'Pay him his money and let him show us the place.'

" 'It is not far from the stores of the Sons of Hanan. On the Mount of Olives. In Gat Shemen. Come with me.'

" 'You must call the Sanhedrin into session at once, and put the man to trial,' I called out.

" 'That is impossible,' they answered.

" 'Why?'

" 'The Sanhedrin cannot be called into session at night to judge a man who faces the death penalty. We must wait till tomorrow morning. We cannot get the Sanhedrin together this night. It is against the law. Its members will be occupied with the Passover sacrifice. The procedure of judgment is bound up with many formalities. The trial will have to be put off till after the festival.'

" 'And I tell you that my orders from Pilate are to deliver the man at once. Tomorrow morning Pilate himself will sit in judgment. Both rebels will be tried, Bar Abba and the Nazarene.'

" 'Bar Abba rebelled against the government. The crime of the Nazarene is of quite a different order. It is a purely Jewish religious affair. We must call together the members of the Sanhedrin, at least the small Sanhedrin of twenty-three. And a certain number of Pharisees must be there, too. Without them we have not a sufficiency of members to deal with a case of this character. But the Pharisees will certainly refuse to attend. I tell you, Hegemon, it is impossible, according to our laws, to push a case like this through hastily, and in the night. It is illegal.'

" 'This is no time for formalities. I warn you that you are playing with fire. Tomorrow morning the Nazarene must appear before Pilate, together with your verdict. Those are his specific orders. You know what that means. I am doing my best to avoid a massacre in the city and, what would be worse, a great deal of—inconvenience for the High Priest. You remember the great procession to Caesarea, when Pilate assumed the authority here.'

" 'You mean when he hung out the Roman images and trophies on the Antonia? I remember,' said old Hanan, and his beard trembled.

" 'It may happen again.'

"The sons of the old High Priest were silent and looked into their father's face. He alone remained calm.

" 'I will talk this matter over with the High Priest—if indeed the situation is as serious as you say, Hegemon. Perhaps our scholars will find a way out. I know only one thing: the Pharisees will never agree to this procedure.'

" 'But neither will we,' exclaimed the oldest son of the High Priest, Eliezer. 'The law is the law.'

" 'My son, act carefully in a time of danger, when so many lives are involved. I say I will talk this matter over with the High Priest. Meanwhile, we must make sure of the man. Let the guard go with Judah to Gat Shemen and make the arrest.'

" 'I will make the arrest in person!' I interjected. 'The Nazarene is a prisoner of Rome not less than of the High Priest. And I rely on no one. I have no confidence in the High Priest's guard. The Nazarene can fool them with one of his magic tricks. They will run away from him or take him and let him go. Wait here, Judah. I will go over to the Procuratorium and return with a cohort of troops. We do not know how many of the rebels are assembled up there and what arms they have.'

" 'Ho, ho, *zeh ishi,* that's my man! Bring the Procurator along, too, and a couple of legates, all the high officers, and half the army, to take my Rabbi prisoner!' Judah, sitting in a corner, playing with the thirty pieces of silver which had been delivered to him, babbled like a man possessed.

"I left the High Priest and his sons arguing fiercely in the guardroom. Some of them were for refusing to obey the Procurator, though at the risk of their lives; others were not so hot-headed. Among them, I felt I could rely on old Hanan, and on his youngest son, Hanan ben Hanan. I knew that once the man was arrested they would carry through Pilate's orders to the end.

"I went over to the Procuratorium and ordered out a cohort made up of Romans, Askelonites, and Syrians. I put on my uniform, and on my corselet hung the Tribune's insignia. When I returned to the High Priest's house, there was already assembled a Priestly guard, with spears, clubs, staves and whips. When I looked at this rabble, and saw the skin on them crawling with fear, saw their knees trembling under them, as if they were about to be taken to be executed, I realized how well I had done to place no reliance on them, and had provided myself with an entire cohort of five hundred men. And later on, in Gat Shemen, when it came to the actual arrest, I congratulated myself a third time on my foresight. You saw how the servants of the High Priest behaved there. Had it not been for the cohort, they would have scattered and fled at the very sight of the Nazarene, just as his disciples scattered and fled at the sight of us.

"We bound him and took him along in our midst. Before we entered the Lower City, I tripled the guard about him, to conceal his identity and avoid trouble. It was an unnecessary precaution. Jerusalem was asleep and the streets were empty. The city did not know that this night we were leading its king, a bound prisoner, to trial.

"And I may as well reveal to you that I know how this man, bound as he was, still terrified the Priests. I was told about it later. For I was not present at the proceedings. I merely delivered the Nazarene to the Priests. I waited outside with my men while they conducted the examination with such members of the Sanhedrin as they were able to get together late in the night. For my orders still stood. I was to deliver the prisoner to Pilate in the morning, with their report on him. As to what happened within, you can tell me, for you were there."

"Yes," I answered, and I took up the thread of my narrative.

CHAPTER TWENTY-THREE

WITH rapid steps we descended the hill and entered the sleeping city, hastening toward the house of study of our Rabbi. We did not encounter a living soul in the streets. All the inhabitants were tired out with the preparations for the festival. Bluish pale moonlight was poured out on the walls of the houses; the stones in the street slumbered, lulled into dreams by the quiet song of the moonlight. It was now the middle of the second watch, and once or twice it seemed to us that we caught at a distance the footsteps of guards in lonely alleys.

We found our Rabbi asleep in his room, which was next to the study house, and we debated with ourselves whether we ought to wake him. On the one hand we were confronted with the laws of respect and affection toward our Rabbi, laws not less stringent than those which apply to one's own parents; on the other hand, a life was in danger, and danger overrides many lives, according to the tradition. But while we hesitated, our Rabbi awoke of himself, and we thanked God that we had not been compelled to break in disrespectfully on his rest.

He had not slept well. He had been fearful of the coming day and what it might bring for the Nazarene; and when we failed to return to the house of study, his uneasiness increased. No doubt he had been waiting even in his sleep for our return, and while we lingered outside his door he started and called us in.

We entered and found him sitting on his bed. When we told him what had happened on the Mount of Olives that night, he sprang up and set his feet on the floor. Never, in all the days through which I was privileged to be near him and serve him, had I seen my Rabbi so perturbed, so filled with indignation and rage. Indeed, it is not easy for me to remember the occasions which have moved him to anger. But it was the holy anger of God which burned in him now, and he was so agitated by it that we found it hard to do our service by him and help him to dress. We brought him a vessel with water, and he washed the sleep of the night from his hands and face. He strode fiercely through the room, this way and that, muttering:

"By what power have they dared to do this thing? The like of it has never been heard in Israel!"

Then he said: "Let me have all my pupils about me!" He wanted to send them to awaken and assemble the members of the Sanhedrin. He wanted us to run to Rabban Jochanan ben Zakkai and Rabban

Gamaliel ben Simon and the other leading Pharisees. He called for an immediate assembly of the Companionship. Then he mastered himself and became calm. He sat down and meditated audibly. "To begin with, they cannot sit in trial in the night. In the second, even if they dared to try him in the night, they cannot pass sentence against him. Thirdly, in matters of this kind they must have at least the complete attendance of the Smaller Sanhedrin, which is impossible without our presence. Fourth, they cannot under any circumstances try him on the eve of a festival. They will not take such a sin upon themselves, for such a judgment would be nothing more or less than the shedding of innocent blood. No. Morning will be time enough. I need not alarm the sages."

But the calmness was momentary. For he rose from his seat and again he strode back and forth through the room, in a manner altogether strange to him. And still he continued to mutter:

"But who knows what the Sons of Hanan and the Sons of Beitus are capable of? They will stop at nothing. They who send out their slaves and servants like mad dogs against the people, will they shrink from attacking an individual? And even like their slaves and servants, the scribes and scholars of the Sadducees will obey to the letter the commands of the Sons of Hanan. Have we not seen them disregard and reject the ruling on the Passover sacrifice handed down to us from the great Hillel? No. My soul can find no rest. Come!" he turned to us. "Let us go up to the house of Kaifa."

He bade us bring him his robe of dignity, the long black mantle of the Pharisaic Rabbi, which came down to the heels of his sandals, and the black head covering of his Rabbinic office. We went forth, Rufus and I bearing the lamps before him, more as the mark of respect due him than to illumine the way, for the moon made the streets almost as bright as by daytime. The other pupils following, we ascended to the Upper City, to the house of the High Priest Kaifa.

The gate was locked and bolted. We smote upon it till the watchman came out and asked us what we wanted.

"Go in and report that Rabbi Nicodemon, a Rabbi of the Pharisees and a member of the Great Sanhedrin, demands admission with his pupils to the session."

A long time passed before the gate was opened for us. It seems that there was a fierce division of opinion on the question of admitting us. Finally, when the watchman returned, it was with two messengers from the Sanhedrin, who invited my Rabbi to enter into the session.

"The sessions of the Sanhedrin are held in the Chamber of the Hewn Stones, in the Temple, and not in the house of the High Priest. I want to know, where is the man who was taken this night?" my Rabbi answered, sharply.

"He is within, at the session with the High Priest."

"Lead us to him!" my Rabbi ordered.

We entered and passed through the outer court. When we reached the inner court we beheld, in the place where the house guards were usually assembled, a strange scene. A wood fire blazed, and about it was gathered a group of guards, servants, housemaids, cooks, and others of the household. They warmed their hands at the fire and talked fiercely of the events of that night. But at the center two guards held a man by the arms, and a housemaid was shrieking into his face. The man shrank from her, seemed to be denying something, and struggled in vain to free himself. When we drew near we recognized him whom they held in the dancing light of the flames. It was Simon bar Jonah. He was white, in mortal fear, and his head shook from side to side in constant negation. The housemaid pointed her finger at him and reiterated:

"You were also with Yeshua the Nazarene! You were also with Yeshua the Nazarene!"

And Simon lifted up his shoulders, shook his head, and answered her, trying to impart to his speech the accent of the Judaeans, but failing:

"I do not know what you are saying!"

"All have abandoned him," my Rabbi groaned. "Even his most faithful disciples." We hastened past and followed the messengers through many rooms and corridors till we came to the large hall where the High Priest would sit in council with the chief officers of the Temple and sometimes try minor cases. This hall was arranged in the manner of the Great Sanhedrin, which is at the Temple entrance, and which is known as the Hall or Chamber of the Hewn

Stones. But here the dimensions were smaller. One end of the hall was built in the form of a half-moon, and twenty-three benches were cut into the wall, the center bench, raised above the others, being reserved for the High Priest. When we entered, about one-half of the benches were occupied. The High Priest, in purple mantle, was there; to his right sat his father-in-law, old Hanan, and Hanan's son, Eliezer; they, as former High Priests, also wore purple mantles, but shorter than that of the regnant High Priest and more like capes. They were full-fledged members of the Sanhedrin. To the left of Kaifa sat his other brother-in-law, Jochanan, who, as chief administrator of the Temple, was entitled to a seat in the Sanhedrin, but did not wear the purple cape. There were also present others in purple capes, all of them former High Priests and sons of the House of Beitus; they, however, were present in their capacity as interpreters of the law for the Sadducees. One of them, an ancient with a long white beard and thick white eyebrows overshadowing his large, blue, watery eyes, was recognized as the sage among the Sadducee scholars, learned above the others in the interpretations according to the Sadducean tradition. In the full sessions of the Sanhedrin, the members along one arm of the half-moon confronted those along the other, but now, the attendance being limited, the participants sat together, and the seats at both ends were empty. To right and left of the raised bench of the High Priest sat the recorders, their steel pens in their hands, their wax tablets before them: one recorder for the prosecution, one for the defense.

A large number of oil lamps hung from the ceiling, and to the light of these were added the flames blazing in fire bowls of red marble. Two servants holding aloft torches stood by the High Priest.

Fronting the seats of the members of the Sanhedrin were rows of benches for the pupils of the Rabbis. It was not only the right, it was also the duty, of pupils to attend their Rabbi at the trial sessions of the Sanhedrin, and to observe him closely throughout the entire proceedings. As pupils we even had the right to take part in the debate preceding the sentence, but only for the defense of the prisoner, never for the prosecution. When Rufus and I and the other pupils of Rabbi Nicodemon entered, the front benches were already occupied by the pupils of the Sadducean Rabbis, most of them the children of rich Priestly families, between whom and us there had always been enmity. On the first bench of the pupils sat also the other sons of Hanan, those who were not entitled to a place in the Sanhedrin; among them, black-haired, tall and energetic, we distinguished the youngest son, Hanan ben Hanan.

In the light of the oil lamps and fire bowls, and against the background of crimson and purple and black vestments, the white robe of the Nazarene struck us the moment we came in. His dress seemed to me to be as white as when I perceived him approaching the house of Hillel the watercarrier, on his way to celebrate the *seder*; but the folds had lost their stiffness and they clung to his body, wetted through by the sweat of the anguish through which he had passed that night. Yet they had lost nothing of their whiteness. He stood before the High Priest as I had last seen him standing in the garden of Gat Shemen, with the same deep and mournful tranquillity on his face, save that perhaps the thin line of his lips, visible through his beard, had become even thinner, more tremulous and touched with deeper pain. I saw now that his earlocks and short beard had become quite gray, and it seemed to me that old age had come upon him in the brief interval since I had seen him. His hands were nerveless, and he held them tight to his body. But the look of mortal terror which we had marked on his face in the garden of Gat Shemen was completely gone; on it were written tranquillity, sorrow and pain. He gazed with large, astonished eyes straight at his judges, and at the High Priest, not in bitterness, but with childlike curiosity, as though all this about him affected everyone but himself.

When the High Priest saw my Rabbi at the entrance to the hall, he proclaimed to the assembled:

"A Rabbi of the Pharisees, a member of the Great Sanhedrin, Rabbi Nicodemon honors us with his presence. We call upon Rabbi Nicodemon to come forward and take his place in the session of the Sanhedrin Court."

My Rabbi answered from the entrance: *"Ishi Kohen Gadol!* My lord High Priest! Before I enter the session, I wish to be informed what kind of session this is which you have called, and what danger compelled you to call it in the night. I see none of the sages of the scribes and Pharisees, but only those of the Sadducees. What does this mean?"

"The Prosecutor will declare the matter to the Rabbi of the Pharisees," the High Priest commanded.

"The session has been called to judge the man who has caused Jews to rebel against the Jewish God. And the session has been called in the night because the matter is urgent. We must issue our sentence before the morning, for the government demands it of us," the Prosecutor stated.

"Judgment of life and death in the night? Who has ever heard the like? It is an accepted and incontrovertible law that such trials must take place precisely during the day, not in the night. It is accepted and incontrovertible law that ample time must be given for the preparation of the defense, and that there shall be no haste. It is likewise accepted and incontrovertible law that the verdict shall be issued without pressure of any kind and from whomsoever it may proceed. Therefore I, as a Rabbi in Israel, declare at the outset that this court has no right to sit in judgment on a case involving life, and that every verdict pronounced by this court is null and void before it is issued. For the trial is being conducted contrary to the law and the justice of the Torah."

A sudden agitation arose among the members of the Sanhedrin and died down. The High Priest paled. He forced himself to be calm and sat playing with the locks of his beard. There followed a long debate between the sages and scholars of the Sadducees.

Eliezer, the oldest son of Hanan, rose:

"My lord High Priest! Even though we Sadducees do not accept the complicated procedure with which the Pharisees have surrounded all trials of capital crimes, I am nevertheless, on this occasion, in agreement with the Rabbi of the Pharisees. For what purpose have we been called hither this night, and what shall be the significance of our judgment and verdict? Shall it be judgment in regard to the laws of the government? Then we have nothing to do with it; let the government render its own judgment. Shall it be judgment in regard to the laws of our court? Then the trial must be held in accordance with the procedure of our court and the verdict rendered in accordance with the laws of the Torah. And if we find the man guilty according to our laws, we shall pronounce sentence against him according to the same laws. But since when have we taken it upon ourselves to conduct the trials of the government?"

The High Priest lifted his hand, and the murmur died down.

"I will ask Rabbi Todros, interpreter of the law, to give his opinion concerning the objections raised by Rabbi Nicodemon and the former High Priest, Rabbi Eliezer."

The ancient with the long white beard rose and answered:

"The Rabbi of the Pharisees and the former High Priest Rabbi Eliezer are correct in their objections also in accordance with the laws of the Sadducees."

The High Priest called out:

"Most just Court! We have heard the statement of our interpreters of the law. I therefore declare that the session which we have called together this night is not a trial session, but a session for investigation and examination. We cannot, according to our laws, issue sentence for the crime of which the prisoner is accused, for the judgment can be executed only by the government. We therefore transform this session into one of investigation and examination."

Now my Rabbi came forward and took his seat with the Sanhedrin; Rufus and I and the other pupils sat down on the pupils' benches.

Now began the investigation and examination. The Prosecutor, who sat next to one of the recorders, rose, and from the document on his lectern read forth the accusation:

"We have all," he began, "been witnesses of the actions of this man who now stands before us, whom the people call 'Rabbi,' and 'Prophet,' and by another name which I will not repeat, when he broke into the Temple courts and—"

Rabbi Nicodemon sprang to his feet.

"My lord High Priest! I protest against the opening remarks of the Prosecutor. We are not witnesses, and we know nothing of what the accused is purported to have done! We have seen nothing and we have heard nothing. The man who stands before us is, in our eyes, as innocent as a new-born child, for until his guilt has been established by reputable witnesses, we must judge him favorably."

The High Priest lifted his hand toward the interpreter of the law, who said:

"The Rabbi of the Pharisees is right. Such is the law also according to the interpretation of the Sadducees."

"In accordance with the objection of the Rabbi of the Pharisees," the High Priest instructed the Prosecutor, "I expunge from the record the accusation read forth."

The Prosecutor continued: "There have come before us sundry reputable witnesses and have testified that the man standing before us, he who is called by the people 'Rabbi' and 'Prophet' and by that other name which I will not repeat, spoke blasphemously and offensively of the Holy One of Israel."

"Call in the witnesses!" the High Priest ordered.

An attendant at the door of the witness chamber called out: "Judah Ish-Kiriot, disciple of your Rabbi, enter and bear witness."

Judah Ish-Kiriot appeared in the doorway. He looked with assurance at the judges, avoiding only the face of my Rabbi. But he did not avoid the face of his own Rabbi, but stared at him with a fixed and obstinate gaze, as though he were quite certain of himself.

"Judah a witness!" my Rabbi roared with the voice of a lion. "That abomination in Israel who delivered a Jewish soul into the hand of heathens? He a witness? He? It would be permitted to rip his body open, like the body of a fish, and that on a Day of Atonement even when it falls on a Sabbath! He may be killed by anyone who encounters him! His name is wiped out from the congregation of Israel! He is cursed with all the curses of the anathema, unto all generations. He cannot testify here, for an informer is not a reputable witness."

Judah covered his face with the hem of his robe.

The High Priest turned to the interpreter of the law:

"Is this in agreement with the interpretation of the law according to the tradition of the Sadducees?"

"We are in agreement with the Rabbi of the Pharisees. An informer is not a reputable witness," answered the ancient.

"An informer is not a reputable witness," agreed the other members of the Sanhedrin.

The attendants seized Judah by the arms and conducted him from the hall.

"There have come before us reputable and acceptable witnesses and have testified that they heard with their own ears how the man now standing before us, known as 'Rabbi' or 'Prophet' or by the name which I will not pronounce, spoke blasphemously and offensively of the Holy Temple!"

"Witnesses!" called the High Priest.

"Witnesses!" repeated the attendants at the door.

There came in a little man with short legs. He held himself erect and proudly, like a peacock displaying its tail. He would have the assembly know that he was acquainted with Writ, for his pen was behind his ear, and from his neck hung the wax tablet. He was led before the High Priest.

"Do you know the Writ?" the High Priest asked him.

"I know the Writ," he answered.

"Do you know the law of the Torah concerning one who bears false witness?"

"He shall receive the punishment which would have been meted out to him against whom he bore false witness."

The scribe was now bidden to turn and confront the accused. The little man tried to stand on tip-toe, that he might be able to meet the gaze of the Nazarene. He said:

"I, with my own ears, heard this man who stands before me, utter with his mouth these words: 'I will throw down this Temple, which has been raised by the hands of men, and in three days I will build another, which shall not be raised by the hands of men.' "

"Where was he then."

"In the Temple court."

"On which side?"

"By the Water Gate."

"Was it in the day or in the evening?"

"It was toward evening, when the Priests bring the afternoon sacrifice, before they close the Temple gates."

"Take away this man to a separate room."

"Two witnesses shall establish a thing," said the High Priest. "Have you another witness?"

"Witnesses!" the attendant called into the witness room.

A second man was led in. As the first witness was small, so this one was exceedingly tall, and he had to stoop in order to meet the gaze of the Nazarene.

"I, with my own ears, heard this man who stands before me say to his disciples, when they asked him to look upon the Temple: 'Do you see that great building? There shall not remain of it one stone upon another, which shall not be cast down.' "

"Where was this?"

"In the Temple court."

"By day or in the evening?"

"It was at the midday hour."

"Who was present?"

"His disciples."

"My lord High Priest!" my Rabbi called, "I declare this witness inacceptable."

"On what grounds, Rabbi of the Pharisees?"

"The witnesses do not speak of one and the same occasion; they report two different expressions which the accused is purported to have used."

"But he may have said both things," old Hanan interjected. "We have testimony for it."

"My lord High Priest! It is written in the Torah: 'Two witnesses shall establish the thing.' The meaning thereof is that each of them shall deliver the same thing, without contradiction. And these witnesses have testified concerning two different expressions which the accused is purported to have used. On these grounds I declare their testimony to be inacceptable."

The High Priest turned to the Sadducee interpreter of the law.

"I am in agreement with the Rabbi of the Pharisees. 'Two witnesses shall establish the thing!' " said the Sadducee interpreter of the law. "The witnesses do not say the same thing, therefore their testimony is invalid."

"The law remains with the Rabbi of the Pharisees," declared the High Priest. He turned to the Prosecutor. "Have you any other accusation to bring against the man who stands before us?"

The Prosecutor read on:

"There came before us reputable and acceptable witnesses and testified that the man who stands before us is a misleader, that he preached rebellion and persuaded the people to turn aside from serving the Jewish God, according to the laws and commandments, and that—"

But here my Rabbi sprang to his feet and interrupted the reading of the Prosecutor:

"My Lord High Priest! I protest against the accusation of the Prosecutor before we have heard the witnesses."

"On what grounds?" asked the High Priest.

"A misleader is one who turns away the people from serving the Jewish God and persuades them to serve idols. Have you witnesses who shall testify before this court that the man who stands before us has made the hearts of the people rebellious against the one living God, and has persuaded them to serve idols?"

The Prosecutor continued:

"We have witnesses who came before us and testified that the man taught them rebellion, that they might not serve God according to the laws and commandments as they have been interpreted by the sages, but according to his own interpretations."

Again my Rabbi rose, and his face flamed. He called out in a loud voice:

"I protest against the accusation, and I demand that it be stricken from the record before we hear another witness."

"On what grounds, Rabbi of the Pharisees?" asked the High Priest.

"My lord High Priest, every Jew has the right to interpret the laws and commandments according to his own understanding, as long as he bases himself on the Torah. That is our privilege. We have sages of various schools: those of the Sadducees and those of the Pharisees. If you assert that the law shall be interpreted only in the spirit of your sages, then you must bring to the judgment all those who accept another interpretation. And then, according to the accusation of the Prosecutor, you could bring to the judgment all the scribes and all the sages of the Pharisees and accuse them of rebellion against God and of preaching idol worship, for which the punishment is death. This is a dangerous precedent which you would set and would open ancient wounds in our people. For hundreds of years now this dispute has continued between you and us. Bethink yourselves, members of the Sanhedrin, whither this accusation may lead you. I therefore demand that the accusation of being a misleader be stricken from the record and it shall be regarded as not having been uttered, before we admit another witness."

There was agitation among the Sadducees, a whispering and conferring. The High Priest restored order with a gesture.

"Let us hear the opinion of our interpreter of the law on the objection of the Rabbi of the Pharisees."

The old Sadducean Rabbi, Todros, did not reply at once. His white head was gathered in the cluster of the heads of the other Sadducean interpreters of the law. After a while he gave his opinion:

"This is an ancient calamity in Israel; and in order to prevent renewal of those disputes, we have decided not to accuse such a one of rebellion against God and the preaching of idol worship, as long as he stands on the foundation of the Torah; not even if he denies the accepted traditions of the sages. Only he who turns away the people from the living God and toward idol worship shall be called a misleader."

"Prosecutor," said the High Priest, "have you witnesses who shall testify against the man who stands before us that he preached rebellion against the Jewish God, and the worship of idols?"

"My lord High Priest!" answered the Prosecutor, "for that accusation against the man who stands before us, I have no witnesses."

"Have you witnesses on any other accusation against the man who stands before us?" the High Priest asked.

"I have no more accusations against this man, High Priest," answered the Prosecutor.

My Rabbi stood up again and in a voice that rang with triumph began:

"It is known unto all that the man who stands before us brought the hearts of the people close to our Father in heaven. I therefore propose to this holy court—"

But at this point the High Priest rose and lifted up his hand with a gesture which was meant to remind us all that the right to initiate a prosecution belonged only to him; my Rabbi acknowledged the prerogative, bowed respectfully and suspended his speech.

The High Priest spoke calmly:

"Most just court! We have heard the decisions of the interpreters of the law concerning the accusation of misleading brought against the man who stands before us. We have also heard from the Prosecutor that he has no further accusations to bring against him. We therefore declare void the accusations of the Prosecutor. But, members of the Sanhedrin," and here the High Priest raised his voice (it seemed to me that he had become much older; he looked older than even his father-in-law Hanan; his beard was gray, his face dark and earnest), "are we concerned with this or that word which the man who stands before us may or may not have uttered? Are we, indeed, concerned with words? We are rather concerned here with matters touching our highest sanctities. Who is he that now stands before us? By what right and with what authority does he do and say these thnigs? With respect to these questions there can be only one whose testimony can enlighten us, and that is—the man himself." Here the High Priest stepped down from his dais and took a step toward the Nazarene; he looked straight into his face, and seemed unable to continue with his speech. He breathed heavily, as if searching for words; then having found them he directed them in a trembling voice at Yeshua:

"I charge you by the living God to tell us whether you are the Messiah!"

The chamber was silent. Everyone in the assembly waited. It was as if time itself had ceased to move and waited with us for the answer of the Nazarene.

And the Nazarene opened his lips and in a clear voice answered the High Priest; but his eyes were not turned upon the High Priest;

they were turned upon empty space, and it was as if his gaze pierced beyond the wall before him.

"*Atah kamarta!* You have said!"

He made a short pause, as to draw breath. Then we heard the same pure voice again:

"But I say to you, from now on you will see the Son of Man seated on the right hand of the power, and sitting in the clouds of heaven!"

There was not one member of the Sanhedrin who could utter a word then. They waited now for the ceiling to be torn away and for the heavens to open, to testify to the words which had just been spoken. Nothing happened. Then suddenly there was heard the sound of tearing. It was the High Priest who had torn his purple mantle in sign of mourning. And after him, one by one, the members of the Sanhedrin tore their mantles—the only sound in the dreadful silence.

"See!" proclaimed the High Priest. "What need have we of witnesses. You have all heard his blasphemy. What is your verdict, most just court?" And he turned to the youngest member of the Sanhedrin.

"Child of death!" The dreadful sentence came from the youngest member of the Sanhedrin, in the sentence seat.

"Child of death!" said after him the second youngest.

But at this point my Rabbi had come to. He was on his feet again. He raised his hand, and cried:

"My lord High Priest! I protest!"

The High Priest signaled to the Sanhedrin to suspend the roll call.

"What is your protest, Rabbi Nicodemon? Have you not yourself heard his blasphemous utterance against the highest sanctity?"

"My lord High Priest, what he said was not blasphemy. The accused did not utter the Ineffable Name. And the law says: 'He that blasphemes is not guilty until he has mentioned specifically the nam of God in all its forms.' The man only used the words 'the power,' and did not utter the Ineffable Name. According to our laws, this is but insolence toward heaven, for which the punishment is the lash."

"We will hear the opinion of our interpreters of the law on the objection of Rabbi Nicodemon," said the High Priest.

On this point Todros held no consultation with his assistants. He answered straightway:

"We do not take account of the laws of the Pharisees in the matter of blasphemy. Here the investigation is being conducted in the spirit of the interpretation of the Sadducees. We have all heard the accused utter blasphemy and offense against the name of the Holy One. He is therefore a child of death!"

"High Priest! We have not come to this session to sit in judgment. We are here only to investigate and examine. We have no right to pronounce sentence!" my Rabbi called.

"We do not pronounce sentence here, Rabbi Nicodemon. We cannot pronounce sentence, neither have we the power to carry it out. Others have that power," the High Priest answered.

"If that be so, let us free him."

"We must deliver him to the government. The government has only placed him in our hands that we might examine and investigate."

"Deliver him to the government! What the government will do with him is their affair, and not ours!" several voices cried.

"But with what accusation, High Priest, will you deliver him to the government?"

"With the accusation which the investigation has uncovered; that which he has brought against himself, by saying that he is the Son of Man, who will sit at the right hand of 'the power,' which means that according to his own word he preaches to the people that he is the Messiah. How else shall we understand his words?"

My Rabbi paled. "Deliver him to the Government with the accusation that he calls himself the Messiah? But that means death! How can we do this? How can we deliver a soul in Israel into the hands of the wicked?"

"Rabbi Nicodemon!" cried the High Priest, and he too had paled. "If we do not deliver the accused to the government, after the words he has spoken and all of us have heard, it would mean that we believe them to be true, and we would have to prostrate ourselves at his feet and proclaim him the King-Messiah. No one, no one in the history of our people, has ever used such words, neither Abraham, nor

Moses, nor King David. Are we to believe, then, that he is higher than they, higher than flesh and blood, higher than all the living and the dead, that he is, indeed (God forbid!) a second authority? Can you believe that there are two authorities?"

"God forbid! God forbid!" voices answered.

The High Priest turned to my Rabbi:

"Are you, Rabbi of the Pharisees, prepared to throw yourself at his feet, and to recognize him as that which he asserts himself to be?"

"God forbid!" my Rabbi exclaimed, like the others. "But it is not incumbent upon me to recognize him as that which he asserts himself to be. And it is not incumbent upon me, either, to deliver him into the hands of the wicked, where he will assuredly be a child of death!"

"Rabbi Nicodemon! We, the Sadducees, do not believe in a heavenly Messiah. But you, a Pharisee, do believe in a heavenly Messiah—how can you speak, then, as you have just spoken? A Messiah performs that which he has said, or else he dies for it. Ask the accused, and he will tell you. If he believes himself to be the Messiah, he will give the proof of it tomorrow before Pilate."

But my Rabbi would not yield:

"My lord High Priest! Our Torah states: 'Thou shalt not be guilty of thy brother's blood.' What is it we are concerned with here? The delivery of a soul in Israel into the hands of the heathen. If this man has transgressed against us, against the Jewish faith, then we will be the judges. Since when does Israel admit strangers into his garden, to do the weeding for him? Israel cleanses his own garden. 'And thou shalt burn out the evil from thy midst.' *Thou*—not a stranger. I therefore demand of the sages and Rabbis here assembled, that they shall not deliver a soul in Israel into the hands of Edom, but that they shall put off the whole matter till beyond the festival. Then we shall call together an empowered court of the Sanhedrin and issue judgment according to the laws and commandments of the Holy Torah."

The words of my Rabbi had made an impression; and they were supported by those of Eliezer, son of the High Priest Hanan:

"My lord High Priest! With the permission of my father the High Priest, I would say that the words of the Rabbi of the Pharisees, Rabbi Nicodemon, are such as I would have spoken. The transgression is directed against the Jewish faith: God's name has been blasphemed, the Temple offended, the Priesthood shamed; that is our affair. Let us hide the whole thing from the government. For what has the government to do with it? The accused shall be brought before the judgment of Israel."

But now arose the old High Priest Hanan, and silence fell. He stroked his beard, and began to speak softly and easily, as was his wont:

"My lord High Priest! With the permission of the Priests and the sages, let me now remind this assembly that we cannot conceal this matter from the government; nor, if we could, have we the authority to do so. Indeed, we have already made the attempt, and have failed. For it is known to all and sundry that for many weeks the accused has haunted the courts of the Temple and taught in them. We have never molested him. No, not though there came to our ears words and parables of his which hinted at his Messiahship. We paid no attention to them, attributing no weight to hints and parables. There were reported to us, likewise, bitter and inflamed utterances of his against the sages and the ancients, both our own and those of the Pharisees. We passed them over in silence and did not proceed against him. We observed his deeds, and we investigated the doctrine which he taught, and we took him to be a Rabbi of the Pharisees, of the school and house of Hillel, who preaches the resurrection and foretells the time of the Messiah. And even though the teachings were not in our spirit, we did not forbid it, for we believed that by means of good parables he brought the hearts of the simple people closer to God, dissuaded them from following evil and guided their footsteps away from the net which Bar Abba spread for them. Thus it was for the duration of the whole winter. But when the winter was over it came to our ears that Bar Abba was preparing a revolt during the Passover days and was assembling arms and men in Jerusalem to that end. We considered it our duty to advise the government, so that the danger of the sword would be lifted from our people, and so that the government should not accuse us all of being fellows in treachery with Bar Abba. And in such a time, when unrest and fever had seized the land, and the government awaited only a pretext in order to flood the streets with our blood, the accused who stands before us permitted himself to be led into Jerusalem amid the proclamations of his kingship. Were this not enough, he broke into the Temple courts and drove out the merchants of doves and the moneychangers whom we have stationed there for the convenience of the pilgrims, and assaulted the order of things as established for many generations. He created wide tumult, called the Temple a den of robbers, spoke with deepest contempt of the Priests, the sages and the scribes. And we sent messengers to him, asking: 'Tell us, by what power do you do these things! Give us a sign of your identity.' To this anxious question he vouchsafed no reply. Do you think, my Rabbis and sages, that the government knows nought of all this? The government knows! It knows even that we, the Priesthood, sent messengers to him, instead of taking him prisoner. Therefore the government includes us in his conspiracy, and it has demanded of us, under threat of dire action, that we seize and deliver him. The government sent a Tribune, the Hegemon of Jerusalem, at the head of an entire cohort, in the company of our men, to arrest him. And now you would conceal the matter from the government? My Rabbis and sages, if Jerusalem is dear to you, and you would prevent the shedding of blood in the Temple courts, if you would not have the Sanctity desecrated with corpses in the days of our festival, deliver this man to the government. If he is that which the people say he is, that which he gives himself out to be according to his speech here, let him prove it." Here the old High Priest turned to my Rabbi. "Rabbi Nicodemon, you have often visited the man, openly and in secret: we know it. You have demanded a sign from him. You demanded a sign in the name of the Jews, even as Moses bade us obtain a sign from one who came to present himself as a prophet. Such a sign he refused to give. But now you have it: let Pilate be the sign."

And voices were heard from the Sanhedrin: "Let Pilate be the sign!"

The pupils on the benches cried: "Let Pilate be the sign!"

Even the attendants in the chamber, the servants and the slaves, took up the cry:

"Let Pilate be the sign!"

"High Priest!" my Rabbi cried. "But that is to try God!"

"No! Not in this case. This will not be trying God, but trying the man," answered the High Priest, pointing to Yeshua. "The people say that he is Elijah the prophet. Let him prove this by doing what Elijah did."

"High Priest! It is forbidden to put the lives of men to the test with miracles!" my Rabbi cried.

"But Elijah the prophet put his life to the test with a miracle. Do you not think, Rabbi Nicodemon, that if Elijah had failed to bring down fire upon the prophets of Baal he would have been a child of death in the hands of Ahab? But in the test Elijah was triumphant. Let the new Elijah perform his miracle before the prophets of the new Baal. And if he cannot, then 'it is better that one man shall perish rather than a whole people.' "

There the decision remained.

The Chief Officer issued a command, and the servants of the High Priest led the Rabbi of Nazareth from the chamber.

When we came forth from the house into the courtyard the gray of the dawn was already about us. A cold wind blew, driving the night clouds before it with rough, raw hands, and a milky mist hung in the air. The wood fire in the courtyard was dying in its smoke.

We saw the soldiers of the cohort, the Tribune at their head, bring forth the Nazarene, his hands bound once more. Among the steel shields, among the corselets and helms and swords, his white robe glimmered in the paleness of the dawn. Still unstained, it looked like a sponge which thirsts to draw in drink, and like a fresh-plowed field which longs to break into flower.

The soldiers and the Nazarene set out for the Procuratorium.

Outside, by the gate of the High Priest's house, we came upon Simon bar Jonah. He stood with his face thrust into the fence, and wept.

From the walls and towers about the Temple we heard the pealing of silver trumpets. The first detachment of Priests was going to the service.

Hegemon, can you relate now what happened to the Nazarene in the trial before Pilate?

CHAPTER TWENTY-FOUR

THE Hegemon began:

"We conducted the accused to the Procuratorium, which had been moved for that season from the Antonia to the Herod palace, which was spacious enough to accommodate several cohorts. The hour was early, and day and night were still struggling in the sky.

"It was a short distance from Kaifa's palace to the Procuratorium, since both buildings were in the Upper City. The Herod palace was the last of the three great edifices on the northern side where the descent begins. Everyone was asleep when we arrived, and we led the prisoner into the dungeons under the encampment in the courtyard. The other prisoner, Bar Abba, was already in a cell.

"There was no time to weld the rings and chains in the wall about the prisoner's hands and legs, as the practice was, for we knew that before long we should have to lead him out again to the trial. We therefore left him there as he was, his hands bound. The place was lightless even at noon; in that early hour it was a black hole. But before we led him down the first ray of the rising sun broke through from the east and illumined his face.

"In the long years which I have passed in the service of the Caesar I have had occasion more than once to see men facing death: I have seen those who were being led forth to crucifixion, those who have been condemned to the galleys, and those who have been flung to the beasts in the arena. But never have I seen on the face of a condemned man such pain, and wretchedness, and helplessness, and longing for life, as lay on the terrified face of my prisoner. Terror laid a violent hand on him and paralyzed his muscles. His eyes expanded, as if they were staring into an abyss which was about to receive his body. And I said to myself: Is this the man who has come to liberate them? Is this their redeemer? A man afraid of death? This is cowardice."

"No, no, it was not cowardice," I broke in. "It was pity."

"Let it be as you say," answered the Hegemon, incredulously. "In any event, he did not remain long in his cell. The trumpets of the first watch sounded, and we saw Pilate, a massive figure, descend the steps from the inner chambers to the Pretorium, in the company of his attendants. The Pretorium was the name given to the open-air platform raised in the interior court of the palace. Here Pilate received public deputations, and conducted public trials. On other occasions when I have seen Pilate try cases in the Pretorium, people were admitted to the court. Today not a single Jew was present. Perhaps they kept away of their own accord, since it was their festival and they were afraid of contaminating themselves for the sacred service by touching something of ours. The servants and messengers of the High Priest, too, did not enter the court but, having conducted the man with us as far as the Procuratorium, remained at the gates. But as the morning light grew, we heard a vast murmuring on the other side of the walls. Apparently the whole city knew what had happened in the night. They were assembling to hear the outcome of the trial and to demand of Pilate the liberation of one of the prisoners; it was a custom with the Procurator to free a condemned Jewish criminal in honor of a festival. It soon became apparent that the gathering crowds consisted of Bar Abbaites, for even before the trial began we could distinguish the shouts of 'Bar Abba! Bar Abba!'

"The preparations for the trial were complete. The high chair of the Procurator stood between the smaller stools of the Tribunes and the scribes. Numbers of troops off duty were drawn to the Pretorium, curious to look on the Jewish rebels who were about to be condemned.

"Pilate was in evil humor that morning. I knew it by the way he drew down his thick, bristling eyebrows and by the suspicious glimmer in his eyes. I was told afterwards that he had had a bad night. There had been a banquet; the Egyptian cook had made a special effort to display his art, and had stuffed the pheasants, which the High Priest had imported from some distant place and sent to the Procurator as a special gift, with a new, heavy filling. Pilate and his guests had washed down the stuffed birds with Cypriot wine and had spoiled their stomachs. (As often as Pilate was in Jerusalem, and feasted there, he and his guests spoiled their stomachs.) Whatever the cause, he was in very bad mood, and wanted to get through the trials as quickly as possible. He was irritated, too, by the bellowing and screeching of the Jews assembled on the platform before the palace façade.

"He sat down in the judgment chair; he opened his wide mouth, which foamed a little at the corners, and made a sign to the officers to begin.

"The guard led out before him the first prisoner, the bandit leader Bar Abba. Bar Abba's enormous head was pulled down earthward by the iron circlet from which a chain was drawn tightly to the leg pieces. He threw his head about like a wild ox. His gigantic chest was uncovered, but we could not see his beard, because of the posture in which he was held by his chains. Pilate did not even glance at him. He asked the Tribune on his right what the crime of the man was.

"The Tribune happened to be old Petronius. He answered that the prisoner was a murderer, a highway robber and a rebel. 'He gathered bands about him and they attacked merchants on the roads. He broke into homes and carried away valuables. He collected arms and was preparing to lead a revolt against Rome during the festival, as we discovered only two days ago. His capture cost us the life of several legionaries.'

" 'The lash and cross! And his body shall hang on the cross to be eaten by the birds!'

"Bar Abba was led away.

"There was a little incident before the second prisoner was brought before Pilate. A slave approached, knelt, and presented him with a tablet. Pilate cast his eyes over the words written on it. He signaled to me, and showed me the tablet. It was a message from his wife, Claudia. I read:

" 'Do not raise your hand against the just man. I have suffered much this night because of him.'

"Now I must explain to you what had been going on elsewhere while I was occupied with the arrest.

"You will remember I once spoke to you of a certain woman named Dark Hannah, whom we had known in Rome, a woman who frequented the highest circles of the aristocracy. She sold love-philters, charms, unguents, perfumes and other Oriental wares, and at the same time won secret adherents to her Jewish God. Her intimacy with the women of the court gave her great influence in Rome. Pilate too, you remember, had made use of her when he was wooing Claudia.

"This same Dark Hannah was now in Jerusalem, and she had become one of the first converts of the Nazarene, whom many women followed. During the brief visit of Pilate and Claudia to Jerusalem I often encountered Dark Hannah in the Procuratorium. She had renewed her old acquaintance with Claudia and had begun once more to supply her with philters. She it was who had filled the mind of Claudia with stories of the wonderful deeds performed by her Rabbi, of the power which he wielded over men and spirits, of his miraculous resurrection of the dead, his curing of the sick and his cursing of trees.

"Claudia had already questioned me several times concerning the Rabbi and that especially since she had caught a glimpse of him on the streets when he went riding by on his ass toward the Temple. The Jewish woman made such an impression on Claudia with her fantastic stories, that when the latter heard of the Rabbi's arrest she was thoroughly terrified; and all that night she was haunted by him as by a vision. In the early morning Dark Hannah was seen to steal into the Procuratorium; she had come to plead with her patroness to intervene—and this note from Claudia was the result.

"I said to Pilate: 'Dark Hannah was here this morning.'

" 'That woman has a frightful effect on Claudia! If she comes here again I'll turn her over to the troops for a whipping,' muttered Pilate, and thrust the slave with the tablet away from him. 'Bring out the prisoner!'

"They brought forth Yeshua the Nazarene. Standing in his white robe before Pilate, he made one think of a child in the clothes of a grown-up person. He looked at everyone except the man who held his life in his hand; it was as if he did not even notice his judge.

"Pilate amused himself awhile scrutinizing the man.

" 'A Galilean?' he asked me.

" 'Yes.'

" 'I thought so.'

"I was the Tribune reporting on the Galilean. I said: 'Bar Abba was the organizer of the uprising, but this criminal was its spiritual leader. He is much more dangerous than Bar Abba. For Bar Abba can be struck down with arms, but this man finds his way into the hearts of his followers, inflames their imaginations, dissuades them from obedience to the Caesar and bids them prepare themselves for another life and another order, in which he will be their Messiah.'

" 'Messiah! Messiah!' said Pilate. 'I have heard the word before. What does it mean?'

"I tried once more to explain. 'The Messiah—it is a fantasy of theirs that one day a liberator will appear, sent to them by God. By means of his magic he will conjure down hosts from heaven, and he will lead them to the conquest of all their enemies. They will destroy Rome—which they call Edom—and slaughter all of us, the Caesar, the generals and the troops. After which this Messiah will rule over them and over all the world.'

" 'And they believe that? They take it seriously?'

" 'They do indeed. They wait every day for the appearance of their deliverer.'

" 'Then all of them ought to be crucified, together with him,' roared Pilate. 'And *he* is supposed to be their Jewish king?'

"Suddenly he burst into convulsive and uncontrollable laughter.

" 'He has had himself proclaimed as such. He had himself conducted into Jerusalem on a little ass, while his followers proclaimed him the Messiah.'

" 'Yes! Yes! Isn't that the man we saw in a big procession, when we were on our way to the theater?'

" 'The same! The next day he burst into the Temple courts and drove out the dove merchants and the moneychangers; whipped them with a rope. We have good grounds for believing that the scholars and even the Priests wanted to keep him out of our hands. It was only because of your strict orders that I was able to arrest him. They all expect him to perform great miracles, according to his promise. When he will have liberated them from our rule they will crown him the Jewish king. They are waiting outside the courts for the moment when he will annihilate us with the breath of his mouth.'

"I looked at Pilate. His face had turned slightly green, partly with rage and partly with fear. I really believe that in the depths of his heart he had become uneasy in the presence of this mystic, incomprehensible person who stood there in his white robe, silent and motionless, steeped in earnestness, as though he could indeed at any moment lift up his arms and command hosts to descend from the skies.

" 'Yes! Yes! These are the things you have told me about him before.' He addressed the prisoner. 'You! Are you the King of the Jews?'

"The prisoner did not look at Pilate. It was as if he had withdrawn into himself to deliver the answer:

" '*Atah kamarta!*'

" 'What is that in our language?'

" 'It means: You have said.'

"He turned to Yeshua: 'You confirm it, then?'

"Yeshua gave him no answer.

" 'Don't you know that it is in my hand to free you or to hang you on the cross? Don't you know before whom you stand?'

"Yeshua did not answer.

" 'Did the Sanhedrin examine him?' Pilate asked me.

" 'Yes, in the night.'

" 'Of what did they find him guilty?'

" 'Blasphemy. They are standing outside. They will not come in for fear of defiling themselves.'

"An ironic smile flickered across Pilate's heavily modeled face.

" 'That being so, I will go out to them,' said Pilate.

"Before the façade of the Procuratorium lay the high level platform, worked with mosaic, where the proclamations and rescripts of the Caesar were read out to the populace. Five wide steps led up to the platform. On the steps stood the messengers of the High Priest, the Prosecutor in their midst. The entire area about the platform was filled with the multitude which had gathered there in the early morning. There were few women in it. Here and there we saw powerful figures, men with blazing eyes, broad shoulders, knotted and muscular limbs; we knew them to be the remainders of Bar Abba's bands. They had come to demand the release of Bar Abba for the festival. Before Pilate had a chance to open his mouth, the murmur of their voices rose into a shout in which was mingled anger and prayer:

" 'Release Bar Abba to us for the festival!'

" 'Give us Bar Abba!'

" 'Bar Abba!'

" 'And what shall I do with the King of the Jews?' asked Pilate, ironically.

"They did not know of whom he was speaking. Most of them were not aware that Yeshua had been taken in the night.

" 'What King of the Jews?'

" 'Your Messiah!'

" 'He who healed our sick?'

" 'The Prophet of Nazareth?'

" 'When was he taken prisoner?'

" 'Do you not see the Sons of Hanan standing there?'

" 'Silence! Let the Procurator speak!'

"Pilate turned to the Prosecutor, standing amidst the messengers of the High Priest.

" 'What evil have you found in this man, whom you call the King of the Jews?'

" 'He declared publicly before the High Priest that he would sit on the right hand of the power and would come with the clouds in heaven,' the Prosecutor read forth.

" 'What does that mean?' asked Pilate, bewildered.

" 'It means he will sit at God's right hand.'

" 'Mad!' exclaimed Pilate.

" 'Our Father in heaven! That is blasphemy against the Most

High! It is punishable with death!' Voices were heard on every hand. 'Did he indeed say that?'

" 'If he cannot prove it, it is blasphemy. No one among us has ever spoken thus, not Abraham, not Moses, not David.'

" 'Of what else is he accused?'

" 'He declared himself to be the King-Messiah!'

" 'What is the punishment therefor?'

" 'If he cannot prove it by a sign, or even if he produce a sign but seek to persuade us to serve idols, the punishment is death.'

" 'He never persuaded us to serve idols! He persuaded us to serve the One and living God!' voices shouted from the crowd.

" 'He cannot show the sign!'

" 'He will show it now, before Pilate!'

" 'Do you want me to release to you your King of the Jews?' asked Pilate of the multitude.

" 'What is that? What does he say?'

" 'The Procurator asks whom shall he release to you for the festival: Bar Abba or the King of the Jews?'

"The multitude paused. Debate broke out in its ranks, the debate grew into wild dispute, hands were lifted, beards were seized. Pilate and his men looked on in amusement.

" 'Look at those little Jews quarreling,' said Pilate to me, laughing, and pointing to the crowd. 'They'll finish up by tearing each other's eyes out.'

"I heard their shouts:

" 'He's not the King of the Jews! He's a blasphemer!'

" 'No! He is a holy man. No one knows who he is. He will show us a sign! You will see!'

" 'He told us to pay tribute to the Caesar! What kind of Messiah is it that bids us pay tribute to the Caesar?'

" 'He healed our sick! He performed wonders every day. He drove the Sons of Hanan from the Temple. That is why they have delivered him to the government!'

"At this point my friend Hanan ben Hanan mounted the steps of the platform and called to the crowd:

" 'How often have you not come before him and asked him to

give you a sign that he is the King-Messiah? Yet he has never given you the sign. Now let him give proof, as Elijah gave proof on Carmel: let him destroy the prophets of Baal!'

" 'Let him destroy the prophets of Baal with the breath of his mouth!'

" 'Let him come riding in the clouds on the right hand of the power!'

" 'Let Pilate be his sign!'

" 'Let Pilate be his sign!'

" 'They are shouting my name! What is it?' Pilate asked me.

" 'They are calling to their Messiah to show them a sign in you.'

"Pilate's face turned purple with rage. The blood pressed into his thick, bulky neck, and I thought he would fall down in an apoplectic fit. But he mastered himself, summoned a smile, and asked the people again:

" 'Do you want me to free the King of the Jews?'

" 'The Messiah will free himself!'

"Pilate did not answer, but it was clear that he had made up his mind. He strode back to the Pretorium and confronted the prisoner. Across the face of the prisoner passed flickers of pain. We marked a movement of his lips, as though he would lift his voice and say something to those assembled without. But the seal of all the sorrow of the world kept him silent.

" 'Do you hear what they say?' asked Pilate.

"The prisoner did not look at him.

"Pilate turned to the Tribune. 'Release Bar Abba!' he commanded.

"Bar Abba's Tribune, old Petronius, who knew the country well, having served under former Procurators, summoned up courage and approached Pilate.

" 'Procurator,' he said. 'Bar Abba is a dangerous criminal. He led a revolt against Rome. Had we not received advance information on it, we would have lost many more soldiers than we did. The man is guilty of several murders. Think of the legionaries we lost when we took him prisoner. But that other man, he whom they call the King of the Jews—against him we have nothing, and know of no crime which he has committed. No blood has been shed because of him. On the contrary, we have information that he bade the people in the Temple pay Caesar the tribute due him. But Bar Abba has always preached the withholding of the tribute and rebellion against Rome. Since when, Pilate, do you yield to the clamor of the mob?'

"Pilate became angry, and as always when rage overcame him, a tide of blood washed over his enormous, hairless head, and his breast expanded with haughtiness so that you feared it would crack open. He pulled down the corners of his mouth, growled furiously, and cast a contemptuous glance at old Petronius.

" 'The Hebrew spirit is much more dangerous for all of us than the Hebrew fist. Go! Deliver this man to the soldiers. Lash him and crucify him! Crown him the King of the Jews!'

"Among the troops which filled the space about the Pretorium there were many German horsemen, auxiliaries which we always drew to Jerusalem from other stations for the festivals. They, of all our soldiers, were most feared and hated by the Jews; the terror and enmity went back to the days of Herod, who had first used the Germans to hold the Jews in subjection. Many of these Germans, when they became old and could no longer remain in the army, went over to the service of the High Priest, who had them circumcised so that he could keep them in Jerusalem as slaves and use them as guards and watchmen. The old Germans were excellent for this purpose, and they received good pay and good food. They were armed with short clubs, which the Jews called *'Eileh,'* and which they celebrated in their ribald songs about the High Priest.

"The commander of the German horsemen was a man with an evil face and cold, murderous eyes. He was the terror of the Jews. His name was Hermanus. It was to Hermanus and his men that the prisoner was delivered.

"I had been watching them during the trial. They stood on their tip-toes, straining like bloodhounds who expect a bone to be flung to them. When thy heard that the pale, thin man was accused of setting himself up as the Jewish king, they burst into wild howls of laughter. And now, when he was delivered to them, they went mad with joy, like wolves to whom a sheep has been thrown.

"Hermanus seized the prisoner by the hand. A grimace passed

over his face, as though he wanted to smile; but the smile was lost in the wooden immobility of his face; so that instead of a smile there issued a dark, miserable grimace. Like a beast, he did not know how to laugh. He made me think of the black, sunless woods among which he had been born; the thick swamps of his childhood had laid their stamp on him. He dragged the prisoner toward the innermost court, and kept shouting to the soldiers:

" 'Come! We're going to crown the King of the Jews.'

"Within, in the court of the camp, there was a tall whipping post, with rings in it, which was always used for criminals condemned to the lash and the cross. What was done there with Yeshua I do not know. We did not follow the soldiers. They remained within a long time. Now and again we heard wild bursts of laughter. But we did not hear a single cry or groan from the prisoner. But we did hear, outside, round the walls of the Procuratorium, the shouting of the multitude, which penetrated the thick walls and gates and reached us in the closed court. It was like the far-off sound of the waves beating on a dam; and it grew from minute to minute, as if the multitude was increasing.

"Finally Hermanus issued, dragging the prisoner by the hand toward the place where Pilate stood with his officers. Hermanus turned, bowed low before the tortured man as before a Caesar, and with the characteristic grimace on his features, proclaimed:

" 'The King of the Jews!'

"We looked at the condemned man. On his graying hair lay a wreath woven of thorns. The thorns had pierced through his hair and penetrated the skin and the bone of his head. Little trickles of blood clotted the hair of his earlocks, ran down his beard, and fell drop by drop onto his throat and naked body. Yes, the King of the Jews stood before us naked, crowned with a crown of thorns, his slender white body covered with the swollen, bluish stripes left by the lashes. But I observed something marvelous. It was not as though he were standing naked before us, but we standing naked before him. The livid welts seemed to clothe his body in royal raiment. He was not ashamed in his nakedness. His eyes, which were directed at us, were filled more with self-pity than shame or bitterness. And perhaps it only seemed so to me, for I must confess that at this moment I began to feel a certain weakness for this Rabbi of theirs; and perhaps I had even felt it earlier, when I had led him into the dungeons and had seen his mournful, unhappy face. Perhaps it had grown in me, unobserved by myself, when I had watched him at the trial, standing before Pilate and answering not a word to the accusations. Yes, I think it was already there, in me, undermining my sense of duty as a Tribune, weakening my resolution and blurring my conviction of the man's guilt, making it impossible for me to proceed against him as vigorously as I should. Then I said to myself: 'Beware, Cornelius! This man is beginning to draw you once more into the circle of his magic.' It was not the attitude and bearing of the man which worked on me; it was something that lay in the essential being of him, in the quiet, sad gaze of his eyes, which pierced through you, and seemed to evoke in you queer Hebraic and Semitic emotions. I had been fighting against them all morning. Now those eyes, lifted toward me from the midst of the trickles of blood which ran down his forehead, were becoming dangerously potent, stirring a softness and weakness in my heart. They were binding me to him, they were pulling me toward his feet; and if I did not remain on guard they would transform me into one of those witless, characterless, sentimental Hebrews. Therefore I pulled away from him; I summoned up my Roman will, and opposed it to his; I called to my help my contempt for the Jews and their God. 'Yes, Pilate is right!' I muttered fiercely to myself. 'The Hebrew spirit is more dangerous for us than the Hebrew fist.' And I joined in the laughter of the others.

" 'It would be an excellent thing,' I said to Pilate, 'to send this King of the Jews to the old fox. I mean as a hint. Let him see what a King of the Jews looks like.'

" 'Excellent thought! Take him, and have him led over to Herod Antipater. By the way, since the prisoner is a Galilean, like Herod, there will be a special emphasis on our meaning. Lead the King of the Jews to him.'

"We took Yeshua, with the crown of thorns on his head, with his hands tied behind his back, and we hung about his neck a tablet with the words: 'King of the Jews.' And thus, surrounded by soldiers, we led him out to the Hasmonean Square. When the crowd which had been waiting outside the Procuratorium saw Yeshua with his crown of thorns and the tablet bearing the inscription 'King of the Jews,' there was a storm of agitation. Voices were heard:

" 'Why have they written: "King of the Jews"? Why not: "He who calls himself King of the Jews"?'

" 'Pilate wants to insult us with this King of the Jews.'

" 'Look, that is Pilate's jest.'

"Part of the crowd accompanied us to the Hasmonean Square, which was in the vicinity of the Procuratorium. I led Yeshua through the vast, impassive gates, and down many long, dark, narrow corridors, for the Palace of the Hasmoneans was an ancient building, Asiatic, and more specifically Babylonian, in style. In the gray, lofty hall to which we were conducted, we found Herod Antipater. He sat on a throne-like chair in the darkest corner of the hall, and though on the square outside there was brilliant sunlight, here within yellow oil lamps were needed. In the half-darkness I was able to mark the unusual pallor on the Tetrarch's face, yellowish in the faded illumination of the lamps, and making the impression of gall sickness. He must have been more than a little terrified by the man whom I led before him, his hands bound, the drops of blood congealed on his face; I saw the Tetrarch's breast rising and falling in agitation under the loose folds of his toga. He even started from his seat, then recalled his dignity, and sank back again. He too, even like their sages and High Priests, expected a miracle. For the unease of spirit which I read in him did not leave him once throughout the interview, nor could he conceal it behind the assumption of curiosity and amusement with which he strove to confront Yeshua.

" 'So!' he exclaimed. 'This is the man of wonders who brings back the dead from their graves! This is he of whom the people say that he is Elijah the prophet!'

"Then suddenly Herod's eyes fell on the tablet which hung about Yeshua's neck. The instant that the words 'King of the Jews' penetrated to his mind, his face became black like a clod of earth. His eyes turned over in their sockets, so that only the whites were visible. He could not utter a single word. As for me I was aware of a singular pleasure in witnessing the wretched discomfiture of this pretender to the Jewish crown. I studied him closely, enjoyed every betrayal of terror, so that I might later describe it in utmost detail to Pontius Pilate.

"That self-betrayal did not last long. The Tetrarch mastered himself; his face became calm, his eyes resumed their normal aspect. But there lingered in them a profound sadness. He looked silently at the man before him.

"The interchange did not last more than a moment. Herod's gaze was dark, troubled and insecure, like a man who strains his sight in darkness and feels the mouth of the pit yawning at his feet. The gaze of the bound man, though overshadowed by pain, was assured, earnest; it asked forgiveness and responded with pity. The interchange ended when Herod's eyes sank suddenly earthward, overcome by the gaze of the bound man who stood before him, his head crowned with thorns, the blood running again down his beard and earlocks.

" 'What is the crime of this man?' asked Herod.

" 'His crime is written on his breast,' I answered.

"Then Herod pretended that he saw the tablet for the first time, and he burst into hysterical laughter. I do not know until this day whether this laughter was intended to deceive me, to throw off the poisonous implication of the inscription, or to deceive himself, to overcome the terror in his own heart. But it may have been both, and the second more than the first. For they were all afraid of the Rabbi of Nazareth. I had never before seen Herod in such convulsions. He rolled about on his stool, he clasped his belly with his hands, the tears began to hop down his cheeks.

" 'The King of the Jews! Good! Very good! Let him be clothed in the purple!' he gasped. 'You!' he shouted at an attendant. 'Bring him the purple!'

"An attendant ran out, came back with a purple mantle, and flung it over Yeshua's shoulders.

" 'A king must go about in kingly raiment, what, Hegemon? Transmit my greetings to the Procurator, and tell him that this rich jest wipes out all the grudges I've ever had against him. Pilate thinks only of my pleasure! Pilate is my friend!'

"By this time he had worked himself so admirably into the game of pretense that even I began to doubt whether he did not really mean what he said.

" 'Take him back, and my greetings to the noble Pilate,' he repeated, with a royal gesture, and dismissed us.

"I led the prisoner back to the Procuratorium.

"When the Jews in the streets saw Yeshua in his purple mantle, and the blood running with renewed strength from under his crown of thorns, they burst into loud lamentation. They shook as if a storm were blowing through them, and they cried:

" 'See, O God, our shame! The mouth of the wicked is filled with laughter for our wretchedness!'

"But when Pilate and his officers saw the King of the Jews in all his glory, they thought the jest excellent.

" 'Give him a scepter!' he commanded. 'Kingship demands a scepter!'

"A soldier stuck a reed into Yeshua's hand.

" 'Greetings and honor, King of the Jews!' the soldiers jested, and they came before him one by one and spat in his face.

"Meanwhile others brought out from the storehouse of the camp a large wooden cross. Pilate looked at it, and bade them bring it closer to him.

" 'Inscribe these words on the cross, in three languages,' he commanded, 'in the three languages of the country, Latin, Greek and Hebrew. "Yeshua, King of the Jews." '

"His instructions were carried out.

" 'Now,' he said. 'Show them their King in all his glory.'

"But scarcely did we appear before the open gates of the Procuratorium, when we perceived that a fierce change had come over the spirit of the multitude. Storm broke out. Hands were stretched out against us, and a fearful cry of rage went up. This was an uprising! It was with difficulty that we managed to rescue from their hands Hanan ben Hanan, the High Priest's youngest son. I have never understood what happened in between our first and our second leading forth of Yeshua as King of the Jews. What brought forth this change? Can you tell me?"

"Yes, I was a witness of the transformation," I said. "But in order that you may understand it, I must tell you first what my

Rabbi did when he returned from the trial in the house of the High Priest."

CHAPTER TWENTY-FIVE

THE spirit of my Rabbi was ill at ease when he returned from the trial of the Rabbi of Nazareth. His heart misgave him, and he was silent all the way to the study house; but for all his silence we could mark how the blood in him was hot. He did not remain long in the study house. He went into his room, and we, his pupils, brought him water in a vessel from the cistern, that he might wash his hands and face. He said the morning prayers, then we prepared the table for him: olives and greens, but no bread, because of the approaching Passover. He touched none of the food, saying that there were urgent tasks before him. At first he bade us stay in the study house and lie down to rest, Rufus and I in particular, for we had been awake now the full twenty-four hours. Likewise there was much work of preparation for us in connection with the sacrifices and the festival. But we pleaded with our Rabbi to take us with him to the Temple, whither he was now preparing to go in order to meet with the other sages. And when our Rabbi yielded to our supplication, we washed and changed our garments and were refreshed; for we were young, and in the fullness of our strength. My friend Rufus confessed that he was expected at home, to help his father Simon Cyrene. At this time of the year his father went out into the fields to pluck the weeds growing between the olive trees, and Rufus would work with him. But because of the importance of the events which we expected, he asked permission of the Rabbi not to return home, and the Rabbi acceded to his request.

Rufus and I accompanied our Rabbi to the Temple. We passed through the market place, where the merchants were beginning to bring out their wares and to clean their measures. Camels came in from the countryside, bearing jars of oil and skins of wine. People were arriving to make their last purchases; they were mostly the poor, who had only just managed to get their money together for the festival preparations. The sun was now issuing in all his strength, promising a magnificent prelude to the festival. We saw men hastening in the direction of the sheep market, the belated purchasers of the sacrifice. Women sat by their baskets of greens and worked over them.

As we hastened by we heard talk among the men; it was said that the followers of Bar Abba were assembling before the Procuratorium to ask for the release of their chieftain. Indeed, we saw some of them (as we guessed) pleading with merchants and purchasers to go with them and swell the demand; but they met with little response, for the people were too occupied with buying and selling for the festival, nor was Bar Abba much beloved among them. Concerning that which had happened in the night with the Rabbi of Nazareth they knew nothing as yet.

The Temple courts were as busy as the market place. Pilgrims rose betimes that morning, to say their morning prayers when the Priests were offering the first sacrifice. They were busy with their own affairs, bringing small offerings, paying their tribute to the Temple, kneeling in the courts and praying during the time when the Priests brought the sacrifice for the peace of the world, the sacrifice for the welfare of the seventy nations of mankind, and the sacrifice for the remission of sins. In the courts too they did not know what had taken place in the night, not even among the sages.

The Rabbis of the Pharisees were assembled to take counsel against the Priesthood, which had chosen this year to carry out their Sadducean interpretation of the law of the Passover sacrifice and to refrain from giving it precedence over the Sabbath. The Pharisees planned to bring their sacrifice according to the law of the Torah, to wit, on the fourteenth day of the month, toward the evening, that is, when the Sabbath had already set in.

When my Rabbi arrived in the chamber set aside for the meetings of the Pharisaic Rabbis, he met Jochanan ben Zakkai, Rabbi ben Simon, their colleagues and pupils discussing the sacrifices which the Priests had offered the day before, on the thirteenth day of the month. It was in their minds to declare these sacrifices invalid.

"They wish to bring back the days of Alexander Jannaeus and persecute us as they persecuted Simon ben Shetah," said one of the Pharisees.

"These are not the days of King Jannaeus," said another, hotly. "The people is with us. We must stir it up, so that it shall storm the courts of the sacrifices this evening."

"We shall achieve more by gentle means. Let us go again to the Priests, and talk with them, and persuade them, lest, God forbid! one-half of the people be deprived of the sacrifice."

My Rabbi drew Jochanan ben Zakkai and Rabbi Gamaliel to a side, and informed them of the events of the night.

When the sages heard of the manner in which the trial of investigation had been conducted, and of the outcome, a shudder passed through them. Rabbi Jochanan ben Zakkai, who was wont to scrutinize every word and not to release it before it had passed through the fine sieve of his mind, broke into sudden and impetuous speech.

"But that is murder! What has the government to do with it? It is our affair! The man is responsible before our court and not before the courts of the government!"

"They say that the government compelled them to it."

"There are three things, according to the teaching of our sages, wherein a man must not transgress, though he must pay with his life," cried Jochanan ben Zakkai. "One of them is the shedding of blood. If any man would force you to shed blood, you must let yourself be killed rather than yield. They should have let themselves be killed rather than deliver the man of Nazareth to the government, for they have delivered a just man into the hands of the wicked. Rabbi Nicodemon! According to your account the trial was not conducted according to the laws of Israel. It was called in the night, and on the eve of a festival. It was carried out one-sidedly, by that section of the court which interprets the law in a manner not recognized by the sages. Therefore no matter what the man of Nazareth has done and said, and no matter what the punishment therefor should be—even though it be death, God forbid!—he is pure and guiltless in our eyes as long as he has not been condemned by a Jewish court called and conducted according to the Torah and all the rules which the sages have transmitted to us in the tradition. I tell you we must therefore move heaven and earth, we must awaken all our forces and invoke all our rights; and though the festival is approaching, we must leave the service and the sacrifice and rescue a soul in Israel from death. For you know that to save a single life is equivalent to saving the whole world. We must leave everything; we must go to the High Priests and wrest that life from their hands."

Rabbi Gamaliel concurred and the three Rabbis set out.

The chamber of the *S'gan* or Chief Officer of the Temple was filled with people, who came on various missions in connection with the services. The Chief Officer himself was not to be seen. He sat apart, receiving no one, and the multitudinous business of the Temple was carried on by his assistants, all of them sons and sons-in-law of the Priestly families. We made our way through toward the private room of the *S'gan* and there, before the door, stood Judah Ish-Kiriot.

His eyes were sunk so deep in the folds of his face that they could hardly be seen. He was holding in his hand a small sack of money, and he was pleading with the assistants before the *S'gan's* door to admit him.

"I have something to tell him...."

"The Chief Officer does not wish to see you."

"I must see him, I must see him."

He had not noticed the entry of the Rabbis of the Pharisees, before whom everyone rose with the exception of the Priestly treasurers, who did not even cast a glance at them. The assistants at the doors greeted the Rabbis respectfully, and entered at once to transmit their message to the *S'gan.*

The *S'gan,* Jochanan, the second son of Hanan, who was next in line for the High Priesthood and held his present position in preparation, came out to the Rabbis. He was dressed in the purple mantle which he had worn at the session of the Sanhedrin.

But before he could address himself to the Rabbis Judah Ish-Kiriot threw himself in the way, held out the sack of money and cried:

"Take it! Take the blood money, the money of abomination!"

"I will have nothing to do with it," answered the *S'gan*. "It is yours. You have earned it honestly."

Assistants came running and seized Judah by the arms. They belabored him with their staves for having dared to cross the *S'gan's* path, and they began to drag him from the chamber. Judah struggled with them, screaming continuously:

"Take back the money of abomination! Take back the blood money!"

And while the assistants were dragging him out, he suddenly looked up and observed the faces of Rabbi Jochanan and Rabbi Nicodemon. He closed his eyes, and his screaming changed to a wailing:

"Woe unto my soul! Woe unto my soul!"

But no one regarded him any more. The sages and the Pharisees stood face to face with the *S'gan*. Jochanan ben Zakkai spoke abruptly:

"The sages and the Pharisees have come before the *S'gan* to ask by what authority and what right the High Priests delivered a soul in Israel into the hands of Edom."

"That soul in Israel spoke blasphemously and contemptuously of the God of Israel, as all of us can testify. That soul in Israel is a misleader and persuaded the people that he is the Messiah. That soul must be wiped out from Israel."

"The judgment is not in your hands, nor in the hands of your father's house. It is in the hands of the sages and the scribes. It is in the hands of the holy court, the court of the Sanhedrin, which alone can issue sentence in such matters."

"Do you dare, Rabbi in Israel, to cast doubt on the honesty of the sentence pronounced by the Sanhedrin of the Priests?"

"As a Rabbi in Israel I not only cast doubt thereon, but declare the sentence of the Sanhedrin of the Priests null and void. The trial was conducted in contempt of the laws of the Torah and of the directions laid down in the tradition for such procedure. The decision is therefore completely void, and I demand the return of the soul which was delivered to the government."

The veins on the throat of the *S'gan* could be seen hammering with the pressure of his blood; nevertheless he maintained his voice at the calm level which he judged to be in keeping with his high office.

"That soul," he said, "has been delivered to the government after examination and trial according to the laws and the procedure accepted by us, the Sadducees, and we accept the responsibility for the action."

"As a Rabbi in Israel I denounce this delivery of a Jewish soul into the hands of the wicked as an act of murder!"

The blood retreated suddenly from the face of the Chief Officer of the Temple. The beautifully woven locks of his coal-black beard shook like a cluster of bells.

The multitude in the chamber had begun to gather about us, and a wave of agitation spread through it as more and more people became aware of the matter that was toward. There were present many followers of the Pharisees, and Jochanan ben Zakkai was greatly beloved among them. When they marked how their leader strove with the *S'gan* their affection and admiration were kindled. The *S'gan*, too, did not fail to observe the sharpening of tempers and the flash of eyes, and he held in his anger, fearing an outbreak in the Temple. The tip of his pointed nose quivered, but his voice was restrained as he answered:

"Rabbi Jochanan ben Zakkai, the soul is no longer in our hands. It was demanded of us again by the government, having been placed in our keeping for examination and investigation. This commission we carried out according to the laws and commandments as our conscience interprets them. We returned him to the government together with our report. It is now for the government to judge him according to its lights; we have no part therein. If you demand your righteous man, who publicly blasphemed against the Holy One of Israel, apply to the government, not to us. And for the word which you let fall concerning us we shall demand an accounting, and action will be taken against you for slandering the good name of the Sanhedrin of the Priests."

"It is from *you* that we demand him," intervened the youngest of the Rabbis, Gamaliel. "Your name will be wiped out in Israel, and your memory will be recalled with imprecation until the end of days!"

The young man started back and scrutinized the Rabbi who had dared to pronounce such a curse on the mighty House of Hanan. He whitened with rage. His lips quivered. He clenched his fists. The two men stared steadfastly at each other. It seemed to us that in another moment the Chief Officer of the Temple would command his assistants to arrest the Rabbi; but this latest generation of the ancient Sadducean house was not equal to the mighty authority which it had inherited. The young man trembled, turned on his heel, and withdrew into his chamber.

No one had expected that Pilate would act with such swiftness and pass judgment in the early morning on the man who had been arrested in the night. Never before had the Procurator issued sentence so hastily. Even Bar Abba, who had been captured, sword in hand, had not been tried at once, but had been held two days in the dungeon.

Nor did anyone expect that Pilate would care to provoke an outburst of popular rage on the eve of the festival, when the Jews were already embittered by the slaughter which had attended the capture of Bar Abba. All of us believed that Pilate would put off the trial of the Nazarene until after the festival. And the sages who approached the *S'gan* for the liberation of Yeshua likewise believed that Pilate would not act before the ending of the festival. Thus even the zealous Jochanan ben Zakkai, like my own Rabbi, considered, after their failure with the *S'gan*, that there was still time to effect the rescue. Returning from the chamber of the *S'gan*, they meditated on whom to send to the government, and my Rabbi at once suggested the name of Joseph Arimathea. A messenger was dispatched, to bid him join the council of the Pharisees in the Temple. But the Rabbis had not yet had time to re-enter their own chamber when they were amazed by the news that Pilate had acted in the earliest morning, that he had condemned Yeshua and released Bar Abba on the demand of the Bar Abba-ites who had assembled betimes before the Procuratorium; the Rabbis learned, moreover, that among those who had encouraged the masses to ask for the pardon of Bar Abba had been Hanan ben Hanan and the servants of the High Priest. Then the hearts of the Rabbis stood still with fear, their eyes sank to the earth, and their spirit failed them.

Rabbi Nicodemon said in low tones:

"Only a miracle from heaven can save the Rabbi now. I will go pray for his soul. You, my sons," he addressed himself to Rufus and myself, "go out now and see how the matter stands, and bring me back the report."

From the Mount of the House to the Herod palace was a distance of a quarter of an hour. The way led downhill, for the Procuratorium stood on the edge of the first wall, overlooking the valley and the road to Bethlehem. Though Rufus and I ran as swiftly as we could through the crowded streets it seemed to us that hours elapsed before we reached the palace. We overtook men and women who had come round the Mount and were hastening toward the same destination. They were the poor folk who lived by the Dung Gate and the Water Gate and the Kidron valley. Women panted and wept into their torn and unclean hair veils, and the eyes of the men were hot with rage. It was only now that these people had learned what had happened to their beloved Rabbi in the night. They flung down their work—the porters left their burdens, the drivers their beasts—and came running through the streets in their tattered sackcloth garments, through which showed the nakedness of their flesh. This was the poverty of Jerusalem, to which the Rabbi was so well known. Some of them led the blind and the halt, trying sorely the patience of those whose passage they impeded. When we arrived before the palace we found assembled a great multitude of the men of Bar Abba and those they had brought with them. On the steps of the platform stood Hanan ben Hanan, surrounded by the messengers of the High Priests. The gate leading into the court of the palace was locked, and there was no one on the summit of the platform. The vast walls loomed up before us, shutting off the secret of what was happening within.

The multitude was tense with excitement and expectation. The silence of a great suspense hung over it, so that even the Bar Abba-ites and the messengers of the Priesthood stood wordless. We learned that Bar Abba had been released; further, that Pilate had sent Yeshua to the Tetrarch with a tablet on his breast bearing the inscription "King of the Jews," to taunt both the Tetrarch and the Jews, and that the Tetrarch had found no guilt in Yeshua and had returned him to Pilate clad in a purple robe. Now, it seemed, nothing could help the Rabbi save a miracle; he had come to the last door, and only the intervention of heaven could rescue him. And they waited, all of them, even the Bar Abba-ites and the messengers of the Priesthood, for the miracle. They stood on the square before the palace, their heads lifted, their necks stretched, their eyes directed toward the summit of the walls. A wave of faith and mystic suggestion had passed through them, and it seemed to many of them that they beheld the beginnings of the miracle; they thought they saw signs in heaven, a darkening in the midst of the brightness of the sun. They thought they heard the far-off rush of mustering hosts, and they expected momently that the heavens would open and a flame would descend; the palace would sink into the earth, as Korah and his congregation did of old, and out of the ruins the Rabbi would rise, riding on a cloud.

They forgot that within, behind the mighty gates, was a man of flesh and blood, agonizing in pain like any man of flesh and blood. The Rabbi had become, in their eyes, a spirit, something not of this world. Even those who had come running in rage, with clenched fists, to storm the palace, were drawn into the circle of expectancy. Their anger died in them, their hands fell; it seemed to them that thus the thing had to be, their Rabbi had to be put to the test—and the miracle would take place. Those that had been weeping on the way forgot their tears, their sighs stayed in their throats, because of the faith that streamed into them from the multitude. So sharp was the expectancy that when Hanan ben Hanan broke the silence and cried, "If he is the Messiah, let him prove it," the assembled masses, those that were the followers of Yeshua and those that had opposed him, cried back:

"Yes, he is the Messiah, let him therefore prove it!"

"We want a miracle!"

"Let him destroy the Baal, like Elijah."

"Let him enter the lion's den, like Daniel!"

Then suddenly silence returned. The mighty gates of the palace swung back slowly. At first only Pilate appeared, a triumphant smile on his fleshy face. He cast a contemptuous glance at the waiting multitude. Behind him came legionaries, swords and shields flashing. Then followed two German auxiliaries in high helmets; they led forth the Rabbi of Nazareth; they placed him against the wall, and we saw. . . .

We saw him whom you crowned "King of the Jews." We saw him. You set him before us. At his back was the gigantic, square wall of the Herod palace. A dumb, towering surface of stone rose behind him, and he stood before it in his glory. We saw the blood running down from the crown of thorns into his beard, and dripping from it onto his naked body. We saw him. He "whose raiment was always white and oil was not lacking on his head" stood before us naked, adorned only in the welts your lashes had raised on his body, the crown of thorns on his head, the purple cape flung on his shoulders. The cross with the inscription "Yeshua, King of the Jews" was planted behind him. And near him stood Pilate. Him we saw too. He looked on the stony, silent multitude, and a cynical smile was on his fat, fleshy face. His thick, short neck laughed, his swollen body shook with inner laughter, as he lifted his hand and asked:

"What would you have me do with him whom you call 'King of the Jews'?"

We already saw what he had done with him whom he called "King of the Jews," and all of us felt the stabbing irony and savagery of his question. We felt the humiliation, the insult and the shame of it. Our eyes turned back to the man of Nazareth. We could see how his inmost parts were turning over in him. They had tortured him so that he could scarcely breathe; his white lips moved quietly, his nostrils quivered as he tried to draw breath. He looked on us and we on him. We had been flung from the summit of hope into the abyss of despair. On him all expectation had reposed. We had thought that now, now, the measure of his suffering had been filled, now the salvation was at hand, now he would lift his head, and his enemies would be utterly destroyed. One hunger had filled our hearts: "Let it happen now! Let God's name be glorified! God's name must be glorified!" But the moment had passed, the miracle had not burst upon us. There only stood before us a tormented and beaten Jew, and at his side his hangman, Pilate.

A choked weeping was torn out of our hearts. Near me a man thrust his fingers into his mouth, bit them, and wailed. I heard in the midst of the sobbing about me fragments of Psalms which issued from writhing lips. Pilate looked on our shame and on our defeated hopes, and as if to mock us again, he called out a second time:

"What would you have me do with him whom you call 'King of the Jews'?"

"Crucify him!" screamed Hanan ben Hanan, who stood, pallid, on the steps of the platform.

And the messengers of the High Priest screamed after him:

"Crucify him!"

Then was heard the loud wailing of women. Men stretched out their hands.

"He is our brother!"

"He is a deceiver and misleader! He said he was the Son of God!" shouted the servants of the High Priest.

Voices called back: "Every Jew has a right to call himself God's son. It is written in the Torah: 'Sons are ye of the Lord your God!' We pray to our Father in heaven!"

"He said he would destroy the Temple in three days!" shouted the servants of the High Priests.

"It is a den of robbers!" the multitude called back. "The Sons of Hanan are lords there! The Sons of Hanan have delivered him into the hands of Edom."

"Who will comfort us? Who will bring joy into our poverty?" a woman wailed, wringing her hands.

A learned man declared: "All is not lost yet! Perhaps he must fulfill the measure of his suffering before salvation comes!"

And the tortured man stood by the wall, the cross planted behind him. It was as though he was bound to the cross by the blood which fell from him and was sucked in by the wood. His face was tired, and his eyes begged forgiveness. Pitying and pitiful he looked on the people, and there was a weaving of looks between him and them, like invisible rays. Then the people forgot what their expectation had been, and they saw only a brother who, sinless, had been delivered into the hands of the wicked. Compassion, immeasurable compassion, awoke in them. Their hands were lifted in impotent rage, and voices cried:

"This is the answer of the Sons of Hanan!"

"He was our brother in the hour of our need, the healer of our sicknesses!" a woman sobbed.

"Because he disturbed their commerce in the House of the Lord! This is their revenge!" an old man yelled from the crowd, and lifted his hand toward Hanan ben Hanan. "See him!"

"No," cried the servants of the High Priest. "Because he blasphemed the name of God. That is why we delivered him. There was a trial!"

"There was no trial! The Rabbis of the Pharisees were not there. They knew nothing of it. They were not called!"

"They alone, they alone conducted the trial," cried a young man with quivering earlocks, and pointed to the messengers of the Priesthood.

The multitude began to crowd about Hanan ben Hanan. Hands were thrust out toward him. Eyes blazed.

"We did not make it a trial," answered the messengers, breathlessly. "It was an investigation. He proclaimed himself the Messiah! If he is the Messiah, let him rescue himself!"

"He did not declare himself the Messiah! He is a Rabbi in Israel! He is free to make his own interpretations of the law!"

"It was the Sons of Eli who turned informers! They told the government that he sought to become King of the Jews."

"We have suffered enough from their evil tongues. Informers are they, all of them!"

"Look! Behold them, they who demanded his blood! They themselves went to the government to testify against him. And it is written in the Torah: 'Thou shall not desire the blood of thy brother'!" an old man quavered, and kept pointing at Hanan ben Hanan on the platform steps.

The shouting grew louder, the outstretched arms drew nearer, the circle closed in. Then a chanting rose from the midst of the people:

"Woe unto us because of the house of the Sons of Hanan! Woe to us for the Sons of Beitus. Woe unto us because of their secret councils! They are High Priests, and their sons are treasurers, and their sons-in-laws are high officers! And their servants smite the people with staves!"

Hanan ben Hanan grew pale. The furious circle was growing narrower, the wild hands were within reach of him. And at that instant Pilate came to the rescue of his friend. At a single word of command the soldiers threw themselves on us like beasts; swords were drawn, blood began to flow, the people scattered and fled with a wild wailing.

They pulled Yeshua back into the court of the palace, and Hanan ben Hanan after him: to torture the one and rescue the other.

CHAPTER TWENTY-SIX

THE people withdrew from the square and went their ways. The sun was climbing toward the midday station, and those among the pilgrims and Jerusalemites who had not yet offered the Passover sacrifice hastened to do so, for they knew that the Priests would seek not to delay the offerings beyond the evening, which was the Sabbath. The square before the Procuratorium was almost empty; only here and there a few men and women lingered, some of them still nourishing the hopes which the rest had relinquished in bitterness of heart, and saying: "It cannot be that we have been so utterly deceived. Let us wait. Perhaps the miracle will come at the last moment."

Among the women I marked the two Miriams, she of Migdal and the tall stranger of whom they whispered that she was the mother of Yeshua. The latter was leaning against the wall of a house opposite the Procuratorium, and her face was pressed to the cold stones. By her were the other two women. Miriam of Migdal was without a veil; the heavy graying hair fell over her shoulders, and between the parting shone her bloodless face. She neither wept nor lamented; her dark eyes, which in this moment of extreme sorrow had acquired again a youthful luster, shone with a strange light. One woman there was who seemed to have retained her courage, and that was Sulamith. Her face was uncovered and her lips were pressed together, but her eyes sparkled like the eyes of an animal which gathers for the leap.

The men who remained on the scene were mostly from among the poorest, such as I had encountered in the house of Simon the Leper. There was Joseph the slave, whom the Rabbi had once comforted in the hostelry of the camel drivers. The ropes of his slavery were tied about him. On his face was the look of a simpleton, or of one who had been clubbed on the head and did not know what was happening. Nearby was Joseph Arimathea, leaning heavily on a staff; and by his side, as always, the convert Abraham ben Abraham. His head was sunk to the earth, and it seemed that his brain had crept into his uplifted hump, which stood out, meditative, seeking an answer to the riddle. Somewhat apart from them was Hillel the watercarrier, silent, withdrawn upon himself like a turtle in its shell. There was neither wonder nor surprise on his humble features; it was as though for him all that had happened was as it should have been. These I marked among others waiting before the gate of the Procuratorium. And turning once, I caught a glimpse of a vast, bushy head peeping round the corner of a mighty wall, and two roving, flashing, frightened eyes. It was Simon. But I did not see all the man, for he hid himself.

After a time the gates of the Procuratorium opened again, and a squad of Roman soldiers under an officer led forth the Nazarene. Now he wore again his white mantle, which in truth was no longer white; for in part it dragged, together with his ritual fringes, along the earth, and it left the red stain of his blood on the stones. The crown of thorns was still on his head. His face was hidden from us, for he was bowed down almost to the ground by the cross which they had laid on his back, tying his arms around it backward. And it seemed to us that the cross was heavy with more than its own weight and that invisible burdens pressed his body down, so that it would break at any moment. He strove forward, thus oppressed, and every step came slowly, with infinite pain, like the splitting of the Red Sea. Behind him walked Hermanus, the terror of the Jews, his face inflamed with fury and drenched in sweat. He flourished a whip in his hand, and the lash came down on the Nazarene. Foam of rage and blood thirst whitened the corners of Hermanus's jaws. The tormented man, on whose body the drops of mortal anguish mingled with the drops of blood, drew forward, his limbs quivering under the load and the lash, his garments, thick with damp, clinging to him. His footsteps left red imprints on the stones.

Miriam "the mother" began to beat her head against the wall, and the other two, Miriam of Migdal and Sulamith, led her away; and Sulamith supported almost her total weight. So the three of them went after Yeshua under the cross. Now I heard the high, nasal wailing of funereal lamentations from the other women. The men were grouped together. Their fists were clenched, curses trembled on their lips, fire smoldered in their eyes; but that which lay on their hearts crushed them into silence, and no sound escaped them. Their eyes rigidly fixed on the ground, they followed.

The wailing of the women, the shouting and jeering of the soldiers, drew the inhabitants to doors of the miserable houses by which we passed. The path of the procession lay through a half-abandoned, neglected quarter of the town, approaching the Golgotha, or Place of Skulls, to the northeast. The women in the doorways wrung their hands when they beheld the tormented man among the soldiers; they turned upon the menfolk and screamed:

"You are not men! You are women! You see the agony of a Jewish soul, and you are silent! Is there no one to rescue him?"

"Woe unto us! It is the Rabbi of Nazareth," a woman lamented and wiped the streaming tears from her face with her hair veil. "How many he has helped in his time, and himself he cannot help!"

Then occurred something which made us all stand still, open-mouthed and breathless. The Rabbi fell under his cross: dragging it along with that invisible burden which lay a-top of it, he stumbled and fell. He could not carry it any further; and Hermanus, like a black bird of prey, hovered above the Rabbi. Gnashing his teeth, the German swung the lash with all his might, and brought it down again and again on the recumbent body. A new burst of wailing went up from the women; the men in the procession began to draw nearer, and a murmuring was heard. Here and there a clenched fist was lifted. But at a word the soldiers turned in sudden fury, flung themselves upon us, and plied right and left with the flat of their swords. I and one or two others were seized and dragged toward the commanding officer, who roared:

"Arrest them! We'll have them tried for attempting to liberate the prisoner."

But he had scarcely finished the words before I twisted myself free from the soldier's hands, and escaped with nothing worse than a ringing blow over the ear. They did not attempt to pursue me.

Meanwhile Yeshua had recovered a little measure of strength. Alone, by the force of will, he rose from the ground, lifted the cross and staggered on. We now followed him at a distance, for the soldiers made a guard behind him, interposing a wall of swords.

Before long Yeshua paused again, gasping for breath. He exerted himself to move forward with his burden, but all the strength was gone out of him, and he strained forward, but could not move. The lash fell on him, but in vain. One knee yielded under him, and the cross, with all the invisible burden which lay upon it, collapsed on him. Still the lash whistled on his flesh, but he could not stir; he had reached the end of his strength. The women in the procession raised a frightful lamenting: "Hold back the hand of the wicked!" The men, in desperation, glared up at the heavens: perhaps the sign was now ready and the thunders and lightnings of the powers would strike the wicked; and the men too began to shout. Some of them drew close to the ranks of the soldiers, and cried: "Let us carry his cross! Let us carry it!" The soldiers paid no attention to them. Still the lash fell on the Nazarene.

Then suddenly Simon Cyrene issued from a side street. He did not seem to know what was afoot and what had happened that night and that morning, for he carried on his shoulder his spade and his pruning hook, as if he were just returning from his fields. And before we knew what had happened, before Rufus had had time to cry out "My father, my father!", Simon had recovered from his amazement, had slipped through the ranks of the soldiers, and had thrown himself at the Rabbi's feet. The soldiers seized him, removed the cross from Yeshua, tied it upon Simon's back, and plied the lash on him to make him rise.

"Father! Father!" cried Rufus across the ranks of the soldiers.

"Rufus!" I called.

"A Jew must always be prepared to carry the cross for another Jew." And Simon Cyrene rose, his tall figure bowed under the burden.

The soldiers were happy to have found a new sacrifice. They drove Simon on now as they had driven the Rabbi of Nazareth, who dragged himself painfully after the carrier of the cross. And the Rabbi, as he followed, was still bowed earthward, as if only the cross had been lifted from him, but not the invisible burden. Thus they went forward, Simon, the Rabbi, the soldiers, the lamenting women and the men.

Golgotha, the Place of Skulls, was the hill, not far from the city walls, where they were wont to crucify those condemned by the government. The name had arisen from the ruling made by the government that all who suffered death upon this hill should remain hanging upon the cross until the birds had eaten their flesh, whereas it was the law of Israel that not even he who had been executed for his crimes should remain unburied for a single day. Time and again the sages had pleaded with the Romans to abrogate this cruel decree, but their efforts were fruitless. "Golgotha" was a word of terror among Jews, like the name of the German, Hermanus, a word denoting abomination and foulness. And though the hill of Golgotha was not far from the city, being hard by the gate at the northeast corner, the Jews avoided it, as though the place bred unspeakable diseases in all who approached. Pilate and his slaves saw to it that the hill should not lack victims. To this place, to Golgotha, they now led the Rabbi of Nazareth.

Among those that followed in the procession there were some who refused to ascend the hill; they remained standing at the foot, afraid to move on lest they stumble against the bones of corpses scattered there, and thus defile themselves. But others, notwithstanding this danger, continued after the Rabbi, and after Simon Cyrene, who bore the cross. From afar they could see the bloodstained robe of the Nazarene, shining among the spears of the soldiers. We could not approach too closely, for the soldiers prevented us. We could watch how they led the Nazarene to the summit of the hill. About it were scattered crosses with bodies nailed to them, and the crosses were encrusted with blood, while the bodies were convulsed and drawn together. Concerning some of them we could not tell whether they still lived or were dead; for their mouths were open and twisted to a side, the tongues protruding, while their eyes were wide open. But some were clearly alive, for they moved, and here and there we even heard the dreadful sound of dying curses. Scattered about the hill were also crosses which had fallen with their burdens, and the bodies were beginning to rot, or had been half-eaten by birds. The hill was sown with human bodies, soaked through and through with the sound of human agonies. Death sighs hung in the air, and above them was heard the last groaning of the still living nailed to their crosses.

I could mark, and those that were with me also marked, how the Rabbi, on the ascent to the summit of Golgotha, drew into himself all the lamentation and pain which filled the slopes and the air which clothed them. When he had reached the end of his journey, he beheld, on the summit, two crosses and on them two tortured men. The soldiers took the cross from Simon Cyrene and laid it on the ground. Then they laid their hands on the Rabbi and brought him to the cross.

We stood at a distance and watched; with hearts tormented by fear we waited. Silence came upon the world, such silence that we could hear the wind moving among the crosses and among the dead bodies on the crosses. We did not dare to breathe, for now, now, we were certain, something was about to happen. Now the Rabbi had come down to the lowest abyss of pain. Now he had reached the narrow boundary dividing life from death; he stood before the last door. His eyes had seen everything, his ears had heard everything, his body had been penetrated by all sorrows, all agonies; it was filled to overflowing with the wine of bitterness. He had drained the cup of tears to the last drop. And we understood why he had let them bring him here, to the summit of Golgotha: it was in order that he might begin the ascent to the highest salvation out of the nethermost pit of human wickedness, from ultimate depth to ultimate glory. And a song trembled on our lips:

"With thee, with thee in the highest!"

And we were certain that when they had led him to the cross, he would lift up his hands, he would turn his eyes heavenward, and the redemption would begin. It was as though we already heard the rushing of countless wings.

Woe unto us! Nothing happened. With head bowed, like a bound calf, he approached the cross. There was no motion in his face. Out of his half-closed eyes stared the horror of death.

"Yours is the power, in your hand is the strength!" a voice cried from the foot of the hill. "Let the Kingdom begin!"

"Call to Elijah! Call down the angels!" a voice responded.

"Save yourself and us!"

"Oh, come, show all your might, if you are he who you say you are!"

But the Rabbi let them strip the clothes from him, the cloak and the shirt, soaked through and through with blood and sweat. And the cloak and shirt were ripped, like Joseph's coat, by the nails of human beasts. He stood naked, as when his mother bore him, a fleshless body, a white skin covered with welts drawn over bones; a body which trembled like the body of any man standing face to face with death. Then he strengthened himself. He closed his eyes and gave himself to the spirit, while his lips moved as if in benediction. They raised the cross behind him, they lifted his arms to its arms, and he stood ready to take death upon himself.

Now! Now! It is the moment! How long shall the wicked rejoice?

But Hermanus, the terror of Israel, lifted a hammer and a nail, and he began to hammer the nail through the Rabbi's flesh, through the palm of his hand, into the cross.

A cry went up from the women, the cry of a tortured child. A cry went up from the men.

His cruel face glowing, Hermanus hammered the nail through the Rabbi's flesh, hammered it slowly, steadily, blow by blow, as if he found delight in the swing of his arm, as if he could not bear the thought that his pleasure would end soon. And the victim on the cross, like any tortured mortal, dug his teeth into his lips; his eyes protruded and became covered with blood. His earlocks trembled. And the commander of the soldiers stood and watched.

"Show us now, show us, show that you are the Messiah! Shatter the might of Edom!" voices called to him.

But the Rabbi was twisted with pain; flesh and blood, he was filled through and through with anguish.

Suddenly we heard the voice of Judah Ish-Kiriot, who appeared from behind a half-fallen cross. Now a great cry was torn out of his breast:

"I understand you now, Rabbi! I see you now!"

He fell down and dug his face into the earth. The tormented one on the cross tried to lift his head, tried to see who called him thus in the last moment. And he saw the prostrate figure of Judah. The anguish vanished for a moment from his face; his eyes were touched again with joy. We saw with utmost clarity the last tear glimmering in the eyes of the Galilean. His lips moved as if in prayer, but we heard no words, for the lash of Herman the wicked fell again on his flesh.

"I see him now; I know now who he is! Woe to my soul!" Judah howled, and rising from the ground he fled toward the city.

Slowly, one by one, the men turned and left the place, saying:

"It is all ended now!"

I too turned and made my way to the city, my heart weighted with pain, to bring the mournful tidings to my Rabbi.

Only my comrade Rufus would not go. He said:

"It cannot be that everything is ended."

And he remained there, with the women, to see what would happen.

CHAPTER TWENTY-SEVEN

WHEN I returned home to my Rabbi, Nicodemon, I found him sitting in silent sorrow, for he had already heard of the tortures which Edom had inflicted on the Nazarene, and of the bitter mockeries they had heaped upon him, and, through him, upon all Israel. Like all of us, Rabbi Nicodemon had awaited until the last moment the miracle whereby God would save the Rabbi of Nazareth from the hands of his tormenters. And when he heard from me that the end had come, and that the soldiers of Edom had nailed the Rabbi to the cross, he cried:

"As long as the soul is within his body, we may not despair."

After a while he said to me:

"Behold the greatness of the righteous man: the greater the pains he bears for the glory of the Lord, the more closely, the more strongly he clings to his Father in heaven. Pain is the spring whence the righteous draw their faith; from this spring God gives drink to His chosen ones."

And again after a while he said:

"Who knows how far this thing will go!"

And my Rabbi stood in a corner of the house of prayer, and he prayed long, silent and apart. But the sighs that broke from him seemed to split the roof of the house of prayer, and his robe became wet with the anguish of his thoughts. Not alone the soul of Rabbi Nicodemon cried to God, but all his body, and we saw that he relived the agonies of the Rabbi of Galilee; for he that petitions God for another must put himself wholly in the condition of him for whom he makes the prayer.

My Rabbi issued from the midst of his supplication and turned to me, saying:

"Now the time has come for the offering of the Passover sacrifice. I will stay no longer in the shadow of sorrow, but will clothe myself in joy for the festival, as it is written: 'I rejoiced and said to myself, I will ascend to God's house.' Perhaps God will bring forth a miracle in honor of the festival and will save the Rabbi of Nazareth at the last moment. With God all things are possible."

Then he washed himself and changed his raiment and prepared to ascend to the Temple and offer the sacrifice; for now the sun had reached its midday station and the time of the sacrifice was near. But before he set forth the door opened, and my comrade Rufus burst into the room with a loud lamenting and fell on my Rabbi's neck.

He was filled with terror, and all his body trembled. And my Rabbi held him close to his breast, as a father holds his son, and he said to him:

"Your face betrays evil tidings, Rufus."

And Rufus remained on the Rabbi's breast, and lamented, and would not come to himself. Then my Rabbi said:

"Strengthen yourself, my son, and tell me all that has happened with the Rabbi of Nazareth; for from the righteous we must learn how to be strong in faith and how to sanctify the Name."

And Rufus said:

"Woe to my eyes that have seen it! There is no torture which they did not inflict on him!"

And he burst again into tears. But my Rabbi said:

"Take heart, my son, and tell me everything, in all detail; tell me what you saw and in what manner the last moment came."

Then Rufus strengthened himself and related:

"When they had nailed him to the cross they took the tablet on which Pilate had bidden them write 'Yeshua, King of the Jews,' and fastened it to the cross, above his head. And they mocked him, crying, 'Now, King of the Jews, save yourself!' But the Rabbi only looked on them in great pity and his lips were twisted in pain. His limbs were too weak to hold his body erect on the cross, and his back yielded and he bent forward. And we thought that every moment his own weight would tear him down from the cross; or that the wind would blow him from it; because a wind rose, and the air was black, and it beat on the cross. Then we thought that the wind unfolded wings and was about to lift the Rabbi and carry him away; and we that were standing there were afraid. We thought that the darkness would be rolled up by the wind, and out of the clear spaces beyond the angels would issue to bear the Rabbi away. But the wind rolled about the Rabbi as though caressing him, and then died down.

"And when the wind was gone we beheld the Rabbi hanging on the cross. His face had changed. His eyes were big, and they were turned toward heaven. His mouth was locked, and his lips were touched with a thin foam, as though someone had made them wet with a drink. And now the pain was written not only on his face, but all his body uttered pain. We saw that he was in dreadful anguish, for his body was twisted this way and that, in convulsions, and his hands were helpless; his breast had fallen in and his belly was swollen. And he exerted himself to maintain his body upright against the cross; for his back was breaking and his head falling on his breast; and he pressed the toes of his feet against the wood to stem himself against the upright. His body was waxen-yellow, withered, dried, yet delicate as ivory. And his pallid face, marked with streamlets of blood, stared out from between his beard and earlocks, and became one single cry to God. Still he strengthened himself and lifted his head from his breast, and turned his eyes toward heaven, as though still awaiting help from above; and the help did not come.

"The women stood before the cross and beheld his anguish. And one of them, the tall Miriam, laid her head on the breast of the other Miriam, who supported her. But the tall Miriam fell nevertheless on her knees and stayed thus awhile. Then suddenly she rose, and stood without help, her face uncovered, and she looked straight into the face of the sufferer on the cross. There were no tears in her eyes; they were big and wide open and dry; her face was like stone, her lips were tight, and there was no movement of any muscle on her face, which was turned toward the sufferer. And it seemed as though his pain and hers moved back and forth between them. We could see the pain of his flesh entering into her. Then suddenly it seemed as though the anguish which she sucked into herself had made her taller, and had given strength and stature to her body and strength to her legs, so that they no longer tottered under her. There was no tear in her eyes, not one moan came from her lips; she grew mighty with the pains which flowed into her through her eyes. And thus it was with her till the end.

"Then he that was on the cross began to twist again in anguish, and foam broke out on his lips; his face was drawn, and it fell once more on his breast. His lips began to murmur something. And the Roman commander that stood there took a sponge from a soldier and dipped it into a liquid; and he lifted the sponge on a staff and lifted it to the lips of the sufferer, amid the laughter of the soldiers.

"Then he that was on the cross turned his eyes fully upon the Roman commander, and his look was filled with pain, and yet it was strong and compassionate, too; and we heard him say:

" 'Father, forgive them, for they know not what they do!'

"When the Roman commander heard these words he took a step nearer to the cross and spoke to the sufferer, but we did not hear the words.

"Then suddenly the Rabbi on the cross lifted his eyes to heaven, and moaned bitterly, and from his lips came the cry:

" 'Eli, Eli, lama sabachthani?'

"And when the woman heard this cry from the tormented lips she lifted up her hands to the cross and called:

" '*Tinoki, tinoki!* My little one! My little one!'

"But the despair and death terror on the Rabbi's face lasted but a moment. He became strong again, and calmness returned to him. The spasms ceased in his body, as though sleep had come upon him. He became small, as if he had shrunk in on himself, and his legs bent slowly. With a last effort he looked up again at the heavens, and in a loud, clear voice called: 'Hear, O Israel, the Lord our God the Lord is One.'

"And therewith he let his head fall again, and he closed his eyes. Then over his lips there passed a forgiving smile. Peace descended on him. We heard him murmur as in a song of sleep: 'Into Thy hands I deliver my soul!'

"And he died in sanctity and purity, the smile upon his lips."

When Rufus ceased speaking my Rabbi said:

"It is written in the Torah: 'Thou shalt love the Lord thy God with all thy heart and with all thy soul and with all thy might.' From this our sages have taught: 'Thou shalt love Him with all thy faculties, and in all conditions. That is, thou shalt thank Him for the bad as well as for the good.' Come, my pupils, let us thank God that He did not let the righteous one suffer long on the cross." And my Rabbi lifted his hands to heaven and cried: "Blessed be the true

Judge!" And to us he said: "Be comforted, my sons; the memory of the righteous shall be invoked with blessing." Then he turned his face to the wall and prayed with great fervor. "Father of all creatures, have mercy on Thy servant, Yeshua ben Joseph, who sought to serve Thee with all his heart and with all his soul, and offered up his life for Thee. He shed his blood for Thee like water, and his body was torn like a sieve with wounds. But he did not rebel against Thee, and he took his sufferings upon himself in love, that Thy Name might be sanctified. Have mercy upon him and accept the soul of the righteous one as a pure offering, and grant rest to his soul, and take him under the wings of Thy *Shekhinah*. Amen!"

Then the Rabbi asked us to bring him water in a vessel, and he went to the door of the house of prayer and washed his hands and said:

"Father in heaven, it is known to you that our hands have not shed this blood. We and our children are innocent thereof."

And to us he said:

"The commandment to do grace by the dead outweighs all the other commandments of the Torah, even the commandment of the Passover sacrifice. And those that die for the sanctification of the Name are counted among us martyrs and pure souls. The Rabbi of Nazareth, who was slain by Edom for the sanctification of the Name, is a martyr in Israel, and to occupy oneself with his burial is the highest of all commandments. Therefore hasten to Joseph Arimathea, and bid him approach the government, for he is well known there, and ask for the release of the body of the saint from the hand of the abomination which slew it; and let him pay whatever price they set upon it, though it be all his fortune, so that we may give Jewish burial to the body of the saint before the sun goes down and the Sabbath arrives. And I myself will go to Golgotha and wait there for him till he bring the authority to take down the body of the saint from the cross."

And my Rabbi took out of his stone coffer the store of precious ointments which was his only passion and his only worldly possession; and he went with his pupils toward Golgotha to prepare the burial of the saint.

CHAPTER TWENTY-EIGHT

JOSEPH ARIMATHEA possessed a pearl of great price which had come down to him by inheritance; and it was the peculiarity of this pearl that when a sinful man looked upon it his conscience lashed him like a whip, and he repented for his sins and desired to turn from evil. It was this pearl which Joseph Arimathea gave to Pontius Pilate in payment for the body of Yeshua. And in a few days Pilate returned the pearl to Joseph Arimathea because he could not bear to look on it.

And Joseph Arimathea took the tablet on which Pilate had set down the order to the Roman commander to release the body of Yeshua, and he set out for Golgotha. At the city gate he found waiting for him my Rabbi and his pupils and the Companionship of my Rabbi. And among them were Hillel the watercarrier and Simon Cyrene and the convert Abraham ben Abraham.

As we drew near from the distance we could already distinguish the body of the Nazarene, for it was of a strange, radiant whiteness; and it chanced that the sun broke through the clouds and its rays fell upon the white body. On the ground at the foot of the cross lay outstretched the woman Miriam of Migdal, and her face was buried in the earth. And she lay so motionless and stony that we could not tell if she were dead or still living, for there was no sign of life in her. Near the cross sat Sulamith, the mother of the Zebedees. Her round, wide-open, simple eyes, red from weeping, were fixed on the body of the Rabbi of Nazareth, and in her look there was mingled motherly sorrow and utter faith, as though she still expected momently that the sufferer on the cross would awaken and perform a miracle. Close by her stood the tall Miriam. The skin of her face had taken on the deathly color of the body of the Rabbi; and she looked steadfastly into the dead face of the Rabbi. Her lips were thin and tight-drawn and turned to stone; they neither moved nor quivered. Only her eyes, soft and living, sucked in the vision of the tortured body. At a little distance from the women stood the commanding officer, by his tired soldiers.

There was no life in the bodies of the two Bar Abba-ites who hung on the crosses to right and left of the Rabbi. But it seemed as if, in their last agonies, they had twisted themselves round so that they might die with their eyes fixed on him. Their tongues protruded from their mouths, and the veins on their bodies were swollen into knots, and it seemed as if, at any moment, the veins would burst and leap forth from the flesh. Their eyes were wide open; they bulged out from the sockets, and they glared in death on the tormented, bloodless and bony Rabbi on his cross. When we arrived, the Rabbi and the pupils and the Companionship, we felt that something had taken place—we knew not what—for there was a stillness and ecstasy in the air; it had taken hold not only of the women, but even of the Roman commander who stood somewhat to a side, caught up in the spirit which still rested on the place. And even the soldiers, now weary with their bloody work, were ill at ease, and their faces reflected dread.

Joseph Arimathea went up to the commander and showed him the order for the release of the body; and we, the Rabbi and the pupils and the Companionship, were permitted to approach the cross. And it was only when we were quite near that we perceived how emptied of all blood, how bony and waxen-yellow the body had become. And yet there trembled upon it a strange freshness, something newborn and childlike. The head hung down on the twisted flesh, above the cry of his open wounds.

My Rabbi began to occupy himself with the body, and he let no one help him save those whom he considered worthy. Silently, with a glance of his eyes, he bade the women withdraw and let the men go about this task; and my Rabbi and Joseph Arimathea and Simon Cyrene and Hillel the watercarrier performed their duty. We, the pupils, were permitted to lift our Rabbi upon our shoulders, that he might withdraw the nails from the flesh of the Nazarene and free him from the cross.

And they busied themselves a long time, for they sought to fulfill all the precepts pertaining to Jewish burial, and they would not leave the smallest fragment of flesh upon the cross or the nails of the cross. And when the hands of the Nazarene had been freed, my Rabbi took him upon his back. A mother carries not her only child, brought forth in weeping and suffering, more tenderly than my

Rabbi bore him who had suffered on the cross and had departed this life upon it. And while my Rabbi stood thus, the body resting on his shoulders, Joseph Arimathea and Simon Cyrene withdrew the nails from the feet. And when the body was wholly freed from the cross, the four men, my Rabbi and Joseph Arimathea and Hillel and Simon Cyrene carried it away a little distance.

And they took the body and laid it on a white sheet, which Joseph Arimathea had brought with him. And the body, lying in its whiteness on the white sheet, was like the body of a child which had been tormented, and which now lay at peace in the arms of its mother, safe from all further pain. But my Rabbi, desiring to shelter the body from the contact of human eyes, and to deliver it unstained, with all its crying wounds, to our Father in heaven, wrapped it hastily in the sheet; and he and Joseph Arimathea lifted it up with great tenderness, and they carried it swiftly down the hill. My Rabbi and Joseph Arimathea carried the body, and Simon Cyrene and Hillel the watercarrier and Abraham ben Abraham followed; and after them we came, the pupils, and the women behind us.

And as we passed by certain crucified men who hung upon their crosses, not yet dead, they strained their bodies and twisted themselves away from the wood, and with protruding eyeballs they followed the procession of the Rabbi of Nazareth, forgetting the agony of their flesh. And even the Roman commander and his soldiers moved to a side to make way for us; and I marked clearly on the face of the commander that his heart had melted like water in him.

And we went forward swiftly, for the heavens were clouded over, and it seemed that night hung behind Golgotha and waited, before descending, until we had brought the body of the saint to burial.

Now Joseph Arimathea had a garden in the neighborhood, and in the garden he had prepared a grave for himself, in a cave. And he said: "I will give my grave to the saint, and let him rest there in peace."

Therefore they carried the body of him who had suffered on the cross into the garden of Joseph Arimathea, and they rolled away the stone from the cave and bestowed the body therein. And my Rabbi took the precious ointments, which he had intended for his own burial, and he placed them in the cave where the body was. And coming forth, my Rabbi called into the cave:

"He is pure! He is pure! He is pure!"

Then they rolled back the stone over the mouth of the cave, and my Rabbi stood up and uttered the Sanctification of the Name. He did not speak of him who had been buried, for the Sabbath was waiting, and we were in haste.

And when we came forth from the garden the heavens were again uncovered and the thick clouds had rolled away; they had been carried off and swallowed up in the blue depths, and only their silver edges were still visible over the rims of the hills. And from the hilltops the sacred Sabbath began to glide over Jerusalem accompanied by the last rays of the setting sun.

And the peace of the Sabbath descended over the world.

Now as we hastened into the city, we came down an empty little street which ran along the wall; and there was a fig tree in the shadows, and in the falling darkness it looked like a cross, and a man was nailed to the cross. And we turned aside and drew near, to see what this was; and we beheld Judah Ish-Kiriot hanging by a rope from one of the branches of the fig tree.

And my Rabbi paused a while near the hanging man, and said: "Judah! Judah! Your impatience has brought death upon you! Behold, it is written: 'He that walketh in the way of simplicity shall be helped, and he that twisteth the path, shall fall!' May God have mercy on your soul!"

CHAPTER TWENTY-NINE

ALL this I read forth to Pan Viadomsky in his room on the Bonaparte Street, Warsaw, during the spring. . . . And it was late one night that I brought to a close the recital of my part in the tragedy which had been enacted in those far-off Passover days in Jerusalem.

For a time now Pan Viadomsky had been ill and confined to his bed. I sat at his side, reading from the paper on which I had set down whatever I could recall out of my experiences in the life that had been; and he listened with closed eyes. Of late his sickness had taken a turn for the worse, and his body was wasted and lean, like the skeleton of a herring. It was, in fact, a human skeleton which lay on the bed. When his eyes were closed the pupils bulged through the thin, sickly network of veins on the lids. His cheeks were sunken, his throat stringy, and his Adam's apple bobbed up and down under the withered skin. His nose, which had retained its form to some extent, was extraordinarily pale; it stood forth in a sort of isolated pride on the ruins of his face, a pillar of antiquity on a mound of the past. Were it not for the faint breath which passed to and fro through the half-open mouth, from which the tongue protruded between toothless gums, he might have been taken for dead. At any rate, he certainly appeared to be in a coma; but every now and again he lifted his eyelids, and fixed upon me a penetrating look of suspicion and inquiry. Was I telling him the truth? Now, when I ended the story of the tragedy, and made a long pause, he opened his eyes, stared at me obstinately, and muttered:

"Well?"

"Well what?" I asked.

"What happened after that?" he demanded, and his scrutiny was loaded with his last strength. "Did you not hear what happened with him whom you call the Rabbi of Nazareth after his death?" And to my astonishment he sat up in the bed.

"That which happened afterwards with the Rabbi of Nazareth in Jerusalem has no relation to me," I answered.

"But . . . Did you hear nothing? Were you not told of what took place in Jerusalem after Joseph Arimathea and your Rabbi took him down from the cross and gave him burial? Do you know nothing about it?"

"I have already told you, and I say it again, Hegemon: that which happened with the Rabbi of Nazareth after his death has nothing to do with me."

"But what did they relate in your circles? Did you hear nothing?"

"Certainly we heard," I answered.

"Aha!" muttered Pan Viadomsky, and drew a deep breath.

"What do you mean?" I asked.

"Will you not tell me what it was they heard in your circles? But the truth!" He looked at me sternly. "Hide nothing."

"I have nothing to hide."

"By the oath of excommunication?"

"Even by the oath of the High Priest's vestments," I replied.

"What did they say?"

"In certain circles in Jerusalem secret rumors were current that the Rabbi had disappeared from his grave, that he showed himself in the life to his disciples, and that he told them what they still had to do. At first these rumors were spread only among his followers, but gradually they spread beyond the circle; and those that had believed in the Rabbi during his life began to assemble and to found companionships; and the reports became louder and more open and more insistent that the Rabbi of Nazareth had in fact been the Messiah, that he was now with God in heaven, and that very soon he would come down upon earth, in order to judge the living and to begin the kingdom of heaven. Those who believed in it went by the name of the Messianists."

"Were there many of them?"

"I do not know. I took no interest in the matter. But I knew some of them, because certain members of my own circle joined the sect of the Messianists. My friend Rufus joined; so did his brother Alexander and the convert, Abraham ben Abraham. I believe Joseph Arimathea joined, too, but I am not sure. But I do know that my Rabbi Nicodemon did not belong to them; for I remember a conversation which I held with my Rabbi concerning this matter. My Rabbi said: 'It is enough that Rabbi Yeshua lived like a righteous man, sought after God, drew men nearer to heaven, and died in utter purity, that I shall bow my head to his memory, and recall him with benediction.' As it is written: 'The memory of the just man is a blessing.' Hillel the watercarrier and the others were of his opinion. About Simon Cyrene I do not know."

"Did you persecute them?" asked Pan Viadomsky.

"Persecute them?" I repeated, in astonishment. "What for? What difference was there between us and them that we should persecute them? My friend Rufus remained the pupil of my Rabbi even later, when he became a Messianist. And just as in former days he used to go with us to the temple, to offer sacrifice. So did all the other Messianists. We said the same prayers; and every day we mentioned in them the coming of the Messiah. And we waited for him, day after day. Because they, just like us, did not know when he would come, and therefore like us they expected him every day, and every hour of the day, and every minute of the hour. They, just like us, said that God might choose any instant for the sending of the Messiah and for our deliverance, and therefore it was incumbent on us to be constantly prepared to meet him: for that very waiting, that expectancy and longing, was the fountainhead of faith. The only difference between us was that in their belief the Messiah had already been once on earth, and was due to return, and we said that this could not be, that the Messiah could not have been on earth and mankind remain unredeemed from evil, but full of wickedness. Our belief was that the Messiah was yet to come, theirs that he was to come again."

"And were there no disputes among you concerning such an important matter?"

"Surely there were disputes concerning this matter in our synagogues and study houses, and sometimes even in the Temple courts. But these were disputes which took place among ourselves; just as there were divisions of opinion concerning other religious matters; but all of us belonged to the sacred congregation of God."

"And was there no split between you and the Messianists, because of this difference?"

"Not in my time; not through all the time which I can remember out of my life in Jerusalem."

"And what happened to the Sons of Hanan?"

"The curse which Rabbi Gamaliel ben Simon pronounced upon them was fulfilled. They and all their party of the Sadducees were wiped out in Israel. There is no remnant of them. And the name of the House of Hanan is remembered with a curse. The word which was current in those days in Jerusalem, 'The Sons of Hanan are the sons of Eli,' clings to them even to this day."

"And can you not tell me what became of my friend, Hanan ben Hanan?"

"He? He became an abomination and a stench. When he, the last of them, became the High Priest, he persecuted the sages. But after he brought about the death of Jacob ben Joseph, who was the brother of Yeshua, who had suffered on the cross, the sages were so embittered against him that they sent a deputation to the King; they even went out to greet the new Procurator, Albinus, on his entry; and they did not rest until King Agrippa deposed Hanan ben Hanan for the murder of Jacob ben Joseph. Later on the Jews took vengeance on him. In the time of the revolt against Rome they discovered him to be a traitor. They tore his body apart like a fish and threw the pieces to the dogs. And with him the Sons of Hanan were wiped out and vanished from Israel. And so may all the wicked be lost, and the righteous flourish like a date palm," I ended.

Pan Viadomsky was silent. He closed his eyes, and sat upon the bed sunk in thought.

"And now permit me to ask you something," I said. "What happened to the Hegemon?"

An ice-cold hand fastened on mine, the bony fingers gripping me like a vise. He fixed a wild, penetrating look on me.

"What happened to me? I am here today, as I was yesterday, as I shall be forever. I am here, and I cannot stop being."

I did not understand him. It seemed to me that Pan Viadomsky's mind was wandering; and my looks must have betrayed my feeling, for Pan Viadomsky added in a resigned voice, as his head fell back on the cushion:

"He laid upon me the curse of being."

"Who?" I asked in a low voice.

"He. On the cross."

"The Rabbi of Nazareth?"

"The Messiah of Nazareth!" he cried.

"You believe it?"

"I have always believed it. I only did not want to admit it."

"And yet?"

"And yet I admit it, I must admit it. Do you understand? I must admit it against my will, against my nature, against everything that I am. I must!" he almost screamed, in a gurgling, enraged voice.

"Who compels you?"

"He!" Pan Viadomsky answered, and he collapsed weakly, closing his eyes.

I did not speak. I let him struggle with his thoughts, and the inner battle was reflected in the play of his features. Finally he conquered himself. He opened his eyes and looked at me mournfully, humbly. And, wonder of wonders! he did not show the slightest shame in his weakness. I pretended not to see. I even wanted to leave him. I said:

"It is late. It is time for me to go."

"Where must you go? To what will you leave me?"

And Pan Viadomsky stretched out his hands to me, and on his face was the supplication of weakness.

"Pan Viadomsky! What ails you?"

(I was astonished that he let pass the use of this name.)

He made a gesture, bidding me remain. Silently I returned to my seat.

"I struggled with him. He conquered me!" He talked as if to himself. "He took me as one takes a pot and breaks it. He broke me. I fought against it until the last moment. I felt myself growing weaker and weaker. I tried to avoid his gaze. I knew that he would overcome me. Every glance of his pierced me, it penetrated to my inmost parts; and it was as if armies had forced their way into me, to break down the structure of my character and my inheritance, to melt away my nature, to tear out the roots of my being. I was molten and poured from vessel to vessel, in new forms. And in order to combat his influence over me I made myself more wicked than I am. And when he asked me for water as he hung on the cross I took a sponge and dipped it in vinegar and lifted it to his lips. And it was then that he seized me! He seized me as a lion seizes its prey. He turned his eyes upon me, and my resistance was paralyzed, my limbs were bound, and it was as if I had fallen at his feet. And still I struggled. I gathered my strength and I called to my help the inheritance of my blood. I tried to stand erect, and to outstare him. Then something happened. His bloodshot eyes took mine captive.

The eyeballs which looked out from under their lids held me fast, like two magic stones. He moved his lips and I heard these words issue from them: 'From this day on let vinegar be your drink!' I tried to make mock of the words. I sought refuge in the laughter of contempt. I knew that if I yielded now I would be fastened to him for all eternity. Therefore I asked him in a jeering voice, though my heart already wept: 'And when will my drink turn to water?' And he answered: 'When a tear of mine will fall into it.' And he turned his eyes from me.

"And still I sought to save myself in laughter. I said to him: 'If you are the King of the Jews, come to your own help!' But the words were spoken in vain. That which he had uttered became like a fiery drink, and from that day on there has been a hot flame in my heart and I have found no rest.

"I struggle against him, but I am like a fish which is caught on the hook. It flings itself hither and thither, but it is hooked on the line. And so I am fastened to him.

"My mouth laughs, and curses pour from it. But my heart trembles before him. The last look with which he pierced me pursues me and is forever with me. I must rebel against him. To free myself from him I do everything in his despite. I am forever in flight, I am forever saving myself from him, and yet I cannot free myself from him.

"And so I pass from incarnation to incarnation, and in every incarnation I struggle against him. I tear myself from him, and cannot tear myself away. I cannot be with him, and I cannot be without him.

"My drink is vinegar. Whatever I take into myself is vinegar, and whatever I give out is vinegar. And I long for the clear water of the brook. Oh, if my drink could only be water again! I am so tired! Oh, God, have mercy on me!"

And then—I could not believe it! it could not be!—the eyes of Pan Viadomsky filled with tears; large tears, full like the buds of violets, rolled from his eyes. At first he tried to hide them from me; he wiped them away with his sleeve. And I, too, turned my gaze aside, pretended to be staring at the lamp, so that he might think I had not seen. And he muttered something which sounded like the beginning of a curse. Then suddenly he yielded utterly; he gave up the struggle, and without resistance he let the tears flow over the waxen-yellow skin of his cheeks, openly, without being ashamed before me.

"Glory to God in heaven, His will be done on earth," his lips murmured.

"Pan Viadomsky! Pan Viadomsky! His tear has fallen into your cup!" I cried joyfully.

He tried to bring a stern expression into his sunken eyes, but it was useless. Only his lips whispered a reproach at me:

"What, Pan Viadomsky?"

"Hegemon of Jerusalem!" I corrected myself.

"Hegemon of Jerusalem," he repeated in a whisper.

After a pause he called to me, as out of his sleep:

"What was it took place there, in the Temple courts, on the last day, between him and your Rabbis? I was told that they reached an agreement concerning the first and most important commandment."

"Yes! The Rabbi and the Pharisees were in agreement that the first commandment was to love God, and immediately after it, but also the same, was the commandment to love one's neighbor. On these foundations stand the pillars of human faith."

"Yes, and then what happened?"

"They parted on the matter of the method by which to reach this goal; but the goal was the same for both."

"It is always thus with you Jews! Never can you reach agreement. And even when you come to an understanding, you still have no understanding. Who knows the ways of you Jews?"

And this was the last reproach which he cast at us. He fell into silence.

I remained sitting at the bedside. His hand was fastened to mine, and his flesh was ice-cold. But his eyes still remained open.

There came in through the window the first rays of the morning sun, which had pierced the barriers of darkness and cobwebs to find their way to the bedside. They were tired, these rays, with their long journey, and with the obstacles which they had overcome, but they were still warm with the benediction of the sun.

He was still living. His eyes were open. His lips moved, as if they were conscious of the taste of the sun. A blissful expression which bespoke peace and security began to play on his face, such an expression as might be seen on the face of a captain whose ship is drawing toward the harbor after a long and perilous voyage.

I bent down my ears to his lips, and I heard clearly his last words:

"God! Have mercy on my sinful soul!"

He stretched himself, and his face turned to stone, a delicately chiseled yellow stone, like ivory.

Later, when the sun had fully risen, and the warmth of it streamed into the room, little Blimele, the daughter of the tailor who lived in the janitor's apartment opposite Pan Viadomsky, entered. Her long, black locks, new-washed, fell down over her face and her slender neck and her young, trembling shoulders. Her eyes were fresh and clear, but still dipped in sleep, as if she had only just awakened. Her naked, childish feet were thrust into the shapeless shoes of a grown-up; and in her hand she held a small bouquet of half-faded, yellow field flowers. She said, in a singing, childlike voice:

"We were at the Jewish cemetery yesterday and we picked flowers. So Mamma told me to take some in to the sick Pan."

I took the handful of poor, half-faded Jewish field flowers and laid them on the calmed heart of Pan Viadomsky.

END